EVERYMAN'S LIBRARY

527

FICTION

Everyman, I will go with thee, and be thy guide,
In thy most need to go by thy side

COUNT LEO NIKOLAIEVICH TOLSTOI, poet, social reformer, and one of the world's greatest novelists, was born at Yásnaya Poliána, Russia, on 9th September 1828. Left an orphan at the age of nine, he was brought up by an aunt and studied first under a French tutor and then at Kazan university. Joining the army in 1851 after devoting some years to pleasure, he fought at Silistria (1854) and at Sevastopol (1855). After leaving the army in 1857 he was prominent in social and literary circles, and in 1862 he married Sophia Behrs. He became estranged from her, left home secretly on 29th October, and died at Astapovo on 8th November 1910. Tolstoi, though holding liberal views, was a strong individualist and so never identified himself with the socialistic movement then growing in Russia.

LEO TOLSTOI
WAR AND PEACE

IN THREE VOLUMES · VOLUME THREE

LONDON J. M. DENT & SONS LTD
NEW YORK E. P. DUTTON & CO INC

PZ 3
.T588W

~~AC 1~~
.E8
~~no~~ 527

T588

THE FRENCH AT MOSCOW

1812—1820

BOOK ELEVEN

CHAPTER I

THE fight at Schevardino had taken place on the 5th September; on the 6th not a gun was fired on either side; the 7th was the day of Borodino. Why and how were these battles fought? We ask in amazement, for no great advantage could result either to the Russians or the French. For the Russians they were a step farther towards the loss of Moscow, which was the catastrophe they most dreaded; and for the French a step nearer to the loss of their army, which no doubt filled them with equal apprehension. However, though both these consequences were self-evident, Napoleon offered battle and Koutouzow accepted the challenge. If any really good reasons had ruled the strategy of the rival commanders, neither ought to have fought then and there; for Napoleon ran the risk of losing a quarter of his men at 2000 versts inside the frontier—the straight road to ruin, and Koutouzow, while exposing his army to the same danger, would lay Moscow open. For Koutouzow it was a plain mathematical calculation; as it would be for me were I to play draughts with one draught less than my opponent: if I exchange I am bound to lose and therefore must not exchange. When my adversary has sixteen draughts and I only fourteen, I am weaker than he is by an eighth, but when I have exchanged thirteen with him he is three times as strong as I am.

Before the fight at Borodino the proportion of Russians to French in the respective armies was as 5 to 6; after it as 1 to 2; or as 100,000 to 120,000 before, and as 50,000 to 100,000 after; and yet Koutouzow, an intelligent and experienced veteran, made up his mind to the struggle, in which Napoleon, an acknowledged military genius, sacrificed a quarter of his men and extended his line. Though some writers have tried to

1

prove that he believed he should close the campaign by taking Moscow as he had taken Vienna, it would be easy to demonstrate the contrary. Contemporary historians tell us that as soon as he had reached Smolensk he was anxious to find an opportunity of stopping; for while, on one hand, he was fully aware of the danger of extending his line over too wide an extent of country, on the other he foresaw that the occupation of Moscow would not give him a favourable position. He could judge of that by the state in which he found the evacuated towns, and by the silence which met his repeated attempts to reopen negotiations for peace. Thus both commanders—one in offering battle and the other in accepting it—acted absurdly and on no preconceived plan. Historians, reasoning from accomplished facts, have drawn plausible conclusions in favour of the genius and foresight of the two leaders, while, of all instruments ever employed by the Almighty to work out events, they were certainly the most blind. The ancients have transmitted to us their heroic poems, in which the whole interest of history lies in the heroes themselves, and we cannot yet get used to the idea, that in our humane times, such history is senseless.

When we come to the question as to how the battle of Borodino was fought, the explanation given by historians is again entirely false, though they affect extreme exactitude. According to them this double engagement took place somewhat as follows: "The Russians retiring and concentrating after the struggle at Smolensk sought the most favourable position for coming to a stand and giving battle, and found it in and round Borodino; they fortified it to the left of the high road from Smolensk to Moscow in a line between Borodino and Outitza, while, to watch the movements of the enemy, they threw up an earthwork on the mamelon of Schevardino. This was attacked and taken by Napoleon on the 5th, and on the 7th he fell upon the Russian forces in the plain of Borodino."
—This is what history tells us: but by giving a little careful study to the matter it is not difficult to convince oneself of the inaccuracy of the statement. It is not true that the Russians were seeking a better position; on the contrary, in their retreat they passed several very superior to Borodino; but—Koutouzow would not adopt one that he had not chosen himself; but—the desire of the country for a pitched battle was not yet strongly expressed; but—Miloradovitch had not yet effected his junction. And there were numerous other *buts*, too many to enumerate.

The fact remains that there were other preferable positions, and that at Borodino was no better than any other that might be pitched upon by chance on the map of Russia. Again, not only had not the Russians strengthened Borodino on the left—that is to say at the point where the battle was ultimately fought— but on the morning of the 6th no one had any idea that it would prove to be the scene of an engagement. As evidence on this point it may be said: 1st, That the redoubt in question did not exist on the 6th. It was only begun on that day and was not finished on the following day. 2nd, The spot chosen for the works at Schevardino, in advance of the spot where the battle was fought, was perfectly absurd. Why should that point be strengthened rather than any other? And why again, during the night of the 5th, should the available forces have been weakened by detaching 6000 men to watch the enemy's movements when a patrol of Cossacks would have been amply sufficient for the purpose? 3rd, Do we not know that on the 6th, the day before the battle, Barclay de Tolly and Bagration regarded the redoubt at Schevardino not as an advanced work but as the left flank of the position? And Koutouzow himself in his first despatch, written while the engagement was fresh in his mind, speaks of it in the same way. Subsequently, when detailed reports of the affair were drawn up, the inconceivable statement was put forward that the works at Schevardino were an advanced defence, while, in point of fact, it was only the extreme angle of the left flank; but this was said to cover the blunders of the commander-in-chief, who must at any cost be proved infallible; and it was stoutly maintained that the Russians had prepared to fight in a position chosen and fortified beforehand, while in truth the battle was quite unexpected and took place in a very exposed spot, almost undefended.

The real course of events was as follows: The Russian right rested on the river Kolotcha, which crossed the high road at an acute angle; its left flank lay towards Schevardino, and its right by the village of Novoïé; the centre facing Borodino at the meeting of the Kolotcha and the Voïna. Anyone studying the battle of Borodino, and forgetting the circumstances under which it was fought, will perceive that the sole object of this position on the Kolotcha must have been to intercept the enemy's advance towards Moscow along the high road from Smolensk. Historians tell us that Napoleon, marching towards Valouïew on the 5th, did not discover the Russians in their position between Outitza and Borodino (which he could not see because it was not there) nor their advanced posts. It was only when, in pursuit of their rear, that he accidentally ran against the left flank and the redoubt at Schevardino, and made his troops cross the river, to the great surprise of the Russians. Consequently, even before fighting had begun, they were compelled to withdraw the left wing from the point it was meant to defend, and retire into a position they had not strengthened nor intended to occupy. Napoleon, marching along the left bank of the river, between it and the high road, forced the future battle from right to left into the plain between Outitza, Séménovski and Borodino, to a plain just as suitable for battle as many other plains in Russia, and here it was the battle was actually fought on the 7th.

If Napoleon had not crossed the Kolotcha on the evening of the 5th, and if he had next day insisted on a pitched battle instead of giving orders to storm the redoubt at once, no one could have said that this outwork was not on the left flank of the position, and the engagement would have been fought as was proposed. In that case the Russian left would of course have resisted more obstinately; Napoleon's centre and right would have been attacked at once, and the great battle would have been fought on the 5th, and on the spot where it had been planned. But as the Russian left was attacked in the evening, in consequence of the retirement of their rear, and as the Russian general would not, and indeed could not, engage so late in the day, the first and the most important half of the battle of Borodino was actually lost on the 5th, and the inevitable result was a defeat on the 7th. By the 7th the Russians had only thrown up slight defences, and they were not finished. The generals aggravated the disaster by not attaching due importance to the loss of the left wing, which necessitated an entire reorganisation of their line, and by leaving their troops spread out between Novoïé and Outitza, which involved them in a movement from right to left after the fighting had begun. In this way the French strength was concentrated all the time on the Russian left, which was not half as strong.

Poniatowski's attack on the French right between Outitza and Ouvarov were quite independent of the general scheme of action.

Thus the battle against the French right of Borodino was fought in a way quite unlike the descriptions given of it, which were written merely to cover the faults of the Russian generals;

and this imaginary picture in fact only dimmed the glory of the army and the nation. It was not fought on a spot carefully selected and strengthened, nor with a small numerical difference: it was forced upon them on an exposed plain, after the redoubt had been taken, against forces twice as great as their own, and under conditions which did not even give them a hope of struggling for ten hours and leaving the day undecided; for it was obviously certain that they could not hold their own for three hours before they would be utterly defeated.

CHAPTER II

PETER left Mojaïsk on the morning of the 6th. On the steep street that leads to the suburbs he left his carriage on a rise to the right, by the church where mass was being performed. A regiment of cavalry led by its singers was following close behind him, and meeting these, came a long row of carts bringing in the men wounded in the fray of the 5th. The peasants leading them were storming at their horses, cracking their whips, and running from one side to the other; the wagons, each carrying three or four men, were desperately shaken over the stones flung down at random to represent a pavement. The wounded men, with limbs tied up in rags, pale, pinching their lips and knitting their brows, held on to the bars, jostling each other; almost all stared curiously at Peter's white hat and green coat.

His coachman roughly ordered the peasants to keep on one side of the road; the regiment coming down the hill occupied the whole of it, and drove the carriage to the very edge; Peter himself had to stop and stand aside. At this spot, just above a bend in the road, the hill formed a brow, which screened it from the sun. In the shade it was damp and chill, though it was a fine, bright August morning. One of the carts full of wounded drew up within a few steps of Peter. The driver in his bast shoes ran up out of breath, picked up a stone to scotch the hind wheel, and arranged the harness; an old soldier with his arm in a sling, who was following on foot, helped with his sound hand, and turning to Peter, said:

"I say, mate, are we to be left to die here, or to be dragged on to Moscow?"

Peter, lost in thought, did not hear the question; he looked
* 527

first at the cavalry regiment, checked by the carts, and then at the wagon that was standing near him. In it were three soldiers. And it seemed to him that here, in these men, he would find the solution of the problem that troubled him. One of them was wounded in the face; his head was wrapped in rags, leaving one cheek bare, swelled to the size of a child's head; his eyes were fixed on the church, and he was crossing himself fervently. The second was a fair raw recruit, so pale that he seemed not to have a drop of blood left in his thin face; he looked down at Peter with a pleasant gentle smile. The third was lying down, and his face was invisible. At this moment the singers of the cavalry regiment came close to the wagon, their cheering strains mingling with the noisy ringing of church bells. The bright sun shone on the platform at the top of the hill, and brightened all the landscape, adding as if yet another note of gaiety; but where the wagon had drawn up, the wounded men, and the panting horse, and Peter standing by them, were in shadow, and mist, and gloom. The soldier with the swelled cheek looked at the singers out of the corner of his eye.

"Well, what a lot of dandies!" he murmured reproachfully.

"I have seen something besides soldiers to-day—I have seen peasants driven to the front," said the man who was leaning against the cart, with a melancholy smile. "They are not so particular now; they are going to throw the whole nation at their head. It has got to be done somehow."

In spite of the incoherence of this statement Peter gathered the sense of it, and nodded affirmation.

The road presently cleared; Peter went down the hill and got into his carriage again. As he drove on he looked out on both sides of the road for someone he knew, but he saw none but strangers, and all stared in astonishment at his white hat and green coat. After travelling abour four versts, he at last saw a face he recognised, and at once hailed it: it was one of the physicians to the commander-in-chief, accompanied by a young doctor; his britzska met Peter's; he knew him at once, and signed to the Cossack who was seated on the box by the side of the coachman, to desire him to stop.

"You, count! What brings you here, excellency?"

"A wish to see what is going on, that is all."

"Aye, aye! Well, you will see plenty to satisfy your curiosity."

Peter got out to talk more at his ease, and expressed his intention of taking part in the battle. The doctor recommended him to speak to the commander-in-chief. "Otherwise you will not be recognised, and get put God knows where. . . . His highness knows you, and will receive you gladly. Take my advice; you will find it to your advantage." The doctor looked weary and hurried.

"Do you think so?" said Peter. "Tell me how our position lies."

"Our position? Oh! that is not in my line; when you have passed Tatarinovo you will see; they are carrying loads of earth; go up the hill, and you will have a view of the whole plain."

"Indeed; but if you . . ."

The doctor broke off, and went towards his carriage. "I would have shown you the way with pleasure, I assure you," he said. "But," he added, with an energetic gesture, "I do not know whether I am on my head or my heels. I am on my way now to the general of the corps, for do you know how we stand? To-morrow we fight a pitched battle; out of 100,000 men we must look for 20,000 wounded, let us say. Well, we have neither stretchers, nor hammocks, nor medical officers, nor surgeons even for 6000; we have 10,000 wagons, to be sure, but, as you may suppose, we require something besides that; and we are told to manage as we can."

Peter stood thinking; out of those hundred thousand healthy men, young and old, some of whom at that moment were gazing in wonder at his white hat, twenty thousand were doomed irrevocably to death or suffering; the thought was acutely painful: "They may be dead to-morrow! How can they think of anything but that?" said he to himself, and a natural association of ideas brought up the picture of the steep street of Mojaïsk, the carts full of wounded, the jangling of bells, the flood of sunshine, and the soldiers' marching chorus. "And the cavalry regiment met all those wounded as it rode on to battle? Each man winks to the wounded and goes on, and never thinks of himself, or of what is awaiting him? but gazes at my hat with surprise—It is strange!" And he went on his way towards Tatarinovo.

On the left stood a handsome country-house, with sentries on guard, and a crowd of carriages, fourgons, and military servants waiting in front. This was the residence of the commander-in-chief; he was absent at the present moment, and had left no representative at home; he and his staff had all gone to a *Te Deum* service. Peter went on to Gorky; having reached the top of the hill, as he went along the narrow village street he saw for the first time a party of militiamen in their white shirts, and caps with the badge of the cross, streaming with heat as they toiled, laughing and talking loudly, at a large earthwork covered with tall grass on the right of the high road. Some were digging, others carrying the soil in wheel-barrows running on boards, while some looked on with their arms crossed. Two officers standing on the top of the mound directed the work. These peasants, who evidently were enjoy-ing the novelty of military employment, reminded Peter of the old soldier's speech: "They are going to throw the nation at the enemy's head!" These bearded labourers, in the heavy boots to which they were not yet accustomed, with their sun-burnt necks and collar-bones showing under their open shirts, made a stronger impression on Peter than anything he had yet seen or heard, and brought home to him all the solemnity and importance of the crisis.

CHAPTER III

PETER mounted this hill, as the doctor had advised. It was now eleven o'clock, the sun, almost overhead, flooded the wide and varied panorama that spread before his eyes in the pure calm atmosphere. On his left the high road to Smolensk zig-zagged up a slope, and traversed a village nestling, with its white church, at about five hundred paces from the foot of the mamelon: this was Borodino. A little farther on the road was carried across a bridge, still mounting to the village of Valouïew, five or six versts away; beyond this village, held just now by the French, it was lost in a dense wood which reached to the horizon. Out of this mass of birches and firs rose a belfry, and a gilt cross twinkling in the sun: these marked the position of the convent of Kolotski. In the blue distance, to the right and left of the forest and the high road, the smoke of the bivouacs could be seen, and the confused masses of Russian and French troops. To the right the undulating ground that bordered the Kolotcha and the Moskva formed a succession of hillocks in which lay the hamlets of Besoukhow and Zaharino; on the left waved endless fields of wheat, surrounding the smoking ruins of Séménovski.

The scene on which Peter looked down on either hand was so ill-defined that nothing answered to his expectations; there was no field of battle such as his imagination had pictured; but meadows, clearings, troops, the smoke of camps and villages, hills, brooks—all so mingled that he could not, in all the smiling landscape, discover exactly what the Russian position actually was, or distinguish their forces from those of the enemy. "I must ask," thought he; and he turned to an officer, who was examining this huge and unmilitary stranger with some curiosity.

"Would you have the goodness to tell me," said Peter, "the name of the village opposite?"

"Bourdino, I believe," said the officer, referring to a comrade.

"Borodino," corrected the other.

The officer, charmed at having an opportunity of talking, went towards Peter.

"And where are our troops?"

"Out there, farther off, and the French, too; don't you see them out there?"

"Where, where?"

"Why, you can see them with the naked eye." And the officer pointed to the smoke rising on the left bank of the river, while his face assumed the grave expression which Peter had already seen on so many others.

"Yes, those are the French?—But down there?" and he pointed to the left of the hill where they stood.

"Well, those are ours!"

"Ours? But beyond again?" And he waved his hand in the direction of a more distant height on which a single tree stood out against the sky, by the side of a village huddled into a hollow where black patches were moving about among thick clouds of smoke.

"'He,' again," [1] replied the officer: it was in fact the out-work of Schevardino. "We were there yesterday, but 'He' is there to-day."

"Then where is our position?"

"Our position?" said the officer, with a polite smile. "I can show you exactly, for it was I who planned the entrenchments. Follow me carefully. Our centre is here, at Borodino," and he pointed to the village. "There is the bridge over the Kolotcha. Do you see a bridge in that little meadow where the hay is lying strewed in heaps? Well, that is our centre. Our right flank is here," and he pointed to the valley on the

---

[1] Napaleon was very commonly spoken of as "*Lui*," both by his enemies and his admirers. A poem of Victor Hugo's begins "*Toujours Lui, Lui partout.*"

right; "out there is the Moskva; you see we have three strong redoubts there. As to the left flank, it is a little difficult to explain"; and he seemed embarrassed. "Yesterday it held Schevardino, where you see that single oak; but we have retired on the left as far as that burnt village and this height," indicating the hill of Raïevsky. "But God alone knows whether the battle will be fought there. 'He,' to be sure, has brought his forces forward on that side, but it is a ruse: he is sure to turn to the right by the Moskva. . . . However, come what may, there will be many missing at the roll-call to-morrow!"

An old sergeant who had come up to them was waiting in silence till his chief had ended his harangue; now, distressed by his last words, he interrupted him, saying gravely, "The gabions must be fetched up."

The officer looked slightly abashed, conscious, no doubt, that though he might be thinking of those that would be missing on the morrow, it did not do to speak of them.

"Very well, send down the third company," he said, sharply. "And who are you?" he went on. "Are you a doctor?"

"No; I only came out of curiosity," said Peter; and he went down the hill again, past the militia party once more.

"Oh, curse them!" said the officer following him, holding his nose and running past the labourers.

"Here she comes! They are bringing her! She is coming! Here she is!" shouted a number of voices.

Officers, regulars, and militia, all rushed to the high road. A procession was coming towards them, up the slope from Borodino.

"It is our Holy Mother, our Guardian, our Mother of Iverskaïa!"

"No, no, it is our Holy Mother of Smolensk," said another.

The militia, the villagers, the fatigue party at work on the battery, all flung down their spades and ran to meet the procession. At the head of it marched the infantry, bareheaded and with arms reversed, along the dusty road; behind them rose a solemn chant. Then came the clergy in full canonicals, represented by one old priest, some deacons, sacristans, and choristers. Some soldiers and officers were carrying a large image with a blackened face in a silver reliquary; this was the Holy Virgin that had been brought away from Smolensk, and that had ever since followed the army. On all sides, before and behind, came the mob of soldiery, marching or running and bowing to the earth.

At last the procession reached the top of the slope. The bearers were relieved by others; the sacristans swung their censers, and the *Te Deum* was chanted. The scorching sun shone straight down, and a light fresh breeze played in the hair of the uncovered heads, and fluttered the streamers that garnished the image; the chant rose heavenward in a soft murmur. A space was left between the officiating priest and the deacons, and here, in the foremost rank, stood the superior officers. One bald general, wearing the cross of St. George, stood stiff and motionless, almost touching the priest—presumably a German, for he did not cross himself, and seemed to be waiting patiently till the ceremony was ended, though he considered it indispensable as reviving the patriotic enthusiasm of the people; another general, a martial figure, crossed himself incessantly while he looked about him.

Peter recognised some of the faces, but he did not think of that; his whole attention was absorbed by the look of rapt devotion with which the soldiers and militia gazed at the miraculous image in their fevered excitement. When the choristers began the invocation to the Virgin—wearily enough, for this was at least the twentieth *Te Deum* they had sung—and the priests and deacons responded in chorus: "Most Holy Virgin, our invisible Bulwark and divine Mediatrix, deliver us thy slaves from disaster when we cry unto Thee!" every face wore that look of solemn feeling which Peter had already noticed in almost everyone he met. Heads were bent, hair thrown back, the men sighed and beat their breasts more vehemently.

Suddenly the whole mass of people moved backward, almost upsetting Peter. A man of high dignity, no doubt, to judge from the eagerness with which all made way for him, came straight up to the image: this was Koutouzow on his way back to Tatarinovo, after reconnoitring the ground. Peter knew him at once. Wrapped in a long military cloak, round-shouldered and bent, with his blind eye, and his broad, fat cheeks, he walked unsteadily into the midst of the circle, paused just behind the priest, crossed himself mechanically, touched the ground with his hand, and bowed his grey head with a deep sigh. Bennigsen and the staff came behind him. Notwithstanding the presence of the commander-in-chief, which had distracted the attention of the generals, the privates and militia continued their prayers without allowing themselves to be disturbed. When the service was over Koutouzow stepped forward, knelt down with difficulty, touched the earth with his forehead, and then tried to rise; but his weight and weakness rendered his efforts futile, and his head shook with short jerks. When at last he had got himself up, he put out his lips as children do and kissed the image. The generals followed his example, then the rest of the officers, and after them the privates and militiamen, pushing and jostling each other.

CHAPTER IV

PETER, borne forward by the crowd, looked vaguely about him.

"Count, Peter Kirilovitch! what brings you here?" said a voice. Peter looked round and saw Boris Droubetzkoï, who came up to him smiling, while he beat off the dust that had clung to his knees in his genuflections. His dress, though suited to a soldier on service, was nevertheless elegant; he wore a long cloak like Koutouzow's, and like him, a whip hanging by a shoulder-strap. Meanwhile, the commander-in-chief had gone into the village of Gorky and was sitting in the shade of a cottage, on a bench that a Cossack had hastily brought out, and that another had covered with a rug. His numerous and splendid suite were standing about him; the procession had gone on its way accompanied by the crowd; and Peter, talking to Boris, found himself within thirty yards of Koutouzow.

"Take my word for it," said Boris to Peter, who had been telling him of his wish to fight, "I shall be happy to do the honours of the count, and the best thing you can do, in my opinion, is to keep with Bennigsen; I am his orderly officer, and I will tell him you are there. If you want to get a good idea of the position, come with us; we are going down to the left flank, and when we come back pray put up at my quarters for the night. We might get a little party together—you know Dmitri Serguéïévitch; he lodges there; and he pointed to the third house in the village street.

"But I wanted to see the right wing. It is said to be very strong; and then I should like to go along the Moskva and see the whole position."

"You can do so, of course, but the left is the more important."

"Can you tell me where to find Prince Bolkonsky's regiment?"

"We shall pass it. I will take you to him."

"What were you going to say about the left?" asked Peter.

"Between ourselves," replied Boris, lowering his voice in a confidential manner, "the left flank is wretchedly placed. Bennigsen had a quite different plan: he was anxious to fortify that mound, out there—but his highness would not have it, for . . ."

Boris did not finish his sentence; he had just seen Koutouzow's aide-de-camp, Kaïssarow, coming their way.

"Paissi Serguéïévitch," said Boris, with an air, "I am trying to explain our position to the count; and I admire his highness's acumen in having guessed the enemy's purpose so well."

"The left flank, you mean?" said Kaïssarow.

"Just so; the left flank is formidable."

Though Koutouzow had reduced his staff, dismissing all the useless members, Boris had contrived to keep his place by attaching himself to Count Bennigsen; who, like everyone else under whose orders Boris had served, entertained a high opinion of him.

The army was indeed divided into two parties—the party of Koutouzow, and that of Bennigsen as chief of staff. Boris managed very skilfully, while he made a show of the greatest respect for Koutouzow, to insinuate that the old man was incapable of the conduct of affairs, and that it was Bennigsen who carried everything with a high hand. They were now on the eve of a decisive event, which must either crush Koutouzow and place the command in Bennigsen's hands, or else, if the Russians gained the day, good care would be taken to make it understood that the honour was due to Bennigsen. In either case rewards of every kind would be rife after the battle, and a number of obscure individuals would be brought to the front. The anticipation put Boris into a state of feverish excitement.

Peter was soon surrounded by several officers of his acquaintance who had followed Kaïssarow; he could scarcely answer all their questions about Moscow, or follow the stories of all kinds that were poured into his ear. The faces round him were anxious and agitated; but it struck him that this agitation was due to matters of purely personal interest, and he involuntarily compared it with that other deep and absorbed expression that he had observed on so many faces;—the look of those who, throwing themselves heart and soul into the national interest, understood that this was a question of life and death to all.

Koutouzow, noticing Peter, sent his aide-de-camp for him; Peter obeyed the summons, but at the same moment a militiaman, slipping in front of him, also approached the commander-in-chief. This was Dologhow.

"And how on earth did that fellow get here?" asked Peter.

"That creature sneaks in everywhere," was the answer. "He was degraded, but he comes up again like a cork . . . he has fifty different schemes in his head, and he made his way as far as the enemy's outposts. He is brave enough, that there is no denying."

Peter respectfully took off his hat as he stood in front of Koutouzow, but Dologhow had got the commander-in-chief's ear.

"I thought," he was saying, "that if I warned your highness, you would pack me off, or say the whole thing was known already."

"Yes, very true," said Koutouzow.

"But, on the other hand, if I should succeed I should be doing a service to my country, for which I am ready to die. If your highness should happen to want a man who is not particular about keeping a whole skin, I beg you will remember me; I might be of use to you."

"Yes, yes," said Koutouzow, looking at Peter out of his one eye, with a smile.

At this instant, Boris, with his courtier-like ease, came forward and stood by Peter, addressing him as if they were in the midst of a conversation: "And you see, count, the militia have got into white shirts to prepare for death. Is not that heroism?"

Boris had spoken with the evident intention of attracting attention; and he had gained his point, for Koutouzow turned to him and asked what he was saying about the militia. He repeated his remark.

"Yes, they are an incomparable race!" said Koutouzow, closing his eye and nodding his head. "Incomparable!" he murmured once more.—"So you want to smell powder?" he went on, addressing Peter. "A very pleasant smell, I have nothing to say against it! I have the honour to stand on the list of your wife's admirers; how is she? My camp is at your service."

As often happens with old people, Koutouzow looked away in an absent manner; he seemed to have forgotten all he had to say, and all he ought to do. Suddenly remembering that he had an order to give, he beckoned Andrew Kaïssarow, the aide-de-camp's brother.

"What are those verses by Marina, the lines about Ghérakow?" he asked. "Repeat them to me."

Kaïssarow repeated them, and Koutouzow nodded his head to the rhythm. When Peter moved away, Dologhow followed him and held out his hand.

"I am delighted to meet you here, count," he observed in a distinct voice, not in the least abashed by the presence of strangers. "On the eve of such a day," he went on with firm solemnity, "of a day when God only knows what awaits each of us, I am glad to have the opportunity of telling you how sorry I am for the misunderstandings that have arisen between us, and I beg you to efface all hatred of me from your heart. —I sincerely ask your pardon."

Peter looked at Dologhow with a smile, not knowing what to say. Dologhow, with tears in his eyes, threw his arms round him. Just then Count Bennigsen, at a hint from Boris, proposed to Peter to accompany a reconnoitring party along the line. "It will interest you," he added.

"Certainly it will," said Peter, and half an hour later Koutouzow made his way home to Tatarinovo, while Bennigsen with his staff and Peter, set off on his round of inspection.

CHAPTER V

BENNIGSEN went along the high road towards the bridge of which the officer had spoken as forming the centre of the Russian position; the hay, lying cut in the meadows on both sides of the river, perfumed the air. Beyond the bridge they rode through the hamlet of Borodino, and then, turning to the left, passed an immense train of soldiers and ammunition wagons coming down in front of a height on which the militia were throwing up earthworks. This redoubt was subsequently known as that of Raïevsky, or the mamelon battery. Peter took no particular note of it; he could not guess that this spot would presently be for him the most memorable point in the battle of Borodino.

They then crossed the hollow that divided it from Sémé-novski: the soldiers were carrying away such timbers as were left of the cottages and barns, and down over the undulating ground they crossed a field of rye, beaten and trampled as if it had been hailed upon, and followed in the path left by the artillery over a ploughed field, to reach the advanced works which were as yet incomplete. Bennigsen stopped and glanced at the redoubt of Schevardino, which had been lost only the day before, and on which a few figures stood out against the sky. Napoleon, the officers declared, or Murat with a staff, and Peter, like them, tried to make out which might be Napoleon. A few minutes later the party went down and disappeared in the distance.

Bennigsen, addressing one of the generals in his suite, explained for all to hear, the position of the Russian forces. Peter did his utmost to comprehend what were the combinations that had given rise to this engagement, but to his great regret he felt that his intelligence was not equal to the task, and that he understood nothing about it. Bennigsen observing his deep attention presently said:

"This cannot interest you, I am afraid?"

"On the contrary," said Peter, not quite truthfully.

Leaving the outworks behind them they got into the high road which went on to the left, winding its way through a wood of birch trees of dense growth but not very tall. In the midst of this wood they started a hare, which sprang into the road at their feet and ran on in front of them for some distance to their great amusement, till it was scared by the sound of horses or of voices, and bolted into a thicket. Two versts farther on they came out on a clearing where Toutchkow's corps were placed to defend the left flank. Having come to the limit of the position Bennigsen stood talking with much vehemence, and Peter concluded that he had come to some supremely important decision. In front of Toutchkow's division there was a knoll which was not occupied by the Russians, and Bennigsen criticised the oversight in strong terms, saying that it was absurd to leave such a commanding spot undefended, and to be satisfied with placing a force in the low ground. Some of the generals agreed with him. One, especially, maintained with military energy that they were exposed to certain death. Bennigsen took upon himself to order the corps to occupy the hillock.

This fresh arrangement of the left wing made Peter feel more than ever his incapacity for understanding the subtle ties of strategy; as he listened to Bennigsen and the generals discussing the question he entirely agreed with them, and was astounded that such a blunder should ever have been committed. Bennigsen, not knowing that the division had been placed there, not to defend the position but to fall upon the foe unawares at a certain juncture, changed the plan without first informing the commander-in-chief.

CHAPTER VI

PRINCE ANDREW, that same afternoon, was lying down in a dilapidated cart-shed in the village of Kniaskovo, at the extreme end of the camp occupied by his regiment. Propped on his elbow he was looking out vaguely, through a crack between the boards, at the line of pollard birches that fenced in the farm, at the field where sheaves of oats lay scattered, and where the smoke rolled up from the fires over which the men's supper was stewing. Sad, dreary, useless, as life now seemed to him, he felt—as seven years since he had felt before Austerlitz—excited and deeply moved. He had given his orders for the morrow; he had nothing more to do; his mind was agitated by curiously vivid, and consequently most gloomy presentiments. He foresaw that this engagement would be the most terrific in which he had as yet borne a part, and the possibility of death rose before him in all its cruel nakedness, apart from its bearings in relation to his present life and from any prospect of the effect it might produce on others. All his past life seemed to present itself, as in a magic lantern, in a long array of pictures which he had never before seen in the true light which now appeared to flood the scenes. "Yes, I see them all, —a series of delusive images which cheated my excited fancy!" thought he, looking at them in the cold relentless glare cast by the presence of death. "I see them plainly now, coarse counterfeits that I once could think beautiful and mysterious. Glory, the public weal, the love of woman and even the love of my country! How grand, how all sufficing they seemed! But in truth everything is colourless, squalid, contemptible, in comparison with the dawn of that day which, I feel, is rising for me!" He dwelt particularly on the three great sorrows of his life: his love for a woman, his father's death, and the French invasion. "Love! That little girl with her halo of charm! How I loved her! and what poetic dreams did I not indulge as I thought of the happiness we were to have together! I believed in an ideal love which would keep her faithful to me during my twelve months' absence; like the pigeon in the fable! Like the gentle dove in the fable she would grow pale and wan in my absence. And it all turned out much simpler. Frightfully simple, and . . . horrible. My father, again, was working and building at Lissy-Gory, confident that everything was absolutely his own: the serfs, the soil, the very air he breathed.

Napoleon came, and without even dreaming of his existence, swept him out of his path like a wisp of straw; Lissy-Gory was engulfed, carrying him with it in its ruin. And Maria persists in saying that it is a trial sent from Heaven! Why a trial— since he is no more; whom is it to try? And Russia, and Moscow—lost! Who knows? To-morrow I may be killed by one of our own men, just as I might have been yesterday by that private who accidentally discharged his gun close to my ear. Then the French will come and take me head and heels, and pitch me into a grave that the smell of my carcase may not make them sick; and then life in general will go on under new conditions, just as natural in their turn as the old ones—and I shall not be there to see!" He looked again at the row of birches whose silvery bark, standing out from the duller tints, shone in the sun: "Well, well, let them kill me to-morrow; there will be an end of it, and no more of me!" He pictured the world without himself; the waving, shadowy birches, the fleecy clouds, the camp-fires; everything suddenly took a terrible and sinister aspect; he shivered and started up to go out and walk about.

He heard voices: "Who goes there?" he cried.

Timokhine, the red-nosed captain, formerly the captain of Dologhow's company, and now for lack of officers promoted to be head of a battalion, came up shyly, followed by the aide-de-camp and the paymaster of the regiment. Prince Andrew listened to their report, gave them instructions, and was about to dismiss them, when he heard a well-known voice:

"Deuce take it!" said the voice.

Bolkonsky turned round and saw Peter, who had knocked himself against a water-spout. It was always distressing to Prince Andrew to come across anyone who reminded him of the past, and the sight of Peter, who had been so much mixed up with the unhappy events of his last stay at Moscow, was keenly painful.

"What! You?" he said. "By what strange chance? I certainly did not expect to see you!" As he spoke his eyes and face assumed a hard, almost a repellent expression; Peter could not fail to observe it, and it changed the warmth of his address into embarrassment.

"I came—well, you know—in short, I came because it is extremely interesting," he replied, using the same phrase for the hundredth time that day: "I wanted to see a battle."

"And your brethren the freemasons? What will they say

to that?" said Prince Andrew ironically. "What is doing at Moscow, and what are my people about? Have they got there at last?" he added more gravely.

"They were there, Julia Droubetzkoï told me so. I went at once to call, but missed them: they had gone on, into the country."

CHAPTER VII

THE officers were about to leave Prince Andrew with his friend, but Bolkonsky, not caring for a *tête-à-tête*, detained them, offering them a glass of tea. They looked with some curiosity at Peter's Herculean proportions, and listened without any excitement to his account of the state of Moscow and of the position of the troops he had seen. Prince Andrew kept silence, and his unpleasant expression led Peter to address himself in preference to Timokhine, who listened to him with frank good humour.

"And you really understood the arrangement of our troops?" asked Prince Andrew, suddenly interrupting him.

"Yes. So far, that is to say, as a civilian can understand such things. I got an idea of the general plan."

"Then you know more about it than any other man alive!" retorted Prince Andrew in French.

"Eh. . . . !" said Peter much puzzled, and looking over his spectacles. "But what, then, do you think of Koutouzow's appointment?"

"It gave me great pleasure. That is all I have to say about it."

"And what is your opinion of Barclay de Tolly? God knows what they don't say of him at Moscow! What do they think of him here?"

"Ask these gentlemen," replied his friend.

Peter turned to Timokhine with the friendly smile that everyone involuntarily wore when speaking to the worthy captain.

"His highness's appearance at the head of the army threw daylight on the matter," replied Timokhine, with a timid glance at his chief.

"How was that?" asked Peter.

"For instance, as to wood and forage. When we began our retreat after Svendziani, we dared not take hay or fuel anywhere, and yet we were leaving it behind. It was all left for 'Him'—was it not, excellency?" he added, turning to "his prince." "And woe to us if we touched it! Two officers of our regiment were tried for offences of that sort. But when his highness took the command, it was all as clear as day."

"But why was it forbidden?"

Timokhine, quite confused, did not know how to answer this question; Peter repeated it, however, turning to Bolkonsky.

"In order not to spoil the country for the enemy," said Prince Andrew, still sardonically. "It was a very wise measure, for pillage must be put down at any cost! And at Smolensk, he judged equally wisely, that as the French were superior to us in numbers, they could no doubt turn us. But what he could not understand," he suddenly broke out, instinctively raising his voice, "was that we were defending Russian soil for the first time, and that our troops fought with a spirit that I have never seen equalled. That we had held out bravely for two days, and that this success increased our strength tenfold, he nevertheless ordered a retreat, and all our efforts and losses were rendered futile! Of course he did not mean to betray us, he had foreseen it all, and did what he could for the best. But that is the very reason why he is good for nothing. He is good for nothing at all, because he thinks too much, and looks at things too closely—all the Germans do. Besides— how shall I explain myself?—Supposing your father has a German servant, an excellent servant, who, under ordinary circumstances, does him a variety of service which you could not render—if your father falls ill you will send the man away, and nurse your father with your own clumsy hands; and you will soothe your father's pain better than any stranger could, however clever. It is the very same thing with regard to Barclay: as long as Russia was well and flourishing, a foreigner could do her work, but in the hour of danger she needs a man of her own blood! At your club, I believe, he was accused of treachery? And what will be the upshot of these fictitious calumnies? Why, we shall rush into the opposite extreme; we shall be ashamed of such an odious imputation, and to make amends we shall treat him as a hero, which will be just as iniquitous. He is neither more nor less than a worthy and pedantic German."

"And yet," observed Peter, "he is said to be a good commander."

"I do not know what that means," said Bolkonsky.

"Well," said Peter, "a good commander is a man who leaves nothing to chance; who can guess what is in his enemy's mind."

"That is impossible," said Bolkonsky, positively, as if this was a point he had settled long ago in his own mind. Peter looked up in surprise.

"And yet," said he. "Do they not say that war is like a game of chess?"

"With this slight difference," said Prince Andrew, "that in a game of chess you can take your time, quite at your ease. Besides, the knight is always stronger than a pawn, and two pawns stronger than one; while in war a battalion is sometimes stronger than a division, and sometimes weaker than a single company. The relations of the strength of two armies is always an unknown quantity. You may depend upon it, that if the result were always directly due to the orders given by the staff, I would have remained a staff-officer, and have given orders with as good a grace as any man; instead of which, as you see, I have the honour to serve with these gentlemen, and command a regiment; and I am firmly persuaded that the issue of to-morrow's engagement will rest with us rather than with them. Victory never can be, and never has been the outcome of position, or numbers, or the character of the arms; least of all of position."

"Of what then?" asked Peter.

"Of the feeling that dwells in me—in him," and he pointed to Timokhine—"in every soldier." Timokhine gazed in amazement at his chief, whose excitement at this moment was in singular contrast with his usual reserve and calm demeanour. It was evident that he could not help giving utterance to the thoughts that crowded on him. "The battle is always won by the leader who is most determined to win it. Why did we lose the battle of Austerlitz? Our losses were not greater than those of the French, but we were in too great a hurry to believe ourselves beaten; and we believed it because we did not care about fighting out there, and were anxious to get away from the field of battle. 'We have lost the game; let us be off'— and off we went! If we had not said that until the evening God knows what the issue might have been;—we shall not say it to-morrow! You say the left wing is weak, and the right too much extended. That is absurd, and not of the smallest consequence; but just think of what lies before us to-morrow. A thousand incalculable chances, any of which may prove decisive in an instant! Our men or theirs may turn and fly—this one or that may be killed! What has been done to-day is mere child's play, and the men who went round with you to inspect the positions, can do nothing to help the march of events; on the contrary, they hinder it if anything, for they look to nothing but their personal interests."

"What! Now at this moment?" asked Peter.

"This moment," replied Prince Andrew, "is nothing to them, but the moment when it is most easy to supplant a rival and clutch at a ribbon or a cross. I, for my part, see just this: a hundred thousand Russians and a hundred thousand French will meet to fight to-morrow. The side that fights hardest and spares itself least will win the day; nay more. I tell you this: come what may, and whatever the antagonism of our generals may be, *we* shall win the day!"

"That is the truth, and the whole truth, excellency," murmured Timokhine, "we must not spare ourselves! . . . Would you believe that the men of my battalion would not touch their brandy? It is not a time for that, they say."

There was silence after this. The officers presently rose, and Prince Andrew went out with them to give his last orders. Just then horses' hoofs were heard approaching along the high road. Prince Andrew, looking round, recognised Woltzogen and Klauzevitz, followed by a Cossack; they passed so close that Peter and Bolkonsky could hear them talking in German.

"The war must spread—that is our only hope."

"Yes," replied the other. "From the moment when the first point is to weaken the enemy, the loss of a few men more or less cannot matter."

"To be sure," said the first speaker.

"Oh! yes, spread the war!" said Prince Andrew, passionately. "That is how my father, my sister, and my boy have gone down before it! Much he cares! That is just what I was telling you: these German gentry are not the men to win the battle, take my word for it. All they will do is to shuffle the cards as much as possible; for that German's head contains nothing but a heap of arguments of which the best is no sounder than an egg-shell, while he has not in his soul one grain of the stuff that is in Timokhine, and which will be needed to-morrow. They have handed over all Europe to 'Him,' and now they want to teach us! A pretty lesson, on my word!"

"And you think we shall beat them?"

"Yes," said Prince Andrew, absently. "But there is one thing I would not have allowed if I could have prevented it, and that is giving quarter. Why take prisoners? It is mere

Quixotism! The French have destroyed my home; they are about to destroy Moscow; they are my enemies; they are criminals! Timokhine and all the army feel the same; they can never be our friends, in spite of all they could say at Tilsit."

"Yes, certainly!" cried Peter, with sparkling eyes, "there I entirely agree with you."

The problem which had been tormenting him ever since he had left Mojaïsk had, in fact, found a clear and final solution. He now understood the meaning and solemnity of the war, and of the battle about to be fought. All that he had seen in the course of the day: the expression of gravity and devotion on the soldiers' faces, the latent heat of patriotism—to use a metaphor from physics—which glowed in each man, were now intelligible to him, and he no longer wondered at the calmness, the positive indifference even, with which they prepared to meet death.

"If no prisoners were taken," Bolkonsky went on, "the aspect of war would alter; and believe me it would be less cruel. But we have only been playing at war; that is where the mistake lies. We play the magnanimous, and such generosity and sensibility are on a par with those of a milksop who turns sick at seeing a calf killed: the sight of blood disgusts his instinctive delicacy; but dress the veal with a savoury sauce, and he will eat it with the rest of us. They preach at us about the laws of warfare, chivalry, flags of truce, humanity to the wounded, and what not! But this is only throwing dust in each other's eyes. I saw some of this chivalry in 1805; we were duped, and we deceived them in our turn. Homes are made desolate, false money is circulated, our fathers or our children are murdered—and then we are to listen to a rhodomontade about the rules of war and generosity towards our enemies! No quarter, I say. Kill without ruth, and be ready to be killed! The man who has come to this conclusion, as I have, through the most cruel suffering . . ." Prince Andrew had worked himself up for a moment into a belief that he could bear to see Moscow fall as Smolensk had done; but he broke off. A spasm in his throat choked him, and he walked on a few steps in silence; when he spoke again his eyes glittered fiercely, and his lips were quivering.

"If there were no such false generosity in war it would not be undertaken but for weighty reasons, with the knowledge that it meant death; not because Paul Ivanovitch had given offence to Michael Ivanovitch! All these Hessians and

Westphalians that Napoleon has dragged at his heels would never have come to Russia, and we should not have gone to fight in Austria and Prussia, without knowing wherefore. The fearful necessity of war ought only to be taken seriously and sternly. There are lies enough in the world as it is. War should be treated as a hard fact; not as a game; otherwise it becomes a mere pastime for the idle and frivolous. There is no more honourable class than the military, and yet to what extremities they are driven to gain their ends! In fact, what is the aim and end of war?—Murder.—And its means?—Treachery and spying.—Its procedure? Pillage and robbery for the maintenance of the men! . . . That is to say, falsehood and dishonesty in every form, under the name of the Art of War.—What, I ask you, is the rule to which military men are bound? To slavery, that is to say, to a rigorous discipline, which condones indolence, ignorance, cruelty, depravity, drunkenness—and yet they are universally respected. Every monarch in the world, except the Emperor of China, wears a military uniform, and the man who has killed the greatest number of his fellow-creatures wins the highest rewards. A million of men meet—as they will to-morrow, for instance—to massacre and maim each other; and what follows next? Why, *Te Deums* and solemn thanksgivings for the great number of slain—though the figures, to be sure, are always exaggerated; and the victory is loudly boasted of, for the more men are killed the more brilliant it is thought to be, and those prayers! How can they be acceptable to God, looking down on the world? Ah! my friends, life has been a grievous burden to me during these last months; I see too far into things, and it goes hard with man when he has eaten of the tree of knowledge of good and evil. However, it is not for long now! . . . But forgive me; my wandering talk will have wearied you—as it has me . . . It is late; go back to Gorky."

"No, indeed!" exclaimed Peter, fixing a scared but sympathetic look on his friend's face.

"Yes, go; we must sleep before fighting," said Prince Andrew, going up to Peter and embracing him warmly. "Good-bye. Shall we ever meet again? God knows!" He pushed him to the door and turned away.

It was now dusk, and Peter could not read the expression of his face. Was it tender or stern? He paused a moment in doubt; should he go in to him again or return to headquarters.

"No, he does not want me; I know that this is our last

meeting," he concluded; and with a deep sigh he set out for Gorky.

Prince Andrew stretched himself on a rug, but he could not sleep. Among the medley of thoughts and memories that whirled through his brain he lingered over one with tender emotion: it was that of a certain evening at St. Petersburg, when Natacha had told him, with wonderful spirit, of how, in the previous summer, she had lost her way one day when she had gone out to gather mushrooms in a vast forest. She had described in broken sentences the silence of the woods, her emotions, and her talk with an old man who kept bees, interrupting herself constantly to say: "No, not exactly that—I can never express precisely what I mean—I am sure you can not quite understand! . . ." And in spite of Prince Andrew's assurances, she was vexed with herself for not being able to give an adequate idea of the lofty and poetic feeling that filled her then. "The old man was quite charming—and the forest was so dark—and he had such good, kind eyes—but oh! I cannot tell you, I can never tell a thing properly!" and she blushed crimson. Prince Andrew smiled at the recollection, as he had smiled at the time when he looked at her. "I understood her then," thought he. "I understood her simplicity and the ingenuousness of her soul; yes, it was her soul that was so dear to me, that I loved so perfectly, so fervently, with a love that made me exquisitely happy!" But he shuddered, suddenly remembering what the end had been. "*He* did not want all that; He could not see nor understand. To him she was nothing but a pretty, fresh creature whom he disdained to link with his fate, while to me——. And *he* is still living and enjoying himself!" But at this reflection he winced as if he had been branded with a hot iron; he started to his feet and again took to walking up and down his room.

CHAPTER VIII

ON the 6th of September, the eve of the battle of Borodino, arrived Monsieur de Beausset, Master of the Household to the Emperor of the French, and Colonel Fabvier, one from Paris, the other from Madrid; they found Napoleon in his camp at Valouiew. Monsieur de Beausset, in court uniform, heralded his approach by sending in a packet addressed to the emperor which he had been charged to deliver. He went into the outer room of the imperial tent and undid the wrapper as he stood talking with the aides-de-camp. Fabvier, pausing at the threshold, was speaking to someone outside. Napoleon was dressing in the inner room, which was his bedroom, turning himself about for his valet to brush him—first his broad shoulders and then his bulky person, with evident enjoyment. Another valet, holding his finger loosely over the mouth of a bottle, was sprinkling his master's fat person with eau de Cologne, with intense conviction that he alone knew how many drops were needed, or exactly where to shed them. The emperor's closely cropped hair clung to his brow with the moisture, and his face, though sallow and puffy, expressed physical welfare.

"Go on, harder, go on," he said to the valet, who brushed away with renewed vigour.

An aide-de-camp, who had come with a report of the engagement of the day before and of the number of prisoners, was awaiting his dismissal in the doorway. Napoleon glanced at him with a sidelong scowl.

"What?" he said. "No prisoners! then they prefer to be cut to pieces. So much the worse for the Russian army!" Then, still turning his wide back and shoulders to the soothing friction of the brush—"Very good; show in Messieurs de Beausset and Fabvier.

"Yes, sire" said the aide-de-camp, hurrying off.

The two valets dressed their master in less than no time, in the dark blue uniform of the Guards, and he went into the larger room with a firm, quick step. Meanwhile Beausset had hastily unpacked the present from the empress, and had placed it on two chairs in front of the door the emperor must come in by; but Napoleon had finished his toilet so promptly that Beausset had not had time to arrange it quite to his satisfaction. It was to be a surprise to his majesty. Napoleon saw that he was embarrassed about something, but, pretending not to have noticed it, he signed to Fabvier to come forward. He listened with his brows knit and in utter silence to the colonel's laudatory report of the troops' fighting at Salamanca—at the other side of the world—who, according to his description of them, had but one absorbing idea: that of proving worthy of their emperor; and but one single fear: that of displeasing him. Nevertheless the result had not been victory; and Napoleon comforted himself by asking sarcastic questions, which tended to show that he expected nothing better when he was not on the spot.

"I must make up for it at Moscow," said Napoleon. "Good-bye for the present"; and he turned to Beausset, who had had time to throw a drapery over the empress's gift.

Beausset came forward with an elaborate French bow, such as none ever learned to make but the old courtiers of the Bourbon days—and handed him a sealed letter. Napoleon sportively pinched his ear.

"You have made haste," he said, "and I am glad of it. Well, and what is the news from Paris?" he added, suddenly looking grave.

"Sire, all Paris bewails your absence," replied the courtier.

Napoleon knew perfectly well that this was merely skilful flattery. In his more lucid moments he also knew that it was false; but the phrase pleased him, and again he pinched Beausset's ear.

"I am sorry," he said, "to have brought you so far."

"Sire, I fully expected to follow you to the gates of Moscow."

Napoleon smiled, and glanced carelessly to the right. An aide-de-camp, with a graceful bow, offered him a gold snuff-box.

"Yes, you are in luck," said he, taking a pinch. "You like travelling, and in three days you will be at Moscow. You did not expect ever to see the Asiatic capital?"

Beausset bowed in gratitude to his sovereign for having invented a taste for him of which he himself had no suspicion.

"Ah! what is that?" said Napoleon, observing the attention of the suite directed to a hanging. Beausset, with the neatness of an accomplished courtier, deftly skipped round and whipped away the curtain, saying:

"It is a present sent by the empress to your majesty."

It was a portrait, painted by Gérard, of the child born of the marriage of Napoleon with the daughter of the Emperor of Austria and who was known as the King of Rome. The lovely little boy, with curly hair and eyes like those of the Infant Christ in Sistine Madonna, was playing with a cup and ball: the ball represented the terrestrial globe, while the cup, reversed, was a sceptre. Though it was hard to say why the artist should have painted the King of Rome as piercing the globe with a spike, the conceit was thought as clear and subtle by all who had seen the picture at Paris, as, at this moment, it seemed to Napoleon himself.

"The King of Rome!" he exclaimed, with a gracious movement. "Admirable!" He had a peculiarly Italian facility

in changing the expression of his face, and he went up to the
portrait with a look of tender pathos. He knew that his
every gesture and word on this occasion would be engraved
on the page of history. Hence it struck him that, in contrast
to such a height of power as could allow of his baby son being
represented playing cup and ball with the world, simply paternal
affection would be the happiest inspiration. His eyes dimmed
with emotion, he stepped forward, glancing round for a chair;
the chair was instantly placed, and he seated himself in front
of the picture. Then at a wave of his hand the bystanders
all retired on tiptoe, leaving the great man to his feelings.
After a few moments of silent contemplation, and after touching
the rough surface of the portrait with his finger, without any
clear idea of why he did so, he recalled Beausset and the aide-
de-camp; he desired that the portrait should be displayed outside his tent, that the "Vieille Garde" might have the pleasure
of gazing on the King of Rome, their adored sovereign's son and
heir. The result was as he had anticipated: while he was at
breakfast—having done Monsieur de Beausset the honour of
inviting him to share the meal—an outburst of enthusiasm from
the officers and soldiers of the Old Guard became audible outside.

"*Vive l'Empereur ! Vive le Roi de Rome !*"

When breakfast was over Napoleon dictated his order of the
day to Beausset.

"Short, and to the point!" was his comment, as he read over
the address which he had dictated without a pause.

"Soldiers!"

"We are about to fight the battle you have so eagerly desired.
Victory depends on you; but victory is indispensable—it will
give us victuals in abundance, good winter-quarters, and an
early return to France. Behave as you behaved at Austerlitz,
at Friedland, at Vitebsk, at Smolensk, so that your remotest
posterity may speak of your conduct this day, and say of each
man among you: 'He was at that great battle!'

"Napoleon."

He invited Monsieur Beausset—who was so fond of travelling—to accompany him, and went out of his tent towards the
horses which had just been saddled.

"Your majesty is too good!" said Beausset, though he
desperately needed sleep and could not ride; but when
Napoleon bowed his head Beausset had no choice but to follow.

As the emperor appeared on the scene the shouts of the

veterans who had crowded round the picture rose to frenzy. Napoleon knit his brows.

"Take him away," he said, pointing to the portrait; "he is too young yet to look on at a battle."

Beausset closed his eyes and bent his head with a deep sigh, testifying by his reverential demeanour his appreciation of the emperor's sentiments.

CHAPTER IX

OUR historian of Napoleon has depicted him as spending the morning of that day on horseback, inspecting the ground, discussing the various plans submitted to him by his marshals, and giving orders to his generals.

The original line of the Russian army along the Kolotcha had been driven back, and part of it, particularly the left flank, had retired after the capture of the redoubt of Schevardino. This wing was therefore no longer protected either by out-works or by the river; it faced an open and level plain. It was as evident to a civilian as to a soldier that the attack must begin on this point. This, it would seem could hardly need any very profound calculations, nor any minute elaboration by Napoleon and his marshals, nor that peculiar insight recognised as genius which is so usually attributed to the Corsican; however, he himself and those who were about his person were not of this opinion, and the historians, who have since described these events, have joined in the chorus.

While he rode over the whole position, examining every detail with anxious meditation, he shook his head—now doubt-fully and now approvingly—and without communicating to his staff the profound reflections which led to his conclusions, he simply expressed those conclusions in the form of commands. Davoust, Prince of Eckmühl, having hazarded an opinion that it would be well to turn the Russian left, Napoleon replied, without giving any reason, that it would be quite unnecessary. On the other hand he approved General Compans's plan, which consisted in an attack on the advanced works, and then pushing forward through the woods, though Ney, Duke of Elchingen, ventured to remark that moving across the forest might be dangerous and disorder the ranks. As he studied the spot facing the redoubt at Schevardino, he reflected in silence for

some minutes, and then pointed out two points where he wished
batteries to be placed on the morrow to fire against the Russian.
works; also the position to be occupied by the field-guns.

These various arrangements which have given rise to the
most unbounded admiration on the part of French historians,
and unanimous approbation among foreigners, were laid down
as follows:

"Two new batteries are to be thrown up during the night
on the plain occupied by the Prince of Eckmühl, and to open
fire, at daybreak, on the enemy's two batteries opposite.

"General Pernetti, colonel of the 1st Artillery Corps, is to
advance with 30 guns of Compans' division and all the howitzers
of the Desaix and Friant divisions; he is to open fire, and throw
his shells on the enemy's battery, which will thus be attacked by

Guns of the artillery of the Guards . .	24
Guns of Compans's division . . .	30
Guns of Desaix's and Friant's divisions . .	8
	—
In all . .	62

"General Fouché, in command of the 3rd Artillery Corps, is
to bring up the howitzers of the 3rd and 8th Corps, in all 16
guns, to flank the battery which is to bombard the work on
the left, thus bringing 40 guns to bear on that redoubt.

"General Sorbier will remain in readiness to advance at the
first word, with all the guns of the Artillery Guards, against
either of the enemy's entrenchments.

"During the cannonade Prince Poniatowski must march
down on the village in the forest and turn the enemy's position.

"General Compans is to go through the forest and seize the
first entrenchment.

"As soon as the action has fairly started on these lines,
further orders will be issued according to the enemy's movements.

"The left wing is to open fire as soon as that of the right
wing makes itself heard. Morand's division of sharpshooters
and the Viceroy's division are to open fierce fire as soon as the
attack on the right is begun.

"The Viceroy must seize the village,[1] crossing its three bridges,
and advancing on the same line as Morand's and Gérard's
divisions, which being led by him, will march on the redoubt,
and join the other troops.

[1] Borodino.

"The whole to be carried out with strict good order, and keeping some troops in reserve as far as possible.

"Given at the Imperial Camp at Mojaïsk, Sept. 6th, 1812."

If the arrangements of such a man as Napoleon may be criticised independently of the influence of his genius, which was almost a superstition, it is very evident that these orders are deficient in conciseness and accuracy. They resolve themselves, in fact, into four lines of action, neither of which could be—or was—carried out. First: *the batteries placed on a spot selected by Napoleon, and strengthened by the guns under Pernetti and Fouché, 102 in all, were to open fire and silence the advance works on the Russian side*. Now it was impossible to effect this, because the French projectiles could not be thrown far enough to fall within the enemy's works, so that these 102 guns were firing in the air till one of the generals took upon himself to send them forward, against the emperor's orders.

The second command, by which *Poniatowski was to march down on the village through the forest, and to turn the Russian left*, could not be obeyed, since Poniatowski was met in the forest by Toutchkow, who barred the way and prevented his turning the position pointed out to him. The third instructed *General Compans's corps to go by the forest and seize the first entrenchment;* but it failed to do so, because, on leaving the forest, it found itself obliged to re-form under the fire of Russian musketry, a circumstance of which Napoleon could not be aware. With regard to the fourth arrangement, by which *the viceroy was to take the village of Borodino, and, after crossing the river by the three bridges, to follow the same line of march as the divisions under Morand and Friant* (it may be noted that what that line was to be is nowhere indicated). *They were, however, to proceed to the redoubt, under his command, and form in a line with the other troops*. So far as it is possible to make anything of this unintelligible order by the light of the efforts made by the viceroy to carry it out, it would seem that he was to make his way to the left towards the redoubt after passing through the village of Borodino, while Morand's and Frian's divisions advanced in front of the line. All this was impossible.

The viceroy got through Borodino, but was beaten on the Kolotcha, and Morand and Friant, after experiencing the same fate, failed to take the redoubt, which only yielded to the cavalry towards the end of the engagement. So that none of the orders was or could have been carried into effect.

It was added that *subsequent commands would be issued according to the movements of the enemy.* It was, therefore, to be presumed that Napoleon would take the necessary measures during the progress of the engagement; but he did nothing of the kind; for, as afterwards transpired, he was himself so far from the centre of the action that he could not follow it, and none of the orders he issued during the fight could possibly be executed.

CHAPTER X

SEVERAL historians have asserted that the Russians won the day at Borodino because Napoleon was suffering from a cold. But for that cold, his combinations would have borne the stamp of genius throughout, Russia would have lost, and the face of the world would have been changed. Such a conclusion, namely that Russia remained great because Napoleon had a cold in his head on the 6th, may be held indisputable by writers who can maintain that the mere sovereign will of Peter the Great transformed Russia; or that the will of Napoleon alone metamorphosed the French Republic into an empire, and bore the arms of France on to Russian soil. If it had indeed depended on him whether the action were fought or not, whether this or that decision were taken or not, that cold, by paralysing his energies, would in fact have been the direct cause of Russia's escape; and the valet who, on the 4th September, neglected to give him waterproof boots, might be called her deliverer. Granting such logic as this, the inference as is plausible as Voltaire's when, in jest, he ascribed the massacre of St. Bartholomew to Charles IX. having a fit of indigestion. But to those who cannot accept this manner of argument, such a reflection is simply absurd, and in obvious contradiction to human reason. To the question as to what is the real causation of historical events, it seems to us much simpler to say that the course of this world is foreordained, and depends on the coincidence of the wills of all those who are concerned in the issues; so that the good pleasure of a Napoleon has only a superficial influence.

And though it may at first seem hard to believe that the great massacre decreed by the desire of Charles IX. was not the outcome of his will, or that the slaughter at Borodino of some 80,000 men was not the act and deed of Napoleon, though the orders were given by them, I feel justified in coming to this conclusion by a due consideration of the dignity of humanity, which convinces me that every man is as much a Man as Napoleon himself; and this is confirmed in many ways by the researches of historians. On the day of Borodino Napoleon neither aimed a gun nor killed a man. Everything was done by his soldiers, who killed their enemies, in obedience, not to his orders, but to their own impulse. The whole army— French, Germans, Italians, and Poles—hungry, tattered, worn out by the marches they had made, felt, as they stood face to face with this other army stopping their way, that "the cork was out and the wine must be drunk." If Napoleon had forbidden them to fight the Russians they would have murdered him and have fought afterwards, for it had become inevitable.

When Napoleon's address was read to the troops, promising them as a compensation for suffering and death, that posterity would say of them that "they too were at that great battle," they had shouted "*Vive l'Empereur!*" as they had done just before in front of the picture of the child playing cup and ball with the world—as they had done at all the nonsense he had ever talked to them. They had in fact no choice but to shout, "*Vive l'Empereur!*" and then fight for the food and rest which, if they won the victory, awaited them at Moscow. They did not, then, kill their fellow-creatures by their master's orders; the battle was not of Napoleon's ordering, since none of his commands were carried out, and he did not know what was going on; hence the question as to whether Napoleon had a cold or no is of no more consequence to history than the cold of the rawest recruit.

Historians also ascribe to this legendary cold the weakness of his arrangements; while we, on the contrary, think the plan was a better one than those by which he had won many another battle; they only seem weaker on looking back because Borodino was the first action in which Napoleon was repulsed. The most learned and ingenious schemes always seem bad and give rise to the severest strictures when they have not resulted in victory, and *vice versa*. Weirother's plans of action at Austerlitz, for instance, were a model of exactitude, and yet they were criticised for this very exactitude and minuteness.

Napoleon played his part as representative of absolute power quite as well at Borodino as at his other battles—perhaps better. He had kept within the limits of strict sagacity. No confusion or contradiction can be imputed to him; he did not lose his head; he did not quit the field of action; and his tact and great experience helped him to fill the part of supreme ruler, as it seemed, in this bloody tragedy, with calmness and dignity.

CHAPTER XI

NAPOLEON was thoughtful as he returned from his tour of inspection. "The pieces are on the board," said he to himself. "To-morrow we play the game." He called for a glass of punch, and then sent for Beausset to discuss certain alterations to be made in the empress's household; and he astonished the courtier by his accurate recollection of the smallest details of the court at home.

He took an interest in all sorts of trifles, and laughed at Beausset for his love of travelling, chatting with cool ease as a great surgeon might as he turns up his cuffs and ties on his apron while the patient is bound to the operating table: "This business is my affair," he seemed to imply. "All the wires are in my hands. When it is necessary to act I shall do it better than anyone—for the present I like to amuse myself. The more I laugh and the cooler I am, the more confident and hopeful you may feel; and the more you ought to wonder at my genius.

After a second glass of punch he went to lie down; the anticipation of the morrow would not allow him to sleep, and though the evening damp had increased his cold, he got up at about three in the morning, and went into the outer room of the tent, which he used as his drawing-room, blowing his nose noisily. He asked whether the Russians were still in position, and was told that the enemy's fires were burning on the same spot. The aide-de-camp on duty came in.

"Well, Rapp, do you think we shall make a good job of it to-day?"

"Not a doubt of it, sire."

The emperor looked at him.

"Do you recollect, sire, what you did me the honour to say to me at Smolensk: 'The cork is drawn and the wine must be drunk.'"

Napoleon frowned and was silent.

"My poor army!" he said after a pause. "It has greatly diminished since Smolensk. Fortune is a fickle hussy, Rapp;

I always said so, and now I am learning it by experience. But the Guards—the Guards are complete are they not?"

"Yes, sire."

Napoleon put a lozenge into his mouth and then looked at his watch; he was not sleepy, and it would not be morning yet awhile; there were no orders to give to kill the time; everything was ready.

"Have the regiments of Guards had their biscuits given out?"

"Yes, sire."

"And rice?"

Rapp said that he himself had delivered the emperor's orders to that end, but Napoleon was not satisfied and shook his head: he seemed to doubt whether the order had been carried out. A valet brought some more punch and Napoleon ordered a glass for the aide-de-camp; as he sipped it he said: "I can neither taste nor smell; this cold is intolerable, and doctors and medicine are preached at me, when they cannot even cure me of a cold! Corvisart has given me some lozenges, but they do me no good! The fact is they do not know how to treat everything, and they never will. Our body is just a living machine. That is what it is made for and that is its nature. Leave life to take care of itself, and it will fight its own battles a great deal better than if you paralyse its powers by weighting it with remedies. Our body is like a good watch, made to go a certain time; but no watchmaker can open it; he can only treat it blindfold and feeling his way. Our body is a living machine, neither more nor less."

Having started on definitions, for which he had a great weakness, he went on suddenly:

"Do you know what the art of war is? It is the talent of being stronger than the enemy at a given moment."

Rapp made no answer.

"To-morrow we shall have Koutouzow to deal with. He commanded at Braunau; do you remember? And for three weeks he has not once got on horseback to inspect his defences! Well, we shall see."

Again he looked at his watch: it was only four o'clock. He did not feel like sleeping; the punch was finished and still there was nothing to do. He rose, walked up and down, put on a greatcoat and went out. It was a dark night; a thin fog filled the air. The bivouac fires of the Guards were hardly visible through the smoke; those of the Russian outposts glimmered in

the distance. All was still: nothing could be heard but the
hollow tramp of the French troops making ready to march down
to their positions. Napoleon went forward, studying the fires
and listening to the growing noise; as he passed a tall guardsman,
on guard in front of the imperial tent—who stood upright and
motionless as a pillar on seeing his majesty—he stopped to
speak to him.

"How many years have you served?" he asked, with the
kindly, military bluntness which he effected in addressing his
soldiers. "Ah! one of the old ones I see! And the rice?
Has it been served out?"

"Yes, your majesty."

Napoleon nodded and walked on.

At half-past five he mounted his horse and rode towards
Schevardino. Dawn was growing from grey to white, the sky
brightening rapidly; one cloud hung over the east. The
deserted fires were dying out in the pale daylight. Then, to
the right, one deep, rolling cannon-shot rang out and died away
into silence again. Soon a second and a third rent the air, then
a fourth and fifth echoed the knell from some nearer spot on the
right. Their growl had not died away when a fiercer roar took
it up on all sides. Napoleon and his suite made their way to
Schevardino and dismounted—the action had begun.

CHAPTER XII

When Peter returned to Gorky after his visit to Prince Andrew,
he desired his servant to have his horses ready saddled and to
wake him at daybreak; then he went soundly to sleep in the
corner that Boris had so obligingly offered him. When he
awoke the cottage was empty, the little panes in the windows
were trembling, and his man was shaking him to rouse him.

"Excellency, excellency!" the servant kept on obstinately
repeating, looking away and shaking Peter by the shoulder,
seemingly having lost all hope of ever waking him.

"Why—what is the matter? Is it begun?"

"Listen to the cannonade," said the man, who was an old
soldier. "They have all been gone a long time; even his
highness."

Peter hastily dressed and ran out. It was a brilliant, delicious
morning, dew-drops sparkled everywhere; the sun sent level

rays through the curtain of cloud, and a shaft of light fell across
the roof and through the hanging mist, on the dusty road just
moist with the dew, on the walls of the houses, the rough wood
palings, and the horses standing saddled at the door. The roar
of the cannon grew louder and louder.

"Make haste, count, if you want to be in time!" shouted an
aide-de-camp as he galloped past.

Peter started on foot, his man leading the horses, and made
his way by the road as far as the knoll from whence he had
surveyed the field the day before. This mamelon was crowded
with military; the staff-officers could be heard talking French,
and conspicuous among them all was Koutouzow's grey head
under a white cap bound with red, his fat neck sunk in his broad
shoulders. He was studying the distance through a field-glass.

As he climbed the slope Peter was struck by the scene that
spread before him. It was the same landscape that he had
seen yesterday, but swarming now with an imposing mass of
troops, wrapped in wreaths of smoke and lighted up by the low
sun which was rising on the left and filling the pure upper air
with quivering rose and gold, while on the earth lay long masses
of black shadow. The clumps of trees that bordered the horizon
might have been hewn out of some sparkling yellow-green gem,
and beyond them again, far away, the Smolensk road could
be made out, covered with troops. Close to the knoll the
golden fields and dewy slopes were bathed in shimmering
light, and everywhere to the right and left were soldiers and
still soldiers. It was animated, grandiose and unexpected;
but what especially interested Peter was the actual field of
battle—Borodino and the valley of the Kolotcha through which
the river ran.

Above the stream, over Borodino, just where the Voïna
makes its way through vast marshes to join the Kolotcha, rose
one of those mists which, melting and dissolving before the
sun's rays, gives an enchanted aspect and colour to the landscape it transforms rather than hides.

The morning light glowed on this mist, and in the smoke
which mixed with it here and there, and sparkled on the water,
the dew, the bayonets, even on Borodino. Through that transparent veil could be seen the white church, the hovel roofs of
the village, and on every side serried masses of soldiers, green
caissons and guns. From the valley, from the heights, and the
slopes, from the woods, from the fields, came cannon-shots,
now singly, now in volleys, followed by puffs of smoke which

wreathed, mingled, and faded away. And strange as it may appear, this smoke and cannonade were the most attractive features of the spectacle. Puff! and a tight round cloud of smoke changing from violet to grey, to milky-white, would be seen, and—*boom*! a second later one would hear the sound; *puff, puff*! two smokes would rise jostling each other and then blending into each other, and—boom, boom!—sound would confirm what the eye had seen. Peter turned to look at the first cloud of smoke, which he had left as a firm round ball, and already in place of it were balloons of smoke drifting aside; and "puff" (a pause) "puff, puff!" three or four more would rise, and to each one with the same pauses "boom, boom, boom" answered a full, firm, fine sound. Sometimes it seemed as if these smokes moved, and at others as if they were stationary and the forests, fields and shining bayonets moved past them. To the left over the fields and bushes, they were constantly appearing, these large puffs of smoke with their majestic echoes, and nearer in the lower ground and in the woods, smaller and more frequent puffs of musket smoke with no time to form into balloon-shapes flashed out, giving also place to smaller echo. Tra-ta-ta-ta-ta rattled the muskets, frequently but irregularly, and thinly, compared to the rich noise of the big guns. Peter was chafing to be there among the smoke, and the sparkling bayonets, in the midst of the movement, close to the guns.

He turned to compare his own feelings with those which Koutouzow and his staff might be expected to feel at such a moment, and found on every face that suppressed excitement which he had noticed before, but which he had not understood until after his conversation with Prince Andrew.

"Go, my friend, go," said Koutouzow to a general standing near him, "and God go with you." And the general who had taken the order went past Peter down the hill.

"To the bridge!" he answered in reply to a question from another officer.

"And I, too," thought Peter, following him. The general mounted his horse which a Cossack was holding, and Peter, going up to his servant, asked which of his two steeds was the quietest to ride. Then, clutching the beast's mane, leaning over his neck and clinging on by his heels, off he started. He felt that his spectacles were going; however, as he would not, and indeed could not, leave go of the bridle or the mane, away he went after the general, past the rest of the officers who gazed at him with amusement.

CHAPTER XII

THE general led the way down the hill and turned off sharp to the left; Peter lost sight of him and found himself riding through the ranks of an infantry regiment; he tried in vain to get out of the midst of the men, who surrounded him on all sides and looked with angry surprise at this fat man in a white hat, who was knocking them about so heedlessly, and at such a critical moment.

"Why the devil do you ride through a battalion?" asked one; and another gave the horse a prod with the butt-end of his musket. Peter, clutching the saddle-bow and holding in his frightened steed as best he might, was carried on at a furious speed, and presently found himself in an open space. In front of him was a bridge guarded by infantry firing briskly; without knowing it he had come down to the bridge between Gorky and Borodino which the French, after taking the village, had come down to attack. On both sides of the river, and in the hay-fields he had seen from afar, soldiers were struggling frantically; still Peter could not believe that he was witnessing the first act of a battle. He did not hear the bullets that were whistling about his ears, nor the balls that flew over his head; and it did not occur to him that the men on the other side of the river were the enemy, or that those who lay on the ground were wounded or killed.

"What on earth is he doing in front of the line?" shouted a voice. "Left! left! turn to the left!"

Peter turned to the right, and ran up against an aide-de-camp of General Raïevsky's; the officer looked furious, and was about to abuse him roundly, when he recognised him.

"What brings you here?" said he, and he rode away.

Peter, with a vague suspicion that he was not wanted there, and fearing he might be in the way, galloped after him.

"Is it here? May I follow you?" he asked.

"In a minute—wait a minute," said his friend, tearing down into the meadows to meet a burly colonel to whom he was carrying orders. Then he came back to Peter.

"Tell me what on earth you have come here for? To look on I suppose?"

"Just so," said Peter, while the officer wheeled his horse round and was starting off again.

"Here, it is not such warm work yet, thank God! but there, where Bagration is to the left, they are getting it hot."

"Really!" said Peter. "Where?"

"Come up the hill with me; you will see very well from thence, and it is still bearable. Are you coming?"

"After you," said Peter, looking round for his servant; then, for the first time, his eye fell on the wounded men who were dragging themselves to the rear, or being carried on litters; one poor little soldier, with his hat lying by his side, was stretched motionless on the field where the mown hay exhaled its stupefying scent.

"Why have they left that poor fellow?" Peter was on the point of saying; but the aide-de-camp's look of pain as he turned away stopped the question on his lips. As he could nowhere see his servant he rode on, across the flat as far as Raïevsky's battery; but his horse could not keep up with the officer's and shook him desperately.

"You are not used to riding, I see," said the aide-de-camp.

"Oh! it is nothing," said Peter, "his pace is bad."

"The poor beast has had his off leg wounded just above the knee—a bullet must have caught him there. Well, I congratulate you, count—it is your baptism of fire."

After passing the Sixth Corps they got, through dense smoke, to the rear of the artillery, which held an advanced position and kept up an incessant and deafening fire. At last they found themselves in a little copse where the mild autumn air was clear of smoke. They dismounted and climbed the little hill.

"Is the general here?" asked the aide-de-camp.

"Just gone," was the answer. The officer turned to Peter; he did not know what to do with him.

"Do not trouble yourself about me," said Bésoukhow. "I will go on to the top."

"Yes, do—and stay there; you will see everything and it is comparatively safe. I will come back for you."

So they parted, and never again met, and only much later did Peter hear that the aide-de-camp had an arm shot off that day. He went up to the battery that held the famous knoll which came to be known to the Russians as the "Mamelon battery or Raïevsky's redoubt"; and to the French—who regarded it as the key of the position—as "the great redoubt," or "the fatal redoubt," or the "centre redoubt." At its foot fell tens of thousands.

The works were thrown up on a mamelon surrounded with trenches on three sides. Ten heavy guns poured forth death through the embrasures of a breastwork, while other pieces, continuing the line, never paused in their fire. The infantry stood somewhat farther back.

Peter had no suspicion of the paramount value of this point, but supposed it to be, on the contrary, of quite secondary importance. He sat down on the edge of the earthwork that screened the battery and looked about with a smile of innocent satisfaction; now and then he got up to see what was going on, trying to keep out of the way of the men who were re-loading the guns and pushing them forward each time, and of those who went to and fro carrying the heavy cartridges. The guns of this battery kept up a constant fire, one after the other, deafening those near and clouding the surrounding country by their smoke. Quite unlike the infantry outside whose duty it was to protect the redoubt, the gunners standing on this speck of earth that was enclosed by its semicircle of trenches, and apart from the rest of the battle seemed bound together in a kind of fraternal responsibility; and the appearance in their midst of a civilian like Peter was by no means pleasing to them. They looked at him askance and seemed almost alarmed at his presence; a tall pock-marked artillery officer came close up to him and looked at him inquisitively, and a quite young lieutenant, rosy and baby-faced, who was in charge of two guns, turned round and said very severely:

"You must have the goodness to go away, sir; you cannot remain here."

The gunners continued to shake their heads disapprovingly; but when they saw that the man in a white hat did not get in the way, that he was content to sit still, or walk up and down in the face of the enemy's fire, as coolly as if it were a boulevard, that he stood aside politely to make room for them with a shy smile—their ill-humour gave place to sympathetic cordiality, such as soldiers are apt to feel for the dogs, cocks, or other animals that march with the regiment. They adopted him, as it were, and laughing at him among themselves gave him the name of "our gentleman."

A ball fell within a couple of yards of Peter, who only shook off the dust with which he was covered and smiled as he looked round.

"And you are really not afraid, master?" asked a stalwart, red-faced artilleryman, showing his white teeth in a grin.

"Well, are you afraid?"

"Ah, but you know they will have no respect for you. If

one of them knocks you down it will kick your inside out! How can you help being afraid?" he added with a laugh.

Two or three more had stopped to look at Peter; they had jolly, friendly faces, and seemed quite astonished to hear him talk like themselves.

"It is our business, master. But as for you, it is not at all the same thing, and it is wonderful . . ."

"Now then—serve the guns!" cried the young lieutenant, who was evidently on duty of this kind for the first or second time in his life, he was so extravagantly anxious to be blameless in his conduct to his chief and to his men.

The continual thunder of guns and musketry grew louder and louder, especially on the left, round Bagration's advanced work; but Peter's attention was taken up with what was going on close to him, and the smoke prevented his seeing the progress of the action. His first impulse of gratified excitement had given way to a very different feeling, roused in the first instance by the sight of the little private in the hay-field. Seated on the earthwork he was now engrossed in watching the faces of those round him. It was scarcely ten o'clock yet; twenty men had been carried away from the battery, and two guns were silenced. The enemy's missiles fell thicker and faster, and spent balls dropped about them with a buzz and a thud. The artillerymen did not seem to heed them; they were full of jest and high spirits.

"Look out my beauty! Not this way, try the infantry!" cried one man to a shell that spun across above their heads.

"Yes, go to the infantry," echoed a second; and he laughed as he saw the bomb explode among the foot soldiers.

"Hallo! Is that an acquaintance of yours?" cried a third, to a peasant who bowed low as a ball came past.

A knot of men had gathered close to the breastwork to look at something in the distance.

"Do you see? the advanced posts are retiring, they are giving way!" said one.

"Mind your own business," cried an old sergeant. "If they are retiring it is because there is something for them to do elsewhere." He took one of them by the shoulders and shoved him forward with his knee. They all laughed.

"Forward No 5!" was shouted from the other end.

"A long pull and a pull all together!" answered the men who were serving the gun.

"Hallo! That one nearly had 'our gentleman's' hat off!"

said a wag addressing Peter. "Ah! you brute!" he added as
the ball hit the wheel of a gun-carriage and took off a man's leg.

"Here, you foxes!" cried another to the militiamen who
had been charged with the duty of removing the wounded, and
who now crept forward, bent almost double. "This is not
quite the sauce you fancy!"

"Look at those crows!" added a third to a party of the
militia who had stopped short in their horror at the sight of
the man who had lost his leg.

Peter observed that every ball that hit, and every man that
fell, added to the general excitement. The soldiers' faces grew
more fierce and more eager, as lightnings play round a thundercloud, and as though in defiance of that other storm that
was raging around them. Peter felt that this glow was
infectious.

At ten o'clock the infantry sharpshooters, placed among the
scrub in front of the battery, and along the Kamenka brook,
began to give way; he could see them running and carrying
the wounded on their gun-stocks. A general came up the
mamelon, exchanged a few words with the colonel in command,
shot a wrathful scowl at Peter, and went away again, after
ordering the infantry men to fire lying down, so as to expose a
smaller front. There was a sharp rattle of drums in the regiment below, and the line rushed forward. Peter's attention was
caught by the pale face of a young officer, who was marching
with them backwards, holding his sword point downwards, and
looking behind him uneasily; in a minute they were lost to
sight in the smoke, and Peter only heard a confusion of cries,
and the steady rattle of well-sustained firing. Then, in a
few minutes, the wounded were brought out of the mêlée on
stretchers.

In the redoubt projectiles were falling like hail, and several
men were laid low; the soldiers were working with increased
energy; no one heeded Peter. Once or twice he was told to
get out of the way, and the old commanding officer walked
up and down from one gun to another, with his brows knit. The
boy lieutenant, with flaming cheeks, was giving his orders more
incisively than ever; the gunners brought up the cartridges,
loaded and fired with passionate celerity and zeal. They no
longer walked; they sprang about as if they were moved by
springs. The thundercloud was close overhead. Every face
seemed to flash fire, and Peter, now standing by the old colonel,
felt as if the explosion was at hand; then the young lieutenant

came up to the chief, and saluted with his hand to the peak of his cap.

"I have the honour to inform you that there are only eight rounds left. Must we go on?"

"Grape-shot!" cried the colonel, instead of answering him; and at the moment the little lieutenant gave a cry, and dropped like a bird shot on the wing.

Everything whirled and swam before Peter's eyes. A rain of ball was clattering on the breastwork, the men, and the guns. Peter, who had not thought much about it hitherto, now heard nothing else. On the right some soldiers were running and shouting Hurrah!—but backwards, surely, not forwards. A ball hit the earthwork close to where he was standing, and made the dust fly: at the same instant a black object seemed to leap up and bury itself in something soft. The militiamen made the best of their way down the slope again.

"Grape-shot!" repeated the old commander. A sergeant in much agitation ran to him and told him, in terrified under-tones, that the ammunition was all spent. He might have been a house-steward telling his master that wine had run short.

"Rascals! what are they about?" cried the officer; he looked round at Peter; his heated face streaming with perspiration, and his eyes flashing with a fever of excitement. "Run down to the reserve, and fetch up a caisson," he added furiously to one of the soldiers.

"I will go," said Peter.

The officer did not answer, but stepped aside. "Wait—don't fire!"

The man who had been ordered to fetch up the caisson ran against Peter.

"It is not your place, master!" he said; and he set off as fast as he could go, down the slope. Peter ran after him, taking care to avoid the spot where the boy lieutenant was lying. Two, three, balls flew over his head, and fell close to him.

"Where am I going?" he suddenly asked himself, when he was within a few feet of the ammunition stores. He stopped, not knowing where to go. At the same instant a tremendous shock flung him face downwards on the ground, a sheet of flame blinded him, and a terrific shriek ending in an explosion and rattle all round him, completely stunned him. When he presently recovered his senses, he was lying on the ground with his arms spread out. The caisson he had before seen had vanished; in its place the scorched grass was strewn with green boards, half-burnt up, and with rags of clothing; one horse, shaking off the remains of his shafts, started away at a gallop; his mate, mortally injured, lay whinnying piteously.

CHAPTER XIV

PETER, half crazy with terror, started to his feet, and ran back to the battery, as being the only place where he could find shelter from all these catastrophes. As he went he was surprised to hear no more firing, and to find the work occupied by a number of new-comers, whom he could not recognise. The colonel was leaning over the breastwork, as though he were looking down at something, and a soldier, struggling in the hands of some others, was shouting for help. He had not had time to understand that the commanding officer was dead, and the soldier a prisoner, when another was killed under his eyes by a bayonet thrust in the back. Indeed he had scarcely set foot in the redoubt, when a man in a dark-blue uniform, with a lean, brown face, threw himself on him, sword in hand. Peter instinctively dodged and seized his assailant by the neck and shoulder. It was a French officer; but he dropped his sword, and took Peter by the collar. They stood for a few seconds face to face, each looking more astonished than the other at what he had just done.

"Am I his prisoner, or is he mine?" was the question in both their minds.

The Frenchman was inclined to accept the first alternative, for Peter's powerful hand was tightening its clutch on his throat. He seemed to be trying to speak, when a ball came singing close over their heads, and Peter almost thought it had carried off his prisoner's, he ducked it with such amazing promptitude. He himself did the same, and let go. The Frenchman, being no longer curious to settle which was the other's prize, fled into the battery, while Peter made off down the hill, stumbling over the dead and wounded, and fancying in his panic that they clutched at his garments.

As he got to the bottom he met a dense mass of Russians, running as if they were flying from the foe, but all rushing towards the battery. This was the attack of which Yermolow took all the credit, declaring to all who would listen to him that his good star and daring alone could have carried it through. He pretended that he had had his pockets full of crosses of St. George, which he had strewn all over the mamelon. The French, who had captured the redoubt, now in their turn fled, and the Russians pursued them with such desperate determination, that it was impossible to stop them.

The prisoners were led away from the spot; among them was a wounded general, who was at once surrounded by Russian officers. Hundreds of wounded, French and Russians, their faces drawn with anguish, were carried off the mamelon, or dragged themselves away. Once more Peter went up; but those who had been his friends there were gone; he found only a heap of slain, for the most part unknown to him, though he saw the young lieutenant still in the same place by the earth-work, sunk in a heap in a pool of blood; the ruddy-faced gunner still moved convulsively, but was too far gone to be carried away. Peter fairly took to his heels: "They must surely leave off now," he thought. "They must be horrified at what they have done." And he mechanically followed in the wake of the procession of litters which were quitting the field of action.

The sun, shrouded in the cloud of smoke, was still high above the horizon. Away to the left, and particularly round Séménovski, a confused mass swayed and struggled in the distance, and the steady roar of cannon and musketry, far from diminishing, swelled louder and louder; it was like the wild despairing effort of a man who collects all his strength for a last furious cry.

CHAPTER XV

THE principal scene of action had been over a space of about two versts, lying between Borodino and the advanced works held by Bagration. Beyond this radius the cavalry of Ouvarow had made a short diversion in the middle of the day, and behind Outitza Poniatowski and Toutchkow had come to blows; but these were relatively trifling episodes. It was on the plain, between the village and Bagration's entrenchment, a tract of open ground almost clear of copse or brushwood, that the real engagement was fought, and in the simplest way. The signal to begin was given on each side by the firing of several hundred cannon. Then, as the smoke rolled down in a thick cloud, the divisions under Desaix and Compans attacked Bagration, while the viceroy's marched on Borodino. It was about a verst[1] from Bagration's position to Schevardino, where Napoleon had posted himself; and more than two, as the crow flies, from those advanced works to Borodino. Napoleon could not therefore be aware of what was going on there, for the whole valley was shrouded in smoke. Desaix's men were invisible as soon as they got into the hollow, and when they had once disappeared they could be seen no more, as the opposite slope was hidden from view. Here and there a black mass, or a few bayonets, might be seen; still, from the redoubt at Schevardino no one could be certain whether the hostile armies were moving or standing still. The slanting rays of a glorious sun lighted up Napoleon's face, and he screened his eyes with his hand to examine the defences opposite. Shouts rose now and then above the rattle of musketry, but the smoke thickened and curtained everything from view. Napoleon, standing on the hillock, looked through a telescope, and in the little circle of the spy-glass saw smoke and moving people—now his own men, now Russians; but where it all was when he looked again with the bare eye he could not tell. He went down from the eminence and walked up and down, stopping now and then to listen to the artillery, and looking at the field of battle; but neither from where he stood, nor from the knoll—where he had left his generals—nor from the entrenchments, which had fallen into the hands of the French and the Russians alternately, could anything that was happening be discovered. For several hours in succession, now the French came into view and now the Russians—now the infantry, and now the cavalry, they seemed to surge up, to fall, struggle, jostle, and then, not knowing what to do shouted and ran forwards or backwards. Napoleon's aides-de-camp, the orderly officers of his marshals, rode up every few minutes to report progress; but these reports were necessarily fictitious because, in the turmoil and fire, it was impossible to know exactly how matters stood, and because most of the aides-de-camp were content to repeat what was told them, without going themselves to the scene of action; because, too, during the few minutes that it took them to ride back again, everything changed, and what had been true was then false. Thus, one of the viceroy's aides-de-camp flew to tell the emperor that Borodino was taken, that the bridge over the Kolotcha was held by the French, and to ask Napoleon whether troops

[1] Two-thirds of a mile.

should be made to cross it or no. Napoleon's commands were
to form in line on the other side and wait; but even while he
was giving this order, and at the very time when the aide-de-
camp was leaving Borodino, the bridge had been recaptured and
burnt by the Russians in the conflict with which Peter had got
mixed up at the beginning of the engagement. Another aide-de-
camp came riding up, with a scared face, to say that the attack
on the advanced works had been repulsed, that Compans was
wounded, and Davoust killed; while in fact, the entrenchments
had been recaptured by fresh troops, and Davoust had only
been bruised.

As the outcome of these reports, which were inevitably
inaccurate by the mere force of circumstances, Napoleon made
fresh arrangements, which, if they had not been anticipated by
prompt action on the spot, must have come too late. The
marshals and generals in command, who were nearer to the
struggle than he was, and who now and then exposed themselves to fire, took steps without waiting to refer to the emperor,
directed the artillery, and brought up the cavalry on this side
or the infantry on that. Often, however, their orders were
only half-executed, or not heeded at all. The ranks that
were ordered to advance flinched and turned tail as soon as
they smelt grape-shot; those who ought to have stood firm,
fled or rushed on as they saw the foe rise up before them; and
the cavalry, again, would bolt off to catch the Russian fugitives.
In this way two regiments of cavalry charged across the ravine
of Séménovski, dashed up the hill, turned right round and
pelted back again, while the infantry performed much the same
feat, allowing itself to be completely carried away. Hence all
the decisions necessitated by the events of the moment were
taken by those in immediate command, without waiting for
orders from Ney, Davoust, or Murat—much less from Napoleon.
They did not hesitate, indeed, to take the responsibility, since,
during the struggle, a man's sole idea is to escape with his
life, and in seeking his own safety he rushes forward or back,
and acts under the immediate influence of his own personal
excitement.

On the whole, after all, these various movements resulting
from mere chance neither helped, nor even altered, the attitude
of the troops. Their attacks and blows did little harm: it was
the round shot and shell flying across the wide plain that brought
death and wounds. As soon as the men were out of range
of the cannon their leaders had them in hand, formed them

into line, brought them under discipline; and, by sheer force of that discipline, led them back into the ring of iron and fire, where they again lost their presence of mind, and fled headlong, dragging one another into the stampede.

CHAPTER XVI

DAVOUST, Murat, and Ney had led forward their troops under fire again and again, in enormous masses and in perfect order, but instead of seeing the enemy take to flight, as in so many previous battles, these disciplined troops turned back disbanded and panic-stricken; in vain they re-formed their ranks, their numbers perceptibly dwindled. About noon Murat sent a message to Napoleon to ask for reinforcements. Napoleon was sitting at the foot of the knoll drinking punch. When the aide-de-camp came up and said the Russians could certainly be routed if his majesty would send a reinforcement, Napoloen looked stern and astonished:

"Reinforcements?" he cried, as if he did not understand the meaning of the request, and he looked up at the handsome lad with long black hair, curled in imitation of Murat. "Reinforcements!" he repeated to himself in an undertone. "What more can they want of me when they have half of the army at their disposal in front of the Russian left wing which has not even an entrenchment? Tell the King of Naples that it is not yet noon, and I do not see my way on the chessboard. Go." The handsome young fellow sighed, and with his hand still up to his shako rode back into the fire. Napoleon rose and called Caulaincourt and Berthier, with whom he discussed various matters not relating to the battle. In the middle of the conversation Berthier's attention was attracted by seeing a general riding a horse covered with foam, and coming towards the mamelon with his staff. This was Belliard. He dismounted, and hastening towards the emperor, explained to him, in loud and positive tones, that the reinforcements must be sent up. He swore on his honour that the Russians would be utterly cut up if the emperor would only send forward one division. Napoleon shrugged his shoulders and said nothing, still walking up and down, while Belliard vehemently expressed his opinions to the generals who stood round him.

"Belliard, you are too hot-headed," said Napoleon. "It is

so easy to make a mistake in the thick of the fray. Go back, look again, and then return!"

Belliard had hardly disappeared, when another messenger arrived from the scene of action.

"Well, what now?" said Napoleon, in the tone of a man irritated by constant importunities.

"Your majesty, the prince . . ."

"Wants reinforcements, I suppose?" interrupted Napoleon with an angry gesture.

The aide-de-camp bowed affirmatively. Napoleon turned away, went forward a step or two, turned back, and addressed Berthier.

"We must send them the reserves—what do you think? Whom can we send to help?" he said, addressing Berthier—"that gosling whom I have made into an eagle," as he called him later.

"Let us send Claparède's division, sire," replied Berthier, who knew every division, regiment, and battalion by name.

The emperor nodded approval; the aide-de-camp went off at a gallop towards Claparède's division, and a few minutes later the regiment known as the Jeune Garde (in contradistinction to the Vieille Garde), which stood in reserve behind the mamelon, began to move forward. Napoleon stood looking at it.

"No," he said suddenly, "I cannot send Claparède—send Friant."

Though there was nothing to be gained by moving the second rather than the first, and in fact, the immediate result was great delay, this order was carried out exactly. Napoleon though he little suspected it, was dealing with his army like a doctor, who impedes the course of nature by the application of remedies: a method he was always ready to criticise severely in others. Friant's division was soon lost to sight in the smoke, with the rest, while aides-de-camp came in from every point of the action, as if they had conspired to make the same demand. All reported that the Russians stood firm in their positions, and were keeping up a terrific fire under which the French were fairly melting away. Napoleon continued to sit in a brown study in his folding chair. Monsieur de Beausset, who was still fasting, went up to the emperor, and respectfully suggested breakfast.

"I fancy I may congratulate your majesty on a victory?" he said.

Napoleon shook his head. Monsieur de Beausset, thinking that his negative referred to the assumed victory, took the

liberty of remarking, in a half-jesting tone, that there could be
no mortal reason against their having some breakfast as soon
as it might be possible.

"Go to . . ." Napoleon suddenly began angrily and he
turned away.

A smile of pity and dejection was Beausset's comment, as he
left the emperor and joined the officers.

Napoleon was going through the painful experience of a
gambler who, after a long run of luck, has calculated every
chance and staked handfuls of gold—and then finds himself
beaten after all, just because he has played too elaborately.
The troops and commanders were the same as of old; his plans
well laid; his address short and vigorous; he was sure of himself, and of his experience, his genius which had ripened with
years; the enemy in front was the same as at Austerlitz and
Friedland; he had counted on falling on him tooth and nail—
and the stroke had failed as if by magic. He was wont to see
his designs crowned with success. To-day, as usual, he had
concentrated his fire on a single point, had thrown forward his
reserves and his cavalry—men of steel—to break through the
Russian lines, and yet victory held aloof. From all sides came
the cry for reinforcements, the news that generals were killed
or wounded, that the regiments were demoralised, that it was
impossible to move the Russians. On other occasions, after two
or three moves, and two or three orders hastily given, aides-de-
camp and marshals had come to him beaming, to announce
with compliments and congratulations that whole corps had
been taken prisoners, to bring in sheaves of standards and eagles
taken from the foe; trains of cannon had rattled up behind
them, and Murat had asked leave to charge the baggage-wagons
with cavalry! This was how things had gone at Lodi, at
Marengo, at Arcola, at Jena, at Austerlitz, at Wagram. To-day
something strange was in the air—the Russian advanced works,
to be sure, had been taken by storm—still, he felt it, and he
knew that all his staff felt it too. Every face was gloomy; each
man avoided catching his neighbour's eye; only Beausset alone
did not perhaps understand what was happening and Napoleon
himself knew better than anyone what was the meaning of a
struggle that had lasted eight hours and had not yet resulted in
victory, though all his forces had been engaged. He knew that
it was a drawn game, and that even now the smallest turn of
fortune might, at this critical moment, involve him and his
army in ruin.

As he thought over this weird campaign in Russia—in which, during two months' fighting, not a battle had been won, not a flag, not a gun, not a company of men had been captured—the dismal faces of his courtiers, and their lamentations over the obstinacy of the Russians, oppressed him like a nightmare. The Russians might at any moment fall on his left wing, or break through his centre. A spent ball might even hit him. All these things were possible. He had been used to look forward to none but happy chances; to-day, on the contrary, an endless series of chances, all against him, rose before his fancy. Yes, it was like a nightmare, in which, one sees somebody approaching with evil intent and strikes out with all one's might, knowing that the blow must destroy, and then feels that the hand is helpless, that it falls limply like a rag, and all the horror of instant inevitable destruction seizes upon one. When he heard that the left wing was, in fact, attacked by the enemy, he was panic-stricken. Berthier came up and suggested that he should ride round and judge for himself of the state of affairs.

"What? What did you say? Ah! yes, to be sure; call for my horse. . . ." And he started towards Séménovski.

All along the road nothing was to be seen but horses and men. singly or in heaps, lying in pools of blood: neither Napoleon nor his generals had ever seen so many slain within so small a space. The hollow roar of the cannon, which had never ceased for ten hours, and of which the ear was weary, made a sinister accompaniment to the scene. Having reached the height above Séménovski he could see in the distance, across the smoke, close lines of uniforms of unfamiliar colours: these were the Russians. They stood in compact masses behind the village and the knoll, and their guns still thundered unremittingly all along the line: it was not a battle; it was butchery, equally fruitless to both sides. Napoleon stopped and relapsed into the reverie from which Berthier had roused him. It was impossible to put an end to the slaughter, and yet he it was who, to the world, was the responsible authority; this first repulse brought home to him all the horror and waste of such massacres.

One of the generals ventured to suggest that the Old Guard should be sent forward; Ney and Berthier exchanged glances and smiled in contempt for so preposterous a notion. Napoleon sat in silence, with his head down.

"We are eight hundred leagues from home," he suddenly exclaimed, "and I will not have my Guards cut to pieces!" Then turning his horse, he galloped back to Schevardino.

CHAPTER XVII

KOUTOUZOW, with his head bent and sunk all into a heap from his own weight, sat all day where Peter had seen him in the morning, on a bench covered with a rug; he gave no orders but merely approved or disapproved of what was suggested to him.

"That is it—yes, yes, do so," he would say, or; "Go and see, my good friend, go and see!" or, again: "That is of no use; we must wait. . . ."

But he listened to all he was told, and gave the requisite orders without seeming to take any interest in what was said. But something else, something in the expression and tone of the speaker seemed to interest him. His long experience and hoary wisdom had taught him that no one man can direct the movements of a hundred thousand others, fighting for life and death. He knew that it was neither the plans of the commander, nor the placing of the troops, nor the number of guns, nor the amount of slain which decide the victory, but that imponderable force called the Spirit of the Army, which he tried to control and guide as far as possible. The calm, grave expression of his face was in startling contrast to the weakness of his aged frame.

At eleven in the forenoon a messenger came to say that the redoubt taken by the French had been recaptured, but that Bagration was wounded. Koutouzow exclaimed loudly and shook his head.

"Go and fetch up Prince Peter Ivanovitch," he said to an aide-de-camp; then turning to the Prince of Wurtemberg he said: "Would your highness at once take the command of the Second Army?"

The prince rode off, but before he reached the village of Séménovski he sent back his aide-de-camp to ask for reinforcements. Koutouzow frowned; then he sent Dokhtourow forward to take the command, instead of the prince, whom he begged to return, as he found that he could not dispense with his advice under such serious circumstances. When he was told that Murat had been taken prisoner he smiled; his staff eagerly congratulated him.

"Wait a little, gentlemen," he said. "Wait. The battle is certainly ours, and the news that Murat is taken is not so very astonishing; but we must not crow too soon."

However, he sent an aide-de-camp to make the fact known to

the troops. Somewhat later Scherbinine arrived to tell him that the outworks at Séménovski had been taken once more by the French, and Koutouzow understood from the expression of his face, and the rumours that reached him from the scene of action, that things were going badly. He rose and led him away.

"My good fellow," he said to Yermolow "go and see what can be done."

Koutouzow was at Gorky, the very centre of the Russian position; Napoleon's attack on the Russian left had been bravely repulsed, but in the centre his troops had not got beyond Borodino, and on his left flank Ouvarow's cavalry had made the French run. By three o'clock the French had given up attacking and Koutouzow could read acute excitement on the faces of those who came up from the field, as well as of those who remained with him. The success was far beyond his hopes, but his strength was beginning to fail; his head drooped, and he kept dropping asleep. Some dinner was brought to him; while he was eating, Woltzogen came to talk to him; it was he who had said in Prince Andrew's hearing that the war must have room to spread, and who was hated by Bagration. He had come by Barclay's request, to report progress as to the military operations of the left wing. The wiseacre Barclay, seeing a crowd of fugitives and wounded, while the farthest line had given way, had come to the conclusion that the battle was lost, and had sent off his favourite aide-de-camp to carry the news to Koutouzow. The commander-in-chief was munching a piece of roast fowl, and he looked complacently up at Woltzogen, who approached him with an air of indifference and a superficial smile, and saluted with affected grace; he looked as though he would convey: "I, as an experienced and distinguished soldier, may leave it to the Russians to offer incense to this useless old dotard, whom I know how to estimate at his true worth!"

"The old gentleman"—the Germans always spoke of Koutouzow as "the old gentleman"—"is making himself comfortable!" thought Woltzogen, glancing at the plate; and he proceeded to report on the situation of the left flank as he had been desired, and as he himself had believed that he had seen it.

"All the chief points of our position are in the enemy's hands; we cannot dislodge them for lack of men. Our troops are flying, and it is impossible to stop them."

Koutouzow ceased eating, and looked up astonished; he seemed not to understand the words. Woltzogen saw that he was much moved and went on with a smile:

"I do not think I should be justified in concealing from your highness what I saw. The troops are completely routed."

"You saw! you saw that?" cried Koutouzow, starting up with a fierce frown; with his trembling hands he gesticulated threats, and almost choking, exclaimed:

"How dare you, sir, tell me such a thing as that? You know nothing about it! Go and tell your general that it is false and that I know the true state of things better than he does."

Woltzogen would have interrupted him, but Koutouzow went on: "The enemy's left is driven back, and his right badly damaged. If you saw wrongly, that is no reason to tell a falsehood. Go and tell General Barclay that I intend to renew the attack to-morrow!" No one spoke; there was not a sound but the old man's hard breathing: "He is repulsed on all sides," he added, "and I thank God, and our brave troops! The victory is ours, and to-morrow we will cast him forth from the sacred soil of Russia." He crossed himself, and ended with a sob.

Woltzogen shrugged his shoulders and smiled sardonically. He turned on his heel, not even attempting to conceal his astonishment at "the old gentleman's" wilful blindness. At this moment another officer—a particularly pleasant-looking man, came up the hill.

"Ah! here is my hero!" said Koutouzow.

This was Raïevsky. He had been all day in the hottest place in the field. His report was that the Russians were holding their own, and that the French did not dare to renew the attack.

"Then you do not think, as some others do, that we are forced to retire?" asked Koutouzow in French.

"On the contrary, highness. In a doubtful action the side that stands steady longest is the conqueror, and in my opinion . . ."

"Kaïssarow!" exclaimed the commander-in-chief, "make out the order of the day for me. And you," he added to another officer, "ride down the lines and say that we attack to-morrow."

Meanwhile Woltzogen had been to Barclay and come back again, and he now said that his chief begged to have the orders he had carried confirmed by writing. Koutouzow, without even looking at him, at once had the order written out, which relieved the ex-commander-in-chief of all responsibility.

By that mysterious moral intuition which is known as *esprit de corps*, Koutouzow's order of the day was communicated instantaneously to the furthest corner of the field. Not, of course, that the original words were exactly repeated; in fact the expressions given to Koutouzow were not his at all; but everyone understood their purport and bearing. They were not the utterance, indeed, of a more or less skilful orator, but they perfectly expressed the feeling of the commander-in-chief—a sentiment that found an echo in the breast of every Russian. All these weary, doubting soldiers, when they were told that they were to attack the foe on the morrow, felt that what they wished to believe was really true; this comforted them and revived their courage.

CHAPTER XVIII

PRINCE ANDREW's regiment was one of those kept in reserve and inactive till about two o'clock, behind Séménovski, under heavy fire. At that time, when the regiment had already lost more than 200 men, it was ordered forward on to the open ground between Séménovski and the mamelon battery. Thousands had fallen in the course of the day on this spot, on which the fire of some hundred of the enemy's guns was now steadily directed. Without stirring an inch or firing a shot, the regiment was soon reduced by a third more. In front, and especially on the right, the cannon were thundering through a wall of smoke, and throwing out a hail of shot and shell without one instant of respite. From time to time the storm passed over their heads, the projectiles singing through the air; but then, again, several men were hit in the course of a few seconds—the dead were laid aside, and the wounded carried to the rear. Each explosion diminished the chances of life for the survivors. The regiment was drawn up in columns of battalions, three hundred paces in length; but, in spite of this length of line, all the men were equally and painfully impressed. They were all gloomy and silent; at most they spoke a few words in an undertone, and even those died on their lips as each ball took effect, and as they heard their comrades calling for the hospital men.

The officers had given orders that the men should keep their ranks sitting on the ground. One was carefully tying and untying the runner in the lining of his cap; another, breaking up the dry clay into a powder, polished up his bayonet with it; a third loosened and buckled the straps of his bag; a fourth was diligently turning down his boot-tops, and pulling them on and off; some were scraping out a hollow shelter in the earth, and some aimlessly plaiting straws. They all seemed absorbed in their occupations, and when a comrade rolled over close by, wounded or dead—when the litters touched their heads—when through the rolling vapour they had a glimpse of the foe, no one took any notice; only if they saw the Russian artillery or cavalry move forward, or fancied the infantry were being marched about, remarks of approval were heard on all sides. Then, the moment after, all their attention was centred once more on trifles that had nothing to do with the drama going on around them. It was as if their moral force was exhausted, and had to be revived by a return to the details of daily life. An artillery train presently passed by; one of the horses harnessed to a caisson had got his leg caught in the traces.

"Look out there, at one of your team—take care! He will be down! Have they no eyes!" was shouted on all sides.

Again, the general attention was claimed by a small brown dog, which had come nobody knew whence, and trotted busily along the line with its tail steadily kept aloft. A ball fell close to him, and he ran off with a melancholy yelp, his tail between his legs, and the whole regiment roared with laughter. But such diversions only lasted a moment, and the men, whose anxious and pallid faces seemed to grow greyer and more pinched as time went on, sat there for eight hours, without food, and in the very jaws of death.

Prince Andrew, as pale as his men, walked up and down the meadow from end to end, his head bent and his hands behind his back; everything that had to be done was carried out without any orders from him; the dead were removed, the wounded taken to the rear, and the ranks closed up. At the beginning of the day he had thought it his duty to encourage his men and walk down the ranks; but he soon saw that he could teach them nothing. All the energies of his soul, like those of every soldier there, were directed to keeping his thoughts off from the horrors of the situation. He dragged his feet over the trampled grass, looking mechanically at the dust on his boots; now and then, taking long strides, he tried to pace the ridges left by the mower's scythe; then he would calculate how many went to a verst; or he would pull the tufts of wormwood that grew by the hedgerow, and bruise them in his fingers, and sniff the bitter wild perfume. All the thoughts of the previous evening had left no trace in his mind; in fact he was thinking of nothing, and listened wearily to the unceasing noise, always the same—the crackling of shells and musketry. Now and then he looked round at the foremost battalion: "Ah! here it comes—straight at us," he would say to himself, as he heard the sharp whistle of a ball through the smoke. "Here is another. Down it comes! No, it has passed overhead . . . There, that one has fallen!" and then he would count his paces once more—sixteen across to the edge of the meadow.

Suddenly a ball flew past and buried itself in the earth, not five yards away. He shuddered involuntarily, and looked down the line; several men had no doubt been struck, for he saw a great bustle close to the second battalion.

"Tell the men not to huddle together so much!" he said to an aide-de-camp.

The order was transmitted, and the aide-de-camp came back to Prince Andrew at the very moment when the major rode up on the other side.

"Look out!" cried a terrified soldier, and a shell came flying down like a bird alighting on the ground, whizzing and shrieking, just at the feet of the major's horse, and not two yards from Prince Andrew. The horse did not pause to consider whether or no it were dignified to betray his fear; he reared, neighing with alarm, and flung himself on one side, almost throwing his rider.

"Lie down!" shouted the aide-de-camp.

But Prince Andrew stood still, doubting; the shell spun round like an enormous top, the fuse smoking and fizzing, close to a shrub of wormwood between himself and the aide-de-camp.

"Can this really mean death?" thought he, looking with a vague feeling of regret at the wormwood plant, and the black whirling object. "I do not want to die—I like life, I like this earth. . . ." These were the words in his mind, and yet he understood only too well what it was that he saw.

"Aide-de-camp," he began, "I should be ashamed . . ."

But the sentence was never finished. There was a tremendous explosion followed by a strange clatter like that of smashing glass; a fountain of fire leapt into the air, and fell as a shower of iron; the air was full of the smell of gunpowder. Prince Andrew was jerked forward with his arms out, and fell heavily on his face. Some officers rushed up; on his right there was a pool of blood; the militiamen were called to help, but waited behind the group of officers; Prince Andrew lay with his face in the grass, breathing hard.

"Come on—come!" said someone. The peasants drew near, and lifted him by the head and feet; he groaned—the men looked at each other, and laid him down again.

"Pick him up; it must be done!" said another.

They raised him once more and got him on to a stretcher.

"Good God! what has happened? In the stomach? Then he is done for!" said the officers.

"It actually grazed my ear!" said the aide-de-camp.

The bearers went off quickly along a path they had kept open to the ambulance in the rear.

"Keep step . . . you!" shouted an officer seizing the men by the shoulders and stopping the unevenly carried stretcher.

"Eh, suit your step, Fedor" said the foremost man.

"That's better," beamed the man at the back having succeeded in suiting his step to that of the man in front.

"Excellency — my prince?" murmured Timokhine, in a tremulous voice, running by the stretcher.

Prince Andrew opened his eyes and looked at the speaker; then he closed them again.

Prince Andrew was carried into the wood where the ambulance carts stood, and the hospital tents, three in number, had been pitched close to a plantation of young birches. The horses were in harness, and very contentedly munching their oats, sparrows fluttered down to pick up the seeds they let drop, and crows, scenting blood, flew from tree to tree croaking impatiently All round the tents, sat, lay, or stood men in blood-stained uniforms; the litter-bearers crowded about them, and could hardly be persuaded to move. They were staring at them with downcast looks; deaf to the commands of the officers, they leaned over the wounded, wondering, as it seemed, what could be the meaning of this appalling spectacle. Inside the tents sobs of rage or pain might be heard, mingled with more plaintive groans; now and then a surgeon rushed out to fetch water, and pointed out which were to be taken in next of the wounded men who were waiting their turn—screaming, swearing, weeping, or clamouring for brandy. Some were already delirious.

Prince Andrew, as a commanding officer, was carried through this crowd to the first tent, and his bearers paused for further orders. He opened his eyes, not understanding what was going on around him: the meadow, the wormwood shrub, the mowed field, the whirling black top, the sudden longing to live that had come over him—all recurred to his mind. Quite near him a tall and finely-built corporal was talking very loud, and attracting everybody's attention; his black eyes shone from under a bandage which half-covered them, and he was propped up against the branch of a tree; he had been wounded in the head and in the foot. He had an eager audience.

"We gave him such a dose of it that he made off, leaving everything behind! We took the king himself prisoner!" he was saying, his eyes sparkling brightly.

"Ah! if the reserves had but come up, there would not have been a man of them left, I swear!"

Prince Andrew heard too, and felt comforted.

"But what can it matter to me now?" he thought. "What has happened to me? And why am I here? Why am I in such despair at the idea of dying? There is something in life after all that I have failed to understand."

CHAPTER XIX

ONE of the surgeons, whose hands and apron were covered with blood, came out of the tent; he held a cigar between his thumb and his little finger in order to keep it from getting soiled. He looked up and away, over the heads of the wounded men; it was evident that he desperately wanted a moment of breathing time; but he almost immediately looked down at the scene at hand. He sighed and half-closed his eyes.

"In a minute," he replied, to an assistant who pointed out Prince Andrew, and he had him carried into the tent.

There was a murmur among the rest of the victims.

"Why, you might fancy these gentlemen were the only folks that have a right to live, even in the other world!"

Prince Andrew was laid on an operating table that had but just been cleared; a surgeon was sponging it down. The prince could not clearly make out who was in the tent. The cries and moans on one hand, and the agonising pain he felt in his side, stomach and back, paralysed his faculties. Everything was mixed up in his mind into one single impression of naked, bloodstained flesh, filling the low tent; and that, again, was one with the scene he had witnessed, that scorching August day, in the pool on the Smolensk road. Yes, it was this very "*chair à canon*" which had then filled him with sickening and prophetic horror.

There were three tables in the tent; two were occupied; Prince Andrew was placed on the third, and left to himself for a few minutes, during which he was at leisure to look at the other two. On the nearest, a Tartar was sitting up—a Cossack it seemed from the uniform that lay near him. Four soldiers were holding him, while a doctor in spectacles was probing under the swarthy skin of his muscular back.

"Oh," roared the Tartar, and suddenly raising his tanned face, with its wide forehead and flat nose, he gave a piercing yell, and flung himself from side to side to shake off the men who held him.

The farther table was surrounded with people. A tall, strongly-built man was stretched upon it, his head thrown back; there was something familiar to Prince Andrew in the colour of his curling hair, and the shape of his head. Several hospital attendants were leaning on him with all their weight to keep him from stirring. One leg—fat and white—was constantly twitching with a convulsive movement, and his whole body shook with violent and choking sobs. Two surgeons, one quite pale and tremulous, were busy over his other leg.

Having finished operating on the Tartar, who was covered up in his cloak, the surgeon in spectacles wiping his hands came across to Prince Andrew; he glanced at him and turned away.

"Take his clothes off! What are you thinking of?" he exclaimed angrily to one of his assistants.

When Prince Andrew felt himself in the hands of the attendant who, with his sleeves turned back, hastily unbuttoned his uniform, all the memory of his childhood suddenly flashed upon his mind. The surgeon bent down, examined his wound, and sighed deeply; then he called another to help him, and the next instant Prince Andrew lost consciousness from the intense agony he suddenly felt. When he came to himself the pieces of his broken thigh, with the torn flesh still clinging to them, had been extracted from his wound and it had been dressed. He opened his eyes; water was being sprinkled on his face; the doctor bent over him, kissed him silently, and went away without looking back at him.

After that fearful torture a feeling of indescribable comfort came over him. His fancy reverted to the happiest days of his infancy, especially to those hours when, after he had been undressed and put into his little bed, his old nurse had sung him to sleep. He was glad to be alive—that past seemed to have become the present. The surgeons were still busy over the man he had fancied he recognised; they were supporting him in their arms, and trying to soothe him.

"Show it me—show it me!" he said; fairly crying with pain. Prince Andrew as he heard him felt ready to cry too. Was

it because he was dying ingloriously, or because he regretted life?
Was it by reason of these memories of his childhood? Or
because he had suffered so acutely himself, that tears of pity rose
to his eyes when he saw others suffer.

They showed the other man his amputated leg, with the
blood-stained boot still on it.

"Oh!" he exclaimed, and wept as bitterly as a woman.

Just then the doctor moved. "My God! What is this?
Why is he here?" said Prince Andrew to himself. He could
see that the miserable creature who lay sobbing and exhausted
by his side, was Anatole Kouraguine.

A hospital servant was lifting him, and holding a glass of
water to the swollen and quivering lips that could not close on
the rim. "Yes, certainly it is he—that man is bound to me by
some painful association—but what is it?" He asked himself,
but could find no reply, till suddenly, like a vision from an ideal
world of love and purity, Natacha seemed to stand before him;
Natacha as he had first seen her at the ball in 1810, with her thin
bust and arms, and her radiant, half-scared, enthusiastic face—
and his own love and tenderness woke up, deeper, warmer than
ever. Now he knew what the link was between himself and the
man whose eyes, red and dim with tears, were fixed on him.
Prince Andrew remembered everything, and tender pitifulness
rose up in his heart which was full of peace. He could not control those tears of compassion and charity which flowed for all
humanity, for himself, for his own weakness, and for that of this
hapless creature. "Yes," said he to himself. "This is the
pity, the charity, the love of my neighbour, the love of those
that hate us as well as of those who love us, which God preached
on earth, and which Maria used to talk about—but I did not
understand it then. This was what I had yet to learn in
this life and what makes me regret it. But now, I feel, it
comes too late!"

CHAPTER XX

THE terrible sight of the battle-field strewn with corpses and
wounded men, the crushing responsibility that weighed upon
him, the news that reached him every few minutes of so many
generals being killed or severely wounded, together with the
loss of his prestige, all made an extraordinary impression on
the Emperor Napoleon. He, who was usually glad to look on

the dead and dying, and fancied that his callousness was a
proof of his magnanimity and fortitude, felt morally defeated;
and he hastened to quit the field of battle and return to Schevardino. His face was yellow and puffy, dull-eyed, with a red
nose and his voice hoarse—seated on his camp-stool he could not
help listening to the noise of the guns, but he did not raise his
eyes. He was awaiting with agonised impatience the end of
this business in which he had been the prime mover, and which
he now was impotent to stay. For a moment, a natural and
human impulse had risen superior to the mirage which had so
long bewitched him, and for once he brought home to himself
the keen apprehension of suffering that had come over him on
the battle-field. He thought of the contingency for himself of
death and anguish, and he ceased to long for Moscow, for glory,
for conquest, he sighed but for one thing: rest, quiet, liberty.
Nevertheless, when he had reached the height above Séménovski,
and the general in command of the artillery proposed to bring
up a few batteries to support the firing on the Russian troops
drawn up in compact masses in front of Kniazkow, he had
agreed at once, and desired to be informed of the result. Not
long after an aide-de-camp came to tell him that two hundred
cannon had been turned on the Russians, but that they held
their own: "Our fire mows them down in rows and they do
not stir!"

"Do they want more?" asked Napoleon huskily.

"Sire? . . ." said the aide-de-camp, who had not heard.

"Do they want more?" repeated Napoleon. "Well, if they
do, give it them." And so he came back into the false world
of chimeras that he had created for himself, and (like a horse
tethered to a rope fancies it is doing what it likes because it is
free to run round as far as the rope will permit) resumed the
painful, cruel and inhuman part that he was destined to fill.

This man, who was no doubt more directly responsible than
anyone else for the events of his time, was, till his dying day,
disabled by his darkened intellect and conscience, from understanding goodness, beauty, truth, and the real meaning of his
actions, so contradictory were they to all goodness and truth,
so far from anything human for him to understand it; and as
half the world approved of these acts, he could not repudiate
them without being illogical, and was forced therefore to repudiate all goodness, truth, and everything human. To-day
was not the first time that he had felt a secret satisfaction at
comparing the number of Russian corpses with the French; it

was not the first time that he had written to Paris that the field of battle was a glorious sight. Why should he say this? Because there were 50,000 dead lying there; and even at St. Helena, where he spent his leisure in recording his past achievements, he could dictate as follows:

"The war with Russia ought to have been the most popular war of modern times: it was on the side of good sense and sound interests, of the peace and security of Europe; it was purely pacificatory and conservative.

"It was, for the great cause, the end of haphazard and the beginning of security. A new horizon and new scenes were about to unfold themselves, bright with ease and prosperity for all. The European system was actually established; all that was wanting was to organise it.

"I myself, satisfied on these great questions and tranquil on all sides, I, too, should have had my Congress and my Holy Alliance. Those ideas were stolen from me. In that great council of sovereigns we should have discussed matters of family interests, and settled accounts with the nations with a high hand.

"In this way Europe would soon have been but one people, and everyone, travel where he might, would have still been in the common fatherland. I should have insisted on all the navigable rivers being free to all, on common rights in all seas, and on the great standing armies being reduced merely to an efficient guard for the various sovereigns.

"On my return home, having made France great, strong, magnificent, glorious, and tranquil, I should have defined her immutable frontier; thenceforth every war would have been purely defensive, and all aggrandisement would have been regarded as anti-national. I should have made my son the partner of my throne; my dictatorship would have been at an end; his constitutional sovereignty would have begun. Paris would have been the capital of the world, and France the envy of all nations.

"Then my leisure and old age would have been dedicated during my son's apprenticeship to making a tour with the empress—driving our own horses and taking our time like a country couple—visiting all the nooks of Europe, receiving petitions, redressing wrongs, sowing good seed wherever we went, and founding monumental benefactions."

Yes, he—the torturer of the nations, foreordained by Heaven

to fill that part—racked his brain to prove that his sole aim had been to do them good, that he could control the destinies of millions and load them with benefits by his arbitrary volition!

"Of 400,000 men who crossed the Vistula," he wrote, "half were Austrians, Prussians, Saxons, Poles, Bavarians, Wurtembergers, Mecklenburgers, Spaniards, Italians, and Neapolitans. The imperial army, properly speaking, contained about one-third of Dutch, Belgians, Rhinelanders, Piedmontese, Swiss, Genevese, Tuscans, Romans, natives of the 32nd military district, of Bremen, Hamburg, etc.; there were hardly 140,000 men who spoke French. The invasion of Russia cost France itself less than 50,000: the Russian army lost four times as many men as the French army, in the course of the retreat, and various actions between Vilna and Moscow: the burning of Moscow cost the lives of 100,000 Russians who perished of cold and misery in the forests; and then, in the march from Moscow to the Oder, the Russian army also suffered from the severity of the season. Only 50,000 men reached Vilna, and less than 18,000 got as far as Kalisch."

So he really believed that the war in Russia depended solely on his will and pleasure, and yet the horrors of the accomplished fact caused him no pang of remorse! He boldly took upon himself the responsibility of events, and his darkened intellect sought justification in the fact that of the hundreds of thousands of destroyed human beings there were fewer French than Bavarians or Russians.

CHAPTER XXI

HEAPS of men in every variety of uniform were lying in confusion, tens of thousands of them, in the fields and meadows belonging to Mr. Davydow and the Crown serfs. On those fields and meadows, for hundreds of years the peasants of the neighbourhood had pastured their beasts and harvested their crops. Near the ambulance tents, for about a dessiatine [1] the ground and grass were soaked in blood; crowds of soldiers, some sound and some wounded, and of different arms, were making their weary way in terror towards Mojaïsk or Valouïew; others,

[1] Nearly three acres.

hungry and worn out with fatigue, mechanically formed in line and followed their officers; while others again stayed on where they had been posted and went on firing. Over the field where, a few hours since, all had looked bright and smiling, where bayonets had glittered and the iridescent mists of morning had veiled the scene, there now hung a dense fog made heavy by smoke and exhaling a strange reek of powder and blood. Black clouds had gathered overhead, a fine drizzle was bedewing the dead, the wounded and the utterly weary. It seemed to be saying to them: "Enough, enough, hapless wretches! Bethink yourselves. What are you doing?" Then a thought seemed to dawn in the minds of the poor creatures, and they began to ask themselves whether they were to go on with this butchery. The idea did not, however, gain ground till the evening; till then, though the struggle was drawing to a close, and the men felt all the horror of their position, a mysterious and inexplicable impulse had guided the hand of the gunner who had survived of the three told off to serve each cannon; and who stood faithful though covered with sweat, powder, and blood. He alone carried the cartridges, loaded the gun, aimed it, and lighted the slow match! The balls met and crossed, carried death to numberless victims, and still the fearful work went on, the outcome, not of any human will, but of the Will which governs men and worlds.

Anyone looking on at the fast dispersing French and Russian armies, might have thought that a very slight effort on the part of one or the other would have sufficed to annihilate the foe. But neither side made that last effort, and the battle died away by degrees. The Russians did not take up the offensive because, having been collected on the road to Moscow, from the first, and charged to defend it, they stayed there till the end. Indeed, if they had decided on attacking the French, the disorder of their ranks would not have admitted of it, for even without quitting their position they had lost half their numbers. The effort could only have been possible—or perhaps indeed easy—to the French, who were kept up by the traditions of fifteen years of success under Napoleon, by their confidence of victory, the comparative smallness of their loss—not more than a quarter of the whole efficient force—the knowledge that behind them lay a reserve of more than 20,000 fresh Guards who had not charged, and their wrath at having failed to dislodge the enemy from his positions. Historians have said that Napoleon might have decided the day in his favour if only he had brought up the

"*Vieille Garde*"; but to say this is to assume that winter may suddenly become spring. The failure cannot be imputed to Napoleon. Every man, from the commander-in-chief to the humblest private, knew that such an effort was out of the question; in point of fact the spirit of the French army was thoroughly quelled by this formidable foe, who, after losing half his force, was as resolute at last as at first.

The victory won by the Russians was not indeed one of those which are bedizened with those rags nailed to a pole which are dignified as flags, or which derive their splendour from extent of conquest; but it was one of those triumphs which carry home to the soul of the aggressor a two-fold conviction of his adversary's moral superiority and of his own weakness. The invading army, like some wild beast broken loose, had been mortally wounded; it was consciously rushing on to ruin; but the first impetus had been given, and now, come what might, it must reach Moscow. The Russian army, on the other hand, though twice as weak, was no less inexorably impelled to resist. At Moscow, still bleeding from the wounds inflicted at Borodino, these efforts were to lead inevitably to Napoleon's flight—to his retreat by the way by which he had come, to the almost total destruction of 500,000 men who had followed him, and to the annihilation of his personal influence, overpowered as it was, even at Borodino, by an adversary whose moral force was so far superior.

BOOK TWELVE

CHAPTER XXII

THE human intellect is incapable of understanding *à priori* the idea of unceasing movement in a body; it can only apprehend it when it is at leisure to analyse the component factors and study them separately; at the same time, it is this subdivision into definite units which gives rise to many errors. For instance, a well-known sophism of the ancients tended to prove that Achilles could never overtake a tortoise crawling in front of him even though he walked ten times as fast as the animal; for, every time Achilles should have picked up the distance between them, the tortoise would have got ahead by a tenth of the space; and when Achilles had covered that tenth the tortoise would again have gained a hundredth, and so on, *ad infinitum*. The ancients regarded this as an unanswerable dilemma; its absurdity lies in the fact that the progress of Achilles and the tortoise is calculated on units with stoppage between, while it is in fact continuous.

By assuming the minutest units of any given motion as a basis of calculation, we may constantly approach a solution without ever reaching it; it is only by admitting infinitesimal quantities and their progression up to a tenth, and adopting the total of this geometrical progression, that we can attain the desired result. The modern science of the value of the infinitesimal solves questions which of old were regarded as insoluble. By admitting these infinitesimals it restores motion to its primary condition of inherent perpetuity, and so corrects the errors which the human mind is led to commit by regarding the separate units of motion instead of motion as a whole.

In our search for the laws of history the same rule must be observed. The onward march of humanity, while it is the sum total of an infinite multitude of individual wills, is nevertheless uninterrupted; the study of these laws is the object of history, and in order to account for those which govern the sum of the wills causing that uninterrupted movement, the human mind admits the theory of independent and separate wills. The first process in history is to take at random a series of successive

68

events, and then to examine them apart from all others; but, in fact, there can be no beginning to them and no end, since each event is the necessary outcome of that which preceded it. In the second place, history studies the actions of a single man —a king or a general—and accepts them as the result of the wills of all men, while this result is never summed up in the actions of a single man, however lofty his position. However minute the units may be which the historian takes into account with a view to getting as near as possible to the truth, we cannot but feel that by isolating them, by assuming an independent cause for each phenomenon, and by supposing that human wills can find their expression in the acts of one single historic personage, he remains in error.

No such historical conclusion can bear the scalpel of criticism, because criticism selects a more or less extensive general view of facts—as it has a perfect right to do. It is only by studying the differential quantities in history, together with the homogeneous currents that carry men onwards, and then finding the integer, that we can ever hope to master its laws.

The first fifteen years of the nineteenth century exhibit an unwonted stir among many millions of men. They are seen to quit their avocations, to rush from one side of Europe to the other, to plunder and kill each other, to triumph for a while, and then in their turn be beaten. During this period all the course of daily life undergoes a complete change, till suddenly this ferment, which at one time seemed as though it must go on increasing, utterly subsides. "What was the cause of this phenomenon? What laws did it follow?" are the questions asked by human reason.

By way of a reply, historians narrate the deeds or report the speeches of a few score of men in a building in the city of Paris; to these acts and speeches they give the name of the Revolution; they next give us an elaborate biography of Napoleon Bonaparte, and of certain other persons who became his friends or his foes; they tell us of the influence these personages exercised on each other, and then they say: "These are the causes of the movement; these were its laws." But human reason refuses to accept such an explanation; nay, it pronounces it faulty, because the cause is obviously inadequate to the effect produced. It is the sum of human energy which entailed the Revolution and Napoleon, as it was that which maintained them, and overthrew them.

"Where there is conquest," says the historian, "there is a conqueror, and every subversion of an empire brings forth great men." Very true—answers human reason—but this does not prove that conquerors are the cause of war, or that the laws which govern war lie in the power of individual action. Whenever the hand of my watch points to X, I hear the neighbouring clocks strike; but I should not therefore infer that the hand of my watch tolls the bell of the church clock. Again, when I see a steam locomotive in motion, I hear it whistle, I see the valves open and shut, and the wheels go round; but I do not conclude that the whistle and the valves make the engine move on. Country people will tell you that at the end of spring a cold wind blows because the oaks are budding; now, though I do not know why the cold wind blows, I cannot agree with the peasants in ascribing it to the budding of the oak-trees. All I find in these phenomena, as in all others, is a concurrence of conditions; and I may study the hand of the watch, or the valve of the engine, or the buds of the oak as long as I live, without discovering the cause of the chimes, of the motion, or of the cold wind. To ascertain these I must altogether change my point of view, and study the laws of steam, of acoustics, and of meteorology. The historian must do likewise—indeed attempts have been made in this direction—and instead of studying only kings and emperors, ministers and generals, must take into account the homogeneous elements and infinitesimal differentials which influence the masses. No one can foresee the degree of truth he may attain by following this method; it is certainly the only right one, and hitherto the human intellect has not given to it the millionth part of the pains it has devoted to the description of sovereigns, warriors, and ministers, and the analysis of the combinations their deeds have suggested.

CHAPTER XXIII

THE united forces of European nations had thrown themselves on Russia; the Russian army and population retired before them, avoiding a collision, from the frontier to Smolensk, from Smolensk to Borodino, and the French troops bore on for Moscow with a momentum of increasing ratio, as a body dropped from a height falls more quickly as it approaches the earth. Behind them lay thousands of versts of devastated and hostile country. Ahead, tens of versts between them and the desired goal. Every soldier in Napoleon's army felt and obeyed the impetus that pushed him forward. Among the Russians, the more decisive the retreat became the more did their hatred of the invader increase and rankle in every heart. We have seen the terrific collision between the two hostile forces that took place at Borodino. Still, neither yielded; and after that conflict the Russians continued their retreat as inevitably as a ball which strikes another with a greater impetus rolls back; and as inevitably, the ball with the greater impetus (though it loses most of its force because of the impact) continues to roll onward for a while longer.

The Russians withdrew to a hundred and twenty versts behind Moscow; the French entered the capital, and halting there as a wild beast squats to lick its wounds when driven into a corner, they spent five weeks without offering battle, to fly afterwards, without any reason, home by the road by which they came. They crowded the road to Kalouga, and in spite of a victory at Malo-Yaroslavetz, made the best of their way back to Smolensk, Vilna, the Bérésina and so on.

By sunset on the 7th of September Koutouzow and the Russian army was convinced that the battle of Borodino was a victory for them. The commander-in-chief announced it to the czar, and issued orders to the troops to hold themselves in readiness for another action, which should finally crush the enemy, not because he wanted to deceive anybody, but because he knew the enemy was vanquished, as did every one of those who took part in the action. But in the course of the evening and next day reports came in of losses that had not been suspected. The army was diminished by half, and a second engagement out of the question. How could they think of fighting again before they had even received complete information, rescued the wounded, carried off the dead, appointed fresh officers and given the men time to breathe and to eat? Meanwhile the French, propelled by that fatal momentum, were driving them back. Koutouzow eagerly desired to renew the struggle on the morrow, and so did his army; but something more than the wish was necessary. It had to be possible, and it was absolutely impossible. On the contrary, a retreat was indispensable; from day to day, from stage to stage till the army arrived under the walls of Moscow, and then it was compelled by circumstances to retire even farther, notwith-standing the vehement feeling against it which was seething in the ranks. Thus Moscow fell into the hands of the foe.

Those who fancy that the plan of a campaign, or of an engage-ment, is elaborated by the generals in the silence of a study, forget or misunderstand the inevitable conditions under which a commander-in-chief carries on his operations. These are not in the least as we imagine them: we suppose him to be engaged in working out a campaign on a map of this or that district, with a known number of troops on each side, on familiar ground, and planning every movement at leisure. The commander-in-chief never enjoys such opportunities. He is never at the *beginning* of an event, as we imagine him to be. He is neces-sarily in the middle of a series of events, each one inevitably flowing from its predecessors. And every moment he is sur-rounded by conflicting interests, anxieties, orders, threats, schemes, and advice, and is always forced to reply to countless contradictory questions.

Military writers tell us quite seriously that Koutouzow ought to have got his troops on the Kalouga road before they had marched so far as the village of Fili; and that such a scheme was actually suggested to him; but they overlook the fact that a commander-in-chief has, in such critical junctures, ten or a dozen schemes proposed to him, each based on theoretical tactics and strategy, and all diametrically dissimilar. It might seem, no doubt, that his task would be to select one among them; but even that becomes impossible, for time and events do not stand still. Supposing, for instance, that on the 9th it is suggested to Koutouzow that he should get the troops together on the Kalouga road, while, at the same time, an aide-de-camp comes up from Miloradovitch to inquire whether he is to attack the French or to retire; he must answer at once, and if he orders the attack, that takes him away from the high-road. The commissariat officers ask him where the stores are to be sent; the head of the hospital department wants to know which way the wounded are to go; a courier rushes in from St. Peters-burg with a letter from the czar refusing to admit the possibility of abandoning Moscow, while a rival—for every commander-in-chief has rivals—comes to submit to him a scheme exactly the contrary of that which he has decided on. Add to this external pressure the minor facts that the commander-in-chief is in need of rest and sleep to recruit his exhausted strength; that he has to attend to the complaint of a general who considers himself slighted—to the petitions of the residents who think they are being abandoned to their fate—to the report of an officer who has been sent to inspect the neighbourhood and who exactly contradicts the last account—while a spy, a prisoner, and another officer give him various pictures of the enemy's position—and the reader may understand that those who fancy that at Fili, within five versts of the capital, Koutouzow was free to decide as to the defence or loss of Moscow, are utterly mistaken.

When was the question really settled? Why, at Drissa, Smolensk, and irrevocably, at last, at Schevardino on the 5th of September, and at Borodino on the 7th. After that every day, every hour, every minute of the retreat sealed the fate of the capital.

CHAPTER XXIV

WHEN Yermolow, who had been sent by Koutouzow to study the position, came back to tell him that it was vain to make a stand under the walls of Moscow, the commander-in-chief gazed at him in silence.

"Give me your hand," he said presently, and he felt his pulse. "You are ill, my friend; think of what you are saying." For he could not acknowledge the necessity of withdrawing beyond this point without another engagement.

Koutouzow got out of his carriage on the hill of Poklonnaïa, six versts from the Dorogomilow gate of the city, and seated himself on a bench; a crowd of officers gathered round him, among them Count Rostopchine, who had just arrived from Moscow. This brilliant party divided into several knots, discussing the advantages and disadvantages of their position, the situation of the troops, the various plans proposed, and the temper of the Muscovites. All were well aware that it was in fact a council of war, though it was not called so. The conversation was confined to generalities; private news was exchanged in an undertone; not a jest, not a smile relaxed these anxious faces, and each one was evidently striving to be equal to the situation. The general-in-chief listened to all the opinions put forward, but took no part in the discussion, and expressed no views of his own. Now and then, after listening to some speaker, he turned away, disappointed at not hearing what he had hoped to hear. Some were talking over the position now chosen, some not merely criticising the choice, but abusing the choosers; a third opined that the mistake lay farther back, that an action should have been risked two days since; while a fourth was giving an account of the battle of Salamanca, of which the details had just come to hand through a Frenchman named Crossart.

This Frenchman, who wore a Spanish uniform, was present with a German prince in the Russian service, and in anticipation of the possible defence of Moscow, was describing, at some length, all the vicissitudes of the siege of Saragossa. Count Rostopchine declared that he and the militia were ready to die under the walls of the ancient capital, and he could not help regretting the obscure inaction to which they had been left; he added that if he could have foreseen the turn affairs had taken he would have acted differently. Some of these gentlemen making a parade of their deep-laid strategical plots, argued over the direction in which the troops ought to move; the greater number, however, talked mere nonsense. Koutouzow's face grew ever more worried and anxious. From all he heard, Koutouzow could draw but one conclusion: namely, that it was impossible to hold Moscow. An order to make a stand and give battle would only have led to dire disorder; for not only did the generals regard the position as untenable, but they had already begun to consider the possibility and consequences of a further retreat, and this feeling pervaded the whole army. While almost all had abandoned the idea, Bennigsen, to be sure, continued to favour it; but the question itself had ceased to be the real point—it was no more than a pretext for discussion and intrigue. Koutouzow quite understood this, and estimated at its true value the patriotic feeling of which Bennigsen made a display with a persistency calculated to provoke the commander-in-chief to the last degree. In case of failure the blame would recoil on him, Koutouzow, for having led his army without a fight, as far as the Sparrow hills; or, in the event of his refusing to carry out Bennigsen's scheme, that officer would wash his hands of the crime of abandoning Moscow.

But all these intrigues were not prominent in the old man's mind; another and far more sinister problem rose before him, to which no answer had suggested itself: "Am I, in fact, responsible for Napoleon's advance to the very gates of Moscow? Which of my movements can have led to such a result?" he asked himself a hundred times. "Was it last evening, when

I sent to desire Platow to retire—or the day before, when I was half asleep, and told Bennigsen to act as he thought best? Well, Moscow must be left to its fate, the army must retreat, we can but submit!" And he felt it equally terrible to have to pronounce this decision or to have to resign his authority; for he not only loved power, which he was accustomed to wield, but he firmly believed himself destined to be the deliverer of his country; indeed, was not this what the country had expected of him when it insisted on his being appointed, in opposition to the wishes of the czar? He believed that he alone could command the army in these critical circumstances, that he alone could face the invincible conqueror without a qualm— but now a decisive step must be taken; at any rate the empty babble of these gentlemen must be put an end to. He called the seniors to him and said:

"For good or for evil I must trust my own judgment—" he got into his carriage and returned to Fili.

CHAPTER XXV

A COUNCIL of war was held at two o'clock in the more roomy of two cottages belonging to a man named Andrew Sévastianow. A crowd of peasants, women, and no end of children stood round the door of the other cottage; only the proprietor's little grand-daughter Malacha, a child of six, on whom his highness had bestowed a kiss and a lump of sugar, had stayed in the big room, perched above the stove and staring with shy curiosity at the uniforms and orders of the staff-officers who came in one by one, and seated themselves under the Holy Images. "The grand-father," as Malacha called Koutouzow, was sitting apart in a dark corner by the stove. He was huddled together in his camp-chair, muttering and nervously tugging at the collar of his uniform, which seemed to throttle him though it was open at the throat. He shook hands with some of those who came in, and bowed to others. Kaïssarow was about to open the curtain of the window facing his chief, but an impatient gesture warned him that Koutouzow wished to sit in the half-light, so that his features might not be too plainly visible. So many officers gathered round the deal table spread with plans, maps, paper and pencils, that the orderlies had to bring in another bench, on which the last-comers took their seat: Yermolow,

Kaïssarow, and Toll. The place of honour, exactly under the images, was filled by Barclay de Tolly, wearing the cross of St. George. His pale, sickly face, with a wide forehead that was all the more conspicuous from being bald, betrayed the ravages of a fever of which the ague fit was at this moment making him shiver. Ouvarow, who sat by him, was telling him something in a low voice with jerky gesticulation; no one indeed spoke above his breath. Dokhtourow, a short fat man, with his hands folded over his stomach, was listening eagerly. Facing him sat Count Ostermann-Tolstoï, his elbow on the table and his head on his hand—a handsome head with large features and bright eyes—lost in thought. Raïevsky, as usual, kept combing his black hair over his temples with his fingers and twisting it into ringlets, while he glanced impatiently now at Koutouzow, and now at the door. Konovnitzine's charming and interesting face was lighted up by a pleasant smile; he had caught Malacha's eyes and was amusing himself by making little signs to her, to which she shyly replied.

They were waiting for Bennigsen, who, under pretence of reconnoitring the position once more, was in fact taking his time over a capital dinner; thus they spent two hours, from four till six, chatting in undertones, without coming to any determination.

When Bennigsen at last made his appearance Koutouzow went up to the table, but still so as to avoid placing himself in the full light of the candles which had just been lighted. Bennigsen opened the proceedings by formally proposing this question:

"Are we to abandon without a struggle the ancient and holy capital of Russia, or are we to defend it?"

There was a long and breathless silence. Every brow was knit, every eye turned on Koutouzow, who, frowning too, was clearing his throat and trying to speak without betraying his agitation. Malacha, too, was watching him.

"The old and holy capital of Russia!" he suddenly exclaimed loudly and angrily, emphasising the words so as to accentuate their fallacious plausibility. "Allow me to remind your excellency that the phrase conveys absolutely no meaning to Russian hearts. This is not the way to formulate the question which I have invited these gentlemen here to discuss. It is simply a military problem, to be stated as follows: Since the safety of the country depends on the army, is it more advantageous to risk its destruction and the loss of Moscow by fighting a pitched battle, or to withdraw without resistance and leave the city to its fate? That is the point on which I ask your counsel."

Discussion at once recommenced; Bennigsen, who would not take a beating, sided with Barclay, who thought that it was impossible to hold Fili; he consequently proposed that during the night the Russian right should be marched across to strengthen the left, and then attack the enemy's right. On this point votes were divided, and the pros and cons were warmly argued; Yermolow, Dokhtourow, and Raïevsky supported Bennigsen. Was it that they thought some sacrifice must be made before Moscow was abandoned, or had they other and personal ends in view? They did not seem to understand that their combination could no longer check the fatal march of events. Moscow was, to all intents, already abandoned. The other officers saw it clearly, and only debated as to the line to be taken by the retreating army.

Malacha, looking on, wide eyed, understood the matter quite differently; she thought that "the grandfather" and "the long-coat," as she called Bennigsen in her own mind, were having a quarrel. She saw that they were certainly irritating each other, and at the bottom of her little heart she was sure that "the grandfather" was right; she caught his keen and cunning glance on its way to Bennigsen, and was charmed to see the old man set his antagonist down. Bennigsen reddened and walked across the room; Koutouzow's words, though calm and few, expressed entire disapproval.

"I could not possibly approve of the count's plan, gentlemen. To change the disposition of an army in the immediate proximity of the enemy is always a dangerous manœuvre. History proves it. Thus, for instance," he paused as if to recall some facts, and then, with a look of affected candour straight into Bennigsen's face he went on—"for instance, at the battle of Friedland—which, as you no doubt remember, count, went against us—the disaster was due to precisely such a change." A silence, lasting perhaps a minute, but which seemed never-ending, weighed on the meeting. Presently the discussion began again, but it was fragmentary; the subject was practically exhausted.

Koutouzow suddenly sighed deeply; the others understanding that he was about to speak, turned to listen.

"Well, gentlemen, I see that I must take it on my own shoulders. I have listened to everyone's opinion; I know that some of you will never agree with me; nevertheless . . ." and he rose—"in virtue of the power placed in my hands by the czar and my country, I command that we shall retreat."

The meeting broke up in solemn silence; it might have been a mass for the dead. Malacha, who had long since been due at supper, crept carefully down backwards from her perch, placing her little bare feet on the projections of the stove; then, gliding almost between the officers' legs, she vanished through the half-open door.

Koutouzow remained a long time with his elbows on the table thinking over this cruel dilemma; wondering again how and when the loss of Moscow had become inevitable, and to whom it could be imputed.

"I did not expect it to come to this," he said to Schneider, the aide-de-camp who came in to see him late at night. "I never could have believed it possible!"

"You must get some rest, highness," said the aide-de-camp.

"Well, we shall see! I will make them eat horseflesh yet, as I did the Turks," cried Koutouzow, thumping the table with his fist. "They shall eat it, they shall eat it!" he repeated.

CHAPTER XXVI

In contrast to Koutouzow, and to digress to a far more serious catastrophe than the retreat of the army—the desertion and burning of Moscow—Count Rostopchine, generally regarded as responsible for it, acted quite differently. All Russia—animated at this day by the spirit which then stirred our forefathers—might have prophesied these events which, after Borodino, were inevitable.

At Smolensk, and in every town and village in the empire, the same spirit prevailed as at Moscow, though they did not come within the influence of Count Rostopchine and his proclamations. The whole nation simply sat waiting for the enemy with stolid indifference, without excitement or disorder of any kind. They awaited him calmly, feeling that when the time came they should act as duty required. As soon as the enemy was known to be near, the well-to-do classes withdrew, leaving their possessions behind them, and the poor burnt and destroyed what was left. A conviction that it was the finger of fate, and that this was and must ever be the course of events, was, and still is, deeply rooted in every Russian heart. This conviction

—nay, I may say a prophetic certainty—that Moscow would be taken, pervaded every grade of society in the town. Those who left in July and August, abandoning their homes and half their possessions, proved that this was so, for they acted under the influence of that latent patriotism which finds no utterance in speeches, or in sacrificing our children for our country's good, or in other actions contrary to human nature, but which is expressed simply and unpretentiously, and so leads to great results.

"It is disgraceful," said Count Rostopchine's addresses, "to fly before danger; only cowards will desert Moscow!" and nevertheless they fled, in spite of being stigmatised as cowards. They fled because they felt that it was to be. Rostopchine had not frightened them with tales of the horrors committed by Napoleon in the countries he had conquered. They knew very well that Berlin and Vienna had not suffered, but that during the French occupation, those capitals had been gay with the fascinating conquerors who had bewitched the men, and even the women in Russia. They fled because, as Russians, they could not remain under French supremacy—good or bad; they could not accept the fact. They fled before the battle of Borodino, and, even farther, after the battle of Borodino, paying no attention to calls for defence; notwithstanding the Moscow military governor's expressed intention of raising the icon of the Iberian Holy Virgin and going with it into battle, or the balloons that were to destroy the French army; notwithstanding all the nonsense that was written by Rostopchine in his proclamations. They knew that the army must fight, and if it could not it was quite impossible to go with the young ladies and the servants to the Three Hills to fight Napoleon, and one had to leave town, however much one regretted leaving one's possessions behind. They fled without dreaming that there was any magnanimity in leaving a splendid and wealthy city to be burnt and plundered—as they knew it certainly would be at once—for it is only too true that to abstain from burning and plundering forsaken homes is a virtue quite out of the ken of the Russian populace, they fled each one for himself, and yet, because they fled, that great event happened that will always be the greatest glory of the Russian people. Hence a great lady, who in the month of June moved away from Moscow, with her negro servants and her buffoons, to take refuge on her estate near Saratow, in spite of the risk of being arrested by Rostopchine's orders, was instinctively determined never to be

Napoleon's subject, and in our opinion she was really and truly helping in the great work of saving the country.

Count Rostopchine, on the contrary—who blamed the fugitives, and sent the courts of justice to sit out of town; who served out bad weapons to tipsy brawlers; who ordered a procession one day, and forbade it the next; who seized all the private carriages and carts, taking 136 carts to move the balloon made by Leppich; who announced that he would set Moscow in flames, and his own house first, and an hour after contradicted himself; who appealed to the inhabitants to seize all spies, and then abused them for doing so; who drove out all the French, and left Madame Aubers-Chalmé, whose house was the great meeting-place for the French colony in Moscow; who without a shadow of a reason, exiled Klutcharew, the worthy old head of the post-office; who assembled a mob on the Three Hills, as he said, to repel the enemy, and then, to get rid of them, handed over a man to their fury; who declared that he should not survive the overthrow of Moscow, and wrote French verses in albums about his own part in the matter—such a man had no conception of the moral strength underlying the events going forward under his eyes. His one idea was to act independently, to startle the world by some heroic stroke of patriotism, and he laughed like a mischievous boy at the desertion and burning of Moscow, while he tried to promote or to check, with his puny arm, the irresistible current of national feeling which bore him, like others, down on its tide.

CHAPTER XXVII

HELEN, when she returned with the court from Vilna, found herself in a delicate position. At St. Petersburg she rejoiced in the protection of a magnate holding one of the most important offices of state; but at Vilna she had made friends with a young foreign prince, and as the two gentlemen each claimed her particular favour, her business was to solve the difficult problem of how to keep up both intimacies without offending either rival. However, what would have seemed perplexing, if not impossible, to any other woman, she accomplished without a moment's hesitation; instead of concealing facts or stooping to subterfuge in order to extricate herself from a false position—which must have been fatal to her success by proving her guilt, she at once took the bull by the horns and, like a skilful diplomatist, put herself in the right.

When the young prince on his first visit loaded her with jealous reproaches, she tossed her handsome head, looking at him over her shoulder.

"That is just like a man's cruelty and selfishness," she said haughtily. "I expected as much: a woman sacrifices herself for you; she is to suffer, and this is her reward. And pray what right have you to exact an account of my friendships? This man has been more than a father to me. Of course," she hastily added, to prevent his interrupting her, "he may not feel towards me as towards a daughter, but that is no reason for turning him out of my house. I am not a man, that I should be so ungrateful. I would have you to know, highness, that I account for my private feelings only to God and my conscience"; and she laid her hand on her beautiful bosom, which heaved with emotion as she raised her eyes to heaven.

"But listen to me, I entreat you. . . ."

"Marry me and I will be your slave!"

"But it is impossible. . . ."

"Ah! you will not stoop so low," and she burst into tears.

The prince tried to comfort her, while she, through her sobs, argued that a divorce was obtainable, that cases had been known—but there had as yet been so few that she could only name Napoleon and some other royal personages—that she and her husband had never been anything to each other, that she had been sacrificed. . . .

"But religion, law! . . ." objected the young man, half-persuaded.

"Religion! Law! what would be the use of them if they could not help in such cases?"

The young prince was startled by this suggestion, simple as it seemed; he asked counsel of the reverend fathers of the Society of Jesus with whom he was on intimate terms. A few days later, at one of the brilliant entertainments which Helen was in the habit of giving at her suburban house in Kammennoï-Ostrow, a fascinating Jesuit priest was introduced to her, a Monsieur de Jobert, whose glittering black eyes were in strange contrast to his hair, which was as white as snow. They sat talking together for a long time in the garden, in the poetic light of a splendid illumination, to the exciting strains of an inspiriting orchestra, discussing the love of the creature for the Creator, for the Redeemer, for the Sacred Hearts of Jesus and

Mary, and of the consolations in this life and the next promised by the only true faith, the Roman Catholic religion. Helen, deeply touched by these words, felt her eyes moisten more than once as she listened to Monsieur de Jobert's voice, tremulous with pious emotion. The conversation was interrupted by a partner who came to find her for a waltz; but on the following day her future director spent the evening with her alone, and from that time frequented the house.

One day he escorted the countess to the Catholic church, where she remained on her knees for a long time in front of one of the altars. The French priest, who though no longer young, was a compound of saintly attractions, laid his hands on her head, and at that imposition she felt as she afterwards stated —a pure, fresh air that seemed to touch her heart. . . . It was the operation of Grace!

Then she was brought into contact with a superior ecclesiastic, who heard her confession and gave her absolution; and the next day carried to her, in her own house, a gold vessel containing the sacred Host. He congratulated her on having entered the bosom of the Holy Catholic Church, assured her that the pope would be informed of her conversion, and that she would ere long be favoured by him with an important communication.

All that was going on around her and in her behalf, the attention of all these priestly personages with their subtle elegance of speech, the dove-like innocence she was supposed to have recovered—figured forth in her person by dresses and ribands of immaculate whiteness—all afforded a delightfully new amusement. At the same time she kept her main object in view, and, as always happens in an affair where the motive force is cunning, the weaker brain stole a march and outwitted the stronger.

Helen perfectly understood that the real end of all these fine speeches and strenuous efforts was merely to convert her to Romanism, and extract money for the use of the Order; hence she never failed to insist on the hastening of the formalities needed to procure her divorce, before acceding to any demands on her purse. So far as she was concerned, all she asked of religion was that it should help her to satisfy her desires and whims within the limits of certain conventional proprieties. So one day, in talking to her confessor, she urged him to tell her precisely how far she was bound by her marriage tie. It was twilight; they were sitting by the open window, and the evening air brought in the scent of flowers. A dress of Indian muslin scarcely veiled the whiteness of Helen's shoulders; the abbé plump and clean shaved, with his white hands modestly clasped on his knees, gazing at her beauty with decorous rapture, explained to her his views on this delicate and interesting question. Helen smiled a little uneasily; it might have been thought that she feared, from her director's look of admiration, lest the conversation should take an embarrassing turn. But, though he felt the spell of the lady's charms, the abbé evidently also enjoyed the pleasure of working out his arguments with art.

"In your ignorance of the duties to which you were pledging yourself," said he, "you swore to be faithful to a man who, on his part, by entering into the bonds of matrimony without recognising its religious solemnity, profaned the sacrament. Consequently, such a marriage is not of full and perfect effect: nevertheless your vow was binding. You have broken it. What then is your sin? Mortal or venial? Venial, beyond a doubt, since you committed it with no evil intent. If in marrying another man you hope to have children, your sin may be forgiven you; but here a fresh question arises. . . ."

"But," interrupted Helen impatiently, "what I ask myself is this: How, after being converted to the true faith, can I remain bound by pledges taken under the false one?"

This remark had the same kind of effect on the father confessor as the solution of the problem of the egg of Columbus; he was astounded at the simplicity with which the difficulty had been settled. Though amazed and delighted at his catechumen's rapid progress, he would not at once give up his chain of argument.

"Let us quite understand each other, countess . . ." he said, trying to find some answer to his spiritual daughter.

CHAPTER XXVIII

HELEN was perfectly aware that the affair was entirely free from all obstacles from the religious point of view, and that the objections raised by her directors were based solely on their fear of the secular authorities. So she made up her mind that society must be gradually prepared for it. She began by exciting her old protector's jealousy, and played the same farce with him as with the prince. He, no less astounded at first than the younger man had been, at the suggestion that he should marry a woman whose husband was still living, was, thanks to Helen's imperturbable impudence, not long in coming to the idea that it was a quite natural possibility. Helen would certainly never have gained her point if she had shown the slightest misgiving, the slightest scruple, or made the smallest mystery; but she told all her intimate friends—that is to say all St. Petersburg—without the faintest reserve, and with the most matter-of-course frankness, that both the prince and the old excellency had proposed to marry her, that she was equally fond of them both, and that she did not know how she could bear to hurt the feelings of either. The rumour of her divorce soon gained a hearing; many good people would have been up in arms at the idea, but, as she had taken care to mention that interesting detail as to her indecisions between her two adorers, those very people did not know what objection to raise. She had shifted the whole question to another footing: it had ceased to be whether such a thing could be, and was now only which of her two suitors offered the greater advantages, and how the court would take her choice. Here and there, of course, there were prejudiced persons who were incapable of rising to such sublime heights, and who spoke of the whole business as a profanation of the marriage sacrament; but they were few, and they demurred only in an undertone. As to whether or no it were right for a woman to marry a second time during the lifetime of her first husband, no one hinted the doubt; that part of the matter, it was said, had been settled by superior authorities, and no one would risk looking like a fool or an ill-bred ignoramus.

Maria Dmitrievna Afrassimow was the only person who allowed herself to express a contrary view for the benefit of the public. She was in St. Petersburg that summer to see one of her sons. She met Helen at a ball, stopped her in the middle of the room, and said in her hard, loud voice, in the midst of a general silence:

"So you are going to marry again while your husband is alive? And do you suppose you have invented a novelty? Not at all, my dear, others have thought of it before you, and it has long been the custom in all . . ." She spoke, rolled back her wide sleeves—an old habit of hers—looked at her sternly, and turned her back on her.

Though everyone was afraid of Maria Dmitrievna, it was often said that she was crazy; her scolding was soon forgotten, all but the insult at the end, and this was repeated in whispers, as if all the salt of the discourse resided there.

Prince Basil, who lately had very much lost his memory, and was constantly repeating himself, would say to his daughter, whenever he met her:

"Helen, I have a word to say to you; I have heard of some scheme, some arrangements—hey, you know? Well, my dear child, you know that I have a father's heart, and should be rejoiced to think—you have had so much to bear—dear child, consult your own heart. That is all I have to say—" and to conceal his affected emotion he would clasp her in his arms.

Bilibine had not lost his reputation as a man of parts; he was one of those disinterested allies which a woman of the world not unfrequently attaches to herself, a man to be trusted never to change his attitude. One day as they were sitting together, he gave her his views on this important subject.

"Listen, Bilibine," said Helen, who commonly called her friends of this type by their surnames, and she laid her white hand, with its blazing rings, on his shoulder: "Tell me, as you would your own sister, what I had better do—which of the two?" Bilibine frowned and reflected.

"You do not take me by surprise," he said. "I think of it constantly. If you marry the prince you have lost the chance of marrying the other for ever; and you will displease the court, for he is, you know, in some way connected. If, on the other hand, you take the old count, you will make his last days happy, and then, as the widow of so great a man, the prince would marry an equal in marrying you."

"You are a true friend!" cried Helen, radiantly. "But the thing is, that I like them both so much; I should not like to pain either—I would give my life to make them both happy!"

Bilibine shrugged his shoulders; he evidently saw no remedy for this misfortune.

"What a woman! One of a thousand!" he said to himself. "That is what I call putting things plainly. Why, she would like to marry all three at once. Tell me," he continued aloud, "what will your husband say to the matter? Will he consent?"

"Oh! he is much too fond of me to refuse to do anything for me," said Helen, convinced that Peter too was in love with her.

"Fond enough of you to divorce you?" asked Bilibine. Helen laughed heartily.

Helen's mother was also one of those who ventured to doubt the legality of the proposed marriage. She was always gnawed by envy of her daughter, and she could not bear to think of such good fortune falling to her lot; so she inquired of a Russian priest as to the possibility of a divorce. The priest assured her, to her great satisfaction, that the thing was impossible, and supported his opinion by a text from the Gospel. Armed with these arguments, which she regarded as incontrovertible, the princess went off to her daughter very early in the morning, to be sure of finding her alone. Helen listened quietly, and smiled with gentle irony.

"I assure you," said her mother, "marriage with a divorced woman is expressly prohibited."

"Oh! mamma, do not talk nonsense; you know nothing about it. I have duties, in my position . . ."

"But, my dear child . . ."

"But, mamma, do you really suppose that the holy father, who has the power to grant dispensations . . .?"

At this instant her lady companion came to announce that the prince was in the drawing-room.

"Tell him I will not see him; I am very angry with him for not keeping his word. . . ."

"Oh! countess, every sinner hopes for mercy!" exclaimed a fair man with marked features, who now appeared in the doorway.

The elder lady rose and made a respectful curtsey, of which the new-comer did not take any notice; she glanced at her daughter and majestically quitted the room. "She is right," said the princess to herself—her scruples had melted in the presence of his serene highness: "Yes, quite right. Why, did we never think of such things when we were young? And it is so simple, too!" and she got into her carriage.

By the beginning of August Helen's affairs were settled, and she wrote to her husband—who was so fond of her—a letter announcing her intention of marrying N., and her conversion to the true faith. She also requested him to carry out the formalities needed for the divorce, and which the bearer of her note was competent to explain to him. "So, praying to God to have you in his holy and mighty keeping, I remain, your friend.   HELEN."

This note reached Peter's house in Moscow on the day of the battle of Borodino.

CHAPTER XXIX

FOR the second time since the fighting had begun Peter fled from the battery with the soldiers as far as Kniazkow. As he crossed the hollow he went past the ambulance tents; but, seeing nothing but blood, and hearing nothing but shrieks and groans, he ran off as fast as he could. He wanted one thing only: to forget as soon as possible all the dreadful scenes he had gone through, to relapse into the groove of common life, and find himself in his room and in his bed; there alone, he knew, could he ever get a clear idea of all he had seen and felt.

But how was he to get there? Balls and shells were not singing along the road he was going, it is true; but at every yard he came on fresh scenes of suffering; he saw the same figures, exhausted or dully indifferent, and in the distance he could still hear the angry growl of musketry.

He walked about three versts on the way to Mojaïsk, and then sat down choked with dust. Night was falling, and the roar of cannon had ceased. Peter, resting his head on his hand, remained a long time watching the shadowy figures that filed past him in the dark; at every moment he fancied that a ball was dropping on him, and he started and half rose. He never knew how long he had been there, when, in the middle of the night, he was roused from his lethargy by three soldiers, who lighted a fire close to him and put on their pot. They crumbled their biscuit into it, and stirred in some dripping, and a savoury odour of frying mingled with the wood-smoke that rose from the camp-stove. Peter sighed, but the men paid no heed to him, and went on talking.

"And who are you?" asked one of them, suddenly addressing him; he wished no doubt to convey that they would give him a share of their mess if he could prove himself worthy of it.

"I!" said Peter, "I am a militia officer; but my detachment is not here—I lost it on the field."

"Hm!" said one of the men, and another shook his head. "Well, here, have some if you like!" and he handed to Peter the wooden ladle which he had just been eating with. Peter went up to the fire and ate with a will; he never had thought anything better. While he swallowed large spoonfuls of the stew the soldier sat staring at his face, lighted up by the blaze. "Where are you going to, tell me that?"

"To Mojaïsk."

"Then you are a gentleman?"

"Yes."

"What is your name?"

"Peter Kirilovitch."

"Well, Peter Kirilovitch, we will go with you if you like," —and they set out together.

It was cock-crow before they reached Mojaïsk and slowly climbed the steep hill. Peter, in his bewilderment, had entirely forgotten that his inn was at the bottom of the street, and might never have remembered it if he had not happened to meet his servant, who was wandering about looking for him. He recognised his master by his white hat visible in the gloom:

"Excellency!" he cried, "we could not think what had become of you. Are you walking? Why, where are you going? Come this way."

"To be sure!" said Peter, stopping short. The soldiers stopped too.

"Hallo! so you have found your people?" said one of them. "Well, good-bye, Peter Kirilovitch."

"Good-bye!" said they all in chorus.

"Good-bye," said Peter, turning back—"I ought to give them something, perhaps," he thought, putting his hand into his pocket. "No, it is of no use," said a voice within him.

The inn rooms were all full, so Peter went to sleep in his travelling-chariot.

CHAPTER XXX

HARDLY had he laid his head on the cushion than he fell asleep; suddenly, with a vividness that seemed almost real, he heard the thunder of guns, the flight of shells, the groans of wounded men; he even smelt blood and powder, and was seized with irrational panic. He opened his eyes and raised his head. All was quiet. An orderly was standing outside talking to the inn-porter; just overhead, in an angle formed by the roughly squared beams of the coach-house, a party of pigeons scared by his moving were flapping their wings; and the strong smell of hay, tar, and manure wafted vague suggestions of peace and rustic toil.

"Oh! thank God it is over; what a shameful thing is fear, and what a disgrace to me to have given way to it! And they

—they stood firm and cool to the last moment." "They" were the soldiers—the men in the battery, the men who had given him food, the men he had seen praying to the holy image. In his imagination they stood out, apart from other men.

"Ah! to be a soldier, a private!" thought Peter, "to live that life in common, to throw myself into it heart and soul, to feel and understand what they feel! But how can I get rid of the infernal and useless burthen that weighs upon me? I might have done so some time ago; I might have run away from my father's house; even after my duel with Dologhow. I might have become a soldier!" and his thoughts went back to the dinner at the club, to Dologhow's insult, to his meeting with the "Benefactor," at Torjok. And then he saw a solemn lodge meeting. This lodge was held in the English club. And some-one very dear to him is seated at the end of the table. But it is he! The Benefactor! But he is dead, thought Peter. Yes, he is dead, and I never knew he was alive. How sorry I am that he is dead, and how glad that he is alive again! On one side of the table sat Anatole, Dologhow, Nesvitsky, Denissow and others (all as vivid in his dreams as those he called "they"), and these people, Anatole, Dologhow, shouted and sang loudly, but through their noise could be heard the voice of the Bene-factor. ceaselessly talking, and the sound of his words was as uninterrupted and full of meaning as the hum on the battle-field, but very pleasant and comforting. Peter did not under-stand what he was saying, but he knew that the Benefactor spoke of charity, of the possibility of being like "they." And on all sides "they" with their kindly, simple faces surrounded the Benefactor. But though they were kind they did not look at Peter and did not know him. He wanted to attract their attention, to speak and as he raised himself he uncovered his legs which felt cold. When he again woke the blue twilight of dawn was peeping in under the roof, and a slight frost was sparkling on the beams outside. "Daylight already!" thought Peter, and he went to sleep again, hoping to find comprehension of the words that the "Benefactor" had spoken in his last dream. They had made so strong an impression on him that he remembered them long after, and he felt all the more convinced that they had been actually spoken to him because he did not feel himself capable of giving such a form to his ideas. "The most difficult thing in life is to submit one's freedom to the will of God," said the mysterious voice. "Singleheartedness consists in submission to the will of God, and 'they' are singlehearted.

They do not argue, they act. Speech is silver, silence is gold—so long as man dreads death he is a slave; he who does not dread it is lord of all. If there were no such thing as suffering man would know no limits to his own will—he would not know himself. . . ." He was still murmuring incoherent words when his servant called him and asked if he should put the horses to.

The sun was shining full in Peter's face. He glanced across the yard, which was full of mud and muck, with a well in the middle; round the well stood soldiers, giving water to weary horses harnessed to carts which were now quitting the inn-yard one after another. Peter turned away with a revulsion of feeling, closed his eyes, and rolled over on the cushions of his chariot. "No," he thought, "I will not behold all these hideous objects; I want to follow out the things revealed to me in my sleep. One moment more, and I should have understood! What is to be done now?" And he was horrified to perceive that all that had seemed so clear and satisfactory in his dream had vanished. So he got up, on hearing from his servant and the gate-keeper that the French were advancing on Mojaïsk, and the inhabitants quitting the town. He ordered his man to follow him with the carriage, and went forward on foot. The troops were in full retreat, leaving behind them 10,000 wounded, who were to be seen on all sides in the streets, and the courtyards, and at the windows of the houses. Nothing was to be heard but lamentations and oaths. Peter, meeting a wounded general of his acquaintance, offered him a seat in his carriage, and they went on together towards Moscow. On his way Peter was informed that both his brother-in-law and Prince Andrew were among the slain.

CHAPTER XXXI

HE got into Moscow on the night of the 30th August (September 10th); he had hardly passed the city gate when he was met by an aide-de-camp of the governor's.

"We have been looking for you everywhere," said the officer, "the count wants to speak with you on a matter of importance, and begs you will go to him at once." Peter sent his carriage home, and himself took a hackney coach, in which he drove to the governor's residence; Rostopchine himself had just come in from the country. The ante-room was full of people. Vas-

siltchikow and Platow had seen Rostopchine, and had assured
him that it was impossible to defend Moscow, and that the city
must be left in the hands of the enemy. Although this was
still kept a secret from the inhabitants, the civil functionaries
and heads of departments had come to ask for orders from the
governor so as to escape responsibility. At the moment when
Peter entered the ante-room a courier from the army came
out of Rostopchine's private room. To the questions which
besieged him this officer only replied by a gesture of despair,
and he hurried through the room without stopping. Peter
gazed with tired eyes on the various groups of officials, civil
and military, old and young, who were waiting their turn;
they were all anxious and agitated. He went up to two who
were talking together, and whom he happened to know. After
a few commonplace remarks the conversation resumed its
course.

"It is impossible to answer for anything in the present state
of affairs," said one.

"And yet he has just written such words as these," said the
other, holding up a printed paper.

"That is quite a different thing! That is for the populace."

"What is it?" asked Peter.

"Look at it. It is his last poster."

Peter took it and read it.

"His highness, the commander-in-chief, with a view to
effecting an earlier junction with the force advancing to meet
him, has traversed Mojaïsk and taken up a strong position
where the enemy will not find it easy to attack him. Forty-
eight cannon with ammunition have been sent to him from
here, and his highness declares that he will defend Moscow to
the last drop of his blood, and is ready to fight even in the
streets of the city. My friends, do not let the closing of the
courts of law occasion any alarm; it was necessary to remove
them beyond all danger. The scoundrel will find someone
here to talk to him, all the same! When the moment is come
I shall call on the brave youth of town and country alike.
Then I shall shout forth a ringing war-cry; till then I am silent.
A hatchet is a good weapon, a boar-spear is a better; best of all
is a pitchfork, and a Frenchman is no heavier than a sheaf of
rye. To-morrow afternoon our Lady of Iverskaïa will be carried
to visit the wounded in St. Catherine's Hospital. They will be
sprinkled with holy water, and get well all the sooner. I am
well. I have had a bad eye, but I can see out of both now."

"But military authorities have assured me," said Peter, "that fighting in the town is out of the question, and that the position . . ."

"That is exactly what we were saying," observed one of his friends.

"And what does this mean about his eye?"

"The count had a stye in his eye," said an aide-de-camp, "and was annoyed when I told him that there had been inquiries made as to his health. By the way, count," added the officer, with a smile, "we heard you had been going through a domestic crisis, and that your wife the countess . . ."

"I know nothing about her," said Peter, with indifference. "What have you heard?"

"Oh! so many things are invented, you know; I only repeat what I hear said. They say . . ."

"Well, what do they say?"

"That your wife is going abroad."

"Very possibly," said Peter, looking about him inattentively. "Who is that man?" he added, pointing to a tall old man, whose white eyebrows and beard were in strong contrast to his florid complexion.

"He? Oh, he is an eating-house keeper, named Vérestcha-guine. Do not you know the story of the proclamation?"

"Is that the man?" said Peter, looking at the resolute calm face, which was certainly not suggestive of treason.

"He did not write the proclamation; it was his son, who is in prison, and I fancy will not get off cheap! . . . It is a very complicated story. The proclamation was brought about two months since. The count had it inquired into. Gabriel Ivanovitch, here, was in charge of the matter; the paper had been passed on from hand to hand. 'Where did you get it?' he asked a man. 'I had it from so and so.' Off he went to the person named, and so by degrees traced it back to Vérestcha-guine, an innocent-looking youth, who was asked who had given it to him. We knew perfectly well that he could only have had it from the head of the post-office, and it was quite clear that they had a secret understanding. 'No one,' says he, 'I wrote it myself.' He was threatened and coaxed, but nothing would make him tell a different story.

"Then the count sent for him: 'Where did you get that proclamation?' 'I wrote it myself.' You may fancy what a rage the governor was in; but you must allow that such an obstinate lie was enough to provoke him."

"Yes, I understand," said Peter. "What the count wanted was that they should betray Klutcharew!"

"Not at all, not at all," said the aide-de-camp, somewhat scared. "Klutcharew had other sins on his conscience, and for those he was dismissed. However, to return to the story, the count was furious. 'How could you have written such a thing? It is a translation, for here is the Hamburg paper that contains it; and, what is more, you have translated wrongly, for you do not know French! Simpleton!' 'No,' says he, 'I did not read it in a newspaper; I wrote it myself.' 'If that is the case, you are a traitor, and I will have you tried; then you will hang for it.'

"There the matter stuck. The count sent for the old man, and he answered as his son had done. Judgment was given; he was condemned, I believe, to penal servitude, and the old man has come to ask for his pardon. He is a thorough blackguard, a spoilt rascal, and a loose fish in every way; he has picked up a little learning somewhere, and thinks himself a cut above everybody. His father keeps an eating-house near the Stone Bridge; there is a picture representing God the Father holding a sceptre in one hand, and the world in the other. Well, would you believe it, he has moved it to his own house, and a wretched painter . . ."

CHAPTER XXXII

The aide-de-camp had reached this point in his narrative, when Peter was called to go into the governor's room. At the moment when Peter entered Count Rostopchine was passing his hand over his frowning brow and eyes.

"Ah! good-day, doughty warrior!" said he. "We have heard of your deeds of prowess; but they are not in print at this moment. Now, between you and me, my dear fellow, are you a freemason?" he added, in a stern tone, conveying at once reproof and forgiveness.

Peter made no answer.

"My information is trustworthy," Rostopchine went on. "However, there are, I know, masons and masons; and I only hope you are not one of those who are ruining Russia under pretext of saving humanity."

"I am a mason," Peter said.

"Well, my dear fellow, you know I suppose that Messieurs Spéransky and Magnitzky have been sent—you can guess where—with Klutcharew, and a few others, whose avowed object was the establishment of Solomon's Temple and the destruction of the National Church. You may be very sure that I should not have dismissed the postmaster if he had not been a dangerous man. Now, I know that you smoothed his journey for him by giving him a carriage, and that he left some important documents in your hands. I have a great regard for you; you are younger than I am, so listen to my paternal advice: break off with that set, and take yourself off as fast as you possibly can."

"But what was Klutcharew's crime?" asked Peter.

"That is my business, and not yours!" exclaimed Rostopchine.

"He is accused of having diffused Napoleon's proclamations. But it was not proved," Peter went on, without looking at the count. "And Vérestchaguine . . ."

"Ah! There you are!" interrupted Rostopchine, in a rage. "Vérestchaguine is a traitor, and will get what he deserves. I did not send for you to pass judgment on my actions, but to advise you—or to order you, if you will have it so—to leave as soon as possible, and break off all connection with Klutcharew & Co." Then, feeling that he had spoken too hotly to a man who was in his own eyes perfectly guiltless, he took his hand, and changed his tone. "We are on the eve of a public catastrophe, and I have no time for civil speeches to all who come to speak to me; my brain is in a whirl. Well, my friend, and what will you do?"

"Nothing," said Peter, without looking up, but he seemed anxious.

"Take a friend's advice, my dear fellow; make off as soon as you can: that is all I have to say to you. A word to the wise, you know. . . . Good-bye. By the way, is it true that the countess has fallen into the clutches of the reverend fathers of the Society of Jesus?"

Peter did not answer, but left the room, looking gloomy and annoyed.

At his own house he found several people waiting to see him, the secretary of a committee, the colonel of a battalion, his steward, his bailiff, and others. Everyone had something to ask him. Peter could not take in what they said, he felt no interest in their business, and only answered their questions in order to get rid of them. When at last he was left alone, he opened his wife's letter, which was lying on his table.

"Singleness of heart consists in submission to the will of God. They are an example of this," thought he after reading it. "We must learn to forget, and to understand! So my wife means to marry someone else. . . ." He threw himself on his bed, and instantly fell asleep without even undressing.

When he woke he was told that a police agent had come from Count Rostopchine to inquire whether he had left; also that several persons were asking to see him. Peter made a hasty toilet, and then, instead of going into the drawing-room, he went down the back stairs, and out at the carriage-gates. From that moment till after the burning of Moscow he disappeared, and in spite of every inquiry no one saw him, or could discover what had become of him.

CHAPTER XXXIII

THE Rostows did not leave Moscow till the 13th, the day before the enemy entered the city.

The countess had been absolutely panic-stricken after Pétia had joined the Obolensky Regiment of Cossacks, and started for Biélaïa-Tserkow. The thought that both her sons were engaged in the war, and liable to be killed, gave her not a moment's peace. She first tried to persuade Nicholas to return; then she proposed to fetch Pétia, and place him in safety at St. Petersburg, but both schemes failed. Nicholas, whose last letter had described his unexpected meeting with Princess Maria, gave no further sign of life for a long time; this added to the countess's terrors, and she ceased to sleep at all. The count racked his brain to soothe her anxiety, and succeeded in getting his youngest son transferred from the Obolensky Regiment into Bésoukhow's company, which was being formed at Moscow; at this the countess was enchanted, and looked forward to watching over her Benjamin. So long as only Nicholas was in danger, she had fancied that she loved him best of all her children, and had reproached herself bitterly for favouritism; but when the youngest—that idle monkey Pétia, with his mischievous, bright eyes, his rosy, downy cheeks, and snub nose—was suddenly taken from her, to live among rough, coarse soldiers, who were fighting and killing, and being killed, she imagined it was he that was her darling, and could think of nothing but the moment when she should see him once more. In her impatience even those nearest and dearest to her only irritated her nerves: "I only want Pétia," she would say to herself. "What do I care for others?"

A second letter came from Nicholas at the end of August, but it did not soothe her anxiety, though he wrote from Voronège, whither he had been sent to buy horses. Knowing that he was for the time out of danger, her alarms for Pétia increased. Almost all their acquaintance had left Moscow and urged the countess to follow their example as soon as possible. Still, she would not think of moving before the return of her darling Pétia, who came at last, on the 9th. But, to her great surprise, the officer of sixteen seemed little touched by his mother's extravagant and morbid devotion: she took good care not to let him suspect her purpose of never allowing him to fly again from beneath her maternal wing. Pétia, however, was instinctively aware of it, and to guard himself against being moved by it—"against being made a molly of," he said—he returned her demonstrative caresses with elaborate coolness, kept out of her way, and spent most of his time with Natacha, to whom he had always been fondly attached.

The count's easy-going indolence was the same as ever; on the 9th, the day fixed for their start, nothing was ready, and the conveyances sent to fetch them from the country-houses at Riazan and the neighbourhood of Moscow never arrived till the 11th. From the 9th till the 12th all Moscow was in a state of feverish excitement; day after day thousands of carts came in bringing in the wounded from Borodino, or went out carrying the townsfolk and all they were able to take with them, meeting at the gates of the city. In spite of Rostopchine's declarations —or perhaps by reason of them—the most extraordinary rumours were afloat. It was said that everyone was forbidden to leave the capital, or, on the other hand, that the sacred images and relics had been placed in safety, and that the inhabitants were to be forced to go; or, again, that a battle had been fought and won since Borodino; it was also asserted that the army had been cut to pieces; that the militia were to go to the Three Hills, the clergy at their head; that the peasants were in revolt; that some traitors had been arrested, and so forth. They were all false reports, but those who left and those who remained were equally convinced that Moscow must be abandoned (in spite of the fact that the council of Fili at which it was decided to abandon Moscow had not taken place yet), and that there was nothing for it but to fly and save what they could. It was felt that a total smash was imminent; however, till the 12th there was no conspicuous change; Moscow by sheer force of habit lived its usual life, as a criminal stares about him on the way to the gallows, in spite of the catastrophe which was about to shake it to its very foundations.

These three days were spent by the Rostows in the fuss and bustle of packing. While the count was running about to pick up news and make vague general plans for leaving, the countess superintended the sorting of their effects, always at the heels of Pétia, who tried to keep out of her way, always jealous of Natacha, from whom he could not be parted. Sonia was the only member of the family who set to work to pack with care and intelligence. For some time she had been sad and depressed. Nicholas' letter, in which he spoke of his interview with Princess Maria, had been enough to fill his mother's head with hopes which she had not tried to make a secret of before Sonia, for she regarded their meeting as a direct dispensation of God. "I never was particularly happy," she said, "to think of Natacha's marrying Bolkonsky, while I have always longed to see Nicholas married to Princess Maria, and I have a presentiment that it will take place. That would be a happy thing!" And poor Sonia was forced to admit that she was right, for was not a rich marriage the only means of raising the fallen fortunes of the Rostows?

Her heart was full, and to divert her mind from her sorrow, she had undertaken the tiresome and fatiguing work of the move; in fact the count and countess referred to her when any orders were to be given. Pétia and Natacha, on the contrary, did nothing to help, but got in everyone's way and hindered progress. Then shouts of laughter and flying steps were to be heard all over the house. They laughed without knowing why, simply because they felt light-hearted and everything provoked laughter. Pétia, who had been but a boy when he left home, gloried in having come back a young man; and he gloried even more in having been brought from Biélaïa-Tserkow, where there was not the smallest hope of a fight, and in being at Moscow, where he would be sure to smell powder. Natacha was gay because she had too long been sad, and there was nothing at this moment to remind her of her grief, and because she had recovered her former brilliant health; nay, and they were gay because war was at the gates of the city, and fighting was close at hand; because arms were being given out, because there were plunderers about, people going and coming, bustle and excitement, and the stir of extraordinary events, which always produces high spirits, especially in the very young.

CHAPTER XXXIV

By Saturday, the 12th September, everything was topsy-turvy in the Rostows' house: doors were set open, furniture packed or moved from its place, looking-glasses and pictures taken down, every room littered with hay, paper, and cases, which the servants and serfs were carrying away with slow heavy steps; the courtyard was full of carts and chariots, some loaded and corded, others waiting empty, while the voices of the busy and numerous household echoed in every corner of the house and yard. The count was out; the countess, who had a sick headache as a result of all the noise and turmoil, was sunk in an arm-chair in one of the drawing-rooms, bathing her forehead with vinegar and water. Pétia had gone off to see a comrade, with whom he hoped to exchange from the militia into a marching regiment. Sonia was in the big drawing-room, superintending the packing of china and glass, while Natacha sat on the floor in her own dismantled room in the midst of a heap of gowns, ribbons and sashes, with an out-of-fashion ball dress on her lap, which she could not take her eyes off—it was that which she had worn at that first ball at St. Petersburg. She had been vexed with herself for being idle in the midst of all this excitement, and several times in the course of the morning she had tried to do something to help, but it was work that bored her, and she had always been incapable of doing any kind of work that did not captivate her, heart and soul. So after a few futile attempts, she had left the glass and crockery to Sonia, to arrange her own belongings. At first she found this amusing enough, giving away gowns and frippery to the maids; but when it came to packing everything she was soon tired.

"You will do it all for me, as nicely as possible, won't you, Douniacha?" said she; and sitting down on the floor, she fixed her eyes on the old ball dress, and fell into a reverie that carried her far back into the past.

She was roused by the voices of the maids in an adjoining

room, and the noise of steps on the back stairs. She rose and looked out of the window. A long train of wounded soldiers had drawn up in front of the house. The women-servants, footmen, and grooms, the housekeeper, and the nurse—all the household, in short—crowded out to look at them. Natacha, throwing a pocket handkerchief over her head, and holding the corners under her chin, went out, too, into the street. The old housekeeper, now pensioned off, Mavra Kouzminichna, went a short way from the little crowd in front of the gate, to a *telega* with an awning of bast mats thrown over it, in which a pale young officer was lying. Natacha shyly followed to hear what she was saying to him.

"Have you no friends in Moscow?" asked the old woman. "You would be so much more comfortable in a room; here, for instance—we are all going."

"But would they allow it?" said the wounded man in a weak voice. "You must ask the officer in charge." And he pointed to a stalwart major a few paces off.

Natacha gave the sick man a scared look, but went straight up to the major.

"Can these wounded men stay in our house?" she asked.

"Which is the one you wish to have, miss?" said the officer, with a smile, raising his hand to his cap.

But Natacha quietly repeated her question; her face and manner were so serious that, in spite of the quaintness of her appearance with the handkerchief thrown over her hair, the major ceased to smile.

"Certainly; why not?"

Natacha bowed slightly, and went back to the old woman, who was still talking to the wounded lad.

"Yes, they may, they may," said Natacha, in a low voice.

The wagon in which the young officer was lying at once turned into the courtyard, and half a score or more men were taken into houses in the neighbourhood. This incident, so completely out of the daily monotony of life, was delightful to Natacha, who made as many of the wagons come into the yard as it could hold.

"But, my dear, you must ask your father," said the old housekeeper.

"Is it worth while?" said Natacha. "It is only for one day, and we can surely go into the drawing-room and give them our rooms!"

"Oh! miss, that is just like one of your notions! Why,

even if we put them in the servants' rooms we cannot do it without leave."

"Well, I will ask."

Natacha flew into the house and went on tip-toe into the drawing-room, where there was a strong smell of vinegar and ether.

"Mamma, are you asleep?"

"How can I sleep?" cried the countess, who had, however, been dozing.

"Mamma, sweet little angel!" exclaimed Natacha, kneeling down by her side and laying her cheek against her mother's. "I beg your pardon for waking you, and I will never do it again. But Mavra Kouzminichna sent me to ask you. There are some wounded men here, men and officers, will you allow them to come in? They do not know where to take them, and I was sure you would"—she ran on, all in a breath.

"What? what officers? Who has been brought here? I do not understand?" said the countess.

Natacha began to laugh and her mother smiled.

"I knew you would be quite willing, and I will go and say so at once!" She jumped up, kissed her mother, and darted off; but in the next room she ran against her father, who had just come in, brimful of bad news.

"We have dawdled about too long!" he began, angrily. "The club is closed, and the police are moving out."

"Papa, you will not be vexed at my having allowed the wounded men . . ."

"To be sure not," said the count vaguely. "That is not the point; you will have the goodness, each and all of you, to have done with idle nonsense and to pack, for we must be off to-morrow, and as fast as possible." And the count repeated his instructions to everyone he met.

At dinner Pétia reported what he had heard: during the morning the people had fetched arms from the Kremlin, and in spite of Rostopchine's declarations that he would give the alarm two days beforehand, it was known in the town that orders had been issued that everyone should go in a body next day to the Three Hills, where there was to be a desperate fight. The countess looked at the boy's eager face with dismay, knowing that if she begged him not to go he would answer with something about being a man, honour, country, some extravagant absurdity that would be fatal to her hopes; so, thinking she might yet induce Pétia to leave town with them, as their protector, she said nothing. After dinner, however, she besought her husband, with tears in her eyes, to start if possible that very evening; and with the artless cunning of affection she, who until this moment had been perfectly cool, assured him now that she should die of fright if they did not get away at once.

CHAPTER XXXV

MRS. SCHOSS, who had been to see her daughter, added to the countess's terrors by the history of her experience. In the Miasnitskaïa, outside a large spirit-store, she had been obliged to take a coach to escape from the drunken crowd, who were roaring and shouting all round her; and the driver had told her that the mob had staved in the barrels, having been ordered to do so.

As soon as dinner was over all the family returned to their packing with vehement ardour. The old count hovered about between the house and the courtyard, hurrying the servants till he completely bewildered them. Pétia, too, gave orders right and left; Sonia lost her head, and did not know what to do first under the count's contradictory instructions. The servants squabbled and shouted and hurried from room to room. But suddenly Natacha threw herself into the fray. At first her intervention was looked on with suspicion; no one thought she could be in earnest, so they would not attend to her; however, she persisted with a steadiness that convinced everyone that she really meant it, and at last got herself obeyed. Her first achievement, which cost her immense labour, but which made her authority paramount, was the packing of the carpets; the count had a very fine collection of Persian rugs and Gobelins tapestry. There were two large cases open before her, one containing these carpets, the other china-ware. There was still a quantity of porcelain to pack, and more was being brought out of closets and pantries: there was nothing for it but to pack a third case full, and one was to be fetched.

"But look, Sonia," said Natacha, "we can get everything into these two cases."

"Impossible, miss," said the butler, "we have tried already."

"Just wait, you will see." And Natacha began taking out the plates and dishes that had been carefully packed in. "We must wrap the china-ware in the rugs," she said.

*D 5²⁷

"But then we shall want three cases only for the rugs," said the butler.

"Wait, only wait," cried Natacha. "Look, we need not take that," and she pointed to the commoner Russian ware. "That is quite unnecessary, while that can go with the carpets," and she pointed to a Dresden service.

"Let it all alone," said Sonia reproachfully. "We can manage it all without you."

"Oh! miss, miss!" lamented the butler.

But in spite of their remonstrances Natacha decided that they need not take the old carpets or the common service; so she went on with her task, leaving out everything that was of no value, and packed all over again. By this arrangement everything worth saving found a place in the two cases; still, do what they would, the box of rugs could not be shut. Natacha determined not to be beaten, altered, pushed, and squeezed, and made the butler and Pétia—whom she had enlisted on this arduous service—weigh down the lid with all their strength.

"You are right, Natacha, everything will go in if you take out one rug."

"No, no, press with all your weight! Press hard, Pétia. Now, on your side, Vassilitch!" and with one hand she wiped the perspiration from her face, while with the other she, too, threw all her weight upon the case.

"Hurrah!" she suddenly exclaimed. The lid was closed, and Natacha clapped her hands in triumph, and tears sprang up in her eyes, but only for a second. Having thus conquered the distrust of the family she set to work at once on another box. Even the old count was resigned now when he was told that this or that arrangement had been made by Natacha Ilinichna. Still, in spite of their united efforts, the packing could not be finished that night; the count and countess, having definitely decided not to start till the morrow, went to their room; the girls lay down on sofas.

That evening Mavra Kouzminichna admitted another wounded man into the house. She supposed, she said, that he must be an officer of high rank, though he was completely hidden by the hood and apron of his travelling-chaise. An elderly man-servant of great respectability rode on the box by the coachman, and a doctor and two orderlies followed in another carriage.

"This way, if you please, the family are leaving at once and the house is as good as empty," said the old woman to the servant.

"God only knows whether he is still alive!" said the man. "We have our own house too in Moscow; but it is some distance off and there is no one in it."

"Come in, you are very welcome here. Is your master very bad?" The man gave a despairing shrug:

"No hope," he said, "but I must let the doctor know."

He went to the second carriage.

"Very good," said the doctor.

The man peeped into the chariot, shook his head, and bid the coachman turn into the courtyard.

"Merciful heaven!" exclaimed the housekeeper, as the carriage drew up, "carry him into the house; the family will not object—" and as it was important to avoid going upstairs they carried the wounded man into the left wing, to the rooms which Mrs. Schoss had occupied till to-day.

The wounded officer was Prince Andrew Bolkonsky.

CHAPTER XXXVI

THE day of doom dawned on Moscow. It was a Sunday—a bright, clear autumn morning; the cheerful clang of bells from all the churches bid the faithful, as usual, to prayer.

No one, even now, would allow that the fate of the city was sealed; the covert anxiety which was fermenting silently only revealed itself in the high prices asked for certain commodities, and the unusual number of the poorer class who were wandering about the streets. A crowd of factory workmen, peasants, and servants, soon to be joined by students, civil officials, and men of all grades, had begun at daybreak to make their way towards the Three Hills. Having reached this point the mob waited for Rostopchine; but when he did not arrive, being convinced that Moscow was about to be handed over to the enemy, they presently dispersed and found their way into the taverns and low resorts of the city. In the course of the day the price of weapons, carts, horses, and gold coin rose constantly and steadily; while paper-money and articles of luxury were to be had cheaper and cheaper as the hours passed. A wretched horse would be sold by a peasant for 500 roubles, while mirrors and bronzes were to be had for a mere trifle.

The excitement and confusion that seethed outside was scarcely felt under the patriarchal roof of the Rostows. Three of their servants vanished, it is true, but nothing was stolen. The thirty vehicles brought in from the country were in themselves worth a fortune, so scarce was every form of vehicle, and several people came to offer the count enormous sums for one of them. The courtyard was still crowded with soldiers sent in by officers who had found refuge in the neighbourhood, and with poor wounded creatures who implored the steward to ask the count to allow them to ride on a cart, just to get safe out of Moscow. Though he was moved to compassion by these helpless beings the steward gave the same answer to all: "He did not dare," he said, "to trouble his master with such petitions. Besides, if he gave up one cart why not all, why not even his own carriages? Thirty carts would do nothing towards saving all the wounded, and in such a general catastrophe it was every man's duty to think first of those nearest to him. . . ."

The count had got up, had left his room on tiptoe so as not to disturb the countess, and had come out on the steps, where he presently became a conspicuous object in a violet silk dressing-gown. It was still very early; all the carriages were packed and standing outside; the steward was talking to an old military servant and a pale young officer with his arm in a sling. As the count came out Vassilitch sternly signed to them to go.

"Well, is everything ready?" said the count, passing his hand over his bald head and bowing kindly to the officer and the orderly.

"Nothing remains to be done, excellency, but to put the horses to."

"Capital! the countess will wake presently and then by God's mercy . . .! And you, gentlemen," he went on, for he was always attracted by new faces, "you will find shelter, at any rate, under my roof." The young officer stepped forward; his face, white with pain, suddenly flushed.

"Count, for God's sake let me find a corner in one of your baggage-wagons. I have nothing of my own, so I shall manage very well."

He had not finished his sentence when the old orderly preferred the same request in the name of his master.

"Of course, of course, only too glad," said the count. "Vassilitch just see that one or two of the wagons are unloaded— you see they are really wanted." And without explaining himself more clearly he looked another way. A bright look of gratitude lighted up the officer's face, while the count, much pleased with himself, looked round the courtyard. Wounded men were crowding in and the windows on both sides suddenly were lined with ghostly faces, looking at him with painful anxiety.

"Would your excellency just step into the gallery," said Vassilitch uneasily. "Nothing has yet been settled about the pictures."

The count went indoors, but he first repeated his instructions that the wounded were to be helped to get away. "After all, we may very well leave a few cases behind," said he in a low voice, as if he were afraid of being heard.

The countess woke at nine, and Matrona Timofevna, a pensioned lady's-maid, who now fulfilled the duties of her domestic police agent, came to say that Mrs. Schoss was very angry, and that the young ladies' summer dresses were being left behind. When the countess inquired as to the cause of Mrs. Schoss's wrath she was informed that it was because her trunk had been taken off one of the carts, and that other waggons were being unloaded and the cases piled in a corner of the yard, as the count had given orders that they were to carry wounded soldiers instead.

The countess sent for her husband.

"What is going on, my dear? They tell me that you are having the luggage unloaded."

"I was just coming to tell you, my dear. Well, the thing is, you see, little countess, some officers came and entreated me to lend some of the carts for the wounded. And all those things are not in the least necessary — what do you say? Besides, how can we leave them here, poor souls? We offered them shelter, you know, and I think that therefore we really ought . . . Why not take them with us? But we need not decide in a hurry. . . ."

The count had jerked out his broken explanation in a timid voice—the voice he spoke in when talking over money matters. His wife, who was used to it and knew it always precluded a confession of some great piece of extravagance, such as the building of a gallery in an orangery, or the arrangement of a party or of amateur theatricals, had made it a rule to thwart him whenever he asked for anything in that tone. So she put on a victimised air and spoke.

"Listen to me, count. You have managed so cleverly that at last you are not to be trusted with a kopeck, and now you are doing your best to sacrifice what is left of your children's fortune. Did you not tell me yourself that our furniture and effects are worth a hundred thousand roubles? Well, my dear, I do not intend to leave it behind; you must do as you choose, of course, but not with my consent. It is the business of government to look after the wounded! Look over there, at the Loupoukhine's house; they have carried away every stick. That is what anyone would do, with a grain of common sense! —but we, we are idiots! Have mercy on your children if you have none on me!"

The count hung his head and left the room, a melancholy man.

"Papa, what is the matter?" asked Natacha, who had stolen into the room at her father's heels and heard the debate.

"Nothing—nothing that concerns you," said her father.

"But I heard it all, papa. Why does mamma refuse?"

"What can it matter to you?" said the count crossly, and Natacha shrank back into a window-bay, disconcerted.

"Papa!" she exclaimed. "Here is Berg!"

CHAPTER XXXVII

BERG, the count's son-in-law, now a colonel wearing the orders of St. Vladimir and St. Anne, still held his snug and pleasant post under the head of the staff of the second division. He had come to Moscow that very morning (the 1st (13th) September) without any particular motive. But as everyone was going to Moscow he did as everyone did, and asked leave "on private business." Berg, who had driven up in his elegant droschky with two handsome horses—the counterpart of a pair he had seen belonging to Prince X—got out and crossed the courtyard, staring with much curiosity at the vehicles which crowded it. As he went up the steps he drew out a pocket-handkerchief of immaculate whiteness and tied a knot in it. Then, hastening his pace, he rushed into the drawing-room, threw himself on the count's neck, kissed Natacha's hand and Sonia's, and eagerly asked after his "mamma."

"Who has time to think of health?" the count growled dolefully. "Tell us what is going on. Where are the troops? Is there to be a battle?"

"God only knows, papa," replied Berg. "The army is full of heroic spirit, and the generals are sitting in council; the result is not yet known. All I can tell you, papa, in general terms, is that no words can do justice to the really heroic valour displayed by the Russian troops in the fight of the 7th. I can tell you this, papa," and he slapped his chest, as he had seen a general of his acquaintance do whenever he spoke of the Russian troops. "I can tell you frankly that we officers never once had to urge our men forward; it was with the greatest difficulty that we could keep back those—those. . . . Well, papa, they were really heroes of antiquity," he hastily concluded. "General Barclay de Tolly did not shirk risking his life; he was always in the front. As to our corps, which was placed on the slope of a hill, as you may imagine. . . ." And Berg went off into a long story, a compilation of all he had picked up from hearsay during the last few days.

Natacha's eyes, fixed on his face as though seeking there the answer to some question in her own mind, visibly disturbed the speaker. "The conduct of the troops was heroic; it is impossible to laud it too highly," he repeated, trying to win Natacha's good graces by a smile. "Russia is not in Moscow, but in the hearts of her children! eh, papa?"

At this moment the countess entered the room; she looked tired and cross. Berg leaped to his feet, kissed her hand, asked her fifty questions about her health, shaking his head sympathetically.

"Ah! yes, mamma, very true; these are cruel times for a Russian heart. But what are you uneasy about? You have plenty of time to get away."

"I really cannot think what everyone is about," said the countess, turning to her husband. "Nothing is ready, no one gives any orders. It is enough to make one wish for Mitenka back again! There will be no end to it!"

The count was about to reply, but he thought better of it, and made for the door.

"Papa, I have a great favour to ask," said Berg, taking out his handkerchief as if to blow his nose and accidentally noticing the knot.

"Of me?"

"Yes. As I was passing the Youssoupow's house just now, the steward came running out to ask me to buy something. I had the curiosity to go in, and I found a very pretty *chiffonier* —you remember I daresay that Vera particularly wished for one, and that we even had quite a little quarrel over it. If you could imagine what a pretty thing it is . . ." Berg went on gleefully, as his thoughts went back to his elegant and well-kept little home, "full of little drawers, with a secret division in one of them—I should so like to take it to her as a surprise. —I saw a troop of serfs down in the courtyard; let me have one of them—I will give him a handsome *pourboire* and . . ."

But the count frowned. "You must ask the countess," said he drily. "I do not give the orders."

"Of course, if it is not convenient, I can do without," said Berg. "It was only because Vera . . ."

"Devil take it. Devil take you all!" exclaimed the count, out of patience. "You are turning my brain among you, upon my soul you are!" and he left the room.

The countess melted into tears.

"Oh! the times are desperately hard," Berg began again.

Natacha had followed her father, but a fresh idea struck her and she flew down the stairs four steps at a time. Pétia was on the outside steps, very busy distributing arms to all who were leaving Moscow. The carts were still standing there with the horses ready harnessed, but two had been unloaded, and in one of them an officer had ensconced himself with the help of his servant.

"Do you know what it was about?" asked Pétia of his sister, alluding to the squabble between his parents. She did not answer. "I suppose it was because papa wanted to let the wounded men have the wagons," the boy went on. "Vassili told me, and in my opinion . . ."

"In my opinion," exclaimed Natacha, suddenly flaring up as she looked at her brother, "it is so mean, so shameful, that it maddens me! Are we Germans?"

She stopped, choked with sobs, and as no one was at hand on whom she could vent her passion, she hastily fled.

Berg, seated by his mother-in-law, was pouring out a stream of respectful consolations, when Natacha, angry and tearful, rushed in, like a hurricane, and went resolutely up to her mother.

"It is horrible, disgraceful!" she said. "You never can have given such an order, it is impossible!" Berg and the countess looked up quite scared. The count, who was at the window, said nothing.

"Mamma, it is impossible! Do you know what is going on in the courtyard? They are to be left behind!"

"What is the matter? Who are to be left?"

"The wounded. Oh! mamma, it is not like you. Dear

mamma, dear little dove of a mother, forgive me, I ought not to speak so—but what do we want with all those things?"

The countess looked in the girl's face, and understood the cause of her excitement, and of her husband's bad temper; the count would not look round.

"Well, well, do as you please—I do not prevent you," said she, not yielding entirely.

"Mamma, will you forgive me?"

But the countess gently pushed her aside, and went to her husband.

"My dear, settle it just as you like; have I ever interfered. . . .?" But she cast down her eyes like a criminal.

"The eggs giving a lesson to the old hen!" said the count, and he kissed his wife with tears in his eyes while she hid her confusion on his shoulder.

"Oh, papa! may we? And we shall have plenty of room for all that is necessary. . . ." The count nodded assent, and Natacha was gone, with one bound to the stairs, and another down into the courtyard.

When she gave the order to unload the vehicles the servants could not believe their ears; they gathered round her and would not do it till the count told them that it was by their mistress's desire. Then they were no less convinced of the impossibility of leaving the wounded than they had been, a few minutes before, of the necessity of carrying away all the property, and they set to work with a will. The sufferers dragged themselves out of the rooms and crowded about the wagons with pale but satisfied faces. The good news soon spread to the surrounding houses, and all the wounded men in the neighbourhood flocked into the Rostows' courtyard. Many of them would have managed to find room among the trunks and cases, but, when once the unloading had begun, who could stop it? And after all, what matter whether the whole or only a part of the things were left behind? The yard was littered with half-open boxes, containing rugs, china, and bronzes—all that had been so carefully packed the day before; and everyone was busy trying to reduce the amount of luggage, so as to convey as many of the wounded as possible.

"We still have room for four," said the steward. "They can have my cart."

"And take the one that has my trunks," said the countess. "Douniacha can sit by me."

The order was immediately carried out, and some more

wounded were sent for from two doors off. All the servants, and Natacha too, were in a state of extreme excitement.

"How can we fasten on this case?" asked some men, who were trying to tie a certain box on to the back of a carriage. "It really wants a cart to itself!"

"What is in it?" asked Natacha.

"The books out of the library."

"Leave them; we don't want them."

The britzska was quite full; there was not room even for Pétia.

"He will ride on the box. You will go on the box, won't you, Pétia?"

Sonia meanwhile had never ceased toiling; but, unlike Natacha, she was putting the things in order that were to be left behind, writing labels for them, by the countess's desire, and doing her best to get as much taken as possible.

CHAPTER XXXVIII

At last, by two in the afternoon the four carriages, packed and loaded, stood, horses and all, in a row in front of the steps; while the waggons full of wounded men made their way out of the courtyard. The travelling-chariot in which Prince Andrew was lying, caught Sonia's attention as she and her lady's-maid were busy trying to arrange a comfortable corner for the countess in the roomy carriage.

"Whose is that chariot?" asked Sonia, putting her head out of the window.

"Do not you know, miss?" said the woman. "It is the wounded prince—he spent the night here, and now he is coming on with us."

"What prince? What is his name?"

"It is Miss Natacha's old *fiancé*, Prince Andrew Bolkonsky," said the maid, with a sigh. "He is dying, they say."

Sonia sprang out, and ran off to the countess, who was walking about the rooms, dressed for the journey, with her bonnet and shawl on, waiting till all the party should have assembled to close the doors, and to say a short prayer before starting.

"Mamma," said Sonia, "Prince Andrew is here, wounded and dying. He goes with us."

The countess stared in astonishment.

"Natacha?" was all she said.

In her mind, as in Sonia's, the fact had at first suggested but one idea; knowing Natacha as they both did, the feelings she must experience at this news were more present to them than the sympathy they had always felt for the prince.

"Natacha knows nothing about it, as yet. . . . But his carriage is coming with ours, that is the thing," said Sonia.

"And he is dying, you say?"

Sonia bowed her head, and the countess, clasping her in her arms, began to cry.

"The ways of the Lord are past finding out," thought she. She felt that the omnipotent hand of Providence was plainly visible in all that was going on around her.

"Well, mamma, is everything ready?" asked Natacha, gaily. "But what is the matter?"

"Nothing. Everything is ready."

"Well, then, come——" and the countess held her head down to hide her tears.

Sonia kissed Natacha, and Natacha looked inquiringly into her face.

"What is it? What has happened?"

"Nothing, nothing."

"Something wrong, and concerning me . . .?" asked Natacha, who was as susceptible as a sensitive plant.

The count, Pétia, Mrs. Schoss, Mavra Kouzminichna and Vassilitch came into the drawing-room; the doors were shut, and all sat in silence.[1] In a few seconds the count rose, sighed deeply and crossed himself conspicuously in front of the holy image. All followed his example; he embraced Mavra Kouzminichna and Vassilitch, who were to stay and take care of the house; while the two old servants seized his hand and kissed his shoulder, he patted them kindly on the back, bade them take care of themselves, and said good-bye with vague benevolence. The countess had taken refuge in her room where Sonia found her, again on her knees in front of the images; though some of them had been removed, as the countess clung to those which were most precious as family heirlooms.

At the entrance and in the courtyard, those who were leaving —their high boots pulled up over their trousers, their coats strapped round the waist with leather belts, armed with daggers and swords dealt out to them by Pétia—were taking leave of those who were to remain behind. As usual, at the last moment, several things had been forgotten or badly packed, and the two

[1] It is an old Russian custom for all to sit down and keep silence for a few minutes before a journey.

running footmen stood for a long time at the doors of the carriage, ready to help the countess in, while the maids were still rushing to and fro for pillows and parcels of all sizes.

"They always forget something," said the countess. "You know very well, Douniacha, that I cannot sit like that." And Douniacha, clenching her teeth to keep silent, once more indignantly arranged the countess's cushions.

"Oh, servants! servants!" muttered the count, shaking his head.

Yéfime, the countess's coachman, the only man she would trust to drive her, sat perched on his high box, and did not even condescend to look back at what was going on. Long experience had taught him that it would be some time yet before he was told: "Drive on and God be with us!" and that even after that he would be stopped at least twice, while some forgotten article was sent for; not till then would the countess put her head out of the window and implore him in Heaven's name to be careful going down hill. He knew it all well; so he waited with imperturbable coolness, and patience far greater than that of his horses, for the near horse pawed and champed his bit. At last everyone was seated in the great coach, the step was put up, the door shut, the dressing-case that had been forgotten was put in, and the countess gave the old coachman the usual injunctions. Yéfime solemnly took off his hat and crossed himself; the postilion did the same.

"God be with us!" said Yéfime, as he replaced his hat. "We are off!"

The postilion whipped up the leaders, the near shaft-horse put his collar to the work, the springs creaked and the heavy vehicle swayed. The footman sprang on the box as soon as they had fairly started, and then the other carriages, jolting over the stones as they turned into the street, followed in procession. All the travellers crossed themselves as they passed the church opposite, and the servants who were to remain behind escorted them a little way, hanging about the carriage doors. Natacha had not for a long time felt so happily excited as at this moment; seated by her mother, she saw the houses and walls of Moscow, which they were abandoning to their fate, slowly glide past. From time to time she put her head out of the window and looked at the long file of wagons which led the way—Prince Andrew's chariot at its head. She had no idea of what that closed hood concealed; but as it was the first of the long line she kept her eyes fixed on it.

As they progressed endless files of the same kind turned out from so many of the cross streets that in the great high street—the Sadovaïa—they formed two lines. In front of the Soukharew Tower, Natacha, who was eagerly watching the passers-by, suddenly exclaimed with joyful surprise:

"Mamma, Sonia, it is he!"

"Who? Who is it?"

"Why, it is Bésoukhow—" and she leaned out of the window to make sure that she recognised a tall big man wearing a coachman's *caftan*; it was easy to see at a glance that it was a disguise. Close behind him walked a little old man with a yellow, beardless face, wrapped in a cloak with a frieze collar.

"It certainly is Bésoukhow," said Natacha.

"What an idea! You are mistaken!"

"I will wager my head that it is he. Stop! Wait!" she cried to the coachman.

But it was impossible to stop; the drivers of vehicles in both directions shouted to him to go on and not to check the tide of traffic. However, the Rostows could clearly make out the tall figure, though some way off; if it was not Peter it was someone strangely like him. The person in question was walking on the footway, with his head bent and a grave face; the old man who looked like a servant, noticing the party in the carriage who were gazing at him so inquisitively, gently and respectfully touched his master's elbow. Peter, lost in thought, did not immediately understand what he wanted; but presently looking round to the spot to which his aged companion was pointing, he caught sight of Natacha, and by an involuntary impulse ran towards the coach. He went about ten steps, and stopped short. Natacha, still leaning out, hailed him with a friendly smile.

"Peter Kirilovitch, come here and speak to us. You really seem to know me again! It is very surprising that you should. And what are you doing in that queer costume?" she added, holding out her hand.

Peter took her hand and kissed it awkwardly, walking along by the side of the carriage, for it had not been able to stop.

"What is this?" said the countess, with kindly intent.

"I—nothing. Why? Ask me no questions, pray," he replied, feeling the bewitching charm of Natacha's bright face sinking into his soul.

"Are you going to stay or to leave Moscow?"

Peter was silent for an instant.

"Moscow?" said he. "Yes, to be sure; I shall stay. Good-bye."

"How sorry I am that I am not a man! I should have stayed with you," said Natacha. "For you are right, I know. Mamma, if you would only let me stay. . . ."

"You were at the battle—you saw the fighting?" asked the countess, interrupting the girl.

"Yes," said Peter, "I was there. There will be another to-morrow."

"But what is wrong with you?" Natacha persisted. "You are not like your usual self."

"Oh! ask me no questions. I do not know—to-morrow. Not another word! Good-bye, good-bye!" he repeated. "What dreadful times . . .!" He let the coach pass on and got back to the footway; while Natacha still gazed after him with her friendly, but slightly satirical, smile.

CHAPTER XXXIX

PETER, since his disappearance two days ago, had been living in the rooms that had belonged to his deceased friend, Bazdéïew. This was what had happened.

When he awoke that morning, after his interview with Rostopchine, he was for a few minutes bewildered to know where he was, or what was being said to him; but when his servant mentioned among the names of those who were waiting to see him, that of the Frenchman who had delivered his wife's letter, one of those fits of gloom and despair to which he was so liable came over him with crushing weight. His brain was utterly bewildered and confused; he felt as if he had nothing left to do on earth—that his whole existence had crumbled into nothingness, and that life had come to a deadlock. Murmuring to himself with a forced smile, he sat on his sofa, altogether lost; now and then he peeped through the keyhole at the people waiting in the adjoining room, or took up a book and tried to read. His butler came a second time, to say that the French gentleman urgently begged for an interview, if only for a few moments, and that a man had come from Mrs. Bazdéïew, who was obliged to go into the country, with a message begging him to take charge of her deceased husband's library.

"To be sure, of course—at once. Go and tell him I am

coming, that will be best," said Peter; and as soon as the servant had left the room he snatched up his hat and slipped away by a back door.

He met no one in the passage, and got down to the lower landing. There he saw the porter on guard at the front entrance, so he turned off down a back staircase leading to the courtyard, and stole across it unperceived. However, in going out of the carriage gate, he was obliged to go past the gate-keepers and coachmen in waiting, who all bowed respectfully. To escape their inquiring eyes, Peter did as the ostrich does, hiding its head in the sand; he looked away, and walked off as fast as he could go.

On mature reflection it seemed to him that the most pressing need was to go and look over the papers and books which were entrusted to him. He called the first hackney-coach he met, and directed him to drive to the widow's house, near the "Patriarch's Pools." He looked about him as he drove on, at the lines of conveyances carrying away fugitives; and he held on tightly, in order not to tumble out of his own ramshackle vehicle which jolted slowly along, creaking with rust; he felt as happy as a boy playing truant from school. He began to talk to the driver, who told him that arms were being distributed at the Kremlin, that all the populace were to be sent out on the morrow beyond the gate by the Three Hills, and that a great battle was to be fought there. When they reached the Pools, Peter had some difficulty in recognising the house, for he had not been there for some time. When he knocked at the door, Ghérassime, the little wrinkled old man whom he had first seen at Torjok five years since, opened the door.

"Is anyone at home?" asked Peter.

"My mistress and the children have been compelled by circumstances to take refuge in their country-house at Torjok."

"Let me go in all the same. I must look through the books."

"Yes, come in, come in, sir. His brother—my master's, God rest his soul—is here still; but as you know, he is very feeble."

Peter also knew that he was half idiotic, for he drank like a fish.

"Well, let me see. . . ." said Peter, and he went into the ante-room, where he found himself face to face with a tall, bald, old man, shuffling about in a pair of slippers, with no stockings on, while his rubicund nose bore testimony to his habits. On seeing Peter he growled out a few dissatisfied remarks, and vanished down a dark passage.

"A powerful mind once, but very feeble nowadays," said the servant. "Will you come into the library?"

Peter followed him. "Seals have been placed on everything, you see. Sophia Danilovna said we were to give you the books."

Peter was in the very room which, during the Benefactor's lifetime, he had entered once with such anxious trepidation. Since the old man's death the room had not been used, and the dust which lay on all the furniture made it look doubly forlorn. Ghérassime opened a shutter and went away. Peter went to a cabinet which contained various manuscripts, and took out a packet of very precious documents: the Constitution of the Scotch Lodges, ennobled and elucidated by Bazdéïew. He laid them out on the table, glanced over them, and then forgot everything in a brown study.

Ghérassime opened the door and peered in once or twice, but found him still in the same attitude. Two hours slipped by; then the old servant allowed himself to make a little noise; but it was in vain, Peter heard nothing.

"Is your driver to be sent away?" asked Ghérassime, at length.

"Ah! yes," exclaimed Peter, rousing himself. "Listen," he added, holding the man by a button of his coat, and looking at him with moist and glistening eyes. There will be a fight to-morrow, you know. Do not betray me, and do as I tell you."

"Very well," said Ghérassime, shortly. "Shall I bring you something to eat?"

"No—I want something else. Bring me a complete peasant's outfit, and a pistol."

"Very well," repeated Ghérassime, after a moment's thought.

Peter spent the rest of the day alone in the library, walking up and down it incessantly; and the old servant heard him talking aloud to himself several times. At night he went to rest in a bed that had been made ready for him. Ghérassime, in a long life of service, had seen many strange things; so he was not particularly astonished by Peter's eccentricity, and was very well content to have someone to wait upon. He had got the peasant's coat and cap by the evening without any difficulty and promised to procure him the pistol next morning. The old drunken idiot came as far as the door of the room twice in the course of the evening, shuffling about with his shoes down at heel; he would stand a few minutes gaping at Peter, but as soon as Bésoukhow looked round he crossed the skirts of his dressing-gown over his shanks, and made off as fast as he could go.

Peter, in his costume as a driver, was on his way to buy a pistol at the Soukharew Tower, with Ghérassime, when he met the Rostows.

CHAPTER XL

DURING the night of September 13th, Koutouzow gave the order that the army was to retire through Moscow to the Riazan road. The march began at night; the first regiments led the way in good order, and without hurry; but when, at daybreak, they reached the Dorogomilow Bridge, and saw in front of them an innumerable multitude, crowding the bridge, covering the heights, and thronging the streets till progress was impossible; when, at the same time, they were hemmed in behind by a mass of men pushing them forward, the ranks were reduced to disorder. The soldiers rushed on to the bridge, to the fords, jumped into boats, and many of them even into the water. Koutouzow himself made his way across the town by the back streets. By ten in the morning, of the 14th, however, only the rear guard remained in the Dorogomilow suburb: the rest of the army had made its way across.

At that same hour Napoleon, on horseback, in the midst of his troops, was standing on the Poklonnaïa Hill,[1] and gazing at the splendid panorama before him. During the memorable and eventful week—from the battle of Borodino on the 7th, till the entrance of the enemy on the 14th—Moscow had enjoyed the lovely autumn weather, which is always taken with gratitude as an agreeable surprise; the sun, though low on the horizon, seems to fill the air with sparkling light, dazzling the eye and giving a more genial warmth than in the spring; the lungs expand and dilate as they inhale the perfumed breeze; the nights are not yet cold, and the darkness is made glorious by showers of golden stars—a mysterious splendour that frightens some and enchants others.

On this day the morning light shed fairy-like beauty on Moscow. It lay at the foot of the hill, with its gardens, its churches, its river, its cupolas glistening like domes of gold, its fantastic and unique architecture—and everything looked as though life were moving there as usual. Napoleon, as he contemplated the scene, felt that mixture of uneasy curiosity and

[1] Salutation Hill, about two miles from Moscow on the Smolensk road.

covetousness which stirs a conquerer as he stands face to face with unknown and alien types. He felt that this great city was instinct with life; nay, he could see ample evidence of that from the height on which he stood: it was as though he heard the panting breath of a vast living body. Every Russian heart as it turns to Moscow, idealises the old capital as a mother; and every foreigner, though its maternal attributes may come not to him, is struck by its essentially feminine character. Napoleon felt it.

"This Eastern city with its numberless churches, Moscow the holy! At last I see the famous spot! It was time!" thought he; he dismounted, had the map of Moscow laid before him, and sent for his interpreter, Lelorme d'Ideville.

"A town held by an enemy is a dishonoured girl" he had said to Toutchkow at Smolensk.

But as he admired the Oriental beauty, prone at his feet, it was chiefly in amazement at finding a dream realised which he had so long cherished, and thought so difficult of attainment. He was excited, almost tremulous, at the certainty of possessing her, and he looked about him comparing the details of the scene with the plan of the city.

"There lies the proud capital, at my mercy! And where is Alexander, and what are his feelings?—I have but to speak the word—to give a sign—and the capital of the czars is destroyed for ever. But my clemency is always great to the conquered! I will be merciful. Messages of justice and conciliation shall be written on those ancient monuments of despotism and barbarism. I, sitting in the Kremlin, will dictate words of wisdom. From me they shall learn what true civilisation means, and future generations of Boyards will be obliged to remember the name of their conqueror with gratitude: 'Boyards'—I will say to them—'I do not wish to take advantage of my triumph to humiliate a sovereign I esteem; I will offer you terms of peace worthy of you and of my peoples!' And my presence will elevate them, for I will speak plainly and magnanimously, as I always do."

"Bring me the Boyards!" he said aloud, turning to his staff; and a general officer rode off in search of them.

Two hours went by; Napoleon breakfasted, and then returned to the same spot to await the deputation. His address was prepared—a speech full of dignity and majesty, at least in his own opinion. Carried away by the generosity he intended heaping on the capital, he already saw himself in fancy in the palace of the czars, surrounded by the magnates of the Russian court meeting those of his own. He was appointing a prefect who should gain him the hearts of the people, distributing largess to the benevolent foundations of the town, thinking that—as in Africa he had felt it his duty to drape himself in a *burnous*, and perform his devotions in a mosque—so here he ought to be open-handed after the traditions of the czars.

While he thus indulged his fancy, growing somewhat impatient at the delay in the arrival of the Boyards, his generals were debating in an undertone; for the emissaries charged to fetch these representatives had returned in consternation, announcing that the city was empty, that everyone was leaving. How was this news to be communicated to his majesty without making him ridiculous—the most disastrous issue conceivable? How was he to be told that, instead of the expected Boyards, there was not a soul to be found but the drunken mob? Some said that a deputation of some sort must be got together at any cost; others recommended that the emperor should be told the truth, with all circumspection and delicacy. It was a critical case.

"Impossible!" said they. "And yet he must know it sooner or later." But no one would be the first to tell him.

Napoleon, who had been so long content to indulge in his dream of magnificence, felt at last, with the subtle instinct of an accomplished actor, that the situation was losing its solemnity by dint of sheer lengthiness. He gave a sign, and a cannon was fired. At this signal the troops assembled in front of Moscow rushed in through the various gates at a double quick march, outstripping each other in the midst of clouds of dust, while the streets rang with their deafening shouts. Napoleon, sympathising in their enthusiasm, rode forward as far as the Dorogomilow Gate; there he stopped and dismounted, proceeding on foot, in confident expectation of meeting the deputation he had sent for.

CHAPTER XLI

MOSCOW was deserted. There was still a spasmodic semblance of life, no doubt; but it was practically empty and moribund, like a hive that has lost its queen. At a little distance it may still seem busy, but if you go close to it you cannot be deceived: this is not how it looks when the bees fly home to it; there is not the fragrance, the hum of life. A tap on the hive does not produce the general and immediate revolt of thousands of little creatures, curling themselves round to sting, buzzing and fluttering with rage, and filling the air with the stir of busy labour, though here and there, in its depths a feeble hum may be heard. At the entrance there is no heavy, aromatic scent of honey, no warm odour of gathered stores. No watchful guards are there, ready to give a trumpet call of warning, and then to sacrifice their lives in defending the commonwealth. There is no peaceful, regular toil betraying itself in a steady murmur; only a fitful and broken buzz. The working bees are no longer to be seen setting forth, light of wing, to forage in the fields for their fragrant booty; only thieving drones creep in and out, all clammy with stolen sweets. Instead of swarming bunches of honey-laden bees, clinging to each other, or brushing off the pellets of gathered wax, only a few torpid and half-dead insects are to be seen at the bottom of the hive, or wandering idly and vaguely about the fragile partitions. Where once there was a smooth floor, clean-swept by the fanning of their wings, the seams neatly caulked with wax, lie scattered crumbs of wax, broken ruins, a few dying creatures with legs still quivering, or corpses left unburied. The upper chambers are no less ruinous; the cells, built up with such exquisite skill, have lost their virgin beauty; everything is desolate, crushed, and defiled. Robber wasps invade the abandoned works, and the dismayed inhabitants—shrivelled, limp and decrepit, drag themselves about, listless and hopeless, with scarcely a spark of life; while flies, hornets, and butterflies come fluttering or blundering round the ravaged treasury. Sometimes one or two may be found faithful to their old habits, cleaning out a cell and instinctively removing a dead bee, while, close by these, two others are fighting or encouraging each other in idleness. A few survivors, finding a feebler victim, crowd round and suffocate it; here an invalid, no heavier than a tuft of down, flies slowly away, but soon falls, one more on a heap of dried-up dead—and where, not long since, thousands of bees stood in circles, and back to back, watching the mysteries of hatching broods, there is only a sprinkling of exhausted workers, and in the cells the hapless dead, who, even in their last sleep seem to be guarding the desecrated and violated sanctuary. It is a realm of death and decay! The few that survive climb, try to fly, cling to the masters' hand, and are too weak even to sting ere they die. He seals up the door, marks it for destruction, and presently takes out the fragments of remaining comb.

This was precisely the appearance of Moscow on that 14th of September. Those who had been left behind came and went as usual with mechanical regularity, making no change in the routine of life; while Napoleon, anxious and fuming, was pacing to and fro at the gate, waiting for the deputation to meet him—an empty ceremonial that he held indispensable. When at last they told him, with every conceivable circumlocution, that Moscow was empty, he scowled furiously at the man who had dared to utter the words, and continued his walk in silence. "The carriage!" he said; he got in with the assistance of the aide-de-camp in waiting, and drove into the town. Moscow deserted! What an incredible climax! Without attempting to go to the heart of the city, he alighted at an inn in the Dorogomilow suburb. The grand effect had missed fire.

CHAPTER XLII

The Russians poured through Moscow from two in the morning till two in the afternoon, closely followed by the wounded and the last remaining inhabitants. While they remained immovably locked on the Stone Bridge, the Moskva Bridge, and the Yaouza Bridge, quite unable to move forward, a mob of soldiers took advantage of the halt to steal back along Vassili-Blagennoï as far as the "Red Square," where they fancied they could help themselves to other people's property without any very great difficulty. The alleys and passages leading to the Gostinnoï-Dvor [1] were also thronged with men prompted by the same desire.

No invitations to buy were to be heard; the itinerant

---

[1] The Bazaar of Moscow.

merchants and their barrows had disappeared with the motley crowd of buyers and haggling women; the mob was exclusively composed of soldiers who had laid down their arms, and were going into the houses empty-handed, to come out loaded with spoil. The few owners who had remained on the spot were wandering about in dismay, opening and closing their shops, bringing out whatever they could first lay hands on, and giving it to their men to carry to some place of safety. On the square in front of the bazaar drums were beating a call to arms, but their rattle was ineffectual to restore discipline among the plundering soldiers, who, on the contrary, made off as fast as they could, while, through the seething mob, a few men in grey coats, with shaven heads, were moving to and fro.

Two officers—one wearing a scarf and riding a wretched iron-grey nag, and the other in a cloak and on foot—were talking at the corner of a street; they were presently joined by a third, also on horseback.

"The general says they are all to be driven out, come what may—half the men have deserted. Where are you off to?" he shouted to three infantry privates who were sneaking past to rejoin the ranks, holding up the skirts of their greatcoats.

"How on earth are we to get them together again? . . . We must make those we have march in double quick time to prevent their joining the others."

"But they cannot get forward; there is a deadlock on the bridge."

"Come—go forward and drive the mob in front of you," said an old officer.

The man with the scarf dismounted, and called the drummer, and they took their stand together under the arcade. A few soldiers began running with the crowd. A fat shopkeeper, with flushed, bloated cheeks, and a look of satisfied greed, went up to the officer, gesticulating eagerly.

"Highness," he said, with a free and easy air, "you must grant us more protection. As far as we are concerned it is a mere trifle; and if all that was expected was just enough to satisfy a gentleman like you, we should be only too glad— a couple of pieces of cloth are always at your service; for, of course, we know. But this is sheer pillage! If there were a patrol at any rate, or if we had had notice in time to shut up. . . ."

Some other shopkeepers had joined the group.

"What is the use of lamenting over such a trifle?" said one

of them very gravely. "Who thinks of crying for his hair when his head is cut off? They may take what they please?" he added to the officer, with a gesture of despair.

"It is all very well for you to talk so, Ivan Sidoritch," said the other angrily. "Come, highness, come this way."

"I know what I am saying," said the old man. "Why, have not I three shops, and above a hundred thousand roubles in goods? But how can we hope to save our property when the troops are taken away? God's will is stronger than ours!"

"Only come," repeated the other, bowing to the officer who looked undecided. "But, after all, what do I care!" he added suddenly, and he strode off.

A great noise of fighting and swearing was audible inside a shop where the door stood half-open. He was on the point of going in to see what was happening, when one of the men with shaved heads, in a grey coat, was flung violently out. The man sprang up very nimbly, and stooping almost double, threaded his way between the officer and the shopkeepers, and was lost in the crowd, while the mob flew at the soldiers, who were forcing their way into the shop.

At the same moment a tremendous outcry came up from the Moskva Bridge.

"What is the matter? What is it?" cried the officer, rushing to the spot with his companion.

Two cannon, removed from their permanent position, were placed at the end of the square, which was full of carts that had been overturned, and of infantry marching down on the people, who were running like mad creatures. Some soldiers were roaring with laughter as they stared at a huge waggon loaded with a mountain of furniture; on the top of it a woman was clinging with desperate shrieks to a child's arm-chair with its legs in the air; four dogs fastened to the wagon were huddled together in alarm. From what the officer could learn, the shrieks of the crowd and the woman's screams had their origin in a sudden panic. General Yermolow, hearing that the soldiers were pillaging the shops, and the inhabitants thronging the ways to the bridge, had had two guns brought down from their positions to make the people believe that he was going to clear the square by firing. Frenzied with terror, the mob had scrambled on to the carts and wagons, had upset them, pushing and yelling, and so had actually left the passage open for the troops who had marched on.

CHAPTER XLIII

In the heart of the city the streets were quite empty; private houses and shops alike were closed; near the taverns, here and there, drunken songs or shouting might be heard, but there was no sound of carriages or horses, and only the footfall of some rare passer-by echoed through the dismal silence. The Povarskaïa was as still as the other streets; trusses of hay, ends of rope, and pieces of board littered the wide courtyard of the Rostows' house—abandoned now, with all its splendid fittings; not a soul was to be seen, but the jingling of a piano came from the drawing-room: Michka, Vassilitch's grandchild, who had been left behind, was amusing himself with strumming on the keys; while the gate-porter, with his hand on his hip, was standing in front of a long glass, and smiling graciously at his own reflection.

"How clever I am, Uncle Ignatius!" cried the boy, patting with his hands on the keyboard.

"Wonderful!" replied Ignatius, still gazing at the broad face that beamed at him from the mirror.

"Oh! idle! Shamefully idle!" said the voice of Mavra Kouzminichna, suddenly coming behind them. "I have caught you! Look at that great face, grinning at its own teeth, while nothing is put away, and Vassilitch can hardly stand, he is so tired."

The porter looked grave at once, pulled down his belt, and left the room with submissive eyes.

"I am resting, little aunt!"

"I daresay, indeed, you little imp! Be off and get the samovar ready for your grandfather."

Then the old woman dusted the furniture, shut the piano, sighed deeply, and took care to lock the drawing-room door behind her.

She was standing in the courtyard, considering what she should do next—should she go and take tea with Vassilitch, or finish her work in the store-room—when hasty steps clattered down the deserted street and stopped at the gate; then someone rattled violently at the latch of the door, trying to open it.

"Who is there? What do you want?" cried the old housekeeper.

"The count—Count Ilia Andréïévitch Rostow?"

"Who are you?"

"I am an officer, and I want to see him," answered a pleasant voice.

Mavra Kouzminichna opened the wicket gate and saw in fact an officer, a lad of about eighteen, whose features were remarkably like those of the Rostow family.

"But they are gone—they went yesterday evening," she said, quite affectionately.

"Oh, what ill-luck! I ought to have come yesterday," said the young fellow regretfully.

Meanwhile the old woman had been looking with sympathetic curiosity at the face—so like those that were familiar to her, at the youth's ragged cloak and worn boots.

"What did you want of the count?"

"Oh! it is too late," said the lad somewhat crestfallen, as he turned to go; but he paused in spite of himself as it seemed. "I am a sort of relation of his; he has always been very kind to me—and you see," he added with a frank smile, as he pointed to his boots and his cloak—"I have not a farthing, and I wanted to ask the count . . ."

Mavra Kouzminichna did not wait till he had finished.

"Wait a moment," she said shortly, and she trotted off to the side-court where her rooms were. The officer stood looking at his boots with a melancholy smile.

"What a pity I have missed my uncle. And what a good old body! Where has she vanished to? I must ask her which is the shortest way to pick up my regiment, which by this time must have got to the Rogojskaïa gate."

He saw Mavra Kouzminichna coming back with a determined though somewhat timid look; she had a checked handkerchief in her hand which, as she came near him, she untied, and took out a twenty-five rouble note, which she awkwardly offered him.

"If his excellency had been at home, he would, of course . . . But as it is . . ."

She paused in confusion, while the young fellow gladly grasped the money and thanked her effusively.

"God be with you," said she, as she showed him out. The young officer darted off, along the abandoned streets, to rejoin his regiment as soon as possible by the bridge over the Yaouza. Mavra Kouzminichna watched him go, and stood for a few minutes outside the gate which she had carefully closed. Her eyes were bright with tears; he was long since out of sight, but she was full of the motherly pity and feeling that had been stirred in her soul by the sight of this young fellow, who was a perfect stranger to her.

CHAPTER XLIV

THE ground floor of an unfinished house in the Varvarka was occupied by a tavern ringing at this moment with drunken shouts and songs. Ten or more workmen were seated round the tables in a low dirty room—all tipsy, with coats unbuttoned and bloodshot eyes—and singing at the top of their voices; but it was easy to see that it was not out of jollity. Their faces streamed with perspiration; it was mere rollicking bravado and defiance. One of them, a fair, tall, young fellow, in a blue smock, might have been thought good-looking if his thin lips which twitched incessantly, and his gloomy, glassy eyes had not given his face a strange and sinister expression. He seemed to lead the chorus, beating time with great gravity, and waving his arm right and left above their heads; his sleeves were rolled back, and the white skin showed almost to the shoulder.

Suddenly, in the midst of the song a sound as of fighting fists was heard, and he abruptly stopped, saying in a tone of command:

"That will do, boys; they are fighting outside"; and rolling up his sleeve, which kept tumbling down over his wrist, he went out followed by his companions.

They, like himself, were workmen, whom the tavern-keeper was treating in payment for some leather of various kinds which they had brought from the factory where they worked. Some blacksmiths, fancying from the noise within that something extraordinary must be going on, had tried to get in; but the tavern-keeper and a shoeing-smith had come to blows in the doorway; the smith was thrown, and went reeling into the middle of the street, where he fell face downwards. One of his comrades immediately flew at the tavern-keeper, got him down and knelt on his chest with all his weight; but at that instant the young man of the rolled-up sleeve appeared on the scene, and dealing the smith a tremendous blow, shouted vehemently:

"Come on lads, they are killing our man!"

The shoeing-smith lifted up a blood-stained face, and cried out in a doleful voice:

"Help this way, help! A man is killed—he¹p!"

"Lord have mercy! they have killed a man!" bleated a woman, putting her head out of the gate next door.

A crowd had gathered round the fallen man.

"You are not content with robbing the poor wretches, and

fleecing them of their last rag, but you must kill a man, rascal!"

The fair man standing in the doorway turned his dull eyes from the tavern-keeper to the shoeing-smith, as if doubtful which he should quarrel with.

"Villain!" he suddenly yelled, flying at the tavern-keeper. "Tie his hands, boys."

"What! Tie my hands?" cried the man; he shook off his enemies with a violent effort, and snatching off his cap, flung it on the ground. It might have been supposed that this action bore some mysterious and ominous meaning, for the men instantly stood quiet. "I am for law and order, lads; and I know what order means better than any of you . . . I have only to go and fetch the police. . . . What! you think I shall not go? You will see. Any row in the streets is particularly forbidden to-day, do you understand?" And he picked up his cap. "Well, come on," he added, and he walked off, followed by the fair man, the shoeing-smith, the workmen, and all the crowd, shouting and yelling with excitement. "Come on, come on!"

At the corner of the street a score of journeymen-shoemakers were standing in front of a house with closed shutters, and a bootmaker's sign-board swinging in the wind; their clothes were shabby, and their dejected faces bore the marks of exhaustion from hunger.

"Now, ought not he to have paid us our wages?" said one, with a scowl. "Not a bit of it; he has drained our blood, and thinks the score is settled; he has fooled us all the week, and now he has bolted!" Then, seeing the other party approaching, he broke off, and he and his comrades joined the new-comers out of mere restless curiosity.

"Where are we going? Oh! we know; we are going to find the police."

"Is it a fact, then, that we are getting the upper hand?"

"Why, what did you suppose? Listen to what they are saying."

While everyone was asking questions, or answering at random, the tavern-keeper took advantage of the hubbub to make himself scarce, and stole home again. The young workman, not noticing the disappearance of his foe, continued his harangue, waving his bare arms, and so attracting the attention of the little mob, who eagerly hoped to hear some explanation that might encourage them.

"He says that he knows what law is, that he knows what order means! But have we not the authorities to tell us that? Don't you say that I am right, boys? How can the world get on without the authorities? Why, everyone will be robbed—and then——"

"Stuff and nonsense!" said a man in the crowd. "Do you believe they would all leave Moscow like that? Someone has been laughing at you, and you have taken it for gospel! Why, you can see what a lot of soldiers there are in the streets; do you think they will let 'him' just march in? The authorities are there to prevent it. Listen to what he says!" he added, pointing to the fair man.

Near the wall of the Kitaï-Gorod a group had gathered round a man who was reading a paper aloud.

"He is reading the ukase—listen, the ukase!" said one and another, and the whole party moved in that direction. The man with the paper, seeing himself the centre of a crowd, seemed somewhat embarrassed; but, at the workmen's request, he began again, in a rather tremulous voice: it was Rostopchine's last proclamation, dated August 31 (September 12th):—

"I am going to-morrow to see his highness — his highness," the fair man repeated in a solemn tone, but with a smile —"to consult with him that we may act in concert, and help the troops to destroy these ruffians, and send them to the devil. I shall be back to dinner, and set to work once more, and then we will act decisively, and give 'him' a thorough licking."

The last words were received in total silence. The young workman stood with his head bent, looking very gloomy; it was evident that no one had quite understood, but that the phrase, "I shall be back to dinner," had produced an unpleasant impression. The feeling of the populace was at such a high pitch of tension, that this commonplace platitude rang false in their ear. Anyone might say such a thing as that; in a ukase from a high authority it was quite out of place. No one broke the gloomy silence—not even the fair lad, though his lips quivered spasmodically.

"Let us go and ask him. Hallo! There he is! He will tell us himself——" cried a number of voices; their attention was attracted to an official personage, whose carriage, with an escort of dragoons, had just appeared in the square. It was the chief commissioner of police, who had just been to set fire to the shipping in the river by Rostopchine's orders. He had brought back a considerable sum of money, which, at the

moment, was snugly deposited in his pockets. Seeing a crowd
moving towards him, he desired the coachman to pull up.

"What is the matter?" he asked of the foremost, as they
timidly approached. "Well, what is it?" he repeated, getting
no reply.

"Your excellency, it is—it is nothing," said a man, in a
cloak. "They are all ready to obey your excellency, and to do
their duty, and to risk their lives. It is not a riot, excellency,
but as the count has sent word . . ."

"The count has not gone. He is here, and you shall not
be forgotten! Drive on," he added to the coachman.

The crowd had stood quiet, pressing closely round those who
were supposed to have heard what the representative of power
had said; but still, it allowed him to drive off. The commissioner looked back in alarm, and said a few words to the
driver, who flogged his horses to their utmost speed.

"We are being deceived, boys! Let us go to the count
himself, and don't let that one go! He shall be called to
account for this! Stop him, stop him!"

And they all rushed, helter skelter, in pursuit of the chief
commissioner of police.

CHAPTER XLV

DURING the evening of the 13th, Rostopchine had had an
interview with Koutouzow, and had come away deeply offended.
As he was not a member of the council of war, his proposal
to assist in defending the city was not even noticed; he was
also extremely astonished at the faith in the tranquillity of
Moscow which prevailed in the camp, some high personages
seeming indeed to regard its loyalty as a secondary and un-
important factor.

On his return, after eating his supper, he lay down, without
undressing, to rest on a sofa; between midnight and one in the
morning a servant woke him with a letter from Koutouzow,
which had come by an express messenger. This announced that
the army was to retire behind Moscow, by the Riazan road,
and begged him to be good enough to send the police force to
facilitate the march of the regiments through the town. This
was not news to the count; he had foreseen this issue even before

his meeting with Koutouzow, nay, the very day after Borodino. In fact all the generals had agreed that a second pitched battle was out of the question, and consequently all the treasure and crown valuables had been conveyed out of the city. Nevertheless this command, in the form of a mere note from Koutouzow, and brought at night to rouse him out of his first sleep, annoyed him to the last degree.

After the event, when he amused his leisure by writing an explanation of all he had done at this crisis, Count Rostopchine stated in several passages in his memoirs that his object throughout had been to keep Moscow quiet, and induce the inhabitants to quit it. If this was, in fact, what he aimed at, his conduct was above reproach. Why was not the wealth of the capital saved—arms, stores, powder, and corn? Why were thousands of inhabitants cheated and ruined by being told that Moscow would not be evacuated? "To preserve tranquillity," says Count Rostopchine. Why were masses of worthless documents removed, and Leppich's balloon, and fifty other things? "In order that nothing should be sacrificed," says the count again. If these views are admissible, everything he did may be justified.

All the horrors of the Reign of Terror in France were, in the same way, intended to secure public tranquillity. What could have given Count Rostopchine any ground for fearing a revolution at Moscow when the inhabitants had left, and the army had retired? Neither there, nor on any other spot of Russian ground, did anything take place which had the faintest resemblance to a revolt.

On the 13th and 14th of September there were still above ten thousand men left in Moscow, and excepting at one moment when the crowd collected in some excitement, by the governor's orders in the courtyard of his residence, there was no sign of a riot. Nor would there have been any reason to fear one, even if it had been announced after Borodino that the city must be abandoned instead of asserting the very contrary, distributing arms, and, in short, taking every step which could conduce to keeping up the effervescence of the mob.

Rostopchine was a man of sanguine and irritable temperament; he had always lived and moved in the higher circles of official administration; consequently, in spite of his very genuine patriotism, he knew nothing of the people, though he flattered himself he could manage them. Ever since the enemy had crossed the frontier he had assumed that he could play the part of supreme and active ruler of the national movement in the heart of Russia. He fancied that he not only governed the actions of the inhabitants, but influenced their impulses by means of his "posters"—proclamations written in a style of vulgar familiarity which the populace hold cheap even among themselves, and which they feel to be derogatory from the pen of a superior. But the part was to his fancy; he had thrown himself into it, and the necessity for laying it down before he could find an opportunity for some heroic exploit took him by surprise. The ground was cut from under his feet, and he did not know what line of conduct to pursue.

Though he had so long foreseen the catastrophe, he resisted the conviction that Moscow must be sacrificed to the very last moment, and would do nothing with a view to such a result. It was against his wish that the inhabitants were quitting the town, and it was extremely difficult to persuade him to authorise the steps necessary to secure the safety of the archives of the law courts. All his energies and all his actions were devoted to keeping alive in the citizens that patriotic hatred of the foe and that self-confidence with which he himself was so thoroughly imbued. As to any measure of the extent to which this energy was understood and shared by the populace no estimate has ever been possible. But when, in the course of their development, events assumed their true historical proportions—when words were too feeble to express the hatred of the nation for the invader, though it was not possible to give it vent in the fury of battle—when self-reliance was no longer sufficient to defend Moscow—when the people rushed away like a torrent, carrying their property with them, displaying by this act of negative determination the strength of their national feeling—then Rostopchine's attitude suddenly became an absurdity; he felt deserted, helpless, and ridiculous, and with the ground cut away from under his feet. Having received on waking the cold and commanding epistle of Koutouzow he felt all the more irritated because he knew himself to be guilty. Everything that Moscow contained had been entrusted to him—everything belonging to the State, and which it was his business to see taken into safety. And now to take it out of town was no longer possible. "And who is answerable?" he asked himself. "Certainly not I. All was in readiness, I held Moscow in my two hands and this is what they have chosen to do. Traitors! Scoundrels!" he cried out in his rage, not identifying the traitors and scoundrels against whom he was railing, but stung with an impulse of hatred towards those who, in his opinion, had placed him in this ridiculous position.

He spent the night in giving orders which everyone came to ask for; his friends and household had never seen him so morose and unmanageable.

"Excellency, here is a message from the Consistory—from the University—from the Senate House—from the Foundling Hospital. . . ."   "The firemen—the governor of the prison —the director of the lunatic asylum want to know what is to be done!"   And so it went on all night.

The count's answers were short and stern, and simply intended to convey that he declined to take upon himself any responsibility for the instructions he gave, but threw it all on those who had nullified his efforts.

"Tell the idiot to take proper care of his archives—and the other one not to worry me with silly questions about his firemen . . . If they have horses let them go to Vladimir.   Does he want to leave them for the French?"

"Excellency, the inspector of lunatic asylums is here, what is he to do?"

"To go of course; to go at once, and turn the madmen loose in the town.   Since the army is commanded by madmen it is only fair that those who are shut up should be set free."

When he was asked what was to be done with the prisoners, the count flew in a rage.   "Do you expect me to give you two battalions to escort them out of the city?   There are no troops, you know.   Well then, set them at liberty."

"But, excellency, there are the political prisoners—Metchkow and Verestchaguine."

"Verestchaguine?   Is he not hanged yet.   Bring him here."

CHAPTER XLVI

By about nine in the morning, when the troops began marching through the town, the count had ceased to be importuned with vexatious questions; those who were leaving and those who were staying no longer needed his advice.   He had ordered his carriage to go to Sokolniki, and while waiting for it sat down with his arms crossed and a scowling brow.

In times of peace, when the humblest administrator complacently believes the lives of those to whom he administrates

depend solely on his care, he finds the rich reward of his
pains in the consciousness of his own indispensable utility. So
long as the calm lasts, the pilot who leads the way in his frail
boat, showing the bulky man-of-war the line along which it
must steer, firmly believes—as is but natural—that his personal
efforts are moving the huge hulk; but if a storm should rise
and the surges drive the ship out of her course, she rides the
waves in majestic independence, and the pilot, who before was
apparently omnipotent, is now feeble and useless. This was
what Rostopchine felt, and he was deeply aggrieved.

The chief commissioner of police—the official who had been
stopped by the crowd—came into the count's room at the same
time as the aide-de-camp, who announced that the governor's
carriage was ready. Both men were pale, and the commissioner,
after reporting to the governor as to the results of his errand,
went on to say that the courtyard was full of a great crowd
who were asking to see him. The count, without saying a
word, went into the drawing-room and laid his hand on the
latch of the glass door that led out on to the balcony; but,
changing his mind, he went to another window, from which he
could watch what was going on outside. The tall, fair man
was still haranguing and gesticulating; the shoeing-smith,
covered with blood, stood at his elbow in sullen anger, and the
sound of voices came through the closed panes.

"The carriage is ready?" asked Rostopchine.

"Quite ready, your excellency," said the aide-de-camp.

"And what do those fellows want?" asked Rostopchine,
going towards the balcony.

"They have assembled, they say, to march against the
French by your orders. They talk of treason too; they are a
riotous crew, and I only just escaped from them. Allow me to
suggest to your excellency. . . ."

"Have the goodness to withdraw; I know what I have to
do"— and he still stood looking out. "This is what they
have brought the country to, and this is what they have
brought me to!" he went on, his passion against those whom
he held guilty rising to a pitch of savage fury beyond his
control. "There they are—the mob, the very dregs of the
people, that they have brought to the top by their folly!
They want a victim perhaps," thought he, as his eyes fell on
the young ringleader, and he wondered to himself on whom he
could pour out the vials of his rage.

"Is the carriage quite ready?" he asked once more.

"Yes, excellency. What orders have you to give with regard to Verestchaguine; he is below."

"Ah!" cried Rostopchine, struck by a new idea; he opened the glass door and stepped out on to the balcony. The crowd uncovered their heads and all turned to look at him.

"Good day, my children," he said loudly and hurriedly. "Thank you for coming. I will be among you in a moment; but first I have to settle with the wretch who has lost us Moscow. Wait." And he went back into the room as suddenly as he had come out.

A murmur of satisfaction ran through the crowd.

"You will see—he will make everything right—and you would have it that the French—" and so on—reproaching each other for want of confidence.

Two minutes later an officer made his appearance at the front door and said a few words to the dragoons who formed in a line; the crowd, eagerly curious, pressed forward towards the portico, where Rostopchine now came out.

"Where is he?" he said wrathfully.

Just then a young man appeared upon the scene, coming round the corner of the house; his neck was thin, his head half-shaved, and he wore a blue caftan, once an elegant garment, and a convict's dirty, shabby trousers; he walked slowly between two dragoons painfully dragging his shrunken legs and heavy chains.

"Put him there," said Rostopchine, pointing to the bottom step; but he did not look at the prisoner. The young man stepped up with difficulty, and the clank of his fetters was heard; he sighed, and dropping his hands, which were not at all like those of a working man, he stood with them folded in a submissive attitude. During this little scene not a sound was heard but a stifling cry here and there in the background where the people were crushing each other in their anxiety to see. The count, frowning, waited till the prisoner was in his place.

"Children!" he began in a sharp, ringing voice. "This is Verestchaguine, the man who has lost Moscow!"

The prisoner, whose pallid features expressed utter prostration of mind and body, held his head down; but as the count spoke, he slowly raised it and looked at him from under his brows; he seemed anxious to speak, or perhaps to catch his eye. All down his slender throat a blue vein swelled like whipcord, and his face flushed. Everyone turned to gaze at him, and he smiled sadly, as though he felt encouraged by a belief in their sympathy; then his head fell again and he tried to stand steady on the step.

"He has betrayed his sovereign and his country; he sold himself to Bonaparte; he is the only man of us all who has disgraced the name of Russian. It is through him that Moscow is perishing!" said Rostopchine in a steady hard voice. Suddenly, with a glance at his victim, he added in a louder voice, "I give him over to you to judge. Take him!"

The crowd, still speechless, packed closer and closer; the press was intolerable, and it became agony to breathe in the malodorous atmosphere while awaiting something awful and unknown. The men in the front ranks, who had seen and understood, stood open-mouthed, their eyes staring with fright —a barrier to the surging of the throng behind them.

"Kill him! Let the traitor perish!" cried Rostopchine. "Put him to the sword—I order it!"

An universal cry rose up in response to the furious tone in which the words were spoken, though they were scarcely articulate; there was a general forward movement, but it was instantly checked.

"Count," said Verestchaguine, timidly but solemnly, during this brief lull, "count, the same God judges us both . . .!" and he stopped.

"Kill him! I command you!" repeated Rostopchine, white with rage.

"Draw swords!" cried the officer in command.

At these words the crowd heaved like a billow, pushing the front ranks against the portico steps. Thus the fair-haired orator was brought quite close to Verestchaguine; his face looked stony—he still held his arm in the air.

"Get it done!" said the officer in a low tone to his men, and one of the dragoons hit Verestchaguine violently with the flat of his sword.

The poor wretch cried out with sheer terror; he hardly felt the blow. A thrill of horror and pity went through the crowd.

"Oh Lord! Oh Lord!" pleaded a voice; but Verestchaguine shrieked, and that shriek sealed his fate. The human feeling which till now had held the frenzied mass in suspense suddenly gave way, and the crime, already half done, could no longer be averted. A dull roar of rage and revenge drowned the last murmurs of pity; like the fatal ninth wave which destroys a sinking ship, a human wave rolled irresistibly onward; the hindmost of the crowd bore down among the front rows, and all were mingled in indescribable disorder. The dragoon who had already hit Verestchaguine raised his hand for a second stroke. The miserable wretch, covering his face with his hands, flung himself among the people. The young ringleader, against whom he fell, gripped him by the throat, and with a yell like a wild beast, fell with the prisoner in the middle of the mob, which rushed upon them both. Some pulled or hit Verestchaguine, others fell upon the lad, and their cries only incited the rage of their enemies. It was long before the dragoons were able to rescue the young workman, who was half dead; and, in spite of the violence they put into their bloody deed, the murderers could not beat the life out of their hapless and hardly breathing victim, for the dense mass crushed and squeezed them as in a vice, so that they had not room to do their hideous work.

"Finish him off with an axe! Is he well pummelled? A traitor! a Judas! Is he not dead yet? He has been paid his score!"

Not till the poor wretch had ceased to struggle, and his chest scarcely heaved with the death rattle, did the mob make way round his bleeding body: then all came in turn to stare, and turned away shuddering and shocked.

"Good God! What a wild beast a mob is! How could he possibly have escaped! And he is quite a young fellow, too! Some shopkeeper's son, no doubt! Oh! the mob! And now they say he was not the right man after all; they gave another a good beating! How can they be so little afraid of such a sin—?" They could all say this now, as they looked at the mangled body and the face all disfigured with dust and blood. A zealous soldier in the police service, thinking that the body ought not to be left to cumber the courtyard of the governor's house, ordered that it should be thrown into the street, and the dragoons dragged it out without ceremony, the head knocking against the stones, while the people shrank back in dismay as the corpse went by.

At the first moment, when Verestchaguine fell and the crowd flew at him, Rostopchine had turned as pale as death, and instead of making for the side door where the carriage was waiting for him, he hurriedly ran into the rooms on the ground floor, he himself knew not why. His teeth were chattering as if with ague.

"Excellency, not that way! Here—!" cried a scared servant.

Rostopchine mechanically followed, found his carriage,

jumped in, and told the coachman to drive to his country residence. He could hear the yells of the mob in the distance; and as he went farther away from it, the recollection of the excitement and alarm he had allowed himself to display before his inferiors annoyed him excessively. "The mob is terrible, hideous!" said he to himself in French. "It is like a troop of wolves that can only be appeased with flesh!"

"Count, the same God judges us both!" he remembered Verestchaguine's words; a cold chill ran down his spine. But it was only for an instant, and he smiled at his own weakness. "Come, come," thought he, "I had a duty to fulfil. The people had to be pacified! . . . public good is merciless on individuals!" and he reflected on his duty to his family, to the capital entrusted to his keeping, and to himself—not as a private resident, but as his sovereign's representative. "Had I been no more than a private gentleman my line of conduct must have been quite different, but under existing circumstances I was bound, at any cost, to protect the life and dignity of the governor-general!"

Comfortably rocked in his chariot, his body recovered by degrees, and as is always the way, with the calming of the body, came calm to the mind. His mind suggested the most flattering arguments to soothe his spirit. They were not new ones; ever since the world was created and men began to kill each other, no man that has ever committed a crime of this character has failed to hush his remorse by reflecting that he was forced to it by his regard for the good of the public. Only those who do not allow their passions to get the upper hand refuse to admit that the good of the public can require such deeds. Rostopchine did not for a moment blame himself for Verestchaguine's death; on the contrary, he formed a hundred reasons for being satisfied with his own tact in punishing a malefactor, and at the same time pacifying the mob.

"Verestchaguine was tried and condemned to death," said he to himself—but, in fact he had only been condemned to penal servitude. "He was a traitor, and I could not let him go unpunished. Thus I killed two birds with one stone."

As soon as he reached his destination he proceeded to various other occupations, and so put to rout any further doubts he might have had.

Half an hour later he was driving across the open ground of Sokolniki, having quite forgotten all previous incidents; thinking only of the future, he made his way to speak with Koutouzow who, as he was told, was to be found at the bridge over the Yaouza. As he rode along he prepared a speech of extreme severity, denouncing the commander-in-chief's disloyal conduct, by which he hoped to make that old "court-fox" feel that he alone was answerable for the woes of Russia and the loss of Moscow. The open plain was quite deserted, excepting that at the opposite side, in front of a workhouse and the lunatic asylum, a number of persons dressed all in white were moving about, some of them shouting and gesticulating. When the count's chariot came in view one of these men ran forward to meet it. The coachman, the dragoons, and Rostopchine himself looked with interest mingled with alarm at this party of mad creatures who had just been liberated, and particularly at the man who was coming towards them with an unsteady gait, his long white dressing-gown flying behind his lank legs. He kept his eyes fixed on the count, and shouted to him unintelligible words, while he signed to him to stop. His haggard and gloomy face was covered with tufts of hair; his eyeballs were yellow, with large, jet-black pupils, and they rolled with a scared and restless glare.

"Stop! Stop!" he shouted, panting for breath: and then he went on with his harangue and his extravagant gesticulations. At last he reached the carriage and ran on by the side of it as it went.

"I have been killed three times, and three times have I risen from the dead! . . . They stoned me, they crucified me. But I shall rise again—I shall rise again! Three times must the Kingdom of God be overthrown, and three times shall I re-establish it!" and his voice rose almost to a scream.

Count Rostopchine turned pale, as he had done when the mob had flung itself on Verestchaguine.

"Go on—faster, faster!" he cried to the coachman, quaking with fear.

The horses dashed onward; but still the madman's cries rang in his ears, as he left him farther and farther behind; and before him rose the blood-stained form of Verestchaguine in his fur-trimmed caftan. Time, he knew, could never dim the clearness of that vision; the fearful traces of that scene, he felt, would sink deeper and deeper into his soul, and haunt him till his dying day. He could hear himself say it: "Kill him— on your heads be it if you do not."

"Why should I have said that? he involuntarily wondered. "I might have held my tongue and nothing would have happened." He could see the dragoon's face with its sudden change from terror to ferocity, and the sad look of timid reproach in his victim's eyes: "But no—I could not do otherwise—the mob—the traitor—the safety of the public. . . ."

The bridge over the Yaouza was still crowded with troops; the heat was intense. Koutouzow, tired and anxious, was sitting on a bench close by and mechanically tracing figures in the sand, when a general in a cocked hat with an enormous plume of feathers got out of a carriage at a short distance off and addressed him in French with a mixed air of irritation and hesitancy. It was Count Rostopchine, and he explained to Koutouzow that he had come in search of him, since, as Moscow had ceased to exist, there was nothing left but the army.

"Matters would have turned out differently," he said, "if your highness had told me that Moscow would be deserted without a struggle!"

Koutouzow looked at him, not paying any particular heed to his words, but simply trying to read the expression of his face, and Rostopchine, abashed, said no more. Koutouzow quietly nodded his head, and without taking his eyes off him said: "No, I will not abandon Moscow without a struggle!"

Was he thinking of something else, or did he speak in full consciousness that the words were meaningless? Rostopchine withdrew, and strange to say this proud man, Governor-General of Moscow, found nothing better to do than to proceed to the bridge and stand there cracking a whip to drive on the carts that crowded the road.

CHAPTER XLVII

At four o'clock in the afternoon Murat's army entered Moscow, preceded by a detachment of Wurtemberg Hussars. The King of Naples himself, with a large suite, came on horseback behind. Having reached the Arbat, Murat waited for information from the van as to the state of the fortress known as the Kremlin. A few idlers gathered round him, staring in amazement at this foreign commander with his long hair, his coat blazing with gold, and his many-coloured plume of feathers.

"I say, is that their king?" said one.

An interpreter rode up to the crowd.

"Take your cap off!" whispered somebody in the crowd.

The interpreter came forward, and speaking to an old gate-keeper, asked him whether it were far to the Kremlin. Puzzled by the Polish accent, which was strange to him, the man did not understand the question, and slunk behind his companions. Murat rode up to the interpreter and told him to ask where the Russian troops were. One of the Russians understood the question and several voices answered together. At this moment an officer came up from the front to tell Murat that the gates of the citadel were shut, and that no doubt those within were preparing to defend it.

"Very good," he said, and he ordered one of his aides-de-camp to bring up three guns. The artillery set out at a trot, and Murat, passing the column which was to follow, crossed the Arbat. When they reached the end of the street the column stopped. Some French officers directed the placing of the guns and examined the Kremlin through a field-glass. Suddenly the bells began to ring for vespers; believing it to be an alarm they took fright, and some infantrymen ran forward to the Koutafiew gates, which were barricaded with beams and planks. As they approached two shots were fired. The general in command of the artillery shouted a few words, and all, officers and soldiers alike, turned back. Three more shots were fired and a soldier was wounded in the foot. Seeing this, a determination to fight it out and face death became visible on every face, taking the place of the calm and easy expression which till this moment they had worn. All, from the field-marshal to the humblest private, understood that this was not merely a street in Moscow, but a field of battle—where a bloody struggle was perhaps imminent. The guns were pointed, the gunners lighted their slow matches, the officer shouted: "Fire!" Two sharp whistles rent the air at once, the grape-shot rattled and sank with a sharp noise into the beams, the stonework, and the barricade, while two puffs of smoke hovered over the pieces. The echo of their discharge had hardly died away when a strange noise was heard in the air: an enormous number of rooks flew up from the walls and soared in a circle, croaking and beating their wings heavily as they rose. At the same moment a solitary shout was heard behind the barricade, and in the midst of the smoke, as it cleared away, the figure of a man stood revealed, bareheaded, wearing a caftan, and aiming at the French with a musket.

"Fire!" repeated the artillery officer, and the crack of the musket rang out at the same moment as the roar of the cannon.

A cloud of smoke hid the gate; there was not another sound; the foot soldiers again went forward. Three wounded men and four dead lay in front of the entrance, while two men fled along under the wall.

"Clear away!" said the officer, pointing to the beams and the bodies.

The French finished off the wounded and threw the bodies over the railings. Who were these men? No one ever knew. Monsieur Thiers alone has even mentioned them. "These wretches had taken possession of the sacred stronghold, seized some muskets out of the arsenal and fired on the French. Some were cut down and the Kremlin was purged of their presence." [1] Murat was now told that the way was open. The French entered the gates and bivouacked on the square in front of the Senate House, while the soldiers invaded the premises and threw the chairs out of windows to make their fires. The different detachments followed in files, marching through the Kremlin to find empty and deserted houses where they established themselves, as it were in camp.

Their uniforms were worn out, their faces haggard and hungry, they were reduced to a half of their original strength, but they nevertheless entered Moscow in good order. But as soon as they dispersed through the abandoned city the army, *quâ* army, ceased to exist, and the soldier was lost in the marauder. These marauders, when they left Moscow five weeks later, carried off loads of objects which they regarded as necessary or valuable. Their aim was no longer conquest but the preservation of what they had stolen. Like a monkey who, after having plunged his hand into a narrow-necked jar and grasped a quantity of nuts will not open his fist for fear of losing his plunder and so risks his life, the French increased the perils of their retreat by dragging after them an enormous mass of booty; which, like the monkey, they would not relinquish.

Within ten minutes of their dispersal, soldiers and officers were indistinguishable. Men might be seen inside the houses, passing across the windows, to and fro, in gaiters and uniforms, examining the rooms with a look of satisfaction, and rummaging the cellars and ice-houses for provisions. They tore down the gates of the stables and coach-houses, and turning up their sleeves to the elbows, lighted the stoves and cooked their dinners, amusing some of the inhabitants that had lingered behind, frightening others, trying to win over the women and

---

[1] "The wretches," as Monsieur Thiers calls them, were the convicts.

children. This sort of men swarmed everywhere—in the shops and in the streets, but of soldiers in the true sense there were none.

It was in vain that repeated orders were sent to the different heads of divisions desiring them to keep the men from running about the town, from using any violence towards the inhabitants, and from pillage; quite in vain was the rule that the roll was to be called daily. In spite of every precaution these men, who only yesterday were an army, were scattered throughout the deserted city, seeking the abundant stores of food and means of enjoyment which it still contained. Like a flock of cattle that wanders off and breaks up as soon as rich pasturage is reached after the desert, so did this army wander off in the rich town; and they were soon lost, as water is lost which trickles away through sand. The cavalry quartered in a rich merchant's house, which had been abandoned with all contents, found adjoining stables of far greater extent than they really needed; but they nevertheless could not be kept from overflowing into the next house which they fancied was more commodious. Some, indeed, took possession of several houses at once, and made haste to write on the doors with a scrap of chalk the names of the occupants; so that finally the men of different corps fell to quarrelling and abusing each other. Even before they settled into their quarters they ran about to inspect the town, and rushed off to the places where, from hearsay, they expected to find articles of value. Their chiefs, after vainly trying to check them, allowed themselves to succumb to the temptation to commit similar depredations. Even the generals crowded to the coachmakers' warehouses to choose, one a chariot and another a travelling-carriage. The few inhabitants who had not been able to get away offered free quarters to the superior officers, in the hope of thus escaping pillage. Wealth was abundant; there seemed no end to the plunder, and the French fancied that they would find even greater treasure in the parts of the town that they had not yet explored. And as when water is poured on dry soil, the water and the dry soil disappear so when a hungry army enters a wealthy town, disappear both the army and wealthy town— the result is mud, fires and pillage.

The French ascribe the burning of Moscow to Rostopchine's savage patriotism; the Russians attribute it to the barbarity of the French; but, in point of fact, neither Rostopchine nor the invaders can be held responsible for it. The condition of the town itself was the real cause. Moscow was burnt, as any town might have been which was built of wood—quite apart from the state of the fire-engines and whether there were any left or no. Moscow was burnt because it was deserted by its inhabitants, and as inevitably as a pile of saw-dust on which sparks have been falling for several days. A town built of wood in which while it was in the possession of its inhabitant-owners and with a police, fires break out every day, cannot but catch fire when the inhabitants are not there, and an army smoking, making bonfires in its squares of the furniture out of the houses and cooking two meals a day, is in possession. When an army, even in time of peace, is encamped in a village, the number of fires increases enormously. What must then be the fate of a town built of wood and in the possession of a hostile army? The savage patriotism of Rostopchine and the barbarity of the French can neither of them be blamed. Moscow was burnt because of the pipes, the kitchens, the bonfires; because of the carelessness of enemy soldiers, the non-owning inhabitants of the houses. If there was any incendiarism (which is doubtful) it cannot be considered the reason, for without it the same result was bound to occur. If it is in any sense true that Moscow was burnt by the inhabitants, it is not less certain that it was not by those who had remained there, but by the fact that so many had left. Moscow was not treated by the French with such respect as Berlin and Vienna, because its inhabitants did not welcome the invaders with bread and salt and the keys of the gates, but preferred to leave it to its hapless fate.

CHAPTER XLVIII

IT was not till the afternoon of the 2nd—14th September—that the tide of invasion reached the quarter where Peter was living. He had spent two days in total solitude and in a very strange manner, and he was in a state little short of insanity. One thought alone so entirely possessed him that he no longer knew how and when it had first come to him. He remembered nothing of the past and understood nothing of the present. All that he saw going on around him seemed but a dream; he had fled from his own house to escape the intolerable complications of daily life, and had sought and found a shelter in the house of Bazdéïew, whose memory was associated in his mind with a whole world of eternal peace and solemn calm, the very opposite

of the feverish excitement which crushed him under its irresistible influence. Leaning on his dead friend's dusty desk, in
the deep silence of his study, his imagination painted with clear
accuracy the events he had witnessed during the last few weeks,
among them the battle of Borodino; and he again felt an indefinable pain as he compared his own moral failure and life of
falsehood with the mighty simplicity of the men whose image
was stamped on his soul, and whom he thought of as "Them."

When Ghérassime roused him from his meditations, Peter,
who had made up his mind to take part with the people in
defending Moscow, asked him to procure him a disguise and a
pistol, and announced his intention of remaining there, in concealment in the house. At first he found it impossible to fix
his attention on the masonic manuscript; it reverted irresistibly
to the cabalistic connection of his own name with that of
Bonaparte.

Still, the idea that he was predestined to put an end to the
power of the "Beast" had as yet only occurred to him as a
vague reverie, crossing his brain without leaving any trace. It
was when chance had thrown him in the way of the Rostows
and Natacha had exclaimed: "You are staying in Moscow!
Ah, that is right—very right!" that he had understood that
he would do well not to go away—even if the town were given
up to the enemy—so as to fulfil his destiny.

Next day, full of the thought that he must prove himself
worthy of "Them," he made his way to the barrier of the Three
Hills; but when he had seen that Moscow would certainly not
be defended, the execution of the scheme he had been vaguely
cherishing for some days rose before him as an inexorable necessity. He must keep out of sight and try to come within reach
of Napoleon; then he must kill him—die with him perhaps—
but at any rate deliver Europe from the man who, in his opinion,
was the cause of all her miseries.

Peter was familiar with all the details of the attempt made
on Napoleon at Vienna in 1809 by a German student. He
knew that the student had been shot; but the danger he must
run in fulfilling his providential task only excited him to greater
zeal. Two feelings acted on him with equal strength: the first
—the wish to sacrifice himself and suffer, which had been roused
in his heart by the sight of the general misery, had carried him
to Mojaïsk and under fire, had driven him to quit his house, to
give up the ease and comfort of his ordinary life, to sleep without
undressing on a hard couch, and share Ghérassime's meagre

fare. The second was that essentially Russian contempt for the accepted formulas of life and all that in the eyes of an immense majority goes to constitute its highest joys in this world. Peter had felt that intoxication for the first time at the Slobodski palace, where he had understood, too, that wealth, power, all that men most value, is in reality worthless but for the satisfaction of giving them up. It is the same instinct which leads the recruit to drink his last copper coin, and the drunkard to break windows and mirrors for no apparent reason, though he is well aware that he must drain his purse to pay for the damage; it is this which makes a man commit the most absurd actions, as if to prove his strength; and which is at the same time plain evidence of a superior Will, guiding human energy wheresoever It listeth.

Peter's physical condition corresponded to this mental state. The coarse food he had eaten during the last few days, the quantity of brandy he had drunk in his abstinence from wine and cigars, the impossibility of procuring any change of linen, his uneasy and sleepless nights on a sofa that was too short for him, all helped to keep him in a state of excitation bordering on frenzy.

It was now two o'clock—and the French were in Moscow. Peter knew this, but instead of acting he only brooded over his scheme, thinking out the minutest details. It was not on the deed itself that his dreams centred, nor on the possible death of Napoleon, but on his own death and his heroic courage, on which he dwelt with melancholy pathos. "Yes, I must do it!" he thought to himself. "I alone, for all—I will go up to him—so suddenly. Shall I take a dagger or a pistol? It matters not. It is not my hand but the hand of God that will deal the blow! . . ." And he thought of what he should say as he killed Napoleon: "Well, take me, lead me away to death!" he said firmly, and holding his head high.

As he stood indulging in these foolish fancies the door of the room opened, and he saw on the threshold the usually placid face of Makar Alexéïévitch, now hardly recognisable. His dressing-gown hung loosely about him, his hot, bleared look, betrayed that he was drunk. As he caught sight of Peter, his expression was one of dull confusion, but he plucked up courage as he saw that Peter too seemed embarrassed, and went towards him, tottering on his weak shanks.

"They were afraid," he said, in a husky, good-humoured

voice. "I said to them: 'I will never surrender'—I did right, didn't I?" Then seeing the pistol lying on the table, he suddenly seized it and rushed out of the room.

Ghérassime and the porter ran after him to disarm him, while Peter looked on with disgust and pity for the half-crazy old man who, setting his face, gripped the weapon with all his might, calling out in a hoarse voice: "To arms! Board her, board her! It is a lie! You shall not have it!"

"Come, come, be quiet, pray. Be quiet!" Ghérassime was repeating, as he tried to take him by the elbows and get him into a room.

"And who are you? Bonaparte? Go, wretch! Do not lay hands on me. Do you see that?" cried the madman, brandishing the pistol.

"Seize it!" cried Ghérassime to the dvornik.

They had succeeded in pushing him into the vestibule, when a fresh shriek, a woman's shrill cry, mingled with the noises they were all making—above them all the drunkard's hoarse voice—and the cook rushed in, dreadfully scared.

"Oh! father—there are four of them—four men on horse-back!"

Ghérassime and the porter let go their hold of Makar Alexéïévitch, and in the sudden silence they heard steps coming towards the front door.

CHAPTER XLIX

PETER—who had made up his mind that until he had executed his project he would reveal neither his name and rank, nor his knowledge of French, and that he would, if need should arise, vanish at the first approach of the enemy—remained standing at the door of the study. The Frenchmen came into the house, and Peter's curiosity kept him riveted to the spot.

There were but two: a tall and handsome officer and a soldier, evidently his servant, a lean and weather-beaten fellow, with hollow cheeks and a stupid face. The officer, who limped, came forward a little way leaning on his stick. He glanced round him, and finding the appearance of things to his liking, no doubt, he turned to some men who had stayed outside the door, and told them to bring up the horses. Then, twirling his moustache with a swagger, and lifting his hand to his cap in brief salute, he said with a jolly ring: "Good day to the company generally!" No one made any reply. "Are you in charge here," he went on to Ghérassime, who looked at him with anxious inquiry.

"Quarteer, quarteer, lodgings!" repeated the officer, good-naturedly slapping him on the shoulder.

"The French are jolly good fellows, I can tell you! Come, what is the good of being angry, my worthy friend. I say, can no one speak French in this shop?" he asked, his eye happening to catch that of Peter.

Peter drew back a step, and the officer again addressed Ghérassime, asking to see the rooms.

"My master is not here—I do not understand," said Ghérassime, trying to make himself clear in these few words of French.

The Frenchman smiled with a half comic gesture of despair, and again looked towards Peter, who was about to withdraw altogether when he suddenly perceived, through a half open door, Makar Alexéïévitch with the pistol in his hand; with the cunning that often characterises madness, he was quietly taking aim at the Frenchman.

"On board!" cried the lunatic, pressing the trigger.

At this shout the French officer suddenly turned round, as Peter rushed upon the madman to seize the pistol. Makar Alexéïévitch had time to fire with his trembling fingers; the crack deafened them, and the room was filled with smoke. The officer turned pale and started back, while Peter, forgetting his purpose of seeming not to know French, eagerly inquired whether he were wounded.

"I do not think so, but I had a narrow escape that time," said the officer, feeling himself all over, and pointing to the scraps of plaster that had fallen from the wall. "Who is that man?" he added, looking sternly at Peter.

"Oh! I am really distressed beyond measure," said Peter, entirely forgetting his part. "He is a wretched madman who does not know what he is doing."

The officer stepped up to the drunken wretch, and seized him by the collar; Makar Alexéïévitch hung his lip, and swayed heavily, leaning against the wall.

"Rascal, you shall pay for it!" exclaimed the Frenchman. "We can be merciful after a victory, but we do not forgive a traitor!" and he shook his fist in energetic threat.

Peter, still speaking French, implored him not to take vengeance on a poor wretch who was half idiotic. The officer listened in silence, still scowling at the foe; but presently he smiled, and turning to Peter he looked at him for a few minutes, and then held out his hand with an excess of benevolence.

"You have saved my live. You are a Frenchman!" he exclaimed.

That was the Frenchman all over: only a Frenchman could do a great action; and this was beyond question one of the very greatest—to have saved the life of Monsieur Ramballe, captain of the 13th Dragoons. But, notwithstanding all the flattery implied by this opinion, Peter hastened to contradict it.

"I am a Russian," he said shortly.

"Tell that to those who will believe it," said the captain, with an incredulous wave of the hand. "You shall tell me all about it by and by. I am charmed to meet a fellow-countryman. But what are we to do with this fellow?" he went on, addressing Peter as a comrade; for since he himself had pronounced that he was a Frenchman, there was nothing more to be said. Peter again explained who and what Makar Alexéïévitch was, and how he had possessed himself of a loaded pistol; and he once more entreated him not to attempt to punish him.

"You have saved my life!" replied the French officer, swelling with majesty. "You are a Frenchman—you ask his pardon, and I grant it you! Lead this man away!" he added, and taking Peter's arm, he went with him into the study.

The soldiers, who had come in on hearing the report of the pistol, seemed very ready to execute justice on the guilty man, but the captain stopped them sternly:

"You will be sent for when you are wanted. Go!"

The men went off, and the orderly who had been paying a visit to the kitchen came up to his master.

"They have a leg of mutton, captain, and some soup. Shall I bring them up?"

"Yes, and find some wine."

CHAPTER L

PETER thought it his duty to renew his assurances that he was not a Frenchman, and he wished to retire, but his companion was so polite, amiable, and genial, that he had not the heart to refuse his invitation, and they sat down together in the drawing-room. The captain declared once more, with much hand-shaking, that he was bound to him for life by feelings of eternal gratitude, in spite of his strange fancy to pass for a Russian. If he had been gifted with the faculty of guessing other men's secret thoughts, Peter at that moment would probably have struck him dumb; as it was, his deficient penetration betrayed itself in an unceasing flow of chatter.

"Whether you are a Frenchman or a Russian prince in disguise," he said, glancing at Peter's fine though dirty shirt, and the ring on his finger, "I owe you my life, and I offer you my friendship. A Frenchman never forgets an insult or a service."

There was so much kindliness and magnanimity—at any rate from the French point of view—in the tone of his voice and the expression of his face and movements, that Peter involuntarily responded by a smile and pressed the hand he held out to him.

"I am Captain Ramballe of the 13th Dragoons, and decorated for the affair of the 17th. Will you do me the honour to inform me with whom I have the pleasure of conversing so agreeably at this moment instead of lying in hospital with a bullet in my body?"

Peter coloured as he replied that he could not tell him his name, and tried to invent some plausible excuse for refusing to satisfy his curiosity.

"Pray, pray—" interrupted the Frenchman. "I can quite understand your reasons; you are no doubt some officer of superior rank. You have borne arms against us. It is no concern of mine. I owe you my life and that is enough. I am yours to command. You are a gentleman—" he added, with a shade of interrogation. Peter bowed.

"Your Christian name? Mr. Peter—nothing can be better; that is all I ask to know."

When the mutton was served, with an omelette, the samovar was brought in and some wine and brandy that had been found in a neighbouring cellar; Ramballe begged Peter to share his meal, and he himself set to work with a will like a hungry and healthy man, smacking his lips and eating with an accompaniment of satisfied exclamations: "Capital, delicious!" His face had gradually flushed. Peter, who was equally hungry, also did honour to the food. Morel, the orderly, brought in a pan of warm water in which he stood a bottle of red wine, placing on the table a bottle of kvass; the French had already invented a name for this national drink, calling it "Pig's lemonade." Morel sang its praises, but as the captain had some good wine before him he left the kvass to his man. He wrapped his napkin round the bottle of Bordeaux and poured out a large glassful for himself and for Peter. As soon as his appetite was satisfied and the bottle empty he began to talk again with fresh vehemence.

"Yes, my dear Mr. Peter, I owe you a votive offering for having saved me from that maniac. You see I have enough bullets in me already; here is one—I got that at Wagram," and he touched his side; "number two I got at Smolensk," and he showed a scar on his cheek. "And this leg which doesn't work is a souvenir of the fight on the 17th at the Moskva. By G——, that was something like! You should have seen it; a deluge of fire. You gave us an uncommonly tough job; and you may boast of that, by G——! And, upon my word, in spite of this cough that it has cost me I would begin all over again to-morrow! I pity those who did not see it!"

"I was there," said Peter.

"No! Were you really? So much the better! And you are a noble enemy, say what they will. The great redoubt held firm, by heaven! and you made us pay for it handsomely. Three times we were right upon the guns and three times you knocked us over like a pack of cards. Oh! it was grand, Mr. Peter! Your grenadiers were superb, by thunder! I saw them close up six times, and march as if it were a review. What fine men! Our King of Naples cried bravo! and he know's what's what. Soldiers to match our own!" he added, after a moment's silence. "Well, well, so much the better. Terrible in battle and gallant with the ladies—that is your Frenchman, eh, Mr. Peter?" and he winked his eye. The captain's high spirits were so naïve and frank, and he was so perfectly pleased with himself that Peter could hardly help winking in return.

The word gallant no doubt reminded the captain of the state of Moscow, for he went on: "By the way, is it true that all the women have left the city? What a monstrous idea! What had they to be afraid of?"

"And would not the French ladies leave Paris if the Russians marched in?" asked Peter.

"Ha, ha!" the Frenchman shouted with laughter as he slapped him on the shoulder. "Ha, ha! That is a good one. Why, Paris, Paris. . . ."

"Paris is the capital of the world?" said Peter, finishing the sentence.

The captain's laughing eyes were fixed on him.

"Well," he said, "if you had not told me that you were a

Russian I would have bet that you were a Parisian. You have the air, the manner. . . ."

"I have been to Paris, I lived there several years," said Peter.

"Oh! that is very evident. Paris! Why, the man who does not know Paris is a savage. You can smell your Parisian two leagues off. Paris is Talma, la Duchesnois, Pottier, the Sorbonne, the Boulevards . . ." then, perceiving that the end of his sentence had no connection with the beginning, he hastily added: "There is but one Paris! And you have lived in Paris and can remain a Russian? Well, I think none the worse of you for that."

Under the influence of wine, and after the lonely days he had just spent with no company but his own gloomy thoughts, Peter involuntarily found real pleasure in his gay companion's small talk.

"To return to the ladies; the Russians are said to be beautiful! What an idiotic notion to go and bury themselves in the steppes when the French army is at Moscow. They have lost a chance, I can tell you. Your moujiks of course are mere dolts; but you of the civilised classes ought to know us better than that. We have occupied Vienna, Berlin, Madrid, Naples, Rome, Warsaw, all the capitals in the world. We are feared, but we are loved! We are capital company. Besides, the emperor. . . ." But Peter interrupted him with a gloomy and bewildered look.

"The emperor," he repeated. "Is the emperor?"

"The emperor is generosity, clemency, justice and genius itself—that is the emperor. And I, Ramballe, say it—I as you see me—was his sworn foe eight years ago. My father was a count and an *émigré*. But the man conquered me, swept me before him! I could not resist him when I saw the greatness and glory he heaped on France. When I understood what he was aiming at, when I saw that he was making us a perfect bed of laurels, you see, I said to myself: This is something like a sovereign! And I gave myself up to him. And here I am! Yes, my dear fellow, he is the greatest man of any age past or to come!"

"Is he in Moscow?" asked Peter hesitatingly, in the tone of a guilty man.

The Frenchman looked at the guilty face and gave a short laugh.

"No, but he will make his entry to-morrow," replied the Frenchman going on with his story. Their conversation was interrupted at this point by a noise of voices at the outer gate, and Morel came in to explain to his master that the Wurtemberg Hussars insisted on putting their horses into the same yard as theirs. The cause of the dispute was the fact that the men could not understand each other. Ramballe sent for the German quartermaster and asked him sternly to what regiment he belonged, and how he dared to take possession of quarters that were already occupied. The man gave him the name of his regiment and that of his colonel; and as he knew very little French, and did not understand Ramballe's last remark at all, he broke out in voluble German, interlarded with a few doubtful words of French, in which he sought to explain that he was the quartermaster-sergeant of his regiment, and that his commander had desired him to find quarters in this street. Peter, knowing German, served as interpreter on both sides; the Wurtemberger was finally overruled and led his men elsewhere.

When the captain came back again, after leaving the room for a moment to give his orders, he found Peter with his elbows on the table, and his head in his hands. His expression was one of suffering; but, painful and bitter as the immediate state of affairs could not fail to be to him, his real grief was not that Moscow was taken and that its fortunate conquerors were making themselves at home there, but in the consciousness of his own weakness. A few glasses of good wine, a few words with this jolly fellow, had been enough to clear his mind of that dark and determined mood which had so entirely possessed him during the last few days and without which he could not carry out his project. His disguise, his dagger, were ready; Napoleon was to enter Moscow on the next day; the killing of the "villain" was no less useful, no less heroic than it had been yesterday, but Peter no longer felt capable of committing the deed. Why? He could not have said; but he felt vaguely that strength failed him, and that all his dreams of revenge, murder, and personal devotion had vanished like smoke at the living contact of the first comer. The Frenchman's chatter, which before had amused him was now intolerable. His manner, his gesticulations, his moustache as he curled it, the tune he whistled between his teeth—everything worried him:

"I will go away, I will not speak to him again," said Peter to himself; but even though he thought it, he did not move. A strange feeling of impotency rooted him to his place; he wanted to rise, and he could not. The captain, on the contrary was radiant; he paced up and down the room, his eyes glistened, and he smiled at some comical fancy of his own.

"A charming fellow, the Wurtemberg colonel," he said, "and a brave man if ever there was one but—a German." He sat down opposite Peter. "Regular brutes the Germans—don't you think so, Mr. Peter? Another bottle of this Moscow Bordeaux. Morel will warm us another bottle."

Morel placed it on the table with the candles, and by their light the captain observed his companion's disturbed expression. Genuine sympathy led him to make advances. He took his hand kindly: "We are very sad?" he said. "Have I hurt you in any way? Have you any bone to pick with me?" Peter's reply was a glance which told the Frenchman on the contrary how deeply he appreciated his sympathy. "On my honour, quite apart from the gratitude I owe you, I feel the warmest regard for you. In what can I serve you? You have only to command me. It is for life or death!" he added, striking his chest.

"Thank you," said Peter. "Nothing."

"Well then, I drink to our friendship!" cried the captain, and he poured out two glasses of wine. Peter took one and swallowed it at a gulp. Ramballe followed his example, pressed his hand once more, and then propped his elbow on the table with a melancholy look.

"Yes, my dear fellow," he began. "These are the freaks of fortune. Who could have ever foretold that I should turn soldier and be a captain of dragoons in Bonaparte's service —as we used to call him then. And here I am with him at Moscow! I must tell you, my dear fellow," he went on, in the sad even tone of a man who has a long story to tell, "that our name is one of the oldest in France. . . ." And the captain went on to relate, with a frank ease, the whole history of his ancestors, the principal events of his early youth, his boyhood and his riper years, omitting nothing of his family connections and relationships. "But all that is the petty side of life: the real foundation of it is love! Love, don't you think so, Mr. Peter? Come, another glass!" he added, cheering up a little.

Peter drank a second glass, and poured himself out a third.

"Oh! women, women!" the captain went on, and his eyes assumed a languishing expression as he recalled his adventures with the ladies; he must have had a great many by his own account, and his conquering air, his handsome face, and the enthusiasm with which he spoke of the fair sex made it probable.

Though his confidences had the licentious taint which, in a Frenchman's eyes, constitutes all the poetry of love, he spoke with such entire conviction, and attributed such powerful charms to women, that it seemed as though he were the only man who had ever really appreciated them.

Peter listened curiously. It was quite clear that love, as the Frenchman understood the word, was not that sensual passion that Peter had once felt for his wife, nor yet the romantic sentiment which he cherished for Natacha—two kinds of love which Ramballe held in equal contempt. "The one," he would say, "is all very well for carters, and the other for nincompoops." To him the chief charm of love lay in odd coincidences and unnatural situations.

Thus the captain narrated a dramatic episode of his double passion for a fascinating marquise of five-and-thirty, and her innocent daughter of seventeen. They had vied with each other in generosity, and their rivalry had ended in the mother's sacrificing herself and offering him her daughter as his wife. This reminiscence, though of the remote past, still agitated the captain. Another story was that of a husband who had played the lover's part while he, the lover, took that of the husband. Then came a series of comical anecdotes relating to his stay in Germany, where the husbands eat too much *sauer kraut*, and the young girls are too colourless. And finally his latest romance, in Poland, of which the impression was still fresh in his mind, to judge by the expression of his mobile countenance when he described the gratitude of a Polish gentleman of rank whose life he had saved—a detail which was not wanting in any one of the captain's gasconades. This gentleman had entrusted his wife, a most enchanting creature, a Parisian at heart, to the captain's keeping when he found himself obliged to leave her and serve in the French army. Ramballe was happy, for the fair Pole had agreed to elope with him, but a chivalrous sentiment had made itself heard; he had restored the lady to her husband, saying: "I saved your life once, and now I have saved your honour." As he quoted himself, he passed his hand over his eyes with a little shudder, as though to throw off an emotion which was too much for him.

Peter, who was feeling the effects of the wine and the late hour, as he listened to the captain's recollections, linked with them a whole series of memories of his own. His love for Natacha suddenly rose before him in a succession of pictures which he compared with those described by Ramballe. When the captain enlarged on the struggle between love and duty, Peter was reminded of every detail of his last meeting with the young girl he loved—though at the moment, it must be owned, that meeting had not particularly impressed him; in fact, he had forgotten it, but now poetical significancy seemed to lurk in every detail. "Peter Kirilovitch, come here, I recognised you!" He fancied he could hear her voice, see her eyes, her smile, her little travelling-hood and a lock of hair blown back by the wind—the vision touched and moved him deeply.

When the captain had finished his description of the charms of his Pole, he asked Peter whether he too had sacrificed love to duty, or had ever been jealous of a husband's rights. Peter looked up, and led on by a craving to pour out his heart, he explained that he looked at love from a different point of view: that in all his life he had never loved but one woman, and she could never be his. "Bless me!" said the captain. Then Peter confided to him how he had loved her from childhood without daring to think of her because she was too young; that he was a natural son, with no name nor fortune; and that since a name and fortune had been given him he loved her so entirely, and regarded her as so far above all the world, and himself included, that he thought it impossible to win her love. At this point in his confession Peter interrupted himself to ask the captain if he understood him. The Frenchman shrugged his shoulders and bid him go on.

"Platonic love! Moonshine!" he muttered to himself.

Was it the effect of the wine that led him to open his heart, or the need to express himself, or the certainty that this man would never know any of the people of whom he was speaking? The fact was that he told him his whole history, with a heavy tongue and his eyes fixed on vacancy; his marriage, Natacha's love for his dearest friend, her inconstancy, and their still ill-defined position towards each other. Nay, under a little pressure from Ramballe, he ended by acknowledging his rank and even his name. And in all the long story what chiefly struck the captain was the fact that Peter owned two fine palaces in Moscow which he had abandoned to their fate to remain in the town in disguise.

The night was mild and clear, and at a very late hour they went out of doors together. On the left the first lurid gleams were rising of the fire that was to devour Moscow. On the right, high up in the sky, shone a new moon, and opposite to it, on the brink of the horizon, blazed the comet which was so mysteriously associated in Peter's mind with his love for Natacha. Ghérassime, the cook, and the two Frenchmen were standing outside the gate; they could hear their loud laughter and noisy conversation in two languages. Their attention, too, was directed to the glare now spreading in the distance, though as yet there was no immediate threat in those remote flames, there was nothing terrible in this far-off fire.

As he gazed at the starry sky, the moon, the comet, the ruddy glare, Peter was deeply moved.

"How beautiful!" he thought. "What more can one want?" And then he suddenly remembered his scheme; he turned giddy, and must have fallen if he had not clung to the paling. Then turning away from his new friend, without even bidding him good night, he made his way with uncertain steps to his own room, lay down on the sofa, and fell asleep.

CHAPTER LI

THE light of the first fire on the 14th September was seen from many sides at once, and produced very different effects on the inhabitants who were escaping and the troops who were forced to retreat.

In consequence of the numerous articles they had forgotten, and had sent back for in succession, the Rostows had not got fairly off till the afternoon; they were consequently obliged to spend the night at about five versts out of town. Next day, having risen rather late, and meeting with obstacles at every turn in the road, they only reached the village of Bolchaïa-Mytichtchi at ten in the evening; there the family and the wounded men found quarters for the night in the peasants' huts. As soon as their work was done all the servants, coachmen, and officers' servants, supped themselves, fed their horses, and gathered in the village street. In one of the huts was Raïevsky's aide-de-camp; his wrist had been smashed, and he suffered horribly, and his groans were dismally audible in the calm, dark autumn night. Countess Rostow, who had occupied the room next to his the previous night, had not slept a wink, and she had now chosen an *isba* farther away from the hapless sufferer.

One of the servants suddenly perceived a second blaze on the horizon; the first they had already ascribed to Mamonow's

Cossacks, who—it was said—had set fire to the village of Malaïa-Mytichtchi.

"Look out, lads; there is another blaze," he said. They all looked round.

"Yes, so there is! They say that Mamonow's Cossacks have set the place on fire."

"Not a bit of it! That is not the village, it is much farther off; it might be Moscow."

Two of the men made their way round a carriage which hid the horizon, and perched themselves on the step.

"It is more to the left—there, do you see the flames dancing up? That is Moscow, my friends, Moscow is burning."

No one took the matter up and they stood gazing at the fresh glare which was spreading rapidly. Daniel, the count's old valet, came out and called Michka. "What are you staring at, gaby? The count will call and there will be no one to answer. Go and put his clothes away."

"I only came out for some water."

"What do you think about it, Daniel Térentitch? Is not that Moscow?"

Daniel did not reply, and no one spoke; the flame rose with increasing violence and spread rapidly.

"Lord have mercy upon us! The wind and this drought——" said a voice.

"Lord, Lord! how it is growing! You can see the daws fly up. Lord have mercy upon us miserable sinners!"

"Don't be afraid; they will put it out."

"Who will put it out?" said Daniel Térentitch suddenly in a solemn voice. "Yes, that is Moscow burning sure enough, my children, Moscow, our white-walled mother."

His voice broke with a sob; and then—as if they had only been waiting for this terrible sentence to understand the fearful meaning of the red glare in the sky—groans and prayers rose from the whole assembly.

CHAPTER LII

THE old valet went to tell his master that Moscow was on fire; the count slipped on his dressing-gown and went out to assure himself of the fact, accompanied by Sonia and Mrs. Schoss, who were not yet undressed. Natacha and her mother were left alone in their room. Pétia had parted from them that morning to join his regiment on the way to Troïtsk. At the news of the conflagration the countess began to weep, while Natacha, sitting, with a fixed gaze, on a bench in the corner near the images, paid no heed to her father's words. She was listening involuntarily to the lamentations of the hapless aide-de-camp, which she could hear distinctly though there were three or four cottages between them.

"Oh! what a fearful sight!" cried Sonia, coming in horror-stricken. "All Moscow is on fire, I believe; the blaze is stupendous. Look, Natacha, you can see from here."

Natacha turned round without seeming to understand what Sonia was saying, and then fixed her eyes on the corner of the stove. She had fallen into a sort of lethargy ever since the morning when Sonia, to the astonishment and great annoyance of the countess, had thought proper to inform her that Prince Andrew was among the wounded who were travelling with them, and had told her what serious danger he was in. The countess had been more furious with Sonia then she had ever been in her life. Sonia, in floods of tears, had implored her forgiveness, and been doubly attentive to her cousin to repair the mischief.

"Do look, Natacha, how it is burning!"

"What is burning?" said Natacha. "Ah! to be sure, Moscow!" and, simply to satisfy Sonia without offending her, she looked out of the window, and then resumed her former attitude.

"But you could see nothing."

"I saw it all, I assure you," she said in beseeching tones which seemed only to crave that she might be left in peace. The countess and Sonia understood indeed that she could just now take no interest in anything. Her father withdrew behind the partition and went to bed. The countess came up to her daughter, felt her head with the back of her hand as she was wont to do when she was ill, and pressed her lips to her forehead to see whether she was feverish.

"You are cold," she said as she kissed her. "You are shivering; you ought to go to bed."

"To bed? Oh! yes, I shall go to bed by and by," she replied. When Natacha had heard that Prince Andrew had been dangerously wounded and that he was travelling in their company, she had asked endless questions as to how and when it had happened, and whether she might not see him. She was told that this was impossible, that the wound was a serious one, but that there was no immediate danger. Being fully convinced that, urge it as she might, she would learn nothing more, she had sat silent and motionless in the back of the carriage, as she was now sitting on the stool in the corner of the room. As she saw her wide open eyes and fixed gaze the countess felt sure from long experience that her daughter was hatching some scheme in her brain; and the decision it might lead to—to her unknown—caused her extreme anxiety.

"Natacha, my child, undress; come to bed with me." Only the countess had a bed; Mrs. Schoss and the girls had a heap of hay on the floor.

"No, mamma; I will lie there on the ground," said Natacha impatiently; she rose, went to the window and threw it open.

The wounded man was still moaning; she put her head out into the damp night air, and her mother could see her shaking with convulsive sobs. Natacha knew that this sufferer was not Prince Andrew; she knew, too, that he was in the hut next their own; but these incessant plaints moved her irresistibly to tears. The countess glanced at Sonia. "Come, my child, come to bed," she repeated, laying her head gently on Natacha's shoulder.

"Oh! yes, at once!" exclaimed Natacha, snatching off her clothes and breaking her strings to be quicker. She put on her sleeping-jacket and sat down on the bed that had been arranged for them; then throwing her hair down over her shoulders she began to undo it. While her slim fingers unplaited and replaited it, her head mechanically following their movement, her eyes, dilated with fever, still stared at vacancy. Having finished, she gently dropped on to the sheet which was laid over the hay.

"Natacha, go into the middle!"

"No, lie down," she said. "I shall stay where I am," and she buried her head in the pillow.

The countess, Sonia, and Mrs. Schoss all undressed, and ere long the pale glimmer of a night-lamp was the only light in the room, though outside, the blazing village only two versts away, shone on the horizon. Confused sounds came up from the village tavern, and the aide-de-camp was still groaning. Natacha listened for a long time to all these noises, taking care not to stir. She heard her mother sighing and praying, and the bed creak under her weight; Mrs. Schoss's piping snore; and Sonia's soft breathing. Presently the countess spoke her daughter's name, but Natacha did not answer. "Mamma, I think she is asleep," said Sonia.

A few minutes later the countess spoke again, but this time Sonia even did not answer, and very soon Natacha knew from her mother's deep breathing that she, too, was asleep. She did not move, though the little bare foot peeping out now and then from under the clothes shivered at the touch of the cold floor. A cricket's shrill chirp was audible from some chink in the beams; he seemed quite proud of being awake when all the rest of the world was asleep. A cock crowed in the distance; another answered close at hand; the shouts in the tavern had ceased—only the wounded man was still moaning.

From the moment when Natacha had heard that Prince Andrew was of their party, she had made up her mind to see him; but while she felt this to be inevitable she also knew it must be painful. The hope of seeing him had kept her up all through the day, but, now that the moment was come, she was a prey to nameless terrors. Was he disfigured or altered, as she pictured the wounded man whose cries haunted her so persistently? Yes, he must be—for in her fancy this heart-rending wailing had got mixed up with the image of Prince Andrew.

Natacha sat up.

"Sonia, are you asleep? Mamma?" she whispered.

No answer. She rose very softly, crossed herself, and setting her light foot on the boards, stole softly across the dirty floor which creaked under her weight, and reached the door as nimbly as a kitten. There she grasped the latch. It seemed to her that the partitions of the cottage rang with blows hit in steady rhythm, while it was her heart that was beating almost to bursting with terror and passion. She opened the door, crossed the threshold, and set her naked feet on the damp floor of the covered way between the two houses. The cold chill roused her; her bare foot just touched a man lying asleep on the ground, and then she opened the door of the hut in which Prince Andrew was lying.

It was dark; behind the bed, which stood in a corner, and on which she could make out a vague form, a candle was burning on a bench, and the tallow had guttered into a sort of hood. As she caught sight of the shapeless mass—taking the feet, which stuck up under the counterpane, for the shoulders—she fancied it something so monstrous, that she stood still in horror; but then an irresistible impulse urged her forward. Stepping with great care she reached the middle of the room, which was crammed with luggage of all kinds, in a corner under the images a man was lying on a bench: this was Timokhine. The doctor and valet were sleeping on the floor. The valet turned over, muttering a few words. Timokhine, who was suffering from a wound in the foot, was not asleep; he fixed his astonished eyes on this amazing apparition of a young girl in a sleeping-jacket and nightcap. His faintly murmured words of alarm: "What is it? Who is there?" only made Natacha move quicker, and she found herself standing by the object that had filled her with terror. However dreadful it might be to look at, she felt that she must see it. At that moment the smoky candle flared up a little, and she distinctly saw Prince Andrew, his hands lying on the coverlet, looking just as she had always known him; but that the bright flush of fever, the glittering eyes that looked at her with rapture, and the delicate throat, like a young boy's, in its setting of a turned-down shirt-collar, gave him an appearance of candid youthfulness that was new to her. She went forward quickly, and with a swift and graceful impulse fell on her knees by his side. He smiled and put out his hand.

CHAPTER LIII

SEVEN days had passed since Prince Andrew had first come to himself in the hospital tent after the operation. The fever and inflammation of the intestines, which had been injured by a fragment of shell, would prove almost immediately fatal, in the doctor's opinion; so that he was amazed on the seventh day to see him eat a few mouthfuls of bread with real enjoyment, and to be able to note a perceptible diminution in the inflammatory symptoms. Prince Andrew had quite recovered his senses.

The night after their start from Moscow had been fairly warm, and he had not been moved from his travelling-carriage; but as soon as they reached this village, he had begged to be carried into a house, and to have some tea; but the anguish of being lifted, only from the chariot into the hut, had brought on a fainting fit. When they laid him on his camp-bed he remained for some time motionless, with his eyes shut, then he opened them again, and asked for the tea. To the surgeon's astonishment he remembered this minute detail; and on feeling his pulse, the doctor found it more regular, to his great regret, for he knew by experience that Prince Andrew was irrevocably doomed, and any extension of his days could only result in prolonged and acute suffering, to end after all in death. Little Timokhine, with the red nose, who was wounded in the leg at Borodino, joined Prince Andrew when they left Moscow. They had also the prince's valet, a doctor, a coachman, and two soldier-servants.

A glass of tea was brought to him, and he drank it greedily, while his eyes, fastened on the door, seemed trying to recover the chain of some confused reminiscences.

"No more," he said. "Is Timokhine there?" The man dragged himself along his bench. "Here, excellency."

"How is your wound going on?"

"Mine? Oh, it is a trifle. How are you feeling?"

Prince Andrew lay thinking, as if trying to remember what he had to say.

"Could they get me a book?" he asked.

"What book?"

"The New Testament—I have not got one."

The doctor promised him a New Testament, and asked him how he was feeling. Though he answered reluctantly, he was perfectly clear. He begged them to place a pillow under his loins to ease his pain. The doctor and valet raised the cloak which covered him to examine the fearful wound, of which the smell made them feel sick. The inspection was not satisfactory; the doctor dressed the wound, and turned the sufferer over a little, but this made him again unconscious, and he then became light-headed; he insisted on having the book at once, and that it should be placed under him.

"What harm can it do you?" he said plaintively. "Give it me, and put it there if only for a minute."

The doctor left the room to wash his hands.

"Good Heavens!" he said to the manservant who poured out the water. "How can he live through such torture?"

When the carriage had stopped at the village of Mytichtchi Prince Andrew had been, for the first time, in full possession of his senses: had a clear recollection of the past, and understood the state he was in. Then the pain of being lifted into the cottage had clouded his mind again till the tea had recovered him, and memory brought back the various scenes of the last few days, especially the delusive mirage of calm bliss which had floated before him in the ambulance tent while listening to the cries of the man he so detested. The same vague and confused thoughts took possession of him once more: he was conscious of the same pervading sense of ineffable happiness, with a feeling that he should find that happiness only in the Gospel he had so eagerly implored to have given to him.

Under the pain of having his wound dressed, and of being moved into a fresh position, he again lost consciousness, and he did not recover it till shortly before midnight. All were sunk in sleep; he heard the chirp of the cricket in the adjoining *isba*; a drunken voice was singing in the street; cockroaches were rustling as they scampered over the table, the images, and the wainscot; a large fly buzzed and blundered into the guttering candle.

A man in health can reflect and feel and remember a thousand things at a time, and select certain facts or ideas on which to fix his attention. He can, at need, rouse himself from deep absorption to speak politely to anyone who addresses him, and then resume the course of his ideas; but Prince Andrew was not in this normal condition. While his moral powers had become more active and keener than of old, they acted without any control from his will. The most dissimilar thoughts and visions crowded on his mind; for a few minutes his thoughts had a clearness and depth which they had never had when he was in health, and then suddenly all sorts of fantastic and unlooked-for images ruthlessly wrecked the work of his brain which he was too weak to begin again.

"Yes—a new type of happiness was revealed to me," he thought, and his eyes, glittering with fever, sounded the gloom of the quiet cottage room, "happiness of which nothing can henceforth deprive me—independent of all earthly influences. The happiness of the soul, of love! All men are capable of knowing it, but God alone has the power of bestowing it on them. How came He to make this law of love? Why did the Son. . . .?" The thread of his ideas was suddenly broken; he thought a voice was humming a tune incessantly in his ear —was it reality or delirium?

As he listened to the confused sounds, he felt a structure, as it were, rising from his face, of fine needles and airy shavings, and he devoted his whole effort to preserving his balance so as to save his aerial edifice from falling; though it vanished now and then to rise once more in rhythm to the cadence of that mysterious murmur.

"It is rising! I see it!" he said to himself; and without taking his eyes off it he could see, flitting across it, the ruddy flame of the half-burnt candle, and he could hear the scuttering cockroaches on the floor, and the buzz of the big fly that bounced against his pillow. Each time the fly brushed his cheek, it burnt him like a hot iron, and he wondered how it was that the touch of its wings did not demolish the strange fabric of needles and shavings that rested on his face. And out there, by the door—what was that sinister shape, that motionless sphinx which seemed to smother him?

"It is my shirt, no doubt, that has been left on the table! But then how is it that everything is swelling and spreading and spinning round me? Why that monotonous voice singing in time?" said the hapless sufferer in aggravated anguish—and on a sudden his thoughts and ideas were clearer and stronger than ever. "Yes—Love! Not selfish love, but love such as I then knew it for the first time in my life, when dying I saw my enemy by my side, and could love even him! It is the very essence of the soul which does not cling to only one object of its affection—and that is what I now feel. Love of one's neighbour, of one's enemy, of each and all, is the love of God in all His manifestations! To love those near and dear to us is human love; but to love one's enemy is almost divine. That was the reason of my gladness when I found that I loved that man. Where is he? Is he still living? Human love may turn to hatred, but divine love is perennial. How many people I have hated in the course of my life! And did I not hate most of all her whom I had loved most of all? . . ."

The image of Natacha rose before him, not in the fascination of her external charms alone; he saw into her soul, he understood her anguish, her shame and repentance; and he reproached himself for his own cruelty in having thrown her off.

"If only I might see her," thought he. "If only I could look into her eyes once more and tell her . . . Oh! that fly!" And fancy again bore him away into the world of hallucination mingling with reality, in which he saw, as through a mist, the structure built up from his face, the candle burning in a red halo, and the sphinx watching near the door.

Presently he heard a slight noise, a breath of cooler air fanned his face, and another white figure, a second sphinx, appeared in the doorway. Its face was pale, and its eyes shone like the eyes of Natacha.

"Oh! how weary I am of this delirium!" thought Prince Andrew, trying to shake off this vision.

But the vision did not vanish—it came nearer—it seemed to be real. Prince Andrew made a great effort to return to the realm of pure thought, but his delusions were too strong for him. The murmuring voice still hummed on; something weighed on his chest—and that strange figure was still gazing at him. Collecting all his strength to recover his wits he moved—there was a ringing in his ears, he saw no more, and lost consciousness. When he came to himself Natacha—Natacha in the flesh—she whom he most longed to love with that pure, divine passion that had just been revealed to him, was there, on her knees, by his side. He recognised her so completely, that he felt no surprise, only a sense of ineffable gladness. Natacha was too terrified to dare to move; she tried to smother her sobs and her pale face quivered.

Prince Andrew gave a deep sigh of relief, smiled, and put out his hand.

"You?" he said. "What happiness!"

Natacha eagerly went closer, took his hand very gently and touched it with her lips.

"Forgive me," she murmured, looking up. "Forgive me."

"I love you," he said.

"Forgive me."

"What have I to forgive?"

"Forgive me for what I did," said Natacha, in a low voice, and with a painful effort.

"I love you better than I did before," replied Prince Andrew, lifting her head to look in her eyes, which were timidly fixed on his, swimming with tears of joy, but luminous with love and pity. Her pale, thin features, and lips swollen with crying, had, at this moment, no trace of beauty; but Prince Andrew saw nothing but her beautiful eyes radiant through tears.

Peter, his valet, who had just woke up, shook the doctor. Timokhine was not asleep; he had seen all that had happened, and now tried to hide himself under his sheet.

"What is the meaning of this?" said the doctor, sitting up. "You must have the goodness to withdraw, miss."

At this moment a maid knocked at the door; she was sent

by the countess to find Natacha. Natacha walked out of the room like a sleep-walker who is suddenly roused, and as soon as she got back to their own quarters fell sobbing on the bed.

From that time, at every stage or resting-place on their journey, Natacha went in to see Bolkonsky, and the doctor was forced to confess that he never could have expected to find in a young girl so much steadiness or apprehension of the care needed for a wounded man. However dreadful the countess might deem it that Prince Andrew should die—as the doctor prognosticated—in her daughter's arms, she could not resist Natacha's determination. Their revived intercourse would certainly under any other circumstances have led to a renewal of their old engagement; but the question of life and death that hung over Prince Andrew's head was no less in suspense for Russia itself; and every other consideration fell into the background.

CHAPTER LIV

On the 3rd (15th) of September Peter rose late. His head ached; his clothes, which he had not taken off, hung heavy on his limbs, and he had a vague impression that he had done some shameful act the evening before: this was his overflow of confession to Captain Ramballe. It was eleven o'clock, the weather was gloomy; he rose, rubbed his eyes, and seeing the pistol, which Ghérassime had replaced on the desk, he remembered at last where he was, and what he was to do that day: "Am I not too late?" he wondered. "No, for he was not to enter the city till midday."

Peter gave himself no time to think of what he had to do; he hastened to act. He brushed down his coat with his hand, snatched up the pistol, and was just going out when it occurred to him to ask himself where he should hide the weapon. He could not stick it in his belt, nor carry it under his arm, nor conceal it in the folds of his caftan; and, finally, he had forgotten to load it. "A dagger will be better after all," thought he, though he had more than once blamed the German student, who in 1809 had tried to stab Napoleon. So he took the dagger, which he had bought at the same time as the pistol, though it was all jagged at the edge, and slipped it inside his waistcoat.

He seemed to be eager, not so much to execute his plan as to prove to himself that he had not given it up. Then tightening his belt, and pulling his cap low over his eyes, he crossed the passage, trying to walk noiselessly, and went down into the street, without meeting the captain.

The conflagration, which he had viewed last evening with so much indifference, had gained ground rapidly during the night. Moscow was burning at several points at once. The Gostinnoï-Dvor, the Povarskaïa, the boats on the river, the timber-stacks by the Dorogomilow Bridge were all in flames. Peter went by the Arbat to the church of St. Nicholas; this was the spot which he had long since fixed upon for the great deed he was meditating. Most of the houses had their windows and doors closed and nailed up. The streets and alleys were deserted; the air was full of smoke and the smell of burning. From time to time he met a few scared and anxious Russians, and Frenchmen of military aspect, who took the middle of the street. They all looked inquisitively at Peter: his breadth and height, and the set expression of pain on his face, puzzled them. The Russians stared at him, unable to decide to what rank of life he belonged, and the French, accustomed to be themselves an object of astonishment or alarm to the natives, also followed him with puzzled eyes, for he paid not the slightest attention to them. Outside the gate of a large house three French soldiers, who were striving ineffectually to make some Russians understand them, stopped him to ask him whether he spoke French. He shook his head and went on his way. A little farther on, a sentinel in charge of a caisson shouted in warning, and it was not till he had called out a second time: "Out of the way there!" in threatening tones—with the click of the gun he was cocking— that Peter understood that he was to go to the other side of the street. He had no thought but for his sinister project, and in his fear of forgetting it again he saw and understood nothing.

But his dark resolve was destined to come to nothing; even if he had not been stopped on his way, it was now impossible to carry it into execution, for the simple reason that Napoleon had already been installed for some hours in the imperial palace in the Kremlin. At this very moment he was sitting in the czar's private room, in a very bad temper, giving orders and taking measures for checking the conflagration and pillage, and for reassuring the inhabitants. Of this Peter knew nothing; absorbed in his one idea, and completely preoccupied, as a man always is who is bent on an impossible enterprise, he was worrying himself, not over the difficulty of carrying it out, but over the fatal hesitancy which, at the critical moment, would perhaps come upon him, paralyse his action, and deprive him for ever of all self-respect. However, on he went instinctively, without looking before him, and he thus came straight to the Povarskaïa. The farther he went, the thicker was the smoke; he already was aware of the heat of the fire, and tongues of flame were dancing up from the neighbouring houses. Here the streets were full of an excited crowd. It dawned upon his mind that something extraordinary was going forward; but still he did not fully understand the state of things. But as he followed a beaten footpath across a plot of open ground, bordered on one side by the Povarskaïa, and on the other by the gardens of a large mansion, he suddenly heard, close to him, a woman's cry of despair; he stopped short, as if roused from a dream, and looked up.

At a short distance on one side all the furniture of a house was piled in confusion on the dry and dusty grass-plot; mattresses, quilts, samovars, and baggage of every description. By the side of one of the trunks crouched a young woman, very thin and with projecting teeth, wrapped in a black cloak and wearing a shabby cap. She was wailing and crying bitterly. Two little girls of ten and twelve, as thin and as frightened as their mother, dressed in wretched little petticoats and cloaks to correspond, stared at her in consternation, while a little boy of seven, with a cap too big for him, was crying in his old nurse's arms. A maid of all work—as she seemed—barefoot and dirty, sitting on one of the cases, had undone her dirty drab plait and was pulling out singed hair, while a broad-shouldered man with clipped whiskers, and his hair neatly brushed over his temples, dressed in the uniform of a humble civil official, was stolidly sorting out his clothes from the general muddle. As Peter passed close to her the woman threw herself at his feet.

"Oh! father—good orthodox Christian! Save me and help me!" she said between her sobs. "My little girl, my youngest baby has been burnt! Oh God! Oh God! Was it for this that I nursed you and . . ."

"That will do, that will do, Maria Nicolaïevna," said her husband coolly; he seemed anxious to make the best of himself before this stranger. "Our sister has taken care of her, no doubt."

"Monster! Stony-hearted wretch!" cried the woman, ceasing to cry in her rage. "You have not heart even for your own child. Any other man would have snatched her from the flames! But he is not a man—not fit to be a father! For mercy's sake," and again she turned to Peter, "listen to me: the fire caught our house from the next one; that girl there called out: 'we are on fire'; we flew to save what we could, and ran away with what we could carry, and all we could save you see there, with that image and our wedding-bed; everything else is destroyed. Suddenly I discovered that Katia was not with us—oh, my child, my child is burnt!"

"But where did you leave her?" asked Peter, and his sympathetic face showed the poor woman that in him she had found help and comfort.

"Oh! for God's sake," she went on, "be my deliverer. Aniska, you little slut, show him the way," and as she spoke she showed her long teeth.

"Come along," said Peter, "I will do all I can."

The little maid came forth from behind the trunk, put up her hair, sighed, and went along the path. Peter, eager for action, felt as though he had been roused from some long lethargy; he raised his head, his eyes sparkled and he strode along, following the girl who led him to the Povarskaïa. The houses were hidden behind a dense black cloud of smoke, rent now and again by shafts of flame. An immense throng stood round, at a respectful distance from the blaze, and a French general was addressing those nearest to him in the middle of the street. Peter, guided by the girl, approached him, but the soldiers stopped him.

"You cannot pass this way."

"Here, here, little uncle," cried the little maid. "Down the side-alley, come."

Peter turned about, hurrying to catch her up; she turned to the left, passed three houses, and went into the gateway of the fourth.

"It is here—quite close."

She crossed the yard, opened a little door, and paused on the threshold, pointing to a small house that was wrapped in flames. One wall had already fallen in, the other was still blazing and the flames were pouring out at every opening—the windows and the roof. Peter involuntarily drew back, suffocated by the heat.

"Which of these houses was yours?"

"That one, that one," shrieked the girl. "That is where we lived. And are you burnt, my darling treasure, my Katia, my

pet!" cried Aniska, reminded by the sight of the fire that she
was bound to express some feeling.

Peter went towards the blazing ruins, but the heat drove him
back; he retired a short distance and found himself in front of
a larger house where the roof was as yet only burning on one
side. Some Frenchmen were prowling about. At first he could
not imagine what they were doing there; however, he presently
saw one hit a peasant with the flat of his sword to snatch away
a pelisse of fox-skin, and then he understood that they were
plundering; but the idea only passed through his mind. The
crash of falling walls and ceilings, the roar of the flames, the
cries of the crowd, the dark twirls of the smoke rent by showers
of sparks and wreaths of flame which seemed to lick the walls,
the feeling of suffocation and heat, and the extreme rapidity
with which he was forced to move, all worked up Peter to that
intensity of excitement which is the usual concomitant of such
catastrophes.

The effect was so sudden and violent as to deliver him at once
from the ideas that had possessed him. He was young, prompt
and nimble once more; he went all round the blazing house,
but, just as he was about to try to enter it, he was startled by a
shout and the thud of something heavy falling on the ground
at his feet. He looked up and saw some Frenchmen who had
just flung out of a window a chest of drawers full of metal
goods. Their comrades, waiting below, at once gathered
round it.

"Well, what does this fellow want?" exclaimed one of them
angrily.

"There is a child in the house," said Peter. "Have none of
you seen a child?"

"What is he talking about? Take yourself off!" said several;
and one of the soldiers, fearing lest Peter should rob him of
his share of the plate and bronzes, went up to him with a
threatening air.

"A child?" cried a Frenchman from the upper story. "I
heard something bleating in the garden. That was his brat,
very likely, poor fellow. We must be humane you know."

"Where was it? Whereabouts?" asked Peter.

"Out there," said the Frenchman, pointing to the garden
behind the house. "Wait a bit; I will come down."

In point of fact, a moment later a Frenchman in his shirt-
sleeves jumped out of the ground-floor window, slapped Peter
on the shoulder, and ran with him into the garden.

"Look sharp, you fellows," he cried to his comrades, "it is getting uncommonly hot!" and hurrying down the gravel path he pulled Peter by the sleeve and showed him a bundle on a bench. It was a little girl of three, in a pink cotton frock.

"There is your brat—a little girl. Well, so that's all right. Good-bye, old boy. We must be humane, we are all mortal you see!" and the Frenchman went back to the others.

Peter, quite out of breath, was about to pick up the child, who was as pale and as ugly as her mother, but she gave a desperate yell, slipped down, and ran away. Peter soon caught the little girl and took her in his arms, while she shrieked with rage and tried to fight free with her little hands, biting him viciously. Her struggles, reminding him of some small animal, revolted him to such an extent that it was only by a great effort that he kept himself from dropping the child. On making his way back towards the house he perceived that he could no longer pass by the way by which he had come. Aniska had vanished, and with a mingled feeling of disgust and compassion he found himself obliged to cross the garden and find another way out, carrying the child, who was still fighting like a little demon.

CHAPTER LV

WHEN, after various turns through courts and alleys, Peter got out with his burthen at the corner of the Povarskaïa and the Grouzinski garden, he could hardly recognise it; the square, usually so deserted, was crowded with people, and piled with objects of every description. Not to speak of the Russian families who had been driven out with all their possessions, there were numbers of French soldiers of various corps. He paid no heed to these, but searched anxiously for the child's parents, to restore her to them and then be ready, in case of need, to effect another rescue. He felt as if there was much left for him to do, and that it must be done quickly. Heated by the running, he felt more than ever that same feeling of youth and resolution which had come over him when he went off to save the child. The little girl, who by degrees had quieted down, clung to his caftan, and crouching close to him like a little scared animal, looked about her in alarm, while Peter smiled down at her quite paternally. He felt interested by the pale sickly little face; but he sought in vain in the crowd that surrounded him—he could see neither the functionary nor his wife.

At this moment his eye was attracted by a family of Armenians or Georgians, consisting of an old man of the noblest eastern type, tall and splendidly dressed, a matron of the same race, and a quite young woman whose finely-arched eyebrows, as black as a crow's wing, ivory skin, and calm, regular features gave distinction to her remarkable beauty. She was sitting on a bale of goods behind the older woman, surrounded by piles of their belongings; and in her rich wrapper of satin, with a violet kerchief on her head, and her large almond-shaped eyes whose silky lashes were persistently downcast, she looked like some delicate exotic plant flung out among the snows: she evidently knew that she was beautiful and her beauty gave her alarms. Peter gazed at her again and again. At length he reached the railings and looked round to get a general view of the scene; his strange appearance, carrying the child in his arms, soon attracted the attention of his neighbours, who gathered round him, asking him:

"Have you lost anyone?" "Are you a gentleman?" "Whose is the child?"

Peter replied that the child belonged to a woman whom he had seen on this very spot a short time since, who wore a black cloak and had three children with her.

"Could no one tell him which way she had gone?"

"It must be the Anférows," said an old deacon, addressing a woman who stood by. "Lord, Lord, have mercy upon us!" he murmured in a low bass.

"Where are the Anférows?" said the woman.

"They went away quite early in the day. Perhaps it was Maria Nicolaïevna—or perhaps the Ivanows."

"A woman, he said; Maria Nicolaïevna is a lady," said a voice.

"You must surely know her," said Peter; "a thin woman with long teeth."

"Yes, then it is Maria Nicolaïevna. They ran away into the garden when these wolves came down on us!"

"Lord, Lord, have mercy upon us!" repeated the deacon.

"If you go that way you are sure to find her. She was crying, crying. Go on, you will find them."

But Peter had ceased to listen to the peasant woman who was speaking to him; he was wholly absorbed by a scene that was being enacted by two French soldiers with the Armenian family. One of them, a brisk little man in a dark-blue greatcoat fastened round his waist with a cord, and a foraging-cap on his head, had seized the old man by the legs, and his victim was making haste to take his boots off. The other, who was fair, lean and long, and very deliberate in his movements, had a stupid face; his garments were a pair of blue trousers stuffed into high boots, and a greatcoat; he stood rooted in front of the young woman, with his hands in his pockets, staring at her, speechless.

"Here, take the child and find her parents! Do you understand?" said Peter to one of the women; he set the child down and turned to the Armenians.

The old man was now barefoot, and the little Frenchman who had appropriated his boots was shaking them together, while the hapless owner murmured a few words with a piteous air. But Peter only glanced at him; his attention was centred on the other Frenchman, who had come close to the lady and had put his hand round her neck. The fair Armenian did not move. Peter had not time to rush forward before the robber had snatched off her necklace, and the young woman, roused from her absorption, was screaming wildly.

"Let this woman alone!" cried Peter, shaking the man by the shoulders; he dropped it and then springing loose fled as fast as his legs would carry him.

His companion threw down the boots, drew his sword and marched up to Peter. "Come, no nonsense!" he said.

Peter, flying into one of those fits of fury which multiplied his strength tenfold and made him unconscious of what he was doing, threw himself on the man, tripped him up, and then belaboured him with his fists. The crowd shouted their applause, when, round the corner of the square, a patrol of lancers appeared on the scene; they came forward at a trot, and gathered round the victor and the vanquished. Peter knew only one thing, and that was that he was punishing his victim harder than ever and being beaten in his turn; then he presently found his hands tied, while a party of soldiers were emptying his pockets.

"He has a dagger, captain!" These were the first words he distinctly understood.

"Ah! a weapon!" said the officer. "Very good; you will report all that to the council of war. Do you speak French—you?"

Peter, glaring with bloodshot eyes, made no answer, and his appearance was not probably such as to inspire confidence, for the officer gave an order in an undertone, and four lancers took him in charge.

"Do you speak French?" repeated the officer, standing at a respectful distance. "Call the interpreter."

A little man in civilian's uniform came from behind the ranks, and Peter recognised him as a French counter-jumper whom he had known in a shop in Moscow.

"He does not look like a common man," said the interpreter, eyeing Peter narrowly.

"One of the incendiaries, no doubt," said the officer. "Ask him who he is."

"Who are you?" said the interpreter. "It is your duty to reply to the authorities."

"I will not give my name," Peter broke out in French. "I am your prisoner; lead me away."

"Ah, ha!" cried the officer, frowning. "March!"

A party of starers, including the woman with the child he had entrusted to her, had gathered round the group.

"Where are they taking you to? And what am I to do with the child if it is not theirs, after all?"

"What does the woman want?" asked the officer.

Peter's excitement at seeing the child he had rescued quite turned his head: "What does she want? She has got my child there, that I had just saved from the flames!" And without knowing in the least what had possessed him to tell this aimless lie, he walked on between the four lancers told off to guard him.

This patrol, and several others, had been sent out by Durosnel's orders to check pillage and to capture the incendiaries who, as the French leaders believed, were setting fire to Moscow. But the only persons on whom suspicion had fallen were a shopman, two students, a peasant, a manservant, and a few marauders. Peter was the most unaccountable character they had yet seized, and when the prisoners were taken to the house used as a guard-house, he was placed in a separate room under strict surveillance.

BOOK THIRTEEN

CHAPTER LVI

AT this period a vehement struggle, in which all the drones of the court, as usual, took part, was being fought in the fashionable world of St. Petersburg between the Roumiantzow party, the friends of France and the adherents of the empress dowager and the czarewitch; although the ordinary round of luxurious living went on as before. For those who lived within the influence of this whirlpool of rivalry and competition of every kind, it was difficult, if not impossible, to form any true idea of the critical position of Russia; here were only the regular official ceremonials, the same balls and French plays, the same sordid interests and court jealousies; only in the very highest circles attempts were made to show the real difficulties of the existing position. Now and again, at most, were a few comments breathed as to the different conduct of the two empresses under these grave circumstances. While the empress-mother, thinking only of protecting the different institutions of which she was patroness, had already taken all the necessary steps for their transfer to Kazan, and had had all their possessions packed for removal, the Empress Elizabeth, with her wonted patriotism, had answered to various applications from all sides that as the institutions of the government were in the czar's hands she had no instructions to give on the subject; but that for her part she should be the last to quit St. Petersburg.

On the day of the battle of Borodino Miss Schérer was giving one of her little soirées, of which the crowning feature was to be the reading of a letter written to the czar by the metropolitan and sent with a gift of an image of St. Sergius. This letter was reported to be a supreme expression of patriotic and religious sentiment. Prince Basil, who flattered himself that he was a very remarkable reader—he had occasionally read aloud to the empress—was to give it the advantage of his talent. This consisted in raising and lowering his voice and passing from solemn to sweet without any regard for the sense of the words.

This reading, moreover, like everything that was done at Anna Paulovna's, was full of political significance; some influential personages were to meet there, and were to be made to blush for shame because they continued to frequent the French theatre. Miss Schérer's room was already full, but she did not yet see those whose presence she deemed necessary before that letter could be read.

The latest subject of conversation was the illness of Countess Bésoukhow, who, for some time past, had ceased to be visible in the assemblies of which she was wont to be the ornament, who received no visits, and who, instead of putting herself under the care of a physician of repute, had placed herself in the hands of an Italian doctor; this Italian was treating her with a perfectly new and unknown remedy. Everyone knew that the handsome countess's disorder arose from vexation at her inability to marry two husbands at once; but in Anna Paulovna's presence no one alluded even to this delicate dilemma.

"The poor countess is very ill, I hear; the doctor talks of angina."

"Of angina! but that is a fearful thing!"

"They say that, thanks to this angina, the rivals are reconciled. The old count is quite pathetic, it seems; he cried like a child when the doctor told him that it was a serious case."

"Oh! she will be a dreadful loss—such a charming woman."

"You are speaking of the poor countess? I have just sent to inquire after her. They say she is a little better. Oh yes, she is the most delightful creature in the world," replied Anna Paulovna, smiling at her own enthusiasm. "We belong to different parties, but that does not prevent my esteeming her as she deserves. And she is so unfortunate!"

An imprudent youth, fancying that this remark raised a corner of the veil that shrouded the countess's secret woes, was so bold as to observe that the Italian quack was quite capable of administering dangerous remedies to his patient.

"You may, of course, be better informed than I am," said Miss Schérer, taking the young man up very tartly, "but I have heard, on the best authority, that this physician is a very learned and skilful man. He is a private physician to the Queen of Spain!"

Having thus demolished him, she turned to Bilibine, who was about to deliver himself of a witticism at the expense of the Austrians.

"It strikes me as really delightful!" he exclaimed, speaking of a certain diplomatic note which had accompanied some Austrian flags that had been taken by Wittgenstein—the hero of Petropolis, as he was called at St. Petersburg.

"What is that?" asked Anna Paulovna, to produce a silence, and so enable him to repeat the sarcasm, which she had already heard.

He hastened to take advantage of it, and quoted the very words of the despatch, which he had, in fact, concocted himself: "The czar begs to return these Austrian colours—the flags of a friend which had lost their way when he found them."

"Charming, quite charming!" exclaimed Prince Basil.

"On the road to Warsaw, perhaps," said Prince Hippolyte, quite loud; and everyone looked round at him, for the words were pure nonsense.

He responded to the general surprise with a look of amiable complacency. He did not know what he meant any more than the others did; but in the course of his diplomatic career he had observed that phrases uttered in this style sometimes passed for wit; he had spoken at random, the first words that came to the tip of his tongue, thinking to himself: "Hit or miss. It may be something good; even if not, someone is sure to take the benefit of it!"

The awkward silence that ensued was broken by the entrance of the personage "who was deficient in patriotism," and whom Anna Paulovna proposed to convert to a better mind. Threatening Prince Hippolyte roguishly with her forefinger, she begged Prince Basil to come to the table, had candles placed in front of him, and handing him the letter, requested him to read it aloud.

"Most august sovereign and czar," Prince Basil began in a solemn tone, and with a glance at the company which seemed to pronounce judgment by anticipation on anyone who should dare to raise his voice against this beginning. No one breathed a word. "Moscow, the New Jerusalem, receives her anointed," he went on, emphasising the pronoun, "as a mother embracing in her arms her ardent sons; and, foreseeing the dazzling glory of your power through the growing darkness, she sings with rapture: 'Hosanna! Blessed is He that cometh!'" There were tears in Prince Basil's voice as he read these words.

Bilibine sat looking at his nails; others looked somewhat embarrassed. Anna Paulovna, taking the lead, murmured in an undertone the next sentence, which she knew by heart: "What matter if this insolent and daring Goliath . . ." while Prince Basil went on reading:

"What matter if this insolent and daring Goliath, coming from the frontiers of France, should bring his murderous terrors to the confines of Russia; humble faith—the sling of the Russian David—shall strike the forehead of his pride thirsting for blood. This image of the Blessed Saint Sergius, the ancient zealot of his country's good, is hereby offered to your imperial majesty. I regret that the infirmities of age prevent my rejoicing in the sight of your majesty. I offer my most fervent prayers to the Almighty that He may vouchsafe to add to the number of the righteous, and fulfil your majesty's pious hopes!"

"What power! what style!" cried one and another, praising the author and reader alike.

Anna Paulovna's guests, fairly startled by the eloquence of this epistle, remained for a long time after discussing the position of the empire, and indulging in every variety of supposition as to the issue of the battle which must certainly be fought about this date.

"You will see," said Miss Schérer, "to-morrow is the czar's birthday, and we shall have some news; good news—I have a happy presentiment!"

CHAPTER LVII

HER presentiments were realised. The next day, while the *Te Deum* was being chanted at the palace, Prince Volkonsky was called out of the chapel, and received a despatch containing Koutouzow's report, written on the day of the battle from Tatarinovo. The Russians, he said, had not yielded an inch; the enemy's losses were greater than theirs; but he was writing hurriedly from the field of battle and had not as yet been able to collect the latest information. Consequently this must have been a victory. Then the *Te Deum* was sung all over again as an act of thanksgiving to the Almighty for His mercy shown to his faithful servants. Anna Paulovna was triumphant, and the joys of a high festival were paramount for the whole morning. Everyone believed in a complete victory; several even talked of the possibility of Napoleon's being taken prisoner, of overthrowing him, and placing a new sovereign on the throne of France.

Remote from the scene, and in the midst of court life, it was difficult to estimate the real importance of events as they occurred, for under such conditions they inevitably group them-

selves round some personal fact. Thus, in this case, the joy of
the court at the announcement of the victory chiefly arose from
the fact that the news had arrived on the czar's birthday; it
was like a pleasant surprise successfully carried out.

Koutouzow also mentioned the losses sustained; naming
among the killed Koutaïssow, Toutchkow, and Bagration; but
regret again was concentrated on one alone: Koutaïssow, an
interesting young officer, known to everyone, and a particular
favourite with the czar. All day the changes were rung on
these phrases: "Is not it strange that the news should have
come just during the *Te Deum*? That poor young Koutaïssow!
What a loss! What a sad thing!"

"Well, what did I tell you about Koutouzow?" Prince Basil
would repeat to all comers, wrapping himself, as it were, in the
prophet's mantle. "Did I not tell you from the first, that
he was the only man who could beat Napoleon?"

The following day passed without any news from the army,
and the public mind began to be uneasy. The court was much
hurt at the ignorance in which the czar was kept: "His position
is most painful," they said; and Koutouzow was already held
guilty of causing him all this anxiety, though only yesterday
they had lauded him to the skies. Prince Basil had ceased to
trumpet the praises of his protégé, and kept ominous silence
when the commander-in-chief was mentioned.

That evening a fresh sensational incident added to the excitement which prevailed in aristocratic circles: Countess Helen
died suddenly of her mysterious disorder. It was officially
reported that it was the result of her angina, but privately
further details were discussed: the Queen of Spain's physician
had prescribed some remedy which, in small doses, would have
had a favourable effect; but Helen, tormented by the old count's
jealousy, and the silence of her husband—that dreadful Peter!
had taken a double dose of the medicine, and died in fearful
suffering before any antidote could be administered. It was
said, too, that Prince Basil and the count had taken the Italian
doctor severely to task, but that on reading certain autograph
letters of the deceased lady's which the physician had been able
to lay before them, they had given up the idea of prosecuting
him. Be that as it may, drawing-room gossips had enough to
occupy them that day with three such distressing themes: the
czar's uneasiness, the loss of Koutaïssow, and Helen's death.

On the day but one after the arrival of the great news, a
landed proprietor from Moscow brought the incredible and

astounding story that the old capital had been abandoned to the French. "How shocking! The czar's position was intolerable! Koutouzow was a traitor!" And Prince Basil assured those who came to condole with him on the death of his daughter, that nothing better was to be expected of this blind and impotent old man: "For my part," he added, forgetting, no doubt, in his grief, what he had said the day before, "I always was amazed to think that the fate of Russia should be entrusted to such hands!"

The news was not official, to be sure, and doubt was still admissible: but on the morrow the fact was confirmed by the following report from Count Rostopchine:

"Prince Koutouzow's aide-de-camp has brought me a letter in which the commander-in-chief requests me to furnish him with a force of police to guide the troops across the city to the high road to Riazan. He affects regret at being obliged to abandon Moscow. Sire, this act decides the fate of the capital, and of your empire. Russia will thrill with indignation on learning that the city which represents the greatness of Russia, and which enshrines the ashes of your ancestry, is in the hands of the enemy. I am following the army, and have sent away all that it was necessary to save."

The czar sent for Prince Volkonsky and dictated the following note to Koutouzow:

"Prince Michael Ilarionovitch, I have no news of you later than the 29th of August (10th of September). I have just received *via* Yaroslaw, under date of September 1st (13th), the painful news that you have abandoned our capital. You may imagine the effect it produced on me, and your silence adds to my amazement. General aide-de-camp Prince Volkonsky is the bearer of this note, and is instructed to take information as to the situation of the army, and the reasons which have led you to such an extreme course."

CHAPTER LVIII

NINE days after the abandonment of Moscow a messenger arrived from Koutouzow with official confirmation of the fact. This envoy was a Frenchman named Michaud—"though a foreigner, in heart and soul a Russian," as he himself declared. The czar received him at once, in his private room at the palace in Kamennoï-Ostrow. Michaud, who had just seen Moscow for the first time in his life, and who did not know Russian, nevertheless felt greatly agitated, as he subsequently recorded, when he appeared before our very gracious sovereign to announce to him the burning of Moscow, which had lighted up his road. Though his grief may have had a different cause than that which weighed on the Russians, he looked so deeply distressed that the czar at once said: "You are the bearer of bad news, colonel."

"Very bad, sire!" he said, sighing and looking down: "The evacuation of Moscow."

"Has my ancient capital been given up without a struggle?" And the angry colour mounted to the czar's brow.

Michaud respectfully delivered Koutouzow's message: "Seeing the impossibility of fighting under the walls of Moscow, there was only the alternative of losing the capital and the army both, or of losing the capital only; and he had been compelled to submit to the latter."

The emperor listened in silence without raising his eyes.

"And the enemy is in the city?" he asked.

"Yes, sire. And by this time Moscow is probably a heap of ashes, for I left it in flames."

Michaud was appalled at the effect of his words. The emperor's breathing became oppressed and painful, his lips quivered, and his fine blue eyes filled with tears, but this was a transient emotion; the czar frowned, seeming vexed with himself for his weakness.

"I see," he said, "from all that is happening, that Providence still requires great sacrifices at our hand. I am prepared to submit to His will. But tell me, Michaud, in what state you left the army which could thus look on without striking a blow while my ancient capital was abandoned? Did you see no signs of discouragement?"

Seeing that his gracious majesty was calm, Michaud, too, recovered himself; but not being prepared with any exact information, he answered, in order to gain time:

"Have I your majesty's permission to speak frankly, as a plain, honest soldier?"

"Colonel, that is what I always insist on. Conceal nothing; I want to know the exact truth."

"Sire," said Michaud, with the faintest suggestion of a smile, for he had had time to formulate his answer in the guise of a respectful jest, "sire, I left the army, from the chiefs to the lowest recruit, in a state of extreme and desperate alarm."

"How is that?" asked the czar, sternly. "Are my Russians cowed and crushed by disaster? Never!"

Michaud had made his point. "Sire," he went on with due submission, "their only fear is lest, out of the goodness of your heart, you should be induced to make peace. They are burning to fight, and to prove to your majesty by the sacrifice of their lives how complete is their devotion!"

"Ah!" said the czar, with a grateful look. "You have relieved my mind, colonel."

He bent his head and remained silent.

"Well then," he went on presently, drawing himself up to his full height with majestic dignity, "go back to the army. Tell our brave men—tell all my loyal subjects wherever you go —that when I have no soldiers left I myself will lead forth my beloved nobles, my gallant peasantry, and so fall back even on the last resources of my empire. I have many more at my command than my enemies suspect," he added, warming as he spoke. "Still, if it be written in the decrees of Providence," and he looked up to Heaven with a softened gaze—"that my dynasty is to cease to sit on the throne of my ancestors, then, after exhausting every means in my power, I will let my beard grow and sit down to eat potatoes with the humblest of my subjects rather than sign the disgrace of my country and of my beloved countrymen, whose sacrifices I can so well appreciate!"

He spoke with strong emotion, and turned away as though to hide his tears. After walking to the end of the room and back he eagerly came up to Michaud and wrung his hand, saying, while his eyes flashed with wrath and determination: "Colonel Michaud, do not forget what I have said to you now; some day, perhaps, we may recall it with pleasure. Napoleon and I can no longer reign together; I know him now, and he will not deceive me again!"

Hearing these words, and seeing the resolute expression which was legible on the sovereign's face, Michaud—"though a foreigner, in heart and soul a Russian"—felt himself carried away by genuine enthusiasm (as he subsequently recorded).

"Sire," he exclaimed, "your majesty at this moment seals the glory of your empire and the salvation of Europe!"

When he had thus given utterance, not merely to his personal feelings, but to those of the Russian nation, whose representative at that moment he considered himself, the czar dismissed him with a bow.

CHAPTER LIX

WHEN Russia, already half-conquered, saw the inhabitants of Moscow flying to distant provinces, while the levies of militia went on without cessation, we—who did not live then—we fancy that every individual, from the greatest to the least, can have had but one idea: that, namely, of sacrificing everything to save the country, or to perish with it. The records of the time, indeed, are full of traits of devotion and love, of despair and anguish, but the reality was far from what we fancy it. The historic interest of those terrible years diverts our attention from the minor personal interests which, by their more immediate pressure, blinded contemporary witnesses to the importance of all that was going on around them. The individuals then living, of whom the great majority were guided by these narrow considerations, were, by that very fact, the most useful agents of their time; while those who endeavoured on the contrary to comprehend the general progress of affairs, and to play their part in them by acts of heroism and self-sacrifice, were the most useless members of society. They looked at everything from the wrong point of view, and what they did with the best intentions was, after all, mere aimless folly; for example, the regiments formed by Peter, and by Mamonow, spent all their time in robbing villages; and, again, the lint prepared by the ladies never reached the wounded for whom it was made.

The speeches of those men who never ceased talking of the situation of the country unconsciously bore the stamp either of false judgment, or of blame and of animosity against men whom they accused of faults for which no one was really responsible.

Those who write history learn the wisdom of the prohibition to touch the tree of knowledge; unconscious agency alone can bring forth fruit. He who plays a part in events is the last to know their real importance; and the moment he tries to seize their purport, and to take a conscious part in them, his actions are barren of result. At St. Petersburg, as well as in the interior governments, all, from the militia to the ladies, bewailed the fate of Russia, and of the capital, and talked of nothing but sacrifice and devotion; the army, withdrawn beyond Moscow, thought nothing of what it was abandoning nor of the conflagration it had left behind—still less of vengeance on the French; it thought of the next quarter's pay, the next halting-stage, of Matrechka, the vivandière, and so forth.

Nicholas Rostow, who was still in the service when the war began, consequently played a real and active part in the defence of the country; but he had no preconceived plan, and he gave himself up to no solemn reflections. If he had been asked his opinion as to the state of the country, he would have answered plainly that it was no concern of his; that Koutouzow and the others were there to think for him; all he knew was this: "the regiments were being steadily recruited, there would be fighting for a long while to come, and under existing circumstances it was very likely that he would be promoted to command a regiment." Thanks to this view of the question, he did not even regret his absence from the last battle, and he had gladly accepted a commission to go to Voronège to buy horses for the division.

Thus, only a few days before Borodino, Nicholas had received the needful instructions and money, had sent the hussars in advance, had taken post-horses and set out.

Only those who have spent several months in the atmosphere of a camp during a campaign can form any idea of the gladness that Nicholas felt as he got beyond the radius pervaded by baggage-trains, hospitals, and forage and victualling stores. When he was fairly out of the camp, and the influence of the inelegant details of everyday camp life; when he found himself among villages, peasants, country houses, fields, herds pasturing at their will, post-houses with their sleepy masters—he felt such an exuberance of joy that he could have fancied he saw it all for the first time. Above all what took his fancy were the young, wholesome-looking women that he met, without the usual train of half a score of officers paying court to them, but flattered and smiling at the civilities of the travelling hussar. Enchanted alike with himself and his fate, he reached Voronège at night, put up at the inn, and ordered everything he had been forced to do without in camp. Next morning, after shaving

with particular care, and putting on his full-dress uniform—
which had not seen the light for many a day—he sallied forth
to pay his respects to the authorities.

The commandant of militia, a middle-aged civilian, promoted
to rank as a general, was quite enchanted with his uniform and
new functions. He received Nicholas with a sternly important
air, which he believed to be the right thing for a real soldier,
and questioned him with alternate approval or disapproval, as
if he had the right of judgment. As Nicholas was in the best
possible humour, this only amused him, and not for a moment
did he think of taking offence. He next called on the governor,
a brisk, busy little man, fat and friendly, who told him of a
stud-farm where he could buy good horses, recommended a
horse-dealer, and mentioned a landowner, whose estate lay
about twenty versts out of the town, and who also had some
capital beasts for sale, promising him every assistance.

"You are Count Ilia Andréïévitch's son?" he added. "My
wife is a great friend of your mother's. We see our friends
every Thursday evening—to-day is Thursday; let us have the
pleasure of seeing you this evening. Quite without ceremony."

On leaving the governor, Nicholas took horses and set off
with his quartermaster to visit the stud-farm of which he had
been told. The owner was an old bachelor, a retired cavalry
officer, a great connoisseur of horses, a furious hunter, and the
owner of some brandy, a century old, besides some fine old
Hungarian wine. Nicholas soon came to terms with him,
acquiring seventeen stallions of the best breed to supply the
future requirements of the regiment, for which he was to pay
6000 roubles. Then, after a good dinner, doing ample justice
to the old Hungarian, and taking a cordial leave of his enter-
tainer with whom he was immediately on the most intimate
terms, he made his way back by the same road, as jovially as
he had come—rating the coachman to hurry him up, for fear
of missing the party.

After sluicing himself from head to foot in a cold bath, in
clean clothes, brushed and scented, he made his appearance,
though rather late, at the governor's house. It was not a ball,
but as it was known that Catherina Pétrovna could play waltzes
and country-dances, and there would be dancing, the ladies had
preferred to come in low dresses. Life went on just as usual
in Voronège in 1812; the only difference was that there was
unwonted stir in the provincial town. Several wealthy families
from Moscow had taken refuge there under pressure of

circumstances, and instead of the usual commonplace gossip about the weather, and their neighbours, they discussed what was going on at Moscow, the war, and Napoleon.

The governor's soirée consisted of the cream of local society, including several ladies whom Nicholas had known at Moscow; and of the men there was not one to compare with this brilliant Knight of St. George, the young hussar, the handsome and agreeable Count Nicholas Rostow. Among the guests was an Italian, a prisoner from the French army, and Nicholas felt that his presence there—a living trophy, as it were—added lustre to his own splendour as a hero. In this simple conviction that everyone must share this sentiment he was cordially polite to the Italian, with an infusion of dignified reserve.

The moment he entered the room in his hussar's uniform, diffusing odours of scent and wine, he was surrounded by an admiring circle, and "Better late than never!" was the word on all sides. As the centre of attraction he felt quite in his element, finding himself once more, to his great satisfaction, in the position of which he had so long been deprived as society's favourite. The ladies, married and single, aimed all their coquettish arts at him, and the dowagers at once laid plots for providing him with a wife—to put an end, as they said, to this dashing young officer's follies. The governor's wife, who received him as a near relation, and already was on familiar terms, was among these. Catherine Pétrovna played her tunes; the dancing became lively, giving Nicholas an opportunity of displaying all his graces. His elegant agility charmed the women, and he himself even was surprised to find himself dancing so well; at Moscow he would never have allowed himself such daring freedom, bordering, it must be owned, on bad style; but here he felt impelled to astonish his public by something extraordinary, a revelation to these provincial souls, and to compel them to accept it as the last fashion from the capital.

He selected as the particular object of his attentions a pretty, fair, blue-eyed young woman, the wife of a government official. In the simple conviction which all young men enjoy when their one object is pleasure, that other men's wives were created for them, he never left his conquest for an instant: he even carried his diplomacy so far as to make up to the lady's husband, as though they already foresaw that they could not fail to come to an understanding though they had not as yet confessed their feelings. The husband seemed to have no mind to lend himself to these manœuvres and met the hussar's advances with marked coldness; still, the young fellow's frank good humour and engaging high spirits more than once thawed his rigidity. Towards the end of the evening, however, in proportion as the wife's face flushed and grew eager, the husband's became darker; it was as though they had only a certain modicum of vivacity between them, and when it rose in the wife it fell in the husband.

CHAPTER LX

NICHOLAS, stretched in an arm-chair, was amusing himself by putting himself into attitudes to show off his neat little feet in their irreproachable boots; and all the while he never ceased laughing and paying inflated compliments to the pretty blonde, confiding to her, as a great secret, that he fully meant to run away with one of the ladies of Voronège.

"Which is it?" she asked.

"Oh! a charming creature—lovely, divine! Her eyes," he went on, looking at his neighbour, "are blue, her lips are coral, her shoulders as white!—Her form Diana's own!"

At this moment the husband came up and asked his wife in gloomy tones of what they were talking.

"Ah! Nikita Ivanitch . . ." Rostow exclaimed, rising politely; then, as if to invite him to share the joke, he told him that he intended to carry off a certain lady, fair and blue-eyed. The gentleman received the communication very coldly; the lady was beaming. The governor's wife, who was an excellent kind woman, came forward with a half-stern, half-smiling face.

"Anna Ignatievna would like to speak to you, Nicholas." And she pronounced the name in such a way as to make him understand that the lady was a person of importance. "Come —come with me."

"Immediately, aunt; but who is she?"

"Mrs. Malvintzew. She had heard of you from her niece whom you rescued. . . . Can you guess who?"

"But I rescued so many!" said Nicholas.

"Well, her niece is Princess Bolkonsky; she is here with her aunt. Dear me! how you blush; what is the meaning of that?"

"Not at all—I assure you. . . ."

"Oh! Very well, mystery-monger!" And she introduced

him to an old lady, very tall and stout, with a blue turban on her head, who had just risen from her game at boston with the magnates of the town.

This was Mrs. Malvintzew, Princess Maria's aunt on her mother's side, a rich and childless widow, who never stirred out of Voronège. She was standing up and paying her losses when Nicholas made his bow. Looking at him from her lofty height and knitting her brows, she went on scolding the general who had won her money.

"Charmed, my dear boy," she said, holding out her hand. "Come and see me."

After a few words relating to Princess Maria and her late father, who had never been in her good graces, she asked for news of Prince Andrew, who was no favourite of hers, either. At last she dismissed him, renewing her invitation to call. Nicholas promised to do so and coloured as he left her, for Princess Maria's name roused an incomprehensible emotion of shyness and even of alarm.

He was going back to the dancing-room when he was stopped by a fat little hand on his arm; the governor's wife had a few words to say to him, and she carried him off into a little room, which her other guests very soon discreetly evacuated.

"Do you know, my dear," she began, and her friendly little face assumed a grave expression. "I have found a wife for you. Shall I arrange a match?"

"With whom, aunt?"

"Princess Maria. Catherina Pétrovna thought of Lili; but I am for the princess. Do you like it? I am sure your mother will thank me. She is a charming girl, and by no means so ugly as people say."

"She is not ugly at all," cried Nicholas, in an injured tone. "As for myself—my ways are a soldier's ways; I force myself on no one and I refuse nothing," he went on, without pausing to consider his reply.

"Then you must remember that it is not a mere jest, and I must say, my dear boy, that you are too attentive to the other lady; her husband is really pitiable to see."

"What an idea! We are very good friends!" said Nicholas, who, in his frank simplicity could not imagine that his pleasant pastime could give anyone umbrage. "I answered the governor's wife like a fool," said he to himself at supper. "Now she will be making up a match for me—and Sonia?"

So, when he was bidding her good-night, and she reminded

him of their compact, with a smile, he drew her aside and said:
"I ought to tell you, aunt, that . . ."

"Come in here, my dear boy, sit down. . . ." And he
suddenly felt an irresistible impulse to confide in this woman
who was almost a stranger to him, and to tell her his most
secret thoughts—thoughts which he would not have told his
mother even, or his sister, or his most intimate friend. When
he afterwards remembered this inexplicable explosion of candour, for which there was no adequate motive and which led
to serious issues, he could only ascribe it to chance.

"This is how matters stand. For a long time mamma has
been bent on marrying me to an heiress; but a marriage for
money is to me supremely objectionable."

"That I quite understand," said the good lady.

"But this is a very different thing. I may honestly confess
to you that Princess Bolkonsky attracts me extremely: she
would suit me perfectly; and since I met her under such painful
circumstances I have often thought it was the hand of fate.
Besides, I daresay you know that my mother has always longed
for this marriage, only, I don't know how it was, but we never
had happened to meet. Then, when my sister Natacha was
engaged to her brother, it was impossible that I should think
of it.[1] Now, I have met her again just as that match is broken
off, and other circumstances. . . . In fact, the long and short
of the matter—I never spoke of it to anyone till this moment,
and it is between ourselves. . . ." The lady listened with added
interest. "You know my cousin Sonia? I love her, and I
have promised to marry her, and I mean to marry her. So you
see, the other is out of the question . . ." he added, hesitating
and blushing.

"My dear, my dear boy, how can you talk so? Sonia has
nothing, and you yourself told me that your affairs were all in
confusion. As to your mother—it would kill her; and Sonia
herself, if she has any good feeling, would certainly not accept
such a life: a mother in despair, a fortune gone to ruin! No,
my dear, you and Sonia both must understand that."

Nicholas was silent, but the inference was not wholly
unpleasing.

"But it is impossible, aunt, nevertheless," he said with a
sigh. "Would Princess Maria have anything to say to me?
Besides, she is mourning; it is not to be thought of."

[1] In the Greek Church connection by marriage is regarded as blood
relationship—for instance, two brothers cannot marry two sisters.

"Do you suppose I am going to take you by the throat, on the spot, and marry you out of hand? There are ways and means."

"Oh! what a match-maker you are!" said Nicholas, kissing her plump little hand.

CHAPTER LXI

On her return to Moscow Princess Maria had found her nephew there, with his tutor; also a letter from Prince Andrew, who implored her to go on as far as Voronège and stay there with her aunt, Mrs. Malvintzew. The worry of moving, the anxiety about her brother, the arrangement of a new life in a new home among strange faces, and the education of the little boy—all for a time smothered the temptations which had tormented the poor girl's soul during her father's illness and after his death, and more especially after her meeting with Rostow. She was sad and anxious; the grief she felt for her father's death was aggravated by her sorrow for the disasters of the country; in spite of a whole month spent in peace and monotony, these painful emotions seemed to increase in intensity. The danger which her brother—her only near relation—must constantly run was always in her mind; and added to this was the care of her nephew's education, a task to which she felt herself quite unequal. But nevertheless she was calm of soul because she was conscious of having suppressed her dreams and the hopes she had at first cherished after her meeting with Rostow.

The day after her party the governor's wife went off to call on Mrs. Malvintzew to communicate her scheme; while she insisted that under existing circumstances any regular courting in due form was out of the question, she represented that there was nothing to prevent the young people being brought together, and she asked her consent, which was heartily given. This point being settled, she spoke of Rostow in Princess Maria's presence, and told her how he had coloured at the mention of her name. Maria, however, instead of feeling any pleasure at hearing this, was indefinably uneasy; she could no longer boast of the calm philosophy of which she had once been so proud, and she felt her hopes, her doubts and remorse waking within her with increased vividness.

During the two days which elapsed between this visit and

Rostow's call, she never ceased thinking of how she ought to behave to him. Sometimes she resolved that she would not appear in her aunt's drawing-room, under the pretext of recent mourning, and in the same breath told herself that this would be a breach of politeness towards a man who had done her a signal service. Sometimes she suspected that her aunt and the governor's wife were plotting round her and Nicholas, and then she reproached herself for having such notions, and ascribed them to her own evil mind. How could they think of arranging a marriage for her when she was still in the deepest mourning? And yet she racked her brain to compose phrases with which to meet him; only, in her fear of saying too much or too little, she could not satisfy herself; besides, would not her emotion betray itself in her embarrassment at seeing him again?

But when, after mass on Sunday, her servant came to announce Count Rostow, her face flushed slightly, and her eyes were brighter than usual; these were the only indications of what was going on in her secret soul.

"Have you seen him, aunt?" she asked, surprised at her own tranquillity.

Nicholas entered the room; Princess Maria looked away a moment so as to give him time to pay his respects to her aunt; then, raising her head, she looked full at him. She held out her delicate soft hand with graceful dignity, and spoke a few words; a feminine tenderness of tone—notes that till now had lain mute —vibrated in the ring of her voice. Mademoiselle Bourrienne, who happened to be present, looked at her in amazement. The most accomplished coquette could not have set to work more skilfully to fascinate her victim: "Is it that black becomes her, or is she really handsomer? And what tact! What charming grace! I never noticed it before," thought the Frenchwoman.

If at that moment Princess Maria could have thought of herself, she would have been even more astonished than her companion at the change that had come over her. No sooner had she looked at the face that had grown so dear to her than a living glow, which made her speak and act quite irrespective of her will, flooded her being. Her features were transfigured and radiant with unlooked-for charm—like a vase whose finely chiselled sculptures seem mere opaque confusion till a light within shines through the opal sides. For the first time the travail through which her soul had passed—her griefs, her aspirations to perfection, her resignation, love, and self-sacrifice, were legible in the brilliancy of her expression, the sweetness of her smile, and every feature of her delicate face. Rostow saw it all as clearly as if he had known her all his life; he understood that he stood face to face with a being different to any he had yet met, different and much better, and, above all, superior to himself.

The conversation turned on various subjects: they spoke of the war, of their last meeting — on which Nicholas would not dwell — of the governor's wife and Rostow's relation. Princess Maria did not allude to her brother, and when her aunt spoke of him she changed the subject. It touched her too deeply to be a theme of a commonplace talk. Nicholas noticed this as he noticed with an unaccustomed penetration, all the shades of her character, which only served to strengthen his conviction that she was altogether an unusual person.

During a pause which ensued Nicholas tried to avert the feeling of awkwardness by speaking to Prince Andrew's little boy, and asking him whether he would not like to be a hussar. He took him on his knee and played with him, and happening to look round at Princess Maria he met her touched and gratified glance; she was shyly watching her darling's contentment in the arms of the man she loved. He appreciated all the significance of that glance and coloured with pleasure as he heartily embraced the child. Still, he did not feel justified in repeating his visits too often, as she was in such deep mourning, though the governor's wife persisted in her scheming, and repeated everything pleasant that Princess Maria said about him, and vice versa. She insisted that he was to explain his intentions, and arranged that the young people should happen to meet at the archbishop's house for that express purpose. Rostow told her again and again that he had no wish to come to a declaration; but he was forced to agree to meet her as had been planned.

Just as at Tilsit, where he had not hesitated to accept what others thought right, so to-day, after a short but honest struggle between his wish to work out his life to his own taste and his humble submission to fate, he took the path into which he felt drawn in spite of himself. He knew that any expression of sentiment to Princess Maria, while he still held himself bound to Sonia, was an act of treachery of which he was incapable: at the same time he had a lurking idea at the bottom of his heart, that by giving himself up to the guidance of circumstances and of other people, he not only would be doing nothing wrong, but would be accepting the fulfilment of an important event in his life. After his interview with Princess Maria he

lived to all appearance the same life as he had always led, but
the pleasures which had amused him hitherto had lost all their
charm; the ideas he associated with her had nothing in common
with those which the society of other girls had suggested to
him, nor with the romantic love that he had indulged for the
image of Sonia. As his instincts were virtuous, whenever he
had connected any woman with his dreams of marriage he had
always seen her sitting behind the samovar in a white morning-
gown, surrounded with children, who called them papa and
mamma, and he had indulged in visions of the minutest details
of family life. But the thought of Princess Maria raised no
such pictures as these; in vain did he try to foresee their future
life together: it was all vague and ill-defined, and the chief
association it brought was a kind of fear.

CHAPTER LXII

THE news of the fearful battle of Borodino, and the enormous
losses to the Russians in killed and wounded, and the still more
terrible news about the loss of Moscow, reached Voronège late
in September. Princess Maria having learnt from the news-
papers of her brother's wound but receiving no definite news
from him himself, made up her mind to start in search of
him; Nicholas, who had not met her again, heard this later
from several people.

All these disasters did not rouse him to a desire for vengeance,
or reduce him to despair, he only felt that it was not fitting
that he should prolong his stay at Voronège. All the talk that
he heard rang false on his ear; he knew not what to think of
these events, and felt that he should not thoroughly understand
them till he found himself once more in the atmosphere of
regimental life. So he hastened to make up his complement of
beasts, and got into rages with his servant and quartermaster
more often than usual.

A few days before his departure there was a solemn *Te Deum*
at the cathedral in honour of the successes of the Russian
armies. He attended the service with the rest of the world, and
took up a position not far from the governor; then, having put
on an officially solemn face, he was at liberty to think of other
things. When the ceremony was over the governor's wife
beckoned to him:

"Do you see the princess?" she said, pointing to a lady in

mourning kneeling apart. Nicholas had in fact seen and recognised her, not from her profile, of which he could but just catch a glimpse under her bonnet, but from the instinctive sympathy and bashfulness which had come over him on first seeing her. Princess Maria was absorbed in her devotions, crossing herself as she was about to leave the church. The expression of her face startled him: the features were the same and bore traces of the struggles of her patient soul; but an inward flame showed them in a new light, and at that moment she was a pathetic embodiment of sorrow, prayerfulness, and faith. Without consulting his monitress, without asking himself how far it was right for him to address her in church, he went towards her to assure her of his sympathy in the new blow that had fallen on her. She no sooner heard his voice than a sudden flash of joy mingled with pain shone in her eyes.

"I wanted to tell you, princess," said Rostow, "that as Prince Andrew is in command of a regiment, if he had been killed the papers would certainly have announced the fact." She looked at him, not heeding his words, but giving herself up to the charm of being sympathised with by him. "I have known many cases in which wounds caused by the bursting of a shell were quite trifling when they were not immediately fatal. We must hope for the best, and I am sure that . . ."

"Oh! it would be too dreadful! . . ." she exclaimed, interrupting him, and then, as her agitation was too great to allow of her saying more, she gave him a grateful look and joined her aunt, bowing gracefully as she turned away: all her movements were graceful under the influence of his presence.

Nicholas remained in his lodgings that evening with a view to concluding his bargains and accounts with the horse-dealers. When this was done—it being too late to go out, and too early to go to bed—he rose and paced his room, thinking over his whole life—a rare thing for him. Princess Maria had made a deep impression upon him at their first meeting at Smolensk. The fact that the manner of it was so unusual and that his mother had already mentioned her as a possible rich wife, caused him to pay special attention to her. In Voronège the impression was even deeper. He was struck by the particular moral beauty which this time he noticed in her. And although he was leaving Voronège, it never entered his head to regret his departure because of losing his opportunities of seeing her. His meeting in the morning with Princess Maria had made too deep an impression on him for his peace. Her thin, colourless, melancholy face, her luminous gaze, her soft and gracious movements, and above all the deep, tender sorrow which seemed to pervade her whole person agitated him and commanded his sympathy. While Rostow could not endure any evidence of lofty moral sentiments in a man—and for this reason had never liked Prince Andrew, whom he chose to regard as a philosophical dreamer—in Princess Maria this depth of sorrow, which revealed to him a spiritual world where he was a stranger, was irresistibly attractive to him.

"What a wonderful woman! She must really be an angel! Why am I not free? Why was I in such a hurry to engage myself to Sonia?" and he involuntarily compared her lack with Princess Maria's abundance of those graces of the soul which he knew that he had not, and which for that very reason he prized so highly. He indulged in visions of how he would have acted if he had been free—how he would have wooed her and have made her his wife; but at the thought a chill came over him, and beyond that all was confusion: it seemed impossible to picture Princess Maria in any smiling domestic scene. He loved her, but he did not understand her, while in thinking of Sonia everything was clear and simple; she had nothing mysterious about her. Thoughts of Sonia were always joyful, amusing, whereas thoughts of Princess Maria were difficult and even a little frightening.

"How she was praying!" said he to himself. "That is the faith that can remove mountains, and I am sure her prayers will be heard. Why cannot I pray like that and ask for everything I need?

"What is it that I need? To be free, to break off with Sonia! The governor's wife is right: my marriage with her can only lead to misfortune, to mamma's despair, to confusion. Oh, what a miserable mess! Besides, I do not love her—as I ought to love her! Oh, Lord! Who can help me out of this desperate dilemma? Yes, prayers will move mountains, but one must believe, and not pray as Natacha and I used to do when we were children for the snow to turn to sugar and then run out to taste it and see if it had turned to sugar. No, it is for something serious that I am praying now."

He laid down his pipe and clasping his hands he stood in front of the Holy Images, his eyes full of tears and his heart full of Princess Maria, and prayed as he had not prayed for many a long day. Suddenly the door opened and Lavrouchka came in, carrying some letters.

"Idiot!" cried Nicholas starting from his devotional attitude. "What business have you to come in without being called?"

"From the governor," said Lavrouchka in a sleepy voice. "A courier has come in. Here is a letter for you."

"Thanks, all right; be off!"

There were two letters, one from his mother and one from Sonia; he read Sonia's first. He turned pale as he read, and his eyes opened wide with joy and alarm: "No! Impossible!" he exclaimed aloud. His excitement was too great to allow him to sit still, and he read the letter striding up and down the room. He read it once, twice, and finally with a shrug of sheer amazement, stood still, his mouth and eyes wide open.

His prayer had been heard! He was as completely astounded as though it had really been the most wonderful thing in the world, and he was tempted to regard such an immediate fulfilment of his wishes as a proof that it was the result of chance and not of the direct interposition of God. The Gordian knot that had fettered his future life was cut by Sonia's letter. She wrote that the Rostows had lost the larger part of their fortune by the recent catastrophes, and that this, added to the countess's constantly expressed wish to see Nicholas married to Princess Bolkonsky, with his silence and coldness had made her determine to release him from his pledge and give him back his word. "It is too painful to me," she added, "to think that I could ever be the cause of trouble or dissension in a family which has loaded me with benefits. As my love can only aim at promoting the happiness of those I love, I entreat you, Nicholas, to consider yourself free, and to believe that come what may, no one will ever love you more truly than

"Your SONIA."

The letter from the countess gave an account of their last days at Moscow, of their departure, of the conflagration, and of the total wreck of their property. She added that Prince Andrew, very seriously wounded, was travelling with them, that the doctor now hoped that his life might be saved; Sonia and Natacha were his nurses.

Nicholas carried this letter next morning to Princess Maria; they neither of them made any comment on Natacha's attendance on the wounded man. This letter made them feel on the footing of relations; Nicholas, indeed, saw the princess off to Yaroslaw, and then rejoined his regiment.

CHAPTER LXIII

Sonia's letter, written from the Troïtsky monastery, was the outcome of several events that had happened in the family. Above every other consideration in the countess's mind, her wish to see Nicholas marry a rich heiress remained paramount; and Sonia, who in her eyes was the chief obstacle, had been made painfully aware of it, especially after she had heard of her son's meeting with Princess Maria. The countess never missed an opportunity of casting some cruel and insulting hint at her. A few days before they left Moscow she had sent for her niece, but instead of reproaching her, she implored her with bitter weeping to release Nicholas from his promise and so pay her debt of gratitude to those who had been parents to her. "I shall never be happy till you have said yes."

Sonia replied, with many tears, that she would do anything that was required of her; still, she could not make up her mind to pledge herself formally. It was natural to her to sacrifice herself for others, and in the existing state of affairs the only way in which she could show her gratitude at all was by constantly sacrificing herself. She felt at the same time that each act of abnegation added to her value in their eyes, and, of itself, made her more worthy of Nicholas, whom she worshipped. But the offering she was now required to make entailed a renunciation of all that she had counted on as the reward of her past life, of everything that made the future worth living for. For the first time her soul was bitter: she turned against those who had rescued her from poverty only to load her with far greater miseries. She turned against Natacha, whose feelings had never been outraged or thwarted—on the contrary, they were a law to all who came within reach of her, and yet who could help loving her? She felt too, for the first time, that her love, till now so placid and pure, was turning to a vehement passion outside the pale of law, virtue and religion. The experience of her life had taught her extreme reserve, so the very violence of this storm led her to reply to the countess in general terms, and she determined to wait till she should see Nicholas, intending not to release him indeed, but to bind him more firmly and for ever.

The anxieties of the last few days in Moscow had diverted her mind from her woes, which she was glad to lose sight of in the whirl of occupations that fell upon her; but when she heard that Prince Andrew was under the same roof, in spite of her sympathy for him and for Natacha, a superstitious gladness came over her. She thought that, in this coincidence, she saw the hand of Providence interfering to prevent her being divided from Nicholas. She knew that Natacha had never really ceased to love Prince Andrew; and she foresaw that now that they were thrown together again their affection would take new life, and that then Nicholas could not marry Princess Maria, who in the event she anticipated would be his sister-in-law. And so, in spite of the grief and distress that she saw on all sides, this visible intervention of Heaven in her private concerns caused her the most soothing satisfaction.

The Rostows halted for a night at the Troïtsky monastery. Three large rooms had been reserved for them in the convent inn; one was given up to Prince Andrew, who was better that day. Natacha was sitting with him while the count and countess were in the next room conversing with the Superior who had received them gladly as old friends. Sonia, who was with them, was wondering what Prince Andrew and Natacha could find to say to each other. Suddenly the door opened and Natacha, greatly agitated, came straight up to Sonia, without heeding the monk who rose to greet her.

"Natacha, what are you thinking of? Come here," said her mother. She went to the Father Superior and received his blessing; he urged her to implore the help of God and of the blessed Saint Sergius. As soon as he was gone she dragged Sonia away into the empty room.

"Sonia, he will live! Don't you think he will? Oh! I am so happy and so miserable! Everything is right between us. If only he might live—but he cannot. . . ." She burst into tears.

Sonia, equally agitated by her friend's sorrow and her own secret anxieties, embraced and comforted her.

"Yes, if only he might live!" she said to herself.

They stole to the door of Prince Andrew's room and opened it a little way; they could see him lie there, his head propped on three pillows. He was resting with his eyes shut, and breathing regularly.

"Oh! Natacha!" Sonia suddenly exclaimed, seizing her hand and starting back.

"What? What is it?" asked Natacha.

"It was that, of course, of course," Sonia went on, turning very pale as she shut the door. "Do you remember," she said, half solemn and half scared, "when I looked in the glass that Christmas, I saw . . ."

"Yes, yes," said Natacha, staring at her and dimly recalling Sonia's vision.

"You remember—I told you and Douniacha at the time. I saw him lying down with his eyes shut, and a pink coverlet over him—just as he is now."

And growing more eager as she spoke she described all the details of the scene as it actually was, referring them to that second sight at Christmas, till her imagination no longer doubted its reality.

"Yes, to be sure, the pink counterpane," said Natacha pensively, and feeling that she had seen it too. "But what can it mean?"

"I don't know—it is most extraordinary," replied Sonia.

A few minutes later Prince Andrew rang and Natacha went in to him; Sonia, overwhelmed by a tender pathos which she very seldom felt, stood looking out of a window, quite bewildered by all these strange coincidences.

An opportunity offered that very day of sending letters to the army; the countess took advantage of it to write to her son.

"Sonia, will you not write to Nicholas?" she said in a rather tremulous voice. The young girl understood the entreaty conveyed in the appeal; she could read in the countess's eyes, as she looked up over her spectacles, all the difficulties that had prompted the hint and the hostility that lurked ready to break out if she refused. She went up to the countess, knelt down by her and kissed her hand, saying: "Mamma, I will write."

Under the prompting of that mysterious presentiment, of which the fulfilment would inevitably prevent a marriage between Nicholas and Princess Maria, she did not hesitate to sacrifice herself as usual. With tears in her eyes and a deep sense of the magnanimity of her own action, she sat down, and frequently interrupted by her own sobs wrote the letter which had so greatly perturbed Nicholas.

CHAPTER LXIV

WHEN they had reached the guard-house the officer and soldiers who had captured Peter treated him with no little enmity, in remembrance no doubt of the struggle they had had with him; but they behaved to him, nevertheless, with a certain degree of respect. They wondered with much curiosity whether they might not have laid hands on some person of importance, and when guard was relieved next day Peter observed that the new-comers had not the same consideration. To them, in fact, this big man in his caftan, was not the authoritative citizen who had rated the chief and awed the patrol, but simply No. 17 of the prisoners left in their charge by superior command. If there was anything particular about Peter it was only his bold and pensive appearance and the fact that he spoke French so extraordinarily well. In spite of this, however, that same day he was put in with the other prisoners, the room he had so far had to himself being wanted by an officer. All the men who were locked up with him were of inferior rank; and they, having recognised Peter as a gentleman and heard him speak French, avoided him.

They all, himself included, were to be tried for incendiarism, and on the third day they were led to a house where a general with a white moustache was holding court-martial, with the assistance of two colonels and some other French officers. He questioned the prisoners with that sharp precision which would seem properly to belong only to a being superior to all human weaknesses: "Who was he? Where had he been going, and what for?" etc.

These inquiries, which had nothing to do with the essence of the matter, and so made the chances of arriving at the truth more and more remote, had the same tendency as a judge's questions invariably have: namely to suggest to the accused the direct way to the desired end, which is that he should inculpate himself. Peter, like every man who has found himself in a similar predicament, wondered with amazement why he was asked such questions; they were, after all, but an empty mockery of benevolent formality. He knew that he was in their power—in the power of that brute force which had brought him before his judges and gave them the right to exact compromising answers.

He was asked what he was doing when he was arrested. He

replied that he was seeking for the parents of a child he had saved from the flames.

"Why had he collared the thief?"

"Because I was trying to defend a woman he had attacked, and it was the duty of every honest man. . . ." He was stopped: this was an unnecessary digression.

"Why had he gone into the courtyard of the burning house?"

"He had come out to see what was going on." Again he was interrupted: He was not asked where he was going but what he was doing there.

When they asked his name he refused to give it.

"Write that down; that does not look well, in fact it is very bad . . ." said the general.

On the fourth day after their arrest the fires reached the quarter where they were imprisoned. Peter and his companions were brought out and locked up in the coach-house of a large warehouse. As they went through the streets they were smothered in smoke; the fire was still steadily gaining ground. Though he could not even now appreciate the magnitude of the conflagration he gazed at the spectacle with horror.

For four days they remained in this new prison, and he learned from the French soldiers that they expected every moment to hear what decision the marshal had come to with respect to their fate. What marshal? They did not know. The days which dragged on till the 8th (20th) of September, when they were again examined, were days of misery to Peter.

CHAPTER LXV

ON that day a superior officer, a very great man it would seem from the respect shown to him by the sentinels, came to inspect the prisoners. He evidently belonged to the staff, and held a list from which he called their names. Peter was put down as "the man who will not give his name!" After looking them down with utter indifference, he ordered the officer on guard to see that they were made tidy enough to appear before the marshal. An hour later a company of soldiers escorted the whole party to Diévitchy-Polé (the Maiden's field).

The day was fine and bright after rain and the air marvellously clear; the smoke did not hang low over the ground, but rose in pillars to the blue sky over the city; though the flames were invisible in the sunlight, Moscow was nothing but an immense heap of burning fuel; on all sides nothing was to be seen but devastated spaces, smoking rubbish, and blackened walls with stoves and tall chimneys still clinging to them. It was in vain that Peter scanned the ruins, he could not recognise any part of the city. Here and there a church stood up intact, and the Kremlin, which the fire had not reached, gleamed white in the distance, with the tower of Ivan Véliki. Close by glittered the belfry of the convent of Novo-Diévitchy, where a loud peal was calling the faithful to prayer. Peter remembered that it was a Sunday, and the festival of the Nativity of the Virgin; but who could be celebrating it in the midst of fire and destruction?

As they went along they met only a few people in rags, who hid themselves in terror at the approach of the French. It was quite clear that the nest of Russia was wrecked; still Peter had an indistinct perception that this wrecking of the nest was preparatory to a new order of things. Everything seemed to bear assurance of it, without his attempting to reason it out: their brisk steady march, the straight file of their escort, the presence of the French official who passed them on the road in a carriage driven by a private, the sound of military music marching to meet him across the square, even the list that had been read out this morning. And he—he was being led he knew not whither; but he could read in the faces of their escort that the orders given as to the fate of the prisoners would be carried out without mercy, and he felt that he was no more than a wisp of straw caught in the cogs of a machine new to him, but working with utter regularity.

He and his companions were conducted a little way beyond the monastery to a large white house in the midst of a fine garden on the right-hand side of the square, and he recognised it as belonging to Prince Stcherbatow with whom he had been intimate; it was at present inhabited by Marshal Davoust, Prince of Eckmühl, as he gathered from the soldiers' talk. The Russians were taken in one by one; Peter was the sixth. He was led along a glass gallery and across a vestibule, into a large low study which he knew very well; an aide-de-camp was standing at the door. Davoust was seated at the farther end of the room, his spectacles on his nose, absorbed in reading a paper that lay on the table: he did not look up.

"Who are you?" he asked, in a low voice, addressing Peter, who was standing close to him.

Peter made no reply; he had not the strength to speak, for to him Davoust was not merely a French general, but a man noted for his cruelty. As he looked at the hard, cold face—reminding him of that of a stern schoolmaster, who condescends to a few minutes' patience while he waits for an answer—he fully understood that every moment's delay might cost him his life. But what was he to say? It struck him as quite useless to repeat all he had said the first time, but it was alike shameful and dangerous to reveal his name and rank. The silence remained unbroken; but presently Davoust raised his head, took off his spectacles, and scowled at him with a fixed stare.

"I know that man," he said in a rough, hard voice, intended to alarm the accused. Peter shuddered.

"No, general, you cannot know me; I have never seen you . . ."

"He is a Russian spy," said Davoust, interrupting him, and speaking to another general.

"No, highness," Peter eagerly repeated; he had just remembered that Davoust was a prince. "No, highness, you cannot know me. I am an officer of militia, and I have not been out of Moscow."

"Your name?" said the marshal.

"Bésoukhow."

"And what is to prove to me that you are not lying?"

"Highness!" exclaimed Peter, in entreaty rather than in anger.

Davoust raised his eyes and fixed them on Peter. They looked at each other like this for several seconds, and this look was his saving. In spite of the war, and the position in which they stood to each other, a human feeling rose up between the two men. At the first glance that the marshal had cast at the list in which the men were so many ciphers, and Peter, as being nameless, a mere incident, he could have ordered him to be shot without dreaming that he could do wrong; but now he recognised him as a man—they were brothers.

"How can you prove that you are telling the truth?"

Peter remembered Ramballe, and mentioned his name, with the number of his regiment, and the street in which he had quartered himself.

"You are not what you represent yourself," Davoust repeated.

Peter in an agitated voice again gave the evidence of his veracity. An aide-de-camp just then came in, and gave the marshal some news which delighted him. He rose to go out, having quite forgotten the prisoner. The aide-de-camp reminded him; he ordered that he should be led away. Whither? Peter could not guess. Where were they going to take him? Back to the coach-house, or to the place of execution, which his companions had pointed out as they crossed the square.

"Yes, of course," said Davoust, in answer to a question from his companion, which Peter had not heard.

Then he was led out.

He never knew how long they were on that march; he went on mechanically, like his companions in misfortune: he saw nothing, heard nothing, and only stopped because the others stopped. One single idea racked his brain: Who was it that had condemned him to death? Not those who had just examined him; they would not, and indeed could not have done it. Not Davoust, who had looked at him with true humanity: a minute more, and he would have understood that he was making a mistake; the aide-de-camp's entrance had forestalled it. Who then had condemned him to die? Who could decide that he should be killed—he, so full of memories, hopes, and ideas! Who could do such a thing? Who was the immediate agent? No one. He saw, he understood that it was the outcome of the order of things, and the inevitable result of circumstances.

CHAPTER LXVI

The prisoners were led from Prince Stcherbatow's mansion across the square, towards a kitchen garden, a little to the left; there stood an upright post; behind it a large ditch had been dug—the fresh earth was thrown up all round it. A crowd stood in a semicircle, gazing into this pit with uneasy curiosity. It consisted of some Russians, with a large proportion of soldiers in the French army, but of various nationalities, and wearing a great variety of uniforms. To the right and left of the stake stood files of soldiers in dark-blue greatcoats, red epaulettes, gaiters, and shakos. The condemned were placed inside the circle in the order of their numbers. Peter again was sixth. A roll of drums was beaten on both sides at once; he felt his soul wrung by the clamour; it deprived him of the faculty of thought. He could scarcely see or hear, and one only desire possessed him: that of getting it over—that dreadful and inexorable "It" which hung over him!

The two men at the end of this row were convicts, one tall and lean; the other a swarthy, muscular fellow, with a broken nose. Next to him, No. 3, was a fine stalwart man, with iron-grey hair, of about five-and-forty. The fourth was a peasant, with a pleasant bright face, black eyes, and russet beard; the fifth a factory hand, pale and sallow, a lad of eighteen or so, wrapped in a long coat. Peter gathered that the French officers were consulting as to whether they should be shot in batches, or one by one.

"Two at a time," said the captain, with cold indifference.

There was a stir in the ranks, evidently not arising from any eagerness on the part of the men to execute a regular order, but from their anxiety to have done with a horrible and incomprehensible task. A civil functionary with a scarf on came forward, and read the sentence to the prisoners in French and in Russian; then four soldiers pinioned the two convicts. While someone was sent for bandages for their eyes they stood looking about them like wild beasts driven into a corner, and watching the approach of the huntsman; one crossed himself; the other scratched his back and moved his lips as if smiling. When their eyes were bandaged, and they were tied up to the post, twelve men stepped out of the ranks, and stood eight paces from the prisoners. Peter turned away, not to see what would happen. Suddenly a volley was fired. To Peter it seemed louder than a thunder-clap; he looked round, and in the midst of a cloud of smoke he perceived a party of Frenchmen, pale and tremulous, who were busy round the trench.

The two next victims were led out; their imploring looks seemed to claim some help, some rescue, as if they could not believe that they were to be bereft of life. Again Peter looked away; a louder report than ever rang in his ear. With a heaving chest he looked round at the men who stood near him—on every face he saw the expression of the same amazement, horror, and disgust that were seething in his soul.

"Whose doing is it? They are all as much sickened as I am," he muttered to himself.

"File of the 86th, forward!" cried a voice.

Then No. 5 was led out alone. Peter was so terror-stricken, that he failed to understand that he and the rest were reprieved; that they had only been brought out to see the execution of these five. The young workman started back as the soldiers touched him, and clung to Peter; Peter, with a shudder, released himself from the grasp of the poor wretch who could not stand alone; they seized him by the arms, and dragged him along. He was shrieking with all his might, but when he was attached to the stake he was silent, as if he understood that cries were useless, or hoped perhaps that he might yet be spared.

Peter's curiosity was stronger than his horror; this time he did not turn away or shut his eyes. The excitement he felt, and which was shared by the crowd, had reached an acute pitch. The victim had recovered himself; he buttoned up his coat, rubbed his bare feet one on the other, and arranged the knot of his bandage; when he was tied to the post he drew himself up and stood straight on his feet, without losing nerve again. Peter watched every movement; he could not take his eyes off him. A word of command was given, no doubt, and twelve muskets fired in obedience to it, but he never could remember having heard them; he suddenly saw the man double up, blood spurted from two wounds, the cords yielded under the weight of the body, the head drooped and the legs gave way, so that the dying man hung in a strangely distorted posture. No one held him up. Those who stood nearest to him had turned pale, and the old moustachioed soldier's lip quivered as he untied the cords. The body fell in a heap; the soldiers clutched it clumsily, dragged it away and pushed it into the trench. They looked like criminals themselves, hurriedly hiding the traces of a murder.

Peter glanced in. He could see the body of the workman with the knees drawn up to the head, and one shoulder higher than the other; that shoulder slowly rose and fell with convulsive jerks—but shovelfuls of earth fell fast all the time, forming a heap that covered him. One of the soldiers called to Peter with angry impatience; he did not hear him, but stood rooted to the spot. When the trench was filled up, another word of command was given. Peter was led back slowly to his place, the soldiers faced half right about, and slowly marched past the stake. The twenty-four soldiers whose guns had been fired, fell in as the files went by them—all but one, quite a lad, as pale as death, who remained, without moving from the spot by the side of the grave where he had stood to fire; his shako had fallen back on to the nape of his neck, and his musket was reversed; he staggered like a drunken man, swaying backwards and forwards to save himself from falling. An old sergeant ran towards him, seized him by the shoulder, and pulled him back to his place. The crowd slowly dispersed; everyone hanging his head in silence.

"That will give them a lesson! Those rascally incendiaries . . . ." said a Frenchman, and Peter looked round to see who had spoken. It was a soldier, evidently trying to reconcile himself to the deed he had just done; but he did not finish his sentence, and went off with a dejected air.

CHAPTER LXVII

PETER was parted from his companions and placed by himself in a little deserted chapel. Late in the day a subaltern on guard came with two soldiers to inform him that he was reprieved and to be allowed to join the prisoners of war. He followed them, without understanding what was happening, to some wooden huts, half-burnt down; and in one of these he was left. It was dark inside, and he found himself one of a party of about twenty, without forming any conception of who they were or what was being done with him. He heard voices—he answered questions—he saw all these faces—but his mind worked only as a machine works.

From the moment when he had seen those hideous murders committed by executioners to order, it was as though the nerve which gave life and sense to all he saw had been torn from his brain, and everything had crumbled into nothingness. Though, as yet, he was not conscious of the process, that hour's experience had extinguished in his soul all faith in the perfection of creation, in the human soul, in his own, in the very existence of God. Peter had been through such a crisis before, but he had never felt its effects so vividly. Formerly the doubts that had assailed him had their source in his own shortcomings, and then he had sought the remedy in himself; but this time he could not blame himself for the collapse of all his beliefs, which had left behind it nothing but shapeless and nameless ruins. He felt that a return of faith was no longer dependent on him.

A place was found for him in a corner of the hovel, in the midst of a group who seemed to be amused and interested by his presence. He sat down on a heap of straw, and remained there silent and motionless, opening and shutting his eyes, and still haunted by the horrible vision of the victims and of the men who, in spite of themselves, had been their executioners. His immediate neighbour was a little man sitting quite doubled up, and whose presence indeed was at first only perceptible by the unpleasant smell of his person. It was so dark that Peter could scarcely distinguish him, but he felt that the little man frequently raised his head to look round at him. So with a determined effort of attention he at last succeeded in perceiving that this man was baring his feet, and the process attracted his interest. The man unfastened a narrow band of linen in which one foot was wrapped, and slowly and carefully rolled it up; then he performed the same operation on the other foot. Finally he hung up his bands of linen on pegs over his head, took out a knife, cut something, shut the knife again and put it away. Having finished, he clasped his knees and sat staring at Peter. His quiet, deliberate movements had a soothing effect on Peter's nerves.

"Have you gone through much misery, master?" he said, and there was such genuine and simple kindliness in his drawling accent, that Peter felt the tears choking him as he was about to reply. The little man guessed as much, and to give him time to recover himself, he went on: "Ah! my friend, do not take it too much to heart! We suffer for an hour and live an age. Thank God we are yet alive! There are good and bad men everywhere." And as he spoke he hastily rose and went across the room.

"What, you old rascal, are you back again?" said the kind voice presently, at the other end of the hut. "Back again, ha, ha! You have a good memory!" he patted a little dog that came leaping after him as he turned to his corner, holding in his hand a parcel wrapped in a handkerchief.

"Here, master—you would like something to eat, would not you?" he said, untying the bundle and offering Peter some baked potatoes. "We had a mess of soup at noon, but these potatoes are capital." The mere smell of them tempted Peter, who had eaten nothing all day; he thanked his friend and accepted one.

"Well, how does that do?" said the little man, also taking a potato. He cut it in half, sprinkled it with some salt out of the handkerchief, and offered some to Peter. "A very good thing is a potato; eat away," and Peter thought he had never eaten anything better.

"All this is a trifle," he said presently. "But why did they shoot those poor wretches? The youngest was not twenty!"

"Hush, hush!" murmured the little man. "Tell me, master, what made you remain in Moscow?"

"I did not think they would be here so soon. I stayed quite by chance."

"And how did they get hold of you? In your own house?"

"I went out to see the fire; there they caught me, and condemned me as an incendiary."

"Where there is judging there is always injustice," said the little man.

"And you—have you been here long?"

"I? Since Sunday. They fetched me out of hospital."

"You are a soldier then?"

"In Apchéron's regiment. I was dying of fever. We had never heard a word about it; twenty of us all lying there, and we knew nothing."

"And here I suppose you are pretty sick of it?"

"How can one help being sick of it! Plato Karataïew is my name," said he, to make conversation easier between himself and his neighbour, "and the men used to call me the little hawk. How can one help being sad? Moscow is the mother of all our cities! But you, master, must have lands and a house; your cup must be full—and a wife, too, perhaps? And an old father and mother—are they alive?"

Though Peter could not see his face he felt that his neighbour was turning to him with a friendly smile, and thought him very much to be pitied when he heard that he had no parents—above all, no mother.

"A wife for good counsel and a mother-in-law for a warm welcome—but nothing can make up for a mother! And have you any children?" Peter's negative evidently distressed him, and he hastened to add:

"But you are both young. God may grant them to you yet. Live on good terms, that is the great thing."

"Oh, I do not care about it now!" Peter exclaimed involuntarily.

"Heh! My good friend, there is no avoiding beggary or imprisonment! You see," he went on, clearing his throat for a long story, "my master's estate was a fine one; we had no end of land, the peasants lived comfortably, and the labourers too, thank God! The corn yielded seven-fold, and we lived as good Christians should; till one day—" and Plato Karataïew told him how he had been caught one day by the forester of a neighbouring wood stealing logs, flogged, condemned and sent to serve in the army. "And what then!" he added with a smile, "it looked like a misfortune, and it was really a blessing.

If I had not gone wrong my brother would have had to go and leave five children behind him. I, you see, only left a wife; I had a little girl once, but God Almighty had taken her back again. I went home once on leave. What can I say about it? They live better than they used, though there are several mouths to fill; the women were at home, two of my brothers were away. Michael, the youngest, was the only one left. My father said to me: 'All my children are just the same to me; it matters not which finger is nipped, it hurts just as much. If they had not caught Plato it would have been Michael.' So then, would you believe it, he led us in front of the images: 'Michael,' says he, 'come here; bow down to the earth before Him, and you women too, and you little ones.' Do you understand, master? That is how fate takes us by chance, and we find fault and complain. Happiness is like the water in a landing-net; you pull it along and it is full—you lift it out and it is empty!" After a short pause Plato rose.

"You would be glad to go to sleep, I daresay?" And he crossed himself repeatedly, muttering: "Lord Jesus Christ, Saint Nicholas, Saint Florus, and Saint Laura, have mercy upon us!" He touched the ground with his forehead, got up, sighed, and laid down on the straw, covering himself with his greatcoat.

"What was that prayer you said?"

"What?" said Plato, already half asleep. "I said my prayers, that is all. Don't you say your prayers?"

"To be sure I do; but what were you saying about Florus and Laura?"

"They are the patron saints of horses. We must not forget the poor dumb creatures. Do you see this little rascal? He has come here for warmth and shelter," he added, stroking the dog, who had curled himself up at his feet. Then he turned over and was sound asleep in an instant.

Outside, in the distance, wailing and shrieks were still to be heard, and the lurid glare of the fires gleamed between the ill-fitting planks of the hut; but within all was calm, dark and silent. It was long before Peter fell asleep; he lay with his eyes wide open in the gloom, listening vaguely to Plato's steady snoring, and feeling that the world of beliefs which had crumbled away in his soul was undergoing resurrection once more, and built up now on immovable foundations.

CHAPTER LXVIII

PETER remained in this hut for four weeks, with twenty-three soldiers, three officers, and two civil officials, all prisoners like himself. They left scarcely a trace on his memory; no one survived from it but the figure of Plato, which he retained as one of his dearest and most vivid recollections—the perfect embodiment of all that is most genuinely Russian, warm-hearted, and true. When, the next morning by daylight, Peter saw his neighbour, the first impression of "roundness" was fully confirmed. Plato's whole figure in its French soldier's coat, cap and bast shoes, was round. His head was quite round; back, chest, shoulders, even arms which he always carried as if he were about to embrace somebody, were round. His pleasant smile and large brown eyes were round.

Plato Karataïew must have been about fifty years old, to judge from the service he had seen; he himself could not have told his age with any precision. When he laughed he displayed two rows of sound, white teeth; his beard and hair had not a streak of grey; his whole physique was characteristic of strength and determination, and above all, of stoicism. Though his face was closely covered with tiny wrinkles, its expression was touchingly simple, youthful, and innocent. As he spoke in his soft, sing-song voice, his words flowed with natural eloquence; he never thought of what he had said or of what he was going to say, and the eagerness and variety of his tones gave them persuasive effect. His physical strength and stamina were such, that during the early part of his imprisonment, he seemed not to know what it was to be tired or ill. Every night and morning, as he lay down and got up again, he never failed to say: "Pray God, let me sleep like a stone and rise like a *kalatch*!"[1] And in point of fact he had hardly laid himself down when he was dead asleep, and he woke in the morning fresh and gay, and ready for anything.

He knew a little of everything, doing all neither very well nor very badly. He could cook, sew, carpenter, mend boots, and, being busy all day, never allowed himself to chatter and sing till the evening. Nor did he sing like a man who expects to be listened to; but as the birds of the air sing: it was as much a need of his nature as walking or stretching himself. His voice was tender, sweet, and plaintive, almost like a

[1] A fine light loaf.

woman's, in harmony with his serious face.   After a few weeks
in prison his beard had grown, and he looked as if he had
shaken off all that was not absolutely native to him—a certain
artificial look that had come to him with his soldier's training
—and had become what he really was: a peasant and a son
of the soil.

"A soldier on leave makes a shirt of his drawers!" he would
say; he was not fond of talking of his long years of service, but
was proud of saying that he had never been punished.   When
he told a story it was generally some episode of his early life
which he loved to dwell on.   The proverbs with which he gave
point to his discourse were not coarse or vulgar, like those of
his comrades, and he was fond of using popular expressions,
which in themselves have no particular force, but which, when
applied appropriately, are striking by their aptness and wisdom;
in his mouth they acquired new value.

In the opinion of the other prisoners Plato was just a soldier,
to be made game of on occasion, and sent to do every kind of
errand; but in Peter's mind he dwelt for ever after as the ideal
type of simplicity and truth: always just what he had felt him
to be from the first night he had spent by his side.

CHAPTER LXIX

PRINCESS MARIA, on hearing from Nicholas that her brother
was at Yaroslaw with the Rostows, decided on going thither, in
spite of her aunt's remonstrances, and on taking her little
nephew with her.   The difficulties of the journey did not
make her hesitate for a moment.   Her duty lay before her: it
was to nurse her brother who was suffering—perhaps dying,
and to take him his child.   If Prince Andrew had not asked
to see her no doubt it was because his extreme weakness
prevented him, or because he feared the long and fatiguing
journey for her and the boy.

A few days sufficed for her arrangements.   Her conveyances
were a large coach, in which she had travelled to Voronége, a
britzska, and a *fourgon*.   Her party consisted of Mademoiselle
Bourrienne, little Nicholas and his tutor, her old nurse, two
maids, old Tikhone, a young footman, and a *heyduc* whom her
aunt lent her as an escort.   It was impossible to take the usual
road through Moscow, so she must make a round by Lipetsk,

Riazan, and Vladimir, where she had not a hope of finding post-horses; and the journey was all the more likely to be dangerous, as the French, it was said, had been seen in the neighbourhood of Riazan. Mademoiselle Bourrienne, Dessalles, and her servants were amazed at her unceasing activity and steady purpose. She was in bed the last and up the first; she allowed no obstacle to hinder her, and thanks to her energy, which kept them all up to the mark, they reached Yaroslaw in a fortnight.

The last part of her stay at Voronège had brought her the greatest happiness of her life, for her love for Nicholas was no longer a torment to her; it filled her soul, and seemed to have become part of her being. The struggle was over; for, without confessing it to herself, ever since her last interview with him, she had felt sure of loving and being loved. She became certain of this at her last interview with Rostow when he came to inform her that her brother was with his people. Nicholas had not alluded to the renewal of the old engagement between Natacha and Prince Andrew, if he should recover, but Princess Maria could guess that it was constantly in his mind. His manner to her—tender, reserved, and thoughtful—did not change; on the contrary, he seemed pleased to think that this possible relationship set him at liberty to give expression to friendship, under which Princess Maria soon discerned love. She felt that she herself loved for the first and last time in her life, and, happy in believing herself beloved, she calmly abandoned herself to that happiness.

This calmness did not prevent her feeling the keenest concern at the desperate situation in which she would find her brother; on the contrary, it left her mind free to think of it more exclusively. The deep anguish of her worn and heart-broken face made them all fear that she would fall seriously ill, but the difficulties and anxieties of the journey seemed to double her strength by occupying her thoughts, and so compelling her to forget, at any rate for the time, the object of her undertaking. Nevertheless, as she got nearer to Yaroslaw, remembering that within an hour or two her worst fears might be confirmed, her agitation was too much for her self-control. She sent forward the *heyduc* to ascertain where the Rostows were lodging, and inquire as to the state of Prince Andrew's health. Having done so, he returned and met the carriage as it was entering the town. He was terrified at his mistress's pallor as she put her head out of the window.

"I have found out all you want to know, excellency. Count Rostow's family live a little way from this, in a house belonging to a merchant named Bronnikow, on the banks of the Volga."

Princess Maria kept her eyes fixed on his face, wondering and fearing at his saying nothing in reply to the main question. Mademoiselle Bourrienne spoke the words.

"And how is the prince?" she said.

"His excellency is with the family."

"Then he is alive!" thought the princess. "And how is he?" she asked.

"The servants say he is going on just the same."

What did that mean? She was afraid to ask, and glanced at the child who sat facing her—he was enchanted at finding himself in a large town. Then her head drooped, and she did not look up again till the heavy vehicle, creaking and rolling on its springs, suddenly stopped. The step was let down with a clatter, and the door opened. On her left she caught sight of a sheet of water—the River Volga; on the right were some steps on which some servants were standing, with a young fresh-coloured girl, her head crowned with wide plaits of black hair, and an unpleasantly strained smile on her lips. This was Sonia.

The princess eagerly ran up the steps, while Sonia, exclaimed: "This way, this way!" Then she found herself face to face with a rather Eastern-looking woman, advanced in years, who hurried forward to meet her. Overcome by emotion, the countess threw her arms round her, and kissed her again and again.

"My child," she said, "I love you dearly—I have known you a long time. . . ."

Princess Maria knew who it must be, and that she must respond to this effusiveness; but not knowing what to say she murmured a few words in French, and then asked: "And he —how is he?"

"The doctor says he is out of danger," replied the countess, raising her eyes to heaven with a sigh that contradicted her words.

"Where is he? Can I see him?"

"Of course; in a few minutes, my dear. And is this his son?" added the countess, as Nicholas came in with his tutor. "What a sweet child! The house is a large one; there is room in it for everyone."

Still petting the little boy, the countess led them into the drawing-room where Sonia was talking to Mademoiselle

Bourrienne. The count came in to pay his respects to Princess Maria, who thought him greatly changed since she had last seen him; then he had been brisk, gay, and confident—now he was broken and bewildered: it was sad to see him. As he spoke to her he glanced stealthily round at the others as if to mark the effect of his words. Since the catastrophe at Moscow and his own ruin, uprooted from the surroundings and habits that made up his existence, he had, so to speak, lost his way and his place in life.

In spite of her eager desire to see her brother as soon as possible, and the annoyance she felt at all these formalities and compliments to herself and her nephew, she took note of what was going on around her. She saw that the least she could do was to conform for the moment to the order of things, and accept the consequences with resignation.

"This is my niece," said the count, introducing Sonia, "I do not think you know her."

She turned and embraced Sonia, trying to smother the impulse of instinctive hostility that she felt at seeing her. All these commonplace civilities, lasting so much too long for her impatience, made a most painful impression on her, which was enhanced by the want of harmony between her own feelings and those of all these people.

"Where is he?" she asked, once more addressing the circle generally.

"He is downstairs. Natacha is with him," said Sonia, colouring. "You are tired I daresay, princess?"

Tears of impatience filled Princess Maria's eyes; she turned away and was on the point of asking the countess in so many words to take her to her brother, when a light step was heard outside. It was Natacha—that Natacha to whom she had taken such a dislike on the occasion of their former meeting; but a glance was enough to assure her that here, at any rate, was one who could feel with her entirely, and who truly shared her sorrow. She hastened to meet her, threw her arms round her, and burst into sobs on her shoulder.

When Natacha, who was sitting with Prince Andrew, had been informed of the princess's arrival, she had quietly left the room to run to meet her. Her agitated face expressed only unbounded affection for her, for him, for all who were near and dear to the man she loved, great pity for everyone else, and an intense desire to sacrifice herself wholly for those who were suffering. The mere selfish hope of joining her life to that of

Prince Andrew had ceased to exist in her heart, and Princess Maria's subtle instinct detected this at the first glance: this discovery mitigated the bitterness of her tears.

"Come to him, Maria," said Natacha, leading her into another room. The princess raised her head and wiped her eyes, but she checked herself as she was about to ask a question. She felt that words were inadequate to formulate it or to reply to it, and that she could read in Natacha's face and eyes all she sought to know.

Natacha, on her part, was anxious and doubtful: ought she, or ought she not, to tell her what she knew? How could she hide the truth from those clear eyes which seemed to see to the very bottom of her soul—eyes which could not be deceived? Her lips quivered, and bursting into loud sobs, she hid her face in her hands. Maria understood. However, she could not resign all hope. She asked in what state the wound was, and how long his general condition had been so much worse.

"You—you will see," said Natacha, through her tears.

"When did this come on?" asked Princess Maria. And Natacha told her how, from the first, the fever and pain had made a fatal issue seem inevitable; how they had diminished, but the doctor had then feared gangrene; how that, too, had been averted; then, on their arrival at Yaroslaw, the wound had begun to suppurate, and the doctor had hoped that it was healing in the regular course, but presently there had been fever again, though not to an alarming degree.

"At last, these two days," said Natacha, swallowing her sobs. "It came on suddenly—a change—I do not know why—you will see for yourself."

"Is he very weak? Is he much thinner?"

"No, nothing of that kind, much worse. You will see. Maria, he is too good, much too good, for this world; he cannot live—and then . . ."

CHAPTER LXX

WHEN Natacha opened the door for Maria to go in first, the princess felt that, in spite of her utmost efforts, she would not have the strength to control herself and see her brother without shedding tears. She knew full well what "it" was that had come over him these two days. She understood that this sweetness of humility and tenderness could only be the precursor of death. In fancy she saw the face of her little Andrew as she had seen it in their childhood, with the gentle, loving look that touched her so deeply when she had seen it once more years after; she expected him to receive her with loving and agitated words, such as her father had spoken on his death-bed, and felt that she must melt into tears in spite of herself. However, it must come to that sooner or later, so she resolutely went forward.

Lying on a wide sofa, on a heap of pillows, wrapped in a dressing-gown trimmed with grey squirrel, very thin, very white, with a handkerchief in one transparent hand, while with the other he smoothed his long silky moustache, Prince Andrew looked at the two women as they came in. Princess Maria instinctively trod more slowly. As she saw the expression in her brother's face and eyes her sobs ceased, her tears did not flow—she felt frightened, like a culprit. "Am I guilty?" she asked herself. "Yes, for you have life and a future before you . . ." answered Prince Andrew's absent, severe eyes; and that deep gaze, sunk as it seemed in self-contemplation, had something hostile in it as he slowly turned it on them.

"Maria, how are you? How did you get here?" he asked, as he kissed her; and his voice, like his gaze, did not seem to belong to him. A scream of despair would have alarmed his sister less than that voice.

"Have you brought the child?" he asked gently, with a visible effort of memory.

"And how do you feel now?" asked Maria, wondering at finding she could say anything.

"You must ask the doctor, my dear;" then, trying to say something kind, he added, speaking in a mechanical way, "Thank you, dear, for having come."

His sister pressed his hand, but the pressure made him frown, though very slightly. He said no more, and she could find no words. In his speech, in his voice, above all in his eyes, she read all too plainly that detachment from life, which is so terrible to see in those who are dying, especially when we ourselves are in health and vigour. He cared no more for it, not because he did not understand it, but because his soul was sinking into the depths of an unknown world, out of the ken of the living, and which parted him from them.

"What a strange fate has brought us together again!" he said presently, breaking the silence and looking at Natacha. "She has nursed me, as you see."

Princess Maria listened in amazement. How could her brother, who was so fastidiously refined in matters of feeling, speak thus in the presence of the woman he loved, and who loved him? If he could have dreamed of coming back to life again he would never have spoken with this torturing calmness. The only possible explanation was that he was indifferent to every consideration, because something else—something supreme —was being borne in upon him. The conversation was strained and painful, and became fragmentary.

"Maria came through Riazan," said Natacha. Prince Andrew was not surprised to hear her speak of his sister by her Christian name alone; indeed Natacha herself perceived for the first time that she had done so.

"Yes?" he said.

"She was told that Moscow is burnt—burnt to the ground, and that . . ." But she stopped, seeing that he was making vain efforts to listen.

"Yes, so they say," he murmured, "it is very sad," and gazing into vacancy, he pulled his moustache.

"And you, Maria, met Count Nicholas?" he said suddenly. "He wrote home that he had been greatly charmed with you," he went on, quite lucidly, but hardly realising the force of the phrase to those who were living the life of every day. "If you like him, too, that would do very well—you might marry him!" he added somewhat quicker, as if glad of words for which he had vainly sought and found at last. And Maria, as she heard, understood how far away indeed he must be from this nether world.

"Why talk of me?" she said very composedly, and she looked at Natacha, who did not raise her eyes. Again there was silence.

"Andrew," said his sister, after a pause, "would you—will you see your boy? He has asked for you incessantly." The faintest smile parted Prince Andrew's lips; Maria, who knew so well every shade of expression on his face, saw with alarm that it was not a smile of gladness, or affection—that it was ironical at the idea of her trying this last means of reviving the emotions which were dying by degrees, as he was dying.

"Yes, I shall be very glad to see him. Is he quite well?"

The little boy was brought in. He was terrified at the sight of his father, who kissed him, and he did not know what to say; but he did not cry, because no one else in the room cried.

When he had left the room, Princess Maria bent over her brother, and unable to control herself any longer, melted into tears. Prince Andrew looked at her steadily:

"You are crying for him," he said. She nodded her head. "Maria, you know that the Gosp . . ." and suddenly became silent.

"What's that you say?"

"Nothing. But you must not cry here," he said, looking at her with the same cold severe look.

He understood that his sister would bewail the fate which would leave his child an orphan, and he even tried to see it in that light.

"Yes, it must seem very sad to her—and yet it is so simple," said he to himself. "The fowls of the air sow not, neither do they reap; yet your heavenly Father feedeth them." He thought he would quote the verse to his sister. "No, it is useless," he reflected, "she would take it differently. The living cannot understand that all these feelings that are so dear to them—all these thoughts which seem so important, really do not matter. No, we have ceased to meet on common ground." And he said no more.

Little Prince Nicholas was seven years old; he knew nothing yet, hardly his letters; but if he had been a man grown and in full possession of all his faculties, he could not have understood more clearly or felt more deeply the significance of the scene he had just witnessed between his father, his aunt, and Natacha. It was Natacha who led him away. He went with her without a word, and creeping up to her looked in her face with his large, shy, thoughtful eyes, and leaned his head on her breast; his short, rosy lips trembled and curled, and he cried noiselessly.

From that day he kept out of the way of Dessalles and of the countess, who loaded him with care and kindness; he preferred to be alone, or to stay with his aunt or Natacha, to whom he was devoted; and he would throw his arms round them and caress them in silence.

Princess Maria left her brother's room quite hopeless; she never again spoke to Natacha of his possible recovery. They took it in turns to sit with him; Princess Maria did not weep, but she prayed fervently to the Infinite and Inscrutable Being, whose presence is so near to the pillow of the dying.

CHAPTER LXXI

PRINCE ANDREW knew that this was death—that he was half-dead already—by his conscious detachment from all earthly interests, and by the strange and radiant beatitude that filled his soul. He lay waiting for the inevitable, without impatience or trepidation. That great, ominous and eternal fact, unknown and far away, which all his life long had dwelt in the background of his thoughts, was near now, close at hand; he could feel it—almost touch it.

Formerly he had dreaded death. Twice had he passed through the fearful gulf of death in agonies, once when his eyes, that had been gazing on the beauty of the woods, the meadows, the deep-blue sky, saw it rushing at him in the spinning, rushing shell. When he first came to himself in the hospital tent, that flower of heavenly love had blossomed in his soul, freed for a while from the burthen of living; and thus delivered from the cares of earth, all fear of death had vanished. The more he allowed himself to dwell on the mysterious future which opened before him, the more he unconsciously lost hold on all that lay near him, and the barrier between life and death, which has no terrors, but in the absence of love, gradually gave way. In what is the meaning of loving all mankind, and of self-devotion through love, unless it is loving no one in particular, and living a divine and spiritual life?

He looked forward to the end with real indifference: "So much the better!" thought he.

But after that night of delirious visions when the woman his heart craved for had come to him, when her lips and tears had touched his hand, the love of woman had revived in him and renewed the ties which bound him to life. Confused thoughts of gladness had crowded on him; he had remembered the moment when he had seen Kouraguine by his side and he felt that he could not again feel towards him as he had then felt. He was tormented by a delirious wish to know whether he still were alive, but could not make up his mind to inquire.

His case had followed the normal course, and the change that had come over him in the last two days, as Natacha had told Maria, was the closing struggle between life and death. Death was the stronger, and the renewal of his love for Natacha was more than an involuntary confession of how precious life was to him, a last revolt of the flesh against the horrors of the unknown.

One evening he had been dozing, and was slightly excited, as he usually was at nightfall, by an increase of fever which lent extreme acuteness to his senses. Sonia was sitting at the table. He dozed. Suddenly he became conscious of a glow of beatific gladness.

"Ah!" thought he, "she has come into the room!"

It was, in fact, Natacha who had stolen in to take Sonia's seat, and he was instinctively aware of her presence. She sat back in an arm-chair, and her head screened her candle from his eyes; she was diligently knitting a stocking, begun one day when Prince Andrew had said no one made such a good nurse as an old woman knitting. The monotonous movement produced, he said, a soothing effect on the patient's nerves. The young girl's nimble fingers worked fast with the long needles, and he studied the pensive profile of her bent head. Suddenly her ball of wool slipped and rolled away. Natacha started, stole a look at the invalid, and putting up her hand to keep the light out of his eyes, stooped, picked up the ball, and returned to her former position. He watched her, but did not stir; he saw her bosom rise and fall while she noiselessly tried to recover her breath. During the early days of their reunion he had owned to her that if he were restored to life he would everlastingly thank God for the wound that had brought them together again; but he had never spoken of that since.

"Can it possibly be so now?" thought he, as he listened to the slight noise of the needles. "Why should Heaven have allowed us to meet once more if only that I should die? Has the one truth of life been revealed to me only that I should be left in a lie? I love her more than the whole world, and can I help loving her?" And he groaned deeply, a habit he had fallen into during his long hours of suffering.

As she heard him Natacha laid her work on the table and leaned over to look at him. Seeing the glitter of his eyes she spoke: "You are not asleep then!"

"No, I have been watching you for a long time; I felt you come in. No one but you brings me that sweet calm—that radiance. I could almost cry for happiness!"

Natacha went nearer, and his face flushed with passion and gladness.

"Natacha, I love you too much; I love you more than all the world."

"And I——" she looked away an instant. "Why too much?" she asked.

"Why too much? Tell me, from the bottom of your heart, what you think: Shall I live?"

"I am sure of it—sure of it!" cried Natacha, seizing his hands with growing excitement. He did not reply.

"How good that would be!" he sighed, and he kissed her hand.

Natacha was happy; but she remembered that too much excitement might be fatal:

"You have not slept," said she, composing herself. "You must try to sleep; I entreat you."

He pressed her hand once more and she went back to her place. Twice she glanced round, and meeting his eye each time she concentrated her attention on her knitting so as not to look up again. Presently he fell asleep. Not for long, however. He woke in a cold sweat. His mind was beginning to hover between life and death.

"Love——" he thought again. "What is love? It is the negation of death, it is life itself. All that I understand at all I understand by love alone. It includes everything. Love is God, and death is the re-absorption of an atom of love—that is myself—by the universal and eternal source of love." And these dreams brought him comfort; but they were no more than dreams that strayed through his brain, without leaving even a shadow of reality; and he fell asleep again, still torn by a myriad of confused and exciting fancies.

He dreamed that he was in bed in the room where he now was, but in recovered health. A long line of unknown persons passed before him. He was talking with them, and discussing various subjects, and thinking of following them he knew not whither, saying to himself all the while that he was wasting time in trifles when he had far more serious matters to attend to; and still he lingered, talking and amazing them by his brilliant quotations, which nevertheless had no sense. By degrees these forms vanished, and his whole attention became concentrated on the closed door. Can he lock it quickly enough? All depends on that. He rises and goes towards it to shoot the bolt, but his legs give way under him: he feels that he must be too late. Gathering all his strength into a final effort he is about to rush forward when a fearful anguish freezes his soul—anguish that is the fear of Death! It is Death that is there waiting at the door, and just as he drags himself breathless to the threshold the hideous spectre pushes it open and looks in. That nameless creature is Death,—

Death is marching down upon him; he must fly, come what may, he must escape. He clutches at the door, he can no longer close it, but by putting forth all his remaining energy he may perhaps succeed in checking "Its" advance? Alas! his strength fails him, he is beating the air; again the door opens a little wider—again he tries to resist the fateful pressure from without. In vain! The spectre comes in, he is here. . . . ! And Prince Andrew died.

But at the same moment he became conscious that he was asleep, and with a great effort he woke. . . . "Yes, it was certainly Death! To die and wake! Is death then an awakening?"

The idea flashed on him like a lightning dream; a corner of the veil which still parted him from the unknown had been lifted from his soul. His body was being released from the bonds that held it to earth, and a mysterious beatitude came over him which from that moment did not desert him.

He woke bathed in chill sweat, and made a slight movement. Natacha came to him and asked him what he wanted. He did not understand her question, but looked at her with strange vacancy. That it was of which she had spoken to Princess Maria.

From that moment the fever took a malignant course, the doctor said, but Natacha was not interested in what the doctor said; she saw these terrible, for her, more indubitable, moral symptoms.

His last days and hours glided peacefully away without any further change in his general condition. Princess Maria and Natacha hardly left him for a moment, but they were fully aware that the sole aim of their care was the physical presence —the mortal hull, which would soon be no more than a dear and far-away memory; that his spirit was no longer of this world. Their feelings were so intense and deep that the terrible advent of death took no hold on their minds. It was useless to indulge their grief, so they did not weep, neither when sitting by him nor when out of the room, and as words were empty and inadequate to express it, they ceased even to speak about him. They saw him sinking slowly, calmly into the unseen; and both felt it was inevitable, and that it was well.

He confessed and received the Sacrament and bade them all farewell. When his little son was brought to him he kissed his cheek and turned away, not out of any regret at dying, but because he supposed that nothing more was expected of him. When they begged him to give his child his blessing he did so, and then looked round inquiringly as if to ask whether there was anything more for him to do; and he breathed his last supported by his sister and Natacha.

"It is over!" said Maria a few minutes later.

Natacha bent down, looked into the dead eyes and closed them.

"Where is he now?" she wondered to herself.

When he had been laid in his coffin all the household came in to see the last of him. The child was startled with painful surprise; everyone cried: the countess and Sonia for Natacha and for him who was gone; the old count for himself—foreseeing that he, too, ere long must cross the same bourne. Natacha and Princess Maria wept too; not for their own grief, but under an influence which made their hearts overflow—the sight of the solemn, simple mystery of Death!

BOOK FOURTEEN

CHAPTER LXXII

THE correlation of causes is a thing incomprehensible by the human mind, but the desire to comprehend them is born with it. Hence those who cannot discern the logic of events jump at the first coincidence that strikes them and exclaim: "This is the cause."

In historical events where the objects of observation are the actions of people, the first cause to which results are ascribed is the will of the gods; later it is the will of those individuals who are most in view, i.e. the heroes of history. But one has only to look deeper into the event (i.e. into the actions of all those taking part in an historical event) to see that not only does the will of the hero not direct it, but on the contrary, is itself directed. It would seem as if the understanding of an historical event this way or that was a matter of no moment. But between the man who says that the people of the west moved eastwards because Napoleon so willed it and him who says that it happened so because it had to, is the same difference as between those who declared the earth to be fixed and the planets moved round it, and those who claimed that, although not knowing what supported the earth they nevertheless knew that certain laws governed its movements as well as those of the planets. Though historical events have in fact no other cause than the primal cause, they are nevertheless governed by laws which are unknown to us, or which we can hardly detect, and which we can never discover until we give up all idea of finding behind them the will of any individual man. Thus a knowledge of the law by which the planets move only became possible when men had given up the notion of the fixity of the earth.

After the battle of Borodino and the evacuation and burning of Moscow, the most important episode of the war of 1812, in the opinion of historians, was the march of the Russian army

when it left the road to Riazan to proceed towards Kalouga
and establish itself in the camp at Taroutino. They attribute
this heroic feat to various individuals, and even the French,
when speaking of this flank movement, praise the genius displayed by the Russian chiefs at this juncture. We, however,
fail to discover, as these historians have done, any deep-laid
scheme, evolved by a single brain, to save Russia and ruin
Napoleon, or to see in it the faintest trace of military genius.
For no stupendous intelligence is needed to perceive that the
best position for an army which is not to fight is in a spot
where it can ensure supplies. The veriest child might have
guessed, in 1812, that the road to Kalouga offered the greatest
advantages after the retreat of the army. By what chain of
argument have these gentlemen discovered that this manœuvre
was such a brilliant scheme? Where do they find that its
direct outcome was the salvation of Russia and the destruction
of the enemy? In point of fact, to argue from the circumstances which preceded it, which were coincident with it, and
which followed it, this flank march might have been the ruin of
the Russians and the saving of the French; and it is by no
means clear that it had a favourable result on the situation of
the army.

But for the co-operation of other circumstances it could have
come to no good issue. What would have happened if Moscow
had not been burnt, if Murat had not lost sight of the Russian
troops, if Napoleon had not sat down in inaction, if the Russian
army had forced a battle on quitting Moscow—as Bennigsen
and Barclay advised, if Napoleon had marched on Taroutino
and attacked the Russians with one-tenth of the energy he
displayed at Smolensk, if the French had gone on to St. Petersburg? etc. etc. Under any of these conditions safety would
have turned to disaster. How is it that those who study
history have shut their eyes and ascribed this movement to the
decision of some one man? No one had prepared and schemed
for this manœuvre beforehand; and at the moment when it was
carried out it was simply the inevitable result of circumstances,
and its consequences could not be seen until it had gone into
the realm of the past.

At the council held at Fili the Russian commanders generally
were in favour of a retreat in a straight line along the road to
Nijni-Novgorod. Ample evidence of this fact exists in the
numerous votes given in favour of this course, and more
especially in the conversation which took place after the council

between the commander-in-chief and Lanskoï, the head of the commissariat. Lanskoï announced in his report that the victuals for the troops were, for the most part, collected along the line of the Oka, in the governments of Toula and Kazan; consequently, in case of a retreat on Nijni the transport of provisions would be intercepted by the river, over which they could not be carried when the winter had once begun. This was the first consideration which led to the abandonment of the original, and, on the whole, the more natural plan. Thus the army was kept within reach of supplies. Then, again, the inaction of the French—who had lost all track of the Russians, the need for protecting and defending the manufactories of arms, above all of keeping within reach of food, drove the army southwards.

After getting out on the Toula road by a desperate move, the generals intended to stop at Podolsk; but the sudden appearance of some French troops, with other circumstances—among them the abundance of victuals at Kalouga—led them to proceed still further to the south and to get off the Toula on to the Kalouga road, marching towards Taroutino. Just as it is impossible to specify the precise moment when the desertion of Moscow was decided on, so it is impossible to say exactly when the march on Taroutino was a settled thing; and yet everyone believed himself to have gone there in virtue of the decision of the generals in command.

CHAPTER LXXIII

THE route thus taken was so self-evidently that which the army must follow that even the pillagers straggled in this direction, and that Koutouzow incurred the czar's censure for having led the army in the first instance towards Riazan instead of setting out at once for Taroutino. Alexander himself had suggested this movement in a letter which the commander-in-chief did not receive till after his arrival there.

In fact, Koutouzow's skill at his juncture lay, not in a stroke of genius, but in a competent apprehension of the accomplished facts. He alone fully appreciated the inaction of the French; he alone understood and maintained that Borodino had been a victory for the Russians; he alone—though as commander-in-chief he seemed called upon to take the offensive—did all he could, on the contrary, to prevent an unnecessary waste of strength in futile struggles. The Wild Beast had in truth been mortally hurt at Borodino, and was still lying where the hunter had left it. Was it past fighting? Was it still alive even? The hunter knew not. But suddenly it gave a cry which betrayed its hopeless plight; this cry was the letter brought by Lauriston to Koutouzow in his camp. Napoleon, no less convinced than ever of his own incapacity of doing wrong, wrote as follows under a sudden impulse:

To Prince Koutouzow.

"I am sending one of my aides-de-camp general to discuss various points of interest with you. I beg your highness to believe all he will tell you; more particularly when he shall express to you all the sentiments of esteem and high respect which I have long felt for your highness. This note having no other object, I pray the Almighty to have your highness in his holy and gracious keeping."

(Signed) NAPOLEON.

Moscow, *October 30th.*

"I shall incur the curses of posterity if I am regarded as the first to take any steps towards a compromise in any form. That is the spirit which at this moment rules the nation," replied Koutouzow; and he continued to do all in his power to direct the retreat of the army.

After a month thus spent in pillage by the French troops, and in rest by the Russians, a great change had come over the temper of the two belligerent forces; entirely to the advantage of the Russians. Although the state of the French army and its number were unknown to the Russians, as soon as the relative strength of the two armies had undergone a change, the necessity of an offensive showed itself in a countless number of symptoms. Such symptoms were the arrival of Lauriston; the abundance of food at Taroutino; the information received from all sides of the inaction and disorder of the French; the filling up of our reserves; the fine weather etc. etc. This long inaction had awakened their impatience and curiosity to know what had become of the French, whom for so many weeks they had lost sight of. The audacious courage of the Russian outposts, who skirmished within reach of them day after day, the reports of small guerilla victories and peasant raids, revived the desire and hope of vengeance which had lurked in every soul during the stay of the foe at Moscow; every soldier felt instinctively that the balance of the opposing forces was no longer the same, and that the superiority was now on the Russian side. Just as the chimes of a clock start to play their tune when the hand has made a round of the dial, so the reflex effect of this general feeling was immediately perceptible in increased activity in the higher circles.   *

CHAPTER LXXIV

THE Russian army was commanded on the spot by Koutouzow and his staff, and directed from St. Petersburg by the czar himself.

Before the news of the evacuation of Moscow had reached his majesty a detailed scheme of the whole campaign had been sent to Koutouzow to make matters easy for him; and the staff accepted this plan in spite of the changed circumstances. Koutouzow himself would only say that plans laid down at a distance were always difficult to carry out. Messengers were continually coming to him with new instructions, to solve the difficulties as they arose, and to report subsequently on his acts and deeds.

Some important changes had taken place in the command of the divisions; substitutes had to be found for Bagration, who was killed, and for Barclay, who had withdrawn in dudgeon at being placed in a secondary position. It became a matter of anxious discussion whether it were better to put A. in D.'s place or D. in A.'s, and so on; as though, in a case of this kind, anything could be gained by it except the pleasure of A. or D.

In consequence of the existing hostility between Koutouzow and his chief of staff, Bennigsen, of the presence of the czar's various confidential envoys, and of the changes which had become inevitable, a far more complicated game was being played at the headquarters of the army. The leaders thought only of thwarting each other, and the object of all these intrigues was the conduct of the military situation which they all believed they were controlling, while, in fact, it was taking its course quite irrespective of their influence, and being the simple outcome of the mutual reaction of masses of men on each other. However, this tangle of combinations in high and powerful spheres was an index of what must inevitably ensue.

On the 2nd (14th) of October, the czar wrote a letter which

did not reach Koutouzow till after the battle of Taroutino, as follows:

"Prince Michael Ilarionovitch:

"Moscow has been in the hands of the enemy since the 2nd (14th) of September. Your latest report is dated the 20th (October 2nd), and since then you have not only taken no steps against the enemy to rescue our principal capital, but you have retreated still further. A detachment of French troops now holds Serpoukhow; and Toula, so important to the army as the headquarters of the manufacture of arms, is in danger. I see by Wintzingerode's despatches that the enemy is marching a body of 10,000 men towards the road to St. Petersburg; another of several thousand is advancing towards Dmitrow; a third occupies the road to Vladimir, and a fourth is concentrated between Rouza and Mojaïsk. Napoleon himself was still at Moscow with his regiments of Guards on the 25th (October 7th). Now that his troops are thus divided into detachments, is it conceivable that you have in front of you a sufficiently numerous body of the enemy to prevent your acting on the offensive? It is to be presumed, on the contrary, that you are being followed up by small parties, or, at any rate, by a smaller body than the army entrusted to your command. It would seem that you might have taken advantage of these arrangements to attack an enemy weaker than yourself and destroy him, or at any rate force him backwards so as to rescue the larger portion of the governments at present held by the foe, and thus protect the town of Toula and the other towns in the interior. If the enemy is strong enough to send forward a considerable mass of troops towards St. Petersburg, while it is to a certain extent weakly defended, the responsibility rests with you; for if you had acted with energy and decision, you ought to have been able, with the forces at your command, to preserve us from this new misfortune. Do not forget that you have yet to account to your indignant country for the loss of Moscow. You know by experience that I have always been ready to reward you, and I am so still; but I and Russia are entitled to expect entire devotion from you, unwavering firmness, and the success which we have a right to hope for from your acumen, your military talents, and the bravery of the troops you command."

By the time this note reached Koutouzow, the battle was

fought; he had found it impossible to withhold the army any longer from taking the offensive.

On the 2nd (14th) October, a Cossack named Schapovalow, beating about in the open country, killed a hare and wounded another; in following up the game he let himself be led on into the depths of a forest, and came unexpectedly on the left wing of Murat's division, who were off their guard. He told the story as a good joke to his comrades, and the ensign, hearing of it, reported it to his superiors. The Cossack was sent for, and questioned; the officers in command determined to take advantage of this lucky windfall to carry off the enemy's horses, and one of them, who was known to the higher authorities, mentioned the fact to a general on the staff. At that moment the tension of feeling happened to be at its height. Yermolow had arrived a few days previously, and had entreated Bennigsen to exert all his influence on the commander-in-chief to induce him to decide on an attack.

"If I did not know you well," replied Bennigsen, "I should have concluded that you wished the very reverse of what you say, for if I advise a step, that is quite enough to make his highness do just the contrary."

The Cossack's story was confirmed, however, by other scouts, and it was clear that everything was ready for a crisis. The springs unbent, the wheels creaked, and the chimes struck. Under the pressure arising from the report sent to the czar by Bennigsen, from the wish of all the other commanders which his majesty was said to share, and from the accounts given by the Cossacks, Koutouzow, in spite of his supposed influence, his wisdom and experience, found himself unable to control the movement. So he gave orders for what he believed to be useless, if not mischievous, and signed his assent to what was already *un fait accompli*.

CHAPTER LXXV

THE attack was to take place on the 5th (17th) October. On the day before, Koutouzow signed the order for moving the troops. Toll read the document to Yermolow, and proposed to him to settle the arrangements to be made.

"Yes, very good," said Yermolow, "but I have not time just now."

The plan of battle as concocted by Toll was a capital one.

As in the battle of Austerlitz it was explicitly stated, though not in German: "The first column will march this way, the second will march that way, etc. etc." These columns, as set forth on paper, were to combine at a given moment, to fall on the enemy, and crush him. Everything was foreseen and provided for, as it always is in a written plan of action; but, as also always happens, not one of the columns reached its position in time.

When several copies of this plan were ready, they were given to an orderly officer of Koutouzow's to carry to Yermolow. The young guardsman, extremely proud of so important an errand, went to Yermolow's lodgings. They were empty.

"The general is gone," said a servant. The envoy rode off to find a general, who was in constant communication with Yermolow: "No one at home," he was told.

To another: the same reply.

"I only hope I shall not be called to account for the delay," thought he. "What devilish bad luck!"

He rode all around the camp. Some told him that Yermolow had just gone on with a party of generals; others said he had just come back. The hapless youth sought him till six in the evening, not giving himself time even to eat. Yermolow was not to be found, and no one knew whither he had gone. The envoy, having taken some refreshment at a fellow-officer's rooms, went forward to Miloradovitch's quarters with the advanced guard. Here he was told, he was probably at a ball which General Kikine was giving, and Yermolow might also be there.

"Where on earth is this ball?"

"Over there, at Jechkine," said a Cossack officer, pointing to the roof of a large country-house in the distance.

"Out there? Why, that is beyond the line of the advanced posts!"

"Two of our regiments have been placed on the very line. They are making merry up there this evening. Two regimental bands and three of chorus-singers!"

The messenger crossed the line. As he went towards the house, he could hear the jovial songs of the soldiers' chorus, almost drowned in the eager voices of the company. The young officer could not help falling into the spirit of the thing, though he was afraid he should be held guilty of the delay in delivering the important message, of which he was the bearer. It was already nine o'clock; he dismounted and went up the steps of a handsome house, standing midway between the French and Russian lines, and which had remained unhurt. In the anteroom and offices he met servants carrying wine and dishes. The singers were placed outside, close to the windows.

As soon as he entered the drawing-room, he saw that all the principal generals of the Russian army were assembled there, and among them the tall and stately figure of Yermolow. They were standing in a semicircle, their uniforms unbuttoned, and their faces flushed, roaring with laughter, while in the centre of the room a remarkably handsome man of middle height was lightly dancing the "*trepak*."

"Ha ha! Bravo, Nicholas Ivanovitch! Bravo!"

The messenger felt himself more in the wrong than ever, for coming at such a moment with an important letter; he wished to wait, indeed, but he was at once observed. One of the bystanders pointed him out to Yermolow, and he, knitting his brows, advanced to meet him, listened to his story, and took the paper without saying a word.

"You fancy that he is here by chance," said a comrade on the staff to Koutouzow's messenger, speaking of Yermolow. "Not a bit of it, my dear boy; it is just a trick he wants to play on Konovnitzine, you will see to-morrow what a mess there will be!"

CHAPTER LXXVI

NEXT day old Koutouzow, having been called very early, said his prayers and dressed, and then got into his chariot with the disagreeable feeling that he had now to direct a battle to be fought against his will. He took the road to Létachevka, at about five versts behind Taroutino, the spot fixed upon for the rendezvous of all the corps. As he went he dozed, and then woke, listening to ascertain whether firing had yet begun. An autumn morning, damp and grey, was just beginning to dawn in the east. As he got near to Taroutino he met some cavalry-men leading their horses to water; he stopped the carriage and asked to what regiment they belonged: it was one that ought long since to have occupied a post in ambush. "Well, perhaps it is some mistake," thought he; but a little further on he saw some infantry, their muskets piled, calmly eating their broth. He called the officer, who told him that no orders of any kind had reached him.

"What!" Koutouzow began; but he checked himself, and sent for the colonel.

Meanwhile he got out of his carriage and walked up and down, his head drooping, and breathing hard. When General Eichen arrived, Koutouzow turned purple with anger, not that Eichen was the guilty man, but he at any rate was someone on whom he could vent his anger. Panting and trembling with rage, in a perfect paroxysm of fury, he rushed at Eichen, threatening him with his fists and loading him with the coarsest abuse. A captain named Brozine came in for a share of it, though he was there only by accident and was entirely innocent.

"And who is this scoundrel? let the wretch be shot!" cried Koutouzow in a hoarse voice, and gesticulating like a maniac. What, was he, the commander-in-chief, who was wont to be told that never before had anyone enjoyed such unlimited power, was he to be made the laughing-stock of his army? Was he to have prayed, to have thought, to have planned, through a sleepless night in vain?

"Why, when I was only a subaltern no one would have dared to mock me so," thought he, "and now . . ."

He felt an actual physical pain as if under corporal punishment, and he could only vent it in cries of rage and anguish. But presently his strength was spent: he grew calm, and understanding that he had been to blame in giving way to such violence, got into his carriage again and drove on in silence.

His fury was spent; he listened passively to the excuses and entreaties of Bennigsen, Konovnitzine, and Toll, who tried to persuade him of the necessity of carrying out on the morrow the manœuvre that had failed to-day. He was finally obliged to consent. As to Yermolow, he kept out of Koutouzow's way for two days.

CHAPTER LXXVII

NEXT day the troops were brought together by the evening and set in motion during the night. The darkness was intense; heavy purple black clouds covered the sky, but it did not rain. The ground was wet, the soldiers marched on in profound silence: only the artillery betrayed itself by the metallic rattle of the gun-carriages. Talking, smoking, striking a light even, were forbidden; the very horses seemed to restrain themselves from neighing. The mystery of the thing lent it a peculiar charm, and the men tramped on in excellent spirits. Some of the columns, when they believed that they had reached their destination, piled their arms and stretched themselves to rest on the cold earth; others—in fact, the majority—marched on all through the night, and naturally reached a point where they had no business to be.

Count Orlow-Denissow, with a small detachment of Cossacks, was the only man to reach the right place at the right time. He took up a position in a copse on the outskirts of a wood, and on one side of the path between the village of Dmitrovsk and Stromilow.

The count had fallen asleep a little before daybreak when he was called to examine a French deserter. He proved to be a Polish non-commissioned officer of Poniatowsky's corps; he said he had deserted because he had been passed over, that he ought long since to have received his commission, that he was the bravest man of them all, and meant to be revenged. He assured them that Murat had spent the night within a verst of the Russians, and that if they would give him a company of a hundred men he would pledge himself to take him prisoner.

Count Orlow held council with his fellow-officers. The proposal was too tempting to be refused, and they were disposed to make the venture. Finally, after much discussion and planning, Major-General Grékow decided on taking two regiments of Cossacks, and allowing the Pole to be their guide.

"But mark my words," said the count to the deserter, "If you have lied I will have you hanged like a dog. If you have told the truth, you shall have a hundred gold pieces."

The Pole did not reply; he sprang into his saddle and rode after General Grékow with a determined air; the party disappeared in the wood. The count, shivering with the chill of dawn and uneasy as to the responsibility he had incurred, went a little way into the open to reconnoitre the enemy's camp, which was just visible about a verst away in the doubtful light of morning and the dying camp-fires. The Russian party were to emerge from the wood on a slope to Count Orlow's right; but he looked in vain, nothing appeared. His aide-de-camp thought he saw signs of waking in the French camp.

"Ah! it is getting late," said he to himself. He was suddenly undeceived, as sometimes occurs, when the personal influence that has deluded us is removed—the Pole was evidently a traitor who had cheated them; the intended attack would come to nothing, in spite of the two regiments which Grékow had led God knows where!

"How can they possibly surprise the commander-in-chief when he is surrounded by such a considerable force? The villain has lied."

"We can recall Grékow," said an officer in his suite, who, like himself, was beginning to have his doubts.

"What do you really think? Must we leave things as they are? Yes or no."

"Send for him to come back."

"Very good; go, someone, and bid him return. But it will be late, it will soon be broad day."

An aide-de-camp disappeared in the forest in search of Grékow. When he had been brought back, Orlow, greatly excited by this change of plan and by vainly waiting for the infantry to come up with the enemy lying in front of him, made up his mind to an attack. "To horse," he said in a low voice.

Every man fell into his place and crossed himself, and they were off. A shout rang through the wood, and the companies [1] of Cossacks, scattering like corn shed out of a sack, rode boldly forward with lances poised, across the brook and down on the enemy's camp.

The warning shout of the French outpost who first caught sight of the Cossacks set the camp astir. All the men, still half asleep and only half dressed, flew to the guns, to the musket-piles, to the horses, rushing wildly in all directions and completely losing their heads. If the Cossacks had gone straight ahead, without heeding what was going on around them, they would infallibly have taken Murat prisoner, as the generals hoped and wished; but it was impossible to keep them from pillaging the camp and seizing the men. No one would listen to orders: 1500 prisoners, 38 cannon, with flags, horses, and accoutrements of every kind were taken and much precious time was wasted in securing the men and beasts and dividing the spoil, with the usual concomitants of quarrelling and shouting. The French, recovering from their panic and seeing that they were not pursued, re-formed, and in their turn attacked Orlow-Denissow; he, expecting reinforcements which did not come up, could make no adequate defence.

Meanwhile the infantry were behindhand. They had started

[1] *Sotnia*, a hundred men, under a Sotnik or centurion.

punctually under Bennigsen and Toll, but had reached a point far from that which they were intended to occupy. The men, who had set out in good spirits, soon lost many stragglers, and the feeling roused by the blunder of their chiefs gave rise to much murmuring which increased when they were led back again. The aides-de-camp sent forward to repair the mischief were sharply reprimanded by the generals, who disputed loudly among themselves, till, tired of quarrelling, they simply marched forward without any definite end in view. "We shall come out somewhere," said they—as in fact they did, but not at the place where they were wanted. Some, to be sure, reached their posts; but it was too late; they were of no use but to receive the enemy's fire.

Toll, who in this engagement played the part which Weirother had filled at Austerlitz, galloped to and fro along the line, and ascertained that everything had been done in exact contravention to orders. Thus, in the wood he met, soon after daybreak, Bagovouth's corps, which ought long since to have gone to the support of Orlow's Cossacks. Toll, desperate and furious at the failure of the movement, and ascribing it to him individually, addressed the commander in terms of insolent abuse, and even threatened to have him shot. Bagovouth, a placid old soldier, whose courage was above a shadow of suspicion, was exasperated by the contradictory orders he was receiving from all sides at once, by the unreasonable delays, and the confusion that prevailed; to the astonishment of all, in direct opposition to his usual demeanour, he gave way to a fit of rage and answered bluntly:

"I will not be lectured by anyone; and I am as ready to die with my men as any other man, be he who he may!"

Then, brave Bagovouth, blind with wrath, not giving himself time to think whether such a diversion were opportune, marched with his division, unsupported, straight into the line of fire. Danger—shell and ball, were in tune with the irritated mood: he was struck by one of the first shots, and a great number of his fine corps fell before those which followed. Thus his men remained for some time, exposed to the enemy's fire, without any useful result.

CHAPTER LXXVIII

ALL this while another column, near which Koutouzow was stationed, was supposed to be attacking the French. He, however, knew only too well that this action, fought against his judgment, must probably result in immense confusion; he therefore kept back his troops as much as possible, and would not allow them to quit their position. Mounted on a stout grey nag, he replied indolently to all the suggestions that were made to him to attack.

"You insist on talking of attacking, but you see we can't make complicated manœuvres," he said to Miloradovitch, who begged to be allowed to march forward. "Why, you could not manage to capture Murat this morning," he said to another. "Also, you were late, so there is an end of it."

When he was told that the French had just been reinforced by two battalions of Poles, he glanced out of the corner of his eye at Yermolow, to whom he had not spoken a word since the day before.

"That is the way," he muttered, "everyone wants to attack, all sorts of schemes are proposed; but when it comes to acting, nothing is ready, and the enemy, warned in time, takes due precautions!"

Yermolow smiled; he understood that the storm had passed over, and that the commander-in-chief would be satisfied with this innuendo.

"He is amusing himself at my expense!" said Yermolow, in a low tone, just touching Raïevsky's knee.

Shortly after he went up to Koutouzow, and addressed him respectfully:

"Nothing is lost, highness, the enemy is still in front of us. Will you not give the word to attack? Otherwise the men will not even smell powder all day."

Koutouzow would not answer. When he heard that Murat was retreating, he made up his mind to move forward, but he ordered a halt of three-quarters of an hour at every hundred yards. Thus the whole affair was reduced to Orlow-Denissow's charge, and the unavailing loss of some hundreds of men. The result to Koutouzow was an order in diamonds, and to Bennigsen a hundred thousand roubles, besides the diamonds, handsome rewards to the superior officers, and promotions and staff appointments without number.

"That is always the way—things are always managed hind part before," said the Russian military authorities, after the battle of Taroutino, just as they do to this day; and they hinted that, then and there, some idiot had intervened to do some particularly stupid thing, which they, severally, never would have thought of doing.

But men who talk like this, either have no clear idea of the engagement they are discussing, or else they consciously misapprehend it. No battle, whether Taroutino, Borodino, or Austerlitz, was ever fought in exact accordance with the calculations of those who direct the operations. That is an essential condition. Man is under no circumstances so nearly independent as he is when the next step is for life or death; and an infinite number of such independent forces influence the course of a battle; a course which can never be foreseen, and can never coincide with that which it would take under the impulsion of a single force. When historians, especially French historians, assert, that their wars and battles have been worked out on a preconceived plan, in which every movement was laid down beforehand, the only conclusion we can arrive at is that their accounts are inaccurate.

It is evident that the battle of Taroutino did not end as Count Toll had intended; that is to say, in the advance of the Russian troops under fire in regular order; nor as Count Orlow had proposed, in the capture of Murat; nor as Bennigsen desired, since he meant to destroy the enemy; nor as the officer hoped, who dreamed of distinguishing himself; or the Cossack, greedy of yet more booty. But if the object aimed at was the accomplishment of the universal desire of the country, to drive out the French, and strike a mortal blow at their strength, the battle of Taroutino was certainly and evidently most needful and opportune at this stage of the campaign, since it achieved that end.

It is difficult—nay impossible—to imagine a more favourable turn of affairs than that which resulted from this action. Notwithstanding the almost unexampled muddle, very great advantages were gained, at the cost of small effort and insignificant losses. The weakness of the French was clearly proveb, and the enemy received a shock which, under existing conditons, compelled them to begin a retreat.

CHAPTER LXXIX

NAPOLEON marches into Moscow after the splendid victory of Borodino (or the Moskova, as it is sometimes called)—it must certainly have been a victory, since his troops remained in possession of the field. The Russians retire and abandon Moscow full of stores, arms, ammunition, and incalculable riches. A month elapses before they resume the offensive. Napoleon's position is obviously brilliant and glorious in the highest degree. No exceptional genius is needed, it would seem, to enable him to throw his superior forces on the wreck of the enemy's army and crush it, to extort an advantageous peace, to march on St. Petersburg, if the Russians prove recalcitrant, to return to Smolensk in the event of failure, or at least to remain at Moscow, and to keep the advantage already won. Nothing can be more simple and easy than to take measures to secure that. Pillage must be prohibited, the army must be provided with warm clothing—easily procurable at Moscow, the distribution of food must be strictly regulated—the French historians themselves admit that there were provisions for six months. And yet Napoleon, the greatest genius ever known, who could—as these same historians assert—bend the army as he would, takes none of these precautions, but, on the contrary, selects the most absurd and fatal course.

Nothing, in fact, could more surely lead to disaster than a stay in Moscow so late as October, allowing the army to pillage at will; then, to leave Moscow without any well-defined plan, to go within reach of Koutouzow without giving battle, to get as far as Malo-Yaroslavetz, leaving it on the right, and making for Mojaïsk without trying the fortune of war once more; finally, to return to Smolensk, blindly wandering across a devastated country. Any able strategist studying this series of facts, would unhesitatingly pronounce that it could entail no other result than the destruction—intentional or fated—of the army thus governed. Still, to say that Napoleon sacrificed it voluntarily or by sheer incapacity is just as false as it is to say that he led his troops to Moscow by the vigour of his will, or the brilliancy of his genius. In either case his personal action had no more influence than that of the meanest private; it had to bow to certain laws, of which the outcome was the resultant fact.

It is a mistake on the part of historians to suppose that

Napoleon's intellect must have failed at Moscow, as the only way of accounting for his disaster. His energy at this time was not a whit less wonderful than it had been in Egypt, in Italy, in Austria, and in Prussia. We Russians cannot form a just opinion of what Napoleon's genius may have been in Egypt —where "forty centuries looked down upon his glory"—or in Austria or Prussia, for we must depend on French and German versions of the facts; and the Germans have always cried up his genius, finding no other way for accounting for his triumphs over army-corps that surrendered without striking a blow, and whole regiments that were taken prisoners without attempting to fight.

We Russians, thank God! need not bow down before his genius to screen ourselves from disgrace. We paid dearly for the right to judge him honestly and without subterfuge, and we are, therefore, not bound to any servile concessions. His vigour while at Moscow was no less than it had always been; plans and orders followed each other without interruption all the time he was there; the absence of the inhabitants, the lack of deputations, the conflagration even, never checked him for an instant. He never lost sight of the enemy's movements, of the well-being of his troops, and of the Russian population close at hand, of the management of his empire, of diplomatic complications, or of the conditions to be discussed, with a view to concluding a peace at an early date.

CHAPTER LXXX

As soon as he arrived at Moscow, Napoleon's first care was to order General Sébastiani to watch the movements of the Russian troops, and to enjoin Murat to discover Koutouzow's position. Then he carefully fortified the Kremlin, and elaborated a capital scheme for a campaign in Russia. Passing from military matters to diplomacy, he sent for Captain Iakovlew, who made his appearance ruined and in rags, explained to him at full length his policy and his magnanimous conduct, and wrote a letter to the Czar Alexander, in which he expatiated to his "friend and brother" on his dissatisfaction at Rostopchine's conduct, and sent off Iakovlew to St. Petersburg. After having in the same way unfolded his scheme, and paraded his high-mindedness to Toutolmine, he sent him off to St. Petersburg to start negotiations. In judicial matters he sought out the incendiaries, punished them, and revenged himself on Rostopchine by having his houses burnt; in affairs of administration, he drew up a constitution which he presented to Moscow, established a municipality, and had the following proclamation posted about the town:

"Inhabitants of Moscow!

"Your sufferings are terrible, but his majesty the emperor and king will put an end to them. He has taught you by some terrible examples that he can punish rebellion and crime. Very severe measures have been taken to check disorder, and re-establish public safety. A municipality will be formed for the paternal administration of the town; the members will be elected from among yourselves, and it will be their duty to watch over you, and take care of your needs and your interests. These members will be distinguished by wearing a red ribbon across the shoulder, and the mayor will, besides, wear a white scarf. During the hours when he is not occupied in the duties of his office, he will only wear a red ribbon round his left arm. The police of the city is re-formed on its old footing, and thanks to its exertions, order is being restored. The government has appointed two high commissioners or heads of police, and twenty commissioners for the various districts of the town; they are recognisable by the white ribbon tied round the left arm. Several churches of various sects are left open, and service in them will not be interfered with. Your fellow-citizens are returning to their dwellings, and orders have been given that they are to find such help and protection as are due to misfortune. These are the steps taken by the government up till the present moment with a view to restoring order and alleviating your situation, but for their ultimate success, it is indispensable that you should second these efforts by your own, that you should forget as far as possible your past sufferings, that you should cherish a hope of a happier future, that you should understand that a shameful death will be the fate of all who attack your persons or your property, and that your property will certainly be secured to you, since such is the will of the greatest and justest of monarchs.

"Soldiers and citizens, of whatever race or nation, aid in restoring that public confidence which is the source of national happiness; live as brethren, help and protect each other; combine to frustrate the designs of the evil-minded, obey authority, whether civil or military, and soon your tears will cease to flow."

With regard to provision, Napoleon issued an order that the troops should come in regular turns to Moscow, and by freebooty, acquire supplies which would suffice to victual each regiment for a certain time. In the matter of religion he decreed that the popes should return and reorganise all the ceremonial worship in the churches. The following manifesto, relating to trade, and the importation of victuals, was also placarded on all the walls:

"Peaceable citizens of Moscow, artisans and factory hands, who have been driven out of town by the recent catastrophes, and you also, peasants and farmers, who are kept from coming in from the country by groundless fears, attend. The capital is restored to order, and peace reigns there; your fellow-countrymen are by degrees coming out of their hiding-places, being assured of protection. Every act of violence to them of their property is immediately punished. His majesty the emperor and king is your protector, and regards none as his enemies but those who rebel against his decrees; he only wishes to put an end to your misfortunes, and restore you to your hearths and families. Respond to his beneficent measures, by returning without fear of danger. Citizens, return to your dwellings in perfect confidence; you will soon find the means of obtaining all you need. Artisans and labourers, take up your trades again; your houses and shops are waiting for you, protected by a patrol, and your toil will receive its reward. You, peasants, come out from the woods where you are lurking in terror, return to your huts, and be assured that you will be protected in them. There are storehouses in the town, where the tillers of the soil may deposit their produce, and the fruits of the earth.

"The Government has adopted the following measures for the regulation of sales: First, from to-day the peasants and farmers of the neighbourhood of Moscow may with perfect security place provisions of every description in the two store-houses in the Mokhovaïa and the Okhotny-riad. Second, These articles of consumption shall be bought and sold at prices to be agreed upon between the seller and the buyer; but if the seller does not receive the price agreed upon, he has a right to carry back his merchandise to his own village, without let or hindrance. Third, Sunday and Wednesday in every week are appointed as market-days, and a sufficient number of troops will be stationed on Saturdays and Tuesdays along the various high roads to a certain distance from the town, to protect the carts and waggons. Fourth, similar means will be taken to protect the peasants and their vehicles on their return. Fifth, the ordinary fairs and markets will be reopened as soon as practicable.

"Inhabitants of town and country, workmen and artisans, whatever your race or nation, you are hereby invited to carry into effect the paternal regulations of his majesty the emperor and king, and so to contribute to the common good. Come to his feet with respect and confidence, and hasten to join us."

To raise the tone and spirits of the army and the people, he held reviews and distributed rewards, showed himself in the streets, spoke comfort to the citizens, and, notwithstanding the cares of State, went to the theatres, which were reopened by his desire. In the matter of beneficent institutions, the fairest gem in a monarch's crown, Napoleon did all that it was possible for a mere human being to accomplish. He had the façades of public asylums inscribed as *"maison de ma mère"* (my mother's home), thus suggesting a happy union of filial piety with beneficent majesty; he inspected the Foundling Hospital, held out his white hand to be kissed by the children he had saved, and expressed himself most graciously to Toutolmine. Then, according to M. Thiers' eloquent narrative, he paid his troops with forged Russian notes. "As a set-off to the adoption of such a course, and as an action worthy of himself and the French army, he ordered that help should be distributed to those who had been burnt out of house and home. But as provisions were too precious to be given away to strangers, most of them hostile to him, he preferred to bestow money, and this too was paid in paper roubles." Finally, with a view to preserving discipline, he continued to give constant orders about severe punishments for infringement of duty, and against all found in the act of plunder.

CHAPTER LXXXI

STILL, strange to say, all these measures, which were in no respect inferior to those he had taken elsewhere under similar circumstances, only affected the surface, as the hands of a clock when detached from the mechanism may be turned round and round without making the wheels act.

M. Thiers, in speaking of Napoleon's remarkable military scheme, observes that "his genius had never devised anything more comprehensive, skilful, and admirable;" and in his dispute with M. Fain he shows that the promulgation of it must be dated not the 4th, but the 15th of October. But this "remarkable scheme" never was, and never could have been carried out, because it was inapplicable to the immediate circumstances. The fortifications of the Kremlin—for which "the Mosque," as Napoleon chose to call the cathedral of Saint Basil, had to be destroyed—came to nothing, the undermining of the Kremlin never served any purpose than that of gratifying the invader's wish to blow up this church on leaving Moscow —like a child who, to comfort himself for a fall, beats the floor against which he has bruised himself. The pursuit of the Russian army which caused Napoleon so much anxiety, ended in an extraordinary result: the French generals entirely lost track of these 60,000 men! And according to M. Thiers, it was only the talent—or perhaps genius—of Murat which was equal to the task of rediscovering this speck, this handful of men.

In his diplomatic efforts Napoleon's arguments to prove to Toutolmine and Iakovlew his generosity and justice were equally thrown away: the czar would not receive his ambassadors, and returned no answer to his messages. As to his judicial administration: after the execution of the supposed incendiaries, the other half of Moscow was burnt to the ground. Nor were his other measures more successful: the establishment of the municipal authority did not check rapine, and benefited no one but the officials appointed; they, indeed, under pretext of re-establishing order, plundered on their own account, or devoted their energies to the preservation of their own property.

In matters of religion, though the imperial visit to a mosque had been a great success in Egypt, such a step had no effect in Moscow. Two or three priests did indeed attempt to obey the imperial mandate, but one had his face slapped by a French soldier while in the act of performing the service; and of another an official wrote as follows: "A priest, whom I found out and requested to resume his duties, cleaned and closed the church. In the course of the night the doors were forced open, the padlocks broken, the books torn, and other mischief done." With regard to trade, the proclamation addressed to the "peaceable artisans and peasants" elicited no response, for the simple reason that there were no peaceable artisans, and that the peasants turned on the messengers who wandered so far as to find them and killed them without mercy.

The plays got up for the amusement of the populace were no less a failure; the theatres, opened in the Kremlin and the Pozniakow-house, were closed again immediately, for the performers were despoiled of all they possessed. His benevolence, again, bore no fruit; the paper money, false and real, so liberally distributed to the sufferers, was a drug in Moscow, and absolutely worthless; indeed, even silver was depreciated to about half its value, for the French would take nothing but gold.

The most signal proof of the absence of vitality in all these arrangements lies in the unavailing efforts made by Napoleon to put a stop to plundering and restore discipline. The proclamations of the military authorities in fact said as much.

"Pillage continues in the city, in spite of repeated prohibitions; order is not re-established; not a tradesman carries on his regular business; only the camp-followers have articles for sale, and those are stolen goods."

"My district continues to be pillaged by the men of the 3rd Corps, who are not content with stripping the poor creatures who have taken refuge in underground cellars, of what little they have saved, but are so brutal as to wound them with sword-cuts; several instances of this have come to my knowledge."

"Nothing new has occurred; the soldiers still venture to rob and pillage the people. (October 9th.)"

"Plunder and pillage continue. In our district there is a band of robbers who must be arrested by an armed force. (October 11th.)"

"The emperor is highly displeased to find that notwithstanding the stringency of his orders, the soldiers who come into the Kremlin are all marauders, though in the Guards; and it grieves him to perceive that picked men, specially chosen to guard his person, and whose duty it is to set an example of obedience, go so far in rebellion as to force open the doors of the cellars made into magazines of stores for the army. Others have fallen so low as to defy the sentinels and officers on guard, to insult them, and even to fight them."

"The high steward of the palace complains bitterly that, in spite of repeated prohibitions, the soldiers commit every kind of nuisance in the courtyards, even within sight of his majesty's windows."

This great army was melting and wasting away under the influence of the place and circumstances, like a herd of cattle run wild and trampling down the fodder that might save them from starvation. It did not recover from its torpor till it was roused by a sudden panic on hearing that some convoys had been seized on the Smolensk road, followed by the news of the fight at Taroutino. This reached Napoleon at the moment he was holding a review. As M. Thiers tells us, it fired him with a desire to punish the Russians. He at once gave orders for the departure which the whole army was longing for.

They fled from Moscow, taking with them all they could carry; Napoleon himself clung to his own private treasure. The enormous baggage-trains that hampered his movements alarmed him, it is true; still, with all his experience, he did not give the order to burn the wagons, as he insisted on one of his marshals doing on the march to Moscow. These chariots and carts full of men and booty found grace in his eyes, because —as he said—they might afterwards be found useful for carrying provisions or the sick and wounded.

Is not the position in which the French found themselves like that of a wounded animal, aware that death is at hand and driven mad by terror? Are not Napoleon's crafty manœuvring and magnificent schemes, from the hour when he entered Moscow till the final catastrophe, strangely like the leaping and convulsions which precede the death of the wounded beast?

Frightened by some noise he rushes forward, on to the huntsman's knife; then, mortally stricken, he flies again, and so hastens his end. Napoleon, under the pressure of his army, did just the same. The rumour of the battle of Taroutino scared him, and he hurried forward; he felt the knife and returned as he had come, only to set out again on the worst chosen and most perilous road, the road he had already traversed and known.

Napoleon, who stands forth as the leader of the movement —just as to savages the figure-head of a vessel represents its guiding mind—was, at this crisis, just like a child who pulls at the straps inside a coach and fancies he helps it forward.

CHAPTER LXXXII

On the 6th (18th) October, Peter stepped out of the prison-shed and stood in the doorway, playing with the little bandy-legged dog that commonly slept at Karataïew's feet; the dog frequently made excursions into the town, but returned faithfully every evening. The Frenchmen named him "Azor"; Plato called him "the grey one" or "Grey." No one had claimed him, and there was no name on the collar. The poor brute did not seem at all distressed at having no master, and being of no particular breed; he carried his feathery tail boldly, and his crooked legs did him such good service that he often scorned to use all four at once, and would trot along on three with one hind paw gracefully picked up. Every incident was a pleasure to him; he would roll on his back, or bask in the sun with a look of pensive importance, or play with a chip of wood or a straw.

Peter's wardrobe now consisted of a dirty, ragged shirt—the last relic of his original garments, a pair of soldier's trousers tied round above the ankles, by Plato's advice, to keep his legs warmer, and a caftan. His appearance was greatly altered; his corpulence had diminished, but his large frame was still the ideal of physical strength; a thick beard and moustache hid the lower part of his face; his long, matted and dirty hair fell from under his round cap; the expression in his eyes was calmer and steadier than of yore, and his easy-going indolence had given place to a look of ready energy. His feet were bare. He stood gazing alternately at the plain, where wagons and men on horseback could be seen moving, at the river sparkling below, at the dog pretending to bite him in play, and at his own bare and dirty feet, and putting them into attitudes—smiling all the while with beatific satisfaction as he thought over all he had endured and learnt during these last days.

The weather was mild and bright. It was St. Martin's Summer,[1] with the light hoar-frosts which give a tonic sharpness to the morning sunshine, and revive and stimulate the frame. That magical crystalline brilliancy which is never seen excepting in the clearest autumn day, shone over all the landscape. Far away rose the Sparrow hills, with the village and the green belfry of the church; the roofs, the sandy roads, the

[1] Equivalent to the Indian summer. The gleam of fine weather which often comes between St. Luke's day, October 18th, and St. Martin's, November 11th. In French *l'Eté de St. Martin*, and in England called St. Luke's Summer.

rocks, the leafless trees stood in sharp outline against the transparent sky. A few yards away from the hovel were the ruins of a half-burnt house, occupied by the French; it stood in a garden of stunted lilac-bushes, and this house, which under a gloomy sky would have been the picture of desolation, under this flood of light looked, on the contrary, peaceful and happy. A French corporal, with his coat unbuttoned, a foraging-cap on his head, and a broken pipe between his teeth, came up to Peter with a friendly wink: "What splendid sunshine! eh, Monsieur Kiril?" (the name by which Peter was called by the French). "It might be spring-time," and leaning against the door-post he asked him—as he did every day, always to be refused—to smoke a pipe with him. "If only we have weather like this for our march!"

Peter anxiously asked him if he had any news. The old soldier told him that the troops were being moved out of the town, and that the order of the day was expected to contain some instructions as to the prisoners. Peter reminded him that one of them, named Sokolow, was dangerously ill, and that some steps must be taken for his comfort.

"Be quite easy, Monsieur Kiril; we have capital ambulance waggons, and the authorities make it their business to provide for all emergencies. Besides, you know, Monsieur Kiril, you have only to say a word to the captain. Oh, he is one of those who never forget. You just speak to the captain when you see him; he will do anything for you."

The captain in question often talked with Peter, and expressed a great liking for him.

"I tell you what, says he to me one day—'Kiril is a well-educated man, and can speak French; he is a Russian nobleman who has got into trouble, but he is a man.' And he knows what he is talking about, he does. 'If he asks for anything,' says he, 'see that he has it.' You see, when a man is a scholar himself he likes to meet with other scholars and men who know what's what. It is for your sake I say it, Monsieur Kiril. In that job the other day, you know—it would have been a worse job if it had not been for you." And having gossiped for some time, away he went.

The "job" he had alluded to was a squabble between the prisoners and the French. Peter had been lucky enough to succeed in pacifying his companions.

Some of them, having seen him talking to the corporal, came up to ask for news; just as he was telling them what he had heard, a French soldier, with a pinched, yellow face, and dressed in rags, joined them. He raised his hand to his cap in salute, and asked Peter whether Platoche, the man to whom he had given a shirt to make, was in this hut. Leather and shirting had been given out to the French army the week before, and they had given them to the Russian prisoners to be made into boots and shirts.

"Here you are, it is quite ready!" said Plato, bringing out the article in question neatly folded up. In honour of the fine weather, or perhaps to work more at his ease, Plato had nothing on but a pair of drawers and a torn shirt as black as soot. His hair was tied up with a strip of bast, as workmen do, and it seemed to give an added charm to his broad good-humoured face.

"Make a bargain and stick to it!" said he,[1] "I promised it on Friday, and here it is."

The Frenchman glanced uneasily round; then, conquering his bashfulness, he took off his uniform and put on the shirt, for he had nothing under his coat but a long and filthy embroidered silk waistcoat, which scantily covered his half-starved body. He evidently was afraid of being laughed at; but no one took the slightest notice of him.

"Just fits you," observed Plato, pulling down the shirt, while the Frenchman put his arms through the sleeves and carefully examined the sewing. "You see, my good friend, this is not exactly a tailor's shop; we have nothing fit to sew with, and you know you must have a weapon even to kill vermin."

"All right—quite right, thank you," said the Frenchman, "but there must be some pieces left."

"It will fit you better when you have worn it a little while," Plato went on, admiring his own work.

"Thank you, old chap—but the pieces?"

Peter, perceiving that Plato was making a point of not understanding French, would not say a word. Plato thanked the Frenchman for his pay, and the Frenchman persisted in asking for what was left of the linen; at last Peter thought he had better explain to Plato what his customer wanted.

"What can he want with the pieces? I might have found them useful; however, if he will have them . . ." And Karataïew, much against his will, pulled out of his shirt front a little packet of scraps neatly tied up, gave it to the French-

---

[1] "Agreement is first cousin to good business."—*Russian proverb.*

man without a word, and then turned on his heel. The man looked at the pieces as if he were debating the matter in his mind; and then he looked inquiringly at Peter, and suddenly colouring up, he said:

"Platoche, I say, Platoche, you can keep this. . . ." And, stuffing it into his hand, hurried away.

"And they say they are not Christian souls—but there goes a kind heart! It is a true saying that a moist hand shows a giver, and a dry hand a niggard—he has hardly a rag to wear, and yet he made me a present. All right, my friend, I shall find a use for it. . . ." And he went into the hut with a smile of content.

CHAPTER LXXXIII

PETER had now been a prisoner for four weeks, and though the French had offered to remove him from the hut where the privates were housed to that given up to the officers, he would not accept. He had to endure the greatest privations; but his strong constitution and robust health were impervious to them, especially as they only came on him by degrees; he even felt a certain pleasure in defying them. At last he found himself possessed of that peace of mind and satisfaction with himself that he had hitherto so vainly longed for. This it was that had struck him in the soldiers at Borodino, and that he had vainly sought in philanthropic efforts, in freemasonry, in the amusements of a wordly life, in drink, in the heroism of self-sacrifice, in his romantic passion for Natacha—and suddenly the horrors of death and Plato's philosophical resignation had given birth in his soul to that soothing moral contentment, of which he had always felt the lack. The intolerable anguish of mind he had gone through while his miserable companions were shot had cleared his brain for ever of the restless thoughts and aspirations which he had formerly believed to be of such supreme importance.

He thought no more about Russia, or the war, or politics, or Napoleon. He understood that nothing of all this concerned him, that he was not required to judge events as they happened; and his purpose of killing Napoleon struck him not merely as preposterous, but as ridiculous, not less so than his cabbalistic calculations of the number of the Beast in the Apocalypse

His wrath against his wife, and his horror of seeing his name dishonoured, appeared futile and absurd. After all, what did it matter to him that the woman should lead the life she liked best, or that it should become known that one of the prisoners was named Count Bésoukhow?

His thoughts often turned to Prince Andrew, who was wont to declare, with a shade of bitterness and irony, that happiness was purely negative, and that all our cravings for real happiness were given us for our torment, since they could never be fulfilled. But at this very time Peter was ready to accept the mere absence of pain, the satisfaction of the elementary needs of life, and consequently a free choice of occupation and mode of life, as the ideal of earthly happiness. Here, for the first time—because he was bereft of them—did he appreciate the joys of eating when he was hungry, of drinking when he was thirsty, of resting when he was sleepy, of warming himself when he was cold, and talking when he longed for human intercourse. He forgot one thing, however: namely, that abundance of wordly goods diminishes our pleasure in using them, and that too much liberty in choosing our occupations, since it arises from education, wealth and social position, renders the choice complicated, difficult, and often useless. All Peter's thoughts centred on the hour when he should again be free; and yet, afterwards, he often looked back on that month of captivity, and would speak with enthusiasm of the vivid and impressive sensation, and even more of the moral peace that had been borne in upon him at that period of his life.

On the first morning of his imprisonment, when he woke at daybreak and stole to the door of the hut to look out at the still dark forms of the cupolas and crosses of Novo-Diévitchi, the white frost glistening on the dusty grass, and the wooded slopes of the Sparrow hills, vanishing in grey mist—as the fresh breeze fanned his cheek, as he heard the flapping of the crows' wings across the fields, as he watched the daylight chasing the night-fogs, the sun rising in glory behind the clouds and the domes of the city, while the crosses, the dew, the distance and the river sparkled joyously in the splendour of his rays—his heart overflowed with emotion. This emotion stayed with him and increased his strength a hundredfold in proportion as the perils of his position increased.

This frame of mind also raised him in the estimation of his companions in captivity. His knowledge of languages, the respect paid to him even by the French, his simplicity, kindli-

ness, steadfastness and humilty in his intercourse with his
fellow-men, even his faculty of becoming utterly lost in deep
meditation, all combined to make him appear a mysterious and
superior being. The very qualities which, in his own rank of
life, were a disadvantage and a hindrance, here made almost a
hero of him, and he felt that the estimation in which he was
held brought with it special duties.

CHAPTER LXXXIV

THE French retreat began on the night of the 6th (18th) of
October; they dismantled their huts and kitchens, wagons
were loaded, troops and baggage-trains were on the move in
every quarter. By seven o'clock on the morning of the 19th,
an escort of French soldiers in marching order—shakos, muskets
shouldered, and knapsacks packed and strapped—were drawn
up in front of the guard-house, exchanging a cross-fire of
questions interlarded with oaths all along the line. Inside
the hut the prisoners were all dressed and shod ready to start
and waiting for the word of command. Only poor Sokolow,
pale and exhausted, was neither clothed nor shod, but lay
groaning miserably. His eyes seemed starting out of the dark
circles that surrounded them, and gazed inquiringly at his
companions, who were not troubling themselves about him.
It was not so much the pain he was suffering—his complaint
was dysentery—as the dread of being left to his fate that was
racking him. Peter—who had got a pair of boots that Plato
had made for him, and had knotted a rope round his waist for
a belt—squatted down on his heels by the bedside.

"Listen to me, Sokolow, they are not going away altogether.
They are leaving a hospital here, and you will very likely be
better off than we shall be in the end."

"Oh, Lord! It will be the death of me—oh, Lord! have
pity!" groaned the soldier piteously. "I will go and speak to
them—shall I?" said Peter, and he rose and went to the door.

Just then a corporal came in with a file of soldiers in marching
order. The corporal—the same who had offered Peter a pipe
the day before—came to call over the roll of prisoners.

"Corporal, what is to become of the sick man?" asked
Peter, who hardly recognised his friend, so different did he look
in his shako and tightly-buttoned collar from the man he had

been accustomed to see. He frowned and muttered some brutal but unintelligible remark; then he slammed the door violently and the hut was almost dark; the drums were beating to arms on both sides, and drowned the sick man's complaining. "Yes, there it is again—I know it well!" thought Peter, with an involuntary shudder. In the corporal's altered mien, in the ring of his voice, in the deafening rattle of the drums, he had recognised the presence of that stolid and mysterious brute force which drives men to kill each other—the force he had been so conscious of during the execution of his companions. To dream of escaping from it, to entreat those who had become its instruments, was, he knew, vain; there was nothing for it but to wait in patience. So he stood at the door and said no more.

When it was next opened, for the prisoners to pass out like a flock of sheep, he got in front and went towards the captain, who, as the corporal had told him, was so well disposed to serve him. The captain too was in marching order, and his face wore the same hard, set look.

"Get on, get on!" he said to the prisoners, as they went past him. Though Peter felt that it was useless he went up to him.

"Well, what now?" said the captain roughly, as though he did not recognise Peter. "He can walk, I suppose, devil take it!" he answered to Peter's inquiry.

"He is dying," said Peter.

"Will you mind . . ." cried the captain, in a rage.

And the drums rattled on, and Peter felt that words would be wasted. These men had sold their souls; they were the slaves of that force.

The prisoners who were officers were separated from the privates, and ordered to lead the way. There were thirty officers, including Peter, and three hundred privates. The officers, who came out of neighbouring huts, were all strangers to Peter and much better dressed, and they cast a doubtful eye on him. In front of him walked a burly major in a plaid dressing-gown, a towel round his waist for a scarf; his face was bloated, yellow, and sour; in one hand he held his tobacco pouch and in the other a long pipe. He was quite out of breath, and kept up an incessant growl: "He was being pushed, they were crowding without reason and astonished without cause."

Another officer, a small, slim man, turned first to one and then to another, asking where they were being taken and how many versts made the first stage. A functionary in felt boots and commissariat uniform turned from right to left as he went, seeing what he could see of the burnt town and making loud comments on what he had seen, telling everybody what part of Moscow was burnt and what was still standing, communicating to all within hearing his feelings as they marched through the wrecked city. A third, a Pole, discussed the matter eagerly, trying to prove to him that he was mistaken in his identification of the different quarters.

"What need you quarrel about?" said the major fractiously. "What can it matter whether it was Saint Nicholas or Saint Basil? You see it is all burnt down. Now, then, what are you pushing me for? it is not for want of room at any rate," he snarled at one of his neighbours, who had not even touched him.

"Oh, Lord, oh, Lord! What have they done!" cried the men, looking about them at the ruins.

"Why, quite half the city must be burnt down!"

"I told you so. It spread to the other side of the river."

"Well, it is burnt, and you know it!" scolded the major. "What is the use of talking?"

As they were marching through one of the few streets that had remained intact the whole file suddenly started back as they passed a church, with cries of horror and disgust.

"Oh! the wretches! the savages! It is a dead body, and they have smeared his face. . . ."

Peter looked round and could make out a figure propped up against the wall of the churchyard. From the exclamations of his neighbours he understood that it was a corpse set up on its feet with the face blackened with soot.

"Move on, will you? Move on!" shouted the officers with thundering oaths, and the French soldiers drove on the mob of prisoners who had stopped in front of the dead man, hitting them with the flat of their swords.

CHAPTER LXXXV

THE whole party came to a halt presently near the depot of stores; the prisoners had met no one so far on their way through the narrow streets with their escort and the wagons, but here they overtook a battery of artillery which could hardly get forward, as a number of private carriages had got mixed up with the fieldpieces and caissons. At the head of the bridge everyone had to wait till their turn came to cross it. In front and behind nothing was to be seen but the endless line of vehicles and the army train, while to the right, where the Kalouga road branched off, an enormous body of troops with their baggage and horses stretched away till they were lost to sight; this was Beauharnais' corps, which had been the first to get out of the town. Behind, along the quays and across the Stone Bridge, came the division commanded by Ney; Davoust's corps, of which the prisoners formed a section, were to cross the Krimski Brod [1] (the Crimea Ford).

Having done so they were again compelled to halt; but after a few minutes' waiting went on again in the midst of a throng of men and vehicles, shoving and jostling on all sides. They were more than an hour getting along the hundred yards between the bridge and the Kalouga road. When they reached the open place where the roads meet, the prisoners were crowded together, and kept there for some hours. The air was full of an incessant roll, like the loud murmur of the sea, caused by the rumble of wheels and the tramp of hoofs, broken by curses and shouts on every side. Peter, flattened against the wall of a burnt-out house, listened vaguely to this uproar, which in his fancy was one with the rattle of the drums. Some of his companions hoisted themselves up and perched on the wall above him.

"What crowds and streams of people. Look what they've loaded on the guns! Furs! All looted! The blackguards! Out there—they are carrying off an image! Great God! Those are Germans you may be certain. The wretches! and they have loaded themselves till they can scarcely drag themselves along. What next? There is one with a drosky! and a man in it sitting on his trunks. They deserve a flogging, that they do! And this will go on till nightfall. Look, look there! Are not those Napoleon's horses? What fine beasts!

[1] This too, however, seems to be in fact a bridge.

and what trappings! With such grand monograms and crowns! Lord! there is no end of it! And there are some girls. Look! Russian girls, sitting in those carriages!"

All the prisoners pressed forward, and Peter, being taller than the rest, could see the carriages that had excited their curiosity, over their heads. Three chariots had got in among the caissons, and were very slowly moving forward; they contained a party of women, painted and bedizened in showy colours, and all screaming at the top of their voices. From the moment when Peter had distinctly recognised the mysterious power which, under given conditions, completely masters men, nothing could startle him: neither the corpse desecrated to be the laughing stock of the mob, nor the women wandering God knows whither, nor the burning of the city. It seemed as though his spirit was preparing for a desperate struggle and would not yield to any emotion that might impair its powers. The women went past, and after them the long line of soldiers, *télègues*, baggage-wagons, carriages, caissons, and then more and yet more soldiers, with here and there a few women.

During these hours of waiting Peter's attention was distracted by the endless general stir, and he noted nothing in particular. All, men and horses alike, seemed to be propelled by an invisible force, and to have but one object: that, namely, of outstripping each other; they jostled, pushed, swore, shook their fists, showed their teeth; and on every face was stamped that same hard, stern look which had struck Peter so forcibly that morning when he had seen its mark on the corporal.

At last the officer in charge saw an opening ahead and got his party as far as the Kalouga road. After this they went on without stopping, and never halted again till sunset. The horses were unharnessed, and the men, swearing, shouting, and quarrelling, prepared to sleep under the stars. A carriage which had kept close to them presently had a shaft driven through the side of one of the officers' chariots; a mob of soldiers rushed across, some to flog the horses, others to snatch at the reins, and each and all to fight on the slightest pretence; in fact, a German was badly hurt by a blow on the head.

It seemed as though a universal and violent reaction had come over all these men after the disorderly excitement of the day's march, as soon as they had halted in the open country under the damp twilight of an autumn evening. They seemed to be just beginning to comprehend that the end of their pilgrimage was unknown to them, and that many miseries awaited them on the way. The soldiers in charge of the prisoners treated them far more brutally than they had done in their town quarters; and here, for the first time, they were fed on horse-flesh. All, from the officers to the privates, displayed a grudging ill-will in strong contrast to their former good-nature. This bad feeling was increased when the names were called over and it was ascertained that a Russian soldier had escaped under pretence of a sharp attack of colic; and Peter saw another beaten by a Frenchman for wandering too far from the high road, while his former friend, the captain, rated the corporal smartly for allowing the man to escape, threatening to have him tried by court-martial. The corporal replied that the man was too ill to walk, and the captain retorted that stragglers were to be shot. Peter felt that the brute force which had once already almost crushed him, again had him in its clutches, and he was afraid; still the nearer he was to the fatal grip the more did his own vital force assert itself in his soul, independently of all external influences.

He supped off rye porridge and a piece of horse-flesh, and sat chattering with his companions. They spoke not a word of the scenes they had witnessed at Moscow, nor of the brutal behaviour of the French, nor of the order to shoot them in the event of their escaping; only of their personal reminiscences, and certain comical incidents of past campaigns;—this was quite enough to put them into good spirits and make them forget for the moment how critical was their position.

The sun had long been set, the stars flashed out one by one, and the round full moon was rising luridly red from the horizon, suggesting memories of the fires; but presently it glided above the grey mists and shed its pale light on the earth. The evening was over but it was not night. Peter got up, left his new comrades, and was making his way between the camp-fires to the other side of the road, where he was told that the common soldiers who were prisoners were encamped. A sentinel stopped him, and he was obliged to retrace his steps; but instead of rejoining the officers he sat down on the ground behind one of the carts, and doubling up his knees bent his head over them and gave himself up to thought. For more than an hour he was forgotten by everyone around him, but suddenly he went off into such an uproarious fit of laughter—that frank, boyish laughter which shook him from head to foot—that everyone within hearing turned round at this strange explosion of mirth.

"Ha, ha!" said Peter, talking to himself. "So he would

not let me pass! I was caught, shut up—I am still a prisoner! I—what is 'I' My immortal soul? Ha, ha, ha!" And he laughed till he cried.

A soldier got up and came to see what could have so tickled this Hercules; Peter stopped laughing; he, too, rose, and turning away from the inquisitive intruder, looked on the scene around him. All was silent in the camp, which a few hours since had been alive with voices and the crackling of the fires which were now smouldering and dying out. The moon rode overhead; the woods and fields, before indistinguishable, were now clearly visible, and beyond the plain and the forest the eye lost itself in the depths of an infinite distance. Peter looked up at the sky where myriads of stars palely twinkled.

"All that is mine," thought he. "All that is in me, one with me! And could they take that, and shut that up in a hut?"

CHAPTER LXXXVI

ONE day in October a messenger delivered into Koutouzow's hand a letter from Napoleon, which hinted at conditions of peace; but it was falsely dated from Moscow, for Napoleon when he wrote it was on the old Kalouga road, only a little way from the Russian van. Koutouzow replied to this letter, as he had to the former one, brought by Lauriston, that he could discuss no terms of peace.

Not long after this it was reported by Dorokhow, who was in command of a corps of skirmishers, that the enemy's forces in position at Fominsk consisted of Broussier's division only, and that this, being detached from the rest of the army, might be easily demolished. Officers and soldiers loudly prayed to be relieved from inaction, and the generals on the staff, remembering the easy victory at Taroutino, implored Koutouzow to accede to Dorokhow's wish. However, the commander-in-chief still refused to act on the offensive. The result was a compromise, a small force went to attack Broussier.

By a singular chance this highly-important undertaking—as it proved to be—was entrusted to Dokhtourow, a man whose modest demeanour had gained for him, without any reason, a character for indecision and want of foresight; so that no one has even thought of speaking of him, as of so many others, as elaborating plans for engagements, rushing on at the head of his regiment, or scattering crosses broadcast on the batteries. Nevertheless this same Dokhtourow was always to be seen in all the wars with France, from Austerlitz down to 1813, and leading all the most difficult movements. He was the last to remain at Aughest after the battle of Austerlitz, re-forming the regiments, and saving all that could be saved in that rout, when there was not a general left with the rear. Though suffering from fever he led 20,000 men to the defence of Smolensk against Napoleon's overwhelming host. No sooner had he got there and lain down to snatch some uneasy slumber, than he was roused by the roar of cannon; but Smolensk held out all that day. At Borodino again, when Bagration was killed, when the Russian left wing had lost nine out of every ten, while the whole strength of the French artillery was directed against it, it was Dokhtourow, "undecided and unforeseeing," whom Koutouzow hastily sent forward, to repair the blunder he had committed in making a worse choice at first. Dokhtourow went, and Borodino was made glorious.

So it was Dokhtourow who was sent to Fominsk, and then to Malo-Yaroslavetz, where, it may be said, without fear of contradiction, that the real disasters of the French began. Many a genius and many a hero of that time has been sung in verse and praised in prose; but very little has been said about Dokhtourow, and when he is mentioned, it is in terms of doubtful praise.

On the 10th (22nd) of October, Dokhtourow stopped half-way to Fominsk, at the village of Aristow, and was preparing to carry out Koutouzow's orders, and on the same day the French army, which, after much disorderly marching and counter-marching, had joined Murat in his position, as if intending to give battle, turned sharply off to the left, down the Kalouga road, without any apparent reason, and marched into Fominsk, which had hitherto been occupied by Broussier. Dokhtourow's whole force consisted of Dorokhow's detachment and two less important corps under Figner and Seslavine.

In the evening of the 11th (23rd), a French soldier of the Guards was brought in, having been taken prisoner; this man asserted that the troops occupying Fominsk composed the vanguard of the French army, that they had left Moscow five days since, and that Napoleon was with them. That same evening a peasant from Borovsk declared that he had seen a huge army entering the town. The Cossacks of Seslavine's detachment, who had seen the French regiments of Guards on the Borovsk road, confirmed this account. Hence it was quite evident that the enemy in front was no longer, as had been supposed, a single division, but the whole French army, quitting Moscow and marching in an unexpected direction.

Dokhtourow, though his orders were to attack Fominsk, hesitated what step to take, not being very clear as to what he ought to do in view of this fresh complication. Though Yermolow urged him to come to some determination, he persisted in thinking it necessary to take further orders from the commander-in-chief. To this end a despatch was forwarded to head-quarters and confided to Bolhovitinow, an intelligent officer, who was to supplement it by verbal explanations. After receiving the packet and his instructions, he set out, followed by a Cossack and two spare horses.

CHAPTER LXXXVII

THE autumn night was dark and mild. After riding thirty versts in an hour and a half, along a road ploughed into mud by four days of heavy rain, Bolhovitinow reached Létachevka at two in the morning, dismounted in front of a cottage surrounded by a dry hedge and wattled fence, on which hung a board bearing the words: "Headquarters." He threw his bridle to the Cossack and went into an ante-room where it was perfectly dark.

"The general on duty?" said he to a shade which started up at the sound of his voice.

"He is very ill; for three nights he has had no sleep," answered the drowsy voice of an orderly.

"Well then, go and call the captain. I tell you it is most urgent; a despatch from General Dokhtourow," said the messenger, feeling his way through the half-open door, behind the servant who went in to wake the captain.

"Excellency! Here is a courier."

"What? What is the matter? From whom?" cried the captain.

"From Dokhtourow. Napoleon is at Fominsk," said Bolhovitinow, perceiving that the voice was not Konovnitzine's. The captain yawned and stretched himself.

"I do not want to wake him, I must confess," said he. "He is not at all well, and it is only a rumour perhaps after all."

"Here is the despatch. My orders are to deliver it immediately to the general on duty."

"Wait till I find a light. Where the devil do you always hide yourself?" he went on, speaking to the servant. "Stay, I have got it, I have found it!" he added, as his hand came against the candlestick.

The speaker was Scherbinine, Konovnitzine's aide-de-camp. By the light of the candle Bolhovitinow recognised him, and at the same time saw in the opposite corner of the room a bed in which lay another sleeper—the general himself. First burning blue and then red the sulphur match flared up. Scherbinine lit a tallow-candle on which the cockroaches had been feasting and examined the courier. Bolhovitinow was covered with mud, and when he wiped his face with his sleeve he smeared the mud all the more.

"Who brought the news?" asked Scherbinine as he took the letter.

"The news is correct enough," said the other. "Prisoners, Cossacks and spies, all say the same thing."

"Then we shall have to wake him," and he went up to the sleeping man, who had on a cotton nightcap and was wrapped in his military cloak.

"Piotr Pétrovitch!" he said softly, but Konovnitzine did not stir. "Wanted at headquarters!" he added louder and with a smile, knowing that the effect would be magical.

In fact, the night-capped head was at once raised showing the grave, handsome face of the general, his cheeks somewhat flushed with fever. The impression of his last dream—far enough no doubt from the reality—passed from his face like a lightning flash; he shivered, and was quite himself in an instant.

"What is it? From whom?" he asked, without the slightest hurry.

On hearing the officer's story he opened and read the despatch. This done he turned and set his feet, in their worsted socks, on the floor, found his boots, pulled off his night-cap, combed out his hair, and put on his military cap.

"How long have you been on the road? We will go at once to his highness."

Konovnitzine had at once perceived that the news was of the greatest importance. For good or for evil? He did not even ask himself. On the whole he little cared; he did not apply his reason or his wit to criticising the course of the war; he thought that quite useless. He was entirely convinced that it must come to a happy termination, and that the only thing needed to bring it about was that each man should do his duty; and he did his own without respite or mercy.

Konovnitzine, like Dokhtourow, is one whose name seems to have been placed on the list of the heroes of 1812 out of mere formality, with Barclay, Raïevsky, Yermolow, Miloradovitch, Platow, and the rest. Reputation spoke of him as a man of limited capacity and knowledge; like Dokhtourow, he had never invented plans; but, like him again, he had constantly found himself involved in critical situations. Since his appointment as general on duty he always slept with his doors open, and insisted on being roused whenever a courier might arrive. He was always the first in front of a fight, and Koutouzow's complaint was that he exposed himself to unnecessary danger; indeed, he avoided giving him a foremost position. In short, he and Dokhtourow were like cog-wheels in a machine, which make neither noise nor show, but are indispensable to its working.

As he went out of his hut into the dark, damp night, Konovnitzine knit his brows, partly because the air increased his headache, and partly because he could foresee the effect that this news would produce on the big-wigs of the staff—above all on Bennigsen, who, since the fight at Taroutino, had been at daggers drawn with the commander-in-chief. However, he felt that the crisis must come, though he could not help taking to heart the debates to which it must inevitably give rise. He went into Toll's lodgings as he passed by, to inform him of what had occurred, and Toll at once proceeded to lay down his views of what should be done, to a general who shared his rooms, till Konovnitzine, who was tired, and said little, reminded him that they must go to his highness.

CHAPTER LXXXVIII

Koutouzow, like most old men, slept but little at night, and often dozed during the daytime. At night he lay down on his bed without undressing, and spent the time in meditation, his large scarred face resting on his hand, and his one eye gazing into the darkness.

Bennigsen, who was the most influential officer on the staff, and in direct correspondence with his majesty, had of late avoided the commander-in-chief, and Koutouzow had consequently felt more at ease, inasmuch as he thus escaped being constantly teased to attack the enemy at inappropriate moments.

"They must see," thought he, as he reflected on the lesson to be drawn from the battle of Taroutino, "that we can only lose by acting on the offensive. Time and patience are my two allies." He was quite certain that when the fruit was ripe it would drop; he was certain, as an experienced huntsman, that the quarry was desperately wounded by the combined efforts of Russia—was the hurt mortal? The question was as yet unanswered. The sending to him of Lauriston and Berthemy and the reports that reached him from all sides led him to think so, but he waited for proof positive. "They suggest manœuvres and attacks! What for? To gain distinction for themselves! It might be supposed that fighting was a delightful exercise. They are a parcel of children!" The unanswered question whether the wound given to the enemy at Borodino was mortal or not had been hanging over Koutouzow for a whole month. On one side there was the fact that the French had taken Moscow. On the other there was this feeling of certainty that the blow was fatal. But proof was wanting, and now for a month he had been waiting for this proof and growing more impatient the longer it tarried. Lying on his bed at night he did what he reproached the "young people" for doing—he imagined all sorts of possibilities, without basing any action upon them, it is true. Though he imagined thousands of possible moves for Napoleon, the actual move of the French army, its senseless, helpless throwing itself about from side to side for the first eleven days after leaving Moscow, he did not foresee. It made possible what Koutouzow did not even dare to think of—the complete destruction of the French.

Dokhtourow's account of Broussier's division, the reports brought in by the scouts, the misery the French army was enduring, the rumours of the evacuation of Moscow—all confirmed him in his belief that the foe was beaten, and was about to retreat. But these were only suppositions, and in his eyes far less plausible than they might be in those of the "young people." His experience had taught him the untrustworthiness of hearsay, and he knew too how readily men incline to draw inferences that fit in with their desires, and to ignore everything that contradicts them. Now the more Koutouzow desired an event the less he allowed himself to believe that it could be at hand. It was his one thought; everything else was subordinate and accessory, such as his daily avocations—among which he included his interviews with his staff, his correspondence with Madame de Staël and his St. Petersburg friends, the reading of novels, and the distribution of prizes. The immediate defeat of the French, which he had been alone in predicting, was his only ardent wish.

He was absorbed in such thoughts as these when he heard a noise in the adjoining room. Toll, Konovnitzine, and Bolhovitinow had just come in.

"Hallo! who is there? Come in, come in. What news?" shouted the marhsal. While a manservant lighted candles Toll told him the news.

"Who brought it?" he asked with a cold severity which amazed Toll.

"There is not the faintest doubt of it, highness."

"Bring him in."

Koutouzow had put one foot on the ground and was leaning back in his bed, his other leg bent under him. His eye, half-shut, was fixed on Bolhovitinow, trying to read the truth he so longed for in his face.

"Tell me, speak out at once, my friend," he murmured in a low voice, and he drew his shirt together over his breast. "Come close. What is this pleasant little piece of news? Has Napoleon really left Moscow? Is it true?"

The officer began to give him the verbal message entrusted to him.

"Make haste, be quick; do not keep me in suspense," interrupted Koutouzow.

The messenger finished his story, and then waited for orders in silence. Toll was about to speak but Koutouzow checked him with his hand, and tried to say something himself. His face twitched and he turned away to the side where the images stood.

"Great God; my Lord and Creator! Thou hast heard my prayer! Russia is saved!" he said in a tremulous voice, clasping his hands. And then he burst into tears.

CHAPTER LXXXIX

FROM this moment till the end of the war Koutouzow resorted to every means in his power—orders, cunning, and even humble entreaty—to prevent the Russian army from acting on the offensive, and exhausting itself in futile struggles with a foe whose destruction was now inevitable. It was in vain that Dokhtourow marched on Malo-Yaroslavetz; Koutouzow delays his orders that the town of Kalouga should be completely evacuated, a retreat beyond Kalouga being apparently quite likely. Koutouzow retreats on every occasion, but the enemy without waiting for him to retreat flees in the opposite direction.

Historians of Napoleon's skilful manœuvres at Taroutino and Malo-Yaroslavetz, suggest a variety of hypotheses as to what would have happened if he had invaded the wealthy governments of the south. They forget that not only was there nothing to prevent his going there if he had chosen; but that had he done so it would not have saved his army, the seeds of death were in itself. These latent elements of dissolution would have prevented his recovering his strength in the government of Kalouga, where the inhabitants were of the same mind as those of Moscow, just as much as in Moscow itself, where he had failed to maintain his footing notwithstanding the abundance of supplies which his men were trampling in the dust. The army was practically disbanded and bent on flying with its leaders—all alike, though they but vaguely understood the situation, were moved by the same desire to get out of a hopeless trap.

At the council of war held, for form's sake, by Napoleon at Malo-Yaroslavetz, General Mouton gave it as his advice that they should retreat as fast as possible, and no one contradicted him—no one, not even Napoleon himself attempted to dispute his opinion. At the same time, while they felt the imperative necessity of immediate flight, a certain sense of human self-respect made it desirable that some pressure from outside should render it obviously and indisputably needful.

This pressure was soon felt. It was what the French called "Le Hourra de l'Empereur." The very day after this council of war Napoleon, having ridden out very early in the morning on a round of inspection with several of his marshals and his usual escort, was surrounded by a party of Cossack freebooters, and only escaped in consequence of that passion for plunder which had proved the ruin of the French themselves at Moscow. The Cossacks, tempted, as they had been at Taroutino, by greed of booty, paid no heed to Napoleon who had time to ride off. When it became generally known that these "Sons of the Don" might actually have captured the emperor in the midst of his army, it was evident that the only thing to be done was to get home by the shortest and most familiar road. Napoleon, who had himself lost some of his daring and energy, saw the whole bearing of this incident, and taking Mouton's advice, gave the order to retreat. But his acquiescence and the homeward march of the troops do not at all prove that he instigated the movement: he acted under the influence of occult forces which the whole army was no less compelled to obey.

CHAPTER XC

WHEN the French entered Russia, Moscow was to them the promised land: when they left it, the promised land was Home. But Home was very far away; a man who has a thousand versts to walk before he reaches his destination, is apt to say he will do forty in the day and rest at nights; the rest makes him lose sight of the distance that still parts him from the goal towards which all his hopes and wishes tend.

Smolensk was the first point at which the French aimed on the road by which they had come; they did not hope, of course, to find reinforcements or fresh supplies there, but nothing but the hope of taking breath there for a moment, gave them strength enough to march on and endure their sufferings.

Besides this common goal that bound all these troops into one body, there was another reason for their being as one—their vast number. This enormous mass by the laws of attraction, drew to itself the individual atoms. Each one of these soldiers had but one wish; that he might be made prisoner and so escape the miseries he was enduring; all were ready to seize every opportunity of laying down their arms, but such opportunities were rare; the rapidity of their march and the immense number of men made it difficult, and the internal lesion of this great body had only a limited effect in accelerating the steady process of dissolution.

With the single exception of Koutouzow, none of the Russian generals understood what was happening. The superior officers were all fired with a desire to give chase to the enemy, to cut off their retreat, to crush them utterly; and all ranks clamoured to attack them. Koutouzow alone, put forth all his powers to thwart this desire—but the powers of a commander-in-chief are often as nothing in such a case; his immediate followers abused him and slandered him without mercy. Indeed, at Viazma, Yermolow, Miloradovitch, Platow, and some others, finding themselves in the vicinity of the French, could not resist the temptation to fight two of their corps. In sending to inform Koutouzow of their purpose, they contrived to enclose a blank sheet of paper instead of a letter; and the attack, which, as they declared, would bar the way to Napoleon's retreat, took place in spite of all the commander-in-chief's efforts to prevent it. Some regiments of Russian infantry made a rush forward with their bands playing, and some thousand men were killed on both sides—but as to barring anyone's way, no one was checked even. The ranks of the French army closed up, and losing a few stragglers by the way, it pursued its fatal march to Smolensk.

BOOK FIFTEEN

CHAPTER XCI

In all history there are few more instructive episodes than the battle of Borodino, followed by the occupation of Moscow by the French, and their retreat without again showing fight.

Historians are very generally agreed in saying that the reciprocal influence of nations in their collisions is expressed in war; and that their political power diminishes or increases in proportion to the military success they may be able to command.

Strange indeed are the official narratives, which tell us how this or that king or emperor, having quarrelled with his neighbour, collects an army, fights that of his foe, wins the victory, massacres a few thousand men and appropriates a whole nation of many million souls. And it is certainly difficult to understand why the defeat of an army, that is to say of a hundredth part at most of a whole country's forces, should entail its submission; nevertheless, facts confirm the accuracy of views of the historians. If the army gains a great victory, the rights of the conqueror are at once asserted to the disadvantage of the vanquished; if on the other hand it is beaten, the nation behind it, as it were, loses its right in proportion to the check it has suffered, and if it is entirely routed, submits entirely. It has always been so—at least so history tells us—from the earliest times to the present day, and Napoleon's wars prove the rule. After the defeat of the Austrian army, Austria's rights were abrogated, while France on the contrary gained; and the victories of Jena and Auerstaedt sealed the fate of Prussian independence.

But in 1812 the French marched as conquerors into Moscow, and instead of striking a death-blow at the existence of Russia, the outcome was the destruction of their own army of 600,000 men and, later, of Napoleonic French. And, say what we will, it is impossible to distort the facts to fit historical theory, to maintain that the Russians remained in possession of the field of Borodino, or that after the French had left Moscow, they were cut up in a series of pitched battles! The whole course of the invasion of 1812, from the battle of Borodino, till the last Frenchman had recrossed the frontier, proves to a demonstration that, in the first place, a victory does not necessarily lead to conquest—is not even a sure promise of it, and, in the second place, that the power which decides the fate of nations is not inherent in conquerors, armies and battles, but has a quite different source.

French writers have told us that, excepting in the cavalry, the artillery, and the baggage-trains, everything in the *Grande armèe* was kept in perfect order; they admit that provender was lacking for the horses and beasts, but that for this there was no remedy, as the peasants burnt their hay rather than sell it.

Hence it must be inferred that a victory had not its customary results, *because* the very peasants who after the departure of the French poured into Moscow to plunder the town—not, it must be said, a proof of any very heroic feeling—preferred burning their fodder to selling it to the invaders, notwithstanding the high price they offered.

Suppose now, that two men are about to fight a duel with swords, by strict rule of fence, and suppose that one of them, finding himself very hard pressed, throws away his weapon and seizes a club wherewith to defend himself. Though he may, no doubt, have found the simplest means of attaining his end, if his chivalrous feeling still induces him to throw a veil over this breach of established rules, and to maintain that he has fought and conquered in due form, it is easy to see how confused the reports of such a duel are likely to be. The Frenchman is the duellist who insists on the combat taking place with proper formality and courtesy; the Russian is the antagonist who flings away the sword for the bludgeon; while the reporters, who try to account for the issue on approved principles, are the historians.

In fact, after the evacuation of Smolensk, the war took a course which cannot be accounted for by any received tradition. The burning of the towns and villages, the retreat after each battle, the club hurled at the foe at Borodino, the pursuit by skirmishers, the guerilla warfare, all were out of the pale of cognisance of law. Napoleon, who had struck the correct duellist's attitude at Moscow, knew this better than any man, and he never ceased complaining of it to Koutouzow and the czar; but in spite of his remonstrances, and of the shame which some high personages may very possibly have felt at seeing the country fight in this fashion, the national bludgeon was lifted, and, without any question as to good taste or correct rule, fell and hammered the French unremittingly, till its stupendous brute force had utterly crushed the invasion.

Happy the nation who, instead of handing the sword hilt to a generous conqueror, boldly seizes the first cudgel that comes to hand, without stopping to think what others would do in the same case, and then never lays it down till rage and revenge have given place to contempt and pity.

CHAPTER XCII

ONE of the most remarkable exceptions to the so-called laws of war, and one of the most important in its consequences, was beyond a doubt the independent action of individuals as directed against the dense masses of the enemy who occupied the country. This class of fighting is always developed in a national war; instead of combining in considerable troops the men divide into small parties, surprise the foe, and melt into nothing as soon as they are met by a superior force, only to resume the offensive on the first favourable opportunity. This was the course pursued by the guerillas in Spain, the mountaineers in the Caucasus, and the Russians in 1812. In calling it partisan warfare, an attempt is made to limit the meaning of the word; since, in truth, it is not warfare strictly speaking, being in direct opposition to the rules of tactics which require that the aggressor should concentrate his forces so as to be stronger in attack than his adversary. Partisan warfare, as history shows, is always successful, though in flagrant contradiction to this rule; and the contradiction has its rise in the theory held by strategists that the strength of an armed force is always in proportion to its number. The greater the number the greater the strength, says military science, consequently large battalions always win the day. But in defending such a proposition, military science is in the same kind of error as a theory of physics would be which, being based on the relation of force to mass, should regard the first as bearing a direct ratio to the second.

But force is the product of the mass multiplied by the velocity. And in war the acceleration of the troops is also the product of the mass, but the multiplier is an unknown quantity.

Military science, finding that history is full of instances in which the number of the troops was not the standard of effective strength, but that in many cases small detachments have been able to rout large ones, does vaguely admit the existence of an unknown quantity as the multiplier, and tries to find it in the mathematical precision of the plans adopted, in the mode of arming the men, or—more frequently—in the genius of the leader. But the results attributable to this multiplier still do not agree with the historical facts; to discover this unknown x we have only to give up once for all the hero-worship which leads us to ascribe extravagant importance to the measures taken by commanders-in-chief.

This x is the spirit of the men, their greater or less eagerness to fight, to face danger; it is quite irrespective of the genius of generals, of a formation in two lines, or in three, or of the number of weapons borne by the men, whether clubs or muskets firing thirty shots a minute. Those who are most eager to fight will always be in the best condition for a struggle. The Spirit of the troops is the multiplier which, taking the mass as the multiplicand, will give the strength as a product. The real problem for the science of war is to ascertain and formulate its value, and it will never be able to do so until it ceases to substitute for this unknown quantity such factors as the commander's plan, or the accoutrements of the soldier; then only, by expressing certain historical facts by equations and comparing their relative value, can we hope to ascertain that of this unknown x.

Ten men, say, or ten battalions fighting against fifteen men or fifteen battalions win the victory: that is to say, they kill or capture the others to the last man, losing only four on their side; thus $4x = 15y$; or $\dfrac{x}{y} = \dfrac{15}{4}$. This equation does not show the sum of the unknown quantity, but it shows the relation of the two unknown quantities, that is to say, of the warlike spirit—x and y—of the contending forces. By applying such a system of equations to various historical events: battles, campaigns, and the duration of wars—a series of numbers can be brought out which certainly include, and may be made to reveal new laws.

The law of tactics which prescribes that masses should be moved to the attack, while a retreat demands sub-division, proves, without knowing it, that the strength of an army depends on the spirit that animates it. To lead men under fire requires greater discipline than to enable them to defend themselves against assailants; now, discipline is most efficient over masses of men in movement. A rule which does not take into account the spirit of the troops most frequently results only in delusive estimates, in all cases when either extreme enthusiasm or great dejection has affected this spirit—as happens, for instance, in a national war.

The French, instead of defending themselves in small detachments during this retreat, moved in compact masses; the spirit of the troops was at a low ebb, and only the strength of the mass could avail to protect the units. The Russians, on the contrary, who, by all the rules of tactics ought to have attacked in masses, became divided, for the spirit of the troops was over-excited; single individuals even fought the French without orders, and exposed themselves without compulsion to the greatest fatigues and dangers.

CHAPTER XCIII

THIS guerilla warfare had begun by the time the French had reached Smolensk in their retreat, before the Russian Government had officially recognised it; thousands of stragglers from the enemy's ranks, of foragers and marauders had been killed by the Cossacks and Russian peasantry, with no more remorse than if they had been so many mad dogs. Denis Davidow deserves the credit of having appreciated by patriotic instinct the task that was to be executed by the terrible bludgeon which, regardless of all military law and etiquette, was belabouring the French without mercy; and the honours of this type of warfare are due to him. It was on the 24th of August (Sept 5th), that Davidow's first detachment of partisans was organised, and many others followed his example in increasing numbers as the campaign lingered to its end.

These guerilla parties destroyed the *Grande armée* piecemeal and swept to perdition the dead leaves which dropped away from the perishing trunk. By the month of October, when the French were hurrying back to Smolensk, there were above a hundred of these detachments, varying in numbers and in character. Some had kept up the appearance of regular troops, had infantry and artillery, and the comforts and decencies of life. Others consisted only of Cossacks and cavalry; others again of a mixture of cavalry and infantry; while some were only parties of peasants and landowners, whose names remained unknown. A certain sacristan was reported to have led such a party, and to have made several hundred prisoners; and the wife of a starosta, a woman named Vassilisa had a good many on her conscience. This kind of fighting had spread to a vast extent by the middle of November, and that period, when the skirmishers amazed at their own daring, expecting at any moment to be surrounded and seized by the enemy, lay hidden in the forests and never unsaddled their horses, was over. This kind of war had now defined itself; it had become clear what could and what could not be undertaken against the French. Once fairly started, each man knew exactly what he could venture on. The small parties which were the first to dog the heels of the French, could do much which the leaders of larger corps could never have risked; and as to the Cossacks and peasants who crept into the very heart of the enemy's troops, they flinched at nothing.

On the 22nd October (3rd November), Denissow, who had thrown himself heart and soul into this guerilla fighting, was early on the march with his little corps. All day he had been stalking a considerable convoy of cavalry baggage and Russian prisoners, making their way to Smolensk under strong escort,— as his scouts reported. He and his men kept under cover of the forest that bordered the high road. Besides Denissow and Dologhow, who also had a small company in the immediate neighbourhood—other chiefs, those at the head of large troops, equipped with a regular staff were well aware of the existence of this baggage-train. Two of them, one a Pole and one a German, sent to ask Denissow, each on his own behalf, whether he would not combine with them to try to seize the plunder which all coveted: "No, thank you, my friend, I have teeth and nails of my own!" said Denissow to himself, as he read their letters; and he informed the German that, notwithstanding his wish to serve under so distinguished and valiant a chief, he could not have that honour, as he was already pledged to the Pole; while he told the Pole that he had promised his support to the German. Denissow had in fact made up his mind to lay hands on the booty, with Dologhow's help, without reporting matters to any superior authority.

On the 22nd (November 3rd), the French convoy was moving from the village of Mikouline towards Schamschew; the forest that iringed the left side of the road came close up to it in some places, and here and there retreated to a distance of a verst. Here it was that Denissow and his men lurked, never losing sight of the movements of the French. Early in the day a party of Cossacks had been lucky enough to seize two fourgons loaded with saddles and harness, which had stuck in the mud. After this achievement they made no attempt to attack, for it was wiser to allow the whole convoy to reach the village of Schamschew, where Dologhow was to arrive that evening, and wait in the forest till they joined him. Then they could fall on the French at daybreak from both sides at once, beat them, and carry off the stores. Six Cossacks were left along the high road to keep a good lookout, and give warning if other columns should be discovered approaching. Denissow had about 200 men with him; Dologhow about the same number, and they had reason to believe that the French escort was about 1500 strong; but these superior numbers did not alarm Denissow. One thing, however, it was indispensable that he should know: namely, what arms the escort bore; and for this purpose he must obtain information, that is to say, capture one of the enemy's men. The two fourgons captured in the morning had been taken so completely by surprise, that the soldiers driving them had all been killed, and no one had been brought in alive but a little drummer who had lagged behind, and who could tell them nothing as to the character of the troops forming the escort. A second seizure would be rash, so Denissow, thought it better to send a peasant, Tikhone Stcherbatow, forward to Schamschew to capture, if possible, one of the quartermasters, who would certainly be sent in advance.

CHAPTER XCIV

It was a thorough autumn day, mild and raining; the sky and earth met on the horizon in one dull tint of grey. Sometimes the rain fell in a fine mist, and sometimes in heavy drops.

Denissow, mounted on a lean, light thoroughbred, and wrapped in a short felt cloak, with an astrakhan cap on his head, the rain streaming off him, bent his head to avoid the slanting showers; his steed, pricking his ears, did the same. The rider was peering uneasily into the distance, anxiety was written on his face, which had grown much thinner, and was covered with a short black beard. He was followed by a Cossack corporal, named Lovaiski, fair, with twinkling light eyes, dressed like himself in a cape and fur cap, and riding a stout Don pony, as straight as a lance, and with a stamp of calm firmness on his face and in his whole bearing. Though it would have been very difficult to define what gave this character to his appearance, it was evident at a glance that, compared with Denissow, who sat on his horse uneasily, Lovaïski seemed riveted in his saddle, and one with his beast.

Their guide was a peasant, wet to the skin in his grey caftan and pointed, white woollen cap; he walked in front, and behind them, mounted on a fidgety, hungry-looking tartar horse with a thick mane and tail, and a mouth flecked with blood, came a young officer in a dark-blue, French military cloak. By his side rode a hussar, who had taken up the little drummer behind him. The lad, whose uniform and blue foraging cap were torn, clung to the soldier with his cold, red hands, and looked about him with bewildered eyes as he beat his bare feet against the horse's haunches. By twos and threes hussars followed along the narrow forest path, and Cossacks, some in capes, some in French capotes, some wrapped, head and all, in a cavalry housing. The drenching rain made the colour of the horses indistinguishable; bays and chestnuts alike looked black, their necks seemed curiously narrow with their clinging manes, and a thick steam rose up from their quarters and flanks. Riders, saddles, and bridles streamed with water, and looked all of a piece with the dreary faded aspect of the soil and the dead leaves that were strewn over it. The men sat close, their arms pressed to their sides to prevent as far as possible any fresh percolation of trickling rain to their skin; in the midst of the party rumbled the two waggons, drawn by French horses, with Cossack saddles, jolting over logs and roots, and plunging through the pools in the ruts.

Denissow's horse presently swerved to avoid a large puddle, and hit his rider's knee against a tree:

"Now, then! the Devil!" cried Denissow, in a rage, and flogging the beast smartly, he brought it round, splashing himself and his companions.

Wet, hungry, and above all provoked at getting no news of Dologhow, and seeing nothing of the man he had sent forward, he sat grumbling to himself: "We shall never have such another chance. It is too great a risk to try it single-handed, and if I put it off till another day, one of the regular detachments will carry off the plunder under my very nose. . . ." And he looked anxiously into the distance, in hopes of discerning, at last, Dologhow's scouts.

Suddenly coming out on a clearing, where a vista opened away to the right, Denissow, pulled up.

"There is someone!" he exclaimed.

The esaoul (captain of Cossacks) looked where he pointed.

"There are two of them, an officer and a Cossack; and it can hardly be the lieutenant-colonel," said he, with a love for using words not in use among his race.

The horsemen they had seen came towards them down a hill; for a moment they were lost in a hollow, but soon reappeared. The officer, his hair blown about, his uniform in holes, his trousers worked up to his knees by his rapid ride, was spurring on his weary steed. A Cossack trotted behind, standing up in his stirrups. This officer was a mere boy, with rosy cheeks and bright eyes; as he came up he handed to Denissow a damp letter.

"From the general!" he said. "Excuse its being so wet. They told us it was so dangerous," he went on, turning to the esaoul, while Denissow, knitting his brows, broke the seal. "So I and my friend Komarow," and he pointed to the Cossack, "took the greatest precautions. We each have two pistols. But what have you there?" and he looked at the little drummer. "A prisoner? Have you had a scrimmage already? May I speak to him?"

"Rostow!" exclaimed Denissow. "Why, Pétia—why did you not tell me at once who you were?" And he held out his hand with a smile.

All the way he had come Pétia Rostow had been making up his mind as to the line of conduct which, in his own opinion, he ought to pursue towards Denissow, as being becoming to an older man, and an officer, and ignoring all their past relations to each other. But at this affectionate greeting his face brightened and his cheeks flushed: forgetting in a moment the formal demeanour he had promised himself to maintain, he told Denissow how he had passed just in front of the French, how proud he was of the commission entrusted to him, and how he had already been under fire at Viazma, where a hussar had distinguished himself greatly.

"I am very glad to see you!" said Denissow, but he was looking anxious again.

"Michael Théoclititch," he said, addressing the esaoul. "This is from the German again; this young man is with him. He wants us to support him;—so if we cannot grab this convoy, to-morrow he will be sure to get it. . . ."

While he was consulting the Cossack, Pétia feeling much dashed by Denissow's inattention to him, and fancying that his rolled-up trousers might have offended him, was doing his best to work them down again, without attracting attention and to give himself a truculent air.

"Have you any orders for me, highness?" said he, saluting in due military form, and putting on the airs of the general's aide-de-camp, as he originally intended. "Or am I to stay here with your highness?"

"Orders?" repeated Denissow, absently. "Look here, can you stay here till to-morrow?"

"Oh! do keep me, I entreat you!" cried Pétia, eagerly.

"But what did the general say? That you were to return immediately, I suppose?" Pétia blushed.

"He did not say anything about it, so may I stay?"

"All right," replied Denissow, and turning to his men he bid them make their way through the wood towards a forester's hut, which was the rendezvous agreed upon. Then he sent off the officer on the tartar horse, who did duty as aide-de-camp, to find Dologhow, and ask whether he would join him in the course of the evening, while he, with Pétia and the esaoul should go to the edge of the forest and reconnoitre the French position, which he hoped to attack next morning.

"And now, old greybeard," he said to the guide. "Take us to Schamschew."

CHAPTER XCV

THE rain had ceased, but the branches of the trees hung heavy, and dripped with mist. Denissow, the esaoul, and Pétia silently followed the peasant, who walked briskly and noiselessly in his birch-bark shoes, paying little heed to the roots which lay across his path. At the top of a slope he paused, looked about him, and then made for a thin screen of trees; there he stood under a large oak not yet stripped of its foliage, and beckoned mysteriously to the others to join him. Pétia and Denissow followed, and from thence espied the French. To the left, behind the wood, spread a field; to the right, beyond a hollow in the ground with scarped sides, stood a little village and a country mansion with the roof in ruins; in the village, around the well and the horse-pond, and along the road leading to the village, moving masses of men could be seen through the fog, and their shouts and adjurations in a foreign tongue could be distinctly heard as they urged their beasts up the hill or called across to each other.

"Bring the prisoner here," said Denissow, in a whisper, without taking his eyes off the enemy.

The Cossack got off his horse, lifted down the little drummer and brought him to the captain, who asked him what the troops were that he saw before him. The little lad, who had stuffed his frozen hands into his pockets, looked up at Denissow with frightened eyes, and got so utterly confused that, though he was very ready to tell what he knew, he could not bring out a word beyond a bare affirmation to every question asked him. Denissow turned to the Cossack, to whom he communicated his views.

"Whether Dologhow comes or not, we must attack them," he said.

"It is a very good spot for the purpose," replied the esaoul.

"We will get rid of the infantry down the slope towards the marsh; they will slip down as far as those gardens; you must come up on the other side, and then, at a given signal . . ."

"But you cannot cross the ravine; there is a bog at the bottom," said the esaoul. "The horses will never get out of it; we must go more to the left."

While they were thus discussing matters in an undertone, they were startled by the crack of a gun; a puff of smoke rose into the air, followed by the cries of a hundred French voices. Denissow and his companion involuntarily started back, fearing that they were the objects aimed at; but the gun-shot and shouts were not for them: a red object was running at top speed across the marsh.

"It is our Tikhone that they have caught sight of?" exclaimed the esaoul.

"No doubt of it—the rascal!" cried Denissow.

"He will get away from them," said the Cossack.

Tikhone had by this time reached the river; he plunged in head foremost, with such a splash that the water flew up on all sides, and after disappearing for a second, he scrambled out, dripping, on the opposite bank; the Frenchmen in pursuit stopped.

"He is a sharp fellow, there's no denying!" cried the esaoul.

"He is an ass!" said Denissow, crossly. "What has he been about all this time?"

"What is it?" asked Pétia.

"Our gunner. I sent him out to catch a straggler."

"To be sure," said Pétia, with conviction, though he was none the wiser.

This man, Tikhone Stcherbatow, one of the most useful members of their party, was a peasant from the village of Pokrovski. When Denissow went thither at the beginning of his raids, and had sent for the head man to question him as usual as to the movements of the French, the man replied—also as usual—that he knew nothing whatever about them. Denissow having explained to him that his object was to attack the French, and to know whether any had been seen in the village, the starosta confessed that the marauders had in fact passed through, and that Tikhone Stcherbatow, who was the only man there to trouble his head about such things, could give him information. Denissow sent for him, and on his arrival complimented him in the head man's presence on his fidelity to the czar and his country, and on the hatred of the invader, which ought to dwell in every son of the soil.

"We did the French no harm," replied Tikhone, somewhat bewildered by Denissow's address, "we only just amused ourselves a bit, as you might say; we killed a score or so of the plunderers, but beyond that we did them no harm."

Next day, when Denissow was starting again, a message was brought to him that Tikhone, whom he had quite forgotten, wished to join his detachment. He agreed, and Tikhone, to whom all the hard work was given at first—such as making the camp fires, fetching water, washing the horses, and so forth—soon manifested a great talent for this kind of warfare. He would go out on the prowl at night, and never come back empty-handed, bringing arms or uniforms, or even prisoners if he had been desired to do so. Then Dennissow relieved him of the dirty work, took him among his Cossacks, and made him follow him on his expedition.

Tikhone did not like riding. He always went on foot, and never lagged behind the horsemen. He was armed with a carbine, but only for form's sake, his weapon was a hatchet, which he wielded as skilfully as a wolf uses his teeth—to crunch either a bone or a flea. He could split the stoutest beam in a straight line with a single blow, or cut out little pins, or carve out a spoon with equal ease. So Tikhone had a standing of his own among his comrades. If any difficult task was to be done—a strong heave of the shoulder given to a cart that had stuck, or a pull of the tail to a horse floundering in a bog—if a walk of fifty versts must be done in the day, or a man was wanted to creep in among the French—it was always Tikhone who must do it.

"Why the devil not? it does not hurt him, he is as sound as a bell," his comrades would say with a laugh.

One day when he had taken a prisoner, the Frenchman managed to send a pistol shot through the fleshy part of his loins. This wound, which Tikhone treated himself with applications—external and internal—of raw brandy, was a subject of inexhaustible pleasantry to the whole detachment, Tikhone lending himself very willingly to the jest.

"Well, old fellow, so you are crook-backed for good now? No more games for you!" the Cossacks would say; and Tikhone, writhing and grimacing, made believe to be really angry this time, and swore at the French with comical vigour. The immediate result was that for the time he rarely took prisoners.

No man was a better judge than he of a favourable opportunity for a raid, no man had killed and rifled so many of the enemy; consequently he was a favourite, both with the Cossacks and the hussars. Thus it was Tikhone, who had been sent off over-night to pick up information at Schamschew. Whether it was that he thought it beneath his dignity to capture a single Frenchman, or that he had slept too late, the fact was that having crept for cover at daylight into a copse, he had been detected there by the enemy, as his chief had been able to see for himself.

CHAPTER XCVI

AFTER discussing the attack to be made on the morrow with the Cossack captain, Denissow retraced his steps.

"Now then, my boy," said he to Pétia, "we will go and dry ourselves." As they got near to the forester's hut, Denissow stopped to look keenly about him. He saw coming towards him between the trees a man with legs like stilts, striding along, his arms swinging by his side; his short jacket, bast shoes and tartar cap were dripping wet; his gun was on his shoulder, his axe in his belt. On seeing Denissow he hastily threw something into the brushwood, and pulled off his cap as he approached; it was Tikhone. His face, marked and seamed by the smallpox, and his little eyes were radiant with glee; he looked up, and seemed hardly able to keep from bursting out laughing.

"Where did you lose yourself?" asked Denissow.

"Where did I lose myself? I went to look for the Frenchman," he answered boldly, in a rather hoarse bass.

"And what made you spend the day scrambling about in the brushwood, idiot? that was not the way to catch him."

"Catch him! I did catch him."

"Where is he then?"

"I caught one, as I tell you, on account as it were," and he straddled his big feet, "and I took him down into the wood— Then I saw he was no good; so says I to myself, 'I must find another who will do the job better.'"

"So that was it; the rascal!" said Denissow, turning to the esaoul. "Why did not you bring him with you?"

"Why not bring him?" said Tikhone roughly. "He was no good, I tell you. Do you think I don't know the man you want?"

"Donkey! Well, what next?"

"What next? I went to look for another one. I crept all along the wood, lying down so"—and he threw himself down on the ground to show how he had crawled—"and I came right upon my man. I jumped up and collared him"—and he suited the action to the word—"and says I: 'Come along, colonel!' But he began to howl, and four men threw themselves upon me with short swords, so then I showed them my hatchet. 'What are you about,' says I, 'in God's name?'"

"Oh, yes, we saw from the hill how they chased you across the marsh."

Pétia was dying to laugh, but as the rest kept their countenance, he did the same, though he could not make out what the meaning of it all was.

"Don't play the fool," said Denissow, getting angry. "Why did you not bring in the first man?" Tikhone scratched his head with one hand and his back with the other, while his mouth, opening in a smile of idiotic complacency, showed his teeth and the gap that had earned him his name.[1] Denissow also smiled, and at last Pétia could enjoy his laugh.

"But what am I to say? Have I not told you that he was no good? He was badly dressed and very rude into the bargain. 'What,' says he, 'I am a *ganaral's* son myself, I won't go.'"

"Brute!" said Denissow, "I wanted to question him."

"I questioned him," said Tikhone, "but he said he did not know much, 'and then,' says he, 'there are a great many of us, but a poor lot.' Set up a shout and you may have them all," Tikhone concluded, fixing his eyes with a determined glitter on Denissow's face.

[1] *Stcherbina* or *Stcherbinka*, a gap or notch.

"I will have you paid out with a hundred [1] all hot!" said Denissow, "to teach you to play the fool!"

"What is the good of being angry?" said Tikhone; "you might think I did not know your Frenchman. Wait till it is dark, and I will fetch you three if you like."

"Come, come!" said Denissow, and he did not get over his ill-humour till they reached the forester's hut.

Tikhone followed quite in the rear, and Pétia heard the Cossacks laughing, and teasing him about a pair of boots he had thrown into the underwood. He understood now that Tikhone had killed the man of whom he had been speaking, and it gave him an uncomfortable feeling; he involuntarily looked at the little drummer, and something made his heart feel very full, but this weakness was but for a moment, he choked it down, raised his head, and began questioning the esaoul with an air of great importance as to the expedition in prospect, so as to keep himself on a level with the company he was in.

The officer Denissow had sent to Dologhow met him on the road, and informed him that Dologhow himself was coming, and that on his part there were no difficulties whatever Denissow's spirits rose at this news to their former pitch; he called Pétia to sit by him:

"Well," said he, "and now tell me what good work you have been doing."

CHAPTER XCVII

PETIA, on leaving his parents at Moscow, had joined his regiment, and had soon after become attached as orderly officer to the colonel in command of a considerable body of troops. Ever since this promotion, and above all since his introduction to active service at the battle of Viazma, he had been in a chronic state of happy excitement at the idea that now he was indeed a man; and his only fear was lest he should miss the smallest opportunity of covering himself with glory. Though greatly delighted with all he had seen and gone through with his regiment, it seemed to him that the greatest deeds of arms were always performed where he was not. So he implored the general, who wanted someone to go to Denissow, to trust him with his message. His chief consented; but, remembering

[1] Blows with a stick.

Pétia's foolhardy behaviour at the battle of Viazma—where, instead of following the road, he rode forward as far as the front line of sharpshooters under the French fire and discharged two pistol-shots—he forbade his taking any part in Denissow's manœuvres. This was the cause of the boy's hesitation when he had been asked whether he could stay: as far as the out-skirts of the wood Pétia had promised himself that he would strictly do his duty and return at once; but at the sight of the French, and after hearing Tikhone's story, he made up his mind with the easy reaction of a youthful mind, that his general, whom till this moment he had greatly respected, was "only a rubbishy German;" that Denissow was a hero, and the esaoul another, and Tikhone a third; that it would be disgraceful to desert them in peril, and that he would take part in the attack.

It was dusk by the time they reached the forester's hut. Through the gloom moved the shadowy forms of the Cossacks' horses, saddled and bridled, and of the hussars pitching their tents in the clearing and lighting fires under cover of the hollow, that the enemy might not see the smoke. In the front room of the little hovel a Cossack, with his sleeves turned up, was cutting up some mutton, while in the inner room three officers were improvising a table out of a door taken off its hinges. Pétia pulled off his wet uniform and offered his services in helping to arrange the supper. In ten minutes the table was covered with a cloth, and spread with a bottle of brandy and one of rum, bread, salt, and broiled mutton. Seated with the other officers and tearing the tender, juicy morsels with greasy fingers, Pétia was in a state of childish excitement which made him feel kindly towards all men, and take their kindness for granted in return.

"Do you really think, Vassili Fédorovitch," said he to Denissow, "that if I stay with you for a day I shall not get into hot water? For you see," he went on, arguing with him-self, "I was told to find out—and I shall be sure to find out if only you will let me go—go where there is most. Not for a prize or a reward, you know; but I really do want—" he set his teeth and tossed his head, and clenched his fist as he looked about him.

"Where there is most—most what?" said Denissow with a smile.

"Give me a command; just the smallest command, that is all I ask—it cannot matter to you, you know. Allow me, my knife is quite at your service," he went on, offering it to an officer who was trying to divide a slice of mutton. The officer thanked him and praised the blade.

"Keep it, pray, I have several. Oh! by the by, I quite forgot; I have some raisins with me, capital raisins too, without pips. There is a new sutler in our detachment and he sells wonderful things; I bought ten pounds; I am used to eating sweets—would you like some?" And Pétia ran off in search of his Cossack, and returned carrying a large basket of raisins. "Take them, gentlemen, don't be modest. I wonder if you want a coffee-pot? I bought a famous one from our sutler—he is a capital fellow, and so honest, too, which is the chief thing; I will send it you without fail. By the way, do you happen to have plenty of flints? I have a hundred here that I bought quite cheap. Would you like to have them?" He stopped short, colouring consciously and fearing lest he had gone too far; he tried to remember whether he had committed any other folly in the course of the day; and as he thought over his adventures the face of the little drummer rose before him: "We are very snug here, but where have they taken him? I wonder if he has had anything to eat even? I hope they are not ill-using him. I have a great mind to ask. But what will they think? that I am a child who pities such another as himself. I will let them see whether I am a child or not, to-morrow! Well, I don't care then, I will ask;" he looked uneasily round at the officers' faces, fearing to see that they were laughing at him, as he said aloud:

"May I call that little prisoner, and give him some food?"

"To be sure, poor little fellow!" said Denissow, who saw nothing to criticise in such humanity. "Call him in—his name is Vincent Bosse."

"I will go and call him," said Pétia.

"Yes, do—poor little man!"

Pétia was already at the door, but turning round he squeezed his way between the other men up to Denissow.

"I must embrace you for that," said he. "My kind friend. How good, how very good of you!" and then he rushed off into the next room shouting as loud as he could: "Bosse, Vincent Bosse!"

"Who is it that you want?" asked a Cossack, from the outer darkness. Pétia explained that it was the French drummer.

"Ah! Vessennï?" said the Cossack, for the little fellow's name had already taken a Russian form, and the word, referring to the spring-time, seemed appropriate to the lad. "He is warming himself out there. Hi! Vessennï, Vessennï!" shouted several voices.

"He is a sharp little fellow," said the man standing near Pétia. "We gave him some food, he was starving." They could hear the boy coming; his bare feet splashed through the ooze.

"Here you are," said Pétia. "Are you hungry? Do not be afraid, no one will hurt you; come in."

"Thank you, sir," said the young voice, and the drummer rubbed his muddy feet on the doorstep.

Pétia longed to say many things to him, but he did not dare, so he only took his hand and pressed it kindly.

"Come in," he repeated quite affectionately. "I wonder what I can do for him," thought he, as he opened the door and pushed him into the room. But in spite of his charitable impulse he took a seat at some distance, fearing no doubt lest his dignity should suffer if he showed him too much attention. But he fumbled in his pockets, counting how much small change he had about him, and wondering whether it would be right to give it to the little drummer.

CHAPTER XCVIII

"VESSENNI," after eating his share of the mutton, was dressed in a Russian caftan that he might not be sent to join the other prisoners; and Pétia's attention was soon diverted from him by the arrival of Dologhow. He had heard a great deal of Dologhow's bravery, and of his barbarity to the French, and from the time when he came into the room, he never took his eyes off him.

Dologhow's appearance was striking to Pétia from its extreme simplicity. While Dennissow wore a *tchekmen* or Cossack pelisse, left his beard untrimmed, and displayed an icon of St. Nicholas on his breast. thus emphatically proclaiming the exceptional character of his present mode of life, Dologhow, who at Moscow had chosen to make himself conspicuous by his Persian costume, was now got up with scrupulous correctness in his uniform of an officer in the Guards, with a clean-shaved chin, the Guards' wadded military cloak, the ribbon of St. George in his buttonhole, and the regulation cap set square over his brow. He tossed his wet riding cape into a corner, and marched straight up to Denissow without noticing anyone else. He plunged at once into business; Denissow explained what his plan was, and told him of the rival eagerness of the larger corps; of Pétia's embassy, his replies to the generals, and whatever he knew of the French convoy.

"That is all very well, but we must find out of what the escort consists, and how strong they are," said Dologhow. "Someone must go and see. Without knowing their numbers we cannot rush blindly forward. I like to be precise. One of these gentlemen, perhaps, will accompany me to the enemy's camp? I could, if he liked, lend him a uniform."

"I—I will! I will go with you," cried Pétia.

"It is quite unnecessary," said Denissow. "I will not allow him to go," added he, turning to Dologhow.

"Why not?" cried Pétia; "why may not I go with him?"

"Because there's no necessity."

"I will ask you to forgive me, but I *am* going, and that's all there is to it. You'll take me won't you?" he said, addressing Dologhow.

"Why not?" Dologhow repeated absently. He was looking at the little drummer. "Has that brat been with you long?"

"Only to-day. But he knows nothing—I mean to keep him."

"And what do you do with the others?"

"What do I do with them? Why I send them in and take a receipt for them," said Denissow, colouring. "I may add," he went on boldly, "that not one lies on my conscience. Why, what is the difficulty of sending thirty or even three hundred prisoners under escort to the nearest town? And is it not better, frankly speaking, than to stain one's honour as a soldier?"

"Such squeamishness would be all very well in this sixteen-year-old count!" said Dologhow, with a frigid smile. "But you ought to have outgrown it by this time."

"But," Pétia put in shyly, "I said nothing of the kind. I only want to go with you."

"I repeat it," Dologhow went on, taking pleasure in annoying Denissow, "we are too old for such fads. For instance, why have you kept that child? Because he moved you to pity? We know very well what the receipts are worth! You send off a hundred men and perhaps thirty arrive; they have died of hunger or been knocked on the head; it is far better to send none at all!"

The esaoul, with a twinkle of his pale eyes, nodded approbation.

"I do not hold myself responsible for that, so I need not discuss how far it is true. You say they die on the road? But, at any rate, I shall not have murdered them." Dologhow laughed aloud.

"Do you suppose that they have not their orders to grab us if they can; and if they catch us, do you think with all your beautiful chivalrous sentiments, that we shall escape the aspen trees? However, it is high time to be doing something," he added, after a short pause. "Tell my man to bring my baggage in. I have two French uniforms. So you are coming with me?" and he turned to Pétia.

"Yes, yes, it is a bargain!" cried the lad, colouring to the roots of his hair; he glanced at Denissow, whose discussion with Dologhow had suggested so many ideas that he scarcely knew exactly what had been said.

"Still," thought he, "if the captains think so I suppose it must be all right. And at any rate it will never do for Denissow to fancy that he can turn me round his little finger—" And in spite of his friend's dissuasion Pétia persisted that he knew his own business, and was afraid of nothing.

"You yourself must see that it is indispensable that we should know the strength of the escort, since our lives depend upon it.—Besides, I particularly wish to go.—Do not detain me; it will be worse in the end."

CHAPTER XCIX

So, after putting on the French uniforms, including the shako, Pétia and Dologhow rode off to the clearing, whence Denissow had reconnoitred the French camp; then they went down into the hollow, where Dologhow ordered their Cossacks to wait for them without stirring, and he and Pétia trotted forward, along the road leading to the bridge. The night was pitch dark.

"They will not take me alive, I swear; if they lay hands on me I have a pistol," murmured Pétia.

"Hold your tongue; do not speak Russian!" said Dologhow hastily; and at the same moment a "Qui vive?" distinctly uttered, was heard a few yards off, followed by the click of a musket being cocked.

"Lancers of the 6th," cried Dologhow, without checking his pace.

The black outline of the sentinel was just visible in the middle of the bridge.

"The password?"

Dologhow drew rein and walked his horse.

"Tell me, is Colonel Gérard hereabouts?"

"The word?" repeated the man, barring the way and giving him no answer.

"You don't ask an officer on his rounds the password! I want to know if the colonel is to be found;" and pushing the man aside with his horse's shoulder, he rode on.

Discerning another shade a little way off he went straight towards it; it was a soldier carrying a sack, who came up in perfect confidence and patted the horse's neck. In reply to Dologhow's questions he answered very frankly that the colonel and officers were farther up the hill, at the farm, as he called the house of the owner of the village.

The men had bivouacked all along both sides of the road; without paying any heed to their laughter and shouts Dologhow stopped in front of a gateway, turned into the yard, dismounted, and went up to a large fire that was blazing in the middle. Some men were sitting around it talking vehemently; a piece of meat was stewing in a small saucepan, and a soldier in a dark-blue cloak and foraging-cap was stirring it with his ramrod.

"He is a famous one to cook!" said an officer who was sitting in the shadow on the further side.

"He will make the rabbits fly!" answered another with a laugh; but then they both were silent, peering into the darkness, as they heard Dologhow and Pétia approaching.

"Is that you, Clément? Where the devil . . .?"

But he did not finish his sentence. Perceiving his mistake he frowned, bowed to Dologhow as a stranger, and asked him what brought him there. Dologhow explained that he and his companion wished to join their regiment, and begged him to tell him whether he knew where the 6th Lancers were to be found. The Frenchmen could tell him nothing about it; and to Pétia it seemed as though the officers were examining them suspiciously. The silence lasted some seconds.

"If you expected to find supper you have come too late," said a chuckling voice behind the stewpan.

Dologhow said they had supped already, and that they were going at once; he threw the reins of his horse, however, to the private who was watching the pot, and sat down on his heels next to the officer who had spoken to him. The Frenchman did not take his eyes off him, and again asked him which was his regiment. Dologhow affected not to hear the question, but to be absorbed in lighting his pipe, and in questioning the other officers as to the safety of the roads, and whether there was any danger of meeting with Cossacks.

"The rascals are ubiquitous," said one of the Frenchmen; to which Dologhow replied that there was no danger from Cossacks, excepting to stragglers like themselves, that they would certainly not dare to attack any considerable detachment. To this no one made a reply.

"When will he move off?" thought Pétia to himself; he had remained standing. But Dologhow went on with the conversation, asking them boldly how many men there were in each battalion, how many battalions in their escort, and how many prisoners.

"It is dreary work dragging all those corpses at your heels. Far better shoot the wretches and have done with it!" he added, with such a shout of laughter that Pétia feared the Frenchmen might find them out.

Dologhow's laugh found no echo, and one of the French officers who had been lying invisible in the shadow, covered with a cloak, whispered a few words to his neighbour. Dologhow rose and asked for his horses.

"Now, will they let us have them or not?" thought Pétia, keeping close to his leader. But the horses were brought.

"Good-night, gentlemen," said Dologhow. Pétia tried to say as much, but he could not utter a word. The officers were still whispering together. Dologhow was some time getting into his saddle, for his horse was restive; but finally he rode off, walking slowly out of the gate, Pétia following. The boy would have liked to look back and see whether they were being watched, but he dared not.

Instead of returning as they had come they crossed the village, pausing for a moment to listen.

"Do you hear?" said Dologhow; and Pétia recognised the voices of Russian prisoners, sitting round a fire.

Then they went back to the bridge, past the sentinel, who did not say a word to them, and into the ravine where the Cossacks were waiting.

"Now, good-bye; you can tell Denissow that I expect him at daybreak, at the first gun fired," said Dologhow, moving away.

But Pétia clasped his hand, exclaiming: "Oh! what a hero you are! How splendid! How much I admire you!"

"All right, all right!" said Dologhow; but as Pétia still held his hand he guessed that the lad was leaning over to embrace him. He submitted with a laugh, and then rode off into the night.

CHAPTER C

ON returning to the forester's hut Pétia found Denissow waiting in the outer room in the greatest anxiety, and blaming himself for having allowed him to go.

"Thank God!" he exclaimed, "thank God! But devil take you, I have not had a moment's sleep, thanks to you!" he added interrupting Pétia's enthusiastic narrative. "Go to bed; we have time yet for a nap."

"I am not sleepy," said Pétia, "and I know myself too well. If I go to sleep there will be no waking me; besides, I am not in the habit of sleeping before a fight."

So he sat down and remained quiet, thinking over his adventurous expedition and dreaming of the morrow, till he saw that Denissow was asleep; then he stole out of the cottage. It was still quite dark; a few drops of rain fell now and then, but he could make out the shape of the Cossack tents and of the horses picketed near; further off loomed the forms of the two captured fourgons, and in the hollow a fire which was slowly dying out. Several of the Cossacks and hussars were awake; the murmur of their voices reached his ear, and the munching of horses over their corn. Pétia went towards the waggons where the riding-horses were tied up and found his own, a stout nag from the Ukraine.

'Well Karabach, my boy," he said, stroking his nose and kissing him, "well, we have work before us to-morrow!"

"What, are you not asleep, master?"

"No, Likhatckow—that is your name, I think? I have only just come in. We have been to call on the French." And Pétia gave him a full account of the expedition, and told him why he had gone, and how, in his opinion, it was better to risk his own life than to let the whole detachment try at a venture.

"But go and get a little sleep," said the Cossack.

"No, it is not my habit. By the way, are you supplied with good flints? I have brought some with me, and if you want any you can have them."

The Cossack put his head out from under the wagon to look more closely at Pétia.

"I say this because it is my way to see carefully to everything. Others let everything go haphazard; they are never prepared, and they regret it. I don't like that myself."

"Very true," replied the Cossack.

"And I want you to be good enough to sharpen my sabre, the edge is turned with . . ." but Pétia checked himself just as he was about to tell a lie, for the sword had never yet been sharpened. "Can you put an edge on it?"

"Why not? Of course I can."

Likhatchow crept out, and felt in the saddle-bags; Pétia perched himself on the waggon to watch his proceedings.

"Are all the men asleep?" he asked.

"Some are, some not."

"And where is the boy?"

"Vessenni? He stowed himself in a corner at the door of the hut and fell asleep out of sheer fright."

For a long time Pétia kept silence, listening to every sound; presently he heard footsteps, and a shade stood before him.

"What are you sharpening, mate?"

"A sabre for the master here."

"A good idea," said the man, who was himself a hussar. "Tell me, did we not leave a bowl over here?"

"There it is, by the wheel."

"It will soon be daylight," added the man, picking up the bowl, and he walked away, stretching himself as he went.

Pétia's fancy, meanwhile, had carried him away into a fairy land, where nothing at all resembled the reality. That large dark object a few yards away—was it really the forester's hut, or was it not the entrance to a cavern leading down to the bowels of the earth, and that red gleam, the single eye of a monster fixed on him? Was this a wagon he was sitting on, or a high tower, from which if he were to drop he might fly during a whole day, or a month perhaps, without reaching the ground. He looked up at the sky; it was as fairylike as the earth: clouds, swept along by the wind, rushed across above the trees, leaving rents through which he could see the myriad stars in the infinite blue, which sometimes looked so far, far away, and sometimes seemed so near that he could reach it with his hand. He involuntarily yielded to sleep, closed his eyes, and swayed from side to side. It was still raining a little; the snoring of the sleeping soldiers, and the neighing of the horses mingled with the rasping of the whetstone on his sword-blade. Suddenly Pétia heard a delicious orchestra playing some unknown hymn of exquisite pathos and beauty. His musical instinct was as fine as Natacha's, far beyond that of Nicholas, but he had never learnt a note, or even thought of it. These mysterious strains, suddenly filling his brain and soul, struck him as beyond everything poetical and intoxicating. The music grew clearer and louder. It was what a scientific musician would have called a fugue; but Pétia had not the faintest idea of what a fugue might be. The air, played first by a violin, was taken up by a horn in plaintive and seraphic tones, and before it was ended was lost in a chorus, where it rose again till it melted into a glorious ensemble—a grave and solemn chant of triumph and victory.

"But I am dreaming," said Pétia to himself, as he nearly rolled over; "my ears are ringing no doubt—or is this invisible music at my beck and call? Come back, sing again!" He shut his eyes once more, and the tones of the hymn, coming nearer or dying in the distance, again fell on his ear.

"Oh! how lovely it is!" thought he, trying to control the heavenly orchestra. "Softly, now softly. . . ." and the music obeyed. "And now quicker, more lively, all together!" and the sounds, swelling in volume, seemed to come from the depths of space. "Now, the voices!" ordered Pétia, and men's and women's voices, at first hardly audible, gradually rose to impressive power. The ring of the instruments mingled with this song of triumph, and with the drip of the rain, the grinding of the sabre, and the whinnying of the horses, but the grand effect was not for a moment disturbed. Pétia listened in rapture to the sublime harmony, and never knew how long it went on. He was still in this rapture, and only regretted that there was no one to enjoy it with him, when Likhatchow's voice suddenly roused him.

"Here it is, highness; you can cut a Frenchman in half with it now!"

Pétia roused himself. Dull daylight was showing between the bare branches, and the horses were gradually emerging from the gloom. He jumped down, took out a rouble, which he gave to the Cossack, examined his sabre, and slipped it into its sheath. The men were untying the horses, and examining the girths.

*K 5*7

"Here is the captain!" said Likhatchow, seeing Denissow, who called Pétia from the door of the hut, and gave the word to make ready to start.

CHAPTER CI

THE horses were saddled in no time, and everyone fell into his place. Denissow gave his last instructions to the party of infantry who were to lead the way, and who soon disappeared among the trees, splashing through the mire, and vanishing in the heavy mist. Pétia holding his horse by the bridle, was, impatiently waiting for the order to start. His morning wash had refreshed him; but his eyes still glittered with unusual brightness, and he shivered.

"Well, is everything ready?" asked Denissow; the horses were led up, and after scolding his Cossack for not tightening the girths enough, he mounted. Pétia put his foot in the stirrup, his horse trying as usual to keep him from mounting; but once up, off he went as light as a bird, looking back to see the start of the long line of hussars.

"Vassili Fédorovitch," said he, going round to Denissow's side. "You will give me a little command—a little job—will you not?"

Denissow, who at that moment had almost forgotten his existence, stared at him in surprise.

"I only ask one thing of you," said he sternly, "and that is to do as I bid you, and not to go where you have no business." And not another word would he say to him throughout the march.

By the time they reached the skirts of the wood it was fairly daylight over the plain; Denissow gave an order to the esaoul; the Cossacks filed past them one by one, and he followed them down the hill. The horses, slipping and clinging with their hind hoofs, soon brought their riders down into the hollow. Pétia, whose attack of shivering was becoming serious, rode on by his leader's side. It was now broad daylight, and only the fog hid distant objects from their view. Denissow again rode ahead, and turning to the Cossack, nodded to him, and said in a low voice, "Fire the signal shot!"

The Cossack fired, and at the same instant the horses were put to a gallop, while other shots rang out on all sides. Pétia flogged his horse, giving him his head, and flew forward, heedless of Denissow, who was calling him back. He felt as though the signal had brought a flash of light, and that the day was as bright as at noon. He reached the bridge, which the Cossacks had already crossed, knocked up against a straggler, and galloped madly on again. In front of him men—Frenchmen, no doubt,—were crossing the road from right to left; one of them slipped and fell under his horse's feet. Further on a party of Cossacks had pulled up in front of a peasant's cottage from whence proceeded a fearful shriek of distress. Pétia went closer, and his eyes fell on the pale face of a terrified Frenchman, clinging with both hands to the shaft of a lance that was pointed at his breast.

"Hurrah, boys!" shouted Pétia, spurring his foaming horse, and riding up the street.

Shots were being fired some little way off; Cossacks, hussars, and Russian prisoners in tatters, were rushing in all directions and yelling like mad. A young Frenchman, bareheaded, was defending himself with his bayonet against two or three hussars. By the time Pétia rode up he was overmastered. "Too late again!" thought Pétia.

He made his way to the spot where the firing was briskest; there was fighting in the courtyard, where he and Dologhow had been the night before; the French had entrenched themselves behind the hedges and clumps of bushes in the garden, and were firing at the Cossacks, who stood in a compact mass in the gate. Through the smoke he saw Dologhow's pale face, shouting to his men:

"Take them from behind. Infantry, do not stir!"

"Not stir! Hurrah!" cried Pétia, and without a moment's hesitation, he threw himself into the thickest of the fray.

A volley rent the air, the bullets whistled round; Dologhow and the Cossacks forced their way in at the gate. Amid clouds of smoke the French could be seen throwing away their arms, or rushing to meet the Cossacks, while others went rolling down the hill to the pond.

Pétia was still tearing round the courtyard; but instead of holding the bridle, he was waving both arms wildly in the air, and leaning heavily over on one side. His horse, suddenly coming on the smouldering brands of the fire, stopped short, and Pétia fell heavily. For a moment his hands and feet moved, his head was rigid. A bullet had entered his brain.

A French officer came out of the house then with a white

handkerchief at the end of his sword, and explained that they surrendered. Dologhow, dismounting, went up to Pétia, who was lying on the ground with his arms out.

"Done for!" said he, knitting his brows, and he went forward to meet Denissow.

"Killed?" cried Denissow, knowing at a distance, from the too familiar attitude, that Pétia must be dead.

"Done for!" repeated Dologhow, as if he found a particular pleasure in using those words; and he went back to the prisoners who were crowding round the Cossacks.

"We can leave him there," he called out to Denissow, who did not answer.

He had lifted Pétia's head with trembling hands, and was looking at the poor, blood and mud-stained face. "I am fond of sweet things—these are capital raisins—take them all. . . ." The words irresistibly recurred to his mind; and the Cossacks looked on in amazement as they heard the short, hard breathing, almost like a dog's bark, that broke from Denissow's oppressed chest. He suddenly turned away and clutched convulsively at the railings.

Among the Russian prisoners just rescued was Peter Bésoukhow.

CHAPTER CII

THE French authorities had taken no steps to provide for the conveyance of the prisoners with whom Peter found himself. Since the 22nd of October (3rd November) they were no longer with the corps that had escorted them out of Moscow. Part of the provision-train which, during the first few days, formed the rear of the moving army, was seized by Cossacks, and the rest had gone on in front. The artillery, which, to begin with, had taken the lead, had now given way to Marshal Junot's enormous baggage-wagons, under the escort of a detachment of Westphalians. The troops had marched in three columns, and in good order as far as Viazma, but the ranks were now broken, and the disorder of which Peter had seen symptoms at the first stage, had now reached a climax. The road on both sides was strewn with the carcases of horses; men in rags, and stragglers from every corps, sometimes came up with them, and sometimes fell behind. False alarms had several times occasioned wild panics;

then the soldiers fired at random, turned on each other, jostled and swore, abusing their comrades for their own crazy terrors.

The cavalry-train and Junot's baggage still formed some semblance of a body of troops, but day by day it was melting away. The hundred and fifty wagons were presently reduced to sixty; the rest had been seized or abandoned, and three of Junot's wagons had been rifled by men of Davoust's corps. Peter had heard the Germans say that this baggage-train was more strongly guarded than the prisoners, and that a West-phalian had been shot by the marshal's orders for being found possessed of a spoon with his arms upon it.

The number of prisoners had greatly diminished: from three hundred and thirty that had started from Moscow, they had dwindled to about a hundred, and they were a greater anxiety to the soldiers in charge than even the cavalry-train and Junot's fourgons. If it was weary work to watch the baggage, it was far more tiresome and intolerable, starving and shivering as they were, to keep an eye on the Russians—who were equally hungry and cold, who died off like flies, and whom they were ordered to shoot if they made the slightest attempt to escape. Fearing to be betrayed into a sentiment of compassion which might cost them dear, they treated them more brutally than ever. At Dorogobouge, the soldiers locked up the prisoners in a stable, while they went off to plunder their own stores. Some of the victims tried to escape through a burrow underground that they managed to scrape out, but they were caught in the act and shot. The order at first observed, by which the officers were kept apart from the privates, had ceased to exist. The able-bodied were all placed in one party, and thus Peter found himself once more in company with Plato Karataïew and his little bandy-legged dog. Karataïew fell ill of fever the third day of their march, and as he grew weaker Peter instinctively held aloof from him, or only kept with him by a great effort, for his constant groaning and the peculiar acid odour of his person were to the last degree repulsive.

While shut up in the hut at Moscow, from all that went on in his mind, and the mode of life to which he was forced, Peter had felt keenly that man is created for happiness; that that happiness is in him, in the mere satisfaction of the daily needs of life; and that misery is the foreordained result not of want, but of superabundance. Another new and consoling truth had also been revealed to him during the last three weeks: namely, that nothing in this world is wholly frightening, but that whereas there is no such condition in life where a man is perfectly happy and perfectly free, there is also no such state when a man is utterly unhappy and a complete slave. He saw that endurance, like freedom, has its limits, and that those limits touch each other; that a man lying on a bed of rose-leaves, of which one is crumpled, suffers as acutely as the man sleeping on the damp earth, who feels the cold creeping into his limbs; that he himself, indeed, had suffered as much in his time from a pair of tight evening shoes as he did now from his bruised, bare feet. Finally, he had learned to see that he was no more free when he fancied he was marrying of his own free will, than he was at this moment, locked up for the night in a stable.

Of all the miseries that weighed upon him at this moment, and which he never forgot till his dying day, the most intolerable was the state of his feet. Even the second day he said to himself, as he examined them, that it would be impossible to walk again next day; but when the order to start was given, he limped and shuffled till his cuts and bruises got warm, and then the pain was less severe. Though every night his feet were in a shocking state, at length he made up his mind to look at them no more, and then he forgot them. Never before had he at all understood the strength of man's vital power of resistance, or the beneficial effect of change of scene, and the relief it gives, like the safety-valve of a steam-engine, which lets off the surplus when the boiler is too full. He never heard the prisoners shot who lagged behind, though above a hundred had already been thus disposed of. He thought no more about Plato, who daily grew weaker, and who would, no doubt, meet the same fate; still less did he think of himself. The more precarious his situation, the darker the future, the more comforting and peaceful were his meditations, and the more his spirit dwelt apart from all that was immediately around him.

CHAPTER CIII

On the 22nd October (November 3rd), Peter was toiling up a muddy and slippery hill-road; his eyes, which were chiefly occupied in picking his way, wandered now and then to his companions in misery. The little dog frolicked along, sometimes on three legs as of old, and sometimes, on all four at once, he would dart off to bark at the crows feasting on the carrion.

There was plenty of it about, corpses of men, and carcases of beasts in different stages of decomposition. The wolves dared not approach while the troops were constantly passing, so the little dog was free to yield to his vagabond propensities. The rain had not ceased all day; if it held up for a few minutes, it was only to come down more sharply than ever after each interval. The earth, completely saturated, could take up no more, and the water ran off in a thousand little rills. Peter was counting off his steps on his fingers, and mentally saying to the rain: "Rain away, rain away; wet me through!"

He would have said that he was thinking of nothing, but his spirit was alert and meditative, and deriving much edification from a story he had heard from Karataïew the evening before. Plato, wrapped in his cloak, had been telling the soldiers in his sing-song, and now weak voice, a legend which he had often repeated in Peter's hearing. It was past midnight, and at that hour his fever left him, and he recovered his wonted spirits. Looking at the thin, pale face, in the glare of the bivouac fire, Peter's heart swelled within him. His pity for the man made him uncomfortable, and he would have been glad to get away; but as there was no other fire for him to sit by, he had no choice but to remain by his side.

"Well, and how are you?" he asked, without looking at him.

"Bewailing one's illness will not bring death!" was the reply, and Plato went on with his story.

Peter, as we have said, knew it by heart. It was one that the little soldier took a particular delight in telling. Peter listened to it this evening with fresh interest. It was the history of a worthy old merchant, living with his family in the fear of God, who one day set out on a pilgrimage with one of his friends. They stopped for the night at an inn, and next morning the merchant's friend was found murdered and robbed. A blood-stained knife was lying under the merchant's pillow, and he was tried and condemned, beaten, his nostrils slit, and then sent into penal servitude, "as was but just," Karataïew added.

"So, my dear friends, for ten years and more the old man toiled in the mines, and never did anyone any harm, but submitted as he ought; but still he often prayed God to let him die. Well, one evening the convicts all sitting round, as it might be us here, began telling each other what they had been sent there for, and what their sins were before God. One confessed that he had murdered a man, another that he had killed two; another had set a house on fire, and another was a deserter; at last they asked the old man: 'And you, grandfather, what were you punished for?' 'I, my children,' says he, 'for my own sins and for those of others. I never killed any man, nor stole his goods, and I gave what I could to my neighbour when he was poor. I was a merchant, my little friends, and very rich—' and then he told them, chapter and verse, how it had all happened. 'And I don't complain,' says he, 'for it was God who sent me here no doubt; but I am sorry for my poor wife and children . . .' And the old man began to cry. Well, and if the very man who had really committed the murder was not among them! 'Where did it happen, grandfather? and when? and how?'

"And lo and behold! the man asks all these questions, and his heart grows full, and he goes up to the old man and falls at his feet: 'It is for me, good old man, that you are punished; it is Gospel truth! he is an innocent soul, friends, who is suffering here. I struck the blow, and I slipped the knife under your pillow while you were asleep. Forgive me, grandfather, forgive me, for Christ's sake!'" Karataïew paused with a pensive smile—and gazing into the fire he piled the logs together.

"And the old man says to him: 'May God forgive you, for we are all sinners together before Him; I am punished for my own sins . . .' and he cried bitter tears."

"Well, what do you say to that, my friends?" Plato asked, his smile lighting up his whole face, as if all the charm of the story was in the sequel.

"The real murderer confessed to the authorities: 'I have six souls on my conscience,' says he—for he was a wicked wretch—'but the old man troubles me most of all: I cannot bear that he should be so miserable on my account.' So they wrote all he told them and sent the paper to the right persons. It was a long way off, and then the trial took some time, and all the papers to be made out—as it always does with the authorities; at last it got to the czar, and the czar gave an ukase: 'Set the merchant free and give him a present, as the authorities have decreed,' and when the ukase came they looked for the old merchant. 'Where is the old man?' they ask, 'the innocent man who is being punished? The czar's ukase has come!' and then they tried again to find him." Here Karataïew's voice grew tremulous. "But God's pardon had come quicker,"

he went on. "He was dead! Yes, so it was, my friends!"
And he relapsed into silence, though the smile lingered long
on his face.

It was the mystical sentiment of the story and the pathetic
rapture on the soldier's face that had filled Peter's soul with
vague and indescribable joy.

CHAPTER CIV

"FORM in line!" said a voice in abrupt command. A sudden
stir at once began amongst the soldiers of the escort and
prisoners; it might have been supposed that they were awaiting
some happy but solemn crisis. Orders passed to and fro, while,
to the left of the party, a troop of cavalry, well mounted and
dressed, rode by. A look of constraint was perceptible on
every face in the expectation of the commander-in-chief; the
prisoners were thrust into the background, and the soldiers
formed in a line. "The emperor! The marshal! The duke!"
A carriage with grey horses was driving at a swift pace immediately behind the guard of cavalry. One handsome, calm, fair
face struck Peter as particularly imposing among the escort.
It was one of the marshals, whose eye fell for a moment on
the colossal figure of this prisoner. He looked away again at
once, but Peter fancied he could detect a movement of compassion, which he vainly endeavoured to conceal. The general
in charge of the convoy and baggage-train looked frightened;
his face was red and he spurred his haggard steed to gallop
behind the carriage. Then a few officers collected together and
the soldiers gathered round them: "What did he say? What
was it?" everyone was anxiously inquiring.

At this moment Peter caught sight of Karataïew, whom he
had not before seen that morning. He was standing with his
back to a birch-tree. The pathetic expression his face had
worn last night when he was telling the story of the man who
had suffered innocently, had now an added look of sweet, calm
gravity. His kind eyes were misty with tears and seemed to
appeal to Peter, but Peter was afraid for himself; he dared not
look and pretended he had not seen. As they were marching
on again, however, he glanced back. Plato was in the same
place by the roadside. Two French soldiers were standing
near him, discussing something. Peter would not look; he

went on, toiling up the steep slope. He distinctly heard a shot behind him—but then he remembered that the passing of the carriage had interrupted his calculation of how many stages they had still to march to Smolensk; and he began to count them again.

Two soldiers, with one of the guns still smoking, ran past to join the ranks; they were both very pale and one looked at Peter out of the corner of his eyes; Peter looked at him, and remembered that this man, only two days since, had burnt his shirt when trying to dry it, to the extreme amusement of all the lookers-on. Then he heard the dog howling round the spot where Karataïew was sitting: "What is the matter with the beast, why is he howling?" said Peter to himself.

The soldiers who were walking on each side of him did not turn round, but they looked black and gloomy.

CHAPTER CV

AT the village of Schamschew the prisoners, the marshal's baggage, and the cavalry-wagons were all brought to a stand-still. The men squatted round the fires and cooking-pots, and Peter, after eating his allowance of horseflesh, lay down with his back to the blaze and slept as he had slept at Mojaïsk, after Borodino. His dream was mixed in strange confusion with the reality, and a voice—was it his or another?—repeated the very same reflections he had then so clearly heard. "Life is everything; life is God. Everything has motion, and that motion is God. As long as there is life there is the happiness of recognising the existence of the Divinity. To love life is to love God. The most difficult and the most meritorious thing in life is to love it in spite of all its undeserved suffering." "Karataïew!" Peter suddenly said to himself, ascribing these ideas to him. Then, in his dream, he saw a little old man whom he had long since forgotten, and who had been wont to give him geography lessons when he had been living in Switzer-land: "Wait," said the old man, and he put a globe before him. This globe was alive, moving; it had no clear outlines marked upon it; the whole surface was covered with drops of water lying closely side by side, and these drops trickled about, some-times running together and sometimes sub-dividing to infini-tude; while trying to occupy the largest possible space they repelled or absorbed each other continually. "This is an image of life," said the old professor. "How simple and how clear," said Peter, "and how is it I never understood this before?" "God is in the midst and each drop strives to spread itself out so as to reflect Him better; it expands, it shrinks, it disappears and comes to the surface again—that is how Karataïew disappeared! Do you understand, my son?" said the professor. "Do you understand, by all that's holy?" cried a voice of thunder, and Peter awoke.

He sat up and saw a French soldier who had just been shaking a Russian prisoner and who was now grilling a piece of meat stuck on to the end of a ramrod. His hairy, strong hands twirled the meat round and round with great dexterity, and the glare of the fire lighted up his tanned face and thick eyebrows.

"Much he cares, the wretch!" muttered he; the prisoner, was sitting a couple of yards off patting the little grey dog which wagged its tail contentedly.

"He has followed us," said Peter, "Plato . . ." but he stopped short, for the picture rose before his fancy of poor Plato sitting under the tree, with the shot he had heard, the dog's howling, and the guilty, frightened look of the two soldiers who had passed him with the musket still hot—and Plato had been absent all the evening. It was dawning on him at last that Karataïew had been killed, when, without knowing how or why, he had a sudden vision of the balcony of his house at Kiew where he had once spent a summer evening with a fair Pole. Making no effort of mind to connect these widely dissimilar images he closed his eyes again, and the reminiscence, merging in his dreams with the fluid globe of the old professor's hands, gave him such a sensation of respite and refreshment that he fancied he was gently sinking in deep waters, clear as crystal, which silently closed above his head.

He was roused before sunrise by loud shouts and the discharge of musketry.

"The Cossacks!" yelled a Frenchman, taking to his heels; and a minute later Peter was in the midst of his fellow-countrymen.

It was long before he could understand what was happening; cries of joy rose on all sides:

"Friends! Brothers! Comrades!" the rescued soldiers were exclaiming, as they wept, and hugged the Cossacks and hussars who crowded round them, offering clothing to one, boots or bread to another.

Peter stood sobbing, and as he could not utter a word in his agitation, he threw his arms round the neck of the first man he saw.

Dologhow, standing at the door of the dismantled house, watched the exit of the disarmed Frenchmen, dusting his boots with his riding-whip. Still burning with indignation under their misadventure, they were discussing it vehemently among themselves: but as they passed him and felt the sinister chill of his cold, stern gaze, the words died on their lips. At a short distance off stood his Cossack, counting the prisoners and scoring off the hundreds on the panel of the gate with a bit of chalk.

"How many?" asked Dologhow.

"Two hundred," said the Cossack.

"*Filez, filez!*" [1] said Dologhow, who had already picked up the word from the French, and a relentless flash glittered in his eyes as they met those of a Frenchman.

Denissow was standing with his hat off, and watched, with a dejected air, a party of Cossacks who were carrying Pétia's body to bury it in a grave they had dug at the bottom of the garden.

CHAPTER CVI

AFTER the middle of November, when the cold had fairly set in, the retreat of the French assumed a tragical aspect. A number of men were frozen to death or were burnt in trying to warm themselves, while the emperor, kings and dukes went on their way in furs and carriages carrying off stolen goods; but the actual flight and demoralisation of the French army continued without any essential difference.

Between Moscow and Viazma the 73,000 men—not including the Guards—who during the whole war did nothing but pillage, were reduced to 36,000. The proportions continued to be mathematically the same: from Viazma to Smolensk, from Smolensk to the Bérésina, from the Bérésina to Vilna the French army steadily dwindled, irrespective of the cold or the pursuit of the Russians, or of other unforeseen difficulties taken singly. After Viazma the three divisions melted into a

[1] Be off, look sharp.

confused crowd and went on thus to the end. Berthier wrote as follows to the emperor—and the amount of licence which generals allow themselves in describing the situation of an army is well known:

"I feel it my duty to inform your majesty of the state of your troops in the different divisions which have come under my observation under various circumstances during the last two or three days. They are almost disbanded. The number of men who march with the flags is a quarter, at most, of almost every regiment; the rest wander on in various directions, each on his own account, in the hope of finding food and escaping discipline. On the whole they look to Smolensk as the point where they may join again. During the last few days several have been observed to throw away their cartridges and arms.

"In such a state of things, whatever your majesty's ulterior purpose may be, the interest of the service requires that you should rally the troops at Smolensk, and begin by getting rid of the non-combatants, such as men who have parted with their weapons, all useless baggage, and the material of the artillery, which is now quite out of proportion to the effective force. Besides this, some days of rest and provisions are indispensable to the men, who are worn out with fatigue and want of food; several have died these last few days on the road and in bivouac. This state of things is getting worse and worse, and there is reason to fear that unless some remedy be promptly applied, we shall lose all hold over the troops, in the event of a struggle.

"November 9th, thirty versts from Smolensk."

On reaching Smolensk, the Promised Land of their hopes, the French fell to killing each other to snatch the food they wanted: they rifled their own provision magazines, and having effected these ravages, set forth again on their homeward march, not knowing where it would end or why they were going on again. Napoleon, the general who had never met his match, knew no more than they did. Still, and in spite of everything, he and his courtiers continued to observe the usual formalities in writing letters and reports, and issuing the order of the day. They called each other: "Sire, my cousin—Prince of Eckmühl, or King of Naples. . . ." But all these documents were a dead letter. No one executed orders which it was impossible to carry out; and, notwithstanding this pomp of titles, each man felt that he had much to answer for, and that the hour of retribution had come. In spite of the care they seemed to be devoting to the troops each one in reality was thinking only of himself—of escaping as fast as he could and securing himself —if possible.

CHAPTER CVII

THE movements of the French and Russian armies during this retreat from Moscow to the Niemen, are like nothing so much as a game of blind-man's-buff, in which two men are blindfolded, and one has a bell to ring, so as to let the other know where he may chance to catch him. At first he rings it boldly, without much fear of his adversary, but as the game gets closer he tries to steal away noiselessly, and generally, when trying to avoid the enemy, blunders into his arms. In the same way, during the early part of the retreat of the French along the Kalouga road, the Russians still knew where to find them; but when they had started again on the way to Smolensk, they held the tongue of the bell, and without suspecting the neighbourhood of Russians, came into collision with them now and again. One army was flying, the other pursuing; and owing to the precipitancy of the flight and the fatigue of the horses the chief method of finding out the whereabouts of the enemy—cavalry patrols—no longer existed. Moreover, owing to the rapid and constant change of position such information as was received was valueless.

On leaving Smolensk the French had a choice of routes; it would be supposed that after remaining there for four days, they might have been aware of the advance of the enemy, and have combined for an effective attack; but it was a disorganised mob, and rushed off in utter disorder, without plan or purpose, on the least safe road of all: that to Krasnoé and Orcha, thus retracing their steps in coming. Believing that the enemy lay behind them and not in front, they spread over such wide distances, that often there was a twenty-four hours' march between the various corps. Napoleon led the flight followed by kings and dukes. The Russian army, thinking that Napoleon would keep to the right of the Dnieper—the only rational course to pursue—did the same, and came out on the Krasnoé road. Thus—as in blind-man's-buff—the French found themselves confronting the Russian van. After a moment of panic caused by this unexpected sight, they stopped; but almost immediately turned and continued their mad flight, abandoning all stragglers and their wounded. In this way, for three days in succession, the divisions of the viceroy, of Davoust and of Ney, each in turn came in front of the Russian troops. Neither thought of waiting for the others, but each, simply shedding their baggage, their artillery, and half their men, thought solely of escaping from the Russians by sneaking round their right flank under cover of the night.

Ney, who had lingered to carry out the useless task of blowing up the walls of Smolensk, like a child who beats the floor that he has fallen on, was the last to come up. He rejoined Napoleon at Orcha with 1,000 men—all that were left of 10,000 under his command, whom he had left strewn all along the road with his guns and waggons, having been obliged to force his way during the night through the forest to reach the Dnieper. From Orcha to Vilna, it was the same game of flight and pursuit.

The shores of the Bérésina were the scene of an appalling disaster: numbers of men were drowned, numbers more surrendered, while those who had the luck to get over started once more across country on their desperate march. As to the great captain their leader, he wrapped himself in furs, got into a sleigh and was off—leaving his companions in misfortune behind him. Some followed his example, while some allowed themselves to be captured, or went to swell the long score of dead.

CHAPTER CVIII

As we consider how, all through this campaign, the French were rushing to their ruin, never bringing their operations in detail or the progress of their march within the scope of any strategic scheme, it is hard to understand how, in describing this retreat, historians can again bring out their theory of the impulsion of masses by a single will. But they have, in fact, written volumes to elucidate the remarkable arrangements made by Napoleon for the guidance of his troops, and to celebrate the military skill displayed by his marshals. They put forward the most specious arguments to explain why he selected as his line of retreat, the road he had already devastated on his march to

Moscow, instead of taking advantage of those which led through districts still amply stocked with food. They praise his heroism at the moment when he was preparing to give battle at Krasnoé, and to lead the troops in person, saying to his suite: " I have played the emperor long enough; it is time now to play the general!"—and in spite of such generous words he turned to fly, leaving his army to its miserable fate. They depict the bravery of his marshals—of Ney, in particular, which consisted in struggling through a forest, spending a night on the banks of the Dnieper, and arriving at Orcha without his flags or his artillery, after losing nine-tenths of his men. Finally, they describe with complacent satisfaction every detail of the emperor's departure, leaving the great and really heroic army behind him.

This action, which in homely language would be plainly designated as cowardly, and held up to children as contemptible, our historians speak of as magnificent, and bearing the hallmark of genius. And when they have come to an end of their arguments to justify an action diametrically opposed to all that human nature can accept as right and good, they gravely invoke the phantom Greatness, as if that could exclude our notions of right and wrong. If we could see things as they see them, there could be no wrong for the great; they could be blamed for no form of atrocity. "It is Great!" cry the historians, and that is enough. Right and wrong have no existence for them; there is no standard but what is great and what is not great; and what is great is to them the necessary attribute of certain men on whom they confer the title of Hero!

As to Napoleon, wrapped in furs, and flying as fast as horses can carry him from the men he brought with him, and whose fate is now irrevocably sealed, he, too, can say to himself with calm conviction that "it is great!" And among all those who for fifty years spoke of him as "Napoleon the Great," not one perceived that to admit that "greatness" is something outside the eternal laws of right and wrong is equivalent to recognising its meanness and moral littleness. As we see things, the standard of right and wrong given by Christ must apply to every human action; there can be no greatness where there is no singleness of heart, no kindliness, and no truth.

CHAPTER CIX

WHAT Russian of us all, as he reads the accounts of the end of the campaign of 1812, is not conscious of a vague but painful impulse of vexation? Does he not ask himself how it was that the Russian army, after fighting at Borodino—where it was inferior in numbers to that of the French—and after surrounding the enemy on three sides, could not cut off their retreat and make them all prisoners; are the French so much our superiors that, having surrounded them by greater numbers, we were unable to beat them? How could this have happened? History —or what calls itself History—tells us that we must look for an explanation to Koutouzow, Tormassow, and others, who failed to take certain essential steps at the right moment. But, if so, why were they not tried and punished? Even if we accuse them of such fatal oversight, it is difficult to understand, as we remember the position of the Russian troops at Krasnoé and the Bérésina, how they could fail to seize the whole French army—marshals, kings, emperor and all, if this were indeed, as we are told, what the highest authorities aimed at. Any explanation of such a phenomenon by suggesting hindrances on Koutouzow's part is perfectly inadmissible, because, as we all know now, in spite of his firm determination not to act on the offensive, he found it impossible to oppose the desire of his troops, both at Viazma and at Taroutino. If it were true that the Russian authorities intended to cut off the retreat of the French army and capture it as one man, so that their purpose was in fact foiled by repeated checks, it is obvious that the French may pride themselves on the close of the campaign as a series of victories, and that Russian writers are wrong in speaking of it as a triumphal march for the national army; since, if they are logical, in spite of their poetical and patriotic enthusiasm, they must in that case admit that the French retreat from Moscow was a course of successes for Napoleon and of defeats for Koutouzow.

However, national vanity apart, this inference contains a self-evident contradiction; these "victories" led to the destruction of the foe, while the Russian "defeats" culminated in the redemption of the empire. The fallacy lies in the circumstance that historians have been content to study events in the letters of emperors and marshals, and in official reports and narratives, and have falsely concluded that there was, in fact, a plan for cutting off Napoleon's retreat and making vast numbers of prisoners. But such a plan never was made—never could have been made, for there was no reason for it. Moreover, it would have been impossible to execute, for Napoleon's army fled with a precipitancy that was almost infatuation, thus hurrying of its own accord to the desired end. It would have been ridiculous to elaborate complicated manœuvres against scattered fugitives, most of whom died on the road; and the seizure even of the emperor and the generals would only have hampered the pursuers in their movements.

The idea of cutting off Napoleon's retreat would have been alike foolish and impracticable, for experience teaches us that the movement of a column during the course of a battle five versts off, never precisely coincides at any given spot with the plan laid down for it. It was all very well to propose for a meeting at a fixed place and hour between Tchitchagow, Koutouzow, and Wittgenstein—it was really improbable and impossible; Koutouzow himself was conscious of this when, on receiving the plan forwarded to him from St. Petersburg, he said that schemes laid at a distance never led to the results that were expected of them. The expression "cut off a retreat" is, in itself, simply nonsense; you may cut off a slice of bread, but you cannot cut off an army. Say or do what you will, an army cannot be cut off, or even barred on its way; there is always some way of getting round, and theoretical tacticians may learn from Krasnoé and the Bérésina how darkness favours unexpected moves. Prisoners, again, are not taken unless they mean to be; like the swallow that can never be caught unless it perches on your hand, or like the Germans who surrender in due form by all the rules of strategy and tactics. The French probably thought there was not much to be gained on either side, for whether fugitives or prisoners they had no prospect before them but death from cold and starvation.

The Russian army had lost 50,000 men in sick and stragglers, on the march from Taroutino to Krasnoé, without fighting a single battle. During this period thay lacked provisions, shoes, and clothing; for months they slept on the snow under fifteen degrees of frost; [1] the daylight lasted only seven or eight hours, the nights seemed endless; discipline was at an end, since each man was constantly engaged in a mortal struggle against death and suffering. And so historians tell us that Miloradovitch ought to have executed a flank movement on one side, while

[1] Reaumur—about −1° Fahrenheit.

Tormassow did the same on the other, and that then Tchitcha-gow would have advanced—through snow above his men's knees!—to demolish the enemy. Why do they not rather tell us that these men, dying of cold and hunger, did all that was possible or necessary for the glory of their nation? It was no fault of theirs if meanwhile some other Russians, comfortably ensconced in warm studies, chose to amuse themselves by concocting impracticable schemes. The strange and inconceivable discrepancies between the events as they happened and the official records arise from the mania among historians for describing the sublime demeanour or pungent sayings of certain leaders instead of giving a prosiac tale of facts. Miloradovitch's fine speeches, the rewards heaped on this or that general for his brilliant strategical combinations, are all they care about; the 50,000 men strewed in the hospitals and country churchyards escape their notice as being unworthy of their learned research. But in truth, is it not simply by setting aside reports and plans of battle, by studying with a curious eye the molecular movement of the millions of individuals who are the immediate agents that we find a solution as clear as daylight of questions which have hitherto appeared insoluble?

BOOK SIXTEEN

CHAPTER CX

When a man sees the death of an animal, however humble, an involuntary horror creeps over him, for he beholds the destruction of a particle of that animal nature by which he too lives; but when the death is that of a fellow-creature whom he loves, besides his terror at the sight of this destruction, he undergoes an internal rending and wounding of the soul. And this wound may kill, or, like any other wound, it may heal; but it is always sensitive and shrinks from the tenderest touch.

Princess Maria and Natacha both went through this anguish when Prince Andrew died. Their spirits had bowed, crushed under the sinister cloud of death that had so long hung over their head, and now they dared not look life in the face; they could only find such courage as might enable them to protect that still bleeding wound against the painful friction from outside. The smallest thing—the rattle of wheels in the street, the announcement that dinner was ready, the maid's inquiry as to what dress they would wear, or, worse still, a commonplace remark, a feeble expression of interest—irritated them, for it interrupted them in their contemplation of that mysterious Beyond of which for an instant they had caught a glimpse. It jarred on the deep peace which was so needful to their souls, and in which they could hearken to the chants of the solemn and awful choir which had left its echoes in their imagination. They spoke little to each other, but it was a real consolation to them to be together; they avoided all allusion to the future, to their sorrow, to the dead; for speaking even was a violation of the grandeur and sanctity of the mystery they had witnessed. This reserve, it is true, only added keenness to their grief; but grief, like joy, cannot be eternal or unqualified.

Princess Maria was the first to look beyond the circle of woe in which, for nearly a fortnight, she had lived and moved. Her responsible and independent position, and her duties as guardian to her little nephew, rendered it necessary. A letter came which must be answered; Nicholas' room was damp and he had caught cold; Alpatitch arrived from Yaroslaw with accounts to be looked into, and so forth. He advised her to return to Moscow and settle in the house there, which had not been injured, and only needed some trifling repairs, and this had to be considered and discussed. Daily life must run its course; nothing can stop that. Painful as it was to Princess Maria to tear herself from her contemplative solitude and to leave Natacha alone, a prey to her regrets, the duties of her position claimed her. She did violence to her feelings and returned to active life; looked through the accounts with Alpatitch, held council with Dessalles over the child, and began her arrangements for returning to Moscow.

Natacha, now utterly lonely, held aloof from Maria, as soon as she had decided to go home; the princess proposed that Natacha should accompany her, and her father and mother eagerly agreed; for seeing their daughter grow perceptibly weaker, they hoped that change of air and the advice of the Moscow doctors might improve her health.

"I will go nowhere," replied Natacha, "I ask only one thing and that is to be left in peace!" and she went quickly out of the room, hardly able to restrain her tears of anger rather then of pain.

She was hurt by Princess Maria's desertion, and spent most of her time alone in her room, sitting in a corner of the sofa and idly playing with anything that fell under her hand, while her eyes were fixed on vacancy and saw nothing. This solitude wearied her, wore her out, but she could do nothing else. When anyone entered the room she started up, changed her position and the expression of her face; snatched up a book or a piece of work, and waited with marked impatience till she was left to herself again. She felt as though she were constantly on the very verge of discovering the secret of the awful problem on which all the powers of her soul were concentrated.

One day, at the end of December, she was half lying, as usual, in the corner of the sofa, mechanically puckering the ends of her sash. She was pale and thin now; her hair was loosely knotted up at the top of her head, and she wore a black stuff gown. Her eyes were fixed on the door as though on the spot where he had vanished. That unknown shore of life of which, till lately, she had never thought, that shore which had always seemed so far away and so doubtful, was surely nearer to her; it was visible, almost within reach, and the ground where she still stood was a desert, barren, vacant, full only of grief and tears. Looking for him where she knew that he must be she could not picture him otherwise than as she had seen him during those last few weeks: she saw his face, heard his voice, repeated his words, and added others which she could fancy she had said. There he is! Leaning back in his deep chair, in his wrapper of fur-lined velvet, his head resting in his slender transparent hand; his chest sunk, his shoulders pushed up, his lips pinched, his eyes strangely bright, while faint wrinkles come and go on his pale forehead. One of his knees is trembling she can see: he is struggling with some intense pain. "What pain is it? What can he be feeling?" she wonders. He had noticed her fixed gaze; he looks at her and says without a smile: "To be tied for life to a man always in pain is a horrible fate; eternal torment—" And he seems to try to read her heart. Then she replies, as she always used to reply: "It will not go on for ever; you will get better—" His stern scrutiny is full of reproachful meaning. "What I said," thought Natacha to herself, "was, that it would be dreadful if he were always to suffer thus, and he gave a wrong meaning to my words: I said it for him, and he thought I meant it for myself—for he longed to live then and dreaded death. I spoke without thinking, or else I should have told him that I should have been happy to watch him always suffering, always dying, rather than feel as I do now!—and now it is too late to set it right—he can never know now!"

Then fancy repeated the scene from the beginning, and now she answered differently: "Yes, horrible for you, but not for me; for you know you are everything to me—even to suffer with you is joy to me!" Then she felt the pressure of his hand, she heard herself pouring out words of tenderness and devotion which she had never uttered then, but that she could speak now: "I love you, I love you!" she repeated, wringing her hands, and her pain became even less bitter as her eyes filled with tears. Suddenly she asked herself in terror, to whom she was speaking. "Who was he? Where is he?" Everything became confused; a fearful apprehension checked her effusiveness, she fell again into a reverie—at last, surely at last, the mystery would be solved.

But at the very moment when it seemed within her grasp, Douniacha, the maid, hurried in with a scared face, and without thinking of Natacha's indignation at the intrusion, exclaimed:

"Come, miss, come quickly, something dreadful has happened! . . . Peter Illitch—a letter! . . ." and she burst into sobs.

CHAPTER CXI

NATACHA'S aversion for all society was most marked towards the members of her own family. Her father, her mother, and Sonia, were so familiar and so near to her, that all they said had a false ring in the ideal world in which she lived. To them she was not merely indifferent, but repellent. She listened to Dcuniacha's words without understanding them. "What dreadful thing? What can have happened to them?—their lives go on day after day in easy contentment!"

When she went into the drawing-room, she saw her father coming out of the countess's bedroom. His face was streaming with tears, and as he saw his daughter, with a gesture of utter despair, he broke down into heart-breaking sobs, that distorted his kind, placid face.

"Pétia—Pétia! Go to her, she wants you." Crying like a child, and hardly able to drag his trembling legs, he dropped into a chair and hid his face in his hands.

Natacha felt as though in that instant an electric shock flashed through her from head to foot, and sent an acute pain to her heart; something seemed to crack within it, and she thought she was dying, but this agony was immediately followed by a sense of deliverance. The torpor that had weighed upon her was gone. The sight of her father, her mother's wild cries of bereavement, made her forget her own woes; she hastened towards her father, but he signed to her with a feeble effort to go to the countess's room. Princess Maria had just come to the door, and was standing there pale and quivering. She seized Natacha by the hand and tried to say something, but Natacha neither saw nor heard; she pushed her aside and flew to her mother's side. There she stopped an instant, as if struggling with herself. The countess, lying back in an arm-chair, was twitching hysterically every muscle and beating her head against the wall; Sonia and the maids were holding her hands firmly clasped.

"Natacha!" cried the countess, "it is not true. It is false— Natacha!" And she pushed away the others. "Tell me that it is not true. Killed! Ha, ha, ha. It's not true!"

Natacha knelt down on a footstool and leaned over her mother; then, raising the drooping head, she pressed her cheek closely against her mother's face.

"Mamma, darling—I am here, I am with you," she

murmured again and again, and throwing her arms round her, she held her firmly but lovingly, putting pillows to support her, making her swallow a little water, and unfastening her dress.

"I am here—mamma, I am here," she went on, kissing her hair, her face, and her hands, though blinded by the torrent of her own tears, which streamed down her cheeks.

The countess clasped her daughter's hand, closed her eyes, and for a moment was calmer. Suddenly raising herself with an effort, she looked about her with haggard eyes, and seeing Natacha, took her head in both hands, clenching them with all her might; then, while she held so tightly as to hurt her, she stared in her face with a look of wild bewilderment.

"Natacha, you love me?" she whispered in a confidential tone. "You will not deceive me, you will tell me the truth?"

Natacha's eyes, dim with tears, seemed to be craving forgiveness.

"Darling mother!" she said, putting forth all her filial feeling to console her mother in some degree for her terrible misfortune. But the countess was unable to realise the truth, still refused to believe that she could survive when her adored son had been killed in the flower of his youth, and her struggles to escape the dreadful reality drove her into the phantasy of delirium.

Natacha could never have told how they got through that first night and the following day. She never slept or quitted her mother for an instant. Her faithful and patient devotion made no attempt at comfort or explanation, but wrapped the unhappy mother in an emanation of tenderness that was like a summons back to life again. The third night, while she had taken advantage of an interval when her mother was dozing to close her eyes, with her head resting on the arm of the chair, she was roused by the bed creaking, and started awake to see the countess sitting bolt upright, and saying in an undertone:

"How happy I am to see you back. You are tired? Will you have some tea?"

Natacha went to the bedside.

"How tall and handsome, Maria, you've grown!" the countess went on, taking her daughter's hand.

"Mamma—what are you saying?"

"Natacha! He is dead, he is dead! I shall never see him again!" And falling on Natacha's neck she burst into tears for the first time.

CHAPTER CXII

It was in vain that Sonia and the count tried to take Natacha's place. She was the only person who could keep her mother from sinking into a state of despair verging on insanity. For three weeks she never left her, sleeping in the arm-chair by the bedside; she gave her food and drink, and was always ready to soothe her with gentle and loving words.

This poor soul's wound could not heal. Pétia's death had bereft his mother of the dearest part of her life. A month later the woman who at the time of her son's death carried the burden of her fifty years lightly and vigorously, crept out of her room old and broken, half-dead, and indifferent to everything in life. The blow that had stricken her so heavily had, on the contrary, roused Natacha from her lethargy: Natacha had thought that life was at an end for her, till this output of affection for her mother had shown her that the real essence of her being, her power of loving, was still alive within her; and love once revived in her soul she too came back to life.

The last days of Prince Andrew's life had closely knit Natacha and Maria, and now this new disaster bound them still more together. Princess Maria postponed her departure, and devoted herself to nursing Natacha, whose strength had been too severely tried in her mother's sick-room, and who had now fallen ill in her turn. Seeing one day that she was shivering severely, Princess Maria carried her off into her own room, made her lie on the bed, drew down the blinds, and was about to leave the room when Natacha called her back:

"I am not sleepy, Maria; stay with me."

"But you are very tired; try to sleep."

"No, no. Why did you bring me away? She will ask for me."

"No, my pet; on the contrary, she is much better to-day."

Natacha, lying on the bed, was examining Maria's face in the dim light: "Is she like him?" she thought. "Yes and no. There is something odd, peculiar to herself about her; but she loves me I am sure, and her heart is goodness itself. But what does she think—what is her opinion of me?"

"Macha," she said timidly, drawing her towards her. "Do not think me quite bad—no, my little soul, I love you dearly, indeed I do; let us be friends, real, perfect friends." And she covered her face and hands with kisses. Princess Maria, though surprised and embarrassed, responded warmly to this effusiveness.

From that day forth they had for each other that lofty and passionate friendship which is only found between women. They would kiss apropos of nothing at all, and call each other by loving names, and spent the chief part of their day together. If one went out or away the other was ill at ease, and was not happy till they were together again. Each was more at peace with herself when they were together than when they were apart; it was a bond stronger than friendship, and so close that life without each other seemed unendurable. Sometimes they would sit together in silence for hours, or else, sharing the same room, would chatter all night through till daylight. Their remotest memories were their favourite theme. Princess Maria would tell long stories of her childhood, of her early dreams, and speak of her father and mother; Natacha, who had hitherto shut her eyes with proud indifference to this life of devotion and submission, of poetical and Christian self-sacrifice which was beyond her comprehension, now that she cared so tenderly for her friend, fell sympathetically in love with her past life, and began at last to understand the secrets of her experience which had so long been a sealed book to her. She, it is true, never thought of practising in her own person this absolute self-negation; she was accustomed to seek enjoyment in other ways; but she appreciated the virtue none the less for not possessing it.

As to Princess Maria, as she listened to Natacha's recollections of her childhood she caught a glimpse of horizons she had never known, of faith in life and in the joy of mere living. Of *him* they spoke but rarely so as not to desecrate—for that was their feeling—the loftiness of their associations; but this determined silence by degrees, in spite of themselves, was doing the work of oblivion.

Natacha had become quite pallid, and she was so weak that it was a sort of pleasure to her when she was asked about her health: but suddenly a revulsion came over her, and a dread, not of death but of feebleness, and of losing her good looks. Looking at herself in the glass she was amazed to see how much she had altered as she sadly studied her features: "It could not be otherwise!" said she to herself; and yet it frightened her and filled her with regret. One day having walked upstairs rather quickly, she was out of breath; she immediately made an excuse to go down and come up again; she wanted to try and measure her strength.   Another day, when she called Douniacha, she found her voice was weak.   Though she could hear the girl coming she called again, as loud as she could, taking a deep breath, as she used in singing, and listened to the ring of her own voice.   Though she did not suspect it, and indeed would not have thought it possible, beneath the thick mould under which she believed that her soul was buried, the tender sprouts of a new spring-time were already stirring, soon to pierce the soil and cover with fresh verdure the grief that had overwhelmed her.   The wound was healing from inside.

Princess Maria started for Moscow at the end of January, taking with her Natacha, for the count insisted on her having medical advice.

CHAPTER CXIII

AFTER the collision between the two armies at Viazma—where Koutouzow had found it impossible to restrain the eagerness of his troops to overthrow the enemy and interrupt his retreat —the flight of the French, and the pursuit by the Russian continued without any more pitched battles.   The flight of the French was, indeed, so headlong that the Russian army could not keep up with them; the artillery-horses dropped exhausted on the road, and the Russian soldiers themselves, worn out by this constant pace of forty versts a day, could not go any faster.

Some idea may be formed of the deplorable state of the national army from the following facts: ever since Taroutino it had lost in killed and wounded no more than 5000 men, of whom hardly a hundred had been taken prisoners; and when it reached Krasnoé it was reduced to about half of the effective force of 100,000 men which had started from Taroutino.   The swiftness of the march had, therefore, a no less fatal effect on the Russians than their flight had on the French; with the difference, however, that they were advancing of their own free will, not crushed like the enemy, by the utter dejection at the prospect of destruction; and that stragglers were hospitably received by their fellow-countrymen, while the French who failed to keep up fell into the hands of their foes.

Koutouzow devoted all his energies not to the hindrance of the French retreat, but to promoting it, on the contrary, and to mitigating the advance of the Russian troops.   After the fatigue and losses they had suffered, yet another reason impelled him to moderate their ardour: the only hope of forcing the French onward in their disorderly course was by keeping at some distance in the rear. Koutouzow knew, as every Russian soldier knew, that the invaders were conquered beyond retrieval by the sheer force of circumstances. But his generals, and especially the foreign ones, were still burning with a desire for personal distinction—to capture a duke or a king—and were bent on hitting on a favourable moment for forcing a pitched battle, though nothing could be more absurd. Hence they were consistently besieging him with schemes which could only result in more harassing marches, and increased fatigue for the men; while Koutouzow's sole purpose, steadfastly pursued from Moscow to Vilna, was to spare the soldiers as much as possible in the miseries of this campaign. But, in spite of his utmost efforts, he was impotent to set a check on the ambitions that were seething all round him, and which came to a head when, quite unexpectedly, the Russian army fell upon the retreating foe.

This was what happened at Krasnoé, where, instead of a fray with a single French column, they came upon Napoleon and 16,000 men. It was impossible for Koutouzow to save his troops from a terrible but useless conflict; the slaughter of the undisciplined and laggard French by the exhausted Russians lasted for three days. Toll wrote out an order of disposition of the troops, and as usual nothing was done in accordance with it. Prince Eugene of Würtemberg shot down flying Frenchmen from the top of a hill and called for reinforcements which never came. The French creeping round the Russians at night, scattering, hiding in the woods, made their way forward each man as best he could. Miloradovitch, who claimed to know nothing about the economic part of his troops, the *chevalier sans peur et sans reproche* as he liked to call himself, was constantly sending messengers to the French to demand their surrender, and acted contrary to the orders he received. "I give you this column, my lads," he would say, riding up to his troops and pointing at the French. And his cavalry after flogging and spurring their weary horses into a trot would ride up to the "gift"—a mob of frost-bitten, starved Frenchmen— and the "gift" would throw down their arms and surrender as they had for a long time been longing to do. Numbers of prisoners were taken, with some cannon, and a stick which was at once dubbed "a marshal's baton." Everyone might believe that he had distinguished himself. After the engagement, however, there was a great hubbub. Everyone blamed everyone else for not having captured Napoleon, or at least one of his marshals. These men, blinded by their passions, were, after all, no more than the instruments of inexorable necessity, though they flattered themselves that they were heroes, and were firmly persuaded that they had behaved with consummate nobility and distinction. Koutouzow was the special object of their animosity; they accused him of having from the first prevented their beating Napoleon, of thinking solely of his interests, of having checked the march of the army at Krasnoé, only because he lost his head on hearing of his presence there, of collusion with him, even of having sold himself to the French emperor, and much besides.

Nor did his contemporaries only judge him thus, under the immediate influence of violent feeling; history and posterity also, while giving to Napoleon the surname "Great," have vilified Koutouzow. Foreigners have held him up as a cunning old man, a corrupt and senile courtier; Russians have described him as a nondescript creature, a sort of puppet, useful in his day, thanks to his thoroughly Russian name.

CHAPTER CXIV

IN 1812 and 1813 he was loudly abused. The emperor was dissatisfied with him, and in a certain history, written not long since, under high authorisation, Koutouzow is spoken of as an intriguing courtier and a knave, quaking at the mere name of Napoleon, and capable of blundering to such an extent as to prevent the actions at Krasnoé and the Bérésina from being splendid victories. Such is the fate of those who are not ticketed "great men"; such is the fate of those isolated individuals who divine the designs of Providence, and submit to its decrees—the mob must punish them for having understood those supreme laws by which the affairs of this world are governed, pursing them with envy and obloquy.

It is a strange and terrible fact; but Napoleon, that infinitesimal tool in history, who at no time, not even in exile, showed any manly dignity, is the subject of endless enthusiasm and wonder to the Russians themselves; he is "great" even in their eyes.

But compare him with Koutouzow, who, in 1812, from first to last, from Borodino to Vilna, was never once false to himself in deed or speech, who is an unprecedented instance of self-effacement, who could foresee with such amazing keenness the bearing of immediate events and circumstances on those of the future. And they represent Koutouzow as a colourless being, worthy at most of pity, speaking of him generally with an ill-disguised feeling of shame! But where, let us ask, is an historical personage to be studied, who has aimed more perseveringly at a single end, or attained it more completely, and in a way more absolutely in accordance with the will of his whole nation?

He never talked of "the forty centuries looking down on his soldiers from the height of the Pyramids," of the sacrifice he had made to his country, of his "schemes or his objects!" Still less did he talk of himself. He played no part; on the surface he was a plain-spoken, simple man, saying nothing of any mark, writing to his daughters, and Madame de Staël, reading novels, liking the company of pretty women, joking with his generals, officers, and men, and never contradicting opinions that were opposed to his own. When Count Rostopchine accused him in the most personal terms for having abandoned Moscow, and reminded him that he had promised not to give it up without a struggle, Koutouzow replied:

"That was what I did." But Moscow was, in fact, already abandoned!

When Araktchéïew came to tell him, from the czar, that Yermolow must be appointed to the command of the artillery, Koutouzow said:

"That is what I have just been saying," though a moment before he had said the very contrary.

What did he care—he, who alone of all this helpless crowd, appreciated the vast issues of the event—whether he or Count Rostopchine were held responsible for the misfortunes of the capital? And above all, of what moment to him was the appointment of this or that colonel of artillery?

In these circumstances, as in all others, the old man who, through a long life, had learnt by experience that words are no true motive power of human deeds, often said things which had no sense—the first that came into his head. And yet this man, who attached so little importance to words, never uttered one throughout his public career which did not conduce to the end he had in view.

Sometimes, however, involuntarily, and notwithstanding his melancholy conviction that he should not be understood, he did give distinct expression to his opinions, and on the most dissimilar occasions. For instance, did he not maintain, whenever he spoke of the battle of Borodino, which was the first cause of differences between himself and his fellow-officers, that it had been a victory for the Russians? He said it, he wrote it, and he repeated it to his dying day. Did he not assert that the loss of Moscow was not the loss of Russia? In his reply to Lauriston, did he not declare that peace was impossible so long as it was in opposition to the desire of the nation? Did not he, singly and alone, all through the retreat, regard manœuvring as absurd, feeling certain that everything would come to a natural conclusion even better than we could hope for: that what we had to do was to make a "golden bridge" (an easy retreat) for the retiring foe: that the engagements at Taroutino, Viazma, and Krasnoé were unnecessary: that as many men as possible must be saved to reach the frontier, and that he would not sacrifice one Russian for ten Frenchmen?

He, who has been described to posterity as a courtier who could lie to Araktchéïew to gratify the czar, was the only man who dared at Vilna to say in plain terms that to prosecute the war beyond the frontier was aimless and exhausting, thus incurring the imperial displeasure. But what need is there to affirm that he saw the critical importance of the situation: his actions are ample proof: he began by concentrating all the strength of Russia before coming to blows with the enemy; he beat him, and finally drove him out of the country, mitigating, as far as in him lay, the sufferings of the army and of the population. He, whose motto was always: "Time and Patience"—he, the sworn foe of vigorous effort—he it was who fought the battle of Borodino with unwonted solemnity of preparation, and who afterwards persisted, in contradiction to the opinion of other generals, and in spite of the forced retreat of his victorious army, in declaring that it was a Russian victory, and in denying the need for fighting any more; who refused to recommence the war, or to set foot outside the frontiers of the empire.

How was it that this veteran could so surely guess, in opposition to everyone else, what the upshot and issue of events must be from the Russian point of view? His marvellous intuition had its source in the patriotic feeling which thrilled in his soul with intense purity and passion. This the people understood;

this it was which led them to demand his appointment, in spite of the czar, as the representative leader of a national war. Called by popular acclamation to this high office, he exerted his utmost powers as commander-in-chief not to hurry men to death, but to spare them, and save them for their country.

This simple and unpretentious figure—"great" in the true sense of the word—could not be cast in the false mould of the European Hero, the so-called "Potentate of the nations," as history has sketched him! There can be no great men for lackeys, since lackeys insist on measuring all men by their own standard.

CHAPTER CXV

THE 17th of November was the first day of the battle of Krasnoé. Shortly before dusk, after endless discussions and delays, caused by generals who did not reach the places where they could act with effect in proper time, and after sending aides-de-camp in every direction with orders and countermands, it became evident that the enemy were retiring, and that a battle was out of the question.

The day was fine and cold. Koutouzow, with a numerous suite, among whom malcontents were in a majority, and riding his stout little white horse, went to Dobroïé, whither the head-quarters had been moved by his orders. All along the road the French prisoners taken in the course of the day—about 7,000—were huddled round camp fires, and as they approached Dobroïé, a crowd of prisoners in ragged clothing were talking vehemently over some French guns that had been unharnessed and seized. As the commander-in-chief came near, the men were silent, and every eye was fixed on him, while one of the generals explained to him where these guns and men had been captured. His face was careworn, and he was hardly listening to the account that was being given to him, while he looked at the most wretched of the men. Most of the French had almost lost the very semblance of humanity; their noses and cheeks were frost-bitten, their eyes bloodshot, swollen, and rheumy. Two of them, one with his face terribly wounded, were devouring some raw meat. There was something fearfully and terribly bestial in the scowl which these hapless wretches cast at the new-comers. Koutouzow, after watching them for a few minutes, shook his head with a melancholy pity. A little further on he came upon a Russian soldier, who was speaking to a Frenchman with a kindly smile: again he shook his head, and his expression did not change.

"What were you saying?" he asked a general, who was trying to attract his notice to a group of French flags that were piled in front of the Préobrajenski Regiment. "Ah! some flags!" he added; and rousing himself with an effort from the subject of his meditations, he looked vaguely about him, and then closed his eyes with a deep sigh. One of his staff signed to the soldier who was holding up the flags to bring them forward, and place them round about the commander-in-chief. For a moment Koutouzow said nothing; then yielding, sorely against the grain, to the duties required of him, he raised his head, looked steadily at the officers standing near him, and said slowly, in the midst of perfect silence, these few words:

"I thank you all for your faithful and laborious service. Victory is on our side, and Russia will never forget us. Glory will be yours in ages to come!" He paused; then, seeing a private with a French eagle, which he was holding low in salute before the Préobrajenski standard, he went on:

"Lower, lower still! He must bow his head. Yes, that is right! Now, then, hurrah! my children!" and he turned to the men.

"Hurrah!" roared thousands of voices. While they were still shouting, Koutouzow, bending over his horse's neck, bowed his head, and a gentle ironical smile dawned on his face.

"That is the way of it, my children," said he, when all was silent once more, and officers and men crowded round to hear what he was about to say. The tone of his voice, the expression of his face were completely changed; he was no longer the commander-in-chief, but simply a veteran soldier addressing his comrades in arms.

"That is the way of it, my children. I know how hard it is, but what is to be done? Have patience; it will not last much longer. We will see our visitors safe off, and then we will rest. The czar will not forget your services. It is very hard I know, but at any rate you are at home, remember—while they—" and he pointed to the prisoners, "see what they are reduced to. Their misery is beyond that of the most abject beggar. When they were strong we did not spare them, but now we may have some pity. They are men like ourselves, are they not, my children?"

He could read the sympathy roused by his speech in the steady and respectful gaze of the men. His face brightened with a benevolent smile on his lips and in his eyes; he looked down, however, and added: "But, after all, who asked them to come? They have no more than they deserve, perhaps."

He touched his horse with his whip, and uttering a tremendous oath, rode away, followed by the hurrahs and laughter of the men, who at once broke up their ranks.

Not all his words, no doubt, had reached the understanding of the troops, and no one could have repeated them accurately; but their solemnity to begin with, and the frank, kindly simplicity that had stamped them at the conclusion, went straight to the men's hearts. Each man, indeed, felt, like his chief, not only the justice of his cause, and the triumph of right, but that honest compassion for the enemy which had found expression in the old man's sound oath; the soldiers' hearty shouts were their response, and they did not cease for some time. One of the aides-de-camp having asked the marshal whether he would not now get into his carriage, Koutouzow apparently still labouring under his emotions, suddenly flushed.

CHAPTER CXVI

TWILIGHT had set in on the 20th of November, the last day of the fighting at Krasnoé, when the troops reached their halting-place for the night. The weather was still calm, there was a hard frost, and though a few flakes of snow fell at intervals, a starlit, purple sky bent over the scene.

The infantry regiment, which had started from Taroutino 3,000 strong, was the first to arrive at the village, now numbering 900. The quartermasters found that every hut was occupied by the sick and dead, by staff-officers or cavalry men. Only one was vacant for the use of the colonel of the regiment, who at once proceeded thither, while the men marched through the village, and piled their arms in front of the farthest houses.

The regiment, like a many-armed polyp, at once set to work to establish itself, and find food. A party of soldiers, plunging through snow up to their knees, made their way to a birch-copse to the right of the road, and in a few minutes it was ringing with their songs and the blows of the axes as they lopped the branches. Another party was busy round the wagons, taking out the cooking-pots, biscuit, and forage for the horses, who were already picketed; others again had dispersed through the village to clear out the lodgings for the officers of the staff, carry off the dead bodies of the French, and secure the thatch off the roofs, with boards and dead brushwood from the hedges, to throw up some form of shelter.

A dozen or so of men were in the act of uprooting a hedge which enclosed a shed off which the roof had already been torn. "Now, then, all at once—push!" cried several; and the hedge, laden with snow, rocked under their efforts, cracking in the darkness with the crisp ring of frozen wood. The stakes yielded, and at last the hedge half gave way, dragging the soldiers down in its fall. The men roared with laughter.

"Hold on there, you two. . . ."

"Here, where is the crowbar?"

"What the deuce are you doing?"

"Now, boys, once more. In time."

They were all silent, and a deep, rich bass set up a song; at the end of the third beat, as the last note died away, all the soldiers joined in with a tuneful shout: "All together, boys! over she goes!" But still the fence held good, and they stood panting for breath.

"Here, you fellows of the 6th, come here, lend a hand; we will do you a turn some day."

Some men of the 6th company who were coming through the village answered to the call, and a few minutes later the tall hedge was borne off in triumph, its tangled and wattled branches bruising the breathless men's shoulders under their weight.

"Look out there! You are stumbling, blockhead!"

"What are you at?" cried a non-commissioned officer in imperious tones, rushing at the party. "The general is in that isba. I will teach you—idiots that you are!" he went on, giving a violent cuff to the first soldier that came under his hand. "Silence there! Not so much row!"

The soldiers were silent, though the one who had been hit growled between his teeth as he saw the sergeant retiring.

"By G——, what a blow! My face is bleeding!"

"And you don't like it? Fancy that!" said a mocking voice. Then walking more circumspectly they went on their way; but as soon as they were beyond the village their spirits were as boisterous as ever, and they began their riotous chatter once more, interlarded with harmless swearing.

The officers, assembled in the cottage and drinking their tea, were eagerly discussing the day just passed and the plans for the morrow; a flank march to the left was projected, to cut off the viceroy's communications and take him prisoner.

While the men lugged their hedge along, stumbling at every step, fires were crackling under the pots, the wood roared and blazed, the snow melted, and the black shapes of men stamping to warm their feet were to be seen moving in every direction. Though no orders had been given, knives and axes were busily at work—on one hand wood was being heaped up for the fires during the night, and tents were being pitched for the officers; on the other, supper was being cooked, guns cleaned and accoutrements brushed up. The hedge, supported by stakes, was erected on the northern side in a semi-circle to screen their fire. The bugles sounded, the roll was called, supper was eaten, and the men crowded round the blaze, some mending their shoes or smoking a pipe, while others stripped to the skin and toasted their fleas or other vermin.

CHAPTER CXVII

THE peculiarly squalid condition and hard lot of these soldiers, who lacked shoes and warm clothing, slept under the stars, and marched through deep snow with a temperature at 18 degrees below freezing, might have given reasonable ground for expecting to see them in the most wretched plight. On the contrary, never, even under the happiest circumstances, had the army been in such good spirits or so well affected. The reason was that every day it was able to shake off the weak or dejected; thus those that were left were the pick of the troops, the strongest in body and in mind.

A number of men of the 8th company had collected under shelter of their hedge. Among others two sergeant-majors had claimed a seat near this fire which burnt better than any other, saying that they had brought logs to it.

"I say, Makééf—are you lost? Have the wolves got you? Bring us some wood, slowcoach!" cried a red-haired soldier with a face scorched by the frost and eyes blinking in the smoke, but who would not stir from his place by the fire.

"Do you go, 'Crow,'" said the man addressed, turning to one of his comrades.

The red-haired man was neither sergeant nor corporal, but his powerful build gave him the right of might to order his companions about. The "Crow," a lean little fellow with a sharp nose, rose submissively but at the same moment the blaze lighted up the figure of a fine-looking young trooper who came forward bent under the weight of a pile of dry wood.

"That's good—hand them here!" The boughs were broken and heaped upon the embers; every mouth was ready to blow, the fire was fanned with the skirts of the men's greatcoats, and in a moment the flame rose, flinging up the sparks. The party crowded round and lighted their pipes, while the young trooper with his hands on his hips danced a measure to warm his frozen feet.

"Oh! little mother, the dew is cold but lovely!" he sang in an undertone.

"Look out, your soles are flying off!" cried the red-haired man, seeing one of the lad's soles hanging loose. "It is dangerous to dance too much nowadays."

The dancer stopped, pulled off the torn leather and flung it into the fire.

"That's a true word!" he said; he took a piece of dark-blue French cloth out of his cartridge-pouch and wrapped it round his foot over his shoe.

"We shall soon have new ones now," said one of the men, "and two pairs apiece perhaps. So Pétrow, the skulking lout, has stayed behind with the stragglers?"

"But I saw him I am sure," said another.

"Well, after all he is only one more. . . ."

"Nine men were missing when the 9th were called over last night."

"That is no news! And what is a man to do when his feet are frozen?"

"What is the use of thinking about it?" muttered the sergeant.

"You would like to try how it feels perhaps?" said an old soldier reproachfully to the man who had mentioned frozen feet.

"What do you take us for?" said a shrill quavering voice from the other side of the fire; it was the man they had called "Crow." "Even if we are not ill we grow thinner and thinner, and at last must die. Like me; I am done for. Send me to hospital," he went on, boldly addressing the sergeant. "I have pains in every inch of me and the fever never leaves me; I shall be the next to drop on the road!"

"Come, come!" said the sergeant coolly.

The "Crow" said no more, and the conversation again became general.

"They have caught a good lot of Frenchmen to-day, but their shoes were not worth mentioning," said a soldier to change the subject.

"The Cossacks took care of that, when they cleared out the house for the colonel and carried them all away. Would you believe it, lads, I could not bear to see them so knocked about! One of them was still alive and mumbling something to himself. And how clean they are, boys, all those men—and so white! As white as that birch-tree yonder. And there are some fine brave fellows among them, I can tell you, and noblemen too."

"What is the wonder of that? They recruit them from all classes over there."

"And yet they do not understand a word we say to them," objected the young soldier. "I asked one of them what crown he was under, and he would only stammer out his own gibberish. They are a queer people!"

"There is some bogey trick at the bottom of it, boys," said the one who had expressed his astonishment at the whiteness of French skins. "The people about Mojaïsk told me that when they carted away the dead, a month after the battle, they were still as clean and as white as paper, and didn't smell a bit."

"Because it was so cold, perhaps?" said one.

"What a blockhead's speech! How could it be the cold when it was hot weather? Besides, if it had been the cold our men would have been the same; while they told me our men were all worm-eaten and they had to cover up their faces while they moved them; but the Frenchmen were as white as a sheet of paper."

"It is the feeding does it most likely," said the sergeant; "they lived like princes."

"And the peasants thereabouts told me," the former speaker went on, "that men were sent out from ten villages, and that for twenty days they did nothing but cart away the dead; and that was not nearly all, for there were many packs of wolves. . . ."

"Ah! that was something like a battle!" said an old trooper. "The others were no good except just to worry the men. The day before yesterday we stumbled on some of them. But, bless you, they don't let you get anywhere near! Down go

their guns, and they flop on their knees crying "Pardon!"
They say that Platow took Napoleon himself twice, but even
when you have him in your hands, he turns himself into a bird
and flies away. And you can't kill him."

"Oh, Kisseleff, you're a great one for lies, now I look at you!"

"It isn't lies. It's absolute God's truth."

"If it were my luck to get him, I'd bury him straight away
and put an aspen stake through him. Think of the people
he's destroyed."

"Ah, well, we'll make an end of him sooner or later. That'll
stop his prowling," said an old soldier, yawning.

The conversation now died away, each man making his own
arrangements for the night as best he might.

"Lord! what heaps of stars! It looks as if the women had
spread their linen out over the sky!" cried the young fellow,
gazing up in admiration at the Milky Way.

"It is a good sign, children; it means a fine harvest."

Snoring was soon audible in the general silence; some turned
over to warm themselves, muttering a few words to each other.
Suddenly a peal of laughter, from another camp fire about a
hundred yards away, fell on their ear.

"What is going on over there, among the men of the 5th?
They have got company there! Look!"

A soldier rose and went to see.

"They are uncommonly jolly over there," said he, coming
back. "Two Frenchmen have come in; one is half-frozen,
but the other is as merry as a grig and singing to them."

"Oh, ho! Well, come along then, we must see the fun."

CHAPTER CXVIII

THE 5th company had bivouacked on the skirts of the wood,
and an enormous fire built up in the middle of the snow threw
its broad light on the boughs that bent under the icicles, when
late in the evening, steps were heard cracking the dry sticks
under the trees.

"Hark, boys! A bear!" said a soldier. All the men raised
their heads and listened. Two human creatures, strange
indeed to look upon, came out of the underwood into the full
glare of the blaze: two Frenchmen, who had been hiding in

the wood. They came towards the Russians, uttering unintelligible words. One, who wore an officer's shako, seemed desperately weak; he dropped rather than lay down by the fire; his companion, a short, square-set man, with his head tied up, was evidently of robuster frame. He raised his comrade's head, and pointing to his mouth said something. The soldiers gathered round him, spread a coat under the invalid, and brought both the wanderers some porridge and some brandy. The officer was Captain Ramballe, with his servant Morel. When Morel had swallowed some brandy and a large bowl of porridge, a morbid jollity came over him; he talked without stopping, while his master, who refused all food, lay in gloomy silence, staring vaguely at the Russians with bloodshot eyes. Every now and then a long, quivering groan broke from his lips. Morel, pointing to his epaulettes, tried to explain that his master was an officer, and that what he wanted was warmth. A Russian officer, coming up, dispatched a man to ask the colonel whether he would give shelter to a French officer who was perishing of cold, and the colonel sent word that he was to be taken to him at once. Ramballe was told to rise, and he tried; but he tottered at the first attempt, and would have fallen back but for a private who lifted him up, and with the help of some others carried him to the hut. Putting his arms round the neck of his nurses, and leaning his head on one of the men's shoulders like a weary child, he kept repeating in a plaintive voice: "Oh! my good, kind friends! What good fellows!"

Morel, left with the men, now took the best place; his eyes were red, inflamed and watery; he had on a woman's pelisse, and had tied a handkerchief over his cap and knotted it under his chin. The brandy had gone a little to his head, and he sat singing a French song in a husky, tremulous voice. The soldiers were holding their sides to laugh.

"Come—let me try to learn it; I shall soon catch the tune. Begin again," said a soldier, whom Morel was clasping in a fond embrace.

"*Vive Henri quatre, vive ce roi vaillant !*" sang Morel.

"*Vive Harica, Vive cerowvalla ! Sidiablaka . . .*" repeated the Russian, who had caught the air.

"Bravo! bravo!" shouted the others, with a hearty roar of laughter, and Morel laughed too as he went on: "*Qui eut le triple talent de boire, de battre, et d'être un vert galant !*"

"It sounds pretty enough. Now, then, Zaletaiew, go on."

"*Iou, iou—le triptala deboi, deba et dettra vergala!*" he sang at the top of his voice, but puckering his lips elaborately.

"That's it, that's it! That's French, sure enough! Give him some more porridge; it will take a good deal to satisfy his hunger," and Morel had soon disposed of his third bowlful.

The young soldiers smiled in sympathy, while the older men, regarding such puerilities as beneath them, remained stretched by the fire, raising themselves now and then to glance good-naturedly at Morel.

"They are men too, after all," said one of them, drawing his coat round him. "And even wormwood has roots."

"Oh! what crowds of stars!" said another. "It is a sign of frost, worse luck!"

The stars, secure from any interference in their affairs, seemed to sparkle with added brilliancy in the dark vault; now disappearing and now lighting up again, and sending a shaft of light through space they seemed to be telegraphing some glad mystery to each other.

CHAPTER CXIX

AND so the French army continued to melt away with regularly increasing rapidity, and the crossing of the Bérésina, about which so much has been written, was but an incident in its destruction, and not, in truth, the decisive episode of the campaign. The reason that so much has been said about it by the French is that all the misfortunes and disasters which they had met with, one by one, in the course of their retreat, combined their forces in one tremendous catastrophe to overwhelm them on that narrow bridge, and left ineffaceable traces on their memory. And if its fame was no less among the Russians, it was because Pfühl, at St. Petersburg—far enough from the seat of war, had devised a project by which Napoloen was to be entrapped in a complex strategical snare which he had laid for him, *ex professo*, on the shores of the Bérésina. Thus, being convinced that everything must happen in exact accordance with this scheme, it was always asserted that the passage of the Bérésina had proved fatal to the French, when, in fact, its results were less disastrous than the action of Krasnoé, as can be proved by the sum total of prisoners and guns that they left behind after that engagement.

The more precipitate the flight of the French van, the more wretched was the condition of the wrecked remains of their army, especially after the Bérésina; while, on the other hand, the more furious was the wrath of the Russian generals, who spared no one, and least of all Koutouzow. Believing that the failure of the St. Petersburg plan would be certainly attributed to him, they made no secret of their disgust, venting it in contempt and sarcasms—veiled, of course, under respectful formalities—which placed him in a position in which he could not answer the accusation. All his suite, blind to his true character, declared that any discussion was out of the question with this wrong-headed old man; that he could never attain to their breadth of view; that he would always repeat his wearisome saying: "We must make a bridge of gold for the French." When he answered, instead, that they must wait for provisions, or that the men were barefoot, these obvious replies to their learned theories were to them only fresh proof that he was an old idiot, while they, who were really skilful and intelligent, had no power to act.

This disaffection and ill-will reached their height after the junction of Koutouzow's army with that of Wittgenstein, the famous admiral and favourite hero of St. Petersburg. Once only, after the Bérésina, did Koutouzow lose his temper, and wrote as follows to Bennigsen, who was the czar's private reporter:

"I must request your excellency, on receiving this letter, to retire to Kalouga on account of the precarious state of your health, and to await there his majesty's further commands."

In consequence of this banishment of Bennigsen, the Grand Duke Constantine, who had been with the troops during the early part of the campaign, and had been set aside by Koutouzow, rejoined the army, and communicated to the commander-in-chief his majesty's annoyance at the smallness of the Russian successes and the slowness of their movements; he also announced that his majesty himself would arrive shortly. Koutouzow, whose experience as a courtier was at least equal to his acumen as a soldier, understood at once that his part was played out, and that the semblance of power he had been allowed to wield was now withdrawn. It was easy to understand. On one hand the campaign which it had been his duty to conduct was at an end, and his function therefore fulfilled; on the other, he was, in fact, physically weary, and his frame, broken by years, needed complete repose.

CHAPTER CXX

HE returned to Vilna on the 29th of November—"his dear Vilna," as he called it. He had already been twice governor of the town, so that he found there not only the ease that could only be had in a city which had happily escaped the horrors of war, but also old friends and pleasant memories. Casting off all the cares of government and of military command, he settled down into a calm and regular life, so far at least as he could in the midst of the intrigues that buzzed around him—as though henceforth he was perfectly indifferent to any events that might occur, however important.

The most indefatigable schemer of military manœuvres was Tchitchagow; it was he who had proposed to carry war into Greece or to Warsaw, and he always objected to going where he was sent. Tchitchagow considered Koutouzow as under obligations to him, because when, in 1811, he was charged with the duty of concluding peace with Turkey, irrespective of Koutouzow, and found that it was already signed, he explained to the czar that the credit of the negotiations was entirely due to Koutouzow, and was himself the first to receive him at the gate of the castle of Vilna, in naval undress, his hat under his arm, and to present him with the report of the state of the troops and with the keys of the town. But now the half-contemptuous deference of the younger generation of men for the old man whom they chose to consider as in his dotage was suddenly and brutally manifest in the behaviour of Tchitcha-gow, who was well aware of the accusations that had been brought against Koutouzow. When Koutouzow told him that the fourgons containing his table-plate, which had been seized at Borissow, would be restored to him intact, Tchitchagow replied:

"I suppose you wish to convey that I have nothing to eat with! But I have, I assure you, all you are likely to require, even if you should wish to give dinner-parties." His instinct was always to make a display of his personal importance, and he ascribed the same feeling to Koutouzow.

"Indeed," replied the elder simply, with a keen and subtle smile. "I only told you because I thought you might like to know, not for any other reason."

The commander-in-chief had detained almost all the troops at Vilna, against the czar's desire. After a short residence there the men about him declared that he had altogether lost his head. Henceforth he troubled himself very little about military matters, and left the generals to act as they chose, leading a life of pleasure till the sovereign should arrive.

On the 11th of December, his majesty and his suite, attended by Count Tolstoï, Prince Volkonsky, and Araktchéïew, arrived in his travelling-sleigh at the castle of Vilna. In spite of the bitter cold, a hundred or so of generals and staff-officers, with a guard of honour of the Séménovsky Regiment, were awaiting him outside the gates. The czar's courier arriving in a troïka driven at breakneck speed, shouted: "He is coming!" and Konovnitzine rushed into the vestibule to announce the czar to Koutouzow, who was waiting in the ante-room. A moment after that he stepped out on the terrace, his breast covered with orders, his sash tightening his burly waist, and his stout, heavy person swaying as he moved; he put on his hat, took his gloves in his hand, and slowly descending the steps, took from an official the report it was his duty to present to his majesty.

A second troïka came flying by, and then all eyes were fixed upon a sleigh that followed swiftly and in which the czar and Volkonsky could be seen sitting side by side.

Though accustomed for fifty years to the nervous excitement that he always felt on receiving an imperial visit, the commander-in-chief was as much agitated as usual: he hastily felt all his medals and stars, and set his hat straight on his head. As the czar stepped out of the carriage he looked up at him; then, taking courage, he presented the report and addressed his majesty in his soft, engaging tones. Alexander glanced at him from head to foot with a slight frown, but at once recollected himself, and opened his arms to embrace him. And, as usual, this friendly accolade, rousing personal secret associations, thrilled him with deep feeling which expressed itself in a sob.

The czar bowed to the officers and to the Séménovsky Guards, and once more pressing Koutouzow's hand, led the way to the castle. When they were alone he did not attempt to dissemble his vexation at the mistakes that had been committed at Krasnoé and the Bérésina, and at Koutouzow's slowness in pursuit of the enemy; he also laid before him a plan for a campaign beyond the frontier. Koutouzow made no remarks nor objections. His face expressed only passive and utter submission—as it had seven years before, when receiving the czar's commands on the field of Austeriitz. When he quitted him, his head bent on his breast, as he crossed the large reception-

room with his heavy, uncertain step, he heard a voice saying:
"Your highness!"

Koutouzow looked up and gazed for some little space at
Count Tolstoï, who was standing before him and offering a
small object on a tray. He did not seem to understand what
he was to do. Suddenly the faintest possible smile dawned on
his large face, and bowing respectfully, he took up the object
thus presented to him. It was the Order of St. George of the
first class.

CHAPTER CXXI

NEXT evening Koutouzow gave a grand banquet, and after it
a ball, which the czar honoured with his presence. From the
moment when it was known that Koutouzow had received the
Star of St. George everyone was eager to do him honour; still,
his majesty's disappointment was no secret from anyone. All
the proprieties were observed, and the czar was the first to set
the example, but it was whispered that the old man was much
to blame and quite childish. When his majesty entered the
ball-room, Koutouzow, with a reminiscence of the traditions of
the days of Catherine, had the enemy's standards bowed before
him in salute, and Alexander with a scowl only muttered a few
words—among others: "Old actor!"

His annoyance with Koutouzow arose from the marshal's not
seeing—or not choosing to see—that the intended campaign
was necessary. The day after his arrival at Vilna, Alexander
had said to the assembled officers: "You have not merely
saved Russia, you have saved Europe!"

They all understood from this that the war was not over.
But Koutouzow would not hear of it: he said very plainly that
a continuance of the war could neither improve the position
nor add to the glory of Russia; that, on the contrary, it would
weaken its prestige. He tried to prove to the czar the impossibility of levying fresh troops, and even ventured to suggest
the possibility of failure.

From this moment it was evident that the marshal was
simply an obstacle to be got rid of. To avoid hurting his
feelings too much, a quite natural arrangement was hit upon;
the power was gradually taken out of his hands and transferred
to the czar, as had been done at Austerlitz. To this end the

staff was somewhat altered, and that of Koutouzow was deprived of all influence. Toll, Konovnitzine, and Yermolow had fresh appointments, and the marshal's shaken health was openly discussed; for the more was said about it the easier it would be to nominate his successor. Just as before, when Koutouzow had been quietly brought back from Turkey to organise the St. Petersburg militia, and from thence sent to the army where he was indispensable, so now, his work being done, fresh wheels were set in motion.

The war of 1812 was no longer to maintain the strictly national character which endeared it to every Russian heart, and was to become of European importance.

And now the movement of the western nations eastwards gave place to a tide the other way. This new war needed a new mainspring, acting under different impulses from Koutouzow's. The man to fill this place was the Czar Alexander, who was as necessary to the restoration of nations and national frontiers as Koutouzow had been to the safety and glory of Russia. Koutouzow had no comprehension of what was meant by Europe, by the balance of power, and by Napoleon's aggressions. To him, as the representative of the Russian people, a Russian himself to the backbone, the work seemed to be finished as soon as the foe was crushed, and his country delivered and placed on a pinnacle of glory. There was nothing left to the champion of his country but to die—and he died.

CHAPTER CXXII

PETER—like most men under similar circumstances—did not feel the full effects of the physical privations and moral tension he had endured during his captivity till it was over. As soon as he was free he started for Orel, and two days after, when he was on the point of starting for Kïew, he was attacked by what the doctors called a bilious fever, which detained him at Orel three months. In spite of their attentions—bleedings and every kind of physic—he recovered his health.

The days that elapsed between his rescue and the time that he fell ill left no trace on his memory but of grey, dull, rainy weather, of physical prostration, of horrible pain in his feet and in his side, of an endless series of troubles and miseries, of impertinent curiosity in the officers who would cross-question him, of his difficulty in finding carriages or horses, and above all of moral and mental torpor. On the day that had brought him freedom he saw Pétia carried by—dead; and he heard that Prince Andrew had just died at Yaroslaw under the same roof with the Rostows. Denissow, who told him this, also alluded to Helen s death, of which he supposed him to be informed; Peter was greatly surprised, but that was all; he was incapable of taking in all the bearings of this event on his own future. His only idea was to get away from this hell-on-earth, where men did nothing but kill each other, to find a refuge somewhere—anywhere; to rest; to co-ordinate his ideas; to reflect in peace on all he had seen and gone through.

When he first completely recovered his wits after his illness, he saw, at the foot of his bed, two of his old servants who had come from Moscow expressly to wait on him, and with them his eldest cousin, who had been living on one of his estates in the neighbourhood of Orel.

The impressions to which he had become inured faded very gradually from his mind during the long process of convalescence; he even had some difficulty in accustoming himself to the idea, as each morning dawned, that he should not be driven forward with a flock in which he was a unit, that no one would take possession of his bed, and that he was certain to have dinner and supper each in due season. And when he fell asleep he constantly dreamed of the scenes and details of his life as a prisoner.

But the happy sense of liberty which is innate in man, and which he had felt keenly enough in the first hours after his rescue, came back to him and possessed him wholly during his convalescence. He could not understand how this merely mental liberty quite apart from external circumstances could be so intense a joy, and give him such exquisite pleasure; it was in fact only the result of his physical freedom. He was alone in a strange town, no one made any demands on him, he wanted for nothing, and the remembrance of his wife no longer haunted him as a perpetual humiliation.

From old habit he sometimes said to himself: "What is there for me to do next?"—and the answer was: "Nothing. To live. Great God! how good that is!" He had no aim in life, and this indifference, which had formerly been his bane, now gave him a sense of unlimited freedom. Why should he have any such aim now that he had faith—not faith in any set of rules or accepted dogmas, but in a living and ever-present

God? Formerly he had sought Him in the duties he had set himself; then, suddenly, as a captive, he had discovered, not by force of logic but by a sort of personal revelation, that there was indeed a God, an omnipotent God; and that the God known to Plato Karataïew was greater and more supremely above human apprehension than the "Architect of the Universe," as acknowledged by the freemasons. Had he not been like a man who looks far away for an object that lies at his feet? Had he not spent his life in staring into vacancy over other men's heads, while he had only to look close before him? In that past time nothing had revealed the Infinite to him; he had only felt that it must exist somewhere, and walked on, resolute to seek it; everything within his reach had been a mere medley of narrow and petty interests devoid of real meaning—such as the social life of Europe, politics, freemasonry, and philosophy. But now he understood the Infinite, he saw it in everything, and wholly admired the ever-changing and ever-glorious picture of life in its endless variety. The awful question which had been wont to confront him at every turn, which had undermined again and again the structures of his mind: "Why?"—no longer haunted him; his soul could reply in all honesty and simplicity that God is, and that not a hair of a man's head can fall without His will.

CHAPTER CXXIII

PETER had changed but little; absent-minded as ever, he only seemed to be under the influence of some constant fixed idea. What had formerly repelled acquaintance in spite of his kind face was his unhappy expression; but now the constant smile which the mere joy of living brought to his lips, and the sympathetic kindness of his eyes, made him everywhere a welcome presence. He had been wont to be argumentative, to fire up readily, and be an unwilling listener; now he was rarely to be tempted into a discussion, he was ready to let others talk, and thus often learnt their most secret thoughts.

His cousin, who had never loved him, indeed, who had sincerely hated him when, after the old count's death, he had laid her under obligations to him, could not get over her astonishment on discovering, after a short sojourn at Orel—whither she came to nurse him in spite of the ingratitude of which she chose to

accuse him—that she felt a genuine liking for him. But he
had done nothing to win her good graces; he had simply studied
her character with some curiosity. Formerly, as she had
always suspected him of indifference or of ironical meaning, she
had shrunk into herself and put forth all her prickles; now, on
the other hand, perceiving as she did, with distrust at first and
then with gratitude, that he was endeavouring to read and
understand her deepest feelings, she unconsciously learnt to
show only the best side of her nature: "In fact, he is a very
excellent creature when he is not under the influence of evil-
disposed persons, but under that of people like myself," said
the lady to herself. The change that had taken place in Peter
was also noticed by his two servants Terenty and Vasska.
They found him considerably aged. Often Terenty in undressing
his master and taking away his clothes to clean, would pause
to see if Peter showed any signs of wishing to converse with
him. And generally Peter would detain him with a question,
and listen to his stories or tell his own, making the servant
conscious of the new friendly relations that existed between
him and his master.

The doctor, who called on him daily, though he felt it incum-
bent on him to explain that every minute of his time was precious
to suffering humanity, would spend hours with Peter, relating
his favourite anecdotes and his observations on the characters
of his patients—especially women. "It's a pleasure to talk to
a man like that. Not like one of our provincial gentry," he
would say.

Several French officers were residing as prisoners at Orel,
and the doctor brought one to call on Peter. He was an
Italian, and soon fell into a habit of going often to see Peter;
and Princess Catherine laughed to herself at the fervent friendship he showed to her cousin. He enjoyed talking to him,
relating his past life and confiding to him all his love affairs,
pouring forth, too, the venom of his hatred of the French, and
especially of Napoleon.

"If all Russians are like you," he said one day to Peter,
"it is really a sacrilege to make war on such a nation. You,
who have suffered so much at their hands, do not even hate
them."

At Orel, Peter also found an old acquaintance, Count Villarsky,
the freemason whom we met before in 1807. He had married
a very rich Russian lady, whose estates were in the government
of Orel, and he was just now temporarily employed in the

commissariat department. Though he had never been particularly intimate with Bésoukhow, he was pleased to meet him again; he was bored to death at Orel, and only too glad to fall in with a man of his own society, taking it for granted that they must have some tastes in common. However, to his great surprise, he found that Peter was remarkably behind the world in his ideas, that he had sunk into what Villarsky took for apathy and egoism.

"You are fossilising, my dear fellow!" he constantly said to him; and yet he would return day after day, and Peter, as he talked with him, wondered how he could ever have thought as this man did.

Villarsky, forced to attend to his duties, his business, and his family, regarded all such personal cares as a hindrance to the real uses of life. Military affairs, administrative politics, and freemasonry were the objects of his interest. Peter did not blame him for this, and never tried in any way to lead him to change his views; but he studied the singular phenomenon with a mildly satirical smile.

A quite new feature in Peter's character, and a generally attractive one, was his recognition of every man's right—as he believed—to think and judge for himself, and of the impossibility of convincing anyone, be it who it might, by mere words. This right, which formerly had irritated him excessively, was now the chief source of his interest in his fellow-men.

This new view of things had its influence, too, on the practical outcome of his life. Formerly all demands for gifts of money had worried and puzzled him. "The man wants it, no doubt," he would say to himself, "but such another wants it even more. And how can I tell that they are not both deceiving me?" Finally, not knowing how to decide, he gave away money right and left, all he had at his disposal. But now, to his great surprise, he no longer felt this perplexity; an instinctive sense of justice, which he himself could not account for, guided him unfailingly as to the right decision in each case. Thus, one day a French prisoner, a colonel, after boasting for some time of his various exploits, ended by requesting, almost demanding, a loan of 4,000 francs, to forward, as he said, to his wife and children. Peter refused without an instant's hesitation, surprising himself by the readiness with which he answered in the negative; and instead of handing the sum to the colonel, he persuaded the Italian, who needed it sorely, to accept it.

He acted in the same spirit with regard to his wife's debts, and the reconstruction of his houses in the town and in the country. His head steward, in laying before him a schedule of his losses by the burning of Moscow—which were estimated at about two millions of roubles, advised him to recoup himself by ignoring the countess's debts, and by not restoring his houses, which cost about 80,000 roubles a year to keep up. At the first moment Peter agreed; but when, towards the end of January, the architect at Moscow sent him an estimate for the works needed to restore the ruined buildings, Peter once more read through the letters he had received from Prince Basil and some of his friends in reference to his wife's liabilities, and did not hesitate to reverse his decision. He made up his mind to rebuild his houses, and to go to St. Petersburg to pay off the countess's debts. This, it was true, would diminish his income by about three-quarters, but as soon as he saw that it was just and necessary, he immediately proceeded to carry it out.

Villarsky having occasion to make a journey to Moscow, he arranged to travel with him, and all the way he went his feeling was that of a schoolboy out for a holiday. Everything he saw on the road appeared in a new light, and his companion's frequently expressed regrets at the poor and backward condition of Russia as compared with western Europe could not diminish his enthusiasm: for where Villarsky saw only deplorable torpidity, Peter, on the contrary, discovered the source of that endurance, strength and vital energy which had supported the nation—a nation fundamentally pure, and unique in its way—in a struggle fought out on snow-covered plains.

CHAPTER CXXIV

It would be as difficult to account for the motives which led the Russians, after the departure of the French, to congregate once more on the spot called Moscow, as to discern why and where the ants rush in such bewildered haste, when an ant-hill is upturned by accident. Some flee, carrying their eggs or minute fragments; others run back to the wreck; they meet, jostle and fight; but if we contemplate the ant-hill closely, we cannot but perceive, from the energy and persistent activity of the myriad inhabitants, that the essential element that gives it strength, has survived its utter ruin; and in the same way, by the end of October, notwithstanding the absence of all authority, of church services, of wealth, and even of houses, Moscow had the same general aspect as it had had in August. Everything had been destroyed excepting its indestructible and vigorous vitality.

The motives which brought back those who first returned were wholly savage; a week later and Moscow had already 15,000 inhabitants, then 25,000; and the number increased so rapidly, that by the autumn of 1813 the sum of the inhabitants was greater than in the preceding year.

The Cossacks of Wintzingerode's detachment, the peasants from the neighbouring villages, and the fugitives hiding in the suburbs were the first to come back, and devoted themselves to pillage—thus carrying on the work begun by the French. The peasants made their way home with carts loaded with objects they had found in the houses and in the streets; the Cossacks did the same, and the owners snatched all they could from each other, under pretence of recovering possession of their own. These plunderers were followed by a crowd of others; as their numbers swelled, the business became more difficult, and robbery took a more organised aspect.

Though the French had found Moscow deserted, a semblance of administration had been kept up; but towards the end of their sojourn this mockery of vital energy died out, giving way to a state of unchecked pillage. The plundering which marked the return of the Russians to their capital brought about the reverse process, for people of all classes, tradesmen, artisans and peasants—some out of curiosity and some out of self-interest or in the interest of their masters—flowed back as the blood flows back to the heart, and brought with them wealth and regular habits of life. The peasants who came in with empty waggons hoping to fill them with booty, were caught by the authorities and forced to cart away the dead; others, warned in time of their companions' miscalculation, brought in corn, hay, and oats, and by natural competition brought prices down to the same level as they had stood at before the catastrophe; carpenters came in crowds, expecting to find work; the burnt-out houses were repaired and rose from their ruins; tradesmen began business; inns and taverns took possession of abandoned premises; the priests reopened the churches that had been spared by the fire; officials set their tables and presses in order in such little rooms as they could find; the superior authorities and the police devoted themselves in distributing the baggage left behind by the French—which gave an opportunity, as usual, for abusing and for buying over the police; petitions for pecuniary assistance poured in from every quarter, and at the same time came the monstrous estimates of the tenders for restoring the buildings belonging to the crown; and once again Count Rostopchine's "posters" were to be seen.

CHAPTER CXXV

PETER came to Moscow at the end of January, and settled himself in one wing of his house, which had escaped injury. He intended to start within two days for St. Petersburg, and he went to call on Count Rostopchine and some other old acquaintances who, in the elation of a final and complete victory, received him with joy and questioned him as to all he had seen. Though he met with great sympathy, he was reserved in his communications, and answered very vaguely when he was questioned as to his future plans. He learnt, among other things, that the Rostows were at Kostroma; but his memory of Natacha was now no more than a sweet reminiscence of a very remote past. He was so happy to be independent of all the ties of life that it was an additional pleasure to feel free from an influence to which, at the time, however, he had yielded with his own full consent.

The Droubetzkoïs told him that Princess Maria was in Moscow, and he went to call on her that same evening. As he went his mind dwelt on Prince Andrew, on his sufferings, on his death, on their friendship, and above all on their last meeting, the evening before Borodino.

"Did he die in the irritation he was then feeling?" said he to himself. "Or was the enigma of life revealed to him in the hour of death, I wonder?" Then he thought of Karataïew, involuntarily comparing these two men—so unlike each other, and yet, to him brought so near by his love for them both.

He was grave and sad as he went into the Bolkonsky's house; though it had recovered its characteristic aspect it still bore traces of the disaster. An old manservant with a stern face, as much as to say that the prince's death had made no change in the rules of the establishment, told him that the princess was in her own rooms, and received company only on Sundays.

"Give her my name; perhaps she will see me."

"In that case take the trouble to walk into the portrait-gallery."

In a few minutes the man returned with Dessalles, to say that the princess would be very happy to see Peter, and to beg him to go upstairs to her. He found her in an upper room—a small, low room, lighted by a single candle. She was in black, and another person, also in mourning, was with her. Peter supposed at first that this was one of the lady companions whom Princess Maria was always glad to have about her, but of whom he had never taken any heed. The princess rose eagerly and held out her hand.

"Yes," said she, as he kissed it, noting the alteration in his appearance, "this is how we meet again. *He* often spoke of you towards the end—" and she glanced at the lady in black with a hesitancy that did not escape Peter.

"The news of your rescue was a great happiness to me," she went on, "the only joy we have known for very long." Again she glanced uneasily at her companion.

"Only fancy, I knew nothing about him," said Peter. "I thought he was killed, and I only heard indirectly through a third person—I know he found the Rostows. What a strange coincidence!" Peter spoke eagerly. He, too, glanced at the stranger, and catching her expression of kindly interest, concluded instinctively that this lady in mourning was charming and amiable, and would not be any check on his frank effusiveness to Princess Maria. She, on her part, was very visibly confused when he alluded to the Rostows, and she looked once more from Peter to the lady in black.

"Do not you recognise her?" she said.

Peter now looked with some attention at the pale, delicate face, the lips so strangely pinched, and the large black eyes of this stranger. Suddenly he found in them that soft radiance so dear to his heart, from which he had so long been shut out.

"Impossible!" he thought. "Can that be she? pale, thin, so much older, with that austere expression. It must be a delusion!" But the princess spoke Natacha's name, and the pallid face, with its solemn, mournful eyes, with effort and difficulty, as a rusty door yields to pressure from without, broke into a smile. The lips smiled, and that smile shed a perfume of happiness on Peter, which seemed to float round him and penetrate his being. There could be no doubt after that smile: it was Natacha, and he loved her. The violence of the impression was so great that it betrayed at once to Natacha, to Maria, and to himself the certainty of a passion which he still found it difficult to confess to himself. His agitation was a mixture of joy and pain; the more he tried to mask it the more it betrayed itself, without the help of words, by a deepening blush: "It is only surprise," said he to himself; but when he tried to resume the conversation, and again looked at Natacha, his heart was full of happiness and shyness. He got confused in his sentence, and broke off short. It was not alone because she was pale and thin that he had failed to recognise her, but because her eyes, that had formerly been bright with the light of life, now expressed nothing but sympathy, kindness, and restless melancholy. Peter's embarrassment roused no response in Natacha; her face shone only with gentle satisfaction.

CHAPTER CXXVI

"She has come to stay with me for some little time," said Princess Maria. "The count and countess are to join us before long. The poor countess is sad to see. Natacha needs medical advice, so I brought her away by force."

"Ah! which of us has not been tried?" said Peter. "You know, of course, that it happened on the day when we were rescued—I saw him. What a delightful boy he was!"

Natacha did not speak, but her eyes dilated and glittered with tears that did not fall.

"There can be no consolation," Peter went on. "None! Why—one cannot help asking—why should he die? that bright young creature, full of life and youth?"

"Yes, indeed; and that is what makes faith more necessary than ever in our time," said Princess Maria.

"Very true," assented Peter.

"Why?" asked Natacha, looking at him.

"Why?" repeated Maria. "The mere thought of that which awaits. . . ."

"Because," said Peter, interrupting her, "only those who believe in the guiding power of God can endure such losses as hers . . . and yours."

Natacha seemed to be about to speak, but checked herself, and Peter turned to Princess Maria with an eager wish to know some details of his friend's last days. His embarrassment had vanished, but with it his feeling of absolute freedom had vanished too; he was conscious that each word he spoke, and everything he did, lay open to a judge whose opinion was the most precious in the world to him. Even as he talked he quaked in his inmost soul as to the effect he was producing on Natacha, and was trying to judge himself from her point of view. Princess Maria made up her mind, though reluctantly, to give Peter the details he wished for; his questions and the interest he took in them, his voice trembling with emotion, persuaded her to retrace by degrees the scenes which she hardly dared call up for herself.

"And so he grew calmer and sweeter. He had but one aim in life, towards which he strove with all the powers of his soul, and that was to be perfectly good. What, then, had he to fear in death? His faults, if he had any, cannot be counted against him. How happy it was for him that you should have met once more!" he added, turning to Natacha, and his eyes filled with tears. She shivered a little and bowed her head, unable to make up her mind whether she should speak of him or no.

"Yes," she said in a low, subdued tone. "It was a great happiness, to me at any rate; and he"—she tried to control her emotion—"he wished it, too, when I went to him."

Her voice failed her, and she reddened, clasping her hands convulsively; then, suddenly raising her head with a visible effort, she went on:

"When we left Moscow I did not know, and I dared not ask after him when Sonia told me he was of our party. I could not think. I could not imagine what state he might be in; I only wanted one thing, and that was to see him."

Then she told them—what she had never before revealed to anyone—all she had suffered during those three weeks of travelling and sojourn at Yaroslaw. Peter, as he listened, was thinking neither of Prince Andrew nor of death, nor of what she was saying. He was conscious only of intense pity for the pain it must be to her to call up the grief of the past; but Natacha was impelled by an irresistible impulse. She mingled the most trivial details with the most sacred feelings, told the same scenes again and again, and did not seem to know how to stop. Just then, however, Dessalles asked from the next room whether the little boy might come in.

"And that is all—that is all. . . .!" cried Natacha, rising hurriedly; and flying out of the door, of which little Nicholas had just raised the heavy curtain, she hit her head against the side, and gave a little cry of pain as she disappeared. Was it physical pain or mental suffering?

Peter, who had never taken his eyes off her, felt when she was gone that he was alone again in the world. Princess Maria roused him from a reverie by attracting his notice to the child, His resemblance to his father agitated Peter so deeply in his pathetic excitement, that, after giving him a kiss, he had to turn away and wipe his eyes. He was about to take leave, but Maria detained him.

"Pray stay," she said. "Natacha and I often sit up till three in the morning. Supper must be ready; will you go down? we will be with you in a few minutes. This is the first time," she added, "that she has spoken of him."

CHAPTER CXXVII

A FEW minutes later Princess Maria and Natacha joined Peter in the large dining-room. Natacha had recovered her composure, and her face had a gravity that he had never before seen. All three were suffering under the awkwardness which commonly ensues after a serious and intimate conversation. They sat down to table without a word; Peter unfolded his napkin, and, making up his mind to put an end to a silence which, if it were allowed to last, must become painful to all, looked round at the two women, who were bent on doing the same. Their eyes shone with some revived joy in living, and an unconscious admission that grief is not eternal, but may still give place to happiness.

"Will you have a little brandy, count?" said Princess Maria; and these simple words sufficed to chase the shadows of the past. "And tell us how you managed to live; it is a perfect romance from what we have heard."

"Oh, yes," he said, with gentle irony. "Things have been invented about me that I never saw even in my dreams. I am quite amazed at it still; I find myself a person of interest, and I do not mind it at all. My friends vie with each other in asking me to their houses, and telling me all the details of my captivity as they have imagined it."

"They say that the burning of Moscow cost you two millions; is that true?"

"Very likely; but I am three times as rich as I was before, nevertheless," replied Peter, who was never tired of saying this to anyone who would listen, in spite of the loss he must incur in paying his wife's debts and rebuilding his houses. "What I have gained for good is my liberty. . . ." But he stopped, not wishing to dwell on his merely personal concerns.

"And you mean to build?"

"Yes. Savélitch advises it."

"Where were you when you heard of the countess's death? Were you still at Moscow?" But the princess coloured as she spoke, fearing lest Peter should attribute a wrong sense to a question which seemed to give point to his observations on having recovered his liberty.

"No, I only heard the news at Orel. You may suppose how astonished I was. We were not a model couple," he went on, looking at Natacha, and guessing that she would be curious to hear what he might say on such a subject; "but her death stunned me. When two people cannot agree there are generally faults on both sides, and one feels doubly guilty towards the dead. . . . She died alone, too, without her friends or consolation. I felt the deepest pity for her. . . ." And he ceased, happy in a feeling that Natacha was approving.

"So now you are a bachelor on your promotion again," said Princess Maria.

Peter blushed scarlet and looked down. When he raised his eyes again, after a long silence, to look at Natacha, he fancied her expression was cold and reserved, almost disdainful.

"And did you really see Napoleon, as we were told?" asked Maria.

"Never," and he burst out laughing. "You might fancy that to be a prisoner was synonymous with being Napoleon's guest. I never even heard him talked about; I was in far too humble company."

"Now confess," said Natacha, "that when you stayed in Moscow it was to kill him. I guessed as much when we met you there."

Peter admitted that this had in fact been his intention; and allowing himself to be led on by their questions, he gave them a full account of all his adventures. He spoke at first with that light irony that tinged all his opinions of others and of himself; but by degrees the remembrance, still so vivid, of the sufferings and the horrors he had witnessed gave his speech the genuine and reticent emotion that is natural in a man who goes back in memory to the scenes of acute interest in which he has taken part.

Princess Maria looked first at Natacha and then at Peter, whose native and thorough goodness of heart was conspicuous throughout his story. Natacha, with her elbow on the table and her chin resting on her hand, followed every detail with varying expression. Her eyes, her exclamations, her brief questions, all showed that she fully entered into the real meaning of what he endeavoured to make them understand; nay, better still, the hidden sense of much that he could not utter in words. The episode of the rescue of the child and of the woman whom he had tried to defend—the immediate cause of his being taken prisoner—he related in these words:

"It was a horrible sight; children deserted or left to perish in the flames—one was saved before my very eyes. Then the women, and soldiers snatching away their dresses and even their ear-rings—" he coloured and paused. "And just then a patrol came along and arrested the peasants and all who were not plundering, myself among them."

"You are not telling the whole story," said Natacha interrupting him. "You would certainly have . . . have done some good action."

Peter went on with his tale. When he came to the execution of his companions he tried to pass it over lightly, so as to spare her such shocking details; but she insisted on hearing everything. Then came the story of Karataïew. They had done supper and rose from table; he paced up and down the room, Natacha watching him.

"You could never guess half of what I learnt from that man, that guileless soul who could neither read nor write."

"And what became of him?" asked Natacha.

"They shot him, almost under my eyes!" And in a voice quivering with emotion, he told them of the hapless creature's illness and death.

He himself had never seen his adventures in the light in which they now appeared. They bore a new meaning for him; and as he narrated them to Natacha he felt the keen pleasure which comes of the sympathy, not of a clever woman whose sole object is to assimilate what she hears and to enrich the stores of her little brain, but of that of a true woman who possesses the faculty of bringing out and taking in all that is best in a man. Natacha, though unconsciously, was all attention. Not a word, not a shade of tone, not a glance, a thrill, or a gesture escaped her; she caught his sentences half-spoken, as it were in the air, and treasured them in her heart, divining the mysterious travail that had taken place in his soul.

Princess Maria was interested by all he said, but another thought filled her mind: she had just begun to understand that Peter and Natacha might love each other and be happy together, and it filled her with deep joy.

It was now three in the morning; the servants came in with long faces to bring fresh candles, but no one heeded them. Peter brought his story to an end. His honest emotion, stamped with some embarrassment, responded to Natacha's gaze, which seemed to be questioning his silence even; and without considering the lateness of the hour, he tried to find a fresh subject of conversation.

"We talk of disaster and suffering," he said, "and yet if any one were to ask me: 'Would you rather be just what you were before your imprisonment or go through all you have endured once more?' I should answer: 'Sooner a thousand times a prisoner's life and horseflesh!' We are prone to fancy that everything is wrecked if once we leave the beaten path; in fact it is then only that Truth and Goodness are revealed to us. While there is life there is happiness. We still have much to look forward to—it is for you especially that I say it," he added, turning to Natacha.

"Very true," she said, but she was answering another thought that had flashed across her mind. "I, too, could ask for nothing better than to live my life over again."

Peter looked at her inquiringly. "No, I could ask for nothing more!"

"Is it really possible?" cried Peter. "And am I wrong in living and in wishing to live; and you too?"

Natacha bent her head and melted into tears.

"Natacha, what ails you?"

"Nothing, nothing," she said, smiling at Peter through her tears.

"Good night, it is bedtime," and Peter rose and left them.

Princess Maria and Natacha talked for some time after in their own room, but neither of them mentioned Peter's name.

"Do you know, Maria, that I often fear, lest in never speaking of him, for fear of profaning our feelings, we should altogether forget him."

Princess Maria's sigh confirmed the accuracy of this observation, which she never would have dared to utter.

"Do you think it is possible to forget?" she said. "It did

me so much good to talk it all over to-day; it was both a comfort and a pain. I felt that he had truly loved him, and so . . . Was I wrong?" she asked, colouring.

"Wrong to speak of him to Peter? Oh no! He is so good."

"Did you notice, Maria," said Natacha presently, with a saucy smile that had not been seen on her features for many a day—"did you notice how neat and well-dressed he was, and how fresh-coloured and rosy? He looks as if he had just come out of a moral bath; I mean—but you understand, don't you?"

"Yes, he has altered very much to his advantage. It was that which made 'him' so fond of him," said Princess Maria.

"Yes. And yet they were very unlike. However, they say that men's friendships are always between those who are contrasts; I suppose it is in the nature of things. Well, good night, good night!" said Natacha, and the merry smile with which she had spoken long remained on her face.

CHAPTER CXXVIII

It was long before Peter got any sleep. He strode up and down his room with an anxious face, shrugging his shoulders, starting, and his lips parting as if to make some avowal. Six o'clock struck and he was still thinking of Prince Andrew, of Natacha, of their mutual love, of which even now he was jealous. He went to bed, agitated but happy, having made up his mind to do everything within the bounds of human possibility to marry her.

He had fixed Friday for his journey to St. Petersburg, and on the following morning Savélitch came to him for orders as to his start.

"St. Petersburg? What, I am going to St. Petersburg? What for?" he asked himself in astonishment. "To be sure, I had settled it long since; before this had occurred. Yes, and perhaps I will really go. What a good face old Savélitch has! Well, Savélitch, would you not like to have your freedom?"

"What should I do with it, excellency? We lived with the old count—God rest his soul! And now we live with you, and have nothing to complain of."

"And your children?"

"My children will do as I have done, excellency. With a master like you there is nothing to fear."

"That is all very well; but my heirs?" said Peter. "If I were to marry, for instance? That might happen yet, you know," he added with an involuntary smile.

"And a very good thing, I make bold to say, excellency."

"How lightly he treats it," thought Peter. "He has no idea what a serious, what a terrible thing it is. . . . It is too soon, or too late."

"What orders, excellency? Will you go to-morrow?"

"No; in a few days. I will let you know when. Forgive me for giving you so much trouble. It is odd," said he to himself, "that he should not have guessed that I have nothing to do at St. Petersburg, and that *this* must be decided first of all. I am sure that he does know it and only makes believe not to. Shall I say anything to him about it? No, it will do better another time."

At breakfast Peter told his cousin Catherine that he had called on Princess Maria the evening before, and that there, to his great surprise, he had met Natacha Rostow. Princess Catherine saw nothing in it to be surprised at.

"Do you know her?" Peter asked.

"I saw her once; there was some talk of her marrying young Rostow: it would have been a good thing for him, for they say that the Rostows are ruined."

"I was not speaking of Princess Maria, but of Natacha."

"To be sure; I heard her story—a very sad one."

"Evidently," thought Peter, "she does not understand, or she does not choose to understand. I had better say no more."

He went to dine with Princess Maria. As he went along the streets, where the ruins of the burnt houses still remained standing, he could not help admiring them. The tall chimneys that towered up in the midst of the rubbish-heaps reminded him of the ruins of the banks of the Rhine, or of the Colosseum. The coach-drivers and riders, the carpenters squaring joists, the shopkeepers and dealers, all the men he met seemed to look at him with beaming glances, and say to themselves, "Ah! here he is back again; now we shall see what he will do next."

When he reached the house, he felt as though he had been the sport of a dream, and had seen Natacha in his sleep; but he had scarcely entered her presence when he felt its influence in a thrill throughout his whole being. Though dressed in black, as she had been the day before, and with her hair done just the same, her face was different; if she had looked like this when they first met, he must have recognised her: she had her childish face, her face of a girl-bride. Her eyes were bright with an inquiring gleam, and a saucy and particularly friendly smile parted her lips. Peter dined with them, and would have spent the evening there, but that the ladies were going to vespers, so he accompanied them.

The next day he called again, and stayed so late that, notwithstanding their pleasure in his company, and the absorbing interest he found in their society, the conversation flagged, and turned on the most trivial subjects. Still, Peter could not make up his mind to leave, though he felt that they were impatient for his departure. Princess Maria, seeing no issue to the dilemma, was the first to rise and bid him good-bye, excusing herself under the plea of a headache. "So you start for St. Petersburg to-morrow?"

"No, I am not going away," said Peter, hastily. "At least I don't know; perhaps. At any rate I will call before leaving in case you have any commissions." He was standing up, and greatly embarrassed.

Natacha gave him her hand, and left the room; then Princess Maria, dropping into an arm-chair, and fixing him with her luminous gaze, watched him attentively. Her fatigue had suddenly vanished; it was evident that she was prepared for a long talk with him. Peter's awkwardness and bashfulness had also disappeared as if by magic when Natacha went away. He hastily pulled a chair forward, and sat down by the princess. "I have a confession to make to you," he began, with controlled emotion. "I want your help, princess—what am I to do, what hope is there for me? I know only too well that I am not worthy of her, and this is an ill-chosen time for addressing her. But might I not be like a brother to her? No," he added quickly, "No. I cannot—I will not. I do not know how long I have loved her," he went on, after a pause, and with a great effort to be coherent, "but I never loved any other woman, and I cannot conceive of life without her. Of course it is particularly difficult to ask her just now to give me her hand; but the thought that she might grant it, and that I may be missing an opportunity is more than I can bear. Dear princess, is there any hope for me?"

"You are right," said Princess Maria, "in thinking this an ill-chosen time for speaking of your . . ." But she stopped; it struck her that the entire change in Natacha made her

objections seem improbable; nay, she felt that she would not
be offended by Peter's declaration of love—that at the bottom
of her heart she longed for it; still, she would not yield to a
mere impulse, and she repeated, "You cannot possibly speak
of it now, trust in me, I know . . ."

"What?" said Peter, breathlessly, with an inquiring gaze.

"I know that she loves you—that she will love you!" The
words were scarcely spoken, when Peter started to his feet,
seized her hand, and wrung it hard.

"You believe it—you say you really believe it?"

"Yes, I do. Write to her parents. I will speak to her
about it, all in good time. I sincerely wish it; and my heart
tells me it will certainly be so."

"It would be too great happiness, too great happiness!"
said Peter, kissing Princess Maria's hands.

"Make your journey to St. Petersburg; that will be best,
and I will write to you, I promise."

"To St. Petersburg! Now? Well, I will do your bidding.
But I may come and see you again to-morrow?"

And Peter went next day to take leave.

Natacha was quieter than she had been these last days;
but he, as he looked at her, felt but one thing—the happiness
that thrilled him, and that increased with every word she
spoke, every movement or gesture of her person. As he clasped
her small, thin hand when they were saying good-bye, he
involuntarily held it for a few seconds. "This hand, that face,
that treasure of delight, are they really to be mine, mine for
ever?"

"*Au revoir*, count," she said. "I shall expect your return
with impatience," she added, in a lower voice.

These simple words, and the look that had accompanied
them, were to Peter an endless source of memories and exquisite
dreams during his two months' absence. "She said she should
expect me with impatience!" and at every hour of the day he
kept saying to himself, "What happiness! What happiness!"

CHAPTER CXXIX

HE felt nothing now of what he had experienced during his betrothal to Helen. He then had remembered with shame every time he had said to her, "I love you." Now, on the contrary, he thought over every detail of his interview with Natacha with exquisite and unmixed delight, repeating her last words to himself again and again. He did not think of asking himself whether he were doing right or wrong; no shadow of a doubt was possible. He dreaded only one thing, lest he should have been the sport of an illusion. Was he not too presumptuous, too sure of his happiness? Was not Princess Maria perhaps mistaken? Might not Natacha say to her with a smile: "How very strange! How can he have failed to understand that he is no more than a man like any other man, while I am so far above him?" Only this doubt constantly worried him. He no longer made any plans for the future. The happiness that was in store for him seemed so extraordinary that there could be nothing beyond it. Everything was bound to end.

The very folly of happiness, which he had believed himself incapable of ever feeling again, possessed him wholly. His own life and the whole world were summed up for him in his love for her, and his hope of being loved by her. He fancied he could discern in every face a sympathy which was only hindered from expressing itself by other interests. He often puzzled those he met by his radiant look and smile of happiness. He pitied those who did not understand, and sometimes longed to explain to them that they were losing their time in common-place futility. When it was proposed to him that he should take some office, or when the politics of the day were discussed in his presence as exerting some possible influence over the happiness of the human race, he listened pityingly, and astonished his listeners by the oddity of his remarks. But in spite of everything the radiance of his soul, throwing its light on all who came in his way, enabled him to detect at once what there was of good or kindness in each. As he read through his wife's papers no feeling but one of deep pity was roused in his heart; and in his eyes Prince Basil—so proud of some promotion at Court, and a new order—was no more than a foolish old man.

At the same time the views he held as to men and events

during this period of his life, remained in his mind incontrovertibly true, and often helped him in after life to solve his doubts, "I was absurd and odd perhaps at that time," he would say, "but I was not such a fool as I looked. My mind was open and keen; I understood what things in life were really worth comprehending, because—because I was happy!"

CHAPTER CXXX

As to Natacha, from the first evening she had spent in Peter's company, she was greatly changed. Almost without her knowing it the sap of life had revived in her heart, and had spread, unchecked, throughout her being. Her demeanour, her face, her look, her voice, all were metamorphosed. Her cravings for happiness had come to the surface, and clamoured to be satisfied. From that day forth she seemed to have forgotten all antecedent events. Not a complaint ever escaped her lips, by no word did she allude to the vanished shades of the past, and sometimes she even smiled over plans for the future. Though she never mentioned Peter's name, a flame, long since extinct, sparkled in her eyes when Princess Maria spoke of him, and she could scarcely control the quivering of her lips.

Princess Maria was struck by the change of which she could easily guess the cause; and it pained her. "Did she love my brother so little that she can forget him already?" But when she saw her she could feel no grudge, could find nothing to reproach her for. This reawakening to life was so sudden, so irresistible, so entirely unforeseen by Natacha herself, that Princess Maria could not feel that she had any right to blame her, even in her most secret soul; and Natacha threw herself so entirely and so sincerely into this new vein of feeling, that she made no attempt to mask the fact that, for her, sorrow had given way to gladness.

When Princess Maria came to her soon after her interview with Peter, Natacha met her at the door. "He has spoken, has he not—he has told you?" she said, with a look of pathos and joy that pleaded for forgiveness. "I longed to listen at the door; but I knew you would tell me everything."

Sincere and appealing as her eyes were, her words nevertheless wounded Princess Maria; she thought of her brother.

"But what is to be done?" said she to herself. "It cannot be otherwise . . ." and then, in a voice which was at once severe and gentle, she repeated her conversation with Peter.

On hearing that he was leaving for St. Petersburg, Natacha exclaimed in surprise; then, guessing that she must have made a painful impression on her friend, she asked: "Maria, tell me what I ought to do; I am so afraid of being horrid: I will do whatever you advise."

"Do you love him?"

"Yes," she murmured.

"Then what have you to cry for?—I am glad . . ." said Princess Maria, but she could not check her tears.

"It will not be very soon, Maria. . . . Think how happy we shall be. I shall be his wife and you will marry Nicholas."

"Natacha, I begged you never to mention it. We need only speak of you." And they were both silent.

"But why need he go to St. Petersburg?" Natacha suddenly asked; but answering her own question she went on: "It is best so—it is best, no doubt. Don't you think so, Maria?"

EPILOGUE

PART I

CHAPTER CXXXI

SEVEN years had passed. The storm-tossed historical sea of Europe had sunk to rest upon its shores. Yet, calm though it appeared, the mysterious forces which move humanity (forces mysterious only because we do not understand the laws which govern their action) still continued operative.

Although the surface of the historical sea seemed motionless—seemed as unbroken as the passage of time—humanity still moved. Different groups of human combinations continued to form or to be dissolved, and the springs which make or unmake states and transpose nations continued to be wound. The historical sea was no longer driven by squalls from shore to shore, but raged only below the surface. Historical figures were no longer carried by its waves from coast to coast, but revolved in stationary eddies. Historical personages who had lately been leading armies and directing the movements of popular masses by issuing commands to war, to campaigns and battles, were now directing those movements by means of political and diplomatic conventions, laws, and treaties.

A part of this kind played by historical personages is what historians call reaction. In describing the parts played by historical personages whom they consider to have been the cause of reaction, historians exercise a strict judgment. All the well-known figures of the period, from Alexander I and Napoleon to Madame de Staël, Schelling, Chateaubriand, and the rest, have been arraigned before that stern tribunal, and acquitted or condemned according as they had contributed to progress or to reaction.

Russia too is described by historians as the scene of reaction, and for this they throw the chief responsibility upon Alexander I—upon the same Alexander I to whom they also give the credit for the liberal enterprises of his reign and for the salvation of Russia.

In Russian letters of to-day there is not a man, from the

gymnasium student to the expert historian, who would not throw a stone at Alexander for one or another ill-considered act at this period of his reign.

"He should have done so and so. On such and such an occasion he did well, but on such and such another occasion he did badly. He bore himself excellently at the beginning, as well as in 1812, but he erred in granting Poland a constitution, in forming the Holy Alliance, in giving Araktchéïew power, in encouraging, first of all, Golitzin and his mysticism, and then Shishkoff and Photius. Also he did wrong in interfering with the *élite* of the army—he made a mistake in disbanding the Séménovsky Regiment," and so forth, and so forth. A dozen sheets of paper might be filled with the faults which historians find with Alexander on the strength of that knowledge of what is good for mankind which only historians possess.

Yet what do these reproaches really amount to? Were not the acts for which they blame him (the Holy Alliance, the re-establishment of Poland, and the reaction of the twenties) due to identically the same sources (the conditions of blood, upbringing, and life which made Alexander's personality what it was) as the acts for which they praise him (the liberal enterprises of the early part of his reign, the struggle which he maintained with Napoleon, the firmness which he showed in 1812, and the campaign of the following year)?

What, then, do these reproaches really amount to? They amount to saying that an historical personage such as Alexander I—a personage who stood at the highest summit of human power—at the focus-point, as it were, of a light which inevitably blinded all historical beams which might be turned upon it; a personage who was subject to some of the strongest influences in the world—the influences of intrigue, chicanery, flattery, and self-deception, all of which are inseparable from power; a personage who was conscious, every moment of his life, of being responsible for all that happened in Europe; a personage who was not an imaginary being, but a man alive like his fellows, and possessed of his own personal habits, passions, and aspirations for good, beauty, and truth—I repeat that those reproaches amount to saying that this personage of half a century ago was, if not wholly destitute of virtue (historians do not accuse him of that), at all events without those particular views on the subject of the welfare of humanity which a present-day professor holds who has applied himself to science from his youth upwards—*i.e.* has applied himself to the reading and hearing of books and lectures, and to the copying out of such books and lectures on paper.

If, then, we are to suppose that Alexander erred fifty years ago in his view of what constitutes the welfare of nations, we have no choice also but to suppose that the historian who judges Alexander may, at this distance of time, also be erring in his view of what constitutes the welfare of humanity. This supposition is the more natural and inevitable in that, as we trace the growth of history, we see that, with each successive year and each successive new writer, a change always takes place in the accepted view of what constitutes the welfare of humanity, so that what seemed good, say, ten years ago may seem evil now, and vice versa. In fact, history reveals to us many contemporary, yet utterly opposed, views of what constitutes good or evil. Thus some persons place the Holy Alliance and the granting of a constitution to Poland to Alexander's credit, while others blame him for those two acts.

Neither of Alexander's nor of Napoleon's conduct can it be said that it was either beneficial or harmful, seeing that we cannot say precisely what benefited from or what was harmed by them. If their conduct does not meet with the approval of a given individual, it does not do so simply because it does not happen to coincide with his limited comprehension of what constitutes good. Suppose I consider to be good the preservation of my father's house in Moscow in 1812, or regard as progress the glory won by the Russian forces, or the flourishing condition of St. Petersburg (or any other) university, or the emancipation of Poland, or the might of Russia, or the equilibrium of Europe, or any given branch of European civilisation, it still remains for me to confess that the conduct of each actor in these events may have had other and more general aims in view—aims which, to me, are unfathomable.

Yet suppose also that what we call science can reconcile all contradictions, and that for historical persons and events it has an unchanging standard of good and evil. Suppose also that Alexander might have done everything differently, and followed the prescription of those who blame him and those who profess knowledge of the ultimate ends of the movements of humanity by ordering his conduct according to the programme of nationality, freedom, equality, and progress (for there would seem to be no other) with which his accusers of to-day would have provided him. Finally, suppose that that programme had been possible, and formulated, and that

Alexander had followed it—well, what then would have become of the conduct of all who *opposed* the policy of the Government of that time—of the conduct which historians declare to have been solely good and useful? That conduct would never have been: life would never have been: nothing would ever have been.

For if we allow that human life is always guided by reason, we destroy the premise that life is possible at all.

CHAPTER CXXXII

IF, also, we allow, as historians do, that only great men enable humanity to attain such ends as the aggrandisement, say, of Russia or France, or the equilibrium of Europe, or the diffusion of revolutionary ideas, or general progress, or anything else, it at once becomes impossible for us to explain the phenomena of history without certain ideas on the subject of *chance* and *genius*.

If the aim of the European wars of the opening years of this century was the aggrandisement of Russia, that aim could have been attained without the preceding wars and without invasion. If that aim was the aggrandisement of France, that aim could have been attained without either the Revolution or the Empire. If that aim was the spreading of ideas, it could have been fulfilled much better through the Press than by soldiers. If that aim was the progress of civilisation, then we may reasonably suppose that there exist other and much more suitable ways of extending civilisation than by the extermination of human beings and their possessions.

Why, then, did these things happen thus, and not otherwise? Simply because they did so happen.

"Chance made the position: genius used it," says history. But what is this "chance," this "genius?"

The terms "chance" and "genius" connote nothing that really exists, and therefore lie beyond definition. They connote merely a degree of comprehension of phenomena. Not knowing why a given phenomenon occurs, I suppose that I cannot know: wherefore I do not wish to know, and merely say to myself: "It is chance." I see a force which produces action out of all proportion to the general characteristics of

humanity, and, not knowing whence it arises, I say to myself:
"It is genius."

The sheep which the shepherd puts into a separate pen every
night, so that that sheep becomes twice as fat as its fellows,
would seem to be a genius; and the circumstance that every
night that particular sheep is put into a separate pen instead
of into the common fold, until at last it becomes sufficiently
clothed in fat to make good mutton, would seem to be a striking
conjunction of the quality known as genius with a series of
fortuitous happenings.

Yet the other sheep need only rid themselves of the idea that
all that is done to them is being done solely for the furtherance
of their sheepish ends, as well as to concede that events affecting
them may have aims beyond their comprehension, for them at
once to see the unity, the consecutiveness, of what is occurring
also to their fattened comrade. Although it may not be given
to them to know to what end he is being fattened, they will at
least know that his fate is not overtaking him casually, and
thus will have no need of the idea either of chance or of genius.

Similarly, as soon as we confess that we do not know what
the aim of those bygone disturbances among the European
nations can have been, but that we know only the hard facts
envisaged in the killings which then took place (firstly in France,
and, later, in Italy, Africa, Prussia, Austria, Spain, and Russia),
as well as that a movement from west to east and from east to
west constitutes the whole substance and aim of those events,
we shall no longer find it necessary to see any exceptionality or
genius in the characters of Alexander and Napoleon, nor be able
to regard those two personages as having been in any way dissimilar to their fellows. Not only shall we have no need to
explain the *accidentalness* of the minor events which made those
men what they were, but it will become clear to us that those
minor events were inevitable.

If, therefore, we renounce all knowledge of the final aim of
things, we shall realise that, just as one cannot invent for a
plant new growths, new seeds or flowers, which shall be the
counterpart of those which it already produces, so it would be
impossible for us to imagine two men with a past corresponding
exactly and in absolute minuteness of detail to the destiny
which it fell to the lot of Alexander and Napoleon to fulfil.

CHAPTER CXXXIII

THE real, the fundamental essence of European events at the beginning of this century lies in the fact that a warlike movement by a massed body of European nations took place from west to east, and again from east to west. For the forces of the west to be able to carry out the warlike movement upon Moscow which they accomplished it was necessary—(1) That they should combine into a military group of dimensions capable of sustaining the shock of collision with the military group of the east; (2) That they should renounce all established customs and traditions; and (3) That for the carrying out of their warlike movement they should have at their head a man able, both for their sake and his own, to justify the lies, plundering, and killing which were to be the concomitants of that movement.

Thus, beginning with the French Revolution, we see an old group of inadequate dimensions becoming broken up, and old customs and traditions being abolished. Next, a group of adequate dimensions becomes formed, new customs and traditions developed, and the way prepared for the man who was to stand at the head of the coming movement, and to take upon himself the responsibility for all the events that were to happen. Finally, a man without convictions, without habits, without traditions, without a name—not even a Frenchman—was, by what would appear to be an extraordinary series of chances, to thrust himself into the midst of the various parties agitating France, and, though not an adherent of any one of them, to raise himself to a unique position.

The ignorance of his colleagues, the weakness and insignificance of his opponents, the wholesale intrigues and splendid self-assurance of this man brought him to the head of the army, while the brilliant personnel of the Italian forces, the unwillingness of his opponents to fight him, and his own childish insolence and belief in himself soon won him military glory. A countless number of so-called chances aided him everywhere. Even the bad odour into which he fell with the directors of France only went in his favour. All his attempts to alter the course to which he was predestined were unsuccessful. Russia would not take him into her service, and his appointment to Turkey was a failure. More than once during the war in Italy he found himself on the brink of disaster, yet he escaped each time by some unlooked for chance. As for the Russian forces—the forces which might have shattered his glory—diplomatic considerations prevented them from entering Europe while he was there.

On his return from Italy he found the Parisian government in that stage of dissolution which means the inevitable suppression and extinction of any man who falls foul of such a government. Nevertheless a means of escape from this dangerous position presented itself in the shape of the senseless, inexplicable expedition to Africa. Again a series of so-called chances attended Napoleon throughout. Impregnable Malta surrendered without a shot, and the most rashly conceived of enterprises were invariably crowned with success. To add to that, the enemy's fleet, which never afterwards let a ship escape it, now suffered a whole army to pass through its lines. In Africa a series of outrages was perpetrated upon the almost defenceless inhabitants, yet the men who committed the deeds, and especially their leader, told themselves that it was splendid, that it was glory, that it was what Cæsar and Alexander of Macedon had done, and that it was right to do so.

The ideal of this leader and of those attached to him was the ideal which consists in never admitting that one has done wrong, but in boasting of one's crime and attributing to it some unknown supernatural meaning. This ideal attained wide development in Africa. Likewise, all that Napoleon did not do was in his favour. The plague never touched him. The guilt for the foul putting of prisoners to death was never brought home to him. His childishly incautious, unwarrantable, and ignoble departure from Africa—that is to say, from his comrades in distress—was reckoned to his credit. Once again the enemy's fleet let him slip through its lines. Finally he returned to Paris—his head turned with the deeds he had performed or had been permitted by fortune to perform—at the very moment when the republican government, which, a year ago, could have destroyed him, had come to the end of its tether, and when his presence—the presence of a man free from parties—might, if anything, help to restore it.

He had no plan to propose and was afraid of everyone, but the parties seized upon him and demanded his co-operation. He alone, with the ideal of glory and greatness which he had formulated in Italy and Egypt, his craze for self-glorification, his pride in his enormities, and his sincerity of deceit, could undertake the direction of what was to be done. He was the only man for the place awaiting him, and therefore, almost involuntarily, and despite his vacillation, his absence of a plan, and his innumerable blunders, he was drawn into a conspiracy which had for its object the seizure of power. That conspiracy was crowned with success.

Yet, when dragged before the directors in council, he was panic-stricken and tried to flee, for he thought himself lost. He pretended to be fainting, and then started babbling nonsense which would have ended his career then and there had not the directors of France, formerly so proud and derisive, been conscious that they were on their last legs, and so had their minds as confused as he. Consequently the word was never spoken which would have destroyed him and retained power in their own hands. It was chance—millions of chances—which invested him with authority, and which made everyone, as it were, conspire to aid in the consolidation of that authority. It was chance which formed the characters of the then administrators of France who gave way to him; it was chance which formed the character of Paul I, who recognised his power; it was chance which formed the conspiracy against him which not only failed to injure him, but even strengthened his position. It was chance which delivered Enghien into his hands and suddenly suggested to him the idea of killing his prisoner as the best and most effective method of convincing the populace that he (Napoleon) had right on his side because he had power. It was chance which made him strain every nerve to effect the invasion of England—the very enterprise which would, in all probability, have ruined him—yet never to carry out that intention, but, instead, to make a sudden movement against Mack and his Austrains, who surrendered to him without a blow. It was chance and genius combined which gave him the victory at Austerlitz, and it was chance which made all men —not only the French, but the whole of Europe except England, which took no part in those events—forget their former horror and detestation of his acts, and recognise both his power over them, the title which he had assumed, and the ideal of glory and greatness which he had invented—an ideal which now seemed to them something reasonable and splendid.

Several times during the years 1805–09 the forces of the west tried and practised their powers by making sallies eastwards, in proportion as their strength and mobility grew. Next, in 1811 a great body of men who had formed a union in France effected a junction with certain nations of central Europe, and became, with them, one large group. As this group increased in strength, so also did the man who stood at the head of the movement increase in power. During the ten years' preparation which preceded the great movement this man held converse with all the crowned heads in Europe. The unmasked rulers of the world had no reasonable, no intelligible, ideal to oppose to the Napoleonic ideal of glory and greatness. One by one they vied in showing him their inferiority. The King of Prussia sent his wife to beg the great man's favour. The Emperor of Austria took it as a favour that the great man should receive to his nuptial bed a daughter of kaisers. The Pope, the keeper of the morals of the nations, thought, forsooth, he served his faith by aiding in the elevation of Napoleon! In short, it was not Napoleon himself who carried out his own training for assumption of sole responsibility for what was happening and to happen, but everyone around him. There was not a blunder on his part, not an enormity nor a petty piece of trickery, that was not at once represented in the mouths of his entourage as a great act. The best fête days the Germans can think of to please him are the celebrations of the victories of Jena and Austerlitz. Moreover, not only was Napoleon himself great, but also his forefathers, his brothers, his stepchildren, his sons-in-law! Everything was done to deprive him of the last vestige of reason, and to prepare him for his unique role. By the time that he was ready for it his forces also were ready.

The invading army pressed eastwards until the final goal, Moscow, was reached. The capital fell, and the Russian army was annihilated even more completely than the enemy's forces had ever been in all the previous battles, from Austerlitz to Wagram. Yet suddenly, in place of the chances and genius which had hitherto attended him with such consistency and in such unbroken progress towards the appointed goal, there began to manifest itself a countless series of *reverse* chances, from the cold in the head at Borodino to the flames which consumed Moscow, while, in place of genius, there showed itself only stupidity, a cowardice, which is without parallel.

The invading force began to flee—was turned back, and again fled, while all the chances were now against it instead of in its favour. A return movement was begun from east to west which bore a striking similarity to the movement which had taken place from west to east. The main operation was preceded by the same tentative sallies westwards as had been made towards the east during the years 1805–09, while we also see the same linking up of forces into a group of huge dimensions, the same adhesion of the mid-European nations to the movement, the same vacillation half-way, and the same headlong rush as the forces approached the goal of their return.

That goal, Paris, was reached, but Napoleon's government and army lay shattered. Napoleon himself seemed to have no further meaning, and all his actions now appear pitiful and mean. Nevertheless, another inexplicable chance was to manifest itself at this juncture. The allies hated Napoleon, in whom they saw the cause of all their misfortunes, so that he ought then to have appeared to them—now that he stood deprived of power and detected in his wiles and villainies—what he had appeared to them ten years earlier—namely, an outlaw and a brigand. Yet a strange chance ordained that no one should see him thus. Evidently his role was not yet finished. The man whom ten years earlier (as also a year later) they had hailed as an outlaw and a brigand they now banished to an island only two days' journey from Paris—an island where he ruled, had his own guard, and was permitted to retain the millions which had been paid him for some reason or other.

CHAPTER CXXXIV

THEN the turmoil of the nations began to subside upon its shores. The breakers of the great storm retreated, and on the calm surface remained only a few eddies in which diplomatists busied themselves, in the belief that it was they who had quieted the disturbance.

Suddenly the tranquil sea became restive again. The diplomatists imagined themselves and their differences to be the cause of this new upheaval of the elements. They looked upon war as bound to break out among their masters, and regarded the present situation as uncertain. Yet the wave which they felt to be approaching was not coming from the quarter expected. It was the same wave as before, and its source the same point as before—namely, Paris. The last phase of the movement from the west was about to be accomplished—the phase which was to decide the seemingly insoluble difficulties of diplomacy, and put an end to the warlike movements of the period.

Alone, without a commission, without soldiers, the man who

had wasted France was returning to her shores. Any gendarme might have apprehended him, yet by some extraordinary chance not only was that never done, but everyone went out to greet with acclamations the man whom yesterday they had abjured, and whom but a month later they were to abjure again. That, man was necessary for the direction of the final, the crowning, operation.

The operation was performed and the last act played. Then the chief actor was bidden divest himself of his costume, and wash the rouge and antimony from his face. He was needed no longer.

For a few years this man, alone on his lonely island, played a sorry comedy to himself, lied and intrigued as he strove to justify his actions now that justification was no longer necessary, and showed the whole world what men had taken for strength so long as it had been guided by an unseen hand.

The Dispenser of all had ended the drama and stripped the chief actor of his motley, so that he stood revealed to the world.

"Look," said the Dispenser. "This is he in whom you have believed. There he stands. See you now that it was not he, but I, who moved you?" Yet so blinded were men by the force of the movement that it was long before they understood this.

The life of Alexander I—of the man who headed the counter-movement from east to west — furnishes us with an equally striking example of consecutiveness and destiny.

What did the man need who towered above all others in the direction of the movement westwards? He had need of a sense of justice, as well as of a close familiarity with the affairs of Europe—a detached familiarity, however, not one clouded with petty interests. He had need also of a moral elevation over his allies, the other rulers of the day, as well as of a benign and attractive personality and a personal grudge against Napoleon. All this Alexander I possessed. All this had been added to him by the countless so-called chances of his previous life—by his upbringing and liberal views, by the councillors who stood near him, by Austerlitz, Tilsit, and Erfurt.

So long as the war was a national one this actor took no part in it, since he was unnecessary, but as soon as ever a general European war was seen to be inevitable, this actor appeared in his place at the proper moment, and, uniting the European nations in one, led them to their goal.

The goal was reached, and, the final battle of 1815 having

been fought, Alexander found himself at the summit of human power. How did he use that position?

The man who was the peacemaker of Europe, who from his earliest years had striven only for the good of his people, who had been the chief defender of liberal innovations in his country, who, now that he possessed the utmost measure of power, possessed also the utmost capacity for benefiting his nation while the exiled Napoleon was making childish, knavish plans for desolating humanity if ever the chance should come to him again—the man, Alexander I, who had thus fulfilled his destiny, felt the hand of God upon him, and, suddenly recognising the nothingness of the evanescent power that was his, turned away from it, and committed it into the hands of men whom he despised, with the words:

"Not unto me, not unto me, but unto Thy Name! I am even such a man as yourselves. Suffer me, therefore, to live my life as a man, and to think of my soul and of God."

Just as the sun and every particle of the ether is a sphere complete in itself, as well as only one atom in a purpose which lies beyond the comprehension of humanity, so also does every personality bear within itself its own purposes, as well as contain them that they may serve general purposes which lie beyond all human comprehension.

If a bee, settling upon a flower, stings a child, the child becomes afraid of all bees, and declares that their purpose is to sting people. The poet, however, loves to see the bee drinking from the chalices of the flowers, and says that the purpose of bees is to gather nectar for themselves. The bee-keeper, on the other hand, remarking how the bee not only gathers pollen, but also carries it away to its hive, declares that the purpose of bees is to make honey, while one of his craft who had studied the life of the swarm more closely says that bees collect pollen in order to feed their young and produce queens, i.e., to continue their species. Finally, the botanist, noticing that the fact of a pollen-laden bee settling upon the pistil of a flower fertilises the plant, concludes that that is the ultimate purpose of the insect. Nevertheless the ultimate purpose of bees is not exhausted by any such purposes as the human mind may conceive of it. The higher the human intellect soars in its conception of possible purposes, the more does it realise that such purposes lie beyond its comprehension.

Man cannot rise beyond a certain insight into the correlation of the bee's life with certain other phenomena of life. So also with the purposes for which historical personages and nations exist.

CHAPTER CXXXV

NATACHA's and Bésoukhow's wedding (which took place in 1813) was the last festive occasion to occur in the ancient family of the Rostows. The same year Count Ilia Andréïévitch died, and, as is usual in such cases, his decease caused the household to decline.

The events of the previous year—the burning of Moscow, the flight from the city, the death of Prince Andrew, Natacha's despair, the death of Pétia, and the countess's grief for him—had descended in successive blows upon the head of the aged count. He seemed neither to understand nor to make an effort to understand the meaning of those events, but, meekly bowing his head, appeared to be waiting only in the hope that further blows of fortune might finish him. He seemed cowed and distraught, yet unnaturally excited and restless.

For a while Natacha's marriage occupied his external self. He ordered the wedding breakfast and dinner, and seemed all the time to be trying to seem cheerful, but his cheerfulness was not as infectious as it had once been, and aroused only compassion in those who knew and loved him. When Peter and his wife had left the house the old count broke down altogether, and fell to bewailing his misfortunes. A few days later he was seized with sickness, and took to his bed. From the first day of his malady he knew that, despite all the doctor's assurances, he would never rise from that bed again. For two weeks the countess never took her clothes off, but spent the nights on a sofa at his bed-head. Each time that she gave him medicine he would burst into sobbing, and silently kiss her hand. On the last day of his life he besought her with tears that she and his absent son would pardon him for his squandering of the family property—the chief fault of which he felt himself guilty, and then, having received the last unction and absolution, passed peacefully away. Next day the throng of acquaintances who came to pay their last respects to the deceased filled the hired flat of the Rostows to overflowing. All these people who had so often danced or dined at his house, as well as laughed at him, now said to themselves with a unanimous feeling of compunction and regret: "Yes, taking him all in all, he was a fine man. We do not often meet such men nowadays. We all have our weaknesses, have we not?" This was because the count's death took place just when his affairs had become so involved that no one knew how things would have ended if they had continued so for another year.

Nicholas was with the Russian troops in Paris when the news of his father's death came. He at once resigned his commission, and, without waiting for the resignation to be accepted, set out for Moscow. The position of the count's affairs was ascertained about a month later, and astounded everyone with the immensity of the aggregate of small debts of which no one had suspected the existence. Indeed, they amounted to twice as much as the property itself.

Relations and friends alike advised Nicholas to surrender the inheritance, but he considered that such a course would look like a slur on the hallowed memory of his dead father, and therefore declined the suggestion, and accepted full responsibility for the liabilities.

The creditors—who had kept silence during the count's lifetime, under the indefinable, yet powerful, spell of his universal benevolence—now suddenly, and with one consent, presented their claims to Nicholas. Emulation of this kind—emulation to be the first paid—is common enough, and the same people who, like Mitenka and certain others, had received presents of bills now showed themselves the most insistent of creditors. They granted Nicholas neither rest nor respite, and the men who had compassion upon the old man who had been the cause of all their losses (if losses they were) now threw themselves pitilessly upon the innocent young heir who had voluntarily assumed responsibility for payment. Not one of the schemes put forward by Nicholas was accepted. The property was sold under the hammer, and fetched about half its value, while fully half the outstanding debts still remained unpaid. Nicholas accepted 30,000 roubles offered him on loan by his brother-in-law, Bésoukhow, for the purpose of paying off those debts which he recognised to be actual monetary obligations, while, as regards the rest, he sought to escape the dungeon with which the creditors threatened him by entering public service again.

For him to return to the army—where he had been next on the rota for the first colonelcy which should fall vacant—was out of the question, since his mother now clung to him as her one joy in life. Consequently, despite his reluctance to remain in Moscow surrounded by people who had always known him, as well as to enter the civil branch of the service, he obtained a departmental post in Moscow, and, doffing his beloved uniform, removed, with his mother and Sonia, to a smaller flat.

At this time Natacha and Peter were living in St. Petersburg, and had but a dim idea of Nicholas' position, seeing that, when he borrowed the money of his brother-in-law, he had striven all he could to conceal from him the real state of affairs. His plight was all the worse in that his salary of 1200 roubles not only had to support himself, Sonia, and his mother, but also to support his mother in such a way that she should never discover that they had become poor. The countess could not conceive life as possible without the conditions of luxury to which she had always been accustomed from her childhood, and, not knowing how hard things were for her son, would keep demanding, first of all a carriage for some friend to be sent for in, then expensive cookery for herself and wines for her son, and lastly, money for her to make surprise gifts to himself, Natacha, and Sonia.

Sonia did the housekeeping, went shopping for her aunt, read aloud to her, bore with her caprices and secret indisposition, and helped Nicholas to conceal from her the state of poverty in which they were now placed. Nicholas felt that he owed her a debt which he could never adequately repay for all she did for his mother. Yet, though charmed with her patience and devotion, he strove to keep away from her. In his heart of hearts he had a kind of grudge against her for being so thorough—for never giving him the least occasion to find fault with her. She had every quality in her which people usually value, yet nothing that could make him love her. He felt always that the more he valued her, the less he loved her. He had taken her literally in the letter by which she had given him his freedom, and now treated her as though all that had been between them had long ago sunk into oblivion and could never possibly be repeated.

His financial position gradually became worse and worse. The idea of saving anything out of his salary now seemed to him only an empty dream. Not only did he save nothing whatever, but the task of satisfying his mother's demands caused him to incur small debts. Nor, for that matter, could he see any way out of his troubles. The idea of marrying a rich heiress—the suggestion of his relatives—was abhorrent to him. Another possible deliverance from his position—the death of his mother—never even entered his head. He wished for nothing, and hoped for nothing, but took a vague, grim pleasure in bearing his lot with resignation. Old acquaintances, with their expressions of condolence and offers of insulting help, he pointedly avoided, and all amusement or distraction he also eschewed. Even at home he allowed himself no relaxation beyond an occasional game at cards with his mother, silent pacings of his room, and the smoking of endless pipes. He seemed determined to preserve the mood in which alone he felt that he could bear his misfortunes.

CHAPTER CXXXVI

EARLY that winter Princess Maria arrived in Moscow. Gossip of the town soon informed her of the position of the Rostows—of the fact that (so said the quidnuncs) "the son was sacrificing himself for the mother."

"It is just what I should have expected him to do," said the princess to herself, feeling a joyous revival of her love for Nicholas. Remembering her former intimate relations—the relations almost of a kinswoman—with his family, she decided that it was her duty to go and call upon the Rostows. Yet when she also remembered her former relations with Nicholas at Voronège, she felt afraid to do so. At length, a few weeks after her arrival in town, she nerved herself to the effort, and went to call upon the family.

Nicholas was the first to greet her, for the countess's room could only be reached through his own. No sooner had he glanced at her than, in place of the expression of pleasure which the princess had expected to see there, his face assumed an air of cold austerity and pride which she had never before seen it wear. He inquired after her health, and then conducted her to his mother's room, where he sat with them for a few minutes, and then departed.

When the princess took her leave of the countess, Nicholas again met her in the ante-room, and escorted her with marked gravity and formality to the door. To some remark of hers about the countess's health he returned no answer whatever. "What business have you here? Leave us in peace," was what his glance seemed to say.

"What can she want here? I cannot bear these grand ladies and their civilities!" he said to Sonia in a burst of anger which he seemed unable to control, immediately that the princess's carriage had driven away from the building.

"Oh, how can you say that, Nicholas?" answered Sonia, scarcely able to conceal her delight. "She is so kind, and mamma likes her so much."

To this Nicholas said nothing, and tried never to mention the princess's name again, but from that day onwards the countess was for ever talking of her, praising her, demanding that Nicholas should go and call upon her, and expressing a wish to see her more frequently. At such times the countess always seemed a little disturbed in her mind.

Nicholas endeavoured to say nothing while his mother was talking in this strain, but his silence only vexed the old lady.

"She is a most excellent and deserving girl," she once said to him, "and you ought to go and see her. At all events you ought to see *someone* occasionally, for I am sure it must be dull for you here with us alone."

"I have no desire to see her, mother."

"Once upon a time you were eager enough to do so, yet now you say, 'I have no desire to see her.' I do not understand you, my dear boy. You find it dull here, yet you suddenly decide to see no one."

"I did not say that I found it dull here."

"Well, at all events you say that you do not wish to see her again. She is a very praiseworthy girl, and you used to like her once upon a time. Yet now you suddenly find reasons for avoiding her. People keep things so secret from me."

"Oh no, mother."

"If I had asked you to do something unpleasant I could have understood your refusal, but I only asked you to go and call upon her. Mere civility demands that. Well, I have asked you, but in future I shall leave you alone since you keep secrets from your mother."

"Well, I will go if you wish."

"Oh, it does not matter to me. I only wished it for your own sake."

Nicholas sighed and bit his moustache. Then he dealt out the cards, in the hope of distracting his mother's attention from the subject. Yet, the next day, and the next, and the next, the same conversation was repeated.

After her visit to the Rostows and the unexpected, cold

reception there accorded her by Nicholas, Princess Maria told herself that she had been right in feeling reluctant to call.

"It was just what I ought to have expected," she reflected as she summoned her pride to her aid. "It was not Nicholas that I wished to see at all, but his old mother, who has always been kind to me, and to whom I am much indebted."

Yet she could not soothe herself with these reflections. A feeling akin to regret disturbed her whenever she thought of her visit. Although she had firmly resolved never to see the Rostows again and to forget the matter altogether, she somehow felt undecided about it. Each time that she asked herself what was worrying her so much, she found herself forced to confess that it was her encounter with Nicholas. His cold, punctilious tone could not proceed from his real feelings towards her (she felt sure of that), but concealed something else. What that something else was she must find out. Until she did so she knew that she would never know peace.

One day in mid-winter she was sitting in the schoolroom and superintending her nephew's lessons when she was informed that Nicholas had called. With a fixed determination not to betray her secret or evince any sign of her agitation she summoned Mademoiselle Bourrienne, and proceeded with her to the drawing-room.

The first glance at Nicholas' face showed her that he had merely come to pay the bare debt which civility demanded, and therefore she made up her mind to adopt the same tone to him as he adopted to herself. They discussed the countess's health, mutual acquaintances, and the latest news of the war, and as soon as the prescribed ten minutes of an afternoon call had elapsed, Nicholas rose to take his leave. With the help of Mademoiselle Bourrienne the princess had sustained the conversation well enough, but just at the last moment, when Nicholas was rising to go, such a weariness of speaking of matters of no moment to her, and such a sense of wonder that life should have so little pleasure to offer her alone came over her that she sank into a fit of abstraction, and sat motionless, with her brilliant eyes staring straight in front of her, and her thoughts oblivious of the fact that he had risen to go.

Nicholas glanced at her, and, not wishing to appear conscious of her reverie, said a few words to Mademoiselle Bourrienne, and then glanced at the princess again. She was still seated motionless, while her tender face bore a look of suffering.

Suddenly he felt sorry for her, and a dim idea entered his mind that perhaps he was the cause of that suffering. He wanted to help her, to say something pleasant to her, but could not think what to utter.

"Good-bye, princess," he said at last.

She recovered herself, sat up, and gave a deep sigh.

"Pardon me," she murmured like one awakening from sleep. "Are you going already? Well, good-bye. Have you got my cushion for the countess?"

"Wait a moment, and I will fetch it," said Mademoiselle Bourrienne, and left the room.

Both remained silent a while, and scarcely even glanced at one another.

"Yes, princess," said Nicholas at last, with a mournful smile. "It does not seem a very long time, yet how much water has flowed away to the sea since you and I first saw one another at Bogoutcharovo! And how unhappy we both seem now! What would I not give to recall that time? Yet it will never come back."

The princess looked him straight in the eyes with her brilliant ones as he said this. She was trying to divine the secret meaning of his words—the meaning which would make plain to her his feelings towards herself.

"Yes, yes," she replied. "But you have no cause to regret the past. If I understand your present life aright, you will always be able to look back upon it with pleasure, since the life of renunciation which you are now leading——"

"No, no, I cannot accept your praise," he interrupted hurriedly. "On the contrary, I blame myself every day. However, this is neither a cheerful nor an interesting conversation," and he broke off, while his face assumed its old stern, cold expression. Yet the princess had seen in him the same man as she had formerly known and loved, and it was to that man that she again addressed herself.

"I had hoped that you would not mind my saying this to you," she said. "I used to know you so well—and your family too, that I thought you would not think my sympathy misplaced: but it seems I was mistaken." Her voice had begun to tremble all of a sudden. "Somehow," she went on, recovering herself, "you seem different now, and——"

"There are a thousand reasons why," he said quietly—and he laid a particular emphasis on the "why." "Nevertheless I thank you, princess. Sometimes things are hard for me."

"Then *that* is why, *that* is why!" cried a voice in the inmost depths of the princess's soul. "Yes, it was not that brave, kind, open-hearted face of his only—that handsome form—that I fell in love with. I guessed also his proud, noble, self-sacrificing character. Yes, he is poor now, and I am rich. *That* is why. If only things were not so!" And as she called to mind his former tenderness, and gazed upon his manly, sorrowful, countenance, she suddenly divined the reason of all his coldness.

"But why, count?—but why?" suddenly came from her almost like a cry as she made an involuntary movement towards him. "Tell me why. You *must* tell me why." (He still remained silent) "I do not understand your 'why.' It is for me—for me—that things are so hard. Yes, I do not mind confessing it to you. For some reason you wish to deprive me of our old friendship, and that hurts me." (There were tears in her eyes and in her voice) "I have so little happiness in my life that every loss hurts me. No, but pardon me—do not mind me," and, suddenly bursting into sobbing, she moved away towards the door.

"Princess! One moment, for God's sake!" he cried as he tried to intercept her. "Princess!"

She looked round, and for a moment they stood gazing silently into one another's eyes. Then all at once what had seemed remote and impossible before became now both possible and inevitable. . . .

CHAPTER CXXXVII

NICHOLAS married the Princess Maria in the autumn of 1813, and went with his wife, his mother, and Sonia to live at Lissy-Gory. Four years later, and without selling any of his wife's property, he had paid off the remainder of his small debts, and, being also left a legacy by a cousin, repaid Peter his principal. By 1820, indeed, he had rehabilitated his money affairs so well as to be able to buy a modest estate near Lissy-Gory, and to enter into negotiations for redeeming the ancestral property at Otradnoë—a project which had long been his cherished dream.

At first his own steward of necessity, he soon took to the pursuit so keenly that it became his favourite, and well-nigh his exclusive, occupation. He was a landowner of simple views, and had no taste for innovations—least of all for the English ones which were then coming into fashion, but laughed at all theoretical experiments in husbandry, and would have nothing to do with machinery, high-priced implements, or sowings of expensive crops. In short, he did not confine himself to one department of agriculture alone. In his eyes there was the one property, with no separate departments to it. He considered the main thing in connection with an estate to be, not the azote or the oxygen which lay in the soil or in the air, nor any special plough or manure, but the chief instrument through which the azote or the oxygen or the manure or the plough were made to act—namely, the workman or moujik. When Nicholas first took up agriculture and entered upon the mysteries of its various branches it was the moujik who especially attracted his attention, for he looked upon him as more than a mere instrument—as an end also and a judge. At first he watched him carefully, in the endeavour to comprehend his needs and his opinions as to what was good or bad, and only pretended to supervise and give orders while really taking lessons of him in different ways of working, in nomenclature, and in opinions favourable or unfavourable to given things. It was only when Nicholas had thus gained an insight into the tastes and aspirations of the moujik, had learnt to speak his dialect, to understand the inner meaning of his sayings, and to feel himself on a level with him, that he began to give him orders with confidence i.e. to fulfil, in his relations with his workmen, the same duty which he required of them. And Nicholas' estate-management proved productive of the most brilliant results.

As soon as he took the estate in hand he unerringly, and as though through some gift of prevision, chose his foremen and headmen from among the very men who would naturally have been chosen by the moujiks themselves, if they had had the choice, so that his officials never needed replacing. Before engaging in the investigation of the chemical qualities of manure or in calculations of "debit and credit" (as he used jestingly to call it) he took pains to ascertain the number of stock held by his peasants, and did everything he could to increase that number. Also, he kept the peasant's families as large as possible, i.e. did not allow them to become divided up, while the lazy, the vicious, and the incapable he sought out and endeavoured to banish from the community. At seed-times and hay and grain harvests he paid equal attention to his moujiks' fields and to his own: with the result that few owners had fields so well sown and reaped, so richly profitable, as had Nicholas.

His indoor servants he preferred to leave alone, and was commonly reported to spoil and pamper them. Whenever he had to make any arrangement with regard to them, and especially in the matter of punishment, he used to be very undecided about it, and only acted after he had consulted the entire household. Yet whenever he saw a chance of surrendering an indoor servant instead of a moujik to military service he never hesitated to do so. Indeed, he was never in doubt concerning his arrangements with regard to his moujiks. Every order of his, he knew well, would meet with the approval of the majority of them, even though one or a few should complain.

Similarly, he never allowed himself to overwork or punish a man just because he felt inclined to do so, nor yet to relieve or reward a man just because his personal wish lay that way. He himself could not have defined this standard of his of right and wrong, yet it was firmly and irrevocably fixed in his mind.

Often he would speak vexedly of some fault or omission on the part of "those Russian fellows of ours," and really imagine for the moment that he could not abide the moujik: yet, as a matter of fact, he loved both "those Russian fellows of ours" and their ways devotedly, and understood and made his own the one method and routine of agriculture which could bring him good results.

Countess Maria was jealous of his love for his moujiks, and regretted that she could not share it, since the joys and disappointments of that (to her) remote and unfamiliar world lay beyond her comprehension. She could not understand why it should make him so brisk and cheerful to rise at dawn, to spend a whole morning in the fields or at the homestead, and to return to her at tea-time after a whole day's sowing, haymaking, or reaping. She could not understand his rapture as he proudly told her (say) of the rich moujik of the estate, Matvei Ermishin, who had been leading grain all night with his family, and had got his corn stacked before anyone else had so much as reaped their fields. She could not understand why he laughed and chuckled so delightedly when he stepped out of the window on to the balcony and saw a fine, warm rain falling upon the ripening oats, nor why, when a threatening cloud was driving up before the wind to moisten the fields of grass and corn, he should come in from the homestead with his face red, his body heated and perspiring, and his hair smelling of vetch and clover, and say as he rubbed his hands together joyfully: "Another day or two like this, and both my stuff and the moujiks' will be in the barn."

Still less could she understand why, for all his kindly heart and constant readiness to anticipate her every wish, he should grow almost distracted when she repeated to him the request of some moujik or old woman who had come to beg her intercession in obtaining for them leave of absence from work; nor why he, the usually gentle Nicholas, should so persistently refuse her plea, and angrily request her not to interfere in his affairs again. She felt that he had a separate world to which he was passionately devoted, and in which laws of its own obtained which lay beyond her ken.

When, also, she sometimes strove to understand him, and to praise him for doing good to those under him, he only grew angry, and replied: "Nothing of the sort. Such an idea never entered into my head. It is not for their good that I do it. That is all poetry and old wives' tales—that sort of talk about one's neighbour's good. I wish our children not to have to roam about the world, and therefore I wish to set this estate in order while I am yet alive. That is all. To do that, a system and discipline are necessary. Yes, that is the thing," he would add, clenching his weather-tanned fist, "—though good treatment also, seeing that if the peasant is poorly fed and clothed and only able to afford one horse he will never do good work either for me or himself."

It may be that Nicholas really never allowed himself to think that he was doing this work for others or out of pure benevolence, but considered it mere work of production. In any case, his means increased rapidly, moujiks came from the neighbourhood round to request that he would buy them, and for long enough after his death the memory of his rule was devoutly cherished among the people. "He was a master indeed," they would say. "First the moujik's property, and then his own. Yet he allowed no liberties to be taken with him. In a word, he was a master."

CHAPTER CXXXVIII

ONE thing which occasionally troubled Nicholas in connection with his estate-management was his hasty temper, aggravated by his old hussar's habit of giving his hands full rein when provoked. At first he saw nothing wrong in this, but during the second year of his married life his view of this kind of discipline underwent a sudden change.

One day in the summer a starosta had to be sent for from Bogoutcharovo—a man who had succeeded the deceased Dron, and now stood accused of various faults and omissions. Nicholas went out to the veranda when he arrived, and the man had scarcely begun to reply to his master's questions before the sound of shouts and blows was heard. When Nicholas returned home at tea-time he, as usual, approached his wife—whom he found seated with her head bent over her embroidery frame—to tell her about all that had occupied him during the day, and, among other things, about the starosta from Bogoutcharovo. Nevertheless the countess did not stir, but kept turning red and pale by turns as she sat there, and pressing her lips tightly together. She neither raised her head nor answered a word to what her husband was saying.

"He was such an impudent rascal!" said Nicholas, growing angry again at the mere thought of the encounter. "If only he had told me that he was drunk at the time and therefore saw nothing of it. But what is the matter with you, Maria?" he added, suddenly breaking off.

The countess raised her head, and tried to say something, but dropped her eyes again almost instantly, and compressed her lips as before.

"What is it? What is the matter, my dearest?"

Maria, though not beautiful, always looked most nearly so when she was weeping. Yet she never wept out of pain or temper—only from grief or pity, and when she did so her brilliant eyes took on an altogether inexpressible charm. As Nicholas took her by the hand she could contain herself no longer, and burst into tears.

"Nicholas, I saw—he may be guilty, but you—you—why should you—? Oh Nicholas!"—and she buried her face in her hands.

Nicholas said nothing, but turned very red, and, moving away from her, began to walk up and down the room in silence.

He understood why she was weeping, but instinctively felt that he could not agree with her in condemning what he had been used to do since a boy. "It is all soft-heartedness on her part and old wives' nonsense," he thought to himself. "Yet can she be right after all?" he added presently. Unable to decide this last question satisfactorily, he glanced again at her pained, compassionate face, and suddenly understood that she was indeed right, and felt ashamed of himself.

"Maria," he said softly as he approached her, "this shall not occur again. I give you my word that it shall not. No, never!" he repeated, his voice shaking like a boy's when asking pardon.

The tears flowed the faster from the countess's eyes, but she took his hand and kissed it.

"When did you break that cameo, Nicholas—to change the subject?" she asked him, looking at his hand, which bore a ring with a Laocoon's head.

"This morning. It's all part of the same. Ah, Maria, do not remind me of it!" He fired up again. "I pledge you my word of honour that it shall never occur a second time, and that this shall always help me to remember my word." He pointed to the broken ring.

From that time forth, whenever he was engaged in explanations with his headman or clerks and the blood flew to his head or his fists began to clench themselves, he turned the broken ring on his finger, and looked away from the man who was angering him. Twice, however, that year he forgot himself, and on each occasion he went straight to his wife, confessed his fault to her, and repeated his promise that that should be the last time.

"You must despise me," he said to her, "and certainly I deserve it."

"You should go away, go away, whenever you feel unable to restrain yourself," she murmured as she strove to console him.

The general society of the district respected Nicholas, but scarcely loved him. District interests had no attraction for him, and so some people thought him proud, and others stupid. In summer he spent all his days, from the time of the spring sowings to harvest-tide, on the estate, and in the autumn he devoted himself to sport with the same enthusiasm as he had done to farming—not infrequently going on hunting expeditions which lasted a month or more. The winters were spent in going the round of the other villages and in reading. As for his reading, it consisted mostly of historical works, to the purchase of which he devoted an annual fixed sum. In this manner he amassed what he called a "serious library," and set himself systematically to read the books which he had bought. It was with great gravity that he would sit down in his study to perform this task—a task which he had begun by setting himself as a duty and had gone on to make a regular habit. In fact it gave him a peculiar pleasure to think that, in so doing, he was engaging in a "serious" pursuit. Except for journeys on business, he spent the greater part of the winter at home with his family, and shared the small interest of his wife and children. He drew ever nearer and nearer to Maria, and discovered every day new mental affinities between himself and her.

Sonia had lived with them since their marriage. Before that, however, Nicholas had told his wife—with many self-reproaches and much generous praise of Sonia—all that had passed between himself and his cousin, and had begged Maria always to be kind and good to her. Maria had felt strongly that her husband was to blame, and consequently felt ashamed in Sonia's presence, for she thought that Nicholas' choice must have been influenced by Sonia's poverty. The countess had no fault to find with the girl, and tried hard to love her, but she simply could not. Indeed, sometimes she found herself cherishing uncharitable feelings towards her, in spite of her utmost efforts to overcome them.

One day she spoke of Sonia and her own unfairness to her friend Natacha.

"Now, you know," said Natacha, "you have a good knowledge of the Bible. There is a passage in it which exactly fits her."

"How so?" inquired Maria in astonishment.

"'To him that hath shall be given, and from him that hath not shall be taken away even that which he hath.' Do you remember it? She is one 'that hath not.' Why that should be so I do not know. Perhaps it is because she has not a particle of egoism in her. At all events she has proved to be one of those from whom shall be taken away even that which they have—for it *has* been so taken away. Sometimes I feel terribly sorry for her. I used to pray that Nicholas would marry her eventually, yet I always had a presentiment that he would not. She is what I call 'a wasted flower'—like the strawberry flower. Sometimes I feel sorry for her, but at other times I think that she does not feel it as we should have done."

Ever after that, in spite of her protests to Natacha that the Bible words were not meant to be so interpreted, Maria felt when she saw Sonia, that she had no choice but to agree with Natacha's reading of them. True, Sonia hardly seemed to trouble herself about her position, and appeared reconciled to her fate as "a wasted flower." She seemed to care less for individual members of the family than for the family as a whole. Like a cat, it was to the household that she attached herself rather than to its inmates. She went shopping for the old countess, petted and played with the children, and was always ready to perform any small service which lay in her power—all of which was accepted with a less than adequate measure of gratitude.

The establishment at Lissy-Gory had now been rebuilt, but on different lines to what it had been in the late prince's time. The rebuilding had been begun in days of poverty, so that everything was exceedingly plain. The great house, though reared on the original foundations of stone, was made only of wood, and plastered only on the inside, while the floors were of unpainted deal, and the furniture composed of the simplest of rough sofas, chairs, arm-chairs, and tables—all of them home-made from birch-trees grown on the estate. Nevertheless the place was roomy enough, and contained accommodation for visitors and their servants as well. Sometimes relatives of the Rostows and Bolkonskys would come and stay there for several months, and bring with them their families, sixteen horses or so, and some dozens of domestics. Likewise, four times a year—on the name-days and birthdays of the host and hostess—quite a hundred guests would arrive to spend a day or two in the house, although for the rest of the year a regular routine of occupations was observed, broken only by meals furnished from the resources of the estate.

CHAPTER CXXXIX

It was the eve of the winter festival of St. Nicholas—December 5th, 1820. That year Natacha, with her husband and children, had been staying with her brother since the early autumn. At the moment Peter was in St. Petersburg, whither he had gone on private business lasting for (so he had said) three weeks, but where he was now spending his seventh. Nevertheless he was expected back every moment. On that same 5th of December the Rostows had a guest in the person of an old friend of Nicholas'—a retired general named Vassili Fédorovitch Denissow.

On the 6th, the festive day, when many guests were to be entertained, Nicholas knew that he would have to take off his smock, put on a frockcoat and tight, narrow-toed boots, and go to the new church which he had erected; after which he would be expected to receive congratulations, to propose toasts, and to make a speech about the civil elections and the crops. The *eve* of the festival, however, he considered he might spend as he liked. Before dinner he checked the accounts of the bailiff of Riazan—accounts in connection with the property belonging to his wife's nephew, as well as wrote a couple of business letters and went round the homestead and horse and cattle stables. Next, having taken precautions against the general drunkenness which he knew would ensue on the occasion of the morrow's festival, he returned home to dinner, and sat down to the long table (laid for twenty persons and surrounded by the whole staff of domestics) without having first exchanged a word with his wife. At the table sat his mother, old Madame Bielova (who acted as her companion), his wife, his three children, the children's governess, their tutor, his nephew, his nephew's tutor, Sonia, Denissow, Natacha, her three children, their governess, and old Michael Ivanovitch (formerly architect to the prince, and now living in retirement at Lissy-Gory.)

Countess Maria was seated at the opposite end of the table to Nicholas, but her husband had no sooner sat down in his place than she divined, from the gesture with which he unfolded his napkin and abruptly swept aside the tumbler and wine glass which stood before him, that he was out of humour. This not infrequently happened with him, especially before he had had his soup, and when he had come straight in to dinner from the estate. Maria knew this mood of his very well, and when she was herself in a cheerful one, she would wait quietly until he had finished his soup, and then begin to talk to him and to make him confess that he had had no reason to be angry. To-day, however, she quite forgot this precaution of hers, for it hurt her and depressed her to think of his gratuitous ill-temper with her. First of all she asked him where he had been, and he told her. Then she asked him whether everything was going on well on the estate, and at this he frowned discouragingly, as though irritated at her unnatural tone, and returned a curt answer.

"So I was not mistaken," thought the countess to herself.

"Yet what can he be angry with me for?" The tone in which he had answered her had told her of ill-will towards herself and a desire to cut short the conversation. She knew that her words had been forced and unnatural, yet she had felt herself unable to refrain from asking the questions she did.

However, the conversation at dinner—thanks to Denissow—soon became general and animated, so that Maria said no more to her husband just then, but when everyone had left the table and gathered round the old countess to pay her their respects, Maria bent over her husband, kissed him, and asked him the reason of his ill-temper with her.

"You are always taking strange notions into your head," he replied. "I was not so much as dreaming of being angry with you." Yet the first word always [1] practically said to her, "Yes, I *am* angry, but I do not mean to tell you the reason why."

Nicholas lived on such good terms with his wife that even Sonia and the old countess—both of whom, from instincts of jealousy, wished to see a difference arise between the pair—could never find excuse for reproaching him. Yet they had their moments of hostility, so that at times, and particularly after a more than usually happy period, a feeling of estrangement and enmity would come over them both. This feeling manifested itself most frequently when the countess was enceinte, and the present was such a time.

"Well, *messieurs et mesdames*," went on Nicholas loudly and in a tone of assumed gaiety (it seemed to Maria that he spoke thus on purpose to offend her), "I have been on my legs since six o'clock. To-morrow we shall all of us have to work, but to-day let us rest," and, without another word to the countess, he went into the small drawing-room, and threw himself down upon a sofa.

"That is always the way," thought the countess. "He will speak to everyone but myself. I can see—yes, I can see it clearly—that I am repugnant to him whenever I am in this condition." She glanced at her figure, and then went to a mirror to look at her sallow, drawn face, with its eyes showing larger than ever. Everything now seemed distasteful to her—both the chattering, and Denissow's laughter, and Natacha's voice, and (above all) the look which Sonia swiftly threw her at that moment. Sonia, indeed, was always the first pretext selected by the countess for being vexed about anything.

[1] In the Russian this word comes first in the sentence.

After sitting a while with her guests and not understanding a word of what they were saying, she quietly left the room, and went to the nursery. The children were riding to Moscow on chairs, and invited her to accompany them. She sat down and played with them for a time, but the thought of her husband and his unreasonable anger troubled her continually. She rose, and walked cautiously on tip-toe towards the small drawing-room.

"Perhaps he is not asleep, and I might have an explanation with him," she said to herself. Andrusha, her eldest boy, was walking behind her on tip-toe, in imitation of her movements, but she never noticed him.

"Chère Marie, il dort, je crois; il est si fatigué," said Sonia, who met her at that moment in the large drawing-room (indeed, to the countess she seemed to meet her everywhere). "Take care that Andrusha does not wake him."

Upon this Maria looked round, and, seeing Andrusha behind her, felt that Sonia was right. That alone was enough to make her angry, and she only just restrained herself from returning a sharp answer. She said nothing, however, but, to show her independence of Sonia, signed to Andrusha to keep quiet (though he still kept following her), and approached the door of the small drawing-room, while Sonia moved away to the door of the larger one. From the room in which Nicholas was sleeping there came the sound of the regular breathing which Maria knew so well in all its tones. As she listened to that breathing she seemed to see the smooth, handsome forehead and temples—the whole face—upon which she had so often gazed as he lay sleeping in the silent watches of the night. Suddenly Nicholas made a movement, and snored, whereupon Andrusha cried out from behind the door: "Papa dear, mamma is standing here." For a moment the countess turned pale with terror as she beckoned to the little boy to hold his tongue. He obeyed her, and for a moment or two there ensued what seemed to Maria a dreadful silence, for she knew how greatly Nicholas disliked to be aroused. All at once another snore came from within, then a movement, and at last Nicholas' reluctant voice said:

"They will not let me have a moment's peace. Is that you, Maria? Why have you brought him here?"

"I only came to look for you, as I did not see you anywhere about. Please excuse me."

Nicholas burst into a fit of coughing, and returned no reply.

Maria moved away from the door, and conducted her little boy back to the nursery. Five minutes later the little black-eyed, three-year-old Natacha, her father's pet, had learnt from her brother that papa was asleep and mamma in the drawing-room, and so had scampered off to her father without her mother's knowledge. The black-eyed youngster pushed boldly at the door, ran to the sofa with a loud pattering of her tiny feet, and, having taken stock of her father's attitude as he lay sleeping with his back towards her, raised herself on tip-toe, and kissed the hand upon which his head was resting. Nicholas turned round with a kindly smile on his face.

"Natacha, Natacha!" came the mother's frightened whisper from outside the door. "Papa wishes to go to sleep."

"No, he doesn't, mamma," answered the little girl in a tone of conviction. "He is smiling."

Nicholas put his legs to the floor, sat up, and took his little daughter up in his arms.

"Come in, Maria," he said to his wife. The countess entered the room, and seated herself beside her husband.

"I had not seen that Andrusha was following me," she said timidly. "I am so sorry."

Nicholas, holding the little girl by one arm, glanced at his wife, and, seeing the contrite look on her face, put his other arm round her, and kissed her hair.

"May I kiss mamma?" he asked the tiny Natacha.

Natacha laughed shyly. "Yes, yes—again," she said with a commanding gesture as she pointed to the spot where Nicholas had kissed his wife before.

"I cannot imagine why you should have thought that I was cross," he said, answering the question which he knew was in Maria's mind.

"Ah, but *you* cannot think how unhappy and lonely I am when you behave like that. To me it always seems that—"

"Never mind, Maria. It was all my folly. How you do worry yourself!" he said cheerfully.

"I am always thinking that you do not love me—that I am ugly, and that I shall always be so. And now—when—when I am like this—"

"How absurd you are! 'Handsome is that handsome does,' you know—not the other way about. Only a Malvina or women of that kind are loved for their beauty alone. Do I love my wife? Well, I do not so much love her as—how can I express it? Without you, and when there is this sort of misunderstanding between us, I should feel lost and able to do nothing. Do I love my own finger? No, but if it were cut off—"

"Oh, but I am not quite the same thing. Yet I understand you all the same. You are not angry with me, then?"

"Yes, terribly angry," he said with a smile as he rose and, smoothing his dishevelled hair, began to walk up and down the room.

"Do you know, Maria, what I am thinking about?" he began, at once resuming his habit of expressing his thoughts aloud, now that he was reconciled to his wife again. He never thought of asking her whether she wished to hear his thoughts or not. That he took for granted. An idea had occurred to him, and of course it had occurred to her also. Accordingly he told her of his scheme of inviting Peter to stay with them until the spring.

The countess listened to him, made a few remarks, and then began, in her turn, to utter her thoughts aloud. They were all of them about the children.

"What a little woman it is!" she said in French as she pointed to the diminutive Natacha. "You accuse us women of being illogical. Well, there she sits—our logic. I told her just now that papa wanted to go to sleep, but she replied, 'No, he is smiling'—and she was right too." Maria laughed happily.

"Yes, yes," said Nicholas, lifting his little daughter up in his strong arms, and setting her upon his shoulders. Steadying the tiny legs with his hand, he began to walk up and down the room with her. The faces both of father and daughter looked almost foolishly happy.

"But, you know, you can be unfair sometimes. You love this one too much, for instance," Maria whispered to him in French.

"Yes, but what am I to do? I try my best not to show it."

At this moment there sounded through the hall and passage the noise of hoof-beats as a carriage-drag was let down.

"Someone has just arrived."

"I expect it is Peter; I will go and see," said Maria as she left the room.

In her absence Nicholas took the opportunity of giving his little daughter a gallop round the room. At last, out of breath, he dethroned the laughing mite from her perch, and pressed her to his heart. His prancings round the room had reminded him of dancing, and as he looked at the round, happy, childish face, he wondered what she would be like when he, an old man, led her out to dance the mazurka with her as his dead father had been used to dance the "Daniel Cooper" with his daughter.

"Yes, it *is* he, Nicholas," said Maria presently, as she returned. "Dear Natacha is in raptures. You should have seen her delight, as well as heard Peter catching it for having overstayed his time. Well, let us go now. As for you," she added with a glance and smile to the little girl clinging to her father, "you will have to part from us now."

Nicholas departed, hand in hand with his daughter, and the countess found herself alone a minute in the room.

"Never, never would I have believed that I could be so happy," she whispered to herself. Her face broke into a smile, yet on the instant a sigh came also, and gentle longing showed itself in the depths of her eyes. It was as though, over and above the happiness which she was now experiencing, there existed another kind of happiness, unattainable in this life, of which she had just been involuntarily reminded.

CHAPTER CXL

NATACHA had been married in the early spring of 1813, and by 1820 was in possession of three girls and a boy. To have a boy had always been her dearest wish, and she suckled him herself. She had filled out and become stouter, so that it was difficult to distinguish in the buxom mother the former slender, active Natacha. The lines of her face were firmer, and always wore an expression of quiet cheerfulness and good nature. Indeed, her face contained none of the constant fire and animation which had formerly constituted its greatest charm, but, on the contrary, often looked one with her body, and evinced no sign of a soul behind it. In short, she resembled a fine, vigorous, productive hen. Yet there were certain rare occasions when the old fire flamed up in her again. Those occasions were when—as now—her husband had returned from a journey, or when one of her children was recovering from an illness, or when she and Maria were recalling reminiscences of Prince Andrew (she supposed her husband to be jealous of the prince's memory, and so never mentioned the latter in Peter's presence), or (most rarely of all) when some unusual occasion induced her to sing—an accomplishment which she had altogether dropped since her marriage.

At such times the revival of the old fire in her ample, but comely, form made her look more attractive than ever.

Since their marriage she and her husband had lived successively in Moscow, in St. Petersburg, at a village near Moscow, and at her mother's, i.e. at Nicholas's. Society saw little of the young Countess Bésoukhow, and those who did see her found her unsatisfactory, since she was neither sociable nor ingratiating. It was not that she liked isolation (though, as a matter of fact, she hardly knew whether she liked it or not—on the whole she thought not) so much as that the duties of bearing, rearing, and feeding children and participating in every moment of her husband's life could not be satisfactorily fulfilled except by renouncing the world. All who had known her before her marriage were astonished at the change which it had wrought in her, as though it were something extraordinary. Only the old countess, whose maternal instinct had always told her that Natacha's waywardness proceeded solely from the need of a family and a husband (as, indeed, Natacha herself had once avowed, less in jest than in earnest, at Otradnoë), was surprised that these people who had never understood her daughter should feel astonishment at the change, and often repeated that she had always known that Natacha would prove an exemplary wife and mother. "Only," the old countess would add, "she carries her love for her husband and children to extreme limits, so that it almost seems silly."

Natacha did not follow the golden rule prescribed by sensible people, and especially by the French, that a woman who gets married ought not to neglect herself afterwards and throw away her talents, but rather that she ought to pay more attention to her appearance even than she had done in girlhood, and so to captivate her husband even more than had been the case when he was a bachelor. Natacha, on the contrary, at once laid aside all her charms, one of the greatest of which had been her singing. Indeed, she laid it aside for that very reason—that it was so great a charm. Nor did she pay any further heed to her manners, nor to her refinement of speech, nor to the art of showing herself to her husband in attractive poses, nor to her toilet, nor to the rule of never demanding anything of her husband. In fact, she contravened every one of these rules. She felt that the charms which her instinct had formerly taught her to use would now look ridiculous in her husband's eyes, since he was the man to whom she had given her whole heart from the very first, and left no corner of it hidden from his

sight. She felt that the bond between her and her husband
rested, not on the poetical sentiments which had attracted him
to her at first, but on sentiments as indefinite—though also as
strong— as the bond which bound her body to her soul.

To arrange her hair *en coiffure*, to wear corsets, and to sing
ballads just in order to attract her husband would have seemed
to her as strange as to deck herself out to please only herself.
To adorn her person to please others might have been agreeable
to her—she did not quite know whether it would or not—but at
all events there was no time for it. In fact the chief reason
why she never paid any attention to her singing or dress or
choice of words was that she never had time to do so.

We all know that a human being may become entirely
absorbed in one subject, however trifling it be. We all know,
too, that no subject is so trifling as to be incapable of boundless
development when the whole attention of a human being is concentrated upon it. The subject which absorbed all Natacha's
faculties was her family, i.e. her husband (whom she meant to
hold so tightly as always to remain her undivided property),
her house, and her children (who, of course, had to be born,
reared, fed, and educated). The further she penetrated—not
only with her intellect, but with her whole soul and being—
into the subject which absorbed her, the more did that subject
develop under her cultivation, and the weaker and more insignificant did her powers to cope with it appear to her: with the
result that, though she concentrated the whole of them upon
that one thing, she never succeeded in doing all that she thought
she ought to accomplish.

Likewise, although discussions and opinions on the rights of
women and on the relations, freedom, and rights of married
couples were not then called "questions" as they are now, they
existed just the same. Yet Natacha not only took no interest
in such questions, but simply did not understand them. Then,
as now, those questions existed only for persons who see in
marriage nothing beyond the pleasure which husband and wife
may derive from one another—who see only the basis of marriage
and not the whole significance of the family. These questions
and opinions of to-day—the questions, for instance, of how to get
the most satisfaction out of one's dinner—did not then exist,
and do not now, for persons of whom the aim of dinner is
sustenance, and of cohabitation a family. If the aim of dinner
is the nourishment of the body, then the human being who
suddenly begins to eat two dinners attains, it may be, great

satisfaction, but not his or her aim, seeing that two dinners are indigestible to the stomach. If, also, the aim of marriage is a family, then he or she who seeks to have a number of wives or husbands attains, it may be, great satisfaction, but can never in any case possess a family. If the aim of dinner is sustenance, and that of marriage a family, the whole question is decided by merely eating no more than the stomach can digest or by having no more wives or husbands than is necessary for the production of a family, i.e. one wife or one husband only. Natacha had needed a husband, and a husband had been given her, and he, in his turn, had given her a family. For any other husband— even for a better one—she saw no necessity, but, inasmuch as all her mental faculties were bent upon the service of that husband, and her family, she could not imagine, nor see any interest in imagining, what things might have been like if they had been otherwise.

She had no love for society in general, and for that very reason she loved the society of her relatives—of the Countess Maria, her brother, her mother, and Sonia—the more. She liked the society of people upon whom she could emerge with great strides from the nursery—clad only in a dishevelled dressing-gown, and her face beaming—for the purpose of showing them a diaper stained yellow instead of green, and hearing their congratulations that the child was so much better. In fact, she became so careless of herself that her dresses, her *coiffure*, her rough and ready expressions, her jealousy (she was jealous of Sonia, of the governess, of every woman, pretty or the reverse) grew to be stock jests among her kinsfolk. The general opinion was that Peter was completely under her thumb, and in very truth it was the case. From the earliest days of their married life Natacha had made her demands upon him plain, and though Peter had been much surprised at this entirely new view adopted by his wife—the view that every moment of his life should belong to her and the family—he had benefited from her insistence, and yielded to it.

The subordination of Peter lay in the circumstance that he dare not speak smilingly to another woman, never to go to a club for dinner *merely* in order to pass the time, never to spend money on whims, and never to go away for long visits except on business affairs (among which his wife included his scientific pursuits—matters of which she knew nothing, but to which she attached the greatest importance). In return, Peter had full licence, when at home, to manage himself and his family as he pleased. There Natacha assumed the position of her husband's slave, and the whole household walked on tip-toe when Peter was engaged in reading or writing in his study. He had only to express a command for it to be obeyed—a wish, and Natacha leapt to fulfil it.

The entire household was ruled by what figured as the orders of the husband, i.e. by Peter's wishes, which Natacha endeavoured always to anticipate. How and where they should live, whom they should know, Natacha's ties and pursuits, the education of the children—not only were all these things ordained according to Peter's expressed will, but his wife likewise endeavoured to draw deductions from any ideas which he expressed in conversation. As a matter of fact, she always guessed correctly the substance of his wishes, and, that done, she held him firmly to what he had chosen. If he tried to change his mind she used his original choice as a weapon for effecting his reduction. Thus, during the tedious and (to Peter) always memorable time which followed upon the birth of their first delicate baby, and when, through being obliged to change its wet nurse three times in succession, Natacha fell ill with worry, Peter one day told her of Rousseau's ideas (with which he was in entire agreement) on the subject of the unnatural and deleterious effects of having wet nurses at all. Accordingly, when the next baby arrived, she resisted both her mother, the doctors, and her husband himself when they urged her not to suckle the child herself (as though it were a thing altogether unheard of and harmful!) but insisted thenceforth in bringing up all her children at her own breast.

It often happened, too, that, in moments of friction, the husband and wife would quarrel, but, if so, it always happened that, long after the actual dispute, Peter would suddenly be surprised and pleased to find his wife expressing, both in theory and practice, the very idea about which they had quarrelled— and not the idea alone, but the idea purged of any personal element which Peter had imported into it during the heat of dispute. Thus, after seven years of married life, Peter was able to feel a comforting, assured conviction that he was not a bad fellow after all. This he could do because he saw himself reflected in his wife. In himself he could feel the good and the bad mingling with and infecting one another, but in her he saw reflected only what was good in him, since everything else she rejected. This power of reflection in her was due to no logical scheme, but constituted a power of quite another—a secret and independent—kind.

CHAPTER CXLI

Two months ago, i.e. since they had come to stay with the Rostows—Peter had received a letter from Prince Theodore, summoning him to St. Petersburg, for the decision of some important questions which were then occupying the minds of the members of an association of which Peter was one of the principal founders. As soon as she had read the letter (she read all her husband's letters) Natacha voluntarily advised Peter to go to St. Petersburg, in spite of her knowledge that she would miss him greatly in his absence. To all that constituted the intellectual, the abstract, work of her husband she attributed (since she did not understand it) an immense importance, and was constantly afraid of being a hindrance to its progress. To Peter's diffident, questioning glance after she had read the letter she replied that he might go so long as he kept strictly to the date of his return, and in the end he obtained four weeks' leave of absence.

The term of that leave had expired a fortnight ago, and Natacha had since been in a constant state of nervousness, grief, and anger. Denissow, the discontented retired general who had been staying with the Rostows throughout those two weeks, had gazed at her with pained surprise, as at a bad portrait of some one whom he knew well. Her despondent, uninterested air, her awkward answers, and her talk about her children were all that he saw and heard in an old flame of his. Natacha had been depressed and irritable during the whole of the two weeks, but never more so than when Sonia or Maria had sought to comfort her by making excuses for Peter or by inventing reasons for his delay.

"That is all mere folly and rubbish," Natacha had answered. "The mischief comes of those intellectual ideas of his, which lead to nothing, and of those idiotic associations of his." This, too, concerning the very pursuits to which she had hitherto attached such immense importance! Then she had departed to the nursery to feed her one little boy, Pétia. Nobody in the world could have said anything so wise, so reassuring, to her as did this little three-months-old being when he was laid at her breast and she could feel the movements of his lips and the nuzzling of his tiny nose. That little being said to her: "You may be angry, you may be jealous, you may be wishing to revenge yourself upon him, you may be feeling frightened on his account, but he is here in me, he is here in me!" To this no answer could be returned, for it was more than true.

So often did Natacha have recourse to her baby during those two weeks of anxiety, and so much time did she spend over him, that she overfed him, and he fell ill. She was horror-struck at this, although it was just what she needed, for, so long as she was looking after him, she found it easier to bear the anxiety about her husband. The evening that Peter's cab sounded at the door she had just fed the baby, when the nurse, who knew how much it would please her mistress, ran softly, but swiftly, and with a beaming face, into the room.

"Has he come, then?" asked Natacha in a hasty whisper, but fearing to stir lest she should waken the sleeping infant.

"Yes, ma'am," was the nurse's whisper in answer.

The blood flew to Natacha's face, and her feet made an involuntary movement under her, but to get up and run to the portico was impossible at that moment. Just then the child opened its eyes and looked at her. "So there you are," it seemed to say, and then lazily smacked its lips again. Gently withdrawing her breast, Natacha rocked him a moment and then handed him to the nurse. The next minute she was speeding towards the door. Yet she had no sooner reached it than she stopped (as though she felt her conscience pricking her for letting her delight take her away from baby so soon) and looked round. The nurse, her elbows stuck out, was just lifting him over the rails of his cot.

"Yes, go, go, ma'am! Do not be disturbed about him," whispered the nurse with a smile and with the familiarity which soon arises between nurse and mistress, and Natacha fled on light feet towards the portico. Denissow, who was just issuing, pipe in hand, from the study into the hall, saw her for the first time in a new guise. A clear, brilliant, joyous light was streaming in abundance from her transfigured face.

"He has arrived!" she exclaimed as she sped past him, and Denissow somehow felt that he too was pleased that Peter had returned, little though he liked him. Running into the portico, Natacha saw there a tall figure clad in a fur coat, and unwinding a scarf.

"Yes, yes, it *is* he!" she said to herself as, flying to him, she embraced him, pressed her head to his bosom, and then, drawing a little away from him again, gazed into his red, frost-coated, delighted face. "Yes, it *is* he!" she exclaimed again. "I am happy now, and contented and——"

But suddenly she remembered all the pangs of waiting which she had to go through during the last two weeks, and the joy which was beaming from her face suddenly vanished. She frowned, and a flood of reproaches and bitter words began to descend upon Peter.

"Yes, it is all very well for *you* to look comfortable and merry, for you have been enjoying yourself; but what about me? A lot you cared about the children! Here have I been feeding them until my milk ran dry! Pétia has been at death's door, while you have been enjoying yourself! Yes, it was all very well for *you!*"

Peter knew that he was innocent in the matter, since he could not possibly have returned any sooner. He also knew that, ugly though this outburst looked, it would pass away in a moment or two. Above all, he knew that he himself was in excellent temper and spirits. He would have liked to have burst out laughing, but had not the hardihood to do so, so he pulled a pitiful, frightened face, and cringed humbly before his wife.

"I swear to God I could not come home sooner. But what has been the matter with Pétia?"

"Never mind. Come in now. You would be sorry if you knew what a state I have been in without you, and how I have been worrying myself."

"Then you are quite well?"

"Never mind. Let us go in," she replied, without letting go of his hands, and the pair departed to their rooms.

When Nicholas and his wife came to look for Peter, he was in the nursery, holding his little son in the huge palm of his right hand, and dandling him up and down. On his broad face, with its enormous toothless mouth, was a fixed and happy smile. The storm had long ago dispersed, and the sun was shining clearly and joyously from Natacha's face as she looked approvingly at her husband and child.

"And did you manage to say all that you wanted to Prince Theodore?" she was asking him.

"Yes, certainly."

"Oh, look how he is holding it!" (by "it" Natacha meant the baby's head). "How he frightened me! And did you see the princess? Is it true that she is in love with that . . ."

"Yes, just think of it!"

At that moment Nicholas and Maria entered the room. Peter went to greet them, his son still resting in his arms; but, although he duly answered his visitors' questions, it was clear that, despite the interesting news he had to tell them, the baby with the cap on its nodding head was absorbing the greater part of his attention.

"What a dear!" exclaimed Maria as she looked at the little one and began playing with it. "I cannot think"—here she turned to her husband—"how you fail to see the beauty of such a bundle of charms as this."

"Well, I cannot see it," said Nicholas, looking coldly at the baby. "Just a lump of flesh, that is all. Come, Peter."

"He is the kindest father in the world, *really*," said Maria in justification of her husband; "though only when they have become a year or two older."

"Peter nurses our babies splendidly," said Natacha. "He says that the palm of his hand is just made for a baby's back. See him."

"Yes—better than for this," remarked Peter with a smile as he took hold of the child and handed it to the nurse.

CHAPTER CXLII

As always happens in a real family,[1] the household at Lissy-Gory contained several entirely different communes which, while preserving each of them their individuality, made concessions to the rest, and thus combined to form a single harmonious whole. Each event which occurred in the house brought equal joy or sorrow, was of equal importance or the reverse, to all those communes, while at the same time each separate commune had its own reasons for rejoicing or sorrowing over a given event. Thus Peter's return was an important and joyful occasion, and was expressed as such by everyone. The servants —the truest judges of their employers, since they judge, not by what they hear them say nor by any expression of sentiments, but by deeds and modes of life—were glad that Peter had returned, for the reason that they knew that, so long as he was at home, the count would cease his daily round of the estate, and be in a better and kinder mood. Likewise there would be handsome presents for them all at festival time. The children and their governesses rejoiced at Peter's return because no one

[1] The author means the old-time patriarchal family of grandparents, with all their married or unmarried descendants.

extended to them a share of the common life so much as he did. He alone could play that one piece of his on the clavichord— the piece which, as he himself said, would do for every sort of dance—while his coming represented rich presents for them as well.

Little Nicolenka, who was now a slim youngster of fifteen, with curly flaxen hair and beautiful eyes, as well as of a delicate and highly-strung temperament, rejoiced at Peter's return for the reason that "Uncle" Peter, as he called him, was the object of his passionate adoration and affection. No one had inspired this immense affection in Nicolenka, and, as a matter of fact, he very seldom saw Peter. His guardian, the Countess Maria, tried by every means to induce the boy to love her husband as she did herself, but, though Nicolenka liked him, his liking had in it just a shade of contempt. Peter, however, he simply worshipped. He had no desire to be a hussar or a knight of St. George as his Uncle Nicholas had been. What he wanted to become was a learned, clever, good-natured savant like Peter. In Peter's presence his face never ceased to beam, and when the great man spoke to him the boy would blush and sigh. Not a word of what Peter was saying would he miss, and afterwards he would recall and puzzle over—either with Dessalles or alone —each separate word that his idol had uttered. Peter's past life; his misfortunes up to 1812—misfortunes of which Nico- lenka had succeeded, through fragments overheard, in forming for himself a dim, legendary picture; his adventures in Moscow; his imprisonment; Plato Karataïew (of whom the boy had heard from Peter himself); his love for Natacha (whom Nicolenka also loved devotedly); and, above all, his friendship for his (Nicolenka's) father, whom the boy could not remember — all this elevated Peter, in his eyes, to the position of a saint and hero. From stray references to his father and Natacha, from the emotion with which Peter spoke of the dead man, and from the subdued, reverent way in which Natacha also mentioned his name, the boy, who was just beginning to guess at love, conceived the idea that his father had once been in love with Natacha, and had committed her, at his death, to his friends' care. That father, of whom the boy had no recollection, appeared to him a divinity incapable even of being imagined, as well as a being of whom he never thought but with a softening of the heart and tears of mingled joy and longing. Thus Nicolenka was pleased when Peter returned.

The guests, for their part, welcomed Peter as a man who

could enliven and knit together any society that he was in. The grown-up members of the family were glad of a friend under whom life went easier and quieter, while the elder ones were pleased with the expectation of presents, and mainly with the fact that Natacha had now recovered her spirits.

Peter, of course, was conscious of these different views taken of himself by the various communes, and hastened to give each of the latter what it expected. He was the most unbusinesslike and forgetful of men, but with the help of a list drawn up for him by his wife he had managed to buy everything that was needed, including his mother's and brother's commissions, a dress for Madame Bielova, and toys for his nephews. In the early days of his married life this requirement of his wife's—that he should remember and purchase every single article which he had undertaken to buy—had seemed to him a strange thing, and he had been greatly impressed by her serious displeasure when, on his first return from an expedition, she found that he had forgotten everything. In time, however, he got used to it. Knowing how careful Natacha was never to entrust him with a commission for herself, as well as to entrust him with commissions for others only when she herself was not going with him, he had taken a special boyish pleasure—a pleasure which surprised even himself—in buying these various gifts for the entire household and forgetting nobody. If he deserved any blame from Natacha it was because he had bought and spent too much. To her many failings, as most people thought them, or her virtues, as Peter considered them to be, Natacha certainly added that of thriftiness. From the time when he had begun to live in a large house and have a family entailing large expenses he had been surprised to find that he spent only half of what he had done before, and that his lately disorganised finances—disorganised chiefly by his first wife's debts—had begun to fall into order. Life was cheaper for him because his life was now restricted. The most expensive luxury in life—namely, the sort of life which is liable to be changed from day to day—he no longer possessed, nor did he wish to possess it again. He felt that his order of existence was now settled once and for all till death—that to change it was not in his power, and that that order was an inexpensive one.

It was with a cheerful, smiling countenance that he now spread out his presents. "Look at it!" he cried as, in shopman's fashion, he turned over a width of material. Natacha, who was holding her eldest girl on her knees, turned her beaming eyes from her husband to what he was showing her.

"Is that for Madame Bielova?" she asked as she fingered the stuff to try its goodness. "It must have cost several roubles, did it not?"

He told her the price.

"Too dear," commented Natacha. "However, how pleased mamma and the children will be! Only, it was no good your buying that thing for me," she added, unable to repress a smile as she gazed admiringly at a comb set with pearls—a kind of ornament which was just then coming into fashion.

"They confused me so at Adèle's. One buys and buys, you know," he said.

"When should I ever want to put it on?"—and she laid the thing aside. "Still, we will keep it for little Masha. Perhaps they will be wearing them again in her day. Now let us go."

Collecting the presents together, they proceeded to the nursery, first of all, and then to see the old countess. She was sitting in her usual place with Madame Bielova, playing patience, when Peter and Natacha entered the drawing-room— their arms piled to their noses with parcels.

The old countess—now over sixty—had grey hair and a cap framing her wrinkled face with a frill, while her upper lip had fallen in and her eyes were dim. Since the deaths of her husband and son, following so closely upon one another, she had felt very much lost in the world, like a being devoid of all purpose or meaning. True, she ate, drank, slept, and conversed, but she did not really *live*. Life brought her no impressions, nor did she ask anything of life. All that she asked for was peace—and peace she would find only in death itself. Nevertheless, so long as death did not come to her, she had to exist, to exert her powers of life. She evinced to a remarkable degree the traits to be found only in very young children and very old people. No outward aim was discernible in her life, but merely the necessity of exercising her various faculties and instincts. She needed to eat a little, to sleep a little, to think a little, to talk a little, to weep a little, to work a little, to lose her temper a little—but only because she possessed a brain, a stomach, muscles, nerves and a liver. All this she did as though moved to it by nothing external and doing it in a fashion altogether different to that of persons hale and hearty who see an end beyond the immediate one for which they are striving. She spoke only because it was a physical necessity to her to use her tongue a little; she wept as a child weeps, i.e., because it is physically necessary for it to use its lachrymal glands; and so on. What, in people possessed of their full health and strength, would seem purpose was, in her, merely pretext.

Thus, in the morning—especially if she had eaten anything very rich overnight — she was apt to feel the need of being cross, and so selected the merest pretext for being so—namely, the deafness of Madame Bielova. She would begin by saying something to her, almost in a whisper, from the other end of the room—such as, "I think it is a little warmer to-day, my dear," and then, when Madame Bielova answered at random, "What? Has he returned?" or something like that, the countess would exclaim angrily: "My God! How stupid and deaf the woman is!"

Another of her pretexts was her snuff, which, on such occasions, always seemed to her either too dry or too damp or badly ground. Before fits of temper of this sort her face would assume a bilious tinge, so that her servants had learnt to know unerringly when Madame Bielova would next be deaf or the snuff too dry. Just as she needed to work off her spleen in this way, so she sometimes needed to exercise another of her faculties—namely, the one of thinking, and for this she took as her pretext the game of patience. Again, when she felt inclined to be lachrymose, her excuse was the late count. When she felt desirous of being nervous, she had resort to Nicholas and his health. When she wanted to speak venomously, she selected as her butt the Countess Maria. When she felt the need of sheer exercise for her tongue (which generally happened about seven o'clock after her post-prandial sleep in a darkened room), she accomplished her object by telling, over and over again, the same stories to the same auditors.

This condition of the old lady's was well-known to the whole household, but no one ever spoke of it. On the contrary, every-one endeavoured by every means to satisfy her demands. Only the exchange of an occasional half-smile between Nicholas, Peter, Natacha, and the Countess Maria expressed this mutual comprehension of her position. Yet those glances said more than that. They said that she had sustained her part well in life; that she was not wholly composed of what she now appeared to be; that all would some day be as she was already; and that it was a pleasure to give way to her, to exercise forbearance towards a personage who once was as valuable and as full of life as the rest of them, but who now was fallen into decay. *Memento mori*—that is what those glances said.

Only the few stupid or unkind members of the household and the little ones did not understand, or were offended at her.

CHAPTER CXLIII

WHEN Peter and his wife entered the drawing-room, the countess was in her usual mood, at that hour, of desiring to exercise her intellect in the game of "grand patience," and therefore, despite the fact that she said the accustomed formula which she always employed when Peter or her son returned from a journey—"It was time, quite time, that you were back, my dear; you have been away too long; but thanks be to God that you are home again," as well as said, when presented with the gifts, her equally stereotyped formula of, "I do not deserve a present, my dear one, but I thank you for remembering an old woman like me," it was clear that Peter's entry at that moment was unwelcome to her, since it distracted her from her unfinished game of patience. Accordingly, she finished her game before looking at the gifts, which consisted of a beautifully worked card-box, a bright blue Sèvres bowl with a lid to it and painted with figures of shepherdesses, and a gold snuff-box engraved with the late count's portrait, which Peter had ordered of a miniature painter in St. Petersburg (the countess had long desired to have this). At that particular moment she did not happen to be in the mood for weeping, so she looked quite calmly at the portrait, and devoted more attention to the card-box.

"I thank you, my dear. You have pleased me greatly," she said, as she always did. "But your own return is the best gift of all. Never have I beheld anything like the way in which your wife has been worrying about you. She was like a mad woman in your absence. But I see and remember little nowadays" (this was another stereotyped formula of the old lady's). "Look, Anna Timotheevna," she added. "See the card-box which my son-in-law has brought me."

Madame Bielova duly praised the gifts, and was in raptures over her own dress-length. Although Peter, Natacha, Nicholas, Maria, and Denissow had much to say to one another which could not very well be said in the old countess's presence—not because any concealment was necessary, but because she was so remote from much of their life that, when they began to speak of anything in her hearing, they had to answer her random questions, to repeat things over and over again, and to say, many times in succession, that such and such a person was married or dead whom she could not in the least recall—they gathered as usual in the drawing-room for tea, Peter had many questions to satisfy her about—questions to which she did not really desire any answer, and which interested no one—to tell her that Prince Vassilii was getting an old man, that the Countess Maria Alexievna had sent her her greetings and remembrances, and so forth.

Conversation of this kind—interesting to no one, but inevitable—lasted throughout the meal. All the grown-up members of the family disposed themselves about the circular table where Sonia presided at the tea-urn. The children, too, as well as their tutors and governesses, had had tea, and could now be heard talking in the adjoining ante-room. Everyone always occupied the same place at that hour. Nicholas always sat behind the little table near the stove where his tea had been brought to him, while on a bench by his side lay an old borzoi with a grey muzzle and large, black, prominent eyes. This was Milka, daughter of the original Milka. Denissow, with grizzled slightly curly hair, moustache, and whiskers, and dressed in an unbuttoned general's tunic, sat beside the Countess Maria. Peter sat between his wife and the old countess, to the latter of whom he was now relating what he knew would be interesting and intelligible to the old lady. That is to say, he was speaking to her of foreign affairs, and of the men who had once composed her circle of intimates—men who had once formed an active and influential coterie, but of whom the greater number were now dispersed over the world, and, having, like herself, outlived their day, were reaping the last ears of the crop which they had sown during their lifetime. Yet to the old countess these former intimates of hers still appeared a real and serious world. From Peter's animation Natacha could see that his journey had been full of interest, and that he had much to say about it which he could not say before the countess. Denissow, who was not a member of the family, and therefore failed to understand Peter's cautions, did not approve of the latter, since he took a great interest in what was going on in St. Petersburg. Consequently he kept asking Peter about the affair of the Séménovsky Regiment, about Araktchéïew, the literary society, and so forth. Sometimes Peter would forget himself, and begin to talk unguardedly, but at such moments Nicholas or Natacha always headed him back to topics like the health of Prince Ivan or the Countess Maria Antonovna.

"Now, about this foolishness—Tatarinow and so on; is it all still going on?" Denissow inquired.

"Is it all still going on?" re-echoed Peter. "Why, it is going on more than ever. The literary society means simply the Government."

"Means simply *what, mon cher ami?*" put in the old countess, who had drunk her tea, and was now casting about for an excuse for a little temper. "What do you refer to when you say 'the Government'? I do not understand you."

"You must know, mamma," interpolated Nicholas, who knew how things were best translated into his mother's language, "that Prince A. N. Golitzin has lately formed a society, and is said to be very strong now."

"Golitzin *and* Araktchéïew," corrected Peter incautiously. "As I say, it means simply the Government. And what a Government! They see conspiracies everywhere, and are afraid of everyone."

"Oh, but who could find fault with Prince Alexander Nicolaevitch, I should like to know?" demanded the old countess in a tone of offence. "He is a man above reproach. I often used to meet him at Maria Antonovna's." Then, growing still more vexed because no one spoke, she continued: "To-day they find fault with everything. The gospel society, for instance—what is there wrong about that?" With this she arose (as also did the others), and departed with an air of dudgeon to her table in the ante-room.

The rather glum silence which ensued was broken by the sound of children laughing and shouting in the adjoining apartment. It was clear that some joyous excitement was afoot there.

"It is ready now, it is ready now!" came in the merry lisp of the tiny Natacha, over-topping all the rest. Peter exchanged glances with Nicholas and Maria (Natacha's eye he always held) and smiled a happy smile.

"That is splendid music to hear!" he said.

"It means that Anna Makarovna has finished the stocking," said the Countess Maria.

"I will go and see the performance," said Peter, jumping up. "Of course you know," he added, halting in the doorway, "why I love that music so. I love it because it is always the first thing to let me know that all is well with the children. To-day, as I was coming home, the nearer I drew to the house, the more nervous I grew: yet I had no sooner entered the portico than behold! I heard Andrusha's voice uplifted about something, and knew at once that all was well."

"Yes, yes; I know the feeling," agreed Nicholas. "But *I* must not go in there, for it may be that the stockings are a surprise of some sort for me."

So Peter departed alone to the children, and immediately the laughter and shouting redoubled.

"Now, Anna Makarovna," Peter's voice could be heard saying, "step this way into the middle of the circle at my command. I shall say 'one, two,' and then you must do it at the word 'three.' You stand there, and you here beside me. Now—one, two," continued Peter as a dead silence fell, "and—*three!*"

Instantly the rapturous din of childish voices resounded through the room. "They *are* two, they *are* two!" they cried. By the "two" they meant the two stockings which, by some secret known only to herself, Anna Makarovna knitted at once and then—to the children's intense delight—solemnly pulled apart when finished.

CHAPTER CXLIV

Soon after this the children came to say good night. They kissed everybody all round, and then their tutors and governesses also took their leave and departed. Only Dessalles and his pupil remained. When the tutor proposed to the boy in a whisper that he should go downstairs with the others, Nicolenka objected.

"No, Monsieur Dessalles, I will ask my aunt to let me stay here," he whispered in return. "Aunt, let me stay here," he continued, running to Maria. His face was charged with entreaty, rapture, and excitement. Maria looked at him, and then turned to Peter.

"When you are here he simply cannot tear himself away," she said.

"I will send him to you in a moment, Monsieur Dessalles," said Peter as he shook hands with the Swiss tutor and smilingly

turned to Nicolenka again. "You and I have not seen enough
of each other yet. What a likeness I see in him!" he added to
Maria.

"A likeness to my father?" asked the boy, blushing vividly,
and surveying Peter with sparkling, enraptured eyes.

Peter nodded an assent, and then continued the story which
the children had interrupted. Maria was working something
on canvas, and Natacha sat with her eyes fixed upon her
husband. Presently Nicholas and Denissow rose, asked for
their pipes, lighted them, and, after procuring themselves fresh
glasses of tea from Sonia where she sat humbly and dejectedly
by the tea-urn, fell to plying Peter with questions. The
delicate, curly-headed Nicholas, with his radiant eyes, sat
unnoticed in a corner, where, as from time to time he turned
his curly head and slender neck with its broad collar in Peter's
direction, he would give a sudden start, and whisper something
to himself, under the evident influence of some new and
overpowering emotion.

The conversation turned on the kind of gossip which emanates
from government circles, and which most people in those days
thought the most important interest in home policy. Denissow
who bore a grudge against the Government because of his failure
in the service, listened gladly to these tales of the (so he deemed
them) foolish goings on which were taking place in St. Petersburg, and commented upon them in strong and sarcastic terms
as Peter proceeded.

"In olden days one needed to be a German," he said, "and
now one needs to dance with Mesdames Tatarinow and Krüdner,
and to read Eckarstrausen and all that kind of thing. If only
someone would release our young friend Bonaparte once more!
He would soon send these fools packing. What, for instance,
is the use of giving the command of the Séménovsky Regiment
to that fellow Schwarz?"

Nicholas had not the same desire to vent his spleen as
Denissow, yet he too thought it both necessary and correct to
criticise the Government, and considered that the appointment
of A to such and such a ministry, or of B to be governor and
commander-in-chief of such and such a place, or for the emperor
to say such and such a thing, or for a minister to say such and
such another, were all of them very important matters. Consequently, deeming that he ought to take an interest in such things,
he helped to ply Peter with questions. After the catechism was
finished the conversation did not wander beyond mere gossip

about the higher circles of government. Natacha, however, knew the whole gamut of her husband's views, and saw that Peter had long been trying—though in vain—to divert the conversation and to expound his pet idea—the idea concerning which he had gone to St. Petersburg to take counsel with his new friend, Prince Theodore. Accordingly she gave him a hand by asking him what his business had been with the prince.

"Yes, what was it?" said Nicholas also.

"The same as before," said Peter, after glancing about him. "Everyone can see that things are going on so disgracefully that they cannot be left as they are, and that all respectable men must oppose them so far as possible."

"But what can respectable men do?" asked Nicholas with a slight frown. "What can they do?"

"They can do this: that—"

"Let us go into the study," interrupted Nicholas. Natacha, who had long been expecting to be sent for to feed the children, heard the nurse's call at this moment, and departed to the nursery. Maria went with her, while the men adjourned to the study—little Nicolenka, unnoticed by his uncle, adjourning with them, and secreting himself in a dark corner near the window, by a writing-table.

"Well now, what would you do?" asked Denissow.

"Keep on with the same old fancies," said Nicholas.

"No, the position is this," began Peter without sitting down but alternately pacing the room and standing still as he lisped out his words and made quick gestures with his hands. "The emperor stands aside from everything, for he is too much given up to this specious mysticism" (Peter could pardon no one for mysticism at that time). "He wants quiet—nothing more; and only men who lack both a faith and a conscience—people who dissect everything, and then dismiss it with a shrug of their shoulders—can give him that. I mean men like Magnitsky, Araktchéïew, and so forth. You agree, Nicholas, do you not, that if you did not care about your estate, but wanted only to be quiet, you would attain your end the better in proportion as your foreman exerted himself?"

"Well, what are you driving at?" asked Nicholas.

"At this. Everything is going to ruin. There is thieving in the law courts and constant flogging in the army. The people are being wearied to death with forced emigration and settlement, and civilisation is being strangled. All that is young and of high principle in the nation is being corrupted. Everyone

can see that things cannot go on much longer like that. Everything is stretched at too high a tension, and must inevitably
break." Peter spoke as men have spoken of the policy of their
governments since governments first came into existence. "One
thing in particular I said to them in St. Petersburg."

"To whom?" asked Denissow.

"You know to whom, answered Peter, with a meaning look
from under his eyebrows. "To Prince Theodore and all the
rest of them, of course. Rivalry in civilisation and good works
is a splendid thing—that goes without saying; but at the present
moment we need something else."

At that moment Nicholas noticed that his little nephew was
present. His face darkened as he strode towards the boy.

"Why are you here?" he asked him.

"Why should he not be? Leave him alone," said Peter,
taking Nicholas by the arm, and then continuing: "As I say,
at the present moment we have need of something else. While
you are standing waiting for the over-tense string to break, and
everyone is looking for the inevitable revolution, it is our duty
to close up the ranks of the people as much as possible if we are
to face the general catastrophe. All that is young and strong in
the nation is being seduced and corrupted. Women are used
to seduce one man, presents another, windy words a third,
money a fourth—and they all go over to the other camp. Of
free, independent men like you and myself there are none left.
What I said, then, in St. Petersburg was: 'Widen the scope of
our society, and let the *mot d'ordre* be not so much *beneficence*
as *independence and activity*.'"

Nicholas left his nephew, gave the bench an angry shove, and
sat down upon it. As he sat listening to Peter he uttered an
occasional grunt of dissatisfaction, and frowned more than ever.

"Yes, but activity to what end?" he cried. "In what
relation do you mean to stand to the Government?"

"In what relation? Why, as its assistants, of course. The
society need not be a secret one unless the Government declines
to recognise it. It is not only a society friendly to the Government, but an association of genuine Conservatives. In fact, it is
a society of gentlemen in the true sense of the word. Its aim is
merely to prevent Pougatchew from coming and cutting your and
my children's throats, and Araktchéïew from sending me to a
military settlement. That is all that we are joining hands
for—for the one aim of the common weal and the common
security."

"Yes, but it is a secret society, all the same, and therefore a militant and harmful one—one that can only breed mischief."

"Why so? Was the *Tugend-bund* [1] which saved Europe" (people did not then dare to assert that it was Russia who had saved her) "productive of anything harmful? On the contrary, it was a society of public benefactors. It stood for love and mutual co-operation. Well, that was what Christ preached upon the Cross."

Natacha, entering the room in the middle of this discussion, gazed approvingly at her husband. It was not what he was saying that she approved of so much. That did not even interest her, for it all appeared to her so extremely simple, and as though she had known it for a long time. It appeared so to her because she knew the whole of what it proceeded from, i.e. the whole of Peter's soul. What she approved of, as she gazed at him, was his animated, enraptured figure.

Still greater admiration of Peter filled the little boy who, forgotten by everyone, sat with his slender neck protruding eagerly above his broad white collar. Every word of Peter's fired his soul to such a pitch that, without noticing it, he kept breaking the sealing-wax and pens on his uncle's writing-table with the nervous movements of his fingers.

"The German *Tugend-bund* was not what you think. It was simply what I have stated."

"Well, my good sir, the *Tugend-bund* may have done well enough for the sausage-eaters, but I do not understand it— although I also do not condemn it," said Denissow in his loud, insistent voice. "Everything here is bad and rotten, I admit, but I still do not fathom that *Tugend-bund* of yours, nor do I care about it. A *bunt* [2]—that is the thing. I should be your man at once."

Peter smiled and Natacha laughed aloud, but Nicholas only frowned the more, and assured Peter that no revolution was to be apprehended, and that all the dangers which he spoke of existed only in his imagination. Peter again asserted the contrary, and since his intellectual powers were the stronger and more resourceful of the two, Nicholas soon found himself nonplussed. This irritated him the more in that in his heart he knew—not by reasoning, but by something stronger than reasoning—that his opinion was undoubtedly the right one.

[1] The Band of Virtue. A German society formed in 1813–15 for the expulsion of the French.
[2] "A revolution" a pun on the final syllable of *Tundge-bund*.

"Well, that is all I have to say," he declared as he rose with some agitation and went to a corner to lay his pipe aside. "I cannot prove it to you, of course. *You* say that everything is going wrong with us, and that we shall soon have a revolution. I do not see it at all. You assert also that an oath is only a conditional affair. Well, in answer to that I have to say that, although you are my best friend, as you yourself know, I for my part know that, should you form a secret society or begin in any way to oppose the Government (no matter what sort of a Government it be), I shall always feel it my duty to obey that Government, and that, should Araktchéïew bid me ride against you with a squadron and cut you down, I shall never hesitate for a moment to do so. You must make what you like of that."

An awkward silence ensued upon these words. Natacha was the first to break it, and she took the line of defending her husband and attacking Nicholas. Her defence was weak and clumsy, yet she attained her object. The discussion began again, but not in that unpleasantly bitter tone in which Nicholas's last words had been spoken. When they rose to go to supper, Nicolenka Bolkonsky approached Peter with a pale face and his eyes radiant.

"Uncle Peter, you—you are not—if papa had been alive he would have agreed with you, would he not?" he asked him.

In a flash, Peter understood what an extraordinary independent, complex, and strenuous process must have been proceeding in the heart and brain of this boy during the discussion. Yet, as he recalled all that he himself had said, he felt vexed that Nicolenka should have overheard it. However, he had to give an answer of some kind.

"On the whole I think—yes," he said reluctantly, and then left the room. The boy hung his head, and then saw for the first time what he had done on the writing-table. He gave a gasp, and walked straight up to Nicholas.

"Uncle, I am so sorry," he said. "I did this without thinking," and he pointed to the broken pens and sealing-wax. Nicholas started irritably.

"Very well, very well," he said as he threw the pieces under the table. Then, evidently restraining his anger with some difficulty, he walked away.

"You ought not to have been here at all," he remarked.

CHAPTER CXLV

AFTER supper the conversation turned no more on politics and societies, but, on the contrary, on the most pleasing of topics to Nicholas—namely, reminiscences of 1812. It was Denissow who first started the subject, and Peter was particularly agreeable and interesting over it. Thus the relatives parted for the night on the best of terms.

After Nicholas had undressed in his study and given his orders to the waiting steward he proceeded in his dressing-gown to his bedroom, where he found his wife still writing at her writing-table.

"What are you jotting down, Maria?" he asked.

The Countess Maria blushed, for she was afraid that what she was writing would not be understood and approved of by her husband. She would gladly have hidden it from him, but at the same time he did not feel altogether displeased that his surprising her at that moment now forced her to tell him what it was.

"It is my diary, Nicholas," she said as she handed him a blue note-book filled with her large, firm handwriting.

"A diary?" queried Nicholas with a shade of ridicule in his tone, and took the book into his hands. It was written in French.

"*December 4th.* To-day Andrusha refused to have his clothes put on when it came to getting-up time, so Mademoiselle Louise sent for me. He was naughty and obstinate. I tried threatening him, but he only grew the more determined. Then I turned away, as though to leave him alone, and began to help the nurse to get the other children up, saying that I did not love him. For a while he was silent, as though surprised. Then, clad only in his night-shirt, he suddenly threw himself upon me, and burst into such a passion of weeping that it was long before I could comfort him. It was clear that what had distressed him most of all was to think that he had vexed me. Afterwards, in the evening, when I gave him his conduct ticket, he cried again most pitifully as he kissed me. Tenderness can do anything with him."

"What is that 'conduct ticket'?" asked Nicholas.

"Oh, I have begun to give the elder ones reports each evening as to how they have behaved during the day."

Nicholas looked at the brilliant eyes gazing at him, and then went on turning the leaves and reading. In the diary there was entered everything in the children's life which had seemed to the mother worthy of note, either as expressive of her children's characters, or as furnishing ideas concerning the best methods of educating them. The entries were mostly the merest trifles, but they did not seem so either to the mother or to the father as he now stood reading for the first time this daily record of the nursery.

For the 5th of December he found entered: "To-day Mitia started to be naughty at table, so papa said that he was to have no tart. Accordingly he was given none, but he looked so wistfully and hungrily at the others as they ate! I think that to punish a child by giving him no sweets only develops greed. I must say so to Nicholas."

Nicholas stopped reading, and glanced at Maria. Her shining eyes were gazing inquiringly at him, as though to see whether he approved of the diary or not. There could be no doubt, not only of his approval of it, but of the delight he took in his wife. Possibly he thought that the whole thing need not have been done so pedantically, or even that it was unnecessary; yet this constant, tireless, heartfelt anxiety of hers for his children's moral welfare pleased him beyond measure. If at that moment he could have analysed his own feelings, he would have found that the chief thing upon which his proud, tender, assured love for his wife was based was just this very wonder at her thoroughness and at the high moral sphere, far above his own powers of attainment, in which she always lived. He felt proud that she should be so wise and so good, while he recognised also his own inferiority to her in the realm of spirituality. Still more did it delight him to think that not only did she belong to him in her heart, but that she constituted an actual part of himself.

"I am very, very pleased with it," he said of the diary with an expressive look. Then, after a moment's silence, he added: "Now, *I* have been behaving badly to-day. You see, you were not in the study to stop me. I quarrelled with Peter, and grew quite heated over it. He is impossible sometimes, he is such a child. I do not know what would become of him if Natacha did not hold him on the bit. Can you guess why he has been to St. Petersburg? Why, they have organised there a—"

"Yes, I know," said the Countess Maria. "Natacha told me of it."

"Oh, so you know, then?" continued Nicholas, warming at

the mere recollection of the dispute. "Well, he wanted to persuade me that every honourable man ought to oppose the Government now, in defiance at once of allegiance and duty. I only wish you had been there. They all set upon me—that is to say, Denissow and Natacha as well. Natacha is absolutely absurd. Why, she holds Peter under her thumb, yet, when it comes to political opinions, she has not a word to say for herself, but just says what he does." Nicholas could not resist the impulse which sometimes leads people to criticise their nearest and dearest friends. He forgot that, word for word, the same might have been said of himself in his relation to his wife.

"Yes, I have noticed it," said Maria.

"When I told him that home duties and the oath of allegiance ranked above everything else he started out to prove to me the Lord only knows what. You should have been there to hear him. What should you have said in my place?"

"In my opinion you were perfectly right. I told Natacha so. Peter says that everyone is being oppressed, interfered with, and corrupted, and that it is our duty to help our neighbour. Of course he is right in that, but at the same time he forgets that we have other and even more intimate duties which God Himself has laid upon us, and that, though we may take risks for ourselves, we may not do so for our children."

"That is just what I said to him," agreed Nicholas, who really believed that it was. "Yet they held to their assertions about love for one's neighbour and Christianity. Moreover, all this was said before Nicolenka, who had managed to follow us into the study, and had sat breaking things on my table there."

"Do you know, Nicholas, Nicolenka is often on my mind," said Maria. "He is such a strange boy! Sometimes I fear that I am neglecting him for my own children. You see, we have our children and relations, but he has no one. He is always alone with his thoughts."

"You have no reason to reproach yourself. All that the tenderest of mothers could do for her son you have done, and do, for him. Of course, I am delighted that it should be so. He is a wonderful, wonderful little fellow. To-night he must have fallen into a kind of trance as he sat listening to Peter, for, just as we were getting up to go to supper, he came to me to say that he had broken everything on my writing-table. Indeed, I have never known him tell an untruth. Yes, he is a wonderful, wonderful little fellow," repeated Nicholas, who was not over-fond of Nicolenka in his heart. yet always tried to think the best of him.

"Oh, but I am not the same as a mother to him," said Maria. "I feel that I am not, and that worries me. He is an exceptional boy, and I am terribly afraid for him. He needs more companionship."

"Oh well, it will not be for long; I am going to send him away to St. Petersburg in the summer," said Nicholas. "Yes, Peter is, and always was, a dreamer," he continued, returning to the conversation in the study, which seemed to have moved him greatly. "Yet what have I got to do with it all—with Araktchéïew being a villain, and so forth? What business was it of mine when I married and had so many debts that I was in danger of being put in prison, and a mother who would not see or understand my difficulties. And then—you, children, my duties. Do I spend my days from morning to night in the office for my own pleasure? No. All I know is that my business is to comfort my mother, to repay you, and not to leave the children such paupers as I myself was."

Maria would have told him that a man ought not to engage solely in bread-winning, and that he (Nicholas) attached too much importance to his estate work, had she not known that it was both useless and unnecessary to do so. Accordingly she just took his hand and kissed it. This caress he took to mean approval of what he had said and assent to his ideas, so, after a moment's silent reflection, he went on thinking aloud.

"Do you know, Maria, Ilia Mitrofanitch" (one of the foremen of works) "came over from the Tambov village to-day, and told me that 80,000 roubles have been offered for the timber there." Then, his face beaming, Nicholas went on to speak of the possibility of very soon redeeming Otradnoë. "Granted another ten years of life," he said, "and I shall leave my children in a good position."

The Countess Maria heard and understood all that her husband was saying, for she knew that when he had been thinking aloud in this way he sometimes asked her afterwards what he had said, and was vexed when she admitted that she had been thinking of something else. Yet to do this she had to make great efforts, since what he was saying in no way interested her. She kept her eyes fixed upon him, and thus contrived only to *feel*, not to think of, something else. She felt a sincere and tender love in her heart for this man who could never understand all that she understood, and the very fact made

her love him all the more—made her love him with a touch
of passionate devotion. Yet over and above that feeling,
which absorbed her whole self and prevented her from fully
comprehending all the details of her husband's plans, there kept
passing through her brain ideas which had nothing in common
with what he was saying. She kept thinking of her nephew
(her husband's account of his agitation at Peter's discourse had
struck her greatly), and different traits in his sensitive, affectionate nature kept presenting themselves to her mind. This
led her on to think also of her own children. She did not compare them with her nephew, but only her own feelings towards
them, and recognised with regret that in her feelings towards
Nicolenka there was something wanting. Sometimes the idea
occurred to her that this difference arose from their different
ages, but, for all that, she felt guilty towards Nicolenka, and
promised herself in her heart to make amends and to do the
impossible, i.e. to love in this life both her husband, her
children, Nicolenka, and her neighbour as Christ loves all
humanity. Maria's spirit tended always towards the infinite,
the eternal, and the complete, and therefore was never at rest.
This strenuous and sublime yearning of soul expressed itself in
the drawn expression of her face and the tenseness of her
frame. As Nicholas looked at her it suddenly occurred to him:
"My God! what would become of us all if she were to die?
Somehow her face makes me feel that that might happen soon."
Then, taking his stand before the ikon, he began to read the
evening prayers.

CHAPTER CXLVI

WHEN Natacha found herself alone with her husband she fell to
discussing matters with him as only a wife can do with her help-
meet, i.e. exchanging ideas with extraordinary perspicuity and
swiftness, as well as by a method at once contrary to all the
known rules of logic and independent of all fixed opinions, conclusions, and deductions—a method, in fact, peculiar to married
couples. Natacha was so accustomed to employ this method
with her husband that, when he began to express his thoughts
to her in logical sequence, she knew infallibly that some difference was looming between them. He had only to begin to
prove things at length and to speak quietly and consecutively

and she to follow his example, for her to scent a quarrel in the distance.

From the moment when they were left alone, and Natacha, approaching him with happy, expectant eyes, had clasped him round the neck with sudden, tender swiftness, and pressed him to her bosom, saying, "Now you are altogether mine, mine! You are not going away again!"—from that moment there began a conversation opposed to all the rules of logic in that it turned at one and the same time upon entirely different topics. This simultaneous embracing of many subjects not only did nothing to impair clearness of mutual comprehension, but, on the contrary, was the truest sign that the pair understood one another. Just as, in a dream, everything may be unreal, meaningless, and contradictory except the feelings which animate the sleeper, so nothing that was said during this irrational communion of husband and wife was clearly expressed—only the feelings which animated them both.

Natacha spoke to Peter of her brother's daily life and affairs, of how she had suffered—indeed, had scarcely lived at all—during the absence of her husband, and of how she loved Maria more than ever, although Maria was in all respects superior to her. In saying this, Natacha was quite candid in her acknowledgment of Maria's superiority, but at the same time she implied that she meant Peter to prefer herself to her sister-in-law or any other woman, and that now, when he had just been seeing so many other women in St. Petersburg, was the moment for his making a fresh confession of his faith. Accordingly Peter declared that he had found all his evening parties and dinners in the company of the ladies of St. Petersburg insupportable.

"I have got out of the way of talking to such fine dames," he said with unaffected weariness. "Moreover, I was so busy at the time."

Natacha looked hard at him, and then went on:

"Maria is so charming! How well she understands children! She seems to see into their very souls. Yesterday, for instance, Mitenka began to be naughty and—"

"How like his father the boy is!" put in Peter.

Natacha knew quite well why he interpolated this remark about Mitenka's likeness to Nicholas. He still felt sore over the recollection of his quarrel with his brother-in-law, and wished to have Natacha's opinion of the subject.

"Dear Nicholas has this weakness," said Natacha, "that,

unless a particular thing is accepted by all, he will agree to
nothing. And you only value 'opening up the quarry,'" she
said, repeating an expression he had used.

"No, the truth of the matter is," said Peter, "that, for
Nicholas, all views and ideas are only an amusement—one
might almost say, only a passing of the time. As you know,
he collects books, and makes it his rule never to buy a new one
until he has read his last purchase—whether it be Sismondi,
Rousseau, Montesquieu, or anything else," added Peter with a
smile. "Well, you know, too, how I—" Here Peter began
to soften the impression of what he had said, but Natacha
interrupted him to show that it wasn't necessary.

"So you say that, for him, ideas are only an amusement?"

"Yes, while for myself *everything else* is only an amusement.
All the time that I was in St. Petersburg I saw everyone as in
a dream. When an idea has taken hold of me, everything else
becomes futility."

"Ah, how I wish I had seen you when you greeted the
children!" was Natacha's next remark. "Which of them was
the most delighted? Lisa, I expect."

"Yes," said Peter, and went on with what was in his mind.
"Nicholas, you know, says that we ought not to *think*. Now, I
cannot accept that. Throughout the whole of my stay in St.
Petersburg I kept thinking (I may say this to *you*) that, but for
myself, the whole thing must come to the ground. Every man
is pulling in a different direction, and it is for me to unite them
all; after which my idea will become clear and simple enough.
Of course I did not say that we need oppose anyone in particular.
All that I said was: 'Join hands all you who value what is
right, and let there be one flag over you—the flag of active
well-doing.' You see, Prince Sergius is a sensible man, and
clever."

Natacha never doubted for a moment that Peter's idea was
a great one, yet one thing confused her. That was the fact that
he was her husband. "Can a man who is so important and
necessary to the community really be my husband? How has
that come about?" Then she tried to explain the difficulty to
herself. "Who are the men who have decided that he is so
much cleverer than the rest of them?" she thought as she ran
over in her mind the people whom he most respected. Of
them, according to what he himself often said, he most respected
Plato Karataïew.

"Do you know of whom I am thinking?" she said. "Of

Plato Karataïew. What about him? Would he have agreed with you?"

Peter was not at all surprised at the question, since he understood the trend of his wife's thoughts.

"Plato Karataïew?" he replied, and then reflected for a moment—evidently trying his best to imagine what Karataïew's opinion would have been on the subject. "He would never have understood it—though, of course, he *might* have done," he thought to himself.

"Oh, I love you so!" cried Natacha suddenly. "Yes, ever and ever so much!"

"No, he would not have agreed with me," went on Peter, still deep in thought. "The kind of thing that he would have approved of would have been this family life of ours. He always yearned to see beauty and happiness and peace in everything, and I could have pointed with pride to ourselves. You know, you talk of separations, but you cannot imagine what an affection I have for you after there has been one."

"Yes, at present," began Natacha.

"No, no! I shall love you always, and could not possibly love you more than I do. That is certain. You know—" He did not finish the sentence, for their eyes met at that moment and told them the rest.

"How stupid people are to think that the honeymoon is the best time!" said Natacha. "The present is far better. If only you would never go away again! What a lot of quarrels we have had in our time! And it was I, always I, that was in the wrong. But what we generally quarrelled about I cannot so much as remember."

"Always about the same thing," said Peter with a smile, "About jeal—"

"Do not say the word—I cannot bear it!" exclaimed Natacha while a cold, vindictive gleam showed itself for a moment in her eyes. "Did you see her?" she added after a moment's silence.

"No. At least, I may have seen her, but I did not recognise her."

They were both of them silent a moment.

"Do you know," went on Natacha, evidently wishing to dissipate the passing cloud, "while you were talking in the study to-night I kept looking at you, and thought to myself how exactly you and the boy" (she meant her little son) "resemble one another. Well, it is time I went to him now—quite time, but I hate to leave you."

For a few moments they remained silent again. Then, suddenly turning to one another, they both of them began to speak at the same moment—Peter eagerly and with self-assurance, and Natacha with a quiet, happy smile. Then, their words clashing, each of them stopped to let the other one speak.

"What were you going to say? You speak first," he said.

"No, no. What were *you* going to say? How stupid of me!" she replied.

Accordingly Peter finished what he had begun, i.e. a fresh instalment of his confident opinions about his success in St. Petersburg. At that moment he felt as though he had been called upon to impart a new tendency to the whole Russian community and the world at large.

"I only wished to say," he explained, "that all ideas which have great results are essentially simple ones. My own idea consists only in thinking that, if the baser sort combine together to form a political force, the upright should do the same. How simple that is!"

"Yes, indeed."

"And what were *you* going to say

"Oh, nothing. I am so stupid."

"No, but tell me."

"Nothing, nothing—mere rubbish," said Natacha, beaming more radiantly than ever. "I only wanted to tell you about Pétia. To-night when nurse came to take him away to bed, he laughed so, and pouted, and clung to me! Evidently the little monkey thought that he was successfully hiding himself. He is so extraordinarily good-tempered. There! I can hear him calling for me now. Well, good-bye for the moment," and she left the room.

Meanwhile in Nicolenka's bedroom a lamp was burning as usual (for the boy was afraid of the dark, and could not be cured of his failing). Dessalles was asleep, propped up on his customary four high pillows, and emitting portentous snores from his nose at regular intervals. Nicolenka had just started up from sleep in a cold perspiration, and was now sitting on his bed with his eyes wide open and gazing fixedly in front of him. It was a horrible dream which had aroused him. In that dream he had seen himself and Peter, clad in helmets such as Plutarch describes, marching at the head of a great army. The army was composed wholly of slanting white threads, which filled the air as the spiders' webs do which float about in the autumn—

the kind of gossamer which Dessalles used to call *fil de la Vierge*. In front of the army lay Glory, also composed of threads, but looking denser. All this while Peter and he were marching with easy, joyous strides towards a goal, when suddenly the threads which had hitherto moved them began to give way and become entangled, so that marching became difficult. Then of a sudden Peter and Nicolenka found themselves confronted by Uncle Nicholas, who was standing in a stern and menacing attitude. "Did you do this?" he said to Nicolenka as he pointed to the broken sealing-wax and pens. "I loved you once, but Araktchéïew has given me his orders, and I am to slay the first one of you who advances a step further." Nicolenka looked about him for Peter, but Peter had disappeared, and in his place stood Nicolenka's father, Prince Andrew, and that father was without shape or outline, yet still there. As Nicolenka gazed at him he became conscious of the weakness of love—became conscious of being without strength, without bones or marrow. His father was caressing and pitying him, yet Uncle Nicholas still kept drawing nearer. At length, carried away by his terror, the boy awoke.

"My father!" he thought to himself. "Yes, my father" (there were two portraits of Prince Andrew in the house, yet Nicolenka had never imagined him in human form) "was with me and being kind to me. He approved of me, too, and approved of Uncle Peter. Whatsoever henceforth he bids me to do I will do it. Mucius Scaevola could thrust his own right hand into the flame: why, then, should I not do the same in my life? I know they want me to become a learned man, and I will become one, but some day, too, I will put aside my books, and *do* things. Only one thing do I ask God—that He will let me do as Plutarch's men did. Yes, and I will do even better than they. Everyone shall know of me, everyone love me, everyone applaud me." All at once Nicolenka felt the sobs rising in his breast, and he burst into tears.

"Are you not well?" he heard Dessalles say.

"Oh, it is nothing," answered the boy as he lay down again upon his pillow.

"He is kind and good, and I love him," he thought of Dessalles; "but Uncle Peter—what a splendid man *he* is! And my father too! Yes, I will do such things as shall please even *him*."

PART II

CHAPTER CXLVII

THE subject of history is the life of nations and of humanity. Yet to describe precisely the life even of a single nation, much less that of all humanity, would appear to be impossible. The older historians had one unvarying method of condensing and describing the life of a given people. They simply wrote of the parts played by the individuals who stood in authority over that people, and let those parts stand for the part played by the nation as a whole. To the two questions of how individuals could contrive to compel whole peoples to act according to their will and of how such will itself was directed those historians replied by saying, firstly, that it was through the Divine Dispensation that nations were brought to submit themselves to the will of one person alone, and secondly, that it was through the same Divine Dispensation that the will of the chosen individual was directed towards a predestined end. In fact, the older historians decided both the one question and the other by expressing their belief in the immediate participation of the Deity in the affairs of men.

By its theory, however, the newer history has upset both these positions. Yet, while shattering ancient belief in the subordination of mankind to the Deity and in some undefined end towards which all nations move, the newer history has not done as might have been expected of it. That is to say, it has not abandoned the study of the phenomena of power for the study of the causes which create power. Consequently, though it has displaced the *theory* of the older historians, it still follows their *practice*. Instead of men gifted with divine authority and moved directly by the will of God, the newer history puts forward men who are either heroes gifted with extraordinary, superhuman attributes or men of any and every degree who have happened to stand in authority over the masses. Instead of the old divinely-approved purposes of nations—of the Jews, the Greeks, or the Romans—which bygone historians considered to be the purposes towards which all humanity moved, the newer history puts forward purposes of its own—purposes such as the welfare of the German, the French, or the English nations —or, in its highest flights, the welfare of all humanity (though by "humanity" it generally means only the few nations which occupy one small north-western corner of a great continent).

Thus the newer history sets aside the views of the older science, yet has no new ones to set up in their place. Consequently the logic of the position of those historians who feign to have rejected the divine authority of rulers and ancient myths of that kind has inevitably compelled them to arrive by another route at the same end—namely, at a recognition of the facts (1) that nations are governed by individuals, and (2) that there exists a given end towards which all nations and humanity move. At the base of every work by these newer historians there lie (for all the seeming differences and novelty of standpoint of those works) two old-established and inevitable positions. In the first place, the historian describes the acts only of those particular individuals whom he considers to have exercised authority over humanity (one writer, for instance, regarding as such only monarchs, leaders of armies, and ministers, while another one adds to that list orators, scholars, reformers, philosophers, and poets), and in the second place, each historian has his own particular end towards which he considers humanity to have been, or to be, moving (one such writer, for instance, believing that end to have been the greatness of the Roman, the Spanish, and the French States, while another one considers it to have been the freedom, equality, and civilisation of one small corner of the world known as Europe).

In 1789 a disturbance arose in Paris. It grew, developed, and found expression in a movement of nations from west to east. That movement took place more than once, and collided with a counter-movement westwards, until in 1812 it attained its ultimate goal—Moscow. Next, a strikingly similar return movement was carried out from east to west — a movement which, like the previous one, attracted to itself the nations of Central Europe. Finally this return movement reached its ultimate goal—Paris, and then gradually died away. During that period of twenty years an immense number of fields were left unploughed, countless homes destroyed, and an enormous volume of trade dissipated. Millions of people became destitute, sick, or exiles, and millions of Christians, professing the law of love for their neighbour, killed one another.

What did it all mean? Whence did it arise? What moved those men to burn houses and to kill men like themselves? What were the first causes of those events? What was the force which compelled those men to act after such a fashion?

Such are the involuntary, elementary, and wholly legitimate questions which humanity asks itself as it pores over the records and traditions of that bygone period of turmoil. For the decision of those questions serious human thought turns to the study of that history which has for its aim the self-realisation of nations and of humanity.

If to this day history had continued to support the views of the older writers it would have answered: "The Deity, to reward or to punish His people, granted power to Napoleon, and directed him, through the exercise of the Divine Will, to the attainment of God-appointed ends:" which answer would have been a full and sufficient one enough. One might or might not have believed in the divine destiny of Napoleon, yet, for anyone who did believe in it, everything in the history of that period would at once have become intelligible and free from contradiction. Yet the newer history cannot answer us thus, seeing that science no longer recognises the views of the older writers concerning the immediate participation of the Deity in the affairs of men. Consequently it has to seek other answers to the above questions.

In fact, the newer history answers something to this effect. "Do you desire to know what was the meaning of that movement of the nations—whence it arose, and what was the force which produced those phenomena? Listen to me, then. Louis XIV was a very proud and a very self-confident man. He had many mistresses and favourites, and ruled France badly. His successors likewise were weak men who ruled France badly and kept an equally large number of mistresses and favourites. At the same period certain men wrote certain books. Also, at the end of the eighteenth century there foregathered in Paris a score of men who started to say that all men were equal and all men free. From this men went on, all over France, to cut one another's throats, and killed even their king. Now, at the same time there chanced also to be in France a man of genius—namely, Napoleon. Everywhere he got the upper hand of everyone. That is to say, everywhere he killed numbers of his fellows for the reason that he was a man of genius. For some unknown reason he set out to kill people in Africa, and did the work so well, and was so cunning and clever throughout, that, when he returned home to France, he was in a position to bid all men subject themselves to himself, and to ensure that they did so. Thus become emperor, he again set out to kill nations in Italy, Austria, and Prussia. There, too, he did his work well. In Russia, however, there was the Emperor Alexander, who decided to re-establish order in Europe, and joined issue with the man of genius. Yet in 1807 he unexpectedly made friends with Napoleon, and remained so until in 1811, the pair quarrelled again, and fell once more to killing their fellow-men. Then Napoleon brought 600,000 troops to Russia, and took Moscow. Next, he began a headlong flight from the city, and the Emperor Alexander, with the help of his advisers (Stein and others), united Europe in an expedition against the disturber of its peace. All Napoleon's allies suddenly turned against him, and it was to attack a Napoleon engaged in recruiting new forces that the expedition marched. The allies beat Napoleon, entered Paris, compelled the man of genius to renounce the throne, and sent him to the Isle of Elba— though without depriving him of all imperial dignity and respect, notwithstanding that, five years earlier, everyone had looked upon the ex-emperor as an outlawed brigand, and was to do the same again a year later. Next, Louis XVIII began his reign—a man at whom the French people, as well as the allies, had hitherto only laughed. Napoleon, after weeping in the presence of the Old Guard, renounced the throne, and went into exile. Next, some astute statesmen and diplomatists (chief among them Talleyrand, who had succeeded at the start in securing himself a good position, and used it to widen the boundaries of France) began a series of conferences in Vienna, and by those conferences to make nations happy or unhappy. Yet of a sudden both monarchs and diplomatists came near to quarrelling—came near to bidding their armies begin destroying one another once more. Before they could do so, however, Napoleon had landed in France with a following, and the French, though detesting him, once more submitted themselves to his influence. The allied monarchs, enraged at this, again declared war against the French. This time the man of genius was beaten, and dispatched to the Island of St. Helena as a convicted brigand. There the exile, parted from all who were dear to him, and from his beloved France, died a lingering death on his rocky eyrie, and bequeathed the memory of his great deeds to posterity. Reaction set in in Europe, and the rulers resumed once more their accustomed role of brow-beating their subjects."

It might almost be supposed that the above has been written as a joke on my part—that it represents a mere caricature of an historical exposition: yet, as a matter of fact, it represents no more than a mild example of the contradictory and irrelevant answers given us by *all* history—from general histories and the newer "histories of civilisation" of the period down to books of memoirs and histories of one particular nation only. The *bizarrerie* of those answers proceeds from the fact that the newer history is like a deaf man who persists in answering questions which no one has put to him. If the aim of history is the description of the movements of humanity and nations, then the first question—the lack of an answer to which would render all the rest unintelligible—should be: "What was the force which moved the nations to their action?" To that question the newer history answers with a rambling story, or else with some statement that Napoleon was a great genius, or that Louis XIV was very proud, or even that such and such a writer of the period happened to write such and such a book!

All that may very well be, and humanity is quite ready to accept the fact: yet it bears no relation whatever to the question which humanity has propounded. Moreover, it would only be interesting if we were to concede that some divine power, based upon itself and always acting alone, ruled nations either through Napoleons, through men like the French kings, or through writers. The existence of such a power, however, we no longer recognise, and consequently, before speaking of Napoleons, French kings, or writers, it is necessary to show that any connection existed between those personages and the national movements of their time. If, on the other hand, not divine power, but some other force, moved them, it should be explained what that new force was, seeing that that is the question in which lies the whole interest of history. History seems to suppose that the force in question was a self-explanatory one, and well-known to all. Yet, with every desire to recognise it as one familiar to the world at large, he who dips extensively into historical works will soon find himself doubting involuntarily whether, in view of the differing representations of that force which he sees put forward by the historians themselves, it can really have been a force of which everyone is aware.

CHAPTER CXLVIII

WHAT, then, was the force which moved the nations?

Writers of biographies and historians of individual peoples understand that force as a power pertaining only to supermen and rulers. According to them, events take place solely through the will of Napoleons, Alexanders, or, in general, all such personages as those of whom biographers treat. The answers which historians of this kind return to the question concerning the force by which events are inspired are satisfactory only so long as there is an historian for each separate event; but as soon as ever historians of different nationalities and views begin to describe the same occurrence, the answers given by them become meaningless, since not only do the conceptions of those writers with regard to the force in question differ, but frequently they contradict one another. One historian will maintain that a given event took place through the will of Napoleon, while another one will assert that it took place through the will of Alexander, and a third that it did so through the will of yet another person. Moreover, historians of this kind contradict one another even in their explanations of the force upon which they assert the power of one and the same personage to have been based. For instance, Thiers, the Bonapartist writer, says that Napoleon's power was based upon his genius and benevolence, whereas Lanfrey, the Republican historian, avers that it was based upon his rascality and hoodwinking of the nation. Thus historians of this species, by mutually annihilating each other's positions, annihilate also any definite idea of the force which produces events, and so return no answer to the essential question of history.

General historians (i.e. those who treat of the affairs of *all* nations) seem to recognise the heterogeneity of these specialists in the matter of the force which produces events. They look upon that force, not as a power pertaining only to supermen and rulers, but as the result of several variously-directed forces. In describing the war-making or the conquest of a given nation, the general historian seeks the cause of a given event, not in the power of any one personage, but in the reaction upon one another of the numerous different personages who were connected with that event. According to this view, then, the power of historical personages is (apparently) the product of several different forces, and therefore not recognisable as a force which, in itself, produces events. Yet general historians almost invariably return to the idea that that power is one which does produce events, and that it stands to events in the relation of cause to effect. We find them saying in the same breath that an historical personage is the product of his own time, and that his power is the outcome of various forces, and that the campaign of 1812 and such other events as they disapprove of were the outcome of Napoleon's misdirected will—that, indeed, it was actually through his initiative that the ideas of 1784 were checked! Revolutionary ideas and the general situation produced Napoleon's power, yet that power stifled revolutionary ideas and the general situation! Yet this extraordinary contradiction is not which occurs merely now and again. On the contrary, we meet with it at every step, while it is out of a consecutive series of such contradictions that the writings of all general historians are composed. In reality the absurdity arises out of the fact that, in entering upon the field of analysis, general historians only go half-way.

To find out what are the constituent forces which are equivalent to an integral, a co-efficient, force it is necessary to make the sum of the constituent forces coincide with the integral force of which they form the component parts. This condition we never find observed by general historians. The result is that, to explain what the co-efficient force is, they are driven also to concede (to make good the deficiency of constituent forces) the existence of another and unexplained force which acts in accordance with the integral one.

The specialist historian, in describing the campaign of 1813 or the restoration of the Bourbons, declares that those events were produced by the will of Alexander. The general historian, however, refutes this view of the specialist writer, and seeks to show that the two events were due, not only to the will of Alexander, but also to the agency of Stein, Metternich, Madame de Staël, Talleyrand, Fichte, Chateaubriand, and others. Evidently, then, the general historian is dissolving Alexander into constituent portions represented by Talleyrand, Chateaubriand, and so forth. Yet the sum of those constituent portions, i.e. the action upon one another of Chateaubriand, Talleyrand, Madame de Staël, and the rest—is not equal to the entire co-efficient, i.e. to the phenomenon that millions of Frenchmen subjected themselves to the sway of the Bourbons. From the fact that Chateaubriand, Madame de Staël, and others spoke certain words to one another there can be deduced their personal relations only, and not the subjection of millions of human beings to a dynasty. Therefore, to explain how the relations of those personages brought about that subjection of millions, i.e. how a few constituent forces equal to a single one A produced an integral force equal to A multiplied a thousand times—the general historian finds himself obliged once more to admit the existence of the very force—namely, power—which hitherto he has denied, as well as to recognise it as the result of other forces. That is to say, he has to concede some unexplained force acting in accordance with the working of the whole. This is what all general historians do: with the result that they not only contradict specialist historians, but likewise themselves.

Country dwellers who are looking for rain or for fine weather, but who possess no clear idea as to the causes of rain, generally say: "The wind has driven away the clouds," or, "The wind is driving up the clouds." So too with these general historians. Sometimes, if it suits their theory, they say that power is the *result* of events, while at other times, when they wish to prove something else, they say that power is the *producer* of events.

A third class of historians—those known as the historians of civilisation, who follow a path first cut out for them by the general historians, but likewise recognise such persons as *literateurs* and *grandes dames* as forces productive of events—understand the force of which we are speaking in a perfectly different manner, for it is in what we call culture or intellectual activity that they declare it to be discernible.

Historians of civilisation are reasonable enough in thus following their progenitors the general historians; for if historical events may be explained by saying that such and such people did such and such things to one another, why should not historical events also be explained by saying that such and such people wrote such and such books? From the infinite multitude of signs which accompany every phenomenon of life such historians select the sign of intellectual activity, and declare it to have been a cause. Yet, for all their efforts to show that the cause of a given event lies in intellectual activity, it is only by making great concessions that one can agree with the assertion that between intellectual activity and the movements of nations there can be anything in common, while it is a sheer impossibility to admit that intellectual activity has invariably directed the doings of mankind. Such phenomena as the brutal murders of the French Revolution (which were the result of harangues on the subject of the equality of man), as well as the cruel wars and massacres which have so frequently arisen out of the Gospel of Love, in no way bear out such an assertion.

But even if we admit that all the cunningly devised pronouncements with which these histories are filled are trustworthy, and that nations are ruled by some indeterminate force called *ideas*, the essential question of history will either remain unanswered, or we shall be forced to add to the old power of monarchs and the old influence of councillors and other persons which the general historians have imported this same new force of ideas— the connection between which and the masses is not very apparent. One may understand that Napoleon had power, and that therefore a given event was accomplished. By making large concessions one may even understand that Napoleon, with other influences, was the cause of a given event. Yet how the book *Le Contrat Social* induced the French people to begin murdering one another is wholly unintelligible without some explanation of the causal connection between this new force of ideas and the event referred to.

Undoubtedly there exists a connection between all persons living at the same period, and therefore also a possibility of discovering some connection between the intellectual activity of mankind and historical movements, just as a connection is certainly traceable between the movements of humanity and trade, handicrafts, agriculture, and other pursuits. Yet how the intellectual activity of mankind can appear to historians of civilisation the cause or the expression of *all* historical movements it is difficult to understand. Historians can only have reached such a conclusion through supposing—(1) That, inasmuch as history is written by scholars, it is a natural and pleasant thing for the latter to imagine that the activity of their own profession is responsible for the movements of all humanity just as it might be a natural and pleasant thing for merchants, agriculturists, or soldiers—I do not say this merely because such men do *not* write history—to imagine the same thing; and (2) That all mental activity, enlightenment, civilisation, and ideas are obscure and indeterminate conceptions under cover of which it is easy to use words even more obscure, and so to bolster up any theory at will.

Nevertheless, without speaking of the internal merits of this species of history (it may be that it has a purpose of some sort and is necessary to someone), historians of civilisation (to whose productions general histories are beginning more and more to assimilate themselves) are remarkable for the fact that in examining seriously and in detail the religious, philosophical, and political ideas of the time as the causes of events, each time that they have to describe an actual historical happening, such as the campaign of 1812, they involuntarily describe it as the result of power, stating directly that this campaign resulted from the will of Napoleon. In thus speaking, these historians of civilisation insensibly contradict themselves by showing both that the new force which they have invented does not express historical events and that the only means which enables us to understand history is the force to which they deny recognition.

CHAPTER CXLIX

LET us suppose a locomotive to be in motion. To the question "How does it move?" one peasant might reply that a devil was pushing it along, a second one declare that it moved because its wheels revolved, and a third one state it as his opinion that the cause of the locomotive's movement lay in the trail of smoke which he saw blown backwards by the wind. The first peasant would be irrefutable—or, at all events, to refute him it would be necessary either to convince him that devils do not exist or for some other peasant to tell him that a mechanic, not a devil, was pushing the locomotive along. Only then would they both of them see, from their mutual contradictions, that both of them were wrong. The peasant, however, who should say that the cause of the movement was the revolving of the wheels of the locomotive would refute himself, since, once he had entered upon the ground of analysis, he would be forced to go further and further, until at length he had explained the actual cause of the wheels themselves revolving; nor, until he had arrived at the ultimate agency of all—namely, the steam compressed in the boiler—would he have the right to desist from his investigations. As for the peasant who should explain the movement of the locomotive by the fact of the wind blowing the smoke backwards, he would be one who, having noticed that the explanation regarding the wheels did not furnish the true case, fastened upon the first external sign which occurred to him, and gave it as his explanation of the phenomenon.

In reality, the only conception which could explain the movement of a locomotive is the conception of a force equal to the whole movement visible. Similarly, the only conception which could explain the movements of nations is the conception of a force equal to the sum of those movements. Yet to different historians such a conception connotes entirely different forces —forces not equal to the movements visible. Some historians discern behind those movements a force strictly pertaining to supermen, even as the first peasant saw in the locomotive a devil. Others of them see a force proceeding from other forces, like the wheels of the locomotive. Others, again, see the influence of intellectual activity, like the trail of smoke pouring from the funnel.

As long as histories are written of *individuals* only— of Cæsars, Alexanders, Luthers, Voltaires, and so forth—who have taken part in given events, and not histories of *all persons without exception* who have participated in them, no description of the movements of humanity will be possible without the conception of some such force as compels men to direct their activities to a common end. The only conception of this kind known to historians is the idea of *power*. This conception is the one handle which can regulate the material of history as now expounded, and the historian who would strip off that handle without first of all devising some other means of dealing with historical material would deprive himself of the last possible means of coping with its intricacies. The imperative necessity of this idea of power for explaining historical phenomena is best illustrated by the general historians and historians of civilisation themselves—by the writers who pretend to deny the idea of power, yet employ it at every step.

Hitherto historical science, in its relation to the questions of humanity, has been like monetary currency—like bank-notes and coin. Biographical histories and histories of a single nation resemble the former. They may pass and circulate everywhere without doing harm, and even to advantage, so long as there does not arise the question of the guarantee upon which they are secured. Similarly, so long as one overlooks the question of *how* the will of supermen produces events, histories by such writers as M. Thiers will be found both interesting and instructive, as well as charged with a certain tinge of poetry. Yet, even as a doubt concerning the effective value of bank-notes may arise, either from the fact that they are so easy to make that many people may begin making them, or from the fact that one may come to prefer gold to notes, so a doubt concerning the effective value of histories of this kind may arise either from the fact that there seems to be so many of them or from the fact that one may take to asking, in the simplicity of one's heart—"Yet what force enabled Napoleon to do so-and-so?"—that is one may desire to exchange current paper money for the pure gold of a working idea.

On the other hand, general historians and historians of civilisation resemble persons who, recognising the disadvantages of bank-notes, decide to mint currency of a less durable metal than gold—currency which is metal, certainly, but no more. Paper money may always deceive the unwary, but metal coin—especially of debased metal—deceives no one. Even as gold is gold only so long as it is employable, not merely for exchange, but for the transaction of commerce, so general historians will rank as gold only when they are able to answer the essential question of history—namely, "What is power?" At present they answer it only with contradictions, while the historians of civilisation put it altogether aside, and answer some other question. Even, also, as tokens similar to gold can be circulated only among business men who have agreed to recognise them as gold or among people who do not know the true properties of gold, so the general historians and historians of civilisation, in returning no answers to the essential questions of humanity, serve, for ends of their own, as mere current coin for universities and the reading public—for those who run after what they term "serious" books.

CHAPTER CL

HAVING set aside the views of the older historians as to the divine subordination of a nation's will to one chosen individual and the subordination of that individual to God, history cannot take a single step forward without contradicting itself—without having to choose between two things: either that it shall return to the old belief in the immediate participation of the Deity in the affairs of men, or that it shall define exactly the meaning of the force which produces historical events and is called power. To return to the old belief is impossible, since it lies shattered. Therefore it remains only to explain the meaning of power.

"Napoleon ordered troops to be mustered and to make war." This assertion has become so habitual with us, so entirely the view with which we have identified ourselves, that the question of why 600,000 men should have gone to war exactly when

Napoleon uttered certain words appears to us absurd. He possessed power, and therefore what he commanded to be done was done. Such an answer would be satisfactory enough if we really believed that his power was given him of God, but, inasmuch as we believe that no longer, it becomes necessary to determine exactly what that power was which this one man exerted over his fellows. It cannot have been the direct power possessed by a physically stronger being over a weaker one—the power which is founded upon the exercise, or the threatened exercise, of physical force, such as the strength of Hercules. Likewise it cannot have been the power which is founded upon the possession of moral force (as certain historians assert, in the innocence of their souls, when they declare that all historical personages are cast in heroic mould—are men gifted with extraordinary strength of mind, intellect, and what we call genius), seeing that, apart from men of heroic stamp like Napoleon— men concerning whose moral qualities opinion is much divided— history shows us that even men such as Louis XI or Metternich, who governed millions of their fellows, were remarkable for no special degree of mental vigour, but, on the contrary, were usually weaker than any of the many whom they ruled. If the source of power lies, not in the physical, or in the moral qualities of the individual who possesses it, clearly that source must be external to the individual, and lie, rather, in the relation of the individual to the masses.

A similar view of power is taken by the science of law—the *bureau d'échange* of history, where the historical theory of power purports to be changeable for pure gold. Power, says that science, is the joint will of the masses, conferred, with their tacit or expressed consent, upon the rulers whom the masses may select. In so far as the science of law is concerned—the science which connotes judgments passed for the ordering of a state and power, all this would be clear enough if matters could always be ordered on similar lines; but, in applying such a definition as the above to history, further explanation is required. The science of law looks upon a state and power in much the same way that the ancients used to look upon fire— namely, as something absolutely existing; but in the eyes of history a state and power represent merely phenomena, just as, in the eyes of the natural physicist of the present day, fire also represents a phenomenon, and not an element.

From this fundamental difference of view between history and the science of law there arises the fact that the latter can lay down in detail what it considers to be the best method of organising power, and what it considers that power to be which is irremovable and independent of time, but can return no answer to history's question as to what that power is which changes and is dependent upon time. If power is the joint will of a people imposed upon its ruler, did Pugachev [1] truly represent the will of the masses? And if not, why did Napoleon do so? Why, again, was Napoleon III, when taken at Boulogne, a criminal, and why, later on, were those persons whom he, in his turn captured, criminals? When *révolutions de palais* occur (which are usually affairs in which some two or more persons are concerned), is the will of the masses transferred to the new ruler? In international relations, is the will of a nation transferred to that nation's conqueror? Was the will of the Rhenish Bond transferred to Napoleon in 1808? Was the will of the Russian nation transferred to him in 1809 when our troops marched with the French against the Austrians? We find these questions answered in three different ways.

Firstly, it is said that the will of the masses has always been delegated unconditionally to the ruler or rulers whom the masses have chosen, and that every rise, therefore, of a new power, every struggle against the power once granted, is to be regarded as an infringement of the true power. Secondly, it is said that the will of the masses has always been delegated to their rulers conditionally, i.e. on fixed and limited terms; after which it is shown that all restrictions upon, collisions with, or annulments of that power have arisen out of non-observance by the rulers aforesaid of the terms on which they received it. Thirdly, it is said that the will of the masses has always been delegated to their rulers conditionally, but on terms which are not wholly clear and definite to us, and that the rise of one or more other powers in the state, their struggles, and their fall have proceeded from over-lax or over-strict fulfilment of the unknown terms on which the original rulers received their power.

In these three ways do historians of this kind explain the relations of peoples to their rulers. Those who adopt the first view, being too simple-minded to understand the question of the meaning of power (they are those local and biographical historians to whom I have already referred), speak as though the joint will of the masses were delegated to historical personages unconditionally: wherefore, in describing a given power,

[1] Leader of a Cossack rebellion during the reign of Catherine the Great.

they appear to suppose that it was the only real and absolute one, and that every force opposing it was not a power at all, but only an infringement of, or assault upon, the true one. This theory of theirs, though convenient for dealing with primitive, peaceful periods of history, has this disadvantage in its application to those complex and stormy periods in the lives of nations when several powers usually arise simultaneously and come into collision with one another—that, while the legitimist historian will assert that the Convention, the Directory, and Bonaparte were all of them mere infringements of power, Republican and Bonapartist historians will assert—the former that the Convention, and the latter that the Empire, was the true power, and that everything else was so much infringement of power. This makes it clear that their mutual contradictions render these historians' explanation of power fit only for children of the tenderest years.

While recognising the falsity of this view of history, the historians who adopt the second of the above views state that power is based upon conditional imposition of the joint will of the masses upon their rulers, and that historical personages hold their power only on condition that they carry out the programme tacitly and unanimously assigned to them by the will of the people. Yet what that programme consists of these historians do not say—or, if they do so, they contradict one another continually. According to his particular view of what constitutes the aim of the movements of a nation, each such historian sees in the programme in question either the greatness, the enrichment, the emancipation, or the enlightenment of the citizens of France or of this, that, or the other state. Yet, passing over the mutual contradictions of these historians as to the scope of that programme, and even admitting that there can exist a programme common to all of them, we still see that historical facts almost invariably controvert such a theory. If the terms on which power is delegated mean the enrichment, the emancipation, or the enlightenment of a nation, why did men like Louis XIV and Ivan IV live out their reigns in peace, while others, like Louis XVI and Charles I, paid a penalty to their people? To this question such historians reply that the policy of Louis XIV—which was contrary to the programme—was visited upon Louis XVI. But why was it not visited upon Louis XIV and Louis XV? Why was it visited upon Louis XVI in particular? And what was the period of that visitation? To these questions no answer can be returned. Equally impos-

sible is it to explain—if we adopt the view under discussion—
the fact that the joint will of a people was delegated for centuries
to certain rulers and their successors, and then suddenly transferred, by turns and during a space of fifty years, to a Convention, a Directory, to a Napoleon, to an Alexander, to a
Louis XVIII, again to Napoleon, to a Charles X, to a Louis
Philippe, to a republican government, and to a Napoleon III.
In explaining these swift transferences of the popular will from
one rule to another, and especially in the matter of international
relations, conquests, and alliances, these historians involuntarily
have to confess that some of those phenomena were not regular
transferences of will, but accidents dependent upon the intrigues, errors, stratagems, or weaknesses of a diplomatist, a
monarch, or a leader of a party. Consequently, most of the
phenomena of history, such as civil wars, insurrections, and
conquests, appear to such historians as resulting, not from
transference of the free will of a people, but from the ill-directed
will of one or two individuals. That is to say, they resulted
from infringements of power. Consequently, also, all historical
events appear to writers of this kind divergences from theory.

The historians who adopt the third of the above views say that
the will of the masses is delegated to historical personages conditionally, but on terms which are not known to us, and that
historical personages hold their power only so long as they fulfil
the will imposed upon them. Yet, even if that be so, and if
the force which moves nations lies, not in historical personages,
but in nations themselves, wherein consists the importance of
those same historical personages? Such personages (answer
historians of this kind) only *express* the will of the masses.
That is to say, their activity serves but to *represent* the activity
of the masses. Yet, even if that be so, the question again
arises: Does all the activity of historical personages serve as
an expression of the will of the masses, or only a given side of
that activity? If all the activity of historical personages serves
as an expression of the will of the masses (as some of these
historians suppose), then the biographies of the Napoleons and
Catherines, with their multitudinous details of court scandal,
serve also as an expression of the lives of their respective nations
—which is manifestly absurd. If, on the other hand, only one
side of the activity of historical personages serves as an expression of the life of nations (as others of such pseudo-philosopher-
historians suppose), then, to define which side of the activity of
an historical personage expresses the life of his or her nation, we

must first of all know wherein the life of that nation consisted. Confronted with this difficulty, historians of the kind I am speaking of invent an abstraction of the most obscure, impalpable and general species possible—an abstraction which may serve to cover the greatest number of events, and say that that invention of theirs contains within it the end of the movements of humanity. The general abstractions most commonly adopted by these historians are freedom, equality, enlightenment, progress, civilisation, and culture. Having thus postulated an abstraction as the aim of the movements of humanity, these historians go on to study those personages in history who have left the greatest number of memorials behind them (such as, for instance, monarchs, ministers, military commanders, authors, reformers, priests, and journalists), but only in proportion as they consider those persons to have contributed to, or to have hindered, the abstraction in question. Yet, inasmuch as nothing has ever yet shown that the aim of humanity lies in freedom, in equality, in enlightenment, or in civilisation, and inasmuch, also, as the connection of the masses with the rulers and enlighteners of humanity is based only upon an arbitrary supposition that the joint will of the masses is always delegated to the personages who are most prominent in history, it follows that the activity of millions who emigrate, fire their houses, abandon agriculture, and exterminate one another will find no expression in a description given of the activity of a score or so of persons who do not fire their houses or kill their fellow-men. History proves this at every step. Can the wanderings of the nations of the west at the end of the last century and their drift towards the east be attributed only to the doings of Louis XIV and his two immediate successors, or to the vagaries of their ministers and favourites, or to the lives of Napoleon, Rousseau, Diderot, Beaumarchais, and others? Can the movement of the Russian nation eastwards towards Kazan and Siberia be expressed in mere details concerning the diseased character of Ivan IV and his correspondence with Kurbski? Can the movements of humanity during the epoch of the crusades be attributed solely to the life and doings of the Gottfrieds and the Louis and their ladies? Even so, we still remain unable to understand the movement of nations from west to east—the movement which began with no aim in particular and no leader, but was carried out at first by a mere band of vagrants headed by Peter the Hermit. Still less can we understand the cessation of that movement at the very moment when the preconceived, sacred aim of the expeditions had been proclaimed by the chief historical personages concerned—namely, the freeing of Jerusalem. Popes, kings, and knights strove with might and main to stir up the people to the rescue of the Holy Land, but the people would not move for the reason that the unknown cause which had set them in motion before no longer existed. Thus it is clear that a history of mere Gottfrieds and Minnesingers cannot comprise a history of the lives of nations, and that a history of Gottfrieds and Minnesingers will remain a history of Gottfrieds and Minnesingers and no more, while a history of the lives of nations and of their impulses has yet to be written.

As for the histories of writers and reformers, they do even less to elucidate the lives of nations. True, histories of civilisation explain the impulses and conditions of the life of a given writer or reformer. For instance, we learn from them that Luther had an irascible temper, and that he delivered such and such orations, as also that Rousseau was of a suspicious nature, and that he wrote such and such books. What we do not learn from them is why (for instance) the nations flew at one another's throats after the Reformation, nor why men slew one another during the French Revolution.

Even if the two sorts of history be combined (as is done by some of the newer historians), they form only histories of monarchs and writers, not a history of the lives of nations.

CHAPTER CLI

The lives of nations could not be comprised in the lives of the individuals named above, for the reason that the connection between those individuals and their respective nations has never been defined. The theory that such a connection exists and is based upon the delegation of the general will to historical personages is altogether hypothetical, and in no way borne out by the experience of history. Possibly the theory elucidates a good deal in so far as the science of law is concerned, and is necessary for some purpose or another, but, in applying it to history, it becomes meaningless so soon as ever we are confronted with revolutions, conquests, and civil wars—in fact, so soon as ever history begins. The reason why the theory seems irrefutable is that the act of delegation of the popular will can never be proved, seeing that it never takes place. Yet, no matter what event takes place, nor who directs it, the theory can always say that such and such a person was in supreme direction because to him there had been delegated the joint will of the masses.

Thus the answers returned by this theory to the questions of history are like the answers of a man who, looking upon a flock of sheep as it roams over a pasture, and leaving out of account both the relative richness of the herbage in different spots and the driving of the shepherd, considers the cause of this or that direction taken by the flock to be due to the fact that a particular animal is heading the rest. "The sheep move in such and such a direction because their leader guides them thither, and because to that leader has been delegated the joint will of the flock." That is what the first of our classes of historians answer —the class of those who support the theory of unconditional transference of will. "If the sheep at the head of the flock keep on replacing one another, the fact is due to the circumstance that the joint will of the rest keeps being transferred from one leader to another, according as the leader does or does not lead them whither they desire to go." That is what those historians answer who assert that the joint will of the masses is delegated to their rulers on terms which they (the historians) regard as indeterminate. This is a point of view which often causes the observer to bolster up the particular theory which he has adopted by recognising as leaders those who have not reached the front at all when the masses change direction, but are still on the flanks, or even in the rear. "If we see that both the leaders and the direction of the flock are constantly being changed, the fact is due to the circumstance that, to attain a given direction, the rest of the animals keep delegating their will to those of their number whose movements strike most upon the eye. Consequently, to study the movements of the flock as a whole, we must watch the animals thus most prominent to our sight, no matter from what quarter of the flock they come." That is what the historians of the third species answer—the historians who recognise as expressions of a given period *all* historical personages, from monarchs to journalists.

The theory of the will of a nation being expressed by its historical personages is only a periphrasis—putting the same question in other words.

What is the cause of historical events? Power. What is power? Power is the sum total of will as expressed by one person. On what conditions are the wills of the masses expressed by one person? On the condition of this one person expressing the wills of the masses. In other words power is power, and power is the word the meaning of which we want to know.

If the province of human knowledge were limited to abstract thought only, humanity, in criticising the explanation of power given by science, would conclude that power is only a verbal expression, and possessed of no actual existence. Yet, for the comprehension of phenomena, man has not only abstract thought, but also the weapon of experience, at his disposal when testing the results of such thought; and experience tells him that power is not a verbal expression only, but a phenomenon actually existent. Without mentioning the fact that, without the idea of power, no description of the joint activities of men would ever be possible, the existence of power is proved both by history and by observation of contemporary events.

Whenever an historical event occurs, one or more persons make their appearance in accordance with whose will the event seems to happen. Napoleon III issued an order, and the French went to Mexico. The Prussian king and Bismarck issued orders, and their troops went to Bohemia. Napoleon I issued an order, and his troops went to Russia. Alexander issued an order, and the French made submission to the Bourbons. Thus experience teaches us that every historical event is bound up with the will of one or more persons who issue orders. Some historians are led by their old habit of recognising divine participation in the affairs of humanity to attempt to see the cause of each such event in an expression of the will of an individual invested with power, but this conclusion is upheld neither by reason nor by experience. On the other hand, reason shows us that expressions of the will of an individual—his actual words—are only part of the general activity expressed in such an event as a war or a revolution: wherefore, unless we recognise some incomprehensible, supernatural force—some miracle, in fact, it is impossible to admit that words can be the immediate cause of the movements of millions, while, on the other hand, even supposing that words can be the cause of events, history shows us that expressions of the will of historical personages have seldom resulted in action, i.e., that frequently the commands of such personages are not only left unexecuted, but produce an effect precisely contrary to the one intended. Consequently, unless we admit that the Deity participates in the affairs of humanity, we cannot assume power to be the cause of events. Power, viewed from the standpoint of experience, is merely a link between the expression of the will of a given individual and the fulfilment of that will by other individuals. In order, therefore, to explain to ourselves the conditions under which it is so, we must first of all establish the idea that expressions of will emanate always from men and not from the Deity. If it were the Deity who issued commands, who expressed His will (as history written by the older school assures us), the expression of that will could never be dependent upon time nor evoked by temporal things, seeing that God is in no way bound up with earthly occurrences. Yet, in speaking of commands, i.e., of expressions of will—emanating from men, the fact that the latter are dependent upon time and closely bound up with one another obliges us to explain the connection between their commands and historical events by postulating: (1) That one inevitable condition must always be that both those events and the individual who commands them to occur move in time; [1] and (2) That there must always be a certain connection between the individual and the agents who fulfil his commands.

CHAPTER CLII

ONLY to an expression of the will of the Deity (who is independent of time) can a series of events covering several years or centuries be attributed, and only to the Deity (who is stirred to action by no temporal agency) does it belong to direct, by His will alone, a movement of humanity. Man is subject to time, as well as himself a participator in historical events.

In establishing the first condition conceded above—the condition of human dependence upon time—we see that no single command can ever be fulfilled without a previous command having been given which makes feasible the fulfilment of the second. No command ever appears spontaneously, nor includes within its scope a whole series of events, but, on the contrary, always arises out of another one, and so far from referring to a series of occurrences, refers always to a single moment in a single occurrence. When, for example, we say that Napoleon commanded his troops to go to war, we combine under a single command a series of subsequent commands—all of them dependent upon one another. It did not lie in Napoleon's power to order the expedition to Russia, and he did not do so.

[1] i.e., are limited by the circumstances and conditions of time.

What happened was that one day he ordered certain documents to be dispatched to Vienna, Berlin, and St. Petersburg, while the following day saw issued decrees, orders to the army, the fleet, the subsidiary corps, and so forth. All these millions of orders went to make up a series of commands which corresponded to a sereis of events such as finally landed the French troops in Russia. On the other hand, the fact that, although, throughout his reign, Napoleon kept issuing orders for an expedition to be carried out against England (and spent upon no single other enterprise so much time and effort as he did upon this one), he never once attempted to execute his intention, but, instead, undertook an expedition against Russia (with whom he had often said that he wished to remain at peace), arose out of the circumstance that his earlier commands did not correspond to the sequence of events, whereas his later ones did.

For a command to be faithfully fulfilled it must be a command actually capable of fulfilment. To know always what commands can be fulfilled and what cannot is impossible, not only in the case of a Napoleonic expedition against Russia (an event in which millions participated), but even in the case of the simplest of operations, seeing that both the one and the other are liable at any moment to find themselves confronted with millions of obstacles. Every command fulfilled is invariably one of an immense number of commands unfulfilled. The impossible commands have no connection with the event concerned, and so remain unexecuted. Only the possible ones become linked into a consecutive series of commands corresponding to a consecutive series of events, and so come to be executed.

Our erroneous idea that any command which precedes an event is the cause of that event arises out of the fact that, when an event has occurred, and only those few (out of, perhaps, a thousand) commands have been fulfilled which were connected with the event in question, we forget all about the commands left unfulfilled for the reason that their fulfilment was impossible. Another chief source of error in this regard lies in the fact that, in an historical exposition, a countless series of different petty events (such as, for instance, the many entailed upon Russia by the French war) may become generalised into a single event, according to the result produced by that series of events, and that the series of commands which corresponded to those various petty occurrences may likewise become generalised into a single expression of will. We say, for example, that Napoleon conceived and carried out the expedition against Russia. Yet, as a matter of fact, nothing is to be found in the whole of his career which in any way resembles such an expression of will. What we find, rather, is a series of commands (i.e., expressions of his will) of the most varied and indefinite tenor possible, and that from that countless series of expressions of will it is customary to select such of his *fulfilled* commands as led up to the expedition of 1812: the reason for this being, not that his fulfilled commands were in any way different to his unfulfilled, but that, as a series, they chanced to coincide with the series of events which finally brought the French troops to Russia. As when in stencilling this or that figure appears, it is not because paint is put on in any particular way, but because it was smeared on from any direction on the figure cut out in the stencil.

Thus, according as we observe the relation of time between commands and events, we see that, although a command can never be the immediate cause of an event, there nevertheless exists between the two a certain definite interdependence. To understand wherein that interdependence consists we must establish also the second of our two conditions [1] governing every command which emanates from man and not from God—namely, the condition that every individual issuing commands must also be a participator in events. It is precisely this relation of an individual who issues commands to those who execute them that constitutes what we call power. Let me explain this.

For the purpose of common action, men always unite in combinations in which, whatsoever the aim of their joint action, the relation between the various individuals participating in the movement is always the same. This relation is such as to bring it about that the largest number of members of the combination take the largest direct part, and the smallest number of members the smallest direct part, in the common action for which they have all of them combined together. Of such combinations, one of the most typical and clearly defined is an army.

An army is made up of a large number of men of the lowest military rank (private soldiers), as well as of a smaller number of men (non-commissioned officers) immediately above them, a still smaller number of men (commissioned officers) above the last-named, and a single individual at the head of all. Thus military organisation might be likened to a cone having for its base the private soldiers, and for its apex the commander-in-chief. The private soldier does the immediate work of pillaging, killing, burning, and robbing, and for the execution of all those acts he receives commands from his superior officers, while he himself never issues a command. The non-commissioned officers do less of the immediate work of war than the private soldiers, since their number is smaller, but they sometimes issue commands. The commissioned officers, again, do even less of the immediate work than the non-commissioned officers, but issue commands more frequently. Lastly, the commander-in-chief bids the troops go to war, and appoints them their goal, but seldom or never uses his personal weapons. Thus the head of an army never takes a direct part in the actual work of war, but only makes general dispositions for the movements of the masses under him. The same relation obtains in every combination formed by men for joint action—whether in agriculture, trade, or any kind of government or administration. Thus, without drawing arbitrary distinctions between the various component parts of the cone—between the ranks of an army, or between the various positions and grades of members of any sort of administration or public body, a law results through which men always seek to accomplish action in common by uniting in such a relation among themselves that, the more directly certain of their members participate in the accomplishment of that action, the less are they permitted to issue commands and the greater is their number, while, the less certain others of their members participate in the common action, the more are they permitted to issue commands and the smaller is their number; until at length we arrive at a single individual who, taking the smallest direct part of all in the work, directs that work more than is the case with any other member, through the commands which he issues. This relation between commander and commanded is what constitutes the essence of the conception which we call power.

Thus, in establishing the condition of time under which all events must take place we have found that commands are fulfilled only when they refer to a corresponding series of events. Also, in establishing the condition of an inevitable connection between the commander and those whom he commands, we have found that every commander is bound by his very office to take the smallest direct part in events—to confine his activity exclusively to commanding.

CHAPTER CLIII

WHENEVER an event is taking place, men always express their ideas and aspirations with regard to it; and inasmuch as the event always arises out of the joint activity of several persons, one of such expressed ideas or aspirations is sure to be fulfilled, or approximately so. When, therefore, an idea has been expressed and becomes realised, it also becomes connected with the event in the guise of an antecedent command.

Let us suppose a number of men drawing a beam of wood along the ground. Each of them may be expressing his ideas as to the best method of doing so and the proper destination of the beam, yet it will generally be seen that they are performing their task at the bidding of another person—of a person who is issuing commands. There we have commands and power in their simplest form. The man who does the most labour with his hands has the least time to think of what he is doing, or to foresee what will come of the common action, or to issue commands. On the other hand, the man who is issuing the greatest number of commands is obviously the least able of the party to perform direct labour with his hands.

In a large aggregate of men directing their efforts to a common end, those of them stand out the most prominently who do the smallest amount of manual work and most confine their activity to the issuing of commands. When a man is acting alone he keeps always before him a stock of ideas which he believes to have regulated his action in the past, to be a justification for his action in the present, and to present a basis for his action in the future. In the same way, aggregates of men entrust certain of their number with the task of conceiving ideas both to justify their joint action in the present and to serve as a basis for similar action in the future. Certain known or unknown causes once led the French people to fall to cutting one another's throats, while at the same time they justified themselves by saying that it was necessary to do so for the welfare of France and the furtherance of freedom and equality. When at length they desisted from killing one another, they again justified themselves on the ground of the necessity of uniting their forces against Europe. Next, they carried out a movement eastwards for the purpose of killing fresh numbers of their fellow-men, and on that occasion again they found their justification in talk about the glory of France and the perfidy of England. Yet history shows us that these various justifications had no significance in common whatever, but, on the contrary, only contradicted one another. Instances of this are to be seen in the statements that the murder of man was necessary for the recognition of his rights, and that the slaughter of millions of people in Russia was necessary for the humbling of England. Yet, as viewed in the light of to-day, those justifications have an important bearing. They relieved the men who committed those acts of moral responsibility. Those temporary pretexts were like the bundles of broom which one sometimes sees tied to the front of a locomotive to sweep the rails. They swept those men's road clear of all moral responsibility. Without such justifications we could never explain the exceedingly simple question which confronts us in our study of historical events, namely, "How do millions of men come to accomplish joint crimes such as wars, massacres, and so forth?" In view of the fixed and complex forms of state and public life in Europe, is it conceivable that an historical event should not be ordained and brought about by the word of a monarch, a minister, a parliament, or a journal? And could any joint action, no matter what, not find justification for itself on the ground of state unity, nationality, the equilibrium of Europe, or civilisation? Every event taking place is bound to coincide with some desire which has been previously expressed, until, justifying itself on one pretext and another, it comes to appear the product of the will of one or more individuals. The prow of a ship always drives a billow of foam before it, and to those on board the ship that billow alone, and not the ship, seems, at first, to be moving. Yet, if they watch the billow closely and point by point, and compare its movement with the movement of the ship, they soon come to realise that each stage of the billow's progress is determined by the progress of the vessel, and that they were mistaken in taking no account of the ship's agency. The same thing is apparent as, stage by stage, we follow the progress of historical personages, i.e. as we gradually verify the inevitable condition that every event moves continuously through time, and also keep in mind the condition that there always exists a connection between historical personages and the masses. Whatsoever events may occur, they always seem to have been foreseen and fore-ordained, just as, no matter in what direction a ship be sailing, there always surges before its bows a billow which in no way aids its progress, yet appears, at first sight, to be moving spontaneously, and even to be directing the movement of the ship.

In looking only to those expressions of will on the part of historical personages which have borne some relation to historical events, as commands, historians have supposed that events depend upon commands. Yet, in observing events and the connection always existent between historical personages and the masses, we have found that such personages and their commands depend upon events. Undoubted proof of this lies in the fact that, no matter what commands be issued, no historical event can take place unless there be other reasons also for its happening, and that its accomplishment subsequently reveals the fact that certain of the many previous expressions of will of historical personages in connection with the said event come to stand to it (through time and subsequent interpretation) in the relation of commands. Once arrived at this conclusion, we are in a position to return a direct and positive answer to the two essential questions of history—namely, "What is power?" and "What is the force which produces the movements of nations?"

Power is such a relation of an individual to other individuals that, the smaller his direct participation in the joint action of those individuals, the more is he free to give expression to ideas, proposals, and justifications with regard to the progress of that joint action. As for the movements of nations, they are due, not to power, nor to intellectual activity, nor to combinations of the two (as some historians have supposed), but to the activity of *all* the persons taking part in an event; the manner of combination of those persons invariably being that those of them who play the greatest direct part in the event take upon themselves the smallest share of responsibility, and vice versa.

Morally, the cause of an event is power: physically, its cause is persons who are subject to power. Yet, inasmuch as a moral agency without a physical one is unthinkable, the cause of an event lies neither in the one nor in the other, but in a combination of both. In other words, to the phenomenon which we may be observing no idea as to its cause is ever really applicable. In all ultimate analysis we approach the circle of infinity—approach the ultimate boundary at which the human intellect eventually arrives, in every department of thought, if it does not trifle with the subject in hand. Thus, electricity produces heat, and heat electricity. Atoms are attracted to one another, and atoms are repelled. Yet, in speaking of the inter-reaction of heat and electricity and of the inter-action of atoms, we cannot tell why these things are so. All that we can tell is that they are so because for them to be otherwise would be unthinkable—because there is a law to that effect. The same with regard to historical phenomena. All that we know is that, to accomplish this, that, or the other action, men unite in a combination in which they all participate. Accordingly we say that it is so because for it to be otherwise would be unthinkable—because there is a law to that effect.

CHAPTER CLIV

IF history had to do with external phenomena only, mere statement of such a simple and obvious law would have been sufficient for our purpose, and our discussion would have ended. But the laws of history refer to man, and, although a mere fragment of substance cannot speak and tell us that it feels no impulse towards attraction or repulsion—that, in fact, we are wrong, man—the subject of history—can tell us to our faces: "I am free, and therefore subject to no laws."

The presence of an unexpressed question as to the nature of the freedom of the human will makes itself felt at every step in history. Every seriously thinking historian has involuntarily touched upon the point. All the contradictions and obscurities of history—the whole fallacious road which that science has travelled—have been based upon the non-decision of the problem.

If the will of every man were free, i.e. if every man could do exactly as he pleased—history would be a mere series of disconnected accidents. If but one man out of several millions had the power, once in a thousand years, to act freely, i.e. entirely according to his own will, it is clear that, should his free action transgress a single law, laws could no longer exist at all for humanity. If, on the other hand, one and the same law were to govern the acts of all humanity, there could exist no free-will, since the will of all humanity would be subject to that law. In this contradiction lies the problem of the freedom of human will which from earliest times had occupied the best intellects of mankind, and has always appeared to them of the deepest importance.

The problem lies in the fact that, if we look upon man as a subject for study only (whether from the theological, the historical, the ethical, the philosophical, or any other point of view), we come upon a general law of necessity to which he, like everything else in existence, is subject; yet, if we look upon him also as something representing our own consciousness, we feel that we are free. This consciousness of ourselves is a source of self-realisation quite apart from and independent of reason. True, it is through reason that man can *survey* himself, but it is only through consciousness that he *knows* himself. Without consciousness of self, both the power of observation and the application of the reasoning faculty would be unthinkable.

In order to understand, observe, and remember, man must first of all become conscious of himself as a living being. He becomes conscious of his vitality primarily through his desires, i.e. through his will. When he becomes aware of his will as constituting the essence of his life, he is bound to recognise it as free. If, in the exercise of his powers of observation, man perceives that his will is governed by one unfailing law (whether by the necessity of his taking food, by the action of his brain, or by any other phenomenon which he may remark), he is unable to comprehend this invariable and uniform direction of his will otherwise than through its limitation. What is not free cannot be limited, and therefore man's will appears to admit capable of limitation for the reason that he feels it to be free. Even though he were to say, "I am not free, yet I can raise and lower my hand," everyone would recognise that seemingly illogical speech as an incontestable proof of his freedom. It would be an expression of consciousness not subject to reason. If the consciousness of freedom were not a source of self-realisation separate from and independent of reason, it would be subject to reflection and experience; whereas, in point of fact, such subjection to reflection and experience is never to be met with, and is altogether unthinkable.

Every man learns from reflection and experience that he, like any other phenomenon observable, is subject to given laws. Accordingly, he submits himself to their working, and makes no attempt to resist any such law when once he has become aware of its existence. Yet reflection and experience also teach him that full exercise of the freedom which he recognises to lie within him is impossible, and that every act of his depends upon his particular organism, his character, and the motives which inspire that character. At the same time, he never wholly accepts the deductions of reflection and experience. Having learnt by experience and reasoning that a stone falls downwards, a man believes it absolutely and in every case expects the working of this law, but, having learnt just as certainly, that his will is subject to laws, he does not and cannot believe it. However often reflection and experience may show a man that, given the same conditions and character, he will always, at a given juncture, do precisely what he did before, he will none the less feel assured, when, for, perhaps, the thousandth time, he engages in action which has hitherto always ended in the same way, that he can act as he pleases. Every man who follows the natural bent of his reflections will feel—despite the many undeniable teachings of reflection and experience that it is impossible for him to conceive of two different courses of action for himself under identical circumstances—that, without such an unreasonable conception (a conception which none the less constitutes the essence of freedom), he could not so much as conceive of the possibility of living at all. He will feel that, however impossible such a conception may be, he has no choice but to conceive it, seeing that, without some conception of freedom, he could never either understand life or endure it for a single moment. The reason why life would be intolerable to him is that all the aspirations of man, all his incitements to live, are so many aspirations towards an increase of freedom. Wealth and poverty, fame and obscurity, power and subjection, strength and weakness, health and sickness, education and illiteracy, labour and ease, plenty and want, generosity and stinginess, are all of them greater or less degrees of freedom. To imagine a man wholly destitute of freedom would be like imagining a man destitute of life.

If, then, reason looks upon the idea of freedom as a contradiction as senseless as the possibility of accomplishing two acts at the same moment of time, or as the idea of action without a cause of any kind, it merely proves that consciousness is not subject to reason. This unshakable, incontrovertible consciousness of freedom—a consciousness which is not subject either to reflection or to experience, and is recognised by all thinkers, and felt by all mankind—is an entity without which no portrayal of humanity would be so much as imaginable.

Likewise, it is an entity which opens up other sides of our question.

Man is the creation of an all-powerful, all-righteous, and all-knowing God. What, then, is sin?—of which the idea arises out of man's consciousness of freedom. Here we have a question of theology. The acts of man are subject to general and immutable laws which can be expressed in tabular form. Wherein, then, does the responsibility of man to the community consist?—another idea which arises out of man's consciousness of freedom. Here we have a question of law. Man's acts spring from his inmost character and the motives which influence it. What, then, is conscience, i.e. the perception of good or evil in acts which arise out of the consciousness of freedom? Here we have a question of ethics. So long as man lives in communion with the general life of humanity, he appears subject to laws determining that life. Yet, living independently of such communion, he appears free. How, then, ought the bygone life of nations and humanity to be regarded? As the product of the free or the restricted activity of man? Here we have a question of history.

Only during this self-confident age of ours—the age of the popularisation of knowledge through the instrumentality of printing (the most potent of weapons though it be against ignorance), has the question of free-will reached the basis when it can no longer remain a question. This era of ours has seen a multitude of so-called "leading men,"—i.e. a crowd of ignoramuses—plunge into scientific investigation, on the system of pursuing one side of a question only in order to arrive at the whole. They say that we have neither consciousness nor freedom, for the reason that the life of man is expressed by muscular motions, and that those muscular motions are conditioned by the working of the nervous system. They say, too, that we have neither consciousness nor freedom for the reason that some unknown period of time has seen us gradually become evolved from apes. Thus they write and speak and print, without so much as suspecting that not only was the very law of necessity which they now strive to prove by physiology and comparative zoology recognised a thousand years ago by all religions and thinkers, but that it has never been denied. They do not see that the proper role of the natural sciences, as regards this question, is to throw light upon one particular side of it, since the fact that, regarded from the strictly scientific point of view, both reason and will are "secretions" of the brain, and that man, following a universal law, has gradually developed from the lower animals, merely proves from *one* point of view only the truth of what was recognised by all religions and philosophical systems so long as a thousand years ago—namely, the fact that, viewed through reason, man is subject to the law of necessity. But it does not further by an iota the solution of the question that has a contrary side, based on the consciousness of freedom.

If an unknown period of time has seen man develop from apes, that at least is as intelligible as that a known instant of time has seen him spring from a handful of dust. However, the question of how man's consciousness of freedom combines with the law of necessity cannot be decided by comparative physiology and zoology at all, seeing that, whereas in the frog, the rabbit, or the ape it is only the muscular-nervous action that lies open to our observation, in man we can observe working, not only in the muscular-nervous action, but also consciousness as well. Purely scientific investigators and their disciples who think that they can finally decide this question are like plasterers who are ordered to stucco the walls of a church, but take advantage of their foreman's absence to show their zeal by smearing their material over windows, ikons, and partition walls alike—satisfied only if, from their plasterer's point of view, everything comes out looking smooth and even all over.

CHAPTER CLV

FOR history, the decision of the question of freedom and necessity has this advantage over other branches of learning in which the question has been finally decided, that, in so far as history is concerned, the question has to do, not with the actual nature of the human will, but with manifestations of that will which we find presented in the past under definite conditions. In deciding this question, history stands to the other sciences in the relation of an experimental pursuit to speculative pursuits. History has for its subject, not the will of man itself, but our *conceptions* of it, and therefore there exists for this science no such insoluble mystery in the union of the contradictory ideas of freedom and necessity as there exists for theology, ethics, and philosophy. History pays regard only to presentments of the life of man in which the union of the two contradictions has become accomplished.

Every historical event in human life, every act of mankind, can be comprehended clearly, exactly, and with no sense of contradiction, even though every such event will be seen to be partly spontaneous and partly dependent upon causes. For the decision of the question of the manner in which freedom and necessity combine, and of what constitutes the essence of those two ideas, the philosophy of history can and must follow a path contrary to the path followed by the other sciences. Instead of first of all defining the actual ideas of freedom and necessity, and then bringing under those definitions all the phenomena of life, history must deduce its definitions of those ideas from the multitude of phenomena which it embraces—phenomena which are always themselves dependent upon freedom and necessity.

Whatsoever presentment of the activity of one or more human beings we investigate, we can comprehend it only as the product partly of man's freedom and partly of the law of necessity. Whether speaking of the great migration of nations and the accompanying raids of the barbarians, or of the dispositions of Napoleon III, or of the act of a man which occurred an hour ago and consisted only of his choosing one of several directions in which to walk, we see no contradictions in those various phenomena—the measure of freedom or necessity which governed those acts of certain individuals is clear and definite to our sight.

Frequently, however, our conception of the greater or less freedom of humanity differs with the point of view from which we observe a given phenomenon. Yet every act of mankind is more or less bound to appear a conjunction of freedom and necessity. In every act observed we see a given measure of the one and a given measure of the other, and, the more freedom there may be perceptible in a given act, the less necessity will there be apparent in it, and vice versa. The ratio of freedom to necessity increases or diminishes according to the point of view from which a given act is observed, yet remains always inversely proportional. A drowning man who clutches hold of another one in the same plight and drags him under, or a starving mother who is exhausted with feeding her baby and steals food for it, or a man who is inured to discipline and so slays a defenceless fellow-creature because he is ordered to do so, will seem to the observer who knows the circumstances in which those persons were placed to have been less guilty—i.e. more subject to the law of necessity—than they will seem to an observer who is unaware of the fact that the man was drowning, or that the woman was starving, or that the soldier was bound to obey orders. To such an observer their acts will seem to have been free rather than subject to the law of necessity. In the same way, to an observer who views a crime some twenty years after its commission the criminal will seem to have been less guilty, i.e. less independent of the law of necessity—than he will seem to the observer who views the crime the day after it is perpetrated. Again, every act of a madman, a drunkard, or a man greatly provoked will seem to the observer aware of the mental condition of the culprit at the time of the deed to have been less spontaneous and more subject to necessity than it will seem to the observer who is unaware of the special factors involved. In all these cases the idea of necessity increases or diminishes with the point of view from which the act is observed. Thus, the greater the estimate of necessity, the smaller the estimate of freedom, and vice versa.

Religion, the trained thought of humanity, the science of law, and history itself all understand this relation between freedom and necessity in the same way. All cases whatsoever in which our conceptions of freedom or necessity are subject to increase or diminution are founded upon three bases—namely, (1) the relation of the doer of the given act to the external world, (2) his relation to time, and (3) his relation to the causes which produced the act.

The first of these bases is what we conceive to be the more or less intimate relation of a man to the external world—our more or less clear conception of the definite place which every man occupies with regard to everything existing at the same time as himself. It is this basis which enables us to perceive that a drowning man is less free and more subject to the law of necessity than a man standing on dry land, as well as that the acts of a man living in association with others and in a populated district—the acts of a man possessing ties of family, of common pursuits and common enterprises—appear less free and more subject to the law of necessity than those of a man living alone and in isolation. If we observe a man living alone and without any connection with his environment, every act of his will appear to us free: yet if we observe any point also in his relation to his surroundings, if we observe his connection with anything whatsoever—whether with a man to whom he is speaking, with a book which he is reading, with work in which he is engaged, with the atmosphere which surrounds him, or with the light which falls upon objects in his vicinity—we see that each of those conditions has an influence upon him, and governs one particular side of his activity. And in so far as we perceive those influences, our conception of his freedom is diminished, and our conception of the necessity to which he is subject increased.

The second of those bases is what we conceive to be the more or less distant connection of a man with the external world in point of *time*. That is to say, it constitutes our more or less clear estimate of the place which the acts of that man fill in the onward progress of time. It is this basis which causes the fall of primeval man—the catastrophe from which resulted the human race—to seem to us less free than the present-day entry of man into wedlock, yet also causes the lives and the doings of men who lived their lives centuries ago (lives, none the less, intimately connected with our own) to seem to us less free than contemporary life, the consequences of which are, as yet, unknown to us. Thus the graduation of our conceptions concerning greater or less freedom and greater or less necessity in this connection depends upon the greater or less interval of time which has elapsed between the commission of an act and our judgment of the same. If I observe an act which I committed a moment ago, and committed under conditions approximately identical with those under which I now stand, my act will seem to me to have been wholly free: yet if I consider an act committed by myself a month ago, I—if now standing under different conditions—will recognise insensibly that, had the act not been committed, much that was useful, agreeable, and even indispensable to me would never have fallen to my lot as its result. If I carry my memory back to an event still more remote—say, to one committed ten years ago, or more —the consequences of that act will seem to me even clearer than those of the one just mentioned, and I shall find it hard to realise what my life might have been like had I never committed the act. The further I carry my recollections back— or (which is the same thing) the further I cast my power of apprehension forward—the more will my judgment concerning the freedom of a given act become doubtful.

The same process of conviction concerning the participation of free-will in the general affairs of humanity is to be found operative in history. An event which takes place in our own time seems to us the undoubted outcome of certain given individuals, but in the case of an event more remote we have had time to observe its inevitable consequences, and could not now imagine them otherwise. Thus, the further we go back in our observation of events, the less do they seem to us to have been spontaneous. The Austro-Prussian war appears to us the indubitable consequence of the cunning action of Bismarck and others. The Napoleonic wars seem to us more doubtful, but none the less the outcome of the wills of supermen. When we get back to the Crusades, however, we see in them an event occupying a definite place as an occurrence without which the modern history of Europe could never have come to be. Yet, to the early chroniclers of that war-like movement, the Crusades must have seemed the outcome solely of the wills of certain individuals. In the case, too, of the great migration of races, it would never now enter into anyone's head to ascribe that resettling of the European world to the mere will of Attila. In short, the further we go back into history for our subjects of observation, the clearer does the law of necessity become.

The third basis is the greater or less extent to which we can trace the endless series of causes in which every phenomenon observed (and therefore every act of mankind) has its place as, for those who preceded it, a result and, for those who came later, a cause. It is this basis which causes the acts of ourselves and of our fellow-men to appear to us the more free and the less subject to necessity in proportion as, on the one hand, we are the more conversant with the physiological, psychological, and historical laws to which man is subject and of which we gain knowledge through observation, as well as the more correctly apprehend the physiological, psychological, or historical cause of a given act, and, on the other hand, in proportion as the act itself was the simpler, and the individual whose action we are studying was the less complex in his character and intellect.

It is when we in no way comprehend the cause of an act— no matter whether it be a cruel or a beneficent act, or an act which is neither the one nor the other—that we recognise in the act in question the greatest measure of freedom. In the case of a cruel act, we look, first of all, for a penalty for its commission; in the case of a beneficent act, we appraise, first of all, its value as such; and when the act is neither the one nor the other, we look, first of all, to its degree of individuality, originality, or freedom. Yet, let but *one* of its countless causes become known to us, and we at once recognise in the act a given measure of necessity. Consequently we demand less retribution if the act was a crime, and recognise in it less beneficence or freedom according as it was an act of beneficence or originality. For instance, the fact that a criminal was reared among wrong-doers goes to mitigate his culpability. The self-sacrifice of a father or mother is more intelligible if its cause is the hope of gain than without a cause at all, and therefore less free and less deserving of sympathy. The founder of a new sect or the organiser of a new party surprises us less when we learn how and through what agency his action came to occur. If we possess a large range of experience, if our observation has been continuously directed to investigating the correlation between causes and effects in the acts of men, then their acts appear to us the more subject to necessity and the less free according as we the more correctly connect effects with causes. If the acts observed are simple and a large number of them is available for observation, our conception of the extent to which they were subject to necessity will be the more complete. The dishonest son of a dishonest father, the lewd behaviour of a woman who has sunk to a certain level of society, the relapse into alcoholism of a drunkard, and so forth, are all of them acts which appear to us the less free according as we the better comprehend their causes. If the human being whose act we are observing stands on the lowest level of mental development (such as an infant, a madman, or an imbecile), we know the cause of his or her action and the defective state of his or her character or intellect, and therefore see so large a measure of necessity and so small a measure of freedom in their action that, as soon as ever we know the cause which was bound to produce that action, we can foretell any given act on their part.

It is upon these three bases alone that both the non-imputability of crime which exists in all legal systems and the circumstances which go to extenuate guilt are founded. The imputability of crime appears to us to be greater or less according to our greater or less knowledge of the circumstances under which the individual was placed, while his or her act is conditioned also in our estimate of it by the greater or less interval of time which may have elapsed between the actual commission of the act and our judgment of its merits, as well as by our greater or less comprehension of its causes.

CHAPTER CLVI

THUS our conceptions of freedom or necessity increase or diminish with the greater or less connection of the individual with the external world, with the greater or less interval of time involved, and with the greater or less dependence of an act upon causes. Accordingly, if we select for observation a point in the life of a man in which his connection with the external world is as intimate as possible, the interval of time which has elapsed since a given act on his part is as great as possible, and the causes of that act are as readily comprehensible as possible, we shall acquire a conception of the greatest possible measure of necessity governing the act and the least possible measure of freedom in the same. On the other hand, if we select for observation a man in the least possible dependence upon external conditions, and observe a given act of his which was accomplished at the nearest possible moment to the present time, and of which the causes are wholly unfathomable by us, we shall acquire a conception of the least possible measure of necessity governing the act and the greatest possible measure of freedom in the same. Yet neither in the one case nor in the other shall we ever be able to imagine to ourselves *absolute* freedom or *absolute* necessity—and that no matter how much we keep changing our point of view, or striving to elucidate the connection between the given individual and the external world, or lengthening or shortening the period of time in the case, or understanding, or failing to understand, the causes of the action of the individual concerned.

Firstly, with regard to the connection with the external world—however much we may imagine an individual excluded from all influences of that world, we shall never gain an idea of freedom *in space*, since every act of every individual is bound to be conditioned by his surroundings, and even by his body. Let us suppose that I raise my arm and lower it again. My action seems to me to have been purely free, yet, if I ask myself whether I can raise my arm in *any* direction, I soon perceive that I only raise my arm in those directions in which the bodies of those around me, as well as the structure of my own body, offer the fewest obstacles to my movement. If of all possible directions I thus choose a particular one, it is because in that direction lie the smallest number of impediments. Therefore, to imagine a person wholly free we must at least imagine him standing outside ˜pace—which is manifestly impossible.

Secondly, with regard to time—however much the moment of the accomplishment of an act may approximate to the moment of our judgment of the same, we shall never gain an idea of freedom in time, seeing that, even though I may observe an act accomplished but a second ago, I am bound to recognise that that act had in it no freedom, for the reason that it was conditioned by the moment of time during which it was performed. For instance, I may say to myself, "Can I raise my hand?" and straightway I raise it. Yet I did not raise it precisely at the moment when it first occurred to me to ask myself the question concerning my freedom. Time has gone by which it was not in my power to restrain, and the hand which I then raised, and the air in which I made the movement, were not the same hand which now hangs passively beside me or the same air which now surrounds my body. The moment at which the movement was accomplished can never return, and during that moment I was able to make one movement and no more, while, whatsoever movement I had made, it could have been the only one. The fact that during the next moment I did not raise my hand did not prove that I *could* not raise it: it merely proved that, inasmuch as any movement of mine could have been *one* only during a single moment of time, my hand could not then have been executing any other movement than what it was executing. To imagine that movement a free movement would mean imagining it as having occurred precisely in the *present*, i.e. precisely at the boundary-line which divides the future from the past, and so outside of time: which would have been impossible.

Thirdly, however much we may strive to comprehend the causes of given acts, we shall never attain to a conception of absolute freedom in the sense of a cause being altogether lacking. However much we may fail to understand the cause of a given expression of will (as manifested in an act of ourselves or of others), the first demand of our intellect is for an hypothesis of, and an investigation into, the cause of that expression of will, since, without a cause, no phenomenon of human life is even imaginable. However much I might raise my hand with the object of accomplishing an act which should be independent of any cause whatever, the mere fact of my having wished to perform the act would become the cause of its accomplishment.

Even if we could imagine a man wholly secluded from

external influences in connection with an act performed by him in the present and derived from no cause whatsoever, we should still have to admit an infinitesimal measure of necessity, even if only equal to a cipher, seeing that a being who was subject to no influence whatsoever from the external world, and stood outside of time, and was independent of causes, would not be a human being at all. Similarly, we could never imagine any human act as altogether destitute of freedom and subject wholly to the law of necessity.

In the first place, however much we may increase our knowledge of the conditions of space under which man lives, that knowledge can never be complete, for the reason that the number of those conditions is as infinite as space is boundless. Therefore so long as we are unable to determine *all* the conditions which influence man, so long can absolute necessity never exist, since there must always be in him a certain measure of freedom.

In the second place, however great be the period of time elapsing between the occurrence of a given phenomenon and the moment of our consideration of it, that period will always be bounded—and time is boundless. Therefore, in this regard also absolute necessity can never exist.

In the third place, however comprehensible be the purpose of the causes of a given act, we can never know that purpose in its entirety, since it is infinite. Once again, therefore, we can never attain to a conception of absolute necessity.

Moreover, if, after admitting only the smallest possible measure of necessity, we should recognise in certain cases (as, for example, that of a dying man, or of an embryo, or of an idiot) complete absence of freedom, we should, by so doing, destroy the very idea of man which we hold at present, seeing that man wholly devoid of freedom is unthinkable. Therefore, any conception of the act of a human being as an act wholly subject to the law of necessity and devoid of any particle of freedom is as impossible as is any conception of a human being as wholly free.

Thus, to imagine a human act wholly subject to the law of necessity, we should have to assume knowledge of all the infinite number of conditions of space, as well as power to understand both the infinitude of time and the infinite range of possible causes. On the other hand, to imagine a human being wholly free and in no way subject to the law of necessity, we should have to imagine a being standing outside of space, of time, and of dependence upon causes. In the one case, if necessity were possible without freedom, we should arrive at a limitation (through laws) of necessity by necessity, i.e. at a form devoid of substance; while, in the other case, if freedom were possible without necessity, we should arrive at unconditional freedom (i.e. freedom independent of space, of time, or of causes), and this freedom, through the very fact of its being unconditional and limited by nothing, would itself be nothing, or substance without form. In general, then, we should arrive at the two bases upon which the whole outlook of man is founded —namley, the unattainable essence of life, and the laws which define that essence.

Reason says: "(1) Space, with all the forms which its perceptibility—i.e. its material—gives it, is boundless, and unimaginable otherwise. (2) Time is an endless progression, without a moment's cessation, and unimaginable otherwise. (3) The connection between causes and effects has no beginning, and can have no end." Consciousness, on the other hand, says: "(1) I am one, and all that exists is I alone. Therefore I include space also. (2) I measure time by the immovable moment of the present, in which alone I am conscious of myself as a living being. Therefore I stand outside of time. (3) I am independent of causes, since I feel myself to be the cause of every phenomenon occurring in my life."

Reason, then, expresses the laws of necessity; consciousness the essence of freedom. Freedom, bounded by nothing, is the substance of life as it appears to man's consciousness; necessity, uncombined with that substance, is man's reason as expressed in the above three formulæ. Freedom is what is observed; necessity is what observes. Freedom is the substance, necessity is the form. Only by separating these two sources of self-comprehension (which are to one another as form to substance) can we gain distinct ideas of freedom and necessity—ideas which, when combined, are both incomprehensible and mutually exclusive. Likewise it is only by uniting them that we can gain a clear conception of the life of man. Apart from these two ideas thus mutually limiting one another when united no conception of life is possible. All that we know of human life is summed up in a certain definite relation of freedom to necessity—of consciousness to the laws of reason. All that we know of the external world of nature is summed up in a certain definite relation of the forces of nature to necessity—of the essence of life to the laws of reason. The forces of the life of nature lie without us, and are not felt by us, although we may call them attraction, inertia, electricity, animal force, and so forth: but the force of human life is felt by us, and we call it freedom.

Yet, just as the incomprehensible force of attraction (which is realised by every human being) is understood by us only in so far as we know the laws of necessity to which it is subject (from our knowledge of the fact that all bodies have weight up to the law of Newton), so the incomprehensible force of freedom (which likewise is realised by every human being) is understood by us only in so far as we know the laws of necessity to which it is, in its turn, subject (from the fact that man is mortal up to a knowledge of the exceedingly complex laws of economics or history). All knowledge is a process of bringing the essence of life under the laws of reason. The freedom of man is distinguished from any other force by the fact that it is a force of which his consciousness is aware, but from the point of reason it differs in no way from other forces. The forces of attraction, of electricity, or of any kind of chemical affinity are distinguished from one another solely by the fact that they are forces differently defined by reason. Similarly, reason looks upon the force of man's freedom as distinguished from all other forces of nature solely by the definition given to it by reason itself. Freedom without necessity, i.e. without the laws by which reason defines it—is in no way distinguishable from attraction or heat or the force of growth. In the eyes of reason it is only a momentary, indeterminate perception of life. Just as the undefined substance of the force which moves the heavenly bodies, or the undefined substance of the forces of heat or of electricity or of any chemical affinity or of life, constitutes the substance of astronomy, physics, chemistry, botany, zoology, and so forth, so the substance of the force of freedom constitutes the substance of history. Just, also, as the subject of any science is the *manifestation* of the unknown substance of life, while the substance itself constitutes the subject only of metaphysics, so the manifestation of the force of human freedom in space, in time, and in dependence upon causes is the subject of history, while to metaphysics alone belongs the study of freedom itself.

In the experimental sciences, all that we know of them we call laws of necessity; what we do not know of them we call the force of life. Yet the force of life is only an expression for what we do not know concerning the substance of life. So too with history. What we know of it we call laws of necessity; what we do not know of it we call freedom. For history, freedom is only an expression connoting what we do not know concerning the laws of human life.

CHAPTER CLVII

HISTORY has to do with manifestations of human freedom in connection with the external world, with time, and with dependence upon causes. That is to say, it defines that freedom by the laws of reason, and is therefore a science only in so far as freedom is capable of definition by those laws. For history, the recognition of human freedom as a force able to influence historical events, i.e. as a force subject to no laws—would be what the recognition of a free force governing the movement of the heavenly bodies would be for astronomy. Such a recognition would destroy the very possibility of the existence of laws, i.e. of there being any such thing as knowledge. If but *one* freely moving body could exist there could no longer exist the laws of Keppler and Newton, nor yet any conceptions concerning the movements of the heavenly bodies. If there could occur but *one* free act of a human being, there could no longer exist any laws of history, nor yet any conceptions concerning historical events.

For history there exist lines of movement of human wills, one end of which is hidden in the unknown, and at the other one moves—both through space, through time, and in dependence upon causes—humanity's consciousness of itself in the present. The more our field of vision becomes extended in this regard, the clearer do the laws of that movement become. To apprehend and to define those laws constitutes the function of history.

From the point of view from which that science now regards its subject, and judging by the route which it now takes in its investigations into the causes of phenomena manifested in the free-will of human beings, the expression of laws is, for history, impossible, seeing that, however much we may set bounds to human freedom, we no sooner recognise it as a force not subject to laws than the existence of any law at all becomes impossible. We have merely to limit that freedom to infinity, i.e. to look upon it as an infinitely small entity—to become convinced of our inability to comprehend the causes of things. Therefore, putting causes aside, history now adopts for its task the investigation of historical laws.

The investigation of those laws was begun long ago, and with the self-destruction which the older history is bringing upon itself as it increasingly abandons research into the causes of phenomena there are becoming evolved new methods of historical thought. By the same road have all the human sciences travelled. To arrive at the infinitely small, even mathematics—the most exact of all the sciences—has resigned the process of resolution in favour of the new process of summarising the various infinitely small fractions which it considers. Abandoning the conception of a cause, mathematics now seeks laws, i.e. qualities common to all the unknown and infinitely small elements of a problem.

A similar course (for, though differing in form, that course has always remained substantially the same) has been followed by the other sciences also. When Newton enunciated his law of attraction he did not say that the sun or the earth could attract. What he said was that every body, from the largest to the smallest, had the quality of seeming to attract others. That is to say, he set aside the question of the *cause* of the movement of celestial bodies, and expressed only a *characteristic* common to all bodies, from the largest to the smallest. That is what the natural sciences do. Setting aside the question of a cause, they investigate laws. Consequently, if history is to have for its subject the study of the movements of nations and humanity, and not merely descriptions of episodes in human life, it must likewise abandon the idea of causes, and apply itself to the laws which are common to all the minute and indissolubly connected elements of freedom.

CHAPTER CLVIII

IMMEDIATELY that the law of Copernicus was discovered and enunciated, the mere recognition of the fact that the sun does not move, but the earth, destroyed the whole cosmography of the ancients. Without that law being controverted, and the old view as to the movements of the heavenly bodies retained, it would have seemed impossible to continue the study of the old Ptolemaic worlds; yet, even after the discovery of the law of Copernicus, those Ptolemaic worlds continued to be studied. Similarly, immediately that the first man declared and proved that the number of births and the number of crimes are both of them subject to mathematical laws, that certain geographical and politico-economic conditions determine this, that, or the other form of government, and that certain relations of population to the soil produce popular movements, the very bases upon which history had rested hitherto were destroyed. Without those new laws being controverted, and the old view of history retained, it would have seemed impossible to continue the study of historical events as though they were the product of the free-will of mankind. For, if such and such a form was established, and such and such a movement of a nation brought about through the agency of such and such geographical, ethnographical, or economic conditions, then the will of the individuals who are represented as having established the given form of government, or as having originated the given movement of a nation, cannot be looked upon as the cause of those phenomena. Yet the older history continues to be studied *pari passu* with the laws of statistics, geography, political economy, comparative philology, and geology—all of which directly contradict its propositions. Long and stubbornly has the struggle between the older and the newer views been carried on by physical philosophy. For a while theology stood guard over the older view, and accused the newer one of impeaching revelation; but when the truth conquered, theology rebuilt its house as firmly as before on the new ground. In history also the present struggle between the older and the newer views is being carried on with stubbornness and persistency—theology, as before, standing guard over the older view and accusing the newer one of infringing revelation. Both in the one case and in the other the contest evokes passions on both sides, and obscures the truth. On the one side it is a struggle evoked by fear and by regret for the learning which the ages have brought forth, while on the other side it is a struggle of a mere passion for destruction. To those persons who are contending against the rising truth of physical philosophy it would seem that, once they recognised that truth, their belief in God, in the creation of the universe, and in the miracle of Joshua, the son of Nun, would be shattered, while to the defenders of the laws of Copernicus and Newton it would seem that the laws of astronomy are essentially subversive of religion. Indeed, Voltaire even went so far as to use the law of attraction as a weapon against all religious belief.

Similarly, some people at the present day suppose that, once they recognised the law of necessity, there would be an end to all conceptions of the soul and of good and evil, as well as to all state and ecclesiastical institutions which are founded upon those conceptions, while, like Voltaire before them, the un-recognised upholders of the law of necessity use it as a weapon against all religion—the truth being that, as, in astronomy, the law of Copernicus, so, in history, the law of necessity does nothing to destroy the ground upon which state and ecclesiastical institutions are based, but, if anything, tends to strengthen it.

As once in the question of astronomy, so now in the question of history, the whole difference of view between the two sides is based upon the recognition or non-recognition of some absolute unit which serves as a standard for visible phenomena. In astronomy that unit used to be the immobility of the earth, while in history it is the independence of personality, or freedom. Just as in astronomy the difficulty of recognising the movement of the earth lay chiefly in the impossibility of denying one's personal consciousness that the earth was stationary, so in history the difficulty of recognising the subordination of personality to the laws of space, of time, and of casuality lies in the impossibility of denying one's personal impression of being independent of those laws. Yet just, also, as in astronomy the new view said, "True, we are not conscious of the movement of the earth, yet if we were to allow that it is stationary we should arrive at an absurdity, whereas if we allow that it moves (though we may not actually feel it doing so), we shall arrive at laws," so in history the new view says, "True, we are not conscious of our independence, yet if we were to allow that we are free we should arrive at an absurdity, whereas if we allow that we are dependent upon the external world, upon time, and upon causes, we shall arrive at laws." In the former case, denial had to be made of all consciousness of an immobility in space which was non-existent, and recognition to be accorded to a movement which was not felt, so now, in the present case, denial must be made of a freedom which is non-existent, and recognition be accorded to a dependence of which we are not personally conscious.

THE END

EVERYMAN'S LIBRARY

A Selected List, arranged under Authors

Anthologies, composite works, etc., are given at the end of the list.

1

January 1954

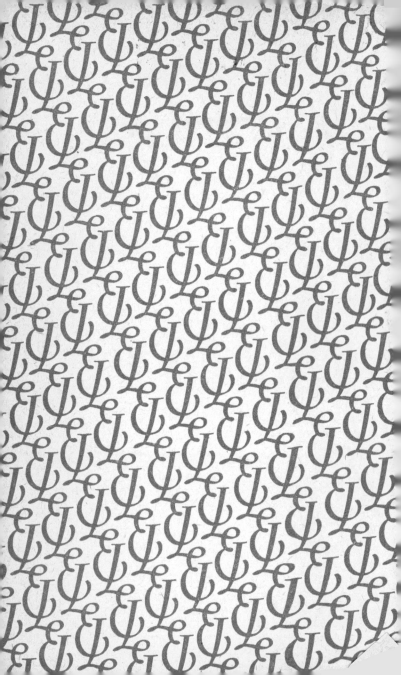